ALSO BY JOHN HERSEY

Men on Bataan   1942

Into the Valley   1943

A Bell for Adano   1944

Hiroshima   1946

These are BORZOI BOOKS
published in New York by Alfred A. Knopf

THE

WALL

THE

WALL

BY

John Hersey

1 9 5 0

ALFRED A. KNOPF
NEW YORK

THIS IS A BORZOI BOOK,
PUBLISHED BY ALFRED A. KNOPF, INC.

Manufactured in the United States of America
Published simultaneously in Canada by McClelland & Stewart Limited

This is a work of fiction. Broadly it deals with history, but in detail it is invented. Its "archive" is a hoax. Its characters, even those who use functions with actual precedent — such as the chairmanship of the *Judenrat*, for example — possess names, faces, traits, and lives altogether imaginary.

THE

WALL

EDITOR'S PROLOGUE

O NE SUNNY DAY IN THE SUMMER AFTER THE END OF THE war, a search party found the Levinson Archive buried in seventeen iron boxes and a number of small parcels, the latter wrapped in rags and old clothes, under the sites of what had been, before the razing of the entire Warsaw ghetto, Nowolipki Street 68 and Swientojerska Street 34. Could but poor Levinson have been there himself that day!

The search party consisted of four survivors of the ghetto, including Henryk Rapaport and Rachel Apt, together with a team of surveyors from the Warsaw municipality, some city employees with digging implements, and a number of government people. Their search was as difficult as if they had been mariners hunting for some Atlantis under an uncharted sea. In hard fact, there was nothing left of the ghetto except the encompassing wall. Within, there was only an immense quadrangle of ruin: scores of city blocks reduced now to a plaza of thoroughly raked-over bits of mortar and crumbled brick, with here and there unaccountably untouched hills of rubble, like careless piles of husks and pollards left around after a threshing. For the most part, the wreckage had been cleared and everything but masonry carted away, as if even the down-pulled ruins of Jewry had been offensive. Among thousands of buildings that had once been ranked on this ground, only one—one building!—was left standing: fittingly, the Gensia Street Jail. Around the prostrate quarter was an eight-foot wall, into the rounded mortar at the summit of which bits of prohibitive glass had long ago been stuck, and Rachel Apt says the walltop sparkled that day in the summer sun, with glints of amber and blue and green.

Thus it was the task of the search party to go out into the huge wrecked space within the twinkling wall and try to find, not only the location of two specific nonexistent buildings, but also the exact situation of their respective former courtyards, and inside those courtyards certain corners, and under those corners the little

3

tombs of Levinson's Archive: like finding a couple of coins dropped into the sands of a wide, dry beach. It is public knowledge that in a matter of hours the party was successful.

Fortunately, the searchers had started out with three specific pieces of guidance as to where they should find the archive: a letter in Noach Levinson's own handwriting, dated November 5, 1942, which Levinson had sent through Hechalutz couriers to Palestine and which had been returned to Warsaw directly after the war; a memorandum by Rachel Apt, written down by her soon after her escape from the ghetto, based on what Levinson had asked her to memorize; and a document that had been sent up to Warsaw from Budapest, notes put down in German by a German underground courier who had visited the ghetto just a month before it was destroyed and had been given Levinson's directions by Rachel Apt. The three documents were in proper accord. Rachel Apt's included one fact the others did not: the depth to which the strongboxes had been sunk (on the average, their tops were said to be half a meter, about twenty inches, down); and Levinson's own letter was more specific than the others, in that it actually dealt in meters *and* centimeters, in telling how far out from the corners—from the courtyard and cellar walls in both cases—box-edges might be found. Long after the archive had been found, other sets of directions were still drifting back to Warsaw from various points of the compass and from as far away as Shanghai; Levinson, a meticulous man, had made certain that his labors would not be wasted.

The morning of the search, the surveyors, equipped with the three documents, with prewar waterworks charts, and with an alidade, triangulated the spire of the Cathedral of St. John, the north side of the Gensia Street Jail, and the skyscraper on Napoleon Square. Gradually they moved toward their objective. Before ten o'clock, the chief of the surveying team, standing by his tripod on a little plateau of brickbats, shrugged his shoulders and said, "Well, try here."

The diggers cleared away surface fragments and found that they were indeed on the flat ground of a former courtyard. With mallets they drove down long, slender star drills until—before noon—one of the workmen hit a box of the Swientojerska cache. The collection in the Nowolipie courtyard was located in mid-afternoon.

Two days' digging brought up the whole treasure. Naturally the search party was nervous about the possibility of missing some units of the archive, especially one or more of the cloth-wrapped parcels which Levinson evidently buried toward the end and in haste. Explorations were therefore made far outside the areas designated in the three documents of guidance. It is practically certain that everything was found.

Most of the archive had been buried for more than two and a half years, yet it was, by and large, in excellent condition. Some of the strongboxes had corroded, and all the cloth around the smaller packages was pretty much rotted; but Levinson and his helpers had packed the archive with affectionate care, and only in the case of one strongbox, about a third of whose contents seemed to have been badly soaked, had any of the documents been rendered totally illegible. Each major manuscript was separately enveloped in several layers of paper and each box and parcel was very tightly crammed or wrapped. One can imagine that the clothing bound about the parcels must have been taken from dead bodies or from deserted apartments.

A forlorn task it must have been, putting this archive to rest: but carried out with what love and zeal!

The Levinson Archive is famous in Poland and in Palestine. So far the Historical Commission has published in the Polish language thirty-seven volumes of material from it, and many more are promised.

What a wonder of documentation! The archive contains all sorts of rich things, mostly intensely moving, simple, personal writings: diaries, novels, notebooks, account books, minutes of meetings, collections of letters, plays, poems, short stories, sketches, musical compositions; as well as a great mass of official records, mostly from the *Judenrat*, every single page of which tells a human story, dry as the intent may have been. Levinson, driven by his obsession that the only legacy the crowds in the ghetto would have to pass on would be their history, collected all this. He kept calling himself, in a rather scornful and half-humorous way, Archivist, or Historian, but he was only interested, really, in separate Jews, in people. He must have been a lonely man.

This volume contains excerpts from Levinson's own document, and a remarkable one (the editor will be pardoned if he feels that) it is.

For eight years Noach Levinson made almost daily entries in a loose-leaf notebook. He tried to write down everything. He nearly succeeded! During the three and a half years with which this book is concerned, he wrote more than four million words—which the editor, with a diffidence he cannot express, has been obliged to reduce, by selection, to one twentieth their original scope. Who knows how many notebook fillers Levinson consumed? His pages alone filled three of the iron filing cases of the archive. He was a paper-thief: this is the only misdemeanor the editor has been able to attach to Levinson.

Levinson wrote in Yiddish in a tiny, beautiful hand—a calligraphy worthy of a scribe of the law. His hand is crystal clear: it is doubtful whether there are a thousand illegible words in all his four million, and considering the tension under which he wrote toward the end, that is a remarkable minimum. Yet he must have written with great speed. Writing was his grace and agility.

Like a living being, the manuscript changed as it grew. Before the troubles in the ghetto, it consisted, as Levinson wrote, mocking himself, of "the slightest kind of personal, diaristic notes for some polite Jewish history I intended in a quiet year to write." Later, it was, he wrote, "only the febrile, hand-tremorous act of recording." Nevertheless, the whole has a unity, which rests upon Levinson's feeling that events were less important than people's reactions to them. Had he ever written his "polite history," it must surely have been a humanistic work, a sociology.

It would be hard indeed to classify what Levinson left behind him: it is not so formidable as history; it is more than notes for a history; it is not fiction—Levinson was too scrupulous to imagine *anything*; it is not merely a diary; it is neither journalism nor a journal in the accepted modes: it has scant precedent. This writing seems to reflect the life and mind of Noach Levinson in troubled times. Yet the editor cannot help feeling that it may be other than it seems.

Levinson never had time to go back over what he had written and revise it. In fact, he chose not to. He refers, in the entry dated July 29, 1942, to "the rule I set myself long ago that I should never destroy anything from this record: the principal value of these jottings for later use will be as a guide to the reactions of the moment, and I cannot help it if they remind me and embarrass me." We can be glad of this rule, for it gives us an opportunity to see the shifting opinions, the inconsistencies, the resourceful self-delusions of a man in final difficulties.

With all his thoroughness, Levinson must have had some prejudices or blind spots. How else account for some of the omissions from his notes? For instance, he never mentions the underground radio transmitter, which broadcast even at the beginning of the final battle in the ghetto under the call letters SWIT. He must have known about it. He must not have *wanted* to write about it. Why?

Although Levinson reveals himself quite thoroughly in the body of this book, as he writes about other people, perhaps a few words about him might be helpful here. The editor, who never met him, must rely on the accounts of Levinson's surviving friends.

In appearance, Noach Levinson was, it seems, not only unimpressive: most accounts agree that there was actually something repellent about his looks. His stature was small. He had the face of an intellectual, narrow and drawn out forward, and upon his unruly nose sat a pair of steel-rimmed glasses whose lenses were so thick that Levinson's eyes seemed, to one who looked into them, far larger than most human eyes. These glasses, and the piscine eyes they gave him, made him look, they say, like a snooper. His hair was seldom tidy. No one has ever spoken to the editor about his clothes, so they must have been drab but in no way disgusting.

Even Levinson's closest friends cannot say exactly how old he was. His skin had the transparency of that of a man with a delicate constitution who has driven his body, by discipline and through hardship, into a kind of toughness. He was probably traversing his early forties during the ghetto years. He had had a hard life. Born of an orthodox, lower-middle-class family in Skierniewice, he was sent to religious schools and went on as a Yeshiva student until he was about eighteen. He then ran away from home, rebelling, as many of his generation did, against the rigidity of his devout parents. He lived in Warsaw, poorly, working as a shoemaker, writing poems and stories, and educating himself in secular subjects. In 1928, or thereabouts, he went to work for the Yiddish paper, the *Togblat*, but resigned four or five years later in some sort of disagreement with the editor. For several years he

7

supported himself as a clerk in a capmaker's shop, but one gathers that his real life was at night, when he studied and wrote. During that period, he published his famous scholarly books, *The Diaspora* and *Customs*. In the early 'thirties, he took work in the secretariat of the *Kehilla*, the Jewish Community Council, which was, under the Germans, transformed into the *Judenrat*. He was there at the time of the beginning of this book.

Levinson began writing in his notebooks late in 1935. Five years later, in the ghetto, they had become, in a sense, his career. At first, in this later phase, he was rather furtive about his writing, though he almost always had his loose-leaf about him. He worked through conversation and observation, letting new material come to him as it would. Evidently he read back over his notes quite a lot, for we find him picking up details that interested him in some event, months after the event took place, tracking down the details and filling them out.

Gradually he lost his inhibitions about his work, to the point where many people considered this persistent and tactless little ferret to be a dreadful nuisance. He would ask anyone anything. People who were fighting for their existence could be pardoned for wondering whether Levinson had nothing better to do than to go around asking personal questions. As his inhibitions fell away, his sense of the need for his work grew. He came to feel that anything that happened to any Jew belonged in his notes. In the midst of the most commonplace conversations, Levinson might be seen sitting there taking notes. Rapaport tells a story, which he got from Dolek Berson, of something that happened one day in the *Judenrat*: Apparently a man named Morgenstern, who worked in the Vital Statistics Department, was paid a visit at his office by his wife. She was very upset about something, and Morgenstern went out into the corridor to talk with her. There the couple fell into a bitter argument. All of a sudden in between husband and wife comes Noach Levinson's nose. He is not there with advice or mediation; no, he is taking notes! (The editor has succeeded in finding the Levinson passage on this incident. The Morgensterns were arguing about an intensely private matter of household finance. The end of the passage is cryptic, but it suggests how some people felt about Levinson's labors. He wrote: "Their fight, though harsh, was satisfactorily concluded when both Mr. and Mrs. Morgenstern were diverted by their alliance in an argument against N.L., the substance of which is not worth recording.")

The editor can do no better than to quote from a letter about Levinson by Rachel Apt:

"He was a queer man, but we loved him. Until he joined our 'family' he was all alone. He had never developed any ties of any kind, and he had no relatives. Thus he had plenty of time for work.

"His voice was always a surprise, it was so deep and strong, coming from that narrow neck, as if a flute could make a noise like a trombone. Sounded very important.

"I remember one time we were walking along Gensia Street, Noach and Dolek and I, and he came right out and said, 'I decided today that I am a coward.' He talked that way, but of course he wasn't. He had too much on his mind all the time to be a coward. His eyes were so strange because of his glasses. The pupils were terribly big, and one had the impression they were actually embedded in the glass. Toward the end we only seemed to see each other's eyes. We didn't look at faces any more, because they were all the same, and everybody's eyes seemed to get bigger and bigger.

"It is funny. He could get anything out of you. Why would people confess intimate things to Noach, who was so impersonal? Well, he was an ear, he would listen, while everybody else was so busy thinking about himself. But there was something else also. There was a timid warmth in Noach. When he recited poetry! He could make us all cry, he could even make Dr. Breithorn cry. I loved him, he was so intense. I never thought him a bother, as some did."

Levinson died of lobar pneumonia in March, 1944, nearly a year after the destruction of the ghetto. Doubtless the physical attrition of the ghetto years had made him too weak to fight off the sickness.

When the Levinson Archive was first dug up, the Historical Commission took it over and spent several months sorting it and selecting the most likely manuscripts for immediate publication. Being so bulky, the Levinson notes were put aside. Finally, in nine months of 1946, they were translated into Polish. It then seemed unlikely, however, and it still seems unlikely, that the Historical

Commission would get around to publishing them for several years, because of their wordage and because they are, in their raw state, rather chaotic.

Thanks to the persistent appeals of Rachel Apt and others, the Historical Commission was finally persuaded, after the Polish translation was completed, to send the original manuscript of the Levinson notebooks to Palestine. Levinson's final notes, which he did not bury but entrusted to Rachel Apt before his death, were also dispatched by her to Palestine. While on a visit to Tel Aviv early in 1947, Mr. A. Breslin, of the Jewish Historical Institute of New York, heard about the Levinson papers, examined them, and managed to have them shipped to the United States. It was at the request of the Institute that the present volume was undertaken. At the time of publication of this work, the manuscript will still be at the library of the Institute, 313 Madison Avenue, where it can be seen by qualified persons. Before long it will doubtless have to be sent back to Israel.

A word about the editing. It has taken two years. It could take twenty, and the editor would still be dissatisfied with the result. The problem, of course, was one of selection. After consultation with others, the editor decided it would be wisest to use for the most part only those passages which concerned the members of the "family" which Levinson joined, and a few others. He wrote just as much about scores of people whose names never appear in this volume. He would write as much as fifty thousand words in separate notes about a man, and all those notes would culminate in a bleak sentence: "Menachem Bavan was taken away today." In having selected a number of people to follow who survived the ghetto, the editor may be guilty of putting too much emphasis on survival in a situation where that was by far and away the exception. Yet Levinson was much interested in survival—and not merely his own.

In the case of each note, the reader will find first the date of the events therein described, and then the date of Levinson's entry. Levinson was careful in every note to designate his source, and these attributions have been kept. Where the note was based on his own observation or opinion, he used, and this volume uses, the initials N.L. The reader will notice that a number of passages are marked with a star (✿). The passages are all taken from the context of a series of interviews that took place on May 9–10, 1943.

At last, the editor must express his gratitude to the two translators, Mendel Norbermann and Mrs. L. Danziger. Both of them worked with feeling. Mr. Norbermann's mother, Sara Norbermann, was deported from the Warsaw ghetto in September, 1942. Mrs. Danziger's brother-in-law died there of typhus. Their task was very difficult: they had to try to convey in English the life of Eastern European Jews without falling into the colloquialisms, word orders, and rhythms which, as taken over and modified by the American Jewish community, have become part of an entirely different culture: the connotations would have been misleading.

It is time to let Noach Levinson speak for himself.

THE EDITOR

THE WALL   PART I

1

Events November 11, 1939. Entry November 17, 1939. N.L. . . . Of all the pleasures in this surprisingly agreeable week in Pawiak Prison, I think the greatest was making the acquaintance of Berson.

He likes to argue. That is fine.

He is what political sophisticates call "a backward man": disinterested in affairs, honest about his confusion. But he has good instincts. He is, above all, zestful. He is both strong and qualmish. He has a powerful physique, but he refused to kill a spider that walked up the wall of our cell one morning: Dr. Breithorn did the job, with some relish, I thought.

I would call Berson a drifter: he lets life carry him along in its stream. He himself said that when we took him into the Community Building off the street the other day, he followed the crowd with a sensation of being dragged and buffeted by the wake of a vessel. He is a drifter, no doubt of it, and that may be why I have become curious about him: we have so many here who let themselves float along in whatever currents.

In one way Berson differs from your commonplace drifter. He is full of gusto, and to him everything is a skylark. He asks a million questions. He even discovered and exploited a certain entertaining quality in ugly little Schpunt. Not that he is all piquancy; he has a moody temper. . . .

Events November 4, 1939. Entry December 3, 1939. From Symka Berson. Froi Berson has finally told me of the events of November 4, from her point of view. Poor girl, she had no idea what was happening.

That day was the Bersons' fifth wedding anniversary. Symka Berson says she set out in mid-afternoon to shop for the party she had planned for that evening. She went down the stairs from her apartment irregularly: that is to say, she walked two or three steps,

13

then somewhat sidewise trotted a few, pleased by the way her red skirt fanned brightly under her open coat, then more carefully took two at a time for a bit with hard, clean blows of her high heels on the wood; and so on, mixing paces. She hurried at the landings. She says she was in good spirits.

At the foot of the stairs she found Tomasz Kucharski, the Polish janitor for the apartment house, very recently stirred, she could see, into low-flickering activity by the telegraphic taps of her footsteps. He moved a broom without conviction across the floorboards of the entrance hall, gently fanning rather than cleaning them. He wore black trousers and an old green sweater, frayed open at the elbows—for bending's sake, as he would say.

Symka, facing the brilliant opening out into the courtyard: —— Isn't this sunlight fine?

Kucharski, breaking off his sweeping with a disgusted sigh, as if the abandonment were a considerable sacrifice, and looking up: —— Be careful out there. Don't get a sunstroke. (The grey-haired janitor smiled, as if his heavy irony needed a signal. It was November and cold.) I'm waiting for the new family. I think these people are rather disorganized. They sent me a note to say they would arrive at nine this morning, and what is it now? Have you a watch?

—— A few minutes past three.

Symka observed to herself that old Tomasz had, as usual, found a way of asking the time. To the janitor, life seemed to be a series of impatient waits between sleeps.

Kucharski: —— I don't think they like moving to this section.

Symka, lightly rejecting a statement that (she now realizes) might have stood some reflection: —— I can't help it.

Kucharski: —— They'll have me carrying things upstairs all evening, I can see that.

The janitor was started now; Symka moved toward the door and down the courtyard steps, half listening and half leaving. Tomasz prattled on and raised his voice as Symka walked away.

—— I hear a family from Praga is going to move in next week. . . .

Now Symka was stepping rapidly across the cobbled yard; she turned and waved a kind of dismissal to the lonely old gossip, who was shouting:

—— This courtyard has been as bad as a hotel for the last month. Coming and going. . . .

Poles going wholesale; Jews coming. Symka did not explore the thought. Walking rapidly along Sienna Street, she says she gave herself up to the mood of sunlight. [NOTE. N.L. I can imagine that in the bright day she looked slightly pinched and sallow; she is a delicate girl, with quick, big, dark eyes and a docile, soft mouth. She has long, black hair, with a wonderful freedom and luster. Outdoors her coat, which is brown, doubtless looked faded. She walks along with short steps, swinging her arms freely, and one can guess that she tilted her head back a little that day to face the friendly sky.]

Symka turned into Wielka Street and walked diagonally across it to Menkes' Bakery, on the far side. As she entered the yeasty shop, a tall, huge man was carrying forward, above his head, a flat pan whose still warm freight was covered over with clean, damp gauze.

—— *Sholem aleichem.*

—— *Aleichem sholem,* Froi Berson. (The baker slipped the pan onto one of the deep shelves lining the shop walls, and did not look around at her.) And how is your big talker since the other night?

—— You shouldn't have baited Dolek so. He doesn't know when he is being teased.

The baker turned toward Symka. His bald head glistened. He wiped his powdered hands on his powdered apron, to no purpose, and said:

—— I wasn't baiting him. We were talking seriously enough, and when your husband began to argue absurdly, as usual, I simply phrased my questions absurdly, for the sake of reciprocity, and he wasn't alert enough to realize it. My Symka, you are married to a baboon.

—— I know, and isn't he a splendid one?

—— No!

Both laughed. Symka said, with mock severity:

—— A loaf of white bread and a dozen sweet buns, if you please, Fraind Menkes.

—— Please, Froi Berson.

The big man turned, reached up for a golden lump from a

15

laden shelf, and slid out from another level a pan on which, when he peeled back its gauze overcast, were discovered many ranges of sugar-capped buns. He broke off twelve, then tossed two extra ones onto the pile.

—— Anything else, Froi Berson?

—— You're coming tonight?

—— Could I miss it?

—— Just think: five years today! It hardly seems possible.

—— Just think! (Like the bullfrog trying to imitate the thrush.) Hardly possible: that you haven't left him yet.

Symka, laughing: —— Six o'clock. . . . Dolek's gone to the Old City, and he said he wouldn't be back till after six. You know what that means, with him. We'll have plenty of time to be on hand to surprise him.

—— If he is capable of being surprised.

Symka let herself out of the door and hurried homeward. In Sienna Street, at the entrance to the courtyard at Number 17, she saw two wagons piled high with furniture and bundles; a number of porters, speaking Polish, were bustling around the wagons, untying cords, arguing, postponing their real work as long as possible. Symka says she realized the "new" family must have arrived. As she turned in at the courtyard gate, Symka met Rabbi Goldflamm. [NOTE. N.L. He is a middle-aged man with a round, young face, in which expressions of patience, gravity, and surprise share an uncomfortable tenancy.]

—— Good afternoon, Rabbi. Don't forget we're expecting you tonight. I hope you haven't given my plans away to Dolek.

—— My dear, you needn't worry about my abusing a confidence. (The rabbi stepped closer to Symka, and she reports that he pointed at the wagons and said, in precisely the tone customarily employed to abuse a confidence:) Expensive furniture. The father of the family is in the jewelry business. The name (he added, with the air of one to whom all the details have been entrusted) is Apt.

Symka, hurrying on: —— I'll expect you at six o'clock.

EVENTS NOVEMBER 4, 1939. ENTRY NOVEMBER 9, 1939. FROM DOLEK BERSON. Today Berson told me how he happened to fall into this situation:

He was going along Grzybowska Street and some distance

ahead of him as he walked, he saw a sudden motion. A small boy darted, as quickly as if he had just committed a theft, from the south to the north side of the street, from the shady to the sunny, stopped abruptly by a high, windowless, brick wall, twisted to one side with the agonized, almost crippled stance of a boy reaching deep for something in a packed pocket, whipped the something out, and, with four or five bold strokes, used it to draw a picture on the wall. Then, pausing only to stuff the something back in his pocket, the boy spurted up the street toward Berson, jerkily turning his head now and then as he ran, as if he expected, or at least imagined, pursuit. The boy ran past Berson, ignoring him entirely; and Berson had a good look in the bright light at the urchin's ugly features: a bumpy, shaved crown, huge eyes in dark sockets, a flat nose, lips drawn back, a sharp chin, like the end of a lemon; and across the whole face, like a cancellation, a pale, sucked-in scar, running from the right temple down between the eyes, over the nose, across the left cheek, and down to the base of the jaw.

Berson quickened his steps to see what urged this disfigured sprinter to such speed. Soon he came to the blank wall. A half-dozen passers-by were already standing and looking at a simple cartoon displayed on the grey bricks in swift, tarry lines: Hitler, amazingly caught in two features—an oval outlining a face, with one end of the stroke curving down over that face's forehead in an unmistakable cowlick; and a tiny, quadrangular mustache. And across the face, insultingly, dismissingly, a huge X.

When the bystanders recognized what they were looking at and realized the possible consequences of their admiration, they turned and fled, too, like the boy, looking over their shoulders, but all in adult slow-motion, at a walk.

Going on, Berson mused about the crossed-out child crossing Hitler out, and he was reminded of the argument he and a friend of his, a baker named Menkes, had had a few nights before. The baker, who is apparently quite a blusterer, had boasted about what he would do in answer to the racial decrees, when they came here in Poland, as they surely would now that the Germans had arrived. Overt opposition. Kill the rats. Show a fist. But, Berson says he asked, whom would the baker fight? Hitler in person? Rosenberg? The S.S. commander for the Warsaw district? Or some individual German citizen, complying, shaking his head but complying? Or, more availably, a Polish citizen, who didn't seem to need the de-

17

crees in the first place? Whom would this baker fight? And with what? Baking powder? Bellows? Berson says he reflected that the boy's cartoon might sustain the boy and might even cheer up a few Jewish pedestrians—but had it any real effect? No, thinks Berson, there is only one resistance: it is inward. It is living one's Jewishness as well as possible, meeting things as they come.

[NOTE. N.L. I may say that this discussion between Berson and his friend could scarcely be called unique, though Berson, with his enthusiasm and wholeheartedness, seemed to regard it as such. Actually, we had all been talking this way, back and forth and in and out, for over a month, ever since the fall of the city on September 29. And with reason enough.]

[NOTE. EDITOR. To clarify what N.L. means by "reason enough," the following inserts are supplied from previous days: ENTRY SEPTEMBER 29, 1939. Well, the siege is ended. The longest twenty-one days I have ever spent. They say fifty thousand were killed in the city, and I can believe it. This beautiful place has been handled roughly. Only the bare walls of the Citadel stand. The Stock Exchange, the Ministry of War, the Lutheran Church are totally ruined. Warsaw University, the Opera House, the Church of St. Mary the Blessed Virgin are badly damaged. Here in the Jewish section, the worst-hit streets are Twarda, Grzybowska, Nowolipie, Nowolipki, Franciszkanska, Dzika, Zamenhofa, and Bielanska. . . . ENTRY OCTOBER 3, 1939. And now we get it. We expected it, but does that make it easier? On a bread line yesterday afternoon, the Jews were rejected. . . . ENTRY OCTOBER 10, 1939. Looting. . . . A row of trucks drove into Gensia Street, which was then closed at both ends. Jews from neighboring alleys were rounded up and forced to load the trucks with goods from those warehouses on Gensia which had not been shelled. H. Perl, the distinguished violinist, was one of these *ad hoc* porters. . . . ENTRY OCTOBER 12, 1939. Leather goods being taken from Franciszkanska Street. . . . ENTRY OCTOBER 23, 1939. It is as if we all expected terrible weather—though the real reason is simply that so many windows were broken during the siege. Windows are being boarded up. Also, a nice new trade: making panes out of pieces of shattered glass leaded or puttied together. We call windows made of such panes Mosaic Views—thinking bitterly with part of our mind of Moses. . . .]

Berson, walking along in this state of mind, now saw ahead

of him on the left side of Grzybowska Street a knot of agitated men, perhaps twenty of them. A couple of bearded Hasidim moved about in their midst, flapping their black kaftans like crows' wings, glossy in the sunlight. Groups within the group coalesced, fragmented, agglutinated again. Hands flew, heads nodded, feet shifted. Berson says that the body of the crowd was shaken, as if by several tics. He was drawn by curiosity to the disturbance; then, coming closer and noticing that it was taking place in front of the Jewish Community Building, he felt aversion toward it: this must be more or less official turmoil, and was not for him.

Just as Berson stepped out into the street to get around the contending men, he was accosted by one of them, who shot out from the crowd and put a hand on his sleeve. Berson describes this man as *a sharp little fellow in a brown suit, carrying a black loose-leaf under his arm and wearing glasses so thick that his eyes looked like two raw eggs.* [NOTE. N.L. I regret to say that this description, which Berson gave me with relish and laughter, was of me. Some day someone will flatter me on my looks, and I will perish forthwith.]

N.L.: —— Excuse me. We need you.

Berson says he felt uneasy. He wanted to remain aloof from the nervousness at the side of the street, especially insofar as it was official and ceremonious, and he said mildly:

Berson: —— I am on an errand.

N.L.: —— Errand or no errand, we need you.

Berson: —— My wife is sick.

(Berson has now told me that this was a lie, and that at the time he immediately wondered why he had said it.)

N.L.: —— Maybe she is dying. I would appreciate your coming with us.

(Berson has also now told me that he felt a coldness about the *sharp little fellow in the brown suit* that he did not particularly like. Well, Berson is frank.)

Berson: —— What is this all about?

N.L. explained that the Germans had called a meeting of the so-called *Judenrat*, that only ten deputy councilors were on hand, and that the Germans had given twenty minutes for assembling the full twenty-four. N.L. told Berson that he would do in lieu of one of the deputies. Just barely. Berson suddenly grew furious and said:

19

—— This has nothing to do with me. You people carry out your own affairs. I have no concern with you.

—— Yes, this has to do with you. With you and your sick wife, too. And with all your *mishpokhe*: it concerns all your family ties. You'd better come.

The *sharp little fellow* turned away, assuming, as imperatively as possible, that Berson would follow him. Some of the group had already gone into the Community Building. Berson listened a moment and then went up to the edge of the remaining clamor; and at once became part of it, in spite of himself. He jumped from knot to knot, trying to piece together the snatches of agitated grammar he heard, but he could make no sense of them: the less he understood, the more nervous and mobile he became. The whole crowd shifted toward the building, and Berson floundered along behind.

At the front door, just inside the dividing line between the brilliance outside and the ancient-fragrant darkness within, Berson was stopped by an elderly, rather formal man, who was apart from all the others in his steadiness and quietness. [NOTE. N.L. This was Felix Mandeltort, our Secretary.]

—— We will need your name and address, I think.

—— D. B. Berson. Sienna Street 17.

—— Is that so? (Felix in his social tone.) I live at Sienna 23.

Berson, who was unprepared for amenities, speaking rather loudly: —— It is my wedding anniversary, my fifth wedding anniversary. I should like to know . . .

Felix, suavely interrupting: —— This shouldn't take long. (Then, after a swift look up the stairs across the hall, creaking under the climbing councilors and deputy councilors and impromptu deputy councilors, he added:) I hope.

Berson, making another try: —— You might tell me . . .

The formal gentleman looked over Berson's head and shouted to the *sharp little fellow*:

—— Have we enough?

—— I think so. I trust so.

EVENTS NOVEMBER 4, 1939. ENTRY NOVEMBER 17, 1939. N.L. The *Judenrat* had been formed a month earlier, to the day. The Germans told us then that the *Kehilla*, or Community Council, would henceforth become the *Judenrat* and would be the instrument of German authority over the Jews. The original directive was explicit and brief: *The Judenrat is required to carry out through its president or vice-president the demands of the German authorities. It will be responsible for their strict fulfillment to the smallest detail. The orders which it issues must be obeyed by all Jews and Jewesses.* M. Sokolczyk, one of the few officials of the *Kehilla* who had not fled Warsaw before the end of the siege, was named Chairman, and was directed to appoint twenty-four councilors and twenty-four deputy councilors. The first order given the *Judenrat* was to make a census of the Jews of Warsaw, together with a special census of professional Jews: doctors, lawyers, engineers, writers, and so on. For an organization that had dealt previously with religious affairs for the most part (the *Kehilla* had owned and administered the Jewish cemetery, synagogues, libraries, hospitals, and certain schools), this census was a highly complex and novel task, and it absorbed our entire energy up until October 28, when it was completed. We had registered 359,827 Jews in Warsaw.

We waited for our next assignment. On the afternoon of November 4, a number of us were sitting in the half-darkened conference room of the Community Building more or less gossiping. We had just heard that in Krakow, brassards marked with the Star of David had been decreed for all Jews. Shortly after four o'clock a half-dozen Germans came hurrying in like a little dust storm, and gave us twenty minutes to gather all forty-eight councilors and deputy councilors. The councilors were all in the building, but we had only ten deputies. We enlisted a few *Judenrat* employees and then went out in the streets to shanghai the requisite remainder. Appropriately enough, we collared three employees of the Rotblat Funeral Parlor, adjoining the Community Building. N.L. was able to impress Berson into service: that was my first meeting with Berson. [SEE ENTRY NOVEMBER 9, 1939.]

EVENTS NOVEMBER 4, 1939. ENTRY NOVEMBER 9, 1939. N.L. When we had gathered our quota, I followed the others upstairs, keeping an eye on Berson, just to make sure that he didn't slip off to his "sick" wife. We walked into the empty lecture hall, whose collapsible seats were stacked against one wall and where, counting the new arrivals, some fifty men were gathered. Down from the walls stared generations of rabbis, austere and impassive

21

behind their decent beards. At the front of the hall, standing before the small stage, was a young German *Obersturmführer*, and beside him a rather fat civilian in a black suit, evidently also German, who from time to time tugged at a watch chain, hanging thick and garish as bunting across his globular vest, and pulled out an enormous watch, the covered face of which he snapped open with a loud click and then snapped shut again, barely looking at the time but reminding the men assembled before him of its passage by the impatient, repeated *click-click, click-click* of the cover. The *Obersturmführer* spoke politely enough to Sokolczyk [NOTE. EDITOR. A tall, elderly, bearded Jew.], who had been walking about with his air of being in charge; and Sokolczyk turned and said in his very loud voice, in Yiddish, as usual betraying his dignity by bawling like a sergeant:

—— Arrange yourselves into formations. Ranks of four. Regular councilors on my right, deputy councilors on my left. Hurry, hurry, we haven't much time!

Click, the huge watch said, and *click*, as if to emphasize these last words.

I saw Berson standing bewildered, as the men sorted themselves out and moved to one side or the other, so I walked by in front of him and said:

—— With me. You are a deputy councilor, more or less.

—— You honor me too much.

Berson said this bitterly, following me, nevertheless, and taking up a position just in front of me in one of the deputy councilors' rows. I was glad to see this sign of humor in him.

Berson turned his head as he heard (and I also heard) the man in the next row just to Berson's right muttering:

—— Everything military, these damned Germans: wooden soldiers: wooden heads.

The mumbler was Fischel Schpunt. [INSERT. FROM ENTRY AUGUST 7, 1939. N.L. Schpunt is our grotesque. He is a minor clerk. He is a very short man of about fifty, with a too-big head and a very sad face, with a short curly beard, a hanging mouth, a bulbous purple nose, a high bowl-shaped forehead, and ears sticking out like sails. He is tragically ugly, and seems to live tragically: he bows and scrapes and appears to be on the verge of tears. I have heard, however, that on two or three occasions he has allowed himself grand fits of temper.] Berson says that on hearing

Schpunt's low growl, he thought to himself that only a man so ugly
would have the stored-up resentments and hatred to utter such
rebellious thoughts, even *sotto voce;* Berson admits he has a certain respect for German thoroughness. Berson asked the ugly man:
—— What is the purpose of this meeting?

Schpunt, turning toward Berson and speaking now with a
quite different expression and attitude, courteous and even servile:
—— Excuse me. We never know the Germans' purpose. I am
only a worker in the Self-Help Department in this building. I
was asked to attend in place of an absent deputy councilor. I
wouldn't know the purpose. (Then, with a flicker of the lugubrious mockery of his earlier muttering:) I have not been consulted
. . . so far.

Click, the enormous watch said. *Click.*

Schpunt, to Berson, in a confidential tone: —— The official
suffers from elephantiasis of the timepiece. See how nervous he is
for those tremendous minutes to pass! [NOTE. N.L. My own
attention had been drawn to the watch, and I confess that I was
reminded, quite irrelevantly, of the Wonder Rabbi Elimelekh of
Lizhensk, who, while reciting the Prayer of Sanctification on the
Sabbath, used to take out his watch every few seconds and look at
it, because he was afraid that his soul would evaporate in bliss,
and so he kept looking at his watch in order, they say, *to steady
himself in Time and the world.* I was brought back from this
thought when I saw Schpunt turn his whole baleful face on Berson in a kind of reproach and heard him say:] Who are you?

Berson, half in apology, half in protest: —— I was only passing in the street. It is my fifth wedding anniversary.

Schpunt, disgustedly: —— Oi, misery, we all have excuses.

Click. Click. The black-suited civilian shouted in sudden,
high-pitched German that time was up. The *Obersturmführer*
spoke quietly again to the tall, bearded, supervisory Sokolczyk.
The latter bellowed in his parade-ground voice:
—— Attention! Will the Secretary please read the roster?

Felix stepped forward, as imperturbable as always, unfolded
a sheet of paper, and began to read:
—— Councilors: Chairman Sokolczyk.

The Chairman, loudly, in a tone as if to say, Of course, *he*
was here: —— Here!
—— Schein.

—— Here!

—— Benlevi.

—— Here!

[INSERT. FROM ENTRY NOVEMBER 10, 1939. FROM BERSON. Benlevi! Berson says he looked at the man who had answered the call: that proud, grey face! He wondered how he could have missed it. Benlevi, the distinguished jurist, winner of the Nobel Peace Prize back in the late 'twenties. Evidently that name had a certain magic for Berson. He tells me that he saw, suddenly, the lecture amphitheater at Bonn, and even smelled the linseed oil on the fastidious panels and heard the clanking of the inadequate steampipes in the frigid hall; and on the podium, Benlevi, his exhalations fogging on the cold morning air: *Justice as an abstract concept, my dear young men, is not nearly so appealing as concrete injustice. . . . The citizen's sense of personal dignity may either grow or wane, as he becomes enmeshed in court procedure. Yes, yes, either is possible.* A foolish style, Berson recognizes; but breathtaking content, he maintains. Berson says he has quoted Benlevi in a thousand arguments. Personally, I respect the old man somewhat less: I consider him rather pompous. Berson, at any rate, says he was deeply moved to find Benlevi answering this rollcall. Benlevi! Here! *The citizen's sense of personal dignity . . . !*]

The roster unfolded. Even now the black-encased German yanked at his oversized watch and: *click, click.* Now the deputy councilors were being called.

—— Breithorn.

—— Here!

—— Levinson.

Berson says that when I answered, he wondered whether I could be Noach Levinson, the historian, author of *The Diaspora* and *Customs.* I could be.

—— Schpunt.

The ugly man, in his servile aspect: —— Here, if you please.

—— Berson.

I saw the red go up Berson's neck. He tells me that his voice caught in his throat, as if his larynx independently resisted the idea of its proprietor's being caught up in . . . in whatever this was. He cleared his throat, and finally managed to answer. The response came out much too loud:

—— HERE!

24

The rollcall flowed on past us and soon ended.

Chairman Sokolczyk, proudly to the fresh-faced *Obersturm-führer*: —— All here, and in twenty minutes.

The *Obersturmführer*, in inoffensive, humdrum German: —— Very good. . . . I have an order to read. You will oblige me by listening carefully.

The officer held up some typewritten copy. One of Felix's clerks began making notes in shorthand as the German read:

—— *To the* Judenrat, W*arsaw. From* Höherer S.S. und Polizei-führer Ost. *Concerning precautions against epidemics of typhus, city of Warsaw: the setting up of a residence area for Jews and Jewesses. Beginning on the date specified below. . . .*

Berson says that he understood the words clearly enough as they came out, but that the general sense escaped him. Was this a tirade on lice? The young officer read, and mostly mispronounced, a number of street names: Zelazna, Wolnosc, Mlynarska, Dzika, Niska, Bonifraterska, Krasinski Place, Zamenhofa, Zelazna Brama, Wielka, Zlota. Boundaries of some sort. The reading seemed to Berson rather dull, he says: the heavy prose of all directives. He looked around. He says he wanted guidance on the meaning of this unexpected, weird session. Schpunt's face seemed vacant, if a visage so crowded with disfigurements could be that; he seemed barely to be listening. The Chairman's face was complacent, but Berson says he had a feeling that that was an expression it could not avoid. Berson glanced over at Benlevi's face, and says he was shocked by its change: it had become taut, hateful, somehow crafty. Berson decided he had better listen more carefully.

—— *And in token of delivery of these orders, as well as to assure their execution, the Deputy Councilors of the* Judenrat, W*arsaw, will be received in temporary custody at the Pawiak, as of today's date, their confinement to be terminated upon satisfactory execution of the above orders. In case the above orders are not carried out within the stated time, the said hostages will be shot. Signed, W*arsaw, November 4, 1939. B. Mondschrift, Colonel *S.S. and Major General of Police, W*arsaw District, Government *General, Poland.* (To Chairman Sokolczyk:) Is this all clear?

Sokolczyk, bowing his head in careful ambiguity, with a certain irony on behalf of his colleagues but also with definite respect for the German: —— Perfectly clear.

Berson says he thought: Clear? Who was that who might be shot? Somebody going to jail in the Pawiak? Not at all clear!

Sokolczyk: —— Not to question these orders, Herr *Obersturmführer*, but simply by way of checking up, might I ask for a statement from one of our deputy councilors, a medical man, Dr. Breithorn?

—— If you wish.

Click, said the enormous watch. *Click: don't take too much time.*

Sokolczyk, too smoothly: —— Dr. Breithorn, would you say that there is danger of typhus in the city?

Breithorn, sourly: —— Danger? There is always danger of typhus in a crowded area. More in summertime than now, however.

Sokolczyk: —— Especial danger among our people, Dr. Breithorn?

Breithorn, staring carefully at Sokolczyk: —— It depends upon the housing. In general, Jews and Poles are equally susceptible. Germans also sometimes come down with the disease. Sometimes.

The *Obersturmführer*, cheerfully: —— You have heard the orders, gentlemen. That will be all.

Sokolczyk, bending in his double-edged obeisance: —— Thank you.

The *Obersturmführer* nodded toward a door at the back of the hall. A squad of six *S.S.* soldiers, absurdly over-embattled under the circumstances, clanked and squeaked into the room and, at a nod from the officer, marched to the deputy councilors' ranks. They began herding us toward the door. Berson asked me:

—— Where are we going?

—— To the Pawiak, my brother deputy.

Berson, excusing himself profusely to one of the soldiers in German, broke away and pushed to Felix Mandeltort, the Secretary, with whom Berson apparently felt he had established, by telling him his name downstairs, some rapport; the soldier followed him closely.

Berson, shrilly: —— My presence here is accidental. My anniversary . . .

Mandeltort (gentle Felix!): —— I'm awfully sorry. We are involved in this all together.

Berson began to argue. The soldier drew him back to our group. He rushed then to me and cried:

—— But what is this about? This is not fair!

N.L., curtly, for by this time I was rather tired of small grievances: —— Calm yourself. Who gave you the idea that there is any question of fairness or not-fairness here?

EVENTS NOVEMBER 4, 1939. ENTRY NOVEMBER 9, 1939. N.L. We were in a cell intended for two prisoners, eight of us who had been brought from the Community Building. Berson, Schpunt, and Dr. Breithorn were in the same cell with me, as well as one bonafide deputy councilor and three others who, like Berson, had been grabbed off the street to stand for absent deputy councilors. One of these, a Rotblat Funeral man, had been making such a bitter and protracted howl (enough to raise the dead, Berson said) about being imprisoned on false identity that Berson and the other two Accidental Public Servants, as they had begun to call themselves, had turned against the howler and had thereby, in championing their predicament, become reconciled to it. Berson was still puzzled more than anything else, and he asked Dr. Breithorn, who was sitting on the floor, huddled against the outer wall of the building, hugging his knees to his chest:

—— Why all that talk about the danger of epidemics?

The doctor merely looked sour and shrugged his shoulders, holding the shrug for some time.

N.L., in my didactic tone: —— Everything is humane. If you find that three hundred thousand people constitute a threat to the public health, you quarantine them, naturally. This is to be a quarantine, you understand, not a ghetto. You heard the *Obersturmführer*. He said: *Seuchensperrgebiet*. Quarantine area.

I was standing at the end of the cell, leaning against the door. Berson was seated with Schpunt on a short bench attached to one wall. We talked on, mostly complaining. Schpunt was silent. After a while Berson turned to me and asked, with a directness that startled me:

—— What is the notebook you carry?

N.L., with a tight casualness that I cannot shake off when I speak of things close to me: —— Just a notebook. Some notes. I am a writer.

Berson: —— Then perhaps you are the Levinson who wrote *The Diaspora?*

N.L.: —— Guilty. Author of *The Diaspora* and a threat to the public health.

I cannot deny that I had taken pleasure from Berson's last question; in his next statement I felt a perverse impulse to erase my pleasure:

—— I didn't like the chapter on the Sephardim.

—— So? And why?

I believe Berson was somewhat surprised to see that, on my part, the pleasure remained; was increased, if anything.

—— It seems to me you pictured them in a sentimental way. I imagine the life of the Jews in Spain as having been just as hard as that of the Jews in Eastern Europe.

Dr. Breithorn, in a kind of whine: —— My God! What a time to discuss literature!

N.L.: —— I thank you for calling it literature. . . . I find any time at all delightful for a discussion of my work. Abstractly, though, what better time than this for a colloquy on the Sephardim and the Ashkenazim? Are you busy, doctor?

Dr. Breithorn sucked his lips and looked at his knees.

Schpunt, without defiance: —— What time do you think they will feed us?

One of the Accidental Public Servants: —— Better ask *what* they will feed us.

The A.P.S. laughed sharply. No one joined in the laughter.

Berson says this discussion of food made him think of the supper he would not be having with his wife, Symka. He knew she would have found something special for him on their anniversary: fish roe, a Camembert, or *lox*, perhaps, which he loves. And now he would not be able to give her the present he had, in any case, not bought! Having put off and put off the purchase of a present, he had worked out an elaborate excuse to get to the Old City this afternoon in order, among other errands, to pick up something. What would he have bought? A wooden present for the wooden wedding anniversary: some small carving, probably, of the kind that Symka likes, he says, one of those cynical little peasant figures from Ciechanów, or perhaps a brightly painted box for kindling (his wife had been asking for one). . . .

Berson, loudly, having suddenly realized for the first time

28

that his wife would have no way of knowing where he was: —— Is it possible to get a message out from this place?

Schpunt, meekly: —— I have heard that the Polish hall-guards welcome bribes and are honorable.

Dr. Breithorn, with what I took to be sarcasm, though perhaps I was too sensitive: —— Maybe Levinson could spare us a page from his history notebook.

I quickly opened my book and tore out a page. At this several of the men in the cell moved toward me. The Rotblat Funeral man who had been protesting so loudly reached me first and raucously began dictating his address.

N.L., waving the back of my hand toward the noisy appellant: —— You will come last.

Dr. Breithorn, rising to his feet with a weary groan: —— Obviously we can send only one message all together. Here, let me co-ordinate this.

I soon could see that Dr. Breithorn, in spite of his mordancy, in spite of the sneer that lives in the cave of his mouth and comes out to sun itself at the opening of the cave all day long, is nevertheless good at managing things. My only previous experience with the doctor had been that time when I suffered that infected hangnail, and then I had the impression that . . . [INSERT. FROM ENTRY SEPTEMBER 10, 1939. N.L. My finger having become much worse, I went to Dr. Breithorn, who has been assigned as the more or less official doctor of the Community Council. He received me with a bitterness that should not, it seems to me, be part of a doctor's equipment. He reproached me with developing a hangnail at the moment when Poland was having its guts clawed out by the German Army, as if I had planned this coincidence, as if I were somehow a malingerer, or a saboteur. I asked around about him afterward, and I learned that he graduated from the medical department of Warsaw University with the highest grades ever earned there, that he became a specialist in the epidemiology of typhus, that he has four times been refused grants for special equipment he had requested of the Polish government, that he was admitted to the Army in March of this year and discharged without explanation in August, exactly nine days before the invasion. I think he is the most disgusted man I have ever seen. Query: did his misfortunes result from his personality, or the other way around?]

The doctor announced that our message would be addressed to Felix Mandeltort, as Secretary of the *Judenrat*, and said that he would allow each man twenty words, address inclusive, to frame a message which the *Judenrat* would be asked to forward. The doctor sat on the bench and spread the paper on the plank beside him, nodded to one man after another, and wrote down what each dictated. When Berson's turn came, Berson deliberately spoke off what he wanted written, and at the end he concluded with a greeting:

—— Happy anniversary.

The doctor looked at Berson queerly, and Berson exclaimed:

—— No, no! Leave that off!

Breithorn, almost pityingly: —— I should hope so.

Berson: —— Write instead: Forgive me.

Breithorn, laughing concisely, apparently pleased with Berson's ineptitude: —— That's not much better.

Berson blushed and turned away. He has since told me that he then began to worry about how his wife would make him suffer for getting into this mess. He imagined her resignation, very feminine and justifiably martyred-looking; her careful, repeated questions about how he let himself be taken. I have told him that I would try to help him prepare a defense. He wondered why he had invented the excuse that his wife was sick, when I accosted him in front of the Community Building. And he remembered the words of the directive: *In case the above orders are not executed within the stated time, the said hostages* . . . He tried to imagine his wife struggling on alone, kissing the little wooden figure he had (not) bought her as an anniversary present, weeping for her dead Dolek. He was amusing and charming as he reported to me this little fantasy of his, which he says he savored until Dr. Breithorn, having finished taking the messages and having slumped down again to the floor at the end of the room, suddenly interrupted him by saying sharply:

—— Berson, go on about the Sephardim.

I could see Berson looking at the doctor's face, evidently searching out mockery; but there was nothing in the doctor's expression, so far as I could see, but tiredness and sourness. Then Berson said, in an attempt at counter-sarcasm, which, he showed by his renewed blush right after speaking, he himself realized was inadequate, flat, and humorless:

—— Perhaps you would like to lecture us on lice.

Breithorn, with a surprising show of sprightliness: —— The louse is a sluggard. (The doctor spoke quite literally in a lecturing tone, portentous and singsong.) Compared with the transient flea, who with his short legs can leap, it is said, seventy-five times his own height, the louse is a homebody who cares very little for change of scenery, so long as he gets plenty of blood to drink. Nevertheless, as we have seen this afternoon, the louse is in a sense a political figure. Perhaps the facts that he has a huge mouth and practically no eyes help him in this career. As he transmits the pathogenic agents of typhus, he . . .

The Rotblat Funeral man, who ever since dictating his message had been standing peering through the broken judas in the door of the cell, now interrupting loudly: —— When does that damned guard come? I have an appointment for an embalming on Karmelitzka Street tonight.

Schpunt, thrown suddenly into his defiant phase: —— Hold your tongue! Dr. Breithorn was just coming to the interesting part, about typhus.

Schpunt meant it. He was very angry and serious, but his ugly face was so contorted by his unexpected and exaggerated emotion that his expression was irresistibly comical, and all the men in the cell laughed hard.

EVENTS NOVEMBER 4, 1939. ENTRY DECEMBER 3, 1939. FROM SYMKA BERSON. The guests in the room were having a good laugh, Symka Berson says. Pavel Menkes, the baker, was putting on a side-splitting imitation of Dolek Berson, presumptively lost down in the area near the Vistula and trying to find his way back to Sienna Street. Thus the big baker was accounting for Berson's lateness. It was nearly eight o'clock. Symka Berson sat in the sofa with her head lying back, laughing till tears formed in her eyes. Dolek *is* absent-minded, she says, and the way Menkes caught Dolek's puzzled squint, when he is trying to remember what he is doing or where he is going, was perfect.

Menkes, imitating Berson, gravely addressing an imaginary policeman: —— Excuse me, is Sienna Street up this way? . . . What! That way! . . . No, I beg your pardon, I believe it is this way. I am almost sure. . . .

Yes, that was his manner, truly! Stopping to ask his way and

31

then arguing about the answer. Symka laughed harder than ever, and felt that she was getting a stitch under her heart.

In general, Symka recalls that she was feeling pleased with herself. The apartment looked exceptionally well. The Bersons have five rooms on the fifth, the top, floor of the second entry in the courtyard at Sienna 17: the least elaborate quarters in the courtyard, but more than adequate for the two of them, in a fine building, and in the best kind of neighborhood, for Sienna Street is the more or less aristocratic avenue here in the Jewish section. I gather that Berson had a certain amount of money from his father. The living room is spacious and has a high ceiling. The furniture, which belonged to Berson's parents, is of a slightly frayed and splintered Gothic elegance, heavy, decorated with inexplicable pendancies, bumps, and scallops, upholstered with tapestries that have achieved, over the years, an other-generation brownness: furniture that gives a comforting sense of continuity. Into this dun background, Symka had, during that day, introduced splashes of brilliant color: some autumnal branches from the venders of Zelazna Brama; a bright blue china pitcher, bought in the thieves' market; and lively green satin covers that she had made for the cushions on the sofa and easy chairs. Through the double doorway into the dining room could be seen the table, with a linen cloth, lighted candles, sparkling silver, and a whole inventory of foods: especially, at the center, a big platter of Dolek's favorite dish—pink *lox* [NOTE. EDITOR. Smoked salmon.], with olive oil, lemon, and even precious capers ready at hand. The guests, too, were just right: few and fond: they were hearty Pavel; Rabbi Goldflamm; Symka's friend Regina Orlewska, a diffident teacher at the big Jewish school on Okopowa Street; Lazar Slonim, a Socialist lawyer who attended Bonn with Dolek; and Meier Berson, Dolek's cousin. It would have been impossible to ask more: because of the curfew it would be necessary for all the guests, except Rabbi Goldflamm, who lived in the same courtyard, to spend the night.

Rabbi Goldflamm, as a sally of laughter at Menkes' impersonation died down: —— Seriously, I wonder where Dolek is. He really should be here by now.

Slonim, with a sharp contemptuousness of which he is capable: —— If Dolek could just organize and discipline himself, he could be of some real use these days.

32

Symka says she suffered; Slonim's implication, that Dolek was of no use as things stood, struck her more forcibly than the praise in what Slonim had said.

Menkes, still acting the part of Dolek, over-modest and gruff: —— No. I have too much to learn. I'm not worthy of public service.

Cousin Meier, glumly: —— He's just lazy.

Symka: —— I think you're all unkind to talk about Dolek behind his back. Wait till he's here to defend himself.

Regina Orlewska went to the piano—the beautiful concert Bechstein of which Berson is so proud—and uncovered the keyboard and played a simple mazurka, the kind of thing one remembers from discontinued childhood piano lessons. She played slowly and haltingly. By the time she had finished, Symka, thinking of Dolek's magnificent playing, and overflowing with annoyance and self-pity, had burst into tears.

Slonim: —— A fine celebration for her! Wouldn't you think that Berson could have made a little extra effort today?

Hearing this made Symka all the more miserable, and she says she cried harder.

Menkes, heartily: —— Nu, we could go ahead and eat. I wager a hundred zlotys that the sound of our chewing will bring Dolek in off the streets.

Symka, with what she hoped was an appealing bravery, suppressing some final sniffles: —— Yes, we should eat.

Menkes, rushing playfully into the dining room: —— Hoorah! Pigs form to the right, behind me! Horses to the left, behind the rabbi!

Cousin Meier, who had followed Menkes rather closely and chanced to be standing right behind him when he gave this command, was discomfited by it, and moved as unobtrusively as he could to the other end of the table.

Symka, already in full possession of herself, hurrying to the table: —— Only please don't take any lox until Dolek comes. That is for him. Anything else, eat your fill.

The abundant food cheered everyone up, and while the guests were eating, no mention of Dolek was even made, except once, when Pavel, repeating his joke, urged Symka to chew loudly so that Dolek would hear her jawbones calling. Menkes apparently more than adequately fulfilled his own admonition; it seems he is

33

a good loud eater. Symka was horrified to see the pile of treats, assembled and prepared at such cost and effort, so diminished in a few minutes. Cousin Meier sat alone in a corner, stoking himself as if his fires were very low. Regina ate primly. After all were finished, and even big Menkes was sated, the group conversed stiffly, with long pauses. Rabbi Goldflamm launched several long and authoritative stories about the situation in the city since the Germans had arrived. This passed the time. Once a loud slamming noise downstairs made Symka jump to her feet: she had mistaken it for the front door banging.

Rabbi Goldflamm, with a knowing nod, as Symka sat down: —— That's the Apts moving in. It is my guess that they have just dropped a beautiful nineteenth-century *troumeau* and have broken it into fifty pieces. I am sorry to have heard the noise.

At a few minutes past eleven, there was a knock on the door. Menkes, who had long since abandoned his buffoonery and had become serious and worried-looking, ran into the hallway and opened the door; Symka was close after him. A shabby, small man who stood outside asked:

—— Is this the Berson apartment?

Symka, pushing in front of Pavel: —— I am Pani Berson.

—— Message.

The man reached into his pocket, pulled out several envelopes, shuffled through them, and finally offered one.

—— From the *Judenrat*. . . . Used to be the *Kehilla*, you know. . . . On Grzybowska Street.

Symka snatched the envelope and ran back to the light of the living room. The poor messenger appeared to be full of information that he was eager to impart; he also appeared to have sniffed the food inside the apartment. Menkes tipped him, muttered some thanks, and closed the door abruptly on the hungry, frustrated face. Symka meanwhile had torn open the envelope and had discovered, on a full sheet of expensive bond paper, these words:

PANI BERSON, SIENNA 17. TAKEN BY BUREAUCRATIC ERROR TO PAWIAK WITH JUDENRAT DEPUTY COUNCILORS. RELEASE UNDOUBTEDLY TOMORROW. FORGIVE ME.

BERSON per MANDELTORT, SECY.

34

Directly she had finished reading, Symka started crying again. Menkes, who had been reading over her shoulder, took the note from her and handed it to Slonim. The others crowded round and read it together. Then everyone exclaimed and began a clamor. Regina, trying to soothe Symka, began to weep herself. Menkes, Slonim, and Rabbi Goldflamm began a heavy speculation as to what had happened, with the rabbi offering certain theories as actual fact. Then, seeing the girls collapsed, the men made strenuous efforts to quiet them. Slonim approached the problem intellectually, arguing loudly against the idea of crying. The rabbi ran off to get a wet towel. Nobody particularly noticed Cousin Meier as he quietly made his way into the dining room and helped himself to several slices of *lox*.

Symka, sobbing: —— At least, Dolek might have wished me a happy anniversary!

EVENTS NOVEMBER 5, 1939. ENTRY DECEMBER 3, 1939. FROM SYMKA BERSON. Early the next morning, Menkes took Symka Berson to the Community Building. At the receptionist's window in the front hall, Menkes asked to see Felix Mandeltort, the Secretary. The girl told him to wait in the room across the hall. There, on some benches, Menkes and Symka found quite a few restless supplicants and complainants of various kinds already waiting. The two friends sat down and waited a long time. Finally Menkes went out again to the window and asked the girl behind it when it might be possible to see Reb Felix Mandeltort. Symka says that in these requests, Menkes spoke politely and respectfully, with none of the bluster he used toward his friends. The girl, herself reflecting some of the pomp of high office, said that Secretary Mandeltort was still busy: please to wait in the room with the benches.

Menkes, humbly: —— We have come to ask him about Berson, one of those who were taken to the Pawiak with the deputy councilors yesterday.

The girl, coming down with a sudden change of attitude, as if she had been rebuked: —— Oi, I'm sorry. Just a minute.

And in just that minute Menkes and Symka were led into Mandeltort's office. [NOTE. N.L. Since one of the desks in it is mine, how well I know that office! I was pleased to hear Froi

35

Berson remark that she noticed that the Secretary's desk was in a slovenly condition, while the unoccupied desk was almost reproachfully neat. Would that my reproach could have some effect on my untidy friend!] As the two entered, Mandeltort rose and said genteelly, as if this were a surprise encounter rather than an announced call following an hour's wait:

—— Pani Berson! Charmed! I believe we are neighbors on Sienna Street.

Symka, who had felt nervous and tired on the bench in the waiting room with all the haggard people there, says that she blossomed under this official sunshine and even began to feel rather attractive. Felix can do that to people. Menkes introduced himself, and as Felix shook the hand that was offered him, he said hesitantly, as if the guess might turn out to be insulting:

—— Menkes? Of the . . . um . . . bakery?

—— Of the bakery.

—— I see.

Symka says that the Secretary's manner toward her now underwent a subtle change, in the direction of, but not quite reaching, condescension. He went into a long speech about the unfortunate affair of the previous day, and particularly about how hard it would be to manage the concentration of three hundred thousand people within one hundred city blocks: none of which, at the time, communicated anything at all to Symka or Menkes, who did not yet know about the ghetto orders.

Menkes, bluntly: —— When will Berson be released?

Mandeltort addressed his answer, which was evasive, to Froi Berson. He spoke of uncertainty. . . .

Menkes, the bullishness coming up in him: —— But as I understand it from what you say, Berson was taken in place of one of the regular deputy councilors. The man for whom he substituted should now be substituted for him.

Mandeltort, going the limit of condescension with the baker:

—— In these things, Menkes, we have learned to leave well enough alone. And now (standing up) I'm afraid I'm rather busy. I believe we have your address. We shall keep you informed.

I was embarrassed for my friend Felix as Froi Berson gave me this account. She felt resentment. With all his fine qualities, one must face Felix's snobbishness.

36

EVENTS NOVEMBER 4–9, 1939. ENTRY NOVEMBER 9, 1939.
N.L. Berson is certainly a talker. All of us in this cell owe him
our gratitude for having kept things going during these days,
which might have been very boring and mournful. He is musical,
and in the evenings especially his quiet songs have given us great
pleasure. His own humor is slow: he has to think quite a while
before he utters a witticism, and then it is liable to a definite
paleness. But he makes the most of others' wit, and with a cheerful guffaw has been able to turn even Breithorn's vehement com-
ments into jokes. He has made us all laugh at poor Schpunt a
good deal. On the other hand, there have been times when he has
sat for a whole hour at a stretch, staring and locked shut.

Though he is a ready talker, when he opens up, he has a
modesty which seems to me unhealthily overdeveloped, and I
have had to ask many questions to find out a few things about
him.

He was born, he tells me, thirty-two years ago, here in Warsaw. His father was religious and stern; a glove manufacturer;
moderately prosperous. Dolek was an only child. His parents sent
him to Heder and Tarbuth schools, but he also had a good secular education, at first from tutors and later in a Polish Gymnasium,
where, he now says, he learned a certain flexibility about his Jewishness: he sometimes defended himself in fistfights and sometimes passed off abuses as if they had not been offered. As a small
boy he was rather fat and was therefore the butt of both Jewish
and Polish teasing. He became, as a consequence, more skillful than
most of us in the use of the timely retort, the opportune lie, the
slow-absorbent insult, and the vituperative retreat. He also practiced
up on boxing, at his father's insistence; this he hated.

He showed a musical talent by the age of seven, when he began piano lessons. Possibly his playground tortures made him more
friendly with the piano than he would otherwise have been; at any
rate, he practiced three and four hours a day when he was only ten.
His diligence at the piano was not, however, altogether spontaneous. He says that when his mother discovered he had some talent,
she pushed him and pushed him and pushed him; she always used
to say she wanted people to know what a Jewish boy could do.

As he grew into young manhood, Berson rebelled more and
more against the religious atmosphere of his home, and so began
to run away, like so many of our generation, from his Jewishness.

37

This was when he went to Bonn to study. While there, thanks partly to his ability in music, he was pretty well assimilated and was accepted by his University acquaintances as a Pole. His mother died while he was out of the country.

After his return from Germany, Berson worked for four years in his father's glove factory, and disliked it: working down from the top, he says. This career was ended by his father's death and the sale of the plant. Berson then tried a number of kinds of work: as a newspaper reporter, a clerk in a millinery store, a messenger for a law firm (he studied at night, thinking he might eventually pass his examinations), and even from time to time in artisan trades, as an apprentice locksmith, as a cartwright, and in a bookbinding plant. All these changes of job account for his wide range of acquaintance, some of it apparently inconsistent with his background and education: his friendship with the baker, for instance. For one black period soon after his father's death—I could not discover the reason for this; there is some mystery—he joined the *Lumpenproletariat*, the world of tramps, moving with them from town to town, eating at charity kitchens, sleeping in fifty-groszy dormitories, begging, stealing, and loafing. Certainly it was not poverty that drove him to this adventure, as he enjoyed a fair patrimony; curiosity, perhaps. Curiosity has in fact grown unusually stout in him. He is one of those people who think they are always learning: *That was good experience*, he says of one job, or, *I feel that that was part of my education*. He has taken up many kinds of out-of-the-way study, such as bookkeeping, electrical mechanics, astronomy, and so on. He remembers surprisingly much of these various bits of nonsense, if one can judge from random conversation in a prison cell.

He married, five years ago, a girl who is frail and delicate, it seems, often sick and usually helpless. Childless.

Berson evidently reads a lot, though there are shocking gaps in his reading. No Goethe. No Gogol. No Peretz. He has read my books. He has read them carefully. (I would not be myself if I did not admit that this may be most of my reason for liking him.) In a long talk one afternoon he discussed what I had to say about the Bar Mitzvah ceremony in *Customs*: a really remarkable memory for details, but here and there he had missed the larger points altogether.

His judgment of people is spotty. Although he seems to be

quickly offended—Breithorn has got under his skin two or three times here in the cell—he seems very trusting and generous, and he hates to believe badly of anyone. Of old Benlevi, for instance, he is extravagantly admiring. He refuses to understand that this once-fine man has been victimized by his fame, to the point where he is now a name, an actor, and even a fraud. I acknowledge here an excessive severity on my own part. I seem increasingly to dislike everyone. Hence my surprise at feeling well-disposed toward Berson. . . .

EVENTS NOVEMBER 5–8, 1939. ENTRY DECEMBER 3, 1939. FROM SYMKA BERSON. During the following days all sorts of reports ran around. The correct version of what had taken place could be heard, and so could many variants, more and less sensational than the facts. The exaggerated stories tended to excite their hearers, the understated ones to make theirs complacent. Rabbi Goldflamm purveyed quite a few of both types to Symka, who decided, finally, to rely on the version she heard from Lazar Slonim; and that, luckily, was almost the true one.

Pavel Menkes was kind: he took much time away from the bakery to go with Symka on various errands, all of them futile—to the Judenrat, several times, to the Pawiak, where they were not able to do anything but stare miserably at the prison from across the street, hoping for an impossible glimpse of Dolek, to the apartment of Sokolczyk, our Chairman, from which they were turned away, and even, once, to the Polish police precinct on Niska Street, which had no jurisdiction over these Jewish affairs.

On the strength of Mandeltort's promise that if anything happened, Symka would be notified at home, a constant watch was kept at the apartment; whenever Symka was out, Regina, if she was free from her duties at the Okopowa school, or Rabbi Goldflamm, if he was not busy studying or visiting, would sit and wait. On the third day a short, impersonal message came from Mandeltort, simply saying that all the prisoners were safe and well.

In the Jewish section of town, meanwhile, public resentment and anxiety were growing. It was rumored that the Judenrat, after several sessions of debate, had just about decided to accede to the German orders. On the fourth day word got around that there would be a mass meeting the next morning in front of the Community Building. Slonim offered to take Symka. Early they went to Grzybowska Street, and, with the help of a *Judenrat* employee whom Slonim knew, they were able to get a place to stand right near the steps of the Community Building, from which the speeches were to be made. Slonim, after a knowing surveyal, told Symka that this might be a lively meeting, as he recognized in the crowd several leaders of Hechalutz, Hashomer Hatsair, and other Zionist organizations, as well as several old Socialists: the *Judenrat* would get a roasting and the Zionists and Socialists would doubtless be at each other's throats. Slonim was cynical:

—— Only the Germans will go untouched today. You'll see.

He was right. The first speech was by Henryk Rapaport, the famous Socialist leader, a handsome, grey-haired man with a fine, resonant voice, who called for a fight against the ghetto idea, for mass solidarity, for a people's solution, and if necessary for a general strike in Warsaw, of Polish and Jewish workers alike. Slonim pointed out that Rapaport did not say whether he had the assurance of Polish unions that they would participate in such a strike; but he spoke with fire and noise and roused the crowd. The next big speech was by Hil Zilberzweig, the leader of Hashomer Hatsair, the left-Zionist youth group, a sober, middle-aged leader of boys, with black hair slicked back over his round head; calm as a stone. He urged resistance but he also urged care. He spoke about hoarding anger for tests to come. Symka says she wondered: What tests? Part of the crowd grew angry at Zilberzweig's advice, and shouted against him, but he went on stolidly. Symka's heart pounded when he said:

—— The authorities have warned that the hostages in the Pawiak will be shot if this order is not carried out. We should know that the authorities are capable of meaning what they say.

After Zilberzweig, several other speakers jumped up, and they argued with each other like hard-faced enemies; but Symka felt that the speeches were full of clichés and false emotion. During a lull, Slonim, who is himself a Socialist, said that he would try to collar Rapaport, the Socialist speaker, after the meeting, and see if he could do anything about Dolek. The old man was influential, Slonim said.

—— The world is organized on a basis of personal friendships. Even the Socialist world. I dabbled in theory when I was at the University, but since then I have learned that friendship is everything.

40

Slonim spoke as if Socialism had been on the curriculum at the University, like chemistry and trigonometry, to be studied cavalierly in those student days, for the sake of a passing mark. But Symka says she never can tell whether Slonim means what he is saying. At any rate, when the meeting exhausted itself inconclusively in a smattering of intra-Jewish tempers, resulting in a few fistfights, Slonim made his way to the old Socialist. Symka saw in Rapaport's eyes a pleasant warmth and friendliness.

Rapaport: —— Wasn't it splendid? I think they are with us!

With a sweep of his arm the old man indicated the listless and apathetic crowd, draining off now into side streets.

Slonim asked directly for help in getting Berson released. Rapaport shrugged and said:

—— One man. . . . (Then, with a shrewd look at Slonim:) If we resist. . . . (Then, his face suddenly sympathetic again:) I'll do whatever I can. . . .

As it turned out, of course, there was nothing he needed to do.

EVENTS NOVEMBER 9–10, 1939. ENTRY NOVEMBER 17, 1939. N.L. The Germans called off their threat of a ghetto as unexpectedly as they imposed it. Very confusing.

On the evening of November 8, the *Judenrat* met and debated, yet again, the question whether they should submit to the German decree. I understand that old Rapaport made a moving appeal to his colleagues and then threatened to resign from the *Judenrat* if they complied. He made this threat with full knowledge of the consequences to himself, in case he should actually resign. [NOTE. N.L. Since the *Judenrat* is an instrument of the Germans, they could not be expected to deal leniently with a councilor who resigned in a protest.] The *Judenrat* then decided to appeal to the German military.

A delegation of four went next morning to Major General Prünn, the *Wehrmacht* commandant for the Warsaw District, and put before him some of the difficulties in the way of carrying out the ghetto orders. The designated area was already badly congested: how introduce 160,000 additional Jews and their belongings to such slums? What about all the Jewish institutions, such as the hospital, the cemetery, the biggest synagogue, and so on, that were left outside the decreed area? What about disruptions in the economic life of Warsaw? Old Rapaport said:

41

—— A city is a living body. How can you sustain the body if one fifth of it, at its very entrails, is suddenly tied off, without circulation or sensation?

At first General Prünn seemed surprised, later he seemed very angry. He burst out at last and said that he had not been consulted by the Gestapo on this huge plan, that he was in command in Warsaw, that we would see who was in command . . . the definition of his command had been in all the papers . . . we would see . . . preposterous. . . .

General Prünn did not look like a military man, the delegates say. They say he was more like a professor.

The general sent the *Judenrat* delegates in to his adjutant to dictate all the details in connection with the ghetto plan. Fifteen minutes later he called them back into his office and, with a nervous German civilian at his side, he told the Jews to do nothing—except on orders from him.

And with that the matter was dropped. And yet, *has* it really been dropped?

EVENTS NOVEMBER 11, 1939. ENTRY NOVEMBER 18, 1939. FROM SYMKA BERSON. At noon on the eleventh, Symka Berson received a message from Mandeltort saying that the deputy councilors would be released from the Pawiak at five o'clock that afternoon. She and Menkes went to the prison and stood in the crowd that was gathered there in the street. A cheer was heard when the heavy door opened and the first figures emerged. Symka stretched for a sight of her husband: she wanted and dreaded the sight: she expected that he would be haggard, whiskery, and filthy. Then she saw him! He was clean-shaven, his hair was neatly combed, and he was chuckling at something *a dried-up little man* beside him was saying. [NOTE. N.L. *Her phrase*, uttered, with a sweet smile, to my face.] She ran up to him, threw her arms around him, and cried out tragically:

—— Oh, Dolek, Dolek! Are you all right?

Berson, grinning: —— We've had a grand time.

2

Events November, 1939. Entry November 24, 1939.
N.L.   I am drawn to Rachel Apt. To begin with, she is ugly; right
there I find a community of interest. I am wrong to say she is ugly;
her face is not pretty—in other respects I judge her handsome.
More: somehow she reminds me of my mother, less in looks or
manner than in the way she makes me feel when I talk with her.
Not that she is aggressively maternal; no, it is just a matter of
comfortableness.

I met her through the Bersons. Since our days in jail, I have
seen quite a bit of Berson and his wife. It is odd: I have been
largely friendless through all the easy years, but now that trouble
has come, I have begun to discover companions. Felix is warmer,
now. Perhaps I should be ashamed to write this: I am rather happy.

Rachel Apt says she dislikes Berson, yet she spends a lot of
time in the Bersons' apartment. She has been there every time I
have dropped in during the past few days, and I have had several
long talks with her; we are already on a confidential basis, since
homely people find straight paths to each other's hearts. With Rachel's sister Halinka, who is very, very pretty, I have scarcely passed
two words, though she is frequently at the Bersons', too. Of course
this pretty Halinka will not look at me. She has a feather in her cap
for Berson, even though he has a perfectly good wife. She is a flirt;
she annoys me. Bibble-bibble-bibble: she talks as I imagine a little
white rabbit would talk. But Rachel, now, she comes out slowly
with what she thinks and feels.

Events November 5, 1939. Entry November 26, 1939.
From Rachel Apt.   Rachel Apt told me of the following incident, which took place the day after she and her family moved into
the apartment under the Bersons' (also the day after Berson and
I and the others were thrown into the Pawiak):

Rachel and her sister had a bitter argument over the hanging
of a mirror.

Such a spat is easy to imagine: I can see the two girls standing
in the middle of a disheveled room, they themselves *looking* as opposite as two sides of an argument.

Rachel Apt has the face of a parrot, with eyes close together, a huge chopper of a nose, and lips and chin running hastily back as if in fear of that nose; yet the sum of her face is not equal to the absurdity of its parts: her face has a certain fire and expressiveness, and one can guess that as temper kneaded it about during that argument, it must have made her look intense and warmhearted. Her body is as beautiful as her face is not. Her bosom is ample but not so ample as to need mechanical assistance in maintaining a proper pride; her waist is like her chin, almost nowhere to be found; her hips curve out but know moderation and retire just in time; and her legs (if I am any judge) are splendid. Her voice seems to have its home down in that soft breast; even in the stridence of a fight, I imagine it kept its ease.

Halinka, younger by a year, is more beautiful by a deal. Her face is broader; its cheekbones push out to break its oval pleasingly, her eyes are widely spaced and helpless, her nose is neat, sharp, tiny, and tightplaned, and her lips are so innocent-looking that one imagines they must have curled in horror at the words which rushed past them during the argument. Her hair falls to her shoulders. The grace of Halinka is all spent on her summit. Her body is angular, straight, and barely adequate as a pillar for that elegant head. Her voice lives in her sinuses, and is as small, defiant, and girlish as her nose.

Rachel: —— It should go on this wall, I tell you! This wall needs it.

Halinka: —— Stupid! A mirror ought to be on the wall where the windows are, so that when you look into it, the light is on your face. . . . But then, you wouldn't know about that!

Rachel: —— I'll kill you!

But as Rachel moved toward Halinka with a clear intention of carrying out her threat, she exploded into tears and stopped, with her hands over her face, sobbing.

From the next room there came a crashing sound, a door burst open, and the girls' older brother, Mordecai, stood at the edge of the room in a fury. [NOTE. N.L. He is a handsome man in his early twenties, showily dressed most of the time, and with his hair usually running every which way, evidently from having been combed and cross-combed by nervous fingers.]

Mordecai: —— Will you two shrews stop your screaming? . . . You know I'm trying to write!

44

Halinka, as if by belittling her brother she could seem the cooler of the two sisters, and thus stand at the top of the shabby heap: —— *Trying* is good!

Mordecai, howling: —— Damn you two!

Mordecai disappeared, slamming the door behind him.

This display of tempers, Rachel now says, was partly a result of the moving, which had upset all the habits of their lives, and of being unsettled in the new apartment, with no rugs yet on the pounding floors and no draperies yet on the echoing walls, torn packing-paper strewn about, books in piles, plates in stacks, silver in bundles, and her father's precious paintings lying crated everywhere; but partly, Rachel also thinks, the turbulent emotions on the part of the children reflected the state of mind of their father. Rachel says she pitied her father for the way he took this move. She also despised him for it. She tells me he said it would ruin his business; he said he had spent years getting himself wholeheartedly and unqualifiedly accepted by Poles and Jews alike, not only as merchant, but as guest, conversationalist, connoisseur of paintings ——yes, and as friend. And now, a *suggestion* from a man who was close to the Gestapo: an empty apartment on Sienna Street: the Apt home urgently needed for officers of the *General-Gouvernement*. A large profit, naturally. But certain ruin, she keeps saying that her father kept saying. To move into the Jewish section, to be clearly labeled, every time a letter would be addressed or a phone call made or an invitation dispatched by messenger! Certain ruin. Rachel says she knows she has contempt for these things her father said. What she admits to me, what she can barely tolerate—and why she thinks the tempers were connected with their father's viewpoint—is the suspicion that she and Mordecai and Halinka secretly, somewhere deeply away but not quite hidden, also *hold* the viewpoint they consciously despise. Rachel says that for herself this is a curiously special paradox: she has Semitism molded into her face, there has never been any duplicity for her. But she confesses, with what seems to be an almost unbearable honesty, that she had been proud of the extent to which her father had been assimilated, had been fiercely proud (in the very moments of fiercest jealousy) of Halinka's having gone out with young Poles, had been proud to hear Mordecai's excited accounts of literary discussions with young Polish writers in the beer houses on Teatralny Place. Only she and the younger brother, David, the seven-year-old, are imprisoned in

45

their so obvious Jewishness. Perhaps that is why she feels so tenderly toward David. She has really been her brother's mother since their own died six years back. Rachel says that in her mind she can articulate a love for her father: she can verbalize about it: she can tell herself why she loves him, and how much. But it seems that around her heart the wordless warmth and pain is all for David, her baby brother. She says that at the time roundabout the argument she worried about him, perplexed as he too must have been by the family's move. David is a scholar in the Jewish school in Okopowa Street (he is *too* Semitic-looking to be sacrificed to the childhood nightmare-life of the Polish elementary schools); he had had some standing among his schoolmates as the son of the famous jeweler and art collector, Pan Mauritzi Apt; but now he was dumped down in the Jewish section like all the rest. Rachel says she made up her mind to have a talk with him.

EVENTS NOVEMBER 27, 1939. ENTRY DITTO. N.L. I took occasion to visit the Apts' apartment today. Ostentatious. Incidentally, the mirror hangs on the outer wall, between the windows, so that when one gazes into it, the light from the windows . . .

EVENTS NOVEMBER 5, 1939. ENTRY NOVEMBER 26, 1939. FROM RACHEL APT. From Rachel I understand that Pan Apt is small, round, handsome, and as agitated as a polka. I have not met him yet. The only clear thing that can be said about Rachel's attitude toward her father is this: it is strongly felt, whatever it is. Rachel holds her father in contempt for some things, as I have already noted herein. [ENTRY NOVEMBER 26, 1939.] At the same time, because her mother is dead, she seems to wish to adore him and to stand in her mother's stead with him; but her father prefers Halinka. This rubs badly.

Rachel tells me a story about her father's reaction to the ghetto threat:

It was nearly dinner time, on the evening of November 5, before Pan Apt came home. He almost broke down the door, like a man pursued, and he trotted halfway through the littered living room before he stopped. He stood panting, surrounded by his four children, who had been sitting in sheet-covered chairs waiting for him, and who now stared at him in a hostile way, since they did not know the bad news of which he was full.

46

Pan Apt: —— Have you heard what they are doing?

Mordecai: —— Which *they* is it this time, Father?

Pan Apt: —— They are throwing all the Jews into a ghetto.

Rachel says that Mordecai has the manner of a clever son—extremely alert for the slightest signs of senility in his parent, and grimly patient about those signs once discovered.

Mordecai: —— Wait a minute, Father. Wait a *minute!* All Jews? Our cousin Albert in New York, too?

Pan Apt: —— I saw Felix Mandeltort. He told me all about it. The thing happened at the Community Building yesterday. They have put some of the Jewish Council people in prison already.

Pan Apt still stood at the center of the room, with his arms hanging stiffly by his sides.

Mordecai: —— Would you please start at the beginning, Father?

By the time the family had eaten and after-dinner *ersatz* coffee had been served, Mandeltort's account had come out whole. There had also emerged Pan Apt's plan, already developed in some detail in his mind, for bribing his way back out of the Jewish section and, if necessary, all the way to Lodz, where he had once had a branch of his business and where he still had numerous friends. Pan Apt seemed to be feeling much better.

Pan Apt: —— I thank God that I've put aside some money in my lifetime. Anyone with enough money can do anything he wants, anything. Mordecai, I wish you'd give up this foolish idea of trying to be a writer. It can only lead to poverty and trouble with women. And you, Halinka, wanting to be a singer: drop that, my dear, and find a husband of some substance. And you, poor Rachel . . .

Rachel says that her father abandoned his line of thought, quite at a loss.

EVENTS NOVEMBER 7, 1939. ENTRY NOVEMBER 27, 1939. FROM RACHEL APT. A further anecdote about Mauritzi Apt from Rachel—with a further revelation of her feelings toward him: her account of her father's progress on his plan:

It seems that Pan Apt was on top of the world.

—— I told you that money would do whatever one wanted it to do. Today my money whispered into Herr Gruber's ear and made Herr Gruber smile and say, *Yes!*

47

[Note. N.L. Herr Gruber is the German trustee, as he is
called, assigned to Mauritzi Apt's jewelry business. I understand
that at first the arrival of this Gruber in the beautiful store on
Miodowa Street threw Pan Apt into a three-day terror. But Gruber
proved to be a soft-voiced, kindhearted, tractable man who did not
know the difference between a garnet and a sapphire, and who kept
assuring Pan Apt that his only function, now and forever in the future, would be as a kind of auditor-protector, as much to guard
Pan Apt against drunken German soldiers as to "review" the
ledger.]

—— After listening to my coins, Herr Gruber said we could
move to the Aryan section of town, or to Zoliborz, or to Lodz, or
to *Berlin*, if we wanted. . . . Herr Gruber is an ironical man.

Mordecai: —— How much did this promise cost, Father?

Pan Apt: —— I never accept promises except as gifts, son. It
would be too sordid to elicit a promise by bribery—and too risky,
Mordecai! Let us say, Herr Gruber and I entered into a sort of contract: in return for certain services there will be a stipulated payment, *when the services have been rendered.* Nothing irregular
about that.

Rachel says she thought: Father is merry, but how much of
the gaiety is simply out on the showcase for us children to see, like
the flashy, tasteless bracelets for which he has such contempt but
which he puts in the center-front counter at the store? Rachel
thought she knew her father well enough to understand that these
accounts of bribery so glib on his tongue must actually sting the
roof of his mouth. He had always boasted that he had never carried
on the immensely profitable side-traffic in uncut stones that every
other jeweler in the city accepted as a matter of course. Rachel says
she had detected cowardice in her father, but no sign of corruption
had she ever seen. He was doing these things, or talking about
them, out of sentimentality, she knew: they were little gifts for the
children.

Mordecai: —— Can Herr Gruber fix me up with a job in the
General-Gouvernement when it comes time for me to register for
forced labor?

Pan Apt: —— We can certainly try him, and we will.

Rachel, disgustedly: —— God, Father! Mordecai was being
sarcastic!

Pan Apt, turning to Mordecai with a questioning look: ——

48

We *must* make arrangements. You are a writer, not a . . . not a hodcarrier!

Mordecai, gloatingly, as if it were a rare pleasure to have caught his father in an inconsistency: —— I thought you didn't want me to be a writer.

Pan Apt, with a sudden and unexpected softness: —— I want you to be whatever you want to be.

Halinka: —— Perhaps Mordecai would be a better writer if he *had* been a hodcarrier for a while.

Rachel says that as Mordecai turned angrily to shout something at Halinka, Rachel herself looked at her father. His eyes were veiled. She said to me, in concluding her story:

—— How sorry I was for Father!

EVENTS NOVEMBER 8 or 9, 1939. ENTRY NOVEMBER 28, 1939. FROM RACHEL APT. Rachel tells me that she worried about how her young brother, David, had taken the move, the ghetto rumors, and their father's new extravagant plans. And when the boy seemed to go along, boyishly, not specially impressed by any of it, and certainly not visibly upset, she became even more worried for him. She was convinced that he must be hiding his feelings. Rachel felt so much that it never occurred to her that David might feel almost nothing.

One day after school, with Mordecai out, Pan Apt not yet back from the store, and Halinka practicing singing in her room, Rachel spoke to her little brother.

Rachel: —— David, do you know why we moved from our house to this apartment?

David: —— They needed a house for a wienerwurst to live in.

Rachel: —— David! Has anyone said anything about it to you at school?

David, looking at the ceiling in a bored but respectful attitude, as if he were being questioned by a teacher: —— No. . . . Oh, yes! 'Hammer' Sliwniak said we were lucky to get into Sienna Street. When his family was pushed into the Jewish section, the best they could do was Chlodna Street.

Rachel: —— Do you know why we've been moved here, and the Sliwniaks and other families from the city?

Rachel says that at this crucial stage in the conversation Halinka's voice ran up and down a coloratura arpeggio in the near-by room. [NOTE. N.L. I have heard Halinka take one of these frightful vocal excursions. It sounds like the voice of a woman with a mouse running up her leg. Halinka has a very sweet voice, really, for little songs; but she should be careful about operatic temptations.]

Rachel, firmly and earnestly: —— Do you know, David?

David, evidently brought to a state of seriousness by what he had heard: —— Of course. The Nazis don't like the Jews. Anybody knows that.

In all the times she had anticipated this conversation, Rachel had never imagined that David would talk like an adult, or have faced even general truths. Suddenly, she tells me, she had a feeling that David might be able to take care of himself better than she could take of herself.

Rachel, veering off angrily: —— Dovidl! How many times have I asked you to tuck your sweater into your trousers-top? Go and wash your face! You're filthy! You look like a *schnorrer!*

Rachel began to cry. David got up from the chair in which he had been sitting and walked to her. Putting his hand on her shoulder, and making the effort of a serious boy to comprehend an adult, he said:

—— What's the matter, sister? What's the matter with you, anyhow?

EVENTS NOVEMBER, 1939. ENTRY NOVEMBER 28, 1939. N.L. The main impression I have of Rachel Apt is one of *attentiveness.* She sits quietly listening; she is alert, and she has a way of cocking her head to one side, like a puppy hearing new sounds.

I imagine that she *is* hearing new sounds. This must be her first experience of Jewish community life. Heretofore she has lived in a kind of isolation in a Polish world; behind the wall of her looks. Now she is, comparatively speaking, out in the open.

She listens to me as if I were the wisest man in the world. Can I rebuke her for that? Can I dislike it?

Because of her father's way of life, Rachel has never learned much about inner Jewishness, about Jewish traditions and aspirations, about our religion, except insofar as Pan Apt has unconsciously transmitted these things. Rachel has never participated in any sort of Jewish community activities, nor in any Zionist organizations. She is *tabula rasa*, a clear slate upon which I feel that the writing must now be succinct and careful. For she is strangely mature; she is overripe for learning. She seems to me amazingly well balanced for one in such a difficult position. In her family she has been given all of the duties, but none of the prerogatives or authority, of motherhood; she has the handicap of her face; she has this turbulent state of mind about her father. Yet she is calm, stately, and (as I have written before) comfortable.

She has a picturesque turn of mind, which may not be odd in a girl to whom romantic experiences have been inaccessible. She uses florid images quite often in her speech. One day she said of her own looks, which she can afford to discuss openly and even lightly with a *sharp little fellow* like me:

—— There has been so much handsomeness on both sides of my family! But the genes played a trick on me, Noach. When I was conceived, the handsome dominants bowed and curtsied and backed away, and the homely little recessives rushed in and danced a figure together: my face!

EVENTS NOVEMBER 11 ET SEQ., 1939. ENTRY NOVEMBER 28, 1939. FROM RACHEL APT. News that the ghetto idea had been indefinitely postponed was received in the Apt family as an anticlimax—almost as a disappointment. The family had all been so keyed up, without realizing it, that their sudden release from confinement-to-be left them somehow aimless, waiting for nothing, and feeling the want of anxiety. Pan Apt seemed almost to have been looking forward to the degradation of bribing Herr Gruber and to the risks and dislocations of moving, perhaps to Lodz; and now all those challenging possibilities had been mown away. Pan Apt became irritable. On some instinct, connected with her father rather than with events in general, Rachel had gone right ahead with the settlement of the Sienna Street apartment. But she, too, felt let down. And she found, as she talked with her new acquaintances—with Rabbi Goldflamm, with Symka Berson, with Symka's friend Regina Orlewska, who teaches in David's school (but an older class), and even with Kucharski, the Polish janitor—that the sense of anticlimax was widely felt in the Jewish section. The Jews still knew that something tremendous was coming; it was inevitable; it was inherent in these times. Yet they had become so tense in expectation of being put in a ghetto that now, with the threat removed, they could not help feeling confused and empty.

51

One odd effect of this episode that Rachel tells me she noticed, so far as she personally was concerned, was that for a few days she took long, idle walks and streetcar rides outside the Jewish section—along the Vistula, to Saxon Garden, to Pototzki Palace, past the Bristol and the Europejski Hotels, even to the suburbs, Praga and Zoliborz and Brudno. It was as if she were trying to memorize the Polish parts of her city, the Polish parts of her life.

3

EVENTS DECEMBER, 1939. ENTRY DECEMBER 11, 1939. N.L. I see fighting ahead. And of the bitterest sort: Jew against Jew. Why is it that whenever men are in danger and have a clearcut, dreadful adversary, they turn on each other in hatred? Thus they defer preparations to meet the enemy, and they meet him, when they do, divided and inwardly rancorous.

The Communists have turned up: that is what started me on this. Eugeniusz Tauber called me down to the labor-registration line the other day to point out Kurtz, Budko, and Hartmann, reunited for the first time since 1936. [NOTE. N.L. Incidentally, what an affectation for the elegant Tauber to come and stand in that line! Just like him. All he needed to do was to send a messenger to buy him an exemption. But no: he must make his pompous little protest; stand in line and wait. I never have trusted Tauber. Sometimes I am tempted to think he works for the Gestapo. And yet he comes and spills bits of his intelligence —which is always accurate—to us at the *Judenrat*. Cannot make him out.] Anyhow, we got interested in the Kurtz-Budko-Hartmann reunion and decided to look into it. . . .

EVENTS DECEMBER 4, 1939. ENTRY DECEMBER 12, 1939. FROM MORDECAI APT. I have the external circumstances of the Communists' reunion from young Apt, Rachel's brother:

It snowed the day Mordecai Apt registered for forced labor. A slow, fine, early-December snow, that might go on for two or three days. The line of men waiting to sign up debouched from the Community Building onto Grzybowska Street and stretched twenty or thirty meters along the street in a westerly direction. Mostly the men in the line were working people, poorly dressed, and in air, melancholy. All of them wore the newly obligatory armbands, bearing the Star of David. Mordecai stood at first at the end of the line, stamping on the packed snow, blowing into his hands from time to time. He says he had left his gloves at home.

[NOTE. N.L. As Mordecai told me this, I glanced at his hands. They are pink and clear-skinned. His fingernails are neatly trimmed. This suggests that the tousled effect he maintains with his hair, which I have already described herein, ENTRY NOVEMBER 26, is an affectation of casualness. Indeed, taking his whole appearance, one sees that he is trying to establish a careless, dandy impression. Not enough that his clothes should have been well made from costly materials: he favors the lively colors. So far as I can discover, his writing has never amounted to anything, and will never. His verse is as clever, as affected, and as immature as his appearance. I don't think much has happened to the boy. His education was entirely Polish and of course secular; if anything, slightly Catholic. Rachel tells me he worries about his health and during these winter months is only content when he has a light case of the sniffles: then he can feel grandly sorry for himself. Has a temper. I have observed his harassment of his father. Rachel says he is sometimes capable of a very nice playful mood. Politically I gather he is, you might say, anaesthetized—and so in a way he was a good one to witness this scene.]

The man ahead of Mordecai in line wore a leather jacket over heavy, corduroy trousers, and he had on a fur-lined cap with the earflaps turned loosely down. The man's skin was wrinkled and weathered, and he coughed in occasional rapid spurts, shooting out little puffs of steam, like a starting locomotive with skidding wheels. This man turned to Mordecai after they had been waiting awhile and said:

—— We bring up the rear.

Mordecai nodded. The man had a benign face, curiously pale for one that had obviously been outdoors a lot: he was evidently a workman of some kind. He spoke again, with an open curiosity, probably roused by Mordecai's getup:

—— What sort of labor will you do?

—— Whatever is needed, I suppose.

—— It is best to have something specific in mind.

53

A short, fat man in a Chesterfield coat and a black caracul hat came up behind Mordecai. His necktie was elegant, he wore grey kid gloves, and his feet were in beautiful German overshoes. Even Mordecai wondered what kind of labor *he* would do. The man nodded to Mordecai politely, surveyed the man in the leather jacket, and, evidently having decided not to greet the latter, asked Mordecai:

— Is the line moving at all?

It is possible to imagine that Mordecai would be gratified by this social differentiation and that he would smile elegantly as he replied:

— Only slowly, I'm afraid.

— Standing in line is the worst feature of a military defeat.

Mordecai says the fat man spoke this as if he had suffered in the forefront of the defense of Warsaw and was now paying the price of his valor. He looked at his watch and frowned. The man in the leather jacket turned away and Mordecai found himself in conversation with the gentleman behind him. More and more men came to stand at the end of the line. Before long the well-dressed man had announced to Mordecai his name—Eugeniusz Tauber—and when Mordecai had told him, in response to a question, that he was a writer, Pan Tauber plunged directly into a discussion of rare books: of old quartos and folios, and of the best oil to preserve leather bindings, and of the pros and cons on boxing books. They were standing in the forlorn, whitened street in the falling snow waiting to sign up for forced labor and the fat man was talking about a splendid mint copy of *The Possessed* which he said he owned—when two men, walking down the line toward the end, came alongside the man in the leather jacket.

— Budko! Hartmann!

The man in the leather jacket shouted these names. The one addressed as Budko, a huge man with long mustaches, bundled in a quilted canvas coat on which were accidental dabs and splotches of many colors of paint, turned at the shout and in a moment threw his arms about the neck of the man in the leather jacket, pounded his back, and roared:

— Kurtz! Kurtz! You dog!

As soon as Tauber heard the name Kurtz, he stopped talking and fixed his attention so closely on the hallooing trio that Mordecai also turned to watch them. Hartmann, a very skinny man in a shabby grey overcoat and a battered grey felt hat, was pumping Kurtz's hand.

Budko: —— What is it? Thirteen years?

Kurtz: —— Twelve. Twelve years, Budko. You haven't changed at all. Still as foul as ever, I see.

Budko: —— I kept hearing rumors that you were dead in jail.

Kurtz: —— In jail but not dead. Mostly Pawiak and the Citadel. A boring life, I can tell you. They let us out to help dig those useless tank traps and ditches in September. What a stiff back I got! . . . And you, Hartmann?

Hartmann: —— I get along.

Kurtz: —— You look hungry.

Hartmann: —— No. The more I eat, the thinner I get.

Kurtz had a coughing fit, and during it Budko glanced around at Pan Tauber and Mordecai, standing in frank audience; Budko murmured something to Kurtz and from then on the men spoke in low tones, audible only to each other. Pan Tauber burst occasionally into conversation, but he dropped his gambits and zigzagged erratically in subject matter. He was clearly upset. Finally the section of the line in which Mordecai stood reached the door of the Community Building, and Budko and Hartmann left for the end of the line.

The registration was taking place at two adjacent desks in a room straight ahead from the main entrance. The line became more and more compressed at its head, and by the time Mordecai had turned to face the first of the desks, he was elbow-to-elbow with Kurtz on the one side and Tauber on the other. The clerk at the first desk was a man of such ugliness as Mordecai had never seen. [NOTE. N.L. It was Schpunt.] The clerk began asking questions in a docile voice:

—— Name?

—— Avigdor Kurtz.

—— Address?

—— Nowolipki 24.

—— Trade?

—— Bricklayer.

—— Next.

Kurtz moved aside to the second desk, and Mordecai stepped before the ugly man.

—— Name?

—— Mordecai Apt.

—— Apt. . . . Apt. . . . There was something, something.

Schpunt had screwed up his amazing face, and he said this in a kind of hum. He opened a notebook bound in marbelized paper, ran a stubby finger down a register of names beginning with A, and, when the finger stopped, said:

—— Apt. Excused.

—— I beg your pardon.

—— Excused from labor duty. Excused, excused. (Then Schpunt read from the ledger, with the exaggerated care of a small child reading from a primer:) *Apt, Mordecai. Excused. Request of Herr Mahlen Gruber, Trustee, Apt Jewelers. Approved, Mandeltort. Excused!* Next!

—— But I don't want to be excused.

Mordecai had leaned forward over the desk to say this. Schpunt's tragic visage tilted back. The bulging eyes looked at Mordecai for a moment, then the face went down again, and Schpunt cried, in a furious tone:

—— Address!

—— Sienna 17.

—— Trade?

—— Bricklayer.

[NOTE. N.L. I asked him why he made that choice. He says it was just an impulse. He says he thought of what Kurtz had said. But in the light of what Rachel had told me (ENTRY NOVEMBER 27), I could not help wondering whether he liked the idea of tormenting his father by becoming precisely a hodcarrier. This theory would admit the possibility that Mordecai also thought he could improve his writing, along the lines of Halinka's gibe that day.]

Schpunt's eyes moved onto Mordecai's pink hands, and his face twisted into a caricature of disgust as he shouted in echo, so loudly and vehemently that all the men for some distance down the line laughed:

—— Bricklayer! Next!

Mordecai blushed, thrust his hands into his pockets, and sidled to the adjacent desk. There his labor slip was made out. Kurtz had received his slip by this time and had moved back down the line to talk with Budko and Hartmann, who were now just inside the door of the building. As Mordecai waited for his slip, he saw Pan Tauber lean forward to Schpunt and heard him say:

—— May I see Noach Levinson, please?

Schpunt snapped his fingers. A bedraggled messenger came from a corner of the room, listened to Schpunt's directions, and disappeared. Mordecai heard Pan Tauber say in a matter-of-fact voice to Schpunt:

—— I would like to buy an exemption.

Schpunt, the vociferousness of his reproach to Mordecai completely vanished, speaking as would a clerk at a theater ticket-window: —— Yes, sir. That will be one thousand zlotys, sir.

Pan Tauber peeled off his gloves, reached in a coat pocket, withdrew a billfold, and counted out ten one-hundred-zloty notes. It was at this point that N.L. approached. Pan Tauber addressed N.L. in a hoarse whisper:

—— Ah, Levinson. I thought you would want to know that Avigdor Kurtz, the Communist, just registered. He and Budko are back together again. You are able to appreciate what that means. I thought you would want to know. (Without seeming to have looked around, he said:) Kurtz is down the line in a leather jacket, talking to Budko now. Hartmann is with them: he is negligible: he has changed, we are given to understand. I thought you would want to know.

N.L., turning my head slowly toward the hallway to look for the three men: —— Thank you.

Tauber: —— Nothing. I thought you would want to know.

Mordecai says the clerk at the second desk was now addressing him:

—— As you can see, your number is 3,747. The day before you are needed, you will get a notice, telling you to report either here or at Grzybowski Place. You will be paid five zlotys per day. Keep your number on your person at all times. . . .

Mordecai turned to go. He says he had a sense of adventure beyond anything he had ever known. [NOTE. N.L. Confirming my suspicion that not much had happened to this youth.] As Mordecai left the building, he walked close past Kurtz and his companions, hoping to overhear something interesting; but he was disappointed: they were mumbling together.

EVENTS DECEMBER, 1939. ENTRY DECEMBER 11, 1939.
N.L. . . . Anyhow, we got interested in the Kurtz-Budko-Hartmann reunion, and decided to look into it. So what did we do?
Felix Mandeltort went to his old friend Rapaport, the Socialist,
and told him about it, and asked him to keep us informed of any
developments the Socialist Bund might notice. Jew against Jew.

Sure enough, Rapaport came up with something: the Communists are organizing a nuclear group. They call it Spartacus.
Their work of recruiting is at the moment very much restricted,
because thanks to the Soviet-Nazi pact the Communists could not
be called exactly popular among the Jews. Mostly Spartacus consists of intellectuals who were Communists before the pact. They
meet in the apartments of three or four young girls from wealthy
families, who are members. One of these is on Przejazd Street.
Their principal work is in the field of education, training, and
propaganda. They study Engels and Lenin, discuss the Jewish
problem, and prepare leaflets, mostly anti-British propaganda fo-
cused on Palestine. So far, aside from a few old hands like Kurtz,
there are almost no working people in Spartacus.

I asked Rapaport how the Bund found these things out—since
such a nucleus would presumably be carefully put together. Rapaport has a grand, oratorical manner, and he waved an arm and
said:

—— We Socialists may not have an experiment involving one
hundred and eighty million guinea pigs going, but we have our
little pack of mice!

I think Rapaport may be using Hartmann: Tauber told me
that Hartmann has changed somehow, yet he is in Spartacus—
so far.

This business developed, on the side, an episode that would
have been a joke, were it not so earnest. Zilberzweig, of Hashomer
Hatsair, the left-Zionist outfit, came in the other day and asked
me, in his mysterious but unexcited manner, to come out and take
a walk with him. Out on Grzybowski Place, speaking even there in
a whisper, he said he had evidence that the Socialists and Communists are banding together, or at the very least setting up a liaison.
But he would not give me the "evidence." Jew against Jew against
Jew. I cannot imagine how the Hashomer organization spied out
the Bund's spying on the Communists and then misinterpreted it,
unless Hartmann is even fancier than I would give him credit for

being, on record. Felix and I had a good laugh over Zilberzweig's report.

Well, there we are. Kurtz of Spartacus is the talented one; Rapaport of the Bund is the humanist; Zilberzweig of Hashomer is the dynamo. These personal qualities, I hasten to say, do not necessarily reflect the qualities of the organizations or the ideologies with which they are associated, though the personalities obviously influence the parties locally.

Now that the Communists are starting up again, we must add one more element to our intra-Jewish contests. Our trouble here in facing the Nazis is that we do not have two great forces, thesis and antithesis, right and left; or even just three, left, center, and right. We are a small France here. We are a spectrum. The picture reads from left to right: Communist, Poale-Zion Left, Bund, Hechalutz, Hashomer Hatsair, Hashomer Hanoir, Dror and Poale-Zion Right, General Zionists, Akiba, Revisionists, Orthodoxy; and goodness knows what interstices I have omitted or do not know about; and goodness knows how many Hartmanns there are, who play several tunes. Throw in your drifters, like Berson, who don't know exactly where they stand, and your officials, like me, who are supposed to represent all factions but cannot help being conservative (I confess it), and your assimilationists, who are not interested, and most of your property-owners, who are understandably interested in their property, and most of your workers, who are too busy surviving to worry about anybody *but* themselves—and you have the Nazis' opponents here: a bundle of twigs instead of one oaken staff; an army to be defeated piecemeal, platoon by platoon.

Why can we not unite? We all wear the same armband. Of course the Nazis decided not to put us in a ghetto—yet! They saw that that might pull us together.

I protest against the divisions, and at the same time I contribute to them. I am the one who, with Felix, began the investigations. I delight in the nonsense, with Felix I laugh and laugh. I recognize that I have too much curiosity, and too much of the theater-lover in me. . . .

4

Events March, 1940. Entry March 17, 1940. N.L. A curious sensation: I am being caught up in something like family life. I, who have always prided myself on standing on my own feet, and on being self-sufficient! This group of people around the Bersons, they seduce me. How? What is happening to me? Can I resist this softening influence?

In the first place, the invitation to be the *learned guest* at the Mazurs' housewarming was flattering. Reb Yechiel Mazur wrote me a formal note in stilted Hebrew, stating that his neighbor, D. B. Berson, had given him my name as being a man who knew the meaning of Jewish ways. Would I come to the housewarming and say a few words, in order to deepen the feeling of this happy occasion? Reb Yechiel Mazur wrote that the Bersons would be there, as well as the Apts, and also a mutual friend of his and mine, Reb Felix Mandeltort.

Events March 14, 1940. Entry March 15, 1940. From Felix Mandeltort. My only preparation for the housewarming, which takes place tomorrow, has been a brief conversation with Felix about the Mazur family. It seems that Felix knew them in the 'twenties, when he was living in Lodz. He says that on the whole the Mazurs are quite old-fashioned. Reb Yechiel Mazur owned four or five cotton-weaving establishments in Lodz, and must be fairly well off, though not so rich as Apt. He is very religious, and tends toward the stubbornly cheerful Hasidic habits of thought. His wife is simple, kind, and strong, Felix says. Felix remembers three children, an exceedingly handsome little boy, a playful girl, and a sickly baby boy; these three must be grown up now.

Events March 16, 1940. Entry March 17, 1940. N.L. The housewarming was scheduled to begin at five o'clock. When I entered the apartment, which is on the same staircase as the Bersons' and just under the Apts', it was about ten minutes before five, and Rabbi Goldflamm and the Bersons and Felix had arrived ahead of me.

The home to be "warmed" was pathetic, by the standards to which Felix had told me the Mazurs are accustomed. The only furniture in the living room was a severe, square table, several cheap, straight chairs, and a bookcase already full of books, and in each of the three bedrooms a couple of mattresses, made up with bedding and lying directly on the floor. I was told that Froi Mazur had insisted upon new mattresses, in order to avoid lice and bedbugs. Crowded onto the table and bookcase were a number of elegant knickknacks, strangely lush in contrast with the ascetic furniture: boxes, candlesticks, pieces of china, and, on the bookcase, a pretty salver containing bread and salt, for prosperity. A small, portable sewing machine stood on the floor against one wall. I assume that the furniture is temporary.

When the Apt family came in, I noticed that Pan Apt, on seeing me, puckered up his face in ill-suppressed distaste and quickly sequestered himself with Felix. For some reason, though I probably shot back a pucker of my own in Pan Apt's direction, this made me feel very shy, and I went over to the bookcase and began to scan the titles. Reb Yechiel Mazur, rushing nervously about, paused by the case at one point, pulled out a copy of *Galilut Erez Yisroel*, by Gershon Eleazar Halevi, and handed it to me. Reb Yechiel Mazur is a middle-sized man with the enigmatic, closed face so many bearded, religious Jews have; he wore a black kaftan. He said:

—— Do you know this book? Fantastic, but very deep, very deep!

Froi Mazur was sitting alone in one of the straight chairs, her hands folded, looking placid.

I riffled through the book, which I know well, pretending to be absorbed in it but listening all the while to a vivacious account of the Mazurs' arrival in Warsaw, delivered with spirit and a charming freedom by the Mazur girl, whose name is Rutka. She was saying:

—— Dignity was no longer a consideration, even for Papa. The important thing now for all of us was simply to reach Warsaw. We had about five more miles to go. As I say, it was raining and we were all tired to death.

[INSERT. FROM ENTRY MARCH 23, 1940. I have learned a bit about Rutka Mazur. She is a good-looking girl, though not really pretty. Her hair is so black that it seems almost blue, and she has

61

a soft, bluish texture around her eyes. Her lips are full and strong, and her mouth has a cheerful look. She is a lively girl, and when she and the zestful Berson get together, the conversation is like two people beating a rug. She seems to have had a happy home life, but she has moved quite far from the stodgy atmosphere of black cloth and blissful thoughts with which her father is surrounded. I gather that she joined Hashomer Hatsair, the Zionist youth movement, when she was about fifteen or sixteen—she is now twenty—and that in spite of the opposition of her father she spent two summers on a Hachsharah (NOTE. EDITOR. A farm for the training of potential emigrants to Palestine.) not far from Wloclawek.]

The Mazurs, said Rutka, had been lucky: they had traveled in style from Lodz: by wagon; indeed, in *two* wagons. Schlome was driving the first wagon. He is a boy of fourteen, a Talmudic scholar, whose sensitive, pale face is framed by drooping religious side-curls. Rutka said that her mother rode behind Schlome, sitting bolt upright on a tarpaulin at the crest of a load of possessions, with a woollen scarf tied under her chin. Stefan—who is eighteen, an extraordinarily handsome boy—was walking along leading the horse of the second wagon. Papa Mazur nodded sleepily atop the pile on that wagon, and Rutka herself lay half asleep and sopping wet, with her hair streaming like seaweed across her forehead, using her papa's thigh for a pillow. According to Rutka, her mother was very worried about the few household goods they were bringing along, and kept calling back from the first wagon:

—— I hope this canvas is really waterproof. The man at Klopper's told me it would hold out rain for a week.

Schlome [NOTE. N.L. This pale boy with the trembling earlocks must have made a strangely insubstantial drayman!]: —— May this drizzle stop!

Stefan was walking at the edge of the pavement whistling a melancholy tune from *Halka* in time with the horse's percussion when suddenly he stopped and shouted up to his father:

—— What was that address?

Rutka said that her father lifted his head and let the question settle awhile in his ears, then said:

—— Sienna 17. That is the third time I've had to tell you, son. Are we in any danger of arriving?

—— You've been leaving everything to me. You may all be sound asleep by the time we reach the city.

Rutka said that she raised her head a bit, saw the water dripping off her papa's beard, and then looked down at Stefan with the disgusted expression of someone who is kept from sleeping by a noisy brawler.

Stefan, angrily: —— Do you think we're going to have a roof to keep this damned rain off our heads tonight?

Papa, mildly: —— Your language, son. (Then, more in the way of a rebuke:) I only know what Mauritzi Apt wrote me: that he *thought* there would be a vacant apartment in his courtyard, and that he was sure some arrangement or other for housing could be made.

Stefan [NOTE. N.L. And here, as, in telling her story, Rutka turned her mischievous eyes on Pan Apt, there began to be a barb to her narrative!]: —— Mauritzi Apt isn't the sort of man to take five wet people into his living room.

Papa: —— He's a good friend, Stefan. I thank the Lord for friends.

[INSERT. FROM ENTRY APRIL 7, 1940. FROM REB YECHIEL MAZUR. I am on fine terms with Mazur now, and tonight I wheedled out of him the letter Mauritzi Apt had sent Mazur in Lodz. I had been curious about this letter ever since Rutka Mazur alluded to it in her story of the arrival, the day of the Mazurs' housewarming. As I remember, she made rather more of a point of it than I did in my notes on her story (ENTRY MARCH 17): she told how her father kept patting his chest, to make sure that his travel permit, corruptly arranged at huge sacrifices of conscience, and Pan Apt's letter, which he seemed to regard as a kind of Open Sesame to Warsaw, were still in his vest pocket. Here is what the letter said:

There is irony in this. Four months ago, as you may have heard, they threatened us here with a ghetto, and I made certain arrangements, which would have proved rather expensive had I gone through with them, to come to Lodz. If we had come, I should certainly have written you, as you have now to me. They dropped the ghetto idea here. And now you say they are to impose a ghetto upon you in Lodz. Turn about.

Apparently they do not dare *to use in Warsaw and the* General-Gouvernement *the kinds of repressive measures they can get away with in Lodz and the Warthegau, incorporated as that region is said to be into the German Reich.*

Naturally, I would be glad to do all I can for you here, if you can arrange to reach this city. Come to us. Three or four Polish families have been moving out of this apartment building, which is adequate, though perhaps not quite equal to what you have become accustomed to, and I think one of the flats in our courtyard may be free. I shall see what can be done. Some arrangement for housing can certainly be made. I have connections in an unexpected quarter. I have had a German "trustee" thrust upon me who has proved surprisingly understanding, a Bremener named Gruber. He has a disgusting habit of mining his teeth with a permanent golden toothpick. Loud sucking noises.

You say you will have to leave most of your furniture: that is painful. I remember your beautiful Jabotinski highboy, and that inlay on your bedroom chests! Still, you will learn that nice furniture can be found here, as the city has been rather seriously disrupted. You were wise to transfer your bank accounts to Warsaw last summer, and though our assets are supposed to be frozen, so that one may withdraw from the bank no more than 250 zl. a week, nevertheless I think it may be possible to arrange the procurement of cash beyond that limit. You probably have some about yourself, in any case.

Believe you will find some good friends in authority here. Weren't you once close to Felix Mandeltort? He is secretary of the Judenrat, and I find his company more and more rewarding. He takes everything so quietly. You know how excitable I am. Sometimes I think my head is going to fall off, it gets aching so badly. Mandeltort acts as if everything were the same as always. My only objection to visiting Felix at his office, as I often do, is that his desk is in the same room with that impudent young man, Noach Levinson, the historian, who is rude to me.

My children are a despair. Only Halinka seems to have any sense. Mordecai has signed up for a labor battalion, in spite of the fact that my trustee, Herr Gruber, had gone to some trouble to get him off. The work will kill Mordecai and serve him right. Rachel is morose and rebellious. She spends a lot of time upstairs with some queer people named Berson. Queer! I have only Ra-

*chel's rather surly testimony. They have reading parties, and Levin-
son is up there all the time. You can imagine. Halinka is sweet as
ever, and as beautiful, and as idle—thank heavens, like her dear
mother.*

Let me know when you are to arrive.]

Late in the afternoon (Rutka continued her story of the arrival), the two wagons drew to a creaking stop in Sienna Street.
The dreadfully weary horses hung their heads: Rutka said that
just looking at them, she felt she had no right to be tired herself.
The wagons had scarcely stopped moving when a man with an
umbrella came hurrying out and shouted up to her papa, in a torrent of Polish:

—— Are you the Mazurs? I saw the wagons. I am the janitor,
Kucharski. This rain is miserable: like a gas: it penetrates. We
have been waiting for you for two days. The Apts are all well.
Young Mordecai got his call for labor duty just today: reports day
after tomorrow. . . . We have an apartment waiting for you.
Second floor, Pan Apt's staircase. Pan Apt handled the down payment.

Papa: —— May He be praised!

Stefan snickered at this, and later he told Rutka that he had
thought it sounded as if his father were addressing his gratitude,
not to the deity, but to Mauritzi Apt.

Rutka's admiration of her mother is touching. The daughter
described how Froi Mazur, already disembarked, stepped up to
Kucharski and asked him to take her to the apartment. After
a brief examination of it, she came back to the wagons with a
favorable report and, in quiet firmness, began directing the unloading of the family's meager goods. Nowobarski took Reb Yechiel
Mazur off to his gatekeeper's lodge, and Froi Mazur stayed behind to work. [NOTE. N.L. I perceive that Froi Mazur holds
the old-fashioned belief that men should be left free, after bread-
winning hours, for exercise of the spirit, for contemplation and
enjoyment of God's kindnesses; and that it is the woman's task to
stay in the background, to do the household work cheerfully and
silently, and thus to give the man his proper freedom. Froi Mazur
does not yet regard her sons as men equally with her husband.]
While Reb Yechiel Mazur was in drying his beard *chez* Kucharski, she put the boys to unloading.

Rutka says her mother's supervision of the unloading was a marvelous performance. She knew, after one brief look at the apartment, exactly where she wanted every chattel put. She timed her orders in such a way as to keep the children separated, as she knows how fractious they become when they are working together. She favored Schlome, who is more frail than the others, even over Rutka. Froi Mazur had Schlome carry in all the objects so dear to his father—the Sabbath Menorah, the Seder plate, the Hanukkah lamp, the ethrog box, the phylacteries and prayer shawls in their embroidered velvet bags, and in a little glass-topped box the golden Kiddush goblet. It fell to Rutka to take in the dishes and pans and pots; and, with special care, the Pesach set. When the janitor came out to watch and gossip, Froi Mazur had the tact not to press him into service. There were so few possessions. Froi Mazur told Kucharski that the family had had to sell nearly everything, and her voice made a careful distinction, Rutka says, between explanation, which this was, and apology, which it was not.

Rutka told how her brother Stefan led the horses off to a near-by stable, to which Kucharski had directed him. The last words her father had spoken before going into the apartment house had been:

—— Take care of the horses. A man may not sit down to eat before he has fed his animals. . . .

. . . At this point in Rutka's story, Rabbi Goldflamm cleared his throat. This was a signal for the housewarming ceremony to begin. In years of dealing with throngs, Rabbi Goldflamm has developed a peremptory rasp in his neck, like a buzzer's cry. A hush fell.

Reb Yechiel Mazur's nervousness suddenly peeled away from him. With a dignity that made him seem a little taller now, he walked to the east wall of the room, picked up a hammer and a nail from a chair there, drove the nail into the wall, and hung on it the family Mizrach. [NOTE. EDITOR. Framed, illuminated verses in praise of God.] Then Reb Yechiel Mazur went out into the hallway, with all of us guests crowding behind. Froi Mazur handed him a tiny bit of parchment, from which, squinting closely, he read the words of the *Shema Yisroel* prayer—as if he had to read it!

Reb Yechiel Mazur rolled up the miniature scroll and put it into a small cloisonné capsule, which, with extreme care, he nailed to the doorpost, driving the nails through two brass ears for the purpose, at the ends of the capsule. He touched his fingers lightly then to the name of God, *Shaddai*, showing through a slot in the capsule, and kissed the ends of his fingers. Then Reb Yechiel Mazur recited benedictions and prayers.

—— Blessed be Thou, our God, King of the universe, who hast made us holy with Thy law, and commanded us to affix the Mezuzah. . . . Master of the universe, look down from Thy holy habitation and accept in mercy and favor the prayer of Thy children who are gathered here to dedicate this dwelling and to offer their thanksgiving. . . . Grant them that they may live in their home in brotherhood and friendship. . . .

My turn came at last. Up to the moment when I stood forward to speak as the "learned man" of the occasion, I had no idea what I would say. I know that just before I began, I felt that I ought to make a conscious effort to twist myself around to the sentimentality and melancholy of the affair; but that idea revolted me. I hesitated, clearing my throat. [INSERT. FROM ENTRY MARCH 17, 1940. FROM DOLEK BERSON. Berson says that behind my glasses I appeared to be *outside* the home, not partaking at all of the housewarming, but peering from a distance through powerful binoculars.] Suddenly I felt a terrible bitterness and I began speaking:

—— What is a home? Is it just a box to contain furniture and people? Is it just a space underneath a roof? Let me tell you about my boyhood home. We were poor. We lived in a single room in a wooden house in Skierniewice: my mother and father, my grandmother, my mother's brother, and six of us children. The room was never clean; its smell is in my nostrils now. I was afraid of my father, who was a cruel and religious man, awfully the master of his castle. My mother was his servant, but she was stupid enough to tolerate her status. My home? A miserable place. I am being honest. . . .

I was in an ugly, cynical mood, and I could see the shock on the faces of all my listeners, who up to this point in the occasion had been given little silver spoonfuls of honey and oats—but now were suddenly fed vinegar and raw peppers.

It is curious how the mind veers back and forth. Ordinarily I suppose I might have been viciously pleased to see the horror on the faces of my audience—at least I was stirring them up!—but this time, for some reason I do not understand (unless it was because of something I saw in Rachel Apt's face), I felt utterly confused by the expressions on those faces. I veered away from my harshness. I felt suddenly, in a most poignant way, a member of this group, this family. . . . *In brotherhood and friendship.* . . . That phrase came leaping out at me, and I was overwhelmingly aware of the pleasure and refuge I have had in recent weeks in the Berson and Apt households, upstairs from these rooms, and I said, softening the tone of my voice:

—— Perhaps too honest, speaking to you who have never suffered such a home. But I call up this memory of mine, of a home that I hated, because I have had a glimpse this evening of the daydream I often entertained as a boy: I have seen a home, in the colors and shape I always fantasied: a home that is not furniture or shelter or rented premises, but is a family. In slight gestures and brief words, I have seen the injunction of the Talmud fulfilled: A *good husband loves his wife as himself but honors her more than himself.* Wisdom and ideals on the bookshelves, cleanliness on the kitchen shelves. The children modest, it seems. A harmony throughout. Above all, I think I have seen the wife and mother of the famous chapter in Proverbs—*a woman of worth.* . . .

I cannot say now whether I meant everything I said then. The speech took hold of me, rather than I of the speech. I know that I had been very much struck by the effect on the Mazur household of a religious atmosphere: everything went by a definite pattern, nothing was accidental. There is nothing so orderly as a life run by ritual. In such a world, life is a bedroom, with everything in its proper cupboard and drawer, fresh-laundered and neatly folded, ready for use at the correct time. The danger (which I think perhaps I ignored in my speech) is that the man who lives in this bedroom may become a happy sleepwalker, unaware of the scratching of the rats in the plaster of the walls. I scarcely know what I felt as I spoke; I was transported. I went on, often citing and quoting (for, after all, I was supposed to be a *learned man*), speaking of the significance of Jewish family and home life, and all that I said was overcast with the bitterness and wistfulness of the memory of my own home.

There was no doubt or ambiguity about Reb Yechiel Mazur's sentiments. He was shedding shameless tears when, at the end of my speech, he signaled his wife to pass glasses of wine. When she had gone around with a tray, he raised his drink and said in a shaking voice:

—— *Lehayim!* To life!

The guests, lifting their glasses, murmured after him:

—— To life! To life!

5

Events March 17–23, 1940. Entry March 24, 1940. From Dolek Berson. Berson is not a religious man. Sarcastically he thanks me for the chance of being at Rabbi Goldflamm's secret service at all yesterday morning, when the Schpunt affair took place. He was there, he says, as a direct result of my housewarming speech.

The speech got him all mixed up. He says it filled him with vague, troublesome aspirations. He reproached himself with those of his faults which he recognizes and kept himself busy trying to correct them. (This is funny, my being cast in the role of a corrective rabbi! Of all the impulses I may have had when I made that speech, one of them was certainly *not* to castigate anybody.) Berson says he hovered about Symka, plaguing her with uxoriousness—until, one morning at breakfast, she begged him to leave her alone: she had had enough of his sweetness. The Drifter amazed Kucharski (and himself) by giving the janitor a present of money, the first time in three years. He went once to Menkes' bakery and asked the baker:

—— Have you any errands in the city, Pavel? I'd be glad to do them for you. I have to go down for Symka.

—— Send *you* on an errand? God! You'd forget what I asked you to do before you got out of the door.

Another result: Goaded by his friend Slonim, and urged also by Mordecai Apt—both of whom work in the bricklayers' labor battalion—Berson has registered for labor, and has signed up, too, as a bricklayer. He might make a good one.

Berson also suffered, during these days, an attack of neighborliness. He remembered (apart from my speech) the pleasant, melancholy tone of the Mazur housewarming, and he dropped in, one afternoon, to see if there was anything he could do to help the family get settled. Froi Mazur came to the door, dressed in a linen smock, her head bound into a dustcloth turban.

Froi Mazur: —— Do you mean it?

Berson: —— Naturally.

Froi Mazur, doubtfully, perhaps suspecting that he must be after something: —— Nu, there is plenty to do.

Having once taken Berson at his word, Froi Mazur made no moves of false propriety. She put him to work. Before Berson realized quite what was happening to him, he had been given a broom with a cloth bag over its operative end, had had a dustcloth tied around his own head, and had been told to stand on a chair and sweep the cobwebs out of the angles between walls and ceilings. The men were out, Froi Mazur said: Schlome starting in at the Yeshiva school Rabbi Goldflamm had recommended, Stefan buying some things for the apartment, and her husband getting the family's various permits and passes from the *Judenrat*. Rutka was working in the kitchen.

Froi Mazur sat in one of the straight chairs in the living room, making handsome armbands for her family. Star-of-David brassards can be bought from street venders for anywhere from fifty groszy, printed on paper, to three zlotys, on white linen, but none of these is good enough, Froi Mazur said. She told Berson that the Mazurs were proud of their Jewishness and were going to advertise it with embroidered stars on satin bands. As Berson worked, Froi Mazur talked along—of the Mazurs' apartment in Lodz; of the ghetto decree there and the scramble for living-quarters within its boundaries; and with an open perplexity about her son Stefan, who makes her, she said, both proud and worried, because of his handsomeness and quick talents, and yet his sullen laziness; and some of the time she sat silently sewing. Once she got up, examined Berson's work, and made him do over again one whole length of wall, where he had left broom-streaks.

While Berson was still working, Rutka came running in from the kitchen with some question for her mother. Berson, startled by her arrival, looked suddenly around, lost his balance on the chair, and went crashing to the floor. The sight of his fall, and then of his head, bundled up like a country grandmother's, made Rutka laugh hard at him. Berson went upstairs nursing his vanity and his right elbow.

In these benign days, Berson even made a gesture toward his cousin Meier, whom he dislikes. He invited his cousin to join him and Symka yesterday morning, to attend prayers at Goldflamm's secret prayerhouse, and to visit them all day. The idea of going to worship, Dolek says, was a direct result of what he calls the bogus religious atmosphere I worked into my speech, which had stirred his conscience.

On the way to the hidden "synagogue," Symka walked ahead with Rachel, who alone in the Apt family occasionally attends prayers. Berson says he was feeling expansive; he talked about the Mazurs. Cousin Meier waited for an opening and said:

—— I have in mind a new business venture.

—— So? A sound one, I hope, this time.

—— I think so. In leather. We have a very good proposition. Only one thing remains.

—— And that is—?

—— We need some cash. Some working capital.

Berson says that the kindliness and humanity in which he had been luxuriating for the past few days suddenly dried up. He spoke harshly:

—— I told you the last time that I would never lend you money again. You owe me two thousand already. Why can't you manage better?

Dolek says he was in a black and misanthropic state of mind as he entered the side door of the glove and hat store that, since the ban on public worship, had served as Rabbi Goldflamm's holy place.

EVENTS MARCH 23, 1939. ENTRY MARCH 27, 1939. N.L. Rabbi Goldflamm's secret prayerhouse, no longer available to us after what happened the other day, was in Sapir's Hats and Gloves, a fairly large shop on Panska Street. We were gathered in the salesroom, all around the walls of which run cupboards and showcases. These used to have glass fronts, but the glass has all been taken out to repair windows broken in the siege of the city. On shelves in these cases are cheap felt hats, a few fur caps, and round black skullcaps; as well as kid and cotton and pigskin gloves. The room was dim, because the corrugated-iron shop front was down and latched from within. We were, I suppose, twenty-five or thirty people. About ten of the men wore prayer shawls and

71

phylacteries. At the back of the shop was a small table covered with a white cloth and with two candles stuck by their own wax onto two tin plates, upside down. The Baal Tefilla, or leader of prayers, a man named Baum with a deep, rich voice, stood at the center of us, reciting petitions, blessings, and Psalms:

—— . . . A brutish man knoweth it not, neither doth a fool understand this: when the wicked sprang up as the grass, and all the workers of iniquity flourished, it was that they might be destroyed forever. . . .

[NOTE. EDITOR. Among Eastern European Jews, prayers are not necessarily conducted by a rabbi. Any *minyan*, or quorum of ten, may hold services, and any Jew may recite the ritual. A rabbi need not even be present. Indeed, it is basic in Judaism that any believer may speak directly to God at any time, and never needs the intercession or good offices of God's mortal bureaucracy. The Rabbinate in Eastern Europe regulates the religious life of the community and devotes itself to the study of sacred literature.]

I myself was in a strange, contemplative mood. Like Berson, I had been somewhat stirred up by my own speech, but in a different way and with a different result. The words that had come out of me, as it were involuntarily, during my speech, had made me realize how important to me I had allowed my contacts with the Bersons and the Apts to grow. After the speech, at home, when my pleasure at having moved my hearers had waned, and when I had begun to be disgusted with the sentimentality of some of the things I had said, I suddenly felt endangered. I felt that if I let myself be drawn deeper and deeper into the pleasant sense of kinship these people gave me, I would become dull, domesticated, and lazy. In consequence, during the next few days, I avoided my new friends, I worked and studied. At the prayerhouse, that morning, Rachel had greeted me with a comforting anxiety:

—— Where have you been all week?

When Berson saw me, he saluted me, I thought, rather irritably. [INSERT. FROM ENTRY MARCH 28. N.L. I now know why Berson gave me the brusque greeting at the prayerhouse: it was his annoyance with Meier and with himself.] But on the whole I was very much surprised by the sharpness of my pleasure at seeing these friends again. And so, during the service, I sat musing about them, and about my dilemma: my desire for privacy and my desire for companionship. Both are so hard to achieve! The Baal Tefilla droned on, meanwhile, like a spiritual reciprocating engine.

——. . . The streams have lifted up, O Lord, the streams have lifted up their voice; the streams lift up their roaring. . . .

A sharp clanging crash cut off the prayer. Our alarmed faces turned toward the iron screen at the front of the shop. Clank! Clank! Some club, some metal-bound heavy object was pounding on the corrugated iron store-drop. Then a straining German voice cried:

—— Öffnen. Öffnen Sie! Open up!

Crash! Crash! Crash! Crash! The club, the gun butt, whatever it was, insisted and would not be denied. It was ugly Schpunt who stood up and walked to the front of the store, unhooked the latch of the iron drop, and with his face reddening turned a crank which lifted the rattling screen. In the doorway stood three German soldiers: a sergeant and two privates. The sergeant stepped forward: a middle-aged man who appeared to be a professional soldier. He asked:

—— Who is the rabbi here?

There was a pause. No one dared look at Rabbi Goldflamm, who was sitting with the rest of the crowd. The sergeant simply waited. The silence was fearful.

—— I. I am the rabbi.

It was Schpunt. Schpunt, with a prayer shawl over his head and the box of a phylactery bound by ribbons to his forehead; he looked like an extraordinary, misshapen, stunted woman. The German voice cracked out as sudden and metallic as the sound of the rifle butt on the iron screen had been:

—— Aha! A handsome fellow! Come outside, please.

I looked over my shoulder and saw the soldiers lead Schpunt out into the middle of the street. Then the soldiers went off to one side, out of my view. Schpunt stood alone, mournful and ridiculous, framed by the doorway.

—— Dance!

The clanging voice echoed in the store. A look of incredulity joined the host of contending expressions on Schpunt's weird face.

—— Dance, Rabbi!

Slowly, with a reminiscent expression, as if to say, *Oh, yes, this is something from my boyhood*, the small man began a clumsy

73

jigging and hopping in the street. His motions were froglike. The
Germans could be heard laughing.
—— Faster!
Schpunt increased his efforts. Hippity-hop, clop-clop-clop. The
fringes of the shawl flapped, the phylactery shook up and down on
Schpunt's forehead. I had to smile, so funny was the sight.
—— More gaily!
An insane, fixed smile moved over Schpunt's face, which, as a
result, became dreadfully comical. I heard laughter all around me
in the hat and glove store, and I myself laughed out loud. Schpunt
seemed to be laughing now, too, as if he were conscious of his
clowning effect.
The entertainment ended as suddenly as it had begun. We
heard the sergeant's laughing voice command Schpunt to stop, and
then the sergeant moved back into view in the doorway. Tears
were running down his cheeks, and the other two soldiers, behind
him, were cackling, doubling over, and thumping each other on
the back. The sergeant cried out to us, punctuating what he said
with guffaws:
—— Go home, good people! Go home! Don't you know that
public worship is forbidden?

EVENTS MARCH 23, 1940. ENTRY MARCH 28, 1940. FROM
DOLEK BERSON. We all walked home together—I with my friends
(and how close I felt to them after what I had seen!). Dolek was
walking with Rachel, and he reports to me the following exchange:
Dolek: —— Why did we laugh? Was it because we had fooled
them, and it wasn't the rabbi at all?
Rachel: —— That made it no less shameful.
Dolek: —— I know. I was just wondering. . . . Of course,
Schpunt was very funny.
Rachel, with sudden vehemence: —— You have no heart at
all, have you? I should think that you would be ashamed of yourself. I saw you laughing in there with the others. You're . . .
you're a fool.
Dolek says he turned in surprise, admiring Rachel's spirit but
at the same time deeply offended. They walked the rest of the way
home in silence. Symka joined Dolek at the bottom of their stairway, and man and wife climbed the flights together. On the top
landing, Berson said:

—— My dear, do you think I am callous?
—— Why, Dolek . . . of course not.
But, says Berson, Symka paused in her answer.

EVENTS MARCH 23, 1940. ENTRY MARCH 27, 1940. N.L.
We laughed; that was our mortification. Berson has a theory that
our laughter was indirectly caused by the fact that the Germans
were tricked: they thought they were hazing a rabbi, and they only
had Schpunt. I think it was not so simple. For one thing, the phylactery on Schpunt's forehead waggled up and down in an absurd
way over his even more absurd face. In that little leather box was
housed our monotheistic faith; the words, *Hear, O Israel, the Lord
our God is one God.* And thou shalt bind these words for a sign
upon thine hand, and they shall be as frontlets between thine eyes.
This our religion, which sets us apart, which keeps us erect in the
face of no matter what affronts, which even maintains the spirits
of those who profess to be faithless, our very Jewishness, the whole
incredible nightmare we are experiencing now—all this bounced
up and down before Schpunt's eyes and ours. And so we laughed—
at the Germans. We were also laughing, I suppose, in relief, for
most of us thought Schpunt was to be shot when the soldiers led
him so somberly out into the street. I have said it was not simple;
it was not. We thought we were laughing at Fischel Schpunt. Indeed, he is endowed with an extraordinarily comical face, and it
seems that the less comical Schpunt's mood, the funnier his face.
The moment he realized he was amusing the other day, and began to laugh himself, something was lost—for us Jews, that is: the
Germans seemed to think him even more hilarious than before.
We were laughing at Schpunt not simply as a clown, however; we
were laughing, I think, at the persecution. That the unimaginative
German should derive such pleasure and reward from the embarrassment of this harmless little scapegoat! Ha ha ha! I laugh now.
And I blush now, too, for Schpunt was also *our* scapegoat, and he
had the courage to elect himself to that honorable post. I envy
him. But then, I would not have been quite so funny in his dancing shoes. I will not say that I am too handsome to be comical. I
am too bitter, rather. . . .

6

EVENTS APRIL 17, 1940. ENTRY APRIL 22, 1940. FROM
LAZAR SLONIM. At Berson's apartment last night, and largely for
Berson's benefit, Slonim opened up. He began by talking about
Menkes, but soon by that route he arrived at a more interesting
topic: the event which has given Slonim a certain small fame
among us — or notoriety, depending on the viewpoint.

[INSERT. FROM ENTRY JANUARY 12, 1940. N.L. Lazar
Slonim is a romantic Socialist. He comes from a wealthy background, and he is in the movement for excitement, mainly. When
he speaks of Polish Socialism, he does not talk of wages, hours,
and rents; no, he tells about how the mountaineer Dembowski fell
resisting the charge of the dragoons in a courtyard in Podgorz, in
the Krakow uprising of 1846, or he quotes from the eloquent letter from the martyrs of the Tenth Pavilion, in Warsaw in 1886.
He has a cynical twist, a bantering manner; he has no enthusiasm
for doctrine. Berson says Slonim is such a clever fellow that it
seems he can never stifle his own brilliance: in every discussion,
his incisive but unsubtle mind displays itself, and almost always
in argument. Slonim uses Socratic questions as if they were bludg-
eons, and he grows surprised and truculent if a single series of
blows does not render his opponent senseless and silent. He has a
narrow face, with juicy but stiff lips, like two sections of a tanger-
ine. A handle of hair, on which he tugs constantly, falls over his
forehead. He mumbles his words. He has a thin, hard body, as if
made of waterpipes and pipe joints. But in spite of his aggressive
manner and strange appearance, he has a kind of charm—a charm
of energy, stubbornness, and romanticism.

Slonim is about thirty years old. His father was a wealthy
leather merchant who died eight or ten years ago, leaving everything to Lazar, who was an only child. Slonim studied in Polish
schools and at Bonn, where he formed a close friendship with Berson: perhaps one should call it a running debate rather than a
friendship. It was at Bonn that he was first attracted to Socialism
—dabbled in theory, as he said to Symka the day of the Community
Building mass meeting (ENTRY DECEMBER 3, 1939). After the
University, he joined the Jewish Socialist Bund, and worked as an

activist and organizer. They say he did splendid work in the printers' union, the strongest here in Warsaw. He is married and has two children, but I gather he almost never produces his wife in public. He is a reserve officer in the Polish Army, but was not called up when the Germans invaded the country: this infuriates him more than most "capitalistic injustices."]

. . . and then he told us how the thing had come to take place:

Rapaport pushed back his chair, shoved his green eyeshade up onto his forehead, stretched his arms, and lit a cigaret. It was nearly midnight, but old Rapaport was apparently far from done with his work. He sat in his room beside a round table, and the smoke-lines from his cigaret ascended like inconclusively swinging fists and reaching hands through the cone of light falling from a single shaded bulb. Before him on the table, glistening and promising, was his pride: a new Polish typewriter, which Slonim says Rapaport had acquired, after months of haggling, from a Polish Socialist comrade. Now the Jewish Socialist Bund, cried Slonim in his sarcastic manner, would march ahead, shoulder to shoulder with every other workers' movement that could afford a typewriter. Except, he added, that Rapaport's stenography, like Rapaport's reasoning, is slow: a longhand revolution would come just as fast.

Slonim: —— You wanted to see me?

Rapaport: —— I did. Two decisions of the Central Committee.

[NOTE. N.L. The Central Committee! The Bund has made no secret of its directorate in the past, and I happen to know that three of the six members of the Central Committee left Warsaw during the siege and have not yet returned, and that one of the other three, Spieser, has been ill. Of all people, Slonim, with his rebellious mind, must have known what Rapaport meant by "the Central Committee."]

Rapaport: —— First. You have heard about the attacks on Jewish stall shopkeepers by Polish hooligans from the trade school on Leszno Street, no doubt. The Central Committee has decided to teach those ruffians a lesson. Day after tomorrow, at six in the afternoon, after the school's late session is recessed, our cadres will intercept the students. The meatworkers and transport-workers have been mobilized. I want you to organize whatever you can among

77

the bricklaying labor battalion, in the district Franciszkanska-Nalewki-Zamenhofa.

Slonim: —— Isn't that treating a symptom?

Rapaport: —— I know. The Poles have reason to hate the Germans, and the Jews have better reason to hate the Germans; so the Jews fight the Poles. But, Slonim, we have to teach these Poles that we are not supine. We will deal with the Germans when we can and as we can. That takes preparation. We have to do this first.

Slonim: —— And what do we use to teach this lesson?

Rapaport: —— You have bricks. From all I have been hearing, you handle them rather well—for an intellectual.

[INSERT. FROM ENTRY APRIL 23, 1940. N.L. I am afraid that Rapaport's gibe at Slonim, about being an intellectual mason, the other day, must have been heartfelt, and therefore pathetic. Rapaport, who is earthy indeed, resents intellectuals, I am told. He is not one himself: he is even slow-witted. Of course this does not prevent him from being a much bigger man than Slonim.

Rapaport is a worker's worker. He came up from the very bottom of the pit. He began as a *chalupnik*, one of those fantastically poor drones who do piece work for tailors, hatmakers, and so on. Rapaport has stated that one employer for whom he worked got things done so cheaply by his *chalupniks* that he was able to export to India. From this beginning, Rapaport climbed so far that at last he went to France to study as an engineer—a rise which cannot be demeaned by the fact that he failed his courses in France. He was a leader in the Jewish Socialist youth movement, Zukunft, and later joined the Bund. He has always been much loved: he speaks the workers' language, and he has a friendly manner. He is an intuitive Socialist, a humanist rather than a strict Marxist. He feels concern for the individual rather than for the mass, and they say that he always has time for the personal problems of a working man. He has a quiet dignity, and always maintains a rigid self-control in rancorous or dangerous situations. They say that in the Semperit strike in Krakow in 1936 he showed great personal courage. Everyone seems to call him "old Rapaport," though I believe he is just past fifty: he has a mane of pure white hair and a lion's face. As is often the case with men who have a wonderfully calm exterior, his turmoil is all internal: he has some kind of bad stomach trouble.]

78

Rapaport: —— The other thing: the Bund foresees food as a difficult problem. . . .

Slonim, breaking in: —— The Bund amazes one!

Rapaport: —— . . . and the Bund intends to enlist as many bakers as possible in its work. They will be invaluable later on. Can you help with any of these?

Rapaport handed Slonim a slip of paper on which was a list of names, typed, with errors, erasures, and eccentricities in the left-hand margin: Abramowicz, Dant, Feiwicz, Haleazar, Menkes. . . .

Slonim: —— Menkes. I will try Menkes.

Rapaport: —— Do you know him well, or do you patronize him?

Slonim says that Rapaport bore down rather heavily on that "patronize."

Slonim: —— He is a friend of a friend.

Rapaport: —— Good. Do not approach him as from the Bund. Try to get him interested in the abstract ideas of resistance and underground. When he has had peripheral testing and then training, it will be time enough to discuss the Bund.

Slonim: —— Do you take me for a novice?

Rapaport: —— As the years go by, one learns to repeat and repeat and repeat; to you, I suppose I should apologize. (With a sudden change in manner, from that of a stiff tutor to that of a warm friend:) Come to me on May Day. I'm having a few comrades in to celebrate.

In telling Berson all this, Slonim had seemed to put most of his emphasis on his own conflict with, and superiority to, Rapaport. But as he finished he said:

—— Rapaport sat there with his chin on his fists and his elbows on the table bracketing the precious typewriter. *That takes preparation,* he had said to me. What a patient fellow! His whole life has been preparation: hardening up the periphery, forming the Groups, always getting ready; and always losing, too, defections to the left and right, death, jail, war — and then preparations to compensate for the losses. And the tortuous road of policy, favoring Marxism and opposing Stalinism: preparation of line and counter-line and counter-counter-line. And "teamwork" with the Polish Socialists, preparation for the brotherhood of the working masses— which, speaking of Pole and Jew, does not, cannot, will not exist. And the preparation of himself, for half a century. Foundations to

79

be put down: sharp and troublesome Slonims to be persuaded, bricks to be laid for Nazis and thrown at Polish hooligans. What a patient man! . . . He gave me some material he had written to read, and before I had finished a page, he had put his white head down on his forearms on the edge of the table and had fallen asleep, with his forehead just touching the cool keys of the new typewriter, whose platen still held the old man's unfinished work. I wonder if he will ever finish anything. . . .

EVENTS APRIL 12–18, 1940. ENTRY APRIL 20, 1940. FROM DOLEK BERSON. There are twenty-two men in the bricklayers' battalion in which Berson and Mordecai Apt and Slonim work. The first day Berson reported, the group marched from its concentration point in Grzybowski Place northward to the ruins of two bombed-out houses on Franciszkanska Street. There some of the men were told to load the fallen brick into handcarts and others were detailed to push the carts to various intersections, mostly streets leading off Franciszkanska and Bonifraterska, and still others were assigned to arrange the dumped bricks into neat piles at those crossways.

Berson stayed close by Mordecai Apt, who had been working with the battalion for some time and would be able to pass on what he had learned. For one thing, Apt told Berson to take it easy at first. He himself, not knowing his capacities, had worked too fast in the beginning, had developed aching shoulders and blisters on his hands, had been in real pain in following days, and had had to exert himself from then on with stiff economy. Berson worked gingerly in any case, for he was extremely nervous about his piano-playing fingers.

Berson, Apt, and Slonim were all assigned to the group that was working on demolishing the ruins. As they lifted bricks onto a handcart, Slonim talked in his self-assured way:

—— Well, my friends, we have chosen an excellent profession! There is a future in *this* trade. In a year when there is lots of rain coming down, be a farmer, or a ditch-digger, or if you have grandiose tendencies, a flood-control engineer. In a year when there have been bombs coming down, select some kind of work close to bricks. The legal profession? I am declassed. There is no sense litigating under a lawless regime. [NOTE. N.L. How right he is! I heard of a Jew the other day who tried to sue the Germans for confiscating his shoestore. The case was tried in a so-called *Sondergericht*. He lost. He was not permitted to summon either Poles or Jews as witnesses. He was not permitted to apply for disqualification of the judge on grounds of bias. He was not permitted to appeal. He was permitted to pay court expenses, however.] I shall work now where I am needed, around bricks. Just like these other intellectuals here. I'll wager there's not a single bricklayer among us. What a structure we will build! Kurtz may have handled bricks before, but I doubt it. [NOTE. N.L. This was Avigdor Kurtz, the Communist, who had registered as a bricklayer, as we have seen (ENTRY DECEMBER 12, 1939).] I've never been near a brick before. Here's the only real workman in the battalion, I imagine. . . .

Slonim pointed to a cheerful, broad-faced man named Fein, who had just brought an empty pushcart back from an unloading, and who came over now to pick up the cart Slonim, Berson, and Apt had nearly filled.

Slonim: —— Tell me, Fein, what is your regular work?

Fein: —— Regular? Pfui! I have been a carpenter, a road-worker, a field hand, everything. I have even worked in the sewers. The only "regular" work is with a needle or a little oilcan—tailor, mechanic, barber, furrier, something like that. In a crowded room. Not for me. I have to move around. So now (he grinned) I move bricks around.

With a ludicrous groan, Fein pushed the loaded cart away. Slonim said:

—— You see, a workman. One workman. The rest of us educated men, with or without political ideas. What social levelers the Germans are! (Slonim was speaking in Polish, and this last remark was ironically aimed in the direction of a sleepy young German sentry who was leaning on his rifle not far from the group.) They have accomplished in a few weeks what we Socialists have been unable to accomplish in years. (The drowsy young German shifted from one foot to the other. Slonim spoke louder:) They are revolutionaries! (The German yawned.) The Germans are Reds! (As there was no sign of life in the German boy, Slonim tried the same remark in Yiddish—a much riskier joke, considering how close the Yiddish phrase is to the German:) The Germans are Reds!

At this the German seemed to come to life, and the Jews bent swiftly over their work—but the sentry's awakening appeared to have been coincidental. . . .

On Berson's fifth day, he, Apt, and Slonim were all shifted to the handcarts. On the first trip Berson made, he was directed to take the cart to a certain corner on Nalewki Street. When he reached the crossing, he saw there a large pile of stacked brick, a cone of sand, some bags of quicklime, a drum of water, a bin with some mortar mixed in it—and then, in front of him, where a group of Jews were at work, he saw, knee-high and growing, and shutting off one whole side of the intersection, a wall.

EVENTS APRIL, 1940. ENTRY APRIL 21, 1940. N.L. What is the meaning of these sections of wall? Here, there, a few blocks apart. Some pattern is forming, I feel sure. I can get no satisfaction from the *Judenrat* committee which has responsibility for supplying the building materials for the wall: its members shrug their shoulders and say they are only responsible for raising money and collecting mortar and sand and so on, they know nothing of plans, they say. The name of the committee may or may not be revealing. *Instandhaltung der Seuchensperrmauern.* Maintenance of Epidemicwalls. Dr. Breithorn, that morose man, says he thinks the Germans are going to try to drive all the lice in Warsaw into a hundred-block area this summer! His way, I suppose, of saying that they may try to set up a real quarantine area. Dr. Breithorn says that the place where the walls are being built actually was one of the worst typhus epidemic sections summer before last, but he points out that another of the worst sections then was in Praga, across the Vistula—no walls being put up there.

One stretch of the wall, on Bonifraterska, is finished. It goes straight from the building on one side of the street to the one on the opposite side. It is a little less than three meters high. [NOTE. EDITOR. About nine feet.] The top is rounded off with mortar, and into the mortar is stuck an ugly barbing of broken glass, pottery, and china. This wall is not just a fence or a marker. This wall is actually intended to keep human beings from passing. At the bottom, there are small gutter drainage holes—too small for the smallest human infant to get through. Rats can get through, though, and rats carry lice. Epidemicwalls?

The occupation authorities are building this wall as they do everything else—section by section, episode after episode, separately, without apparent sequence. Here and there, now and then. Casual looting of Jewish property; kosher slaughter forbidden; *Kehilla* disbanded and *Judenrat* formed; public worship forbidden; census; registration for labor; ghetto decree; ghetto decree called off; armbands; bank accounts frozen; limitations on change of residence; registration of Jews' jewelry; schools closed; restrictions on travel; registration of property; Jews barred from trolleys and buses; restrictions on postal savings; prohibition of purchase of gold; wall sections built. Each episode comes at a different time. Each affects a different group. And when each group raises a clamor, all the other Jews cry:

—— Hush! Do you intend to endanger the majority? Hush, friends!

Yet I think we are all going to wake up one of these mornings, hear a loud click in the sky, and see all these puzzle-parts fall into place around us. I wish I could understand the real meaning of the sections of wall. . . .

EVENTS APRIL 19, 1940. ENTRY APRIL 23, 1940. FROM PAVEL MENKES. Menkes has told me, with a blustery indignation, how Slonim approached him the other day on the subject of underground work:

Slonim: —— May I walk home with you, Menkes?

Menkes: —— It's not on your way, is it?

Slonim: —— I want to talk with you.

It was Sunday afternoon. Slonim, Menkes, the young Apts, the Mazur girl, and one or two others had gathered at the Bersons' apartment to hear Dolck play the piano. Menkes says he was not made for music: in broad daylight, and in all that clangor, he had to wrestle frightfully with sleep, until his jaw and throat ached from their resistance to yawns. On the stairs, as he descended with Slonim, he finally surrendered to one, a huge and voluminous one:

—— Awum-hum-hum-hum!

Slonim: —— Am I boring you?

Menkes: —— You haven't started talking yet. . . . Don't be offended until you actually hear snoring.

The two men walked in silence for a while through the far-from-silent streets, which were crowded with idle, Sunday chatterers. Menkes says he waked up now; he says he always feels stimulated and amused by the constant activity of the streets in the Jewish section: they have a nervous vibration, as if every commonplace moment were exciting and even desperate: remarks on the weather are uttered in a tone of conspiracy, greetings are shouted like arguments, hands are thrown to the head in utter amazement at trite remarks, beards are pulled rabbinically to ease the most trivial thoughts, feet hurry even in slowness, and all about one hears or sees tappings, twitchings, noddings, chuckles, wails, exclamations, whistles, and sharp, melancholy bursts of high-pitched laughter. Slonim, tugging at his forelock and walking jerkily, like ambulatory plumbing, fitted well into this agitated scene, Menkes says. As they walked, the baker regarded his companion with a mixture of interest and envy. He says he envied Slonim's adaptability: here was a highly trained man, a professional, who had faced up to events as he met them, had thrown over his whole career, and had taken up physical labor, and did not seem to be angry or upset over the loss of his habits. [NOTE. FROM DOLEK BERSON. It is natural that this aspect of Slonim would interest Menkes, since the baker is himself a creature of routine, according to Berson. Menkes is a conservative in this sense: he lives by, loves, and depends upon his habits, and therefore resists any change. Up at three in the morning, a session over the mixing tub, a wrestling match with batter, the shaping of loaves, the setting of the dough to rise, the clean, quick, long-stroked work with the oven-shovel, and so through the patterned day, indistinguishable from yesterday and the day before, and exactly like a well-assured tomorrow. Change one fixture in the daily exercise, and the next day at once seems less certain, less dependable. Menkes is nearly forty. He is over six feet tall, bald as a light bulb, and a little bit round, as is suitable for a man so intimate with bread. The rigidity of his routine does not prevent him from being jovial and, as I have noted before (ENTRY DECEMBER 3, 1939), full of bluster and mockery.] At last Slonim spoke out, in his blunt way:

—— What I wanted to talk with you about, Menkes, was our situation as Jews. What do you intend to do? Have you thought at all about joining the underground?

One can imagine the reaction of a habit-ridden man to this direct approach: No! Preserve the daily routine! Keep exhausting oneself in the familiar! No such adventures! Menkes says he asked cautiously:

—— What do you mean?

—— I mean that we cannot just sit around listening to piano-playing while we are engulfed. . . . You're a huge, powerful man. You would be very useful in the work of resisting our enemies.

—— I am a baker. Baking takes all my time.

—— They need bakers.

—— Not this one. I would be a hindrance. I am an open man.

—— Most of the bakers will be joining.

Menkes says he thought he heard some kind of threat in that remark. He said:

—— Leave me alone! Let me do the best I can!

—— Can a man your size be afraid?

This question, which Menkes should have expected from Slonim, made the baker furious, and he burst out:

—— You can't shame me! I have nothing to be ashamed of. I am honest. Nobody can say that I ever cheated them. Now leave me alone! I warn you, Slonim: leave me alone.

—— Very well, Menkes. . . . But remember what I told you: most of the bakers will be joining.

EVENTS APRIL 21, 1940. ENTRY APRIL 22, 1940. FROM DOLEK BERSON. Berson says that both he and Mordecai Apt had for several days noticed a marked change in Slonim. He had grown more serious, and even dull. He had dropped his jocular manner, and he had talked, soberly and long-windedly, two or three times, about Jewish history and about the place of the Jews in Poland's economy. He was out of character: he was a torrent of facts.

—— Jews paid thirty-five per cent of all taxes in Poland in 1930, though we were only ten per cent of the population. . . . Of all the tailors in Poland five years ago, eighty per cent were Jewish. Of all the shoemakers, forty per cent Jewish. Of the glaziers, one third Jewish. Of the capmakers . . .

Mordecai, once when he was alone with Dolek: —— He's a *nudnik,* he's a bore. I wish we could get away from him.

Dolek —— I don't know. Something's bothering him.

Early in the afternoon of the twenty-first, during one of their rest periods, Slonim suddenly said to Dolek and Mordecai, all in a rush:

—— Listen! Make it your business to be passing the corner of

Nalewki and Franciszkanska with loaded carts at exactly six fifteen this evening. Both of you!

Modecai: —— But we stop work at six.

Slonim: —— Take one extra trip today. (With a brief return of his twisted smile:) Load up that time with broken bricks—with bad little pieces.

Later in the afternoon, Dolek and Mordecai discussed whether they should obey or ignore Slonim's strange command. Slonim avoided them all afternoon. Mordecai was inclined to be cautious, Dolek to be curious. Mordecai said they might be arrested, if trouble started, and arrests these days were dangerous; Dolek said they had legs, they could run. . . .

At five minutes past six, the two young men were on their way along Franciszkanska Street, eastward toward Nalewki, pushing carts loaded with brick fragments. Dolek was a hundred yards ahead of Mordecai. [NOTE. N.L. I shall give the rest of this account as I got it FROM MORDECAI APT, as his telling of it made a certain point.] Fein, the cheerful workman, ran up behind Mordecai and said:

—— Hey! Don't you know when it's time to stop work?

Mordecai, between his teeth: -—— Last trip.

Fein, walking along beside: —— Want a hand? . . . That's a rotten load you have.

Mordecai: —— No, thanks.

Mordecai saw Rapaport hurrying along the opposite side of the street. At exactly six fifteen, the two carts bracketed the intersection of Franciszkanska and Nalewki. Dolek and Mordecai both stopped, as if to rest. Mordecai saw Slonim talking with a stranger on the opposite corner. Fein paused with Mordecai.

Fein: —— Something is doing. Why have you come this way? None of our routes come by here. What are you trying to do?

As Mordecai tried to think of an answer, he saw that it would not be necessary to answer. Out of Nowolipki Street, a couple of blocks down Nalewki, a gang of young Poles ran, shouting and singing. They turned up Nalewki. Their leaders darted from side to side, just like bloodhounds, Mordecai thought. Jews ducked from the street before the pack, like scattering ground-animals. One of the Poles out in front gave a whoop when he came to a candler's stall, about fifty yards from the corner of Franciszkanska.

The others gathered around. Candles flew out over their heads. Fists beat on the sides of the stall. Mordecai saw a small, Hasidic vender, his beard flopping and his black gown being ripped, handed out overhead by the strong boys. They let the screaming man down on the pavement.

Fein, muttering: —— The dirty bullies!

Mordecai wanted to run away. He looked across at Dolek, and saw the husky, strong-faced man standing beside his pushcart, with a piece of brick in each hand. Mordecai realized in fear the part he would have to play.

The Polish students were playing with the vender, plucking at his beard and tearing off his kaftan. Suddenly the stranger who had been talking to Slonim across the way ran down Nalewki toward the hurly-burly, and began shouting something in Polish at the Poles. The students turned toward him, by twos and threes, until at last the whole mob, dropping the vender, surged toward the cursing Jew. He moved away from them toward the corner— a decoy, Mordecai realized. Mordecai looked across at Slonim, who put his fingers to his mouth, whistled shrilly, and ran toward Dolek's cart. Mordecai felt himself pushed aside and nearly knocked down, and saw five or six big men, all wearing Star-of-David brassards, swarm around his pushcart, grabbing for pieces of brick, and throwing them.

Fein, shrieking: —— Oi, misery, the bastards!

The round-faced workman, with an expression of delight, reached for a missile and hurled it, in a stiff, wheeling delivery.

Mordecai leaned back on the wall against which he had been thrust, panting. He looked across at Dolek and saw his husky, musical friend, with a distorted, demoniac expression, throwing again and again. Mordecai's eyes swept across the street to Rapaport, standing near the corner watching, with his hands in his pockets, his face weirdly calm. Mordecai's look swung back toward the mob, and he had a glimpse of one amazed Polish face just as a fragment hit it. Blood started from the cheek, and the startled mouth screamed.

Within Mordecai, all at once, he says, was released an intolerable sense of shame and resentment. He saw himself as a boy at the Polish Gymnasium (*I have always tried to give you the best that was available*, his father often has said, according to Mordecai); he remembered that he had almost never been beaten up, had seldom been openly teased; always he had wondered why he was being spared—whether it was because of his respected father, or because he did not look particularly Semitic, or because of his own ways of avoiding trouble, or because the Poles simply weren't as cruel as they were supposed to be. Now, suddenly, seeing the blood on the astounded Polish face, Mordecai realized he had not, at last, been spared: today, vicariously, in the body of the shrieking vender, he, Mordecai Apt, had been tortured and brutalized for mere Jewishness. At last!

He pushed himself away from the wall. In a frenzy, he scrabbled in the cart for objects suitable for throwing. He found two, straightened his back, drew his arm for a pitch—and threw. Only then did Mordecai see that the pack had turned and was running down Nalewki again, away from the ambuscade. His brickbat fell short. He was too late with his anger.

EVENTS MAY 1, 1940.   ENTRY MAY 3, 1940.   FROM LAZAR SLONIM.

Little sun, beautiful eye, eye of the beautiful day,
Your ways are not those of our overseer.
You get up when your proper time comes,
While he would have you rise at midnight,
Little sun!

The old Socialists at Rapaport's May Day party were softly singing laborers' songs. Slonim says that he was feeling on top of the world. The old hands had all congratulated him warmly for his organization of the Franciszkanska-Nalewki ambush, which had been talked about all over Warsaw. No more raids by the Polish hooligans. How close a thing the ambush had been, Slonim says he thought, as the famous Bundists patted him on the shoulder: it had all depended on the acquiescence of the two men with the ammunition-carts, his friend Berson and young Apt, and he had staked everything on putting a mysterious idea into the mind of Berson and then staying away to let Dolek's curiosity do the job. This had worked, thank God; and now Slonim was himself a famous Bundist, in a manner of speaking. Now he had a romantic story of his own.

But as the party wore on, Slonim felt the flattery and the congratulations curdling in him. [NOTE. N.L. I have this FROM DOLEK BERSON, to whom Slonim apparently speaks with utter frankness.] After he had been permitted to retell his story of the ambush, he had been left out of the conversation, to a certain extent, and the talk of his Socialist elders, trivial and personal, trading animosities and scraps of scandal, had alienated him, and made him feel that the glowing adventure of party work was being cheapened and dulled by these people. Especially by Rapaport. Slonim says he wondered whether Rapaport had gone along all those years on his appearance: he certainly looked the part of a great, iron-hearted revolutionary, with his white mane and his leathery, deep-lined skin, his hard lips and his warm, friendly eyes. In the past few weeks, though, Slonim had caught Rapaport in so much procrastination, had seen him put off so many important decisions, had heard him make, and waited to see him break, so many promises, that his respect for the "old man" had been diminished.

Slonim says he wondered whether Rapaport had come, so late in his career, to that state which is fatal for a Socialist: doubt. Doubt that the hopeful abstraction for which he had been working so many years could be brought into being by individuals like Rapaport and himself. No single man could possibly be absolutely selfless. Concert the inconsistencies, the lapses of faith, the unconsciously selfish acts of many men—and you had the weaknesses of the Bund, of the Party, of the Idea itself. Rapaport liked holding the reins of the Bund in Warsaw; and why not? Who would not? But when would he relinquish them to younger men with more vigor and at least a fresher zeal? Slonim says he recollected his own pride and satisfaction, at the beginning of this day's celebration, when the old Socialists here had crowded around him and praised him: he says he had thought for one vindictive moment of what it would be like to command these others, to be in charge of old Rapaport. The germ of the invitation of power had been there. Now, with an astringent resolve, Slonim consciously killed the germ—or says he thinks he did.

Rapaport was in a wild mood. He threw his head back, and with an evil and comical grin, holding his voice down to a simulated shout, sang the bitter song of the contract wage-laborers in the fields, the song of the Polish *fornals*:

He is well off, he is well off,
Who knocks someone on the head.
But he is better, better off,
Who gouges out someone's eyes!

7

EVENTS JULY–AUGUST, 1940. ENTRY AUGUST 14, 1940. FROM DOLEK BERSON AND RACHEL APT. One afternoon about three weeks ago, the House Committee for Sienna 17 gathered in the Mazurs' living room. I don't think I have had occasion to note that the severe, cheap wooden furniture has all been removed from the Mazurs' apartment, so that it has lost the austere and barren look it had on the day of my housewarming speech; now the living room is fully furnished in an elegant and somewhat crowded fashion. Berson, Rachel Apt, and Rutka Mazur represented their staircase on the House Committee. Rabbi Goldflamm, one of the nine members from the rest of the courtyard, had been chosen to preside. The windows were wide open; the weather was bland. Shouts of venders and the sounds of the shunting of distant trains drifted in from outdoors. Rabbi Goldflamm was being, according to Berson, highly parliamentary:

—— We have a rather heavy agenda. . . . Do you wish to speak to that motion, Reb Yankel? . . . Are we ready for the question? . . . Do I hear a second? . . . Carried, by unanimous consent. . . .

How foolish a little authority can make otherwise sensible people, Berson says he thought. This goodhearted man, with his problems of garbage disposal, inoculations, replacement of glass panes in cellar windows, was playing at presiding over the Sejm of Poland! As a member from one of the other staircases delivered a long and emotional harangue on the faulty knob and hinges on his staircase door, as if the entire Jewish problem were somehow to be found within those bits of failing machinery, Berson says he recalled one occasion when he himself had been a president. It was at the Gymnasium here in Warsaw, before he had gone to Bonn. He had been appointed by the faculty—he states he would hardly have been elected by his Polish classmates—to run a committee on something or other; he could not even remember its province, now. And he had sat haughtily in the chair, dealing out rebuffs and peremptory procedural commands: *Out of order, Kowalski! Tabled, Beck! Overruled, Pruszow!* He says he is ashamed now when he thinks of it. His classmates had caught him on the way home that afternoon and had taunted him: *Come to order, Berson! You don't have the floor, Berson! You are adjourned, Berson!* He says he hated terribly to be laughed at.

Rutka Mazur began to speak. Berson says he had regarded her as a sensible and likable girl ever since her sprightly account of the Mazurs' wagon-voyage from Lodz at the housewarming. [ENTRY MARCH 17, 1940.] He remarks that she has her mother's handsome forehead and cheeks, but that her eyes, with the soft, bluish look around them, are her own; he also says that she is skillful in smiles of all meaning (I am not quite sure of *his* meaning there). She had said in her introduction that she wanted to put two ideas before the House Committee:

—— We in the Zionist movement have always been eager to train our young people for their life, some day, in Palestine. We are anxious to continue and even increase the facilities for that training now, even though these walls they are putting up may stand between us and Palestine, and even though we are obliged to do our work surreptitiously. I should like to propose, therefore, first, that we set up an illegal school in this courtyard, and second, that we organize a young people's club. . . .

Rutka had worked out her presentation carefully: there were nineteen children of elementary-school age in the courtyard, she said, and if the five parental families would offer their apartments for use in rotation, the work could be safely done. . . . Berson says he was impressed by Rutka's tranquil manner: like her mother's, except not quite so calm and settled; after all, she is only a girl of twenty. Berson admits that her proposals interested him in the proceedings of the Committee for the first time, and he broke his silence. He said he had a candidate for someone to organize and run the school: Rachel Apt. Berson says that Rachel jumped as if she had been pinched when he spoke her name, and then she blushed and squirmed. I asked Berson why he had proposed Rachel for the job. He hardly knows, he says; perhaps it was because he thought a plain girl ought to have something to keep her busy, he says. Rachel's name was unanimously accepted (Berson reports that of all who were present, only Rutka, for some reason, showed by her bearing that she was skeptical of Rachel as a choice), and Rachel declared diffidently that she would do the best she knew how.

It is my guess that Rachel had never been so happy in all her life as she was in the following days. She wrestled with the problem of the illicit school as if it were a risky love affair. Her first. She trysted—with those from whom she wanted things. She sought advice like a lovelorn girl. She tells me that she lay awake nights, her heart pounding at the thought of what she was doing. Her appetite was enormously variable. She wept without knowing why, and she sang without knowing why. She says she felt everything far more deeply than she ever had before. And I write this very small: for the first time in her life she felt equal to Halinka.

At the beginning Rachel's work went very well. She arranged, through Symka Berson, to call on Regina Orlewska—Symka's friend who taught at the big Jewish school at Okopowa 55A until the school was shut down on December 4, 1939—to ask whether Frailin Orlewska would take on the job of teaching the secret school. Rachel found a modest, quiet girl who, behind a pair of glasses, was quite pretty, though prematurely grey. Orlewska seemed never to speak above a murmur, and yet she could put into a gently delivered speech an intensity that raised its effect almost to that of a shout: and it was with just such a joyous shout—unsmiling and barely audible—that she greeted Rachel's proposal.

Orlewska: —— Yes, I would like to try to do the work. . . . I've missed my children so!

Rachel: —— It may prove dangerous.

Rachel says that she was thrilled at her own casualness in making this remark.

Orlewska: —— What is the meaning of danger these days? It's dangerous to walk on Sienna Street, because the people who live on the upper storeys in the apartments facing the street may not have fastened their window boxes carefully, and one might fall on you. Is that the sort of danger you mean?

Rachel: —— Yes, that's what I mean!

Often, during the days when she was "building the school," as she used to say, Rachel talked with her small brother, David, about it. David teased her, even mocked her, as she asked him grave questions, but she felt that the important work was being done: David was coming to understand why he must study this next year in the home courtyard, practically in hiding. One day when she and her brother were alone together, she talked of the school with him:

Rachel: —— What do you want to study when Frailin Orlewska is here in September?

David: —— Her ears . . .

Rachel: —— Dovidl!

David: —— . . . to see if they're clean.

Rachel: —— Will you miss the Okopowa School?

David, fondly, as if he were suddenly sorry for his sister: —— No. I don't think so. Anyhow, Rochele, I'll be able to learn more here at home.

Rachel spoke to the two Mazur boys, Rutka's brothers. She asked the handsome Stefan about the problem of sports and games in the narrow confines of the courtyard, and when he tried to put her off with a few brusque suggestions [NOTE. N.L. I can see that a homely girl like Rachel would not seem worth much of Stefan's time.], she kept after him, until at last he rather grudgingly agreed to supervise her program of games. Rachel asked pale Schlome about the problem of religious instruction, but he spoke, in his other-worldly voice, of much-too-adult things to be learned —of Maimonides, of the significance of the Maccabees, of the sayings of the Great Maggid, Dov Baer of Mezrich. Rachel also went to Berson, asking him if he would tell the children something about music, and play for them, on Sundays. Berson agreed, but he said:

—— My Sunday is getting to be like a woman's purse at the end of the day: crammed with everything but money.

Not once, for some reason, did Rachel consult Rutka Mazur, whose idea the school had been in the first place.

Rachel made her mistake, as a girl would in love, by going too far.

Rutka Mazur had proposed the school in the first place as a Zionist project. In a sober-minded effort to find out the implications of the proposal from that point of view, Rachel asked for, and was granted, an interview with Hil Zilberzweig, the leader of the left-Zionist youth movement, Hashomer Hatsair. In a stiff, unfruitful conversation, Rachel questioned Zilberzweig about Zionist

93

education, and she had the impression that the busy, slick-haired man could not make out what this little, odd, fish-faced girl (he made her feel that way, she says) was driving at, unless she was thinking of embracing Zionism, in which case she scarcely would need to take up *his* time; he hurried from answer to answer and dismissed her as soon as an opening presented itself.

That was all right. But one evening at the Bersons', while Rachel was absorbedly discussing teaching methods, Berson, to pull her leg, said:

—— Why don't you talk with Professor Benlevi? He has won a Nobel Prize. He should be able to help you!

Rachel said thoughtfully that that idea had not occurred to her.

Berson, who tells me he hadn't the heart to press home his jest, went on, following a more serious line, about Benlevi—what the old man had been like at Bonn, and how he had taken the trouble, after Berson's imprisonment with us deputy councilors last autumn, to invite him to tea, and how charming he had been. Berson says he intended in this way to divert Rachel from his bad joke; instead, it seems, he made her take it the more seriously. That was her error. . . .

EVENTS AUGUST 9, 1940. ENTRY AUGUST 14, 1940. N.L. At last I have tracked down the details of the incident on the staircase, at the end of the evening when Berson suggested the Benlevi interview. This occurrence was in itself trivial, but it seems to me to shed some light on a timorousness—a *detachment*—I have observed in Rachel. Poor Rachel! If only I could help you see how unimportant this was!

[FROM HALINKA APT.] It took a bit of courage to go after Halinka Apt on this matter: I was afraid she would regard my questions as invasion of her privacy. Not at all. She talked quite freely, even a little boastfully, I thought, as if she wished to humiliate me. She told me she was talking with Stefan:

Stefan: —— You sang wonderfully last night.

Halinka, with her sly femininity: —— I just rode along on Dolek's accompaniment.

The two young people were lingering on the staircase, before saying goodnight. They were on the blank landing, halfway between the Apts' landing and the Bersons', at the top. One can picture the scene: a single, bare bulb, their moon, throwing its cold, yellow light onto their flushed faces and onto the plaster walls of their garden of love. For the staircase was the only place they could be alone in all Warsaw, except at great risk, because of the curfew. The couple turned their heads as they heard a rustling on the Apts' landing, the next below. They smiled at each other, but made no move to discover who was down there: that would have violated the Code of the Staircase. They moved a bit closer together, and spoke in murmurs.

Stefan: —— You're lucky: you will be a professional singer on the stage. I wish I could be an actor. I think I would look all right, but I'm so stiff when I try to act. You know, Halinka [NOTE. N.L. Here I believe I detect a deliberate ambiguity on the part of this rascal.], I can think of nothing so fine as giving pleasure.

Halinka, with somewhat less imagination than the situation required of her: —— I too.

A door could be heard opening upstairs, and footsteps on the Bersons' landing. Halinka says that she and Stefan moved apart and waited. . . .

[FROM RACHEL APT.] Rachel's attitude, as she told me what had happened from her point of view, seemed to be more disgust than anything else. All the same, she made quite a point of telling me about it.

Rachel says she walked out onto the landing and started downstairs, humming a tune, a Strauss waltz. She tells me she was thinking that Dolek Berson is a puzzling, contradictory man. For the first time, this evening, he had been considerate and truly kind. He had talked about House Committee problems with Rachel, and he had seemed genuinely interested in the difficulties in connection with the school and respectful of Rachel's opinion about them. He had treated her, she says, as an equal, not as a stupid child.

At the half-landing, Rachel saw them: Halinka, not looking at her, but staring quizzically at Stefan; Stefan's eyes, too, averted. Rachel says she ran, skirting the banister closely, and hurried down the next flight. There, in the somewhat darker door of her own home, blocking her way, so lost in each other that they had not even heard her approaching, were two people embracing and kissing. Suddenly they wrenched apart from each other. In the dim

95

light: Mordecai and Rutka. Mordecai opened the door for Rachel, and said, rather breathlessly:

—— Excuse us.

This is where Rachel's account ended, but this was not the end of the incident.

[FROM HALINKA APT.] . . . Twenty pleasant minutes later, having heard the rustlers below descend one flight, Stefan took Halinka down to her landing and, with what she says was a charming shyness, took her hand and kissed it. Halinka then opened the apartment door and slipped within. At the side of the double doorway between the foyer and the living room Rachel stood, leaning her forehead against the doorframe, covering her misfortunate face with her hands, obliviously weeping. Humming a tune, Halinka glided past Rachel and into her own room. It was only when she had closed the door of her room behind her, Halinka says, that she realized she had been humming the very Strauss waltz that had been on Rachel's lips up on the staircase a few minutes before. She says that if there was malice in this coincidence, it was entirely unconscious. I wonder.

EVENTS AUGUST 13, 1940. ENTRY AUGUST 15, 1940. FROM RACHEL APT. Rachel called on Benlevi in his office at the *Judenrat*, and she went in high hopes, expecting the great man to be as gracious to her as he had been to Berson.

After a long wait, she was let into Benlevi's office. She began deferentially:

—— I was recommended to you by Dolek Berson. He worships you.

The distinguished man nodded, acknowledging the validity of both the introduction and the veneration. Rachel said at once:

—— In our courtyard, we are organizing an illegal school.

Benlevi, abruptly: —— Then I have no desire to hear any more. You ought to have more sense than to come here on such an errand. The *Judenrat* is the instrument of legality in the Jewish section. If you wish to break the law, go to the world of smugglers, bilkers, and bribers for help. You'll find plenty of company there.

[NOTE. N.L. This was *bad* of Benlevi. Ha! I must tell Berson about this, who thinks Benlevi such a model man. Himself an educator, how dared he crush this enthusiastic girl? He knows very

well what the Jews are doing against the law to teach their young.]
[INSERT. FROM ENTRY JULY 20, 1940. N.L. Secret schools are
springing up everywhere: in attics, in cellars, in CENTOS kitchens, in homes. Our fine institutions are being reproduced in miniature here: the Lodz Gymnasium is hidden away among us, and
some of the teachers of the greatest rabbinical school in Europe,
the Academy of Learned Men of Lublin, came here after the
place was destroyed last spring. Everything is taught, even Greek
and Latin. We have clandestine laboratories for chemistry and
physics, where students use kitchen pots and tumblers for vials
and beakers. The incredible range of learning that is being done in
the closet, so to speak, goes all the way from primer reading for
tiny children to Hellenistic studies, Midrash, demography, homi-
letics, and Talmudic archeology for advanced scholars. There is
risk in all this. One secret school was discovered in June; the teachers were shot and the students were taken off we know not where.
Naturally parents are afraid to commit their children to this peril,
but the drive to educate them is even stronger than fear. In middle
school classes, there is much absenteeism, for the students have
to go off to smuggle food.]

Rachel says she tried to tell Benlevi that she had only come
for personal advice, but Benlevi flew into an exaggerated, pompous
rage, and roared at the trembling girl that he would call the Gestapo if she didn't get out at once. Rachel left, in tears.

One could understand old Benlevi's having been annoyed by
a foolish interruption; but his anger over Rachel's innocent visit
sustained itself, for some silly reason. The following day Secretary
Mandeltort called Pan Apt to the *Judenrat* and told him how incensed old Benlevi was at his daughter's indiscretion; and N.L.
sent a letter [NOTE. N.L. I curse myself!] to Berson, forwarding
Benlevi's chiding. That evening Rachel suffered the dreadful embarrassment of a dressing down by her father, spoken by him as if
she were a ten-year-old girl. Even more chagrining was Berson's
patronizing comment:

—— My suggestion about Benlevi was a joke, girl!

Worst of all, somehow, Rachel tells me, was the reproach that
Rutka Mazur delivered in ill temper yesterday:

—— I hear you've been chattering about our school idea to
Zilberzweig and Benlevi and everybody's brother's cousin. Don't

97

you realize this could very well be a matter of life and death?

Rachel protests to me:

—— Of course I realized it! That's precisely why I wanted the best advice I could find.

Rachel is going on with her plans for the school, but she is less enthusiastic than before. So much the pity. She actually tells me that she wonders whether there would have been any fumble at all, were she a pretty girl.

EVENTS AUGUST, 1940. ENTRY AUGUST 16, 1940. N.L.
. . . I am timid. I am obliged every day to face my inescapable timidity and cowardice.

The other day, when Benlevi came storming in to Mandel-tort and me about poor Rachel Apt, I felt at the time I should have told him that he was excited about nothing, that he knew all about illegal schools being formed in the Jewish district, that, in fact, as an official of the *Judenrat* and as a great Jew, it should have been his duty quietly to encourage her. Instead, what? I kowtowed and said: *Yes, Pan Benlevi!* Worse, at Benlevi's command, I dispatched a note to the Drifter, since Benlevi had seemed so miffed about Berson's having sent Rachel to him. But for my timorousness, I might have let the note slide. I find it quite easy to be sarcastic to Rachel's ineffectual father; but to Benlevi, to whom as a famous man and a superior official I have double reason to be resistant, I accede, scrape, rub my hands, and act like a man trying to sell something.

And when my puzzlement about the sections of wall was resolved by that obscure little notice, some time ago, commanding Jews who moved "for any reason" to go and live within the wall, I knew with my mind that I should have grown angry and I should have taken some action. Instead, what? I sat at my desk, glad. Yes, actually glad and relieved. I was pleased that all the Germans wanted was to have us Jews living more or less together. I find really a kind of security and comfort in this arrangement, compressive as it may prove to be. We will be together, without the constant, sandy rub of life among the Poles and Germans. I welcome what we resisted last October. This is simply fearfulness and isolationism on my part, I realize. But I *am* glad! I share with others here a feeling that this is perhaps not far from the end of our trouble. They are putting us to one side and they will be glad to remove from their minds such an unpleasant subject as we are to them.

The question is: how serious a weakness is my timidity? I do not possess it alone. I see signs of a similar prudence in my colleagues. Every time a German walks into this office, there is a kind of organized cringing around here. Even our Chairman, Sokolczyk, who has the personal courage of a Gandhi, becomes unctuous in the presence of a minor German functionary. This is especially curious when you consider how far superior he is to his visitors; I myself feel superior to those who frighten me.

One reason, perhaps, for my caution and servility, and for that of my colleagues, is the principle of collective responsibility for which the Germans are so famous. If one does "wrong," all are punished. As a corollary, each of us feels, to some degree, a personal responsibility for the welfare of all.

The Drifter and I had a long talk about this the other night. He says his eyes were opened to this matter of the collective conscience by the Schpunt affair. Up until then he had felt that his relationship with the Germans was personal, and that he could best deal with them personally by being the finest Jew he knew how to be: shame them. The result of that, he now admits, was that he was constantly shaming himself by his minor failures to live up to his idea of a worthy Jew. Schpunt's jig moved him one step. He now feels that it is important to participate in Jewish activities, particularly of a self-help type. Even these shame him in a small way, from time to time, he says: both intrinsically, by their occasional fatuousness, or inadequacy; and subjectively, by the sense they give him of the smallness of one man's efforts; but I have learned that Berson is nothing if not dogged: once he has taken a position, he will stick to his guns, long after his ammunition is gone or their mechanism is jammed.

I tried to point out to Berson that the borderline between exemplary personal behavior and participation in self-help activities, and between the latter and minor resistance work, and between that and the active underground—all these borderlines are shadowy, vague, and constantly shifting. No, says Berson, there's a sharp difference between being *for* something (a set of ethics) and *against* something (the Nazi doctrine). But, says Levinson, what if something is *against* what you are *for*? Must you not go *against* the *against*? No, says Berson, you must be more *for* the *for*.

99

Timidity. I think this is all timidity on Berson's part, which he rationalizes very nicely. I argue with him, but I have to face my own craven spirit. I am especially disgusted with myself for what I did about Rachel and her school work. . . .

8

EVENTS NOVEMBER 15, 1940. ENTRY DITTO. N.L. . . . I have been tense and expectant for many days, but I never anticipated this thing that has happened. Until I went out in the streets today and saw it with my own eyes, I did not believe it, and still this evening my belief is strained.

Many of my colleagues in the *Judenrat* have remained optimistic until this very day, but I have been lugubrious and a spoilsport ever since late in September—ever since that Polish janitor left Sienna 17.

[INSERT. EDITOR. The departure of Kucharski from Sienna 17 had been unexcitedly noted by N.L., almost a month earlier, on SEPTEMBER 23, as follows:

FROM RACHEL APT. Out in the courtyard, day before yesterday morning, stood Kucharski, intercepting every passer-by to make sure he had said goodbye. The janitor had suspended all work for two days, in order to say goodbye to everyone in a proper manner. Kucharski was reluctant to leave, or at least he pretended to be. He was forced to leave under the edict forbidding Poles to work for Jewish establishments. Of course, Jews can work for Poles. The question: from what are the Poles being extricated in this way? Kucharski had considered it necessary, apparently, to set traps for the heads of households, in order to catch them alone, in the seclusion of staircases or foyers, so that they could tip him without the embarrassment of public show. With the ladies it was different: the more audience the better, from the old janitor's point of view. When Rachel crossed the courtyard on an errand, he called out:

Kucharski: —— My dear Panna Apt!

Rachel: —— I was sorry to hear you are leaving us.

Kucharski: —— My favorite young lady!

Rachel: —— You say that to all of us.

Kucharski: —— No! No! (He granted, however, with a ro-
guish laugh, that he adored all the young ladies.) You are special,
Panna Apt. I like the way you went to work on the secret school.
And I like the way you treat your little David. You seem capable
of taking care of everybody.

Rachel says she blushed. The janitor's reference to the school
frightened her. She thought perhaps she had been too free with
her tongue. Should this Pole know about the school—especially
now that he was leaving? (NOTE. N.L. I *think* Kucharski can
be trusted. He has worked in this courtyard for years, and he
seems a loyal and friendly fellow. One can never tell for sure, of
course. He seems above everything else to be lazy; I conceive that
to be a non-political trait. He has always done a bare minimum of
work, and has made up for his sloppy habits with the tenants by
being cheerful and full of gossip—particularly with the young
ladies.)

Kucharski: —— If there is anything I can do for you or for
your friends, Panna Apt, you must let me know. I don't have the
attitude of some Poles, you know, Panna Apt. I am deeply fond
of your people.

Rachel says she felt the embarrassment that always afflicts her
when a gentile becomes too effusive toward the Jews in general.

Kucharski: —— I will send you my address, when I am
settled. And now I imagine you have a thousand things to do.
Goodbye, my dear young lady!]

I suppose I put a disproportionate emphasis on Kucharski's
departure, but for some reason, I attached great importance to
that minor indication; indeed, it marked the turning point in my
spirit. Probably my alarm over this event was simply the culmination of many impressions I myself scarcely knew I had received.
Since then I have been increasingly apprehensive.

Oddly enough, I missed entirely the point of the explicit warning the Germans gave us: the decree of October 16, making it
mandatory for all Jews and all Jewish enterprises remaining outside the Jewish district in Warsaw to move inside forthwith. No
more hypothetical moves "for any reason"; now all would move,
willy-nilly. The deadline was set at October 31, then it was twice
postponed—to, finally, November 12. Nothing happened on November 12. Only today—

I considered this decree to be just another of many episodes

I had been noting. I had no sense of its finality. I paid it scant attention, for I was occupied with my own lines of thinking; my own little occupations loomed large. So with all of us: we let our small personal concerns blind us to the huge thing that was going to happen to everybody together. Berson's case—his being so wrapped up in Pan Apt's affairs that he missed this other thing entirely, and *still* scarcely knows it has taken place—is so typical that I think I will explore it, beginning with the day when I first suggested . . .

EVENTS OCTOBER 23, 1940. ENTRY NOVEMBER 16, 1940. N.L. Mandeltort and I had been told to try to solve a number of personal and familial problems which had penetrated the *Judenrat* through influence, kinship, or acuteness. Felix had the case histories on his desk, and we had reached a pause, being rather sated with distress.

N.L.: —— Aha! I have an idea.

Felix, drily: —— That in itself is measurable progress.

N.L.: —— My thought is to harness my friend Berson. He was telling me just the other night that a Jew ought to participate in self-help work. Let's give him Mauritzi Apt, who can't seem to help himself. That will teach Berson! He already knows Apt's problem; Apt dragged him into it already, he told me.

Felix, thumbing the work-sheets on his desk: —— Very good, very good. Can't we throw in a bonus, too, if Berson is so anxious?

N.L.: —— We could give him Jablonski, who doesn't want to be helped.

Felix: —— Levinson, one of these days you are going to maneuver my job right away from me with your brilliant ideas.

N.L.: —— God forbid! I'd rather sell herring.

And so Berson was called in to us, right from his work with the brick detail, by messenger, and we explained how we wanted him to help. Pan Apt's problem, with which he had been pestering everyone in the *Judenrat* from Chairman Sokolczyk down through Felix and me to Pintricz the office boy, was the year-old question whether he could maintain his jewelry store in the "Aryan" part of town.

N.L.: —— Your assignment, Berson, is simple: just keep Apt out of the *Judenrat*. We can do absolutely nothing for him.

[INSERT. EDITOR. Berson's familiarity with Pan Apt's distress dated back at least to the previous June, when we find the following entry:

EVENTS JUNE 26, 1940. ENTRY JUNE 27, 1940. FROM DO-LEK BERSON. Berson answered a knock at the door of his apartment, and found Pan Apt, wearing house slippers, holding a newspaper in his hand, on the landing. (NOTE. N.L. One would have to say that Pan Apt is a cultured man. He knows as much about painting as any man I have ever talked with—though he seems sometimes more interested in the appraised value of a work of art than he is in the pleasure it gives the eye. He is also a student of European history, and can draw you the plans of all of Napoleon's major battles. He has fascinating bits of knowledge—on certain diseases, on the social life of insects, whose reactionary and rigid labor systems are a great comfort to him, on minerals and mining, on weather, on furniture. His is an eclectic culture. He wants to be a Western European, and seems reluctant to admit that he is Jewish, even here, among us. He is an entertaining man and could be a jolly one if anyone would join him in his casual attitude. He loves his children without understanding them: it is pathetic how much he loves them. They are aware of his making efforts for them: I have already quoted [ENTRY APRIL 22, 1940] Mordecai's appreciation of his father's having given the best that was available in everything. Yet the children are dutiful toward him, rather than affectionate.)

Pan Apt: —— May I speak to you a moment?

Berson: —— Certainly. Come in.

Pan Apt: —— No, here is all right. I don't want to disturb your family. I just wondered whether you had seen this.

Pan Apt folded the newspaper, the *Gazeta Zydowska*, back on itself, twice, until it was a quarter its full size, and then held it up and pointed to an obscure block of small type among the public notices. It was one of the dully worded "V. Bl. G. G." decrees, pertaining to Jews. (NOTE. EDITOR. These initials were used for *Verordnungsblatt des General-Gouverneurs*.) It said that Jews and Jewesses moving to Warsaw from other living-places must take up residence in the area bounded by the new sections of wall; and that Jews and Jewesses living in Warsaw outside that area, upon moving for any reason, must go inside the area. Reading this, Berson reflected with some relief, he says, that since he already lived within the walled area, this notice did not particularly concern him, and he said:

—— No, I hadn't seen it.

Pan Apt: —— I don't like that phrase, *upon moving for any reason*. (Berson says that Pan Apt seemed calm and spoke ingratiatingly.) They made us move into this section for one of those "any" reasons. And now, if they find another such reason for me to move my store, I am finished. Absolutely cut off. You can understand that. *Nu*, I was wondering if I could count on you for a very slight favor. I thought you might be so good as to intervene on my behalf with your cousin to use his influence. . . .

Berson: —— My cousin?

Pan Apt: ——Meier Berson is your cousin?

Berson: —— Yes, but what influence—?

Pan Apt: —— Meier Berson is since last week my trustee's house-Jew. (NOTE. N.L. A "house-Jew" is a Jew taken in by a German official in a factotum capacity: servant, buyer, seller, accountant, guide, informer, pander, and jester.) Herr Gruber has been very kind—so kind, in fact, that I feel I would upset the delicate balance between us if I were to ask him directly for favors. Since your cousin is now his confidant . . . I thought perhaps a nudge from an impersonal quarter. . . . All I need is assurance that *upon moving for any reason* will not apply to my store. . . .

Berson says he was completely muddled by what Pan Apt had said. He had not seen his cousin Meier but once since the day of Schpunt's dance, when Meier had gone to the clandestine prayerhouse with him and had asked for the loan.

Berson: —— Meier told me he was going in the leather business. . . .

Pan Apt: —— You'll do what you can?

Pan Apt is a man who would speak of helping others and of helping himself in exactly the same benevolent, good-doing, and urgent tone.

Berson, still fumbling: —— Of course, I'll try to help. . . . A house-Jew!]

[NOTE. EDITOR. An entry dated AUGUST 6, 1940, indicates that Berson did in fact get an oral assurance through his cousin that Pan Apt's store would not be moved. The new decree of October 16, however, commanding *all* Jewish enterprises to move at once obviously undermined the assurance of August and made the whole question sharply pertinent anew.]

The Jablonski case was more complex. We explained that this man was a *meshummed*, a convert. Jan Jablonski, *né* Isaac Zeligstein, had become converted to Catholicism in 1921, for reasons of his own. He had also changed his name at that time. He now regarded himself as a Pole, and saw no reason why he should move to the Jewish section. The Germans, however, had taken a different view: they classified him, as they did all converts to the second generation at least, as pure Jewish. Jablonski had been appealing for some dispensation, which could not be given him. We handed Jablonski's address—he lived in a solidly Polish section of Zoliborz —to Berson and also gave him a pass as a *Judenrat* courier.

N.L.: —— Do what you can. Console him if you want to. Let him cry. But keep *him* out of here, too.

Berson took all this with his usual cheerful enthusiasm, and left us.

N.L.: —— Well! At least those two problems are solved.

Felix, with a lifted eyebrow: —— Solved?

EVENTS OCTOBER 23, 1940. ENTRY NOVEMBER 16, 1940. FROM DOLEK BERSON. Pan Apt was indeed wild, but his wildness was canny and thorough. Berson's visit to him, on returning from work that evening, struck Pan Apt as felicitous.

Apt: —— Telepathic, my dear Berson, telepathic! I was just thinking about coming up to see you. (In his excitement, says Berson, Pan Apt seemed elated.) We are going to have to go back to your cousin for another little talk.

Berson: —— I don't know how far Meier's influence will stretch.

Apt: —— This time we will not talk favors. We will talk business. I want you to find out how much I would have to pay Herr Gruber, either in zlotys or stones, for the right to keep my store open outside the Jewish section. Authorized in writing.

Berson says he noticed that Pan Apt spoke with none of the humble politeness he had worn the first time he had asked for intervention with Meier; rather, he was speaking as if to an employee—and Berson was quickly granted the meaning of this tone:

Apt: —— If we are successful, ten per cent of the payment,

over and above it, will go to you and to your cousin, as a legitimate commission.

Berson: —— No. Don't speak of that.

Apt: —— We'll discuss it later.

Berson said he would call on Meier as soon as he could.

EVENTS OCTOBER 25, 1940. ENTRY NOVEMBER 16, 1940. FROM DOLEK BERSON. Before Berson left the Jewish section to go out to the suburb of Zoliborz, to see Jablonski, he removed his armband, for he felt confident that his face would not betray him as a Jew, and he decided he wanted an undisturbed trip through the Polish city. He took streetcar No. 21 to the Krakowski Przedmiescie transfer and then No. 17 to Wilson Place. On the latter car, he suddenly wondered whether his impulse to take off his Star-of-David brassard had been due to the fact that he was to call upon an apostate Jew; he decided, at any rate, to leave it off while talking with Jablonski. Man to man, Pole to Pole.

Jablonski came to the door when Berson rang. He was a broad and florid fellow with an abnormally large jaw, as if mastication were his only exercise. His mouth was wide, and his eyes were clear and friendly.

Jablonski: —— From the *Judenrat*?

Berson: —— Yes. From the *Judenrat*.

Jablonski: —— Were you able to make arrangements?

Berson, bluntly, looking at Jablonski's coat buttons, not at his face: —— No.

The buttons moved back, and Jablonski's voice, dull and slow, as if its battery were running down, said:

—— Come in. I'd like to talk with you.

Jablonski sat Berson down in a cheaply furnished but pleasant living room and began talking about himself. Jablonski evidently wanted a Jew to talk to, any Jew. Berson says he reflected after a few minutes that he should, after all, have been wearing his armband.

Jablonski: —— I took up Catholicism because I believed in it. . . . No one seems to understand that. My wife died in childbirth and left me a son who looks Semitic but has been brought up Polish in every way. He cannot speak a word of Yiddish. This is all very embarrassing. Your official people seem to think I am trying to evade something, but that's not true. I was converted nineteen

years ago, before anyone ever heard of Adolf Hitler. I believe in
the faith, it is part of me now. This is very hard for Wladislaw—
my boy.

Jablonski seemed confused and talked in circles, his great jaw
working between sentences, as if he were chewing hard thoughts.
Berson thought it would be tactful simply to keep still, and gradually, painfully, Jablonski came around to the crux of his trouble:

Jablonski: —— Two months ago they told me that the power
plant was putting on an economy drive, and that my job was one
of those which would have to be eliminated "for budgetary reasons," although I had worked there faithfully for sixteen years. I
had always been accepted as a Pole. . . . I wondered at the time.
. . . I had saved very little, my boy's education. . . .

Berson waited.

Jablonski: —— I am told that getting an adequate apartment
requires large sums of key money. I could not bear to subject
Wladislaw to those slums on Smocza Street. I have looked at some
rooms. My savings . . .

Berson: —— Then you have resigned yourself to moving into
the section?

Jablonski: —— If I am said to be a Jew. . . . If the law says
I am a Jew. . . .

[NOTE. N.L. The law does. The official German definition
of a Jew is any man who has had at least three Jewish grandparents, or two Jewish grandparents providing 1) he is active in any
Jewish communal organization or 2) he has a Jewish wife. Jablonski
had four Jewish grandparents.]

Berson: —— In that case, I think we can take care of you.

Berson says he pitied Jablonski; he saw how easy it would be
for a sincere man to get into Jablonski's position. He says he had
thought of a solution, but it involved Symka—and this time he
remembered to speak to her first.

EVENTS OCTOBER 25–28, 1940. ENTRY NOVEMBER 16, 1940.
FROM DOLEK BERSON. Berson says he felt that his cousin Meier
was allowing himself to be uncharacteristically high-minded.

Meier: —— I'm not sure that a bribe would work. Herr Gruber is surprisingly fastidious for a German, you know.

Berson: —— What would make you sure that a bribe would
work? A percentage of it?

Meier, grinning: —— That might help.

Berson said he was authorized to offer five per cent. Meier agreed to try his best. That very evening he came to Dolek to say that the bribe could be arranged, but that the details would have to be worked out with Gruber's financial agent, a man named Edek Hartmann.

Meier: —— You may hear that this Hartmann is or used to be a Communist. I give you my word that for this matter he is reliable, positively reliable.

Berson says he remembered Mordecai Apt's excited account of the reunion of Kurtz, Budko, and Hartmann, and vaguely he recalled some remark to the effect that Hartmann had "changed." [ENTRY DECEMBER 12, 1939.] Berson went to see Hartmann after work the next day in a dingy tobacconist's stall on Nowolipki Street. Hartmann was as thin as a twig, and Berson says his face was almost expressionless, so taut was his skin over the framework beneath. Hartmann was abrupt, to say the least. He named a price, with no preliminaries whatsoever: one million zlotys. [NOTE. EDITOR. At this time, the zloty was worth about two cents on the black market.]

Not having thought this enterprise through to its conclusion, Berson was shocked, he says, when he came face to face with the actual image of the bribe. He began, defensively and clumsily, to bargain. His very confusion, along with his stubbornness, helped him to baffle Hartmann, who burst out once:

—— What are you—a second-hand-clothes dealer? I have never seen such haggling.

The price finally reached was six hundred thousand zlotys net: that is to say, including Hartmann's and Meier's shares. Berson agreed to deliver the cash to Hartmann two days later, at the tobacconist's stall, at seven o'clock in the evening.

Pan Apt went along to the palm-crossing. He was childishly happy, and he was unusually friendly toward Berson, whom he now seemed to regard as a practical man. At the stall, Hartmann held up Gruber's letter between his daddy-longlegs fingers for Pan Apt to read. It was the authorization Pan Apt thought he needed and, more importantly, it was in Gruber's own handwriting. Pan Apt put forward a roll of bills in a trembling paw. Hartmann counted them and nodded. Berson says the whole transaction was a pantomime. On the way home, afoot, Pan Apt was paternal:

—— Dolek, you were a good boy to arrange that for me. (He cleared his throat.) Regard this as a present from a grateful man.

He held out three or four bills. Berson says he raised a traffic-policeman's restraining hand and refused. Pan Apt began pressing. Berson blushed and protested.

Apt: —— All right. Take half. Take these.

Berson, confused and agonized: —— I haven't done anything.

Apt: —— Here! It is only your due.

Berson: —— Too much, too much.

Berson says he does not know why he said that. He does not understand how he let himself be pushed from refusing into bargaining; he was deeply mortified; he was also touched by Pan Apt's evident gratitude and relief; he wanted, above all, an end to this embarrassing impasse. Pan Apt put away all but one bill and said:

—— All right then, just a token.

Fumbling, having no idea of the denomination of the bill, Berson took it and stuffed it roughly into his jacket pocket.

Pan Apt, apparently considering himself out of the affair cheaply, was merrier and fonder than ever, as he cried:

—— I wish my Mordecai were more like you. He's so rebellious!

When Berson arrived home, he found that the note in his pocket was for five thousand zlotys.

EVENTS NOVEMBER 5–8, 1940. ENTRY NOVEMBER 16, 1940. FROM DOLEK BERSON. Berson worked around to the proposal with great caution, speaking of the overcrowding that had already existed in the Jewish quarter, of the hundred-odd thousand who must now enter it, of his and Symka's good fortune in having had an extra bedroom; he told Symka, sympathetically, of his visit to Jablonski. Then at last he made his suggestion, and Symka straightaway shrugged her shoulders and said:

—— Why not?

And so, on November 8, four days before the final deadline for moving, the effusively grateful Jablonskis came to live with the Bersons. [NOTE. N.L. Wladislaw is twenty, a narrow-faced, intelligent-looking boy who must have had his Polishness questioned time and again.] At first the father was stiff and quiet, and his great jaw remained firmly clamped. But gradually, as he saw that the Bersons took their own Jewishness quite for granted, were not

109

themselves particularly religious, and had no interest at all in *his* religion, he began to relax. In spite of the overworked masseteric muscles in his bundle of a jaw, which seemed to indicate a habit of tension, he turned out, on the contrary, to be of a generally happy temperament, and in a few days he began to open up now and then with a huge, raucous laugh.

EVENTS NOVEMBER 12, 1940. ENTRY NOVEMBER 16, 1940. FROM DOLEK BERSON. Much on Berson's mind was the money he had accepted from Pan Apt. When he told Symka about it, she said:

—— Nonsense! You earned it. It's a commission. You say he expected to pay you much more than that, and he would have been obliged to, to anyone but you. You saved him money. Forget it!

But Berson could not, he says. On the morning of November 12, the day of the final deadline, he was in an agony of anxiety about Pan Apt's store. Would it be closed? Would Pan Apt be allowed to manage it and take his profits out? How good was Gruber's word? These worries finally troubled him so much that, using his courier's pass and talking glibly, he got himself excused for a few hours from the brick detail and went out through one of the gates in the wall, to Miodowa Street, and walked past Pan Apt's store, on the opposite side of the street. The shop was open; he saw a beautiful woman in a sable jacket enter; Berson paused; in the window, against which the sunlight slanted, a startling display of jewels shimmered and glistened, almost alive in the brightness, he says he thought (and what thoughts one can admit in times of crisis!), as if each flashing object were a hint of something to come —of one woman's vanity and of another's despair in her senescence, of one man's blossoming sentimentality and of another's lust, of an anniversary remembered, a birthday forgotten, an adulteress nearly abandoned, a daughter dearly loved. He says he thought for a moment of Symka, and of the day they became engaged, when, sitting in broad daylight in Saxon Garden under a whispering birch; he had clumsily given her a ring, bought from this store; the ring had been cold on the counter and dead in the gift-box, but suddenly, on her finger, it had come to life—a life full of hope.

Berson walked across the street and entered the store. He must have been a sight in his working clothes! He says a pretty Polish

salesgirl came up to him and spoke to him as deferentially as if he
were dressed in black coat and striped trousers:
—— Can I help you?
—— Is Pan Apt in?
—— No. Pan Apt is not here.
—— Has he been in this morning?
—— Oh, yes. He's gone out to the bank. Is there any message?
—— No, thank you. A personal matter. No, thank you. . . .
And Berson fled from the store, crazily relieved. That evening
he went down to the Apts' apartment and waited for Pan Apt to
come home. The jeweler arrived ebullient, and when he saw Ber-
son's anxious face, he shouted:
—— What's the matter, Dolek, my boy? You look like a man
who has just lost his mother—well, anyway, his mother-in-law. Ha!
Ha! Ha!

EVENTS NOVEMBER 15, 1940. ENTRY NOVEMBER 16, 1940.
FROM DOLEK BERSON.   For some reason, the fact that the bribe to
Gruber had worked made Berson feel even worse than before
about his "commission." By the morning of the fifteenth, three
days after the deadline, he had determined to give the money back.
He went downstairs, early in the morning, to catch Pan Apt before
he left for the store. Rachel came to the door, and said that her
father had just left a half minute before—that if Dolek hurried, he
might catch him in the courtyard.
Berson says he did hurry, but Pan Apt was out of the courtyard by the time he reached it. He went out into the street and
could just see Pan Apt's fat little back and shoulders, almost a
block away, jouncing up and down in a near-trot, in evident eagerness to get to the beloved store; Pan Apt was about to turn up
Wielka. Berson set out in pursuit, taking long strides and rehearsing the speech he would make.
As he walked, Berson noticed that there seemed to be an unusually large number of people in the streets, considering the hour.
Pan Apt was heading for the Panska Street opening in the wall,
and Berson saw that as the jeweler and he approached Panska, the
crowd became increasingly dense. Even though Dolek was catching up, he had a harder and harder time keeping track of his
quarry, dodging through the press, especially as Pan Apt was short.
But the packed mob near the wall slowed Pan Apt down, and Ber-

son finally came up with him; Berson had the five-thousand-zloty note in his hand, ready. He looked up then for the first time and saw what had caused the crowd to gather.

A barbed-wire barrier had been thrown most of the way across Panska Street. Near the middle of the roadway, two sentry boxes had been set up; between them there was a small gap; and that was blocked by a group of German soldiers, who were letting no one pass.

Pan Apt wriggled and forced his way toward the gap, and Berson, held back by politeness, fell behind him at first. By the time he had reached Pan Apt again, the small man was in excited conversation with a young S.S. lieutenant, who simply shook and shook his head. Pan Apt took out his note from Gruber and gave it to the lieutenant. The German read the letter, handed it back to Pan Apt, and said:

—— Worthless.

Pan Apt, looking about in bewilderment, saw Berson, and grabbing Berson's sleeve in his pudgy fist, he shouted:

—— Tell him! Tell him!

Berson, slowly: —— Tell him what?

Pan Apt, suddenly changing back: —— Come on! Let's go to the Grzybowski Place exit.

And the jeweler began fighting his way out of the crowd. Berson followed confusedly. As they ran along Bagno Street northward, Berson, drawing abreast, held out the bill and said breathlessly:

—— I wanted to tell you . . .

Pan Apt, interrupting: —— Look! There is a crowd in the square, too.

Indeed, there was a blockade at the Grzybowski Place exit, just like the one at Panska Street. Pan Apt burrowed through to the officer in charge of the guard, presented his letter from Gruber, and promptly received it back again.

—— No good.

Pan Apt, turning his panic-twisted face to Berson: —— Let's try Krochmalna.

A bearded Hasid, standing behind Pan Apt, shook his head mournfully and said:

—— No use. All the entrances are closed.

Pan Apt stood still a moment in the hubbub, trying to understand what was happening. Then, his cheeks red and his eyes starting, he turned to Berson and waved the Gruber note in the young man's face.

Pan Apt: —— *You* arranged this! You spent my money for this!

Horrified, Dolek grasped Pan Apt's left hand in his own two hands, forced it open, put the five-thousand-zloty note in it, folded the hand closed, and, with a heave, backed away into the crowd.

EVENTS NOVEMBER 16, 1940. ENTRY DITTO. N.L. It was almost exactly a year ago that I first met Berson, at that queer time when the Germans threatened to put us in a ghetto. What pleasant days those were, when we were locked in our little cell! And now, we have our ghetto. In all my thoughts of a ghetto—and in this Berson concurs—I never dreamed we would be *locked* within our wall.

THE WALL   PART II

1

Events early December, 1940.   Entry December 16, 1940.   N.L.   I try and try and try to comprehend this word: ghetto.

We Jews are shut up together; that is evident. The closure is complete. There are, I believe, eleven gaps in the wall, and now one can only call them entrances, for they are certainly not exits. Guards are on duty day and night, and passes are very hard to get. The wall itself is firm and whole, and wherever it surrenders its function to the side of a building, former doors, windows, and accesses of every kind have been bricked up. Berson worked as a bricklayer on this our containment, yet he seems happy enough. Indeed, I apprehend that he is much happier than usual, and more complacent. He used to hate anything official: I remember his desire to detour the nervous crowd in front of the Community Building the day a year ago when the Germans threatened us with a ghetto, because, as he said, that was *more or less official turmoil.* [Entry November 9, 1939.] Yet now that we have a ghetto, he is thinking of *becoming* an official. He has talked with me about quitting the brick detail and joining the Jewish police.

Only being in a ghetto could have brought such a change. But what is this *being in a ghetto*? Is it simply being within the wall?

Events early December, 1940.   Entry December 16. From Dolek Berson.   Talked with Berson today about the paradox of his wanting to get into the world of office-holders. He has about decided to enlist in the police. He recognizes the irony. He thinks the main reason why he considers becoming a policeman is that he yearns for order. The name of the police force appeals to him very much: *Jüdischer Ordnungsdienst.* Jewish Order Service. He wants to help restore order. I had not previously noticed any strong tendency toward tidiness in Berson, I must confess; though I can see how our present circumstances might have brought out this hidden quality, if he had it at all, since up to now the most

114

obvious definition of *being in a ghetto* is: disorder. The Jewish district is, above all, chaotic. Only now do we begin to understand what has happened during the past four or five weeks. Eighty thousand Poles moved out of this area, and one hundred and forty thousand Jews moved in. The street scenes have been dreadful: crowds and crowds of Jews with all their goods on small pushcarts wandering through the streets looking for homes: no, looking for less than that: looking for mere corners in crowded rooms. The office the *Judenrat* set up as a clearing-house for apartments was overwhelmed; one saw hand-written placards advertising for living space on the walls of coffee-shops and even in the streets. One could see lines of people waiting in the streets for God knows what for days on end. One saw bargaining and arguing everywhere. Groaning was our music. Everything was transacted in a whine. Dr. Breithorn's many years of sourness were justified in one terrible event: the transfer of the Czysta Street hospital within the boundaries of the ghetto—the parade of the sick and dying from a modern building, with the finest medical equipment, to two drafty buildings on Leszno Street. Instruments and laboratories had to be left behind. One can see hunger-panics in the streets every day. The Poles, against whom the Germans discriminate in rations, still get delicacies, such as 250 grams of artificial honey, 62.5 grams of margarine, 100 grams of dried peas, and one lemon, every week. Our people get bread and groats and, if they are wealthy, a little saccharine. Smuggling has begun, of course, but smuggling brings high prices. How long will our money last? Is there any wonder that Berson craves a little neatness?

Berson will not say so, but I believe he is still distressed about his entanglement with Pan Apt. Berson flew into that mess enthusiastically, wanting only to help; he came out of it abused and blamed by Pan Apt. So far as we can learn, the jewelry store is in German hands. Pan Apt has been flat on his back with influenza ever since the day the ghetto was locked. Rachel has been taking gentle care of him. Berson dares not stop in, and Rachel says she has not seen him at all. Even Rachel blames Berson as a meddler: I tell her this is unfair. Thus there is disorder also in our personal relationships.

EVENTS DECEMBER, 1940. ENTRY DECEMBER 19, 1940. FROM DOLEK BERSON. Interesting! Another reason why Berson has decided (now it is definite) to sign up with the police: he thinks that in this way he will be able to resist the Germans a tiny bit. He has been persuaded that the Jewish Order Service will actually be able to alleviate the lot of the Jews and even restrain the Germans in small ways. Slonim has evidently been arguing against this idea: he tells Berson that the Jewish police will only be German tools. Berson thinks otherwise.

I reached my impression that Berson has this motive in an indirect way—through a story Berson told this evening; or rather, through the manner in which he told it. One definition of *being in a ghetto* is: being in a conversation. We talk, talk, talk, talk, talk. For want of meat, we eat gossip. And last night Berson gave us the following tidbit with such relish, with such sparkle in his eye, that I reached the above conclusion:

Fischel Schpunt has a new game. It seems that the grotesque little bureaucrat, realizing his comic power as a result of his performance the day the secret prayerhouse was discovered, is now going out of his way to trick and insult the Germans—and he does it in such a way that the Germans only laugh at him; the Jews laugh, too, long after each prank. For the past few days, Schpunt has been touring the blockaded streets, visiting one after another the eleven gates in the wall, and whenever he sees a German soldier on duty, he approaches casually, catches the German's eye, and then tips his hat with such friendly alacrity, or reaches out to shake hands with such apparent sincerity, that the German is usually tricked into thinking he has encountered an acquaintance, responds, realizes he has simply been accosted by a very funny-looking Jew, and bursts out laughing. Schpunt has developed a kind of claque of idle people who follow him around. Berson saw one of Schpunt's salutations this afternoon. He laughed as he told us about it:

—— His face! His face hated the German so, and the German couldn't see that part of it: the German could only see the funny part.

EVENTS DECEMBER 21, 1940. ENTRY DECEMBER 22, 1940. FROM DOLEK BERSON. Well, Berson had his first official day yesterday, and the reaction is curious. Very curious.

The police force was set up by the *Judenrat*. Chairman Sokolczyk asked for two thousand volunteers between the ages of twenty-one and thirty-five, and he couched his appeal, in a poster, in formal language, but in language that hinted the Jewish police would be able to help their fellow Jews and protect them. (In one sense, they can, as Berson points out: they will at least save the Jews from being policed exclusively by Germans and by "Navy-blues"—Polish gendarmes.) The police were incidentally offered extra rations. A great number of volunteers turned out, especially professionals and intellectuals who now would have no other work: the declassed and the "golden youth." Indeed, by the time Berson decided definitely to join, four days ago, it was necessary to pull wires in order to land an appointment; of course it fell upon me to do the pulling.

Berson applied at the *Judenrat* day before yesterday morning; I had pulled; he was accepted. He was told to report the next morning and was given his "uniform": a cap, a belt, a wooden truncheon, and insignia. He took his things home, put on a black suit, and decked himself in his new plumage. Above the visor of his dark blue military cap there was a Star of David, which he says seemed proud and defiant in this setting, and on the blue ribbon around it a single round tin disk, designating his rank: the lowest: ordinary policeman. Berson says his wooden club swung *authoritatively* from his belt. Besides his white Star-of-David brassard he also sported a yellow armband with *Jüdischer Ordnungsdienst* stamped on it. And on his chest he wore a simple badge with his number: 217.

When Symka saw him, he says she exclaimed that he was beautiful, playfully shoved the cap onto the back of his head, and kissed him on both cheeks, with a formal accolade, as if she too were somewhat official.

On Berson's first day of duty, yesterday, under a cold, crisp, sunny sky, he was assigned to traffic direction at the busy corner of Karmelitzka and Dzielna. Here the flow consisted of wagons full of furniture, pushcarts with personal goods, vendors' trundle-carts, wheelbarrows, bicycles, and pedestrians by the thousands. Berson says he felt that his signals were strong and clear without being pompous. The surging, heavy currents in the streets responded promptly to his commands, and he felt immensely powerful. He went home last night giddily happy, and he sang and cavorted absurdly before Symka's merry eyes.

But when Berson went to his room to take off his trappings,

117

he looked in a mirror—and he says he was frightened by what was reflected. He saw in the glass an apparition of cruelty. He suddenly remembered what it had been like to have a club in his hand all day. He remembered chasing a group of beggars away from his corner. He remembered what had happened when some Germans had come along: the only thing he had resisted was his own impulse to hobnob with them.

Berson has a theory. He thinks that because cruelty—and there, in one word, I suppose, is the definition for this ghetto I have hunted for—because cruelty has been inflicted on him, he now feels the need to pass the cruelty on to someone else. He said tonight:

—— I am like a cup. I've been poured full with a too hot fluid. It *has* to be poured out of me, before I crack.

2

EVENTS PASSOVER, APRIL, 1941. ENTRY APRIL 15, 1941. N.L. . . . and this attitude of concentration on Reb Yechiel Mazur's part as he conducted the Seder ceremony added to the general serenity.

That evening my attention was drawn yet again to Rachel Apt. It is impossible to dismiss Rachel, as I have heard Berson do in very recent days, as a girl who never learned to live with her face. True, she is not good-looking; but I am reminded how often in the last few weeks I have heard "the Apt girl" discussed—and this phrase always refers to Rachel, not to the pretty nonentity who is her sister. Something about Rachel causes her to be remembered and talked about. The other night she showed real courage, and I must confess I exulted inwardly at the rebuke she handed Benlevi. In passing, she included me in her censure, and I fear that in that, as in almost everything she said, she was absolutely just. . . .

EVENTS PASSOVER, APRIL, 1941. ENTRY APRIL 16, 1941. N.L. . . . Later in the evening, when the ceremonies of the first night of Passover were finished and the guests were sitting around talking, Dolek Berson abruptly asked, with a smile:

—— Professor Benlevi, do you remember how angry you got when Frailin Apt here came to you—when was it, Rachel? late last summer?—about the secret school we were starting up here in our courtyard?

It was hard to tell from what motive Berson had brought this up: apparently not out of malice; the remark seemed merely to be an idle, somewhat humorous recollection.

Benlevi turned his stately head toward Rachel, beside him, and for one indecisive moment he seemed torn between acknowledging the folly of his petty temper or standing upon his dignity; when the moment of assessing his audience had passed, he shook his head and said, crushingly:

—— Foolish girl!

I saw Rachel go on a sudden hunt for help. She looked briefly in my eyes, but I suppose my curtains were drawn. She looked at Rutka. Then I intercepted a strange look, deep and strong, between Rachel and Froi Mazur. It was as if they had some understanding with each other. At once Rachel turned to Benlevi. Her face was slightly pale, but otherwise she was quite natural. Her voice was quiet, untrembling, and confident, as she said:

—— Forgive me. I think the foolishness was yours.

Everybody listened. Ugly little Rachel, in a retort to the Nobel Prize winner!

Benlevi, grandly amused: —— So?

Rachel: —— I think it was foolish of you—not of you, personally, Professor, but of all of you in the *Judenrat*—to be blind to what was happening here in Warsaw. Instead of hiding behind legality, it should have been your business to make sure that every Jewish child received proper training, even if it meant risking your official lives. I know: you said, and Sokolczyk and Mandeltort said, and even you, Noach, said: There's no use stirring up the Germans. Every step they took to close in on us, all of you said: Let's not anger them. Let's not fight. Let's not have secret schools. Let's not endanger the majority for the sake of the minority affected by this decree or that decree. . . . No, Professor Benlevi, I think you were the foolish one, not I.

Well, the look on Benlevi's face! By God, I even saw Berson look at Rachel gravely and with something like respect, and he said to Benlevi:

—— Do you know, I think she is partly right?

Rutka Mazur, hotly: —— *Partly* right? Where is she wrong?

Quickly Froi Mazur put an end to a potentially unpleasant situation by saying:

—— Let's leave the table and go and sing some Pesach songs.

Then I saw Froi Mazur glance again, ever so fleetingly, at Rachel, and in that sidelong blink I thought I noticed once more something compelling and rewarding. Rachel looked as if she were under a spell.

EVENTS PASSOVER, APRIL, 1941. ENTRY APRIL 16, 1941. FROM RACHEL APT. I have already noted here that I detected some kind of accord between Rachel and Froi Mazur that night. Indeed, I had the impression that Rachel got the courage to do what she did mostly from Froi Mazur. I asked her about this. She told me that the harmony I had spied out had been achieved only that night—during and just after the Seder ceremony; as follows:

Rachel was placed beside Professor Benlevi at table. At first this embarrassed her terribly [NOTE. N.L. I had observed that myself.], but the theatrical old gentleman seemed to have forgotten all about the ill-considered visit to him at the *Judenrat*, and he nodded and spoke to her benignly.

The Mazurs had asked in some friends for the Seder meal: Berson and Symka, Rabbi Goldflamm, Regina Orlewska, the three older Apt children, Benlevi, and N.L. Rachel says she watched Froi Mazur, as she brought her husband his cushions, and then fetched a plate with three pieces of unleavened bread and another plate containing the ceremonial foods—a roasted shank bone of lamb, a roasted egg, ground nuts and cinnamon moistened with wine, some onion, a horse-radish root, and a dish of salted water. She moved, Rachel thought, with the majesty of one in command of thousands of inferiors, and yet she seemed to have humility; she seemed to wish to stay in the background. When all was arranged, she sat down opposite Reb Yechiel Mazur, who had assumed the traditional half-reclining position. Froi Mazur turned to Schlome, the youngest person present, and said:

—— All right, son, your father is ready.

Schlome turned his grave face toward his father. His side-curls shook as he moved his head. He stated the "Four Questions":

—— Why is this night different from all other nights? On other nights we eat leavened bread, but on this night, only unleavened bread. On other nights we eat both sweet and bitter herb;, but on this night, only bitter herbs. On other nights we dip food in liquid once, but this night we dip twice. On other nights, Father, you sit straight, but this night you sit leaning on cushions.

While Reb Yechiel Mazur answered and then went on with the *Hagadah*, as if explaining to his delicate son the history of things, Rachel sat watching Froi Mazur gazing into the face of Schlome, inquiring, it seemed, whether he was taking it all in— even though the mother must have known that her son had long since memorized the words and wrestled with the sense of the *Hagadah*. Rachel saw a look of anxiety and love: a look of absolute, all-absorbing maternity in Froi Mazur's eyes, and suddenly, re- membering her own flighty and temperamental mother, Rachel yearned, she almost ached with yearning, for such a look directed at herself. Or—for she says there was this strange alternative—for a chance to direct such a look at someone else. With the religious words still droning like summer flies about her ears, Rachel became deeply aware of the ambiguous, frustrating desire Froi Mazur inspired in her.

Rachel says she was abstracted by these uneasy thoughts at the time when Berson came out with his question to Benlevi, and Benlevi with his condescending remark to her. Rachel says she looked around for support. She says she looked first at me to bring herself back to earth. She looked at Rutka, who has been more or less coaching her in Zionist beginnings. Then, almost fearfully, she looked at Froi Mazur.

In Froi Mazur's eyes Rachel saw, full and strong, the look the mother had directed at her pale son, now bathing her. She turned away quickly. She answered Benlevi. . . .

ENTRY APRIL 23, 1941. N.L. I have been thinking about Rachel. I have been remembering things.

I remember something that happened at an earlier Mazur ceremony—at the housewarming where I spoke. [ENTRY MARCH 17, 1940.] I was nervous that day, on account of the part I was playing, but I do remember one brief flurry of conversation after the formalities were over. The younger people were discussing mu- sic, and Berson, who as a pianist presumably knew more about the subject than anyone else, said he thought the second movement of Beethoven's Fourth Piano Concerto was one of the greatest love scenes in music—with the orchestra masculine, the piano feminine. Rachel remarked that her idea of a love scene was not simply a situation where a woman talks a man to sleep. I recall that this dry statement aroused my curiosity to such an extent that I borrowed a recording of the concerto from Felix Mandeltort the next day, played the second movement, and found Rachel absolutely right. I now reflect that the remarkable thing about her observation was not its precision, but the fact that she made it at all—the fact that Rachel Apt, with her unlucky features, should have possessed an *idea of a love scene.*

I remember also the day of the raid on Goldflamm's secret prayerhouse, when Fischel Schpunt discovered that he was comical, dancing on the cobblestones. I glanced at her face when we were all laughing: she was not! I cannot be sure whether this indicated a lack of farcical humor in her, or a surplus of unspent compassion; I suspect the latter. She did not even smile at that very funny sight.

Then there is something Berson said, another time. I believe he was speaking of the intensity with which she organized the courtyard school, and I remember that he broke off to say:

—— The curious thing is that although your first impression of Rachel is that she is dreadfully ugly, you find on acquaintance that she isn't bad-looking at all.

I have been careful to give Rachel every possible chance to vindicate this judgment, but I am afraid I cannot agree. She continues to seem plain—at least, through my thick glasses: I have never thought her "dreadfully ugly."

Then one night at Berson's apartment Rachel questioned me in a feverish way—literally, so that I wondered whether she was suffering from grippe—about the subtle gradations of politics in the various Zionist organizations. I have written in this record of her eagerness to learn, of her *attentiveness.* [ENTRY NOVEMBER 30, 1939.] But this was more than that. There was a kind of desperation in these questions. Perhaps she was looking for an outlet for her energies.

I remember seeing her one day with her little brother David— toward whom, if toward anyone, she can direct looks like Froi Mazur's; and it seemed to me that Rachel was not entirely in control of the situation. Indeed, at one point David laughed at her, and said:

—— Sister, you are too sober-sided!

Every contact I have had with Rachel Apt has left me in a haze of recollection and reflection: she has always made me think. She has a strange *impersonal* magnetism.

I have decided this about "the Apt girl": I think that if I were ever to fall in serious trouble, I should go to her for advice and help. I have seen that she has no wish to mother me, and I am rather grateful, as I have had one mother and one is probably enough. Bolder thoughts enter my mind from time to time, but they drift away, like gentle mists. Yet how comfortable it is to have Rachel there!

3

EVENTS MARCH, 1941. ENTRY MARCH 27, 1941. N.L. How tenacious we are! We refuse to admit that our circumstances are changed. We cling stubbornly to our habits of life. We want to *go on as usual*. We pretend that the wall is not there. Yet it is most assuredly around us, and its existence affects all our small private motions and emotions.

These reflections stem from a talk I had last night with Rutka Mazur. It seems that there are designs on our capable Rutka. Mordecai Apt pursues her, and I think she is rather conscientious in flirting with him. I remember how Rachel, that bitter night when she blundered down the love-cluttered staircase from Berson's apartment, found Mordecai and Rutka embracing; at the time I considered this simply a matter of physical entertainment: young, healthy, magnetized bodies. Evidently I was wrong: Rutka *wants* a grand passion. But the wall—our belted life, and the conflicting anxieties and hopes we feel—the wall inhibits her, she says. She cannot enjoy a traditional romantic love affair while the fears and pressures of this life within the wall come at her from every direction. She is a worker for Hashomer Hatsair, the Zionist youth organization, and now she is torn, too, by Zionism: the *work* engrosses her, the *idea* seems futile. She told me how she worried one day last week, at school.

Rutka goes to one of the *Judenrat* industrial schools, which were authorized by the Germans in January. These schools offer courses in engraving, watchmaking, graphic design, architectural

design, textile design, electrical engineering, locksmithing, metal-
lurgy, cosmetics, and cigaret manufacture. Pupils take a six-month
course, which will be terminated by official examinations. They
pay twenty-five zlotys a month in tuition, and there are scholar-
ships for poor but qualified students. Classes in most of the schools
run from nine to two thirty each day. When the schools opened,
Rutka applied for the course in the manufacture of cosmetics, not
because she felt that that was the most important industry in the
world, but because among the few studies open to women, this
seemed somehow the most defiant, the most optimistic, and the
most comforting. Learn how to be beautiful!

Rutka says, however, that the other day, with what she had on
her mind, she found it hard to take her teacher, "Professor" Kamenhorn, very seriously. She sat back in the hard chair fastened to
her desk and looked out the window at the drab, stone-framed, net-
curtained windows across the way: someone's home.

"Professor" Kamenhorn wrote in large letters on the black-
board:

$$H_2Mg_3(SiO_3)_4$$

Kamenhorn: —— Hydrous magnesium silicate. Remember the
chemical name of that unctuous material. You all wear it, my
dears. (Rutka says that "Professor" Kamenhorn, formerly a teacher
of elementary chemistry in a Praga middle school, brings to Basic
Cosmetic Theory a dry, castrated coquetry.) On your noses. Remember this formula. It is talc. Simple talc. . . .

What lies, Rutka says she wondered, looking across the street,
behind those net curtains across the way? Is there any happiness in
those rooms? A man and wife? How many years married? Is the
physical part still strong? Do they still cling to each other and feel
the gentle, electric warmth of the touch of face to face? Or has it
all gone cold and commonplace, since the wall was built? Do arguments, breaches of faith, and weariness live behind those curtains now? . . .

Rutka says she thought of the excitement she had felt, years
ago, at the Hachsharah farm near Wloclawek, when she had decided, one sunny day working the beet rows, in a heat that made
it possible to imagine that she was actually in Palestine, that she
would never marry. She would be a dedicated woman, like her in-
structress on the farm, Tosia Zimmern, that keen, flint-hearted

maiden to whom there was nothing, absolutely nothing, on either side of the road to Palestine. And she remembered the mystical excitement she had felt, when the flames had come out of the mouths of the speakers at the Zionist Congress in Geneva, just before the war, where she had represented Hashomer for Warsaw. But now . . . now Palestine was so far away, on the other side of such a high wall; and here, just the other side of a woollen coat in the dark doorway on the cold staircase, here was Mordecai, imperious, pleading, hot, hurt, bitter, jealous, remorseful; complicated, needful, and strong. His arms strong from lifting bricks!

And yet: How long would love last—within a ghetto wall?

Thus her debate, in its simple terms. Now it has been complicated by something that happened today:

It has been cold during the past month, and none of us have enough fuel for heat. In Sienna 17, one room is kept heated; the children spend most of their time there; adults rotate, and spend one hour at a time in the warmth. This afternoon after school Rutka sat in the Mazurs' unheated living room, bundled up in an overcoat and wrapped in a quilt, with a book lying jilted on her lap, waiting with all her attention for the sound of Mordecai's heavy boots on the staircase. She says Mordecai has been pressing her for an answer as to whether she will marry him.

At a few minutes past six—too few minutes after six for Mordecai, she decided, looking at the clock on the mantel—she heard the clatter of the staircase door downstairs, and then the sound of footsteps, heavy but rapid, climbing the stairs two at a time. Her brother Stefan, she thought it must be. And it was. He burst in at the apartment door with a red face and excited eyes.

Stefan: —— Is Mother around?

Rutka: —— No.

Rutka says she returned to her book now in pretended earnest, hoping that Stefan would go into his room. But he was full of something.

Stefan: —— Where is she?

Rutka: —— Out shopping.

Stefan: —— Good! I want to talk to you. . . .

Rutka put down her book.

Stefan: —— Baby sister, I've tumbled into a nest of hornets— and I've been offered a sting. Listen! The other day, at the office [NOTE. EDITOR. Stefan was working at this time for Eugeniusz

125

Tauber's Special Commission for the Fight Against Speculators, an organization nicknamed The Thirteen after the address of its office, Leszno 13], one of Pan Tauber's assistants, a man named Prilutzki—I always thought he was just a messenger of some kind, he looks like a small, brown badger—he called me into one of the storerooms, and the first thing he asked me was whether I put any value on my skin. Naturally I said I did, and he threatened me that if I told anyone what he was about to tell me—even my mother or my wife—but you're neither one, Rutkele!—then my skin wouldn't be worth three groszys. Then he said that Pan Tauber had been noticing my work and he liked me and he wanted to help me, and that if I kept my head I might make a lot of money and, he said, *be safe*. So I didn't say anything, and he told me that The Thirteen had built up a business—he called it a *business*—which consists of offering storekeepers and factory-owners permanent protection from the Gestapo for money, and that there was nothing dishonest about that because The Thirteen actually did have an arrangement with the Gestapo to stay away from men who subscribed—I'm using his words—and even to assist those who subscribed extra. Well, I asked him, how assist? And he said that importations into the ghetto are very carefully supervised by the Gestapo and I could see the implications of *that*. . . . Besides all this, Prilutzki said, there were other lucrative activities into which I might be able to gain promotion, by industry and discretion. He said that important smuggling is taking place, and this can be considered very altruistic work; also that both the Gestapo and the *Judenrat* are interested in certain types of information; also that The Thirteen is setting up a kind of apartment rental bureau. . . .

Rutka says she was horrified by what Stefan was telling her.

Stefan: —— Wait! Wait till you hear this: Tauber's in on it, of course; he's the "Director." Gruber's in on it: I've seen him around the office several times: that shows the connection with the Germans. Somebody at the *Judenrat* must be in on it. Hartmann's in on it—he's the ex-Communist that Pan Apt had to bribe about his store. Dolek Berson's cousin Meier is in on it, with Hartmann. And listen: Pan Apt is in on it. He went straight to Gruber about his store and Gruber cooled him off and got him into this. Prilutzki says Gruber and Apt are as friendly as a pair of bandits—he used *that* expression, too! Wouldn't it make you laugh?

No, Rutka says, it would not make her laugh. She says she felt
sick. The very mention of Pan Apt's name—of Mordecai's father's
name—in this connection made her feel giddy and nauseated.

Rutka: —— Are you sure about Pan Apt?

Stefan: —— I saw him in Tauber's office today.

Rutka: —— Are you going to resign?

Stefan: —— Resign! Certainly not! I don't dare. . . . And besides (Stefan laughed, as if the consideration were merely humorous), I might want to accept Prilutzki's bid!

Rutka, tentatively: —— Doesn't Pan Apt's part in this affect
the way you feel about Halinka?

Stefan, empty-faced: —— Why should it?

Rutka, shaking her head: —— I don't know. I don't know.

Rutka says that the news about Pan Apt and The Thirteen
certainly has affected the way she feels about Mordecai—not that
she thinks Mordecai himself capable of any dishonesty. It is just
that all this—so close to her—makes her uneasy. . . .

EVENTS APRIL 4, 1941. ENTRY APRIL 7, 1941. FROM
RUTKA MAZUR. At first I wondered a bit whether Mauritzi Apt
actually was involved in the games of The Thirteen. I thought it
possible that young Stefan was blowing up some kind of story from
a single visit Apt might have paid the office in an effort to salvage
his store. But I guess I was wrong. There now seems to be plenty
of evidence that Apt is working with The Thirteen. For example,
this story, told to Rutka by Stefan, on the evening of the fourth,
and now relayed by her to me:

Stefan was sitting in on his first conference in Tauber's office.
The atmosphere in the office was congenial, according to Stefan.
Tauber sat behind a large desk, with a pretty secretary by his side.
Agents of The Thirteen were seated around the room in sofas and
armchairs: mostly good-looking young men, dressed in "uniforms"
quite similar to those of the Jewish police: their brassards were
green instead of yellow, and they were inscribed: *Fight Against
Speculators.* Around the walls of the office were signed photographs
of both *Judenrat* officials and German officers and administrators:
Sokolczyk hung there, and Mandeltort, as well as Mondschrift of
the *S.S.* and the Governor General himself. These portraits had a
curious effect. Not only did they seem to lend Eugeniusz Tauber
an official sanction, an air of having been approved all around; they

also seemed to make the *Judenrat* officials very friendly with the Germans. Sokolczyk beamed beside the smiling Governor General. The pictures seemed to credit Tauber and discredit the *Judenrat,* subtly.

[NOTE. N.L. Eugeniusz Tauber was a professor of Hebrew in a Yeshiva in Radom before the war. He was an active Zionist. They say he was restless and tremendously energetic, but he showed none of the "prosperous" tendencies that blossomed the moment he came to Warsaw in 1938. He then began to make money hand over fist, yet so far as anyone could see, he had no business—though he had plenty of business connections. In fact, he *was* a business connection. So now. He can fix anything: he is Pan Fix. Everyone on the Jewish side is afraid of him, because he *seems* to have the Gestapo behind him. Perhaps the Germans are somewhat afraid of him: he even gives that impression. He is a pompous little man. He dresses very carefully, usually in dark suits and conservative neckwear. With this formality he combines the gentle manner of a religious teacher, and he is a master of humble flattery. When a man with these qualities becomes rich, powerful, and influential, one can be sure that the result is an analytic and subtle tyrant.]

The purpose of the conference that morning was to give new recruits into The Thirteen some idea of their duties. Tauber was explaining the technique of "soliciting business" in the protection line. Apparently he made this extortion sound like a benevolence. Finally he came to the matter of method of payment:

Tauber: —— The purpose of our organization—to fight against speculators—will best be served if we accept payment in installments, rather than in lump sums: in this way we depress the spending power of our customers over a period of time and do not create an immediate emergency which may lead them to take illegal and speculative risks. Do you follow me? Now, a special problem. We have been finding that many of our people have put their savings into the most compact and disposable of all forms of property—jewelry. Your customers may wish to pay in gems. . . . Panna Weizel, will you ask our appraiser to step in for a moment? . . . If this is the case, it will be necessary to evaluate the payment in an orderly manner. You can understand the need for this! I can see that you young men appreciate the sparkle of a diamond on a young lady's finger—but how many of you could say for sure that the diamond was not made of glass? . . . Ah, here is our expert. . . .

It was Mauritzi Apt. Stefan reports that he looked very pleased with himself, very confident, walking a little on his toes. He says Tauber introduced Pan Apt around the room, and when it was Stefan's turn, Pan Apt came straight over and shook hands with a surprised cordiality, as if he had not seen this young friend for a long time—though in fact Stefan, while visiting Halinka the night before, had had quite a chat with Pan Apt. Pan Apt seemed to want to show that he had connections of his own, and one has the impression that Stefan was not displeased to be singled out: very likely he, too, was as effusive over that handshake as if he were greeting a long-absent uncle.

Tauber: —— We will have to ask you to bring any gems offered in payment to Pan Apt, who as you know is the distinguished jeweler of Miodowa Street. Mauritzi Apt is an old friend of mine [NOTE. N.L. This Rachel categorically denies.], and he is a man of several talents who will have a number of functions in our great fight against speculators; I therefore beg you, gentlemen, if you have gems for Pan Apt to examine, make your business as quick as possible. He is no ordinary appraiser, you know. . . .

EVENTS APRIL 19, 1941. ENTRY DITTO. FROM PAVEL MENKES. I have seen Menkes the baker windy and vehement many times, but usually he bluffs. This evening he was really angry. We were at the Bersons', and Menkes was telling us how young Stefan Mazur had called on him this morning to get him to "subscribe" to the Fight Against Speculators. Here is what Menkes says he shouted at Stefan:

Menkes: —— Are you interested in what I think, boy? I think it's blackmail! You ask each owner of a business to contribute two thousand zlotys a month in order to prevent speculation, smuggling, and the black market. You say it's official, endorsed by the *Judenrat*. You say I will be repaid by protection from unfair and illegal competition, and by protection from the Gestapo. And by whom are these protective marvels to be administered? By Eugeniusz Tauber! The biggest speculator, the biggest smuggler in Warsaw! Listen, boy, do you want my advice? Why don't you join the police, like Berson? Berson has good sense: he stands on a street corner all day long waving to the horses who pass by: he associates with his friends and equals. But you: you're out of your class with those refined swindlers. . . .

I think that what had made Menkes so furious was the fact that young Stefan had somehow threatened him. Menkes passionately wishes to be left alone in his habit-sure life.

EVENTS MAY 3, 1941. ENTRY MAY 5, 1941. FROM DOLEK BERSON. Rutka stood at the door with a saucepan in her hand when Berson answered the knock.

Rutka (with the excessively cheerful mien of someone taking contributions for charity): —— Collections for the Spoon Committee! [NOTE. EDITOR. One of several organizations which gathered food for orphans and indigent refugees.]

Berson: —— Come in. . . . What is it this week?

Rutka: —— Flour.

Berson: —— Symka! . . . Come into the kitchen, Rutka.

Rutka followed Berson. Symka was sitting on a stool in the kitchen, leaning forward over a book that lay open on an oilcloth-covered table. Another open book lay at the other end of the table. There was a small pile of books on the kitchen floor. Berson closed the kitchen door.

Symka (speaking just above a whisper): —— Hello, Rutka. You see we have taken sanctuary in the kitchen. We enjoy our houseguests only a certain number of hours a day.

Rutka: —— So? What's the matter with your "gentile" friends?

Symka: —— Big Jablonski's too digestive and small Jablonski's too long-winded.

Rutka: —— So you hide in the kitchen in your own home.

Berson (shrugging): —— *Nu*, we are near the food supply.

[NOTE. N.L. I have seen the growing estrangement between the Bersons and their convert tenants. It is mutual boredom more than anything else, I think. They have nothing in common. Jablonski is an electrical engineer; Berson is a . . . well, a drifter. There is also Jablonski *père's* appetite.]

Symka stood up and went to a heavy crock on a low shelf by one wall. She lifted the earthenware lid, looked inside, and groaned.

Symka: —— I know that we are supposed to give a teaspoonful per head, but do we really have to donate for the eater and the talker?

Rutka let the Bersons off for the converts' share. Then, hesitatingly, she began talking about Stefan and his work for The Thirteen.

Rutka: —— I hear that Pavel was angry with Stefan for approaching him about the Fight Against Speculators.

Berson: —— Pavel gets angry at any kind of intrusion.

Rutka: —— I don't know whether to be ashamed or not, that Stefan is doing such work. . . . Pan Apt, too. Our staircase is well represented.

Berson says Rutka spoke bitterly. He says he guessed what was troubling her, and Symka did, too. But he himself still goes on the defensive whenever the subject of Pan Apt comes up, and he now became vague:

Berson: —— It is true that prices are high. Perhaps it is worthwhile to fight the speculators.

Rutka: —— How can it be worthwhile to get dirty hands?

Symka handed Rutka back her saucepan, with the Bersons' two teaspoonfuls added, and Rutka left.

[FROM RACHEL APT, CONTINUING EVENTS MAY 3.] On the floor below, Rachel went to the door and found Rutka there.

Rachel (almost sullenly): —— My brother's not in.

Rutka: —— I'm not pursuing Mordecai. I'm scavenging.

She put the saucepan forward. Rachel took it and without saying anything more went to the kitchen for the Apts' five teaspoonfuls of flour. Rachel tells me she had a strange feeling about Rutka. Rachel's own pride had been hurt by Rutka's superior manner at the time of her run-in with Benlevi about the secret school; she considered Rutka brusque and haughty. But she felt that Rutka's cocksureness came from unsureness. She wanted to like Rutka, she says. When Rachel came back to the living room from the kitchen, she found Rutka sitting on the arm of a chair.

Rutka: —— May I rest a minute? I've climbed so many stairs!

Rachel, in an indifferent tone, not sitting herself: —— Surely, make yourself comfortable.

Rutka: —— Is your father out, too?

Rachel: —— No, he's reading in bed.

Rutka: —— Oh. . . . (Casually:) What is he doing these days, now that he can't go to the store?

Rachel, without hesitation: —— He's working for The Thirteen.

Rutka: —— Is that as satisfactory as running a jewelry business?

Rachel says she thought she detected both condescension and sarcasm in that question; she thought Rutka must be in her superior vein. She felt snappish.

Rachel: —— You have a brother working for it. You should know.

Rutka: —— That doesn't mean that I approve of it. I'm not Stefan's supervisor. Anyhow, he's only a kind of errand boy for them.

At this point Rachel suddenly reached to the core of the matter. [NOTE. N.L. I bless her! She is a gentle girl. She knows the right thing to do.]

Rachel: —— I think you're worried about Mordecai.

Rutka was taken completely off guard. Tears gathered quickly in her eyes, and she blurted:

—— I am, I am! What is he really like?

Rachel: —— Why don't you try to understand what makes my father do what he is doing? Don't you think you might work with *anyone* if it meant a chance of recovering part of your life that you had lost? Because that's what the store was to my father. Anyhow, what makes you think Mordecai is like him? Are you like Stefan?

[NOTE. N.L. In all this, I have been interested in how Rutka reacted. Yet how difficult this interview must have been for Rachel, who feels so deeply about her father! She is a strong girl, I am sure of it.]

Rutka brightened up eventually, Rachel says. She told a couple of funny stories on Mordecai, and she seemed quite friendly. After a bit she began to talk about her work for the Zionist youth organization, Hashomer Hatsair, and she urged Rachel to try some of it, and Rachel agreed. [NOTE. N.L. And what good news that is! If Rachel goes ahead with this, I think she will very soon feel at home in our Jewish community.]

When they parted, Rachel felt that Rutka had settled her mind to rest about Mordecai, and yet . . .

EVENTS MAY 7, 1941. ENTRY MAY 10, 1941. FROM RACHEL APT. Mordecai Apt has fallen sick. One might think, as I did at first, that he had simply caught the heavy, prolonged case of influenza from which his father was so long recovering. But Rachel, who is tending Mordecai, and who seems in truth doomed to a career of nursing, for she is gentle and patient—Rachel thinks that Mordecai suffers only from contusions of the vanity. She says he has always taken to his bed whenever his feelings were hurt. I get this from Rachel, who got it straight from Mordecai on his sickbed:

Mordecai, still in his working clothes, with smudges of brick dust on his face, stood with one foot on the landing and one foot on the first stair. Rutka was in the apartment doorway. The door was closed.

Mordecai: —— Have you decided?

Rutka, her head down: —— Don't ask me to decide today.

Mordecai leaned against the wall of the stairway, as if he had been physically pushed. Hollow-eyed with dust, he must have had a tragic look.

Mordecai: —— Wait! Wait! Wait! That's all you can say.

Rutka: —— Don't ask me today. Not today.

Rutka put her hands to her face and began weeping silently. With childish petulance, Mordecai turned and stamped upstairs.

The next morning he had a high fever.

EVENTS JUNE 22, 1941. ENTRY JUNE 24, 1941. FROM RUTKA MAZUR. Now Rutka has come to me with inner questionings about Zilberzweig, the leader of the left-Zionist youth faction, Hashomer Hatsair. What a *receptacle* I have become! Because I listen patiently, because I ask penetrating questions in a sympathetic tone of voice, people have begun, not only to trust me, but also to use me as a vessel into which to pour their anxieties and privacies. Thus Rutka brings me her doubts about Zilberzweig, even though she knows I am not a Hashomer person, nor even a convinced Zionist. As follows:

Rutka cranked the hectograph, and the counseling sheets floated out one by one from the roller of the duplicating machine. On the sheets was printed Hil Zilberzweig's editorial on the German attack against Russia. Rutka says she was working to the limit of her capacities, alertly, smoothly, and, she permits herself to hope, attractively; for Zilberzweig himself was pacing up and down the cellar room, waiting for the job to be finished. It was not often that Rutka had the privilege of working under the sharp eyes of the Chairman of Hashomer, her Zionist idol, and she wanted to make the most of the chance—even if this "most" was only a matter of mechanical efficiency: crank, slide, crank, slide, crank, slide, as uninterruptedly as possible.

[INSERT. FROM ENTRY MARCH 10, 1941. N.L. Hil Zilberzweig is forty-three years old. He is beginning to put on weight, and his hair is falling out—what is left lies slicked back on his ovoid head. I think he must have had a friendly face to begin with, but being a youth leader and therefore *professionally* friendly, this look of amicability has become congealed, fixed, and waxy. He is rigidly, unwaveringly pleasant—and to me this is very unpleasant. However, it must be said that his followers, the youth of Hashomer Hatsair, admire him very much. Maybe I am no longer youthful enough for this sort of man.

Zilberzweig was brought up in Lodz. I am told that he joined the Hashomer organization when he was fourteen, and though he did not show the qualities of a leader at first, organizational work began very soon to dominate his time and thoughts. He eventually became secretary of the Lodz Hashomer circle—the secretaryship there being peculiarly a job that required a plugger and a zealot rather than an imaginative leader. Summers he worked on the *Hachsharah* known as *Kibbutz baMinchara*, near Rowno, a farm where the life of a Palestinian collective was as closely reproduced as the generally damp atmosphere and clayey soil of Poland permitted. Evidently he really intended to go to Palestine, and his parents, who were religious middle-class people, were prepared to make this possible. When he came up for his final examinations for his degree at teacher-training school, he wore his Hashomer uniform—so singleminded and unselfconscious was he. The Director flunked him, not because he answered the questions lamely, but because he had "injected politics into the academic sphere." And then, with the aptitude of any bureaucracy to discourage its own enthusiasts, Hashomer assigned Zilberzweig, who wanted only to go to Palestine, instead to training work in Poland! This drove him into teaching. He could not teach in the regular Tarbuth schools, because he lacked a teacher-training degree; he worked in various primary schools. I gather that he became first resigned, then even dedicated, to Hashomer work in Poland. He got this look of glazed agreeableness. He also got a following, and wound up, five or six years ago, as General Chairman of Hashomer Hatsair. As I have written, he is revered by his young followers.]

Out of the corner of an eye, Rutka watched the Chairman, and once, when he seemed abstracted—he had picked up a paper-backed book from a table and was turning it over and over in his hands—she stopped the machine a moment to say:

—— This is a wonderful editorial.

—— You read it?

—— Of course. I typed the matrix.

—— I am not satisfied with it.

—— I liked especially the paragraph addressed to uncommitted people.

[NOTE. N.L. Rutka tells me that when she had first read this paragraph, she had decided that she must get it into Berson's hands. I have the passage from his copy:

To you who have not made up your minds, you many who have just tried to live along, hurting no one, unhurt yourselves—to you I say this: here in the ghetto you have an opportunity now to be happy and effective—at the very moment when you believe contentment and usefulness quite impossible. As things stand, your lives consist of fitful struggles to keep occupied. Activity, any activity that engages the greater part of your attention, so that you are less conscious of the awful realities of your lives, that is your whole desire. As a friend of mine recently said, you are busy trying to be busy. We in Hashomer offer you plenty of work, abundant activity. But we also offer, without making extravagant promises, a goal: we urge you to work for the establishment of a Jewish nation in Palestine. Survival is not enough. Now that it is certain that our oppressor will be defeated (it is certain because, by his attack on Russia, he has shown that his appetite encompasses the whole globe: he wants too much, and anyone who cannot de-limit his desires sooner or later overreaches and destroys himself), now that this is certain, the possibilities for our survival and future in Palestine are no longer illusory and fantastic. They are real. Join us. Work with us. Survive with us. Come to Palestine with us.]

Zilberzweig approached the machine, picked up one of the printed sheets, and glanced at the paragraph Rutka had praised. He said:

—— Do you know where I got that phrase about being "busy trying to be busy"? I got it from Schpunt, that idiot at the *Juden-*

135

rat who teases the Germans. Day before yesterday morning, just after we heard the news of the German attack on Russia, Schpunt came up to me in the hallway on the ground floor of the Community Building, where I had been on an errand, and he held a fist actually against my chest; he had a *Nowy Kurjer* in the other hand, and he shook it out so I could see the headline:

WAR AGAINST RED PLAGUE.

He said—and he sprayed me with saliva in the violence of his speech—*You are a religious scholar. I try to be religious, but sometimes my thoughts run away with me. You are a scholar: you know the Torah. Does this mean we must suffer seven plagues before we can be free?* I smiled at the fool, but I can tell you that I had confused feelings, what with the momentous news, and all it might mean—and then this excited Schpunt. I said: *You'll have to ask your rabbi.* Schpunt said: *Ach, my rabbi is himself a plague. I am at war with him.* I said: *Excuse me, I am busy,* and I skirted around the ugly little man, to get away. To my receding back, Schpunt said: *Yes, busy. Busy trying to be busy!* . . . And I had to ask myself whether he was justified or not. And he was. You know: it is true. For me. I spend a lot of my time just trying to keep occupied. This paragraph is all very well, but I have no certainty that Hitler will be beaten in time for us. . . . I doubt it, really. I am certain of one thing—that I, for one, will never get to Palestine: I lost my chance to go. . . . I am afraid this editorial is a cheat against our readers.

Rutka says she felt angry with Zilberzweig for saying these things. She had worries enough of her own. She began cranking the machine again. What was he trying to do? Cry on her shoulder? There was a kind of sensuous appeal in the Chairman's confidences that offended Rutka. She says she had the distinct impression that he was considering whether or not to try to embrace her. She decided she preferred his written words to his spoken words —even if the written words were untrue. At least they were noble falsehoods.

Rutka finished her work, took the five copies she was to distribute, shoved them under her blouse, bid good afternoon to the Chairman, and left. On the way to Sienna Street, she stopped at a kiosk and bought five copies of the German-sponsored Jewish paper, *Gazeta Zydowska.* At home, on the staircase, she interfolded the Hashomer sheets into the copies of the newspaper.

Then she climbed to the top floor, and when Berson came to the door, she put one of the papers in his hand and said softly:

—— Return this to me within forty-eight hours without fail. Hide it. Say nothing to anyone about it.

Berson, seeing only that he had been given a copy of the *Gazeta*: —— What's this?

Rutka: —— Do what I ask.

And she ran downstairs.

EVENTS JUNE 25, 1941. ENTRY JUNE 26, 1941. N.L.

Berson: —— The weakness of the Hashomer position is that it doesn't deal with the real question: why prepare for Palestine within a wall—a prison—in Warsaw?

N.L.: —— These people are optimists. They don't think this is going to last forever.

Berson: —— Still, shouldn't you think about how to get out of prison before you think about sitting in the sun in your old age?

N.L.: —— The Hashomer people are resisting the Germans. They are doing as good a job as anyone else. Why do you attack them so? What got you started on this, anyhow?

—— The Mazur girl gave me an underground newspaper the other day with an editorial by Zilberzweig.

—— You have no business telling me that.

—— Why not?

—— Don't you realize you may be endangering her life, and your own, too?

—— But I trust you, Noach. My God, you're my friend. I trust you.

—— You shouldn't.

—— Nonsense.

—— Really, you shouldn't. [NOTE. N.L. I think I frightened Berson a little by the harsh way I said this—as if I were a Tauber operative or something! To be honest, I am heartily sick of having people trust me. It is too burdensome. And yet, I keep on asking for it—to wit, what I said next to Berson:] . . . But now that you have spilled this to me, you might as well show me the paper.

EVENTS JUNE 30, 1941. ENTRY OCTOBER 26, 1941. FROM RUTKA MAZUR. [NOTE. EDITOR. It should be observed that

N.L. did not get the following from Rutka Mazur until October, four months later.]

The examinations were conducted with a prewar pomp—but with a surreptitiousness that was pure ghetto. The sessions were held in the apartment of the Director of the Trade School, Professor Winter. Curtains were drawn. Students stood guard, both at the staircase door and at the gate of the courtyard. Four examiners—Professors Winter and Kamenhorn, Hil Zilberzweig, and Felix Mandeltort—sat behind a table covered with green baize; they were dressed somberly, and their faces were stern; and as they questioned the candidates for degrees in Advanced Cosmetics, Rutka thought them laughably grave. It seemed to her quite humorous to put on such a show for an examination on face-creams, powders, rouges, actors' paints, and other such frivolities; but when her own turn came before the four solemn rooks, she suddenly felt nervous and serious herself. She did well, and later, during the ceremony of bestowing typewritten diplomas, she was specially commended for her work. There was a "reception" afterward—a session of handshaking, punctuated by sallies of stiff conversation. As it broke up, Zilberzweig said to Rutka:

—— If you have nothing better to do, walk with me awhile.

In the street, Zilberzweig marched along with a heaving, padding pace, as if he were a two-legged camel. He was silent quite a distance, then said:

—— Learning how to make yourself pretty must have come easily to you, Frailin Mazur.

So he wished to be personal. [NOTE. N.L. Rutka reminds me that at that time she was on the edge of being disillusioned with Zilberzweig, who had been a great hero to her for several years. (SEE ENTRY JUNE 26, 1941.)]

Zilberzweig: —— You may have noticed that during the examination I asked you some particular questions about theatrical make-up. I was glad to hear you answer me so clearly and thoroughly. You may have some use for your knowledge that you did not expect. (Rutka says she thought: This is a queer approach.) Frailin Mazur, the Hashomer Executive Committee wishes to send you on a dangerous mission outside the ghetto.

Rutka says that terror flashed on the wires of her body—not from the force of what had just been spoken, for that had not sunk

in; but from something else: Rutka suddenly remembered, for
some collateral reason, that Berson had never returned the editorial to her, and she had forgotten to go back for it, as she had
meant to do. She asked with a trembling voice, her mind only
half on the topic:

——— Where do you want me to go?

——— Someone else will give you instructions. . . . You will go?

——— I don't know whether I am capable. I make mistakes.
. . . I forget things.

——— Your face is "safe," and you have done good work in the
past. If we are willing to risk everything on you, perhaps you will
be willing to take chances for us.

Rutka says she thought then about Mordecai, and she asked:

——— When do you want me to go?

——— We are not sure. Perhaps soon. Perhaps not for four or
five months.

Rutka says she looked at the ungainly walker beside her, and
all at once she believed in him again. If he had moments of bitterness and cynicism, perhaps he had good reason. Perhaps her impression of his sensuality had been, after all, unfair.

——— I'll go.

——— You will get instructions from someone who will ask you
if you know Zilberzweig's first name, and you will answer: *Some
call him Hillel, but Hil is correct.*

4

EVENTS APRIL 2–8, 1941. ENTRY APRIL 8, 1941. N.L.
We have a scandal. The whole Berson staircase is enjoying its
scandal. It seems that Halinka Apt, Rachel's and Mordecai's beautiful sister, is having some sort of an affair with a German. The
story popped out today.

EVENTS APRIL 2–8, 1941. ENTRY APRIL 9, 1941. N.L.
On the staircase they are whispering that Halinka's German is
Gruber himself. Really, I doubt it! How could such a flower find
its way into the maw of such a rhinoceros?

EVENTS APRIL 2, 1941. ENTRY APRIL 10, 1941. FROM
DOLEK BERSON. I have learned, at least, how the story about Halinka got started:

Symka leaned toward Dolek and slipped her hand over the
crook of his arm on the between-rest of the wooden seats at the
Femina Theater. The curtain went up with a jerk, the heavy bar
along its foot bouncing and nodding.

Symka: —— She's beautiful!

Berson says that Halinka was indeed extraordinarily pretty in
the envelope of light on the stage: she looked thinner than at
home, and her nervousness made her seem alert, sensitive, and delicate. (Berson takes a dig at Symka: if pretty Symka had the charity to call Halinka beautiful, he says, then Halinka *must* have been
a sight.) This was a matinee of YITA, an amateur theatrical club.
Halinka's skit was uninspired, a sentimental scene of a prewar
flirtation in Krasinski Garden, which is now outside the ghetto
limits; but Halinka sang her part sweetly and with restraint. The
audience, which was also amateur, being made up predominantly
of friends and relatives of the players, clapped wildly for her, and
Berson confesses that he clapped as hard as any.

There were two more numbers and the revue was over. Dolek
and Symka went out into the unreasonable daylight of a Sunday
afternoon and walked around to the back of the theater, where,
after some argument with a doorkeeper, they were admitted to go
to the dressing rooms. Halinka, they discovered, shared a large
room with six other girls. Families were already assembled, and
each proud mother surveyed adjacent groups to see whether the
people there were stealing sidelong looks at her particular little
canary. Berson says that Symka kissed Halinka, and that he, too,
with an extravagant gallantry about which Symka slyly questioned
him later, gave Halinka a kiss on her fragrant, grease-painted cheek.
Then others came in: Mauritzi Apt, weeping and carrying a carnation for Halinka that he had acquired from God knew where;
young David Apt, his eyes as big and as tensely regulated as wristwatches; Rachel, grave and accidental-looking among the pretty
singers. Mordecai was conspicuous by his absence: one would have
thought him capable of paying his sister this small tribute. [NOTE.
EDITOR. This was a full week before Mordecai fell sick.] Stefan,
too, was absent, for he was on duty.

At the height of the storm of compliments, Meier Berson appeared at the edge of the group. He waited awhile and then moved closer to Halinka. He told her she had been exquisite. She thanked him. Meier leaned closer and said, in a voice whose inflections were confidential but which was loud enough to be heard all up and down the dressing room:

—— Herr Gruber was out front this afternoon. He invites you to tea next Wednesday afternoon at his apartment at Kredytowa Street 15, at four o'clock. (Bending over even closer, but no less loudly:) Outside the ghetto! I will arrange permits—if you wish. (Straightening up, and glancing sidelong at Mauritzi Apt, evidently to see whether an impression was being made:) You needn't answer now. Send me a message at Leszno 13.

After Meier's departure, the group around Halinka became muted and wooden. Symka and Dolek Berson excused themselves and left. They took a ricksha. [Note. Editor. These were ingenious vehicles, mostly for two passengers, combining, as cart and horse, the Oriental ricksha and the Occidental bicycle. Even unemployed intellectuals were at this time motivating rickshas.] On the way home:

Berson, sarcastically: —— That was in fine taste on Meier's part!

Symka, compensating, as Berson points out, for her earlier tribute to Halinka's beauty: —— All the same, I'll wager that Halinka goes.

Berson: —— I hardly think so.

Events April 2–8, 1941. Entry April 11, 1941. N.L. Now, Halinka Apt is so pretty that I actually feel like holding my breath when I am near her. Fortunately she almost never speaks to me, so I am not forced to try my tongue before her. Yet in a way I can see that Halinka's beauty is a handicap to her, especially here in the ghetto. She wants to be taken seriously in a mental way: she would rather be talented than so pretty. I understand from Rachel that Halinka used to have quite a few Polish boyfriends; in those days frivolity was in itself both rewarding and exhausting. But now in the ghetto we have very few parties. Ingenuity and resourcefulness are more admired than charm. I have seen Halinka several times try hard to gain admission to an intellectual conversation, only to be frozen out (by men like me, I may say, who tremble at her beauty). Consequently she tries all sorts of things to get attention: she sings in public, she indulges tinny outbursts of temper, she dresses modishly, and she gets herself gossiped about.

Rachel says that when the Apt children were young, Halinka was the energetic, sprightly, and prankish one of the family. She was an Angel of Roguishness. She was always the center of attention when the children were exhibited to relatives. She was also forever slightly sick or pretending to be: the most trivial scratch required bandages, kisses, and admiration—but not iodine, which cures. (In more mature years, it is Mordecai who has the sickly flair.) Rachel has grown up bitterly envious of Halinka, and yet only a stranger can see how much luckier Rachel is than Halinka, in many ways.

EVENTS APRIL 2–8, 1941. ENTRY APRIL 11, 1941. N.L. Ha! The so-called scandal was all a malicious untruth. There is absolutely nothing to it. I have this from Meier Berson. I shall write everything down tomorrow.

EVENTS APRIL 7, 1941. ENTRY APRIL 12, 1941. FROM MEIER BERSON. I suppose the question can be asked: Is Meier Berson reliable? He may have some reason for protecting Halinka. All in all, I choose to believe him. He tells this:

First Meier presented his exit-pass at the gate, then Halinka hers. Everything was in order. The sentry stood to one side and let the pair through. It was but a short walk to Herr Gruber's apartment—not far along Krolewska, to the corner of Saxon Garden, then down to Kredytowa and along it for two blocks. At one point along the way, Halinka asked:

—— What am I to expect?

Meier, mischievously: —— From Herr Gruber, anything.

Halinka: —— Will you stay with me?

Meier: —— Of course, girl! Did you think this was to be a seduction scene? You will be disappointed, my dear. This is to be just what you were invited for—a tea party.

The day was cold but clear and glistening, and the mere sight of even a snow-bleak Saxon Garden—where Halinka must have spent many careless afternoons before the war—seemed to fill her with the reflection of an old gaiety.

Halinka, apparently fighting down her high spirits: —— Outside the ghetto and inside look about the same, after all.

Meier: —— In the streets, yes. Indoors I think you may find a difference. Heat, for one thing. And wait till you taste Herr Gruber's *zakanski*.

There were about twenty people in Herr Gruber's apartment. Among them was one German officer, and Meier saw Halinka start at the sight of his uniform; the other guests seemed to be mostly Poles. Halinka and Meier seemed to be the only two Jews; he had no doubt that Halinka could get along without being found out, and he says he knows how to take care of himself. Greeting Halinka, Herr Gruber took her right hand in both of his and said, in an almost fatherly way:

—— I'm glad you came. I wanted to pay my respects to that excellent voice. In that collection of would-be actresses last Sunday, you shone like a true planet in a firmament of kerosene lanterns. Congratulations. Now let me take you around to meet some friends. Bronek! This is Panna Um-hum-hum . . . Bronek Janta. . . .

All around the room Herr Gruber swallowed and burbled Halinka's name, and that was the only acknowledgment of her Jewishness the whole afternoon: the concealing of it. Meier says that *this tour was also the last Halinka saw of her host, except for a brief farewell at the end of the party.* [NOTE. N.L. Thus Halinka's "affair"!]

Meier stayed by Halinka. He says that she slid into the heart of the party with no effort. The young man named Janta, a tall, curly-haired Pole wearing a turtle-necked sweater under his jacket, took possession of her. Meier says that it was easy to see in Janta's eyes that Halinka was being a success: and her face glowed and was pliant to her vivid reactions.

Janta: —— Have you been to the new cabaret in the Europeiski—since it was done over, I mean?

Halinka: —— I don't have time for dancing these days.

Meier says Halinka gave this answer with a lilt to the word *dancing* that suggested her time was taken up with entertainments compared to which dancing was a nursery pastime.

Janta, his teeth glistening: —— You should take the time!

Janta told Halinka he was an industrial designer, that his was a world of tiny objects, of micrometry and niceties to the ten thousandth of an inch. He had formerly built cotton machinery for Lodz textile plants; now he was "getting some orders for things from the G.G." Halinka, aware that these letters stood for *General-Gouvernement* and that that stood for Germans, evidently thought it best not to press for more details.

Janta: —— And you?

Halinka, accurately, with a vague wave of her hand: —— I languish!

Meier says that during the course of the party he moved Halinka about the room, and in each group she was gay and spoke up. As if to tease her, Meier took her right up to the German lieutenant colonel, who turned out to be a dull regular *Wehrmacht* man. Meier says he had been right about the appetizers: a tray was on a sideboard at the colonel's elbow: tiny black caviar, smoked salmon, herring paste, stuffed eggs, and creams and cheeses without name or limit. But when the officer invited Halinka to take some, she refused—she seemed not to want to be thought hungry. [NOTE. N.L. One can guess from his reputation that Meier had no such compunction.]

Colonel Hoff, to Halinka, his mouth full: —— Did you see the news from Yugoslavia?

Halinka: —— Ah, colonel, I have a hard enough time keeping up with what is happening right here in Poland.

Colonel Hoff: —— My dear girl, *nothing* has happened here in Poland since September 28, 1939, when the campaign ended.

Halinka, helping herself to just a tiny piece of smoked salmon: —— Of course. How stupid of me!

It was almost curfew time when Meier delivered Halinka back to Sienna 17.

Halinka: —— Thank you, dear Meier, for escorting me.

Meier: —— A pleasure.

Halinka: —— It was a harmless afternoon, wasn't it?

Meier —— Yes, girl. Most harmless! What did you expect? Are you disappointed?

EVENTS APRIL 2–8, 1941. ENTRY APRIL 15, 1941. N.L. As I look back, I think I was too eager to clear Halinka Apt from the gossip about her. And yet: How eager everyone was to blame her! How vicious people become when they are helpless! I do not even wish to speculate as to how that story grew so absurdly. Obviously someone must have seen Meier bringing Halinka back that afternoon—someone who had been backstage at the theater or someone who had heard about what took place there. . . . But I said I was not going to speculate. I think I have exceeded propriety in my efforts for Halinka. She is a silly girl. The scandal may have been precisely what she wanted.

5

EVENTS APRIL 9, 1941. ENTRY APRIL 10, 1941. FROM DOLEK BERSON. Berson says he kept edging out into the pinched early-April sunlight. His overcoat, which had seemed perfectly adequate the previous autumn and early in the winter, had been feeling thin and porous in the marrow-searching weather of February and March. Now, at the first hint of the warmth of spring, he wanted to swim in that congenial suggestion. But his duties, as defined by a Polish "Navy-blue," who took his orders in turn from a bored but testy German corporal, kept pulling him into the shade on the south side of Elektoralna Street.

For several weeks, Berson had been assigned to sentry duty at the various gates to the outside world, and in recent days he had been posted at the Elektoralna gate. At this gate there is a single sentry box, a booth about four feet square, with a peaked roof, an arched door, and a bench and a desk inside. The structure is brightly painted with black and white stripes which slant into V's on each wall. On the Aryan face of the box is a sign: WOHN–GEBIET DER JUDEN—BETRETEN VERBOTEN. Within the gate, narrowing the opening still further, are three or four barricade-horses, strung and coiled with barbed wire. There are two German guards—the corporal and a private—in greatcoats and boots and peaked caps with wreath-and-wing badges on them. About ten feet inside the gate stand two Navy-blues. The Jewish policeman, who yesterday was Berson, stands ten or fifteen feet further yet from the gate. His work is to check passes, inspect brassards, and in general make sure that nothing out of order gets even so far as the Navy-blues.

For a few minutes just after noon yesterday, traffic dwindled and almost stopped, and Berson was able to take several fairly long intervals in the sunlight. He was thus drinking warmth in the middle of the street when a group of about twenty Jews turned into Elektoralna from Orla, a block from the gate. They walked down the middle of the street and were going right past Berson, when he said, in the rather harsh tone of Yiddish that had become his habit while on duty:

—— Stop here for inspection, please!

A short man at the head of the group turned toward Berson, and Berson recognized the miserable gnarl that serves Fischel Schpunt for a face.

Schpunt, in German: —— I beg your pardon, I am *meshummed*—a convert. I don't speak Yiddish.

A titter could be heard in the group. Berson says he thought he remembered having heard Schpunt speak Yiddish but realized he might be mistaken, so he said in German:

—— Inspection here before the gate.

Schpunt, politely, speaking this time in Polish: —— Excuse me, I was born and raised right here in Warsaw—Ceglana Street —all my life. My German is rusty. Excuse me.

Dolek heard open laughter in the group of men who had been following Schpunt, and who had now fallen back in an audiencelike semicircle. Berson blushed and said sharply in Polish:

—— Your documents.

Schpunt began fumbling hurriedly and humbly in his pockets. He asked in German:

—— Do you mean my work card? Or my ration card? Or . . . my *Judenrat* pass? I beg your pardon. . . . Or my birth certificate? Here! Here is my birth certificate! I was born in Warsaw. . . .

The audience was growing, and its laughter increasing. Berson says he now realized in a rush what was happening. He was being made the butt of Schweikism—the feigned ignorances, alleged misunderstandings, and regretful language difficulties of Jaroslav Hasek's *The Good Soldier Schweik*. Berson says he felt like a schoolboy with a pack of bullies around him, but the sensation now was queer: the bullies were Jews.

Berson saw that the Polish policemen were becoming interested in the crowd and were moving toward it, and he said, with all the vehemence of a child who has just comprehended mockery:

—— Take your humor to the Navy-blues!

In Berson's awareness, the sport was broken, and Schpunt and his followers hurried off away from the gate before the Navyblues reached them.

146

Berson says he stood in the sunlight for a few moments and then, as abruptly as if he were executing a right-face-and-forward-march on a parade ground, he turned and walked along Elektoralna, away from the gate and his duties. Then he began to run. It was eight blocks to the Community Building. After three blocks and a bit, breathing hard, he slowed to a walk again, and as he walked he hastily took off his police insignia. He ran some more on Grzybowska. He hurried into number 27 and up to my office. He threw his insignia on my desk and said breathlessly:

—— Take my name off the register! Destroy the records, Noach!

EVENTS APRIL 9, 1941. ENTRY APRIL 10, 1941. N.L. I cannot say I was either amazed or upset by Berson's eruption from the police force. Indeed, I had been confidently expecting it. He had had four months of it, approximately. As I noted here [ENTRY NOVEMBER 29, 1940], the sense of power his position gave him lasted only part of one day. From then on, a disturbing sense of wrong-doing seemed to grow on him. Schpunt lit his fuse. . . .

EVENTS APRIL 20, 1941. ENTRY DITTO. N.L. Berson is so happy, it is wonderful to see.

Indeed, a new mood has come over us all, for spring has announced itself in the swelling buds of the delicate birches and old horsechestnut trees outside. The new mood is not exactly hope. It is more nearly a state of patience: mere patience, like this warmer weather we are having, is a comfort. Today has been Sunday. This morning, in the Jewish cemetery, which is within the wall at the northwesterly corner of the ghetto, four of us were working. We were planting garden vegetables in the ground between the headstones—radishes, lettuce, onions, carrots, and beets —for, apart from the few dusty squares where houses have been bombed out, that is the only open land available in the ghetto. We staked out our small plot, where some Bersons are buried, and put up a little sign: *Sienna 17—Berson*. Berson and I were digging, and with us were Rabbi Goldflamm and the son of the convert who lives with the Bersons, the Jablonski boy, Wladislaw.

It was pleasant in the cemetery under the open sky: there, with no buildings jostling each other for air, and only a handful of living people and a gathering of the hushed and fortunate dead, it was peaceful, spacious, and quiet—quiet, that is, but for Wladislaw Jablonski's rattling tongue. This boy apparently does not know the meaning of quiet. Even the rich and busy voice of Rabbi Goldflamm was stilled in the face of this competition. Wladislaw was saying:

—— That was the fun! We would start out across the Vistula and through Praga into the farmland on the road to Lublin, and we'd carry just what it took to live for two days—some blankets, waterproofs, cooking utensils, and a little food and wine. We'd hike as far as we wanted and then we'd give a farmer a few zlotys for the right to fix ourselves a place in one of his fields. And we'd camp there around a fire, singing songs and telling stories. I'll never forget waking up with the dampness of the night fragrant on the ground all around, and then the smell of the wood fire when we first lit it up again. Walking in the fields: Jesus! These pavements!

[NOTE. N.L. Young Jablonski is the only one among us who feels qualified to invoke the Nazarene, and he does so, frequently; perhaps he believes that this gives him some special position among us, or perhaps he keeps this word on his lips as a kind of insurance, in hopes of preferential treatment in Heaven after death, in case . . . I am not a theologian, I had better not get into this.]

Jablonski, continuing: —— And then some of us used to take boat rides up the Vistula: we would hire a skiff, three or four of us, we'd row upstream all morning—we'd take our time, no hurry—and about noon we'd tie up by the banks and swim: that was the reason we went upstream: we had a saying: *Above Warsaw, God's water and His sediment. Below Warsaw, only men's.* And we'd dry ourselves in the sun, and then eat a picnic and drink some wine, and then drift downstream in the late afternoon and evening. . . .

Berson, interrupting, leaning his mattock against a gravestone and mopping his forehead: —— This is fine! Our pleasures. Give way, Wladislaw, let someone else have a chance. Rabbi, what used to be your greatest pleasure?

Goldflamm, with a kind of giggle: —— You know how I love to gossip!

Berson: —— You still can and do gossip. No, a pleasure before the ghetto.

148

Goldflamm: —— I have a very simple confession to make. My greatest pleasure was eating. I didn't know it then, but I do now—now that my diet has become so narrow and dull. I remember a lamb ragout Froi Goldflamm used to make for me. The meat was so tender that it seemed that only the *approach* of a fork-edge was necessary to make it part: as when Moses lowered his rod onto the water: miraculous. And the sauce, in which there was wine from the Crimea, was itself almost a wine! Oi misery, I remember once Froi Goldflamm shrieked in the kitchen, and I ran out, thinking that she had at least cut a finger off. All that had happened was that she had mistakenly dropped into the stew a spoon she had been using to mix a soup containing milk. You may not know our rule with hot dishes, Jablonski, that if anything containing or having touched milk gets into anything containing meat, the latter must exceed the former by sixty times, else it is not kosher—and *vice versa*. Well, I measured the exact displacement of the spoon by using two glasses and some water, and then I measured the stew, by ladling it into a similar glass and transferring it to another pot: and the stew (it was only for the two of us) was only forty-eight times the spoon. So it was *terefah*. We had to throw it all into the garbage. When I think of that now! I suppose I'd have to do the same thing even today, but if it happened in the ghetto, I think I'd throw Froi Goldflamm into the garbage, too, if she were living, may the Lord bless her angelic spirit!

Goldflamm looked, with a poignant, involuntary grimace, toward the section of the cemetery where his wife is buried. She died eight years ago.

Berson: —— Your turn, Noach!

N.L.: —— I'm afraid I will make you angry. I am happier in the ghetto than I was before. I have many friends now, and my mind has been opened up to all sorts of new things. I will tell you: when I worked as a clerk in the capmaker's shop and was writing *The Diaspora* at night, I used to sit on a hard bench from seven o'clock in the morning until six in the afternoon, adding figures, mostly, then I went to a room where I lived with two janitors, and they used to drink beer and talk about machinery all evening—magnetos and eccentric cams and . . . oh, they were experts, only they never could do anything except be janitors—while I would try to keep awake and write my history. A pleasure? It's more pleasure to be digging here in the sunlight. Except that even here in the sunlight, there is a shadow. . . . Are you people conscious of it?

Wladislaw: —— Jesus, Levinson! We were having a good time. . . .

N.L.: —— I was afraid I would spoil everything.

Berson, briskly: —— I've found a new pleasure, too! Listen!

Stepping over to the edge of the cultivated area and reaching into a kitbag that contained, among other things, a piece of bread and a bottle of boiled water, Berson took out a small, hexagonal concertina. He said with a grin:

—— I bought it from an old lady in the street. Six zlotys. A crime to take it from her for that, but that was what she wanted.

Berson sat on a headstone that was slightly askew and began playing, in the penetrating but sweet notes of the trembling reeds, *This Is How We Danced the Hora in Amech*.

EVENTS APRIL 26, 1941. ENTRY APRIL 27, 1941. FROM DOLEK BERSON. Berson says he suffered once again last night a recurrent dream he has been having lately. He stirred in his sleep, woke with a jump, felt the perspiration at his neck and on his face, and turned over to try to go back to sleep. But he had a hard time falling off again: the dream, still clear in his mind, troubled him, and also he felt a vague sensation of pain.

In the center of the dream, he, Berson, had advanced at the head of a warm and friendly group of people. A girl, who seemed to be Rachel, was near him: some of the time she pushed him from behind, whispering in his ear, while some of the time she was behind him, walking very close to him but not touching him. He and the group approached the ghetto wall, and then there was a gap in the wall, and then he was in front of two German sentries, who pointed bayonets at him. Suddenly he was the "good soldier Schweik," politely stupid, obsequiously confused, maddeningly witty, a master of Socratic irony. The crowd laughed and praised him, the girl patted him on the cheek, the Germans did not know what to do. The most vivid thing, wonderful and yet somehow fearful, was that he and the girl and the people in the crowd wore no armbands: the Germans wore white armbands with an inscrutable emblem of inferiority.

Berson tossed in his bed. He says he finally realized that the sensation he had, which was more a pulling than a pain, was in his stomach. He knew at last what it was. He was hungry.

[NOTE. EDITOR. The following incident, which had taken place the previous December, is entered here as background for subsequent entries:]
EVENTS DECEMBER 22–27, 1940. ENTRY DECEMBER 28, 1940. N.L. I have had a romantic adventure. A member of the Bund pointed out to me last week, in my capacity as *Judenrat* librarian and as a notorious book-lover, that the building at Leszno 13 is at the edge of the ghetto and backs up to the Bronislaw Grosser Library, now just outside the ghetto walls. I hurried over to Leszno Street and, pretending to be an electrical worker, went into the basement of No. 13. I satisfied myself that the foundations were of old brick and decided upon the adventure.

Four Bundists, including the one who made the original suggestion, agreed to help me. I also asked Berson, as he is such an ox—and as his police insignia might be a protection. A man in the labor department of the *Judenrat* got us some tools, two kerosene lanterns, and a power-company chart that showed the relationship between the basements of Leszno 13 and the Grosser Library. It was easy to bribe the janitor of Leszno 13, which is an office building, to give us a master key.

On Monday night we began. Berson called for the rest of us at the *Judenrat* long after curfew hour, and "escorted" us to Leszno 13. We were challenged only once on the way, and that was by another Jewish policeman; when he saw Berson, he hurried us along.

We had worked out on the chart the simplest place, theoretically, to penetrate. We chiseled a hole about three feet in diameter in the brick foundations of Leszno 13, and beyond the wall we hit Warsaw's subsoil, which is damp, sandy, hard-packed earth. Digging it out was simple. We were nervous about a cave-in, but Berson arranged a series of ingenious shores. We had one large rock to detour. We worked two nights digging. The moment when we reached a solid brick wall, about eight feet out, was fantastically exciting. There again the removal of bricks was not hard, and at three thirty on the second morning, I squeezed through and found that we had reached the library basement, all right. We enlarged the library "door" somewhat and then quit for the night.

151

On Wednesday night we began the real work. I think I know every inch of every library in Warsaw, and with a hooded lantern in my hand I hopped about like a monkey, picking out the books and records to be taken. The men dragged them through to Leszno 13 in boxes and sacks—and that is the way we worked for four nights. By day my muscles ached! The task of getting the books away from the basement of Leszno 13, where they are stored with the knowledge of our venal friend the janitor, and of taking them to the *Judenrat* library and to our various personal bookshelves, has only begun; it will probably take weeks, as we must work with small bundles; but the books are in the ghetto—that's our little victory. Already I see on my shelves some of my oldest and best friends: Chatos Naarim's *Sins of My Youth,* the *Wonder Tales* of Reb Nachman Bratzlawer, *The Nag* and *The Wanderings of Benjamin the Third* by Mendele Moicher Sforim, a complete Peretz, several feet of Yehoash, Reisin, Pinski, Sholem Aleichem, Gorin, Asch, Nomberg, Boraisha, and others. I'm going to start a lending library of my own.

We had some weird scenes: I on my hands and knees with my head and shoulders in the tunnel, where one of the lanterns hung, drinking in *Three Gifts,* until one of the draggers tapped me from behind and forgave himself for interrupting me but pointed out that we had only reached the P's. And: two of us lost for a few minutes in the stacks, until I came across the *Hatekufa* shelves, which I immediately recognized as if they were houses along a street where I had once lived. And: powerful Berson, when a sack that he was dragging broke, picking the books up out of the dirt daintily one by one between the tips of his thumbs and forefingers, so as not to soil them, with his little fingers elevated to the teacup position. . . .

EVENTS APRIL 28, 1941. ENTRY DITTO. N.L. Walking down Twarda Street this morning, I met Berson, wheeling a pushcart. The pushcart was full of books.

N.L.: —— Where are you going with those?

Berson: —— To the bookstore up beyond Panska. I'm going to sell them.

—— Wait! You can't sell those.

—— These are my own. None of these came from the Grosser Library.

—— That's not what I mean. I don't care about that. I mean that you have no right to think of selling books. Would you sell *me*? Would you sell Symka?

—— I need a thousand zlotys. I've read these books.

—— You've read them! Did you marry Symka and make love to her only once?

—— I've read some of them twice.

Berson half-smiled directly he had said this: he must have reflected that Symka would not have relished his answer to my question.

N.L.: —— No, I won't let you sell your books, Berson. Anything else. Turn around, we're going back.

Berson and I have had long talks about books, and he worked with me in rescuing the books from the Grosser Library; he knows and I guess respects my feeling about them, though he does not seem to share it. However, I sensed that he knew, standing in the busy street with the traffic dividing on either side of his idle pushcart, that the force of my opinions on the subject—the force of my great eyeballs behind my bookman's lenses—would turn him back. Yet he stood.

Berson, driven to confession: —— I can't go back. I want to buy Symka a labor exemption, and I need leeway financially. I can't take these back and tell her I've changed my mind.

N.L.: —— Sell something else! Sell a couple of those antique ikons you have on your wall: you don't pray in front of them. Or sell that box on the sideboard, or a couple of pieces out of your father's silver set you showed me once.

Berson: —— But I'll want those things after the war.

N.L.: —— Can you really believe that? If you'll want anything, you'll want *continuity*: you'll want your books. (Berson seemed to be hesitating.) If you can't face Symka, bring your books to my apartment, sell something else quietly, and that will be that. Come on!

Slowly the pushcart began moving. So it is that my library is even larger this evening than before.

EVENTS APRIL 27, 1941. ENTRY APRIL 29, 1941. FROM DOLEK BERSON. Berson has told me of the conversation that led to his trying to sell his books:

Symka: —— But what shall I do?

Dolek: —— There are only two choices. Either take a job or register for forced labor. Look around you: Rutka, Halinka, and Rachel have all taken jobs.

Symka: —— You could buy me an exemption.

[NOTE. N.L. I can imagine the way Symka would say this, as if an exemption were something sparkling to wear on the lobes of her dainty ears.]

Dolek: —— We can't afford it.

Symka: —— Can't afford it! We have hundreds of things here in the apartment we could sell. And yet you say we can't afford to keep me out of the Kielce quarries!

Dolek: —— They don't send the women to the quarries. . . . Well, I'll think about it. . . . The only thing is (he says he added this somewhat petulantly, having, in his previous sentence, clearly surrendered the substance of the argument), I don't think it looks well.

Symka: —— Can you worry about appearances these days?

Dolek, attempting to recover the face he had lost in the argument by taking *some* position: —— Yes, I think it's extremely important not to seem degraded, even if we are beginning to be. By appearances, it may be possible to sustain realities, or at least to prolong them. . . .

EVENTS APRIL 30, 1941. ENTRY MAY 2, 1941. FROM DOLEK BERSON. One thing Berson says he decided promptly was that he would not go back to his cousin Meier again. He decided to try out Stefan Mazur's connections. Two days after I caught him trying to sell his books, he waited on the staircase for the good-looking young man to come home from work, and intercepted him there.

Berson: —— Stefan! Could you give me some advice and help?

Stefan, with Tauberesque humility: —— I'd be glad to do what I can.

Berson, hurriedly: —— I have to raise a thousand zlotys. I wondered if you might know any way for me to sell something outside the ghetto.

Stefan: —— Are you going to get rid of the Bechstein piano at last?

Berson, smiling: —— No, something more suitable for smuggling.

Stefan, with an air of importance: —— I think I can put you in touch with someone. . . . Listen. I have a date tonight at the Britannia, and I believe we can find someone there to do the job. Come there at about ten o'clock. Do you know where it is? . . . Nowolipie 20.

—— But what about the curfew?

—— Don't leave *all* the ingenuity to me, Berson.

Berson's ingenuity, when the time came, consisted in lying to Symka and in baldly taking his chances in the streets. Whenever he saw anyone, he ducked into a dark doorway and waited, and when the coast was clear he hurried on. The trip took nearly half an hour, but it seemed endless. When at last he approached the night-club, a score of apparitions suddenly glided out from the walls at him, whispering urgently. He was terrified at first, but soon recognized the sneaking, susurrant crowd as a group of beggars. In a manner more lordly than he thought he likes to assume (still, he assumed it), he brushed them aside and deafened his ears to their hissing.

He pushed the door open and another world exploded into view. [NOTE. N.L. It is a world maintained by smuggling. The Britannia, like the Sztuka, the Modern, the Hirschfeld, and other nightclubs, is a small island of luxury in our sea of woe. Here gather, besides wealthy innocents who crave escape, the daring elements of the ghetto: smugglers and their mistresses, informers for the Gestapo, young Poles looking for Jewish girls, young Jewish girls looking for a square meal—and, on the theory that the safest place to hide is under the enemy's nose, or, if possible, right in his nostrils, workers for the various underground organizations. Former society ladies wait on table. Former symphonists play in the jazz orchestras. Goose livers, succulent pies, the rarest liqueurs are to be had, at smugglers' prices; and at the entrances of some of these clubs, doormen with staves beat back the beggars so that customers can come and go unmolested.] A girl took Berson's coat and a headwaiter asked him how many he was. Gusts of smoke and laughter came at him, and in the distance he could hear, as a tasseled fringe on the edge of the general fabric of noise, threads of piano music. Faces were happy, flushed, sensuous, and sluggish: there were glinting wine and golden cognac on the tables. Couples were dancing in a confined square.

Berson: —— I am looking for Pan Stefan Mazur.

He craned his neck as if to prove the truth of this assertion.

Headwaiter: —— Pan Mazur. Certainly, Pan Mazur is right over here.

Stefan was apparently a familiar of the place. Berson found Stefan and Halinka at a corner table, looking indeed very much at home. Stefan jumped up and greeted Berson, the latter thought, with somewhat more than the necessary courtesy—a café congeniality, tumescent, bloodshot, grinning. He took Berson by the arm and said:

—— Right over here, I think we'll find what we want. Excuse us, Halinka.

Stefan led Berson to a round table where a number of middle-aged men and younger girls were sitting; and Berson's heart sank, he says. Cousin Meier. Hartmann. Gruber. Eugeniusz Tauber. Berson, coming into the presence of these familiar figures, felt as if this were a memory, not a current experience.

Herr Gruber, sociably: —— Related to *our* Berson?

Meier, unabashed by the all-too-justified possessive: —— *I* will admit the kinship!

Hartmann, evidently recalling Berson's bargaining over Pan Apt's bribe: —— Oh yes, I remember you. (To Tauber:) This fellow could haggle the horns and hooves right off a cow.

Tauber, on this high praise of Hartmann's accepting Berson into the circle: —— So? Well, join, us, young man.

Berson says he felt giddy, as if he were descending a spiral staircase too fast.

Stefan: —— This particular Berson has a problem.

Embarrassed, driven after all into his cousin's repulsive confidence, Berson leaned over and mumbled to Meier, beginning to tell what he wanted.

Meier: —— You'd better speak to Pan Tauber.

Berson moved to Tauber and began to mutter his needs again.

Tauber: —— Speak louder. We all understand each other here.

When Berson had explained what he wanted, the dapper little man said:

—— Nothing in the world could be easier. Matter of fact, we're expecting a young fellow in just a few minutes who'd be glad to take care of this, I'm sure. Sit down! Bring your pretty Halinka over here, Stefan.

First names, Berson thought. As Stefan went after Halinka, Berson squeezed into the circle.

Berson says that after a while a tall, curly-haired Pole came to the table and was introduced all the way around. Berson says that he was wearing a turtle-necked sweater under his jacket. His name was Janta. [NOTE. N.L. In the light of ENTRY APRIL 12, 1941, concerning the party outside the ghetto at which Halinka met Janta, this information naturally interested me.] Tauber indicated to Berson that this was the young man he had spoken about, and in due course Berson was able to get beside him and bring up his business.

Janta: —— And may I see the object?

Berson reached into his fob and pulled out a large, thin, gold watch, with a long stem, an elliptical, fluted winding knob, and a delicately engraved flap over the face. He handed the watch to Janta.

Berson: —— My father gave it to me. It was his.

Janta, after examining the watch with the cold, clueless face of a physician: —— Your father had exquisite taste. We can get you four thousand zlotys for this.

Berson, blurting: —— I need only one thousand.

Janta: —— My dear fellow, it's a good thing I keep my promises. You shouldn't say things like that.

Berson: —— You misunderstood. I meant: I don't know whether I should sell the watch. . . . Would you take care of this in person?

Janta: —— Heavens, no. Do you realize how dangerous smuggling is just now? I have a little helper.

In the end Berson decided to sell the watch. [NOTE. N.L. Casually, as we talked along, I asked Berson whether Janta and Halinka seemed to know each other. He said at first he thought not; later, on thinking it over, he said they did dance together.]

EVENTS MAY 4, 1941. ENTRY DITTO. FROM HALINKA APT. I confess I went to Halinka expecting to be told to mind my own business. I risked that because I thought that someone ought to warn her that playing with Janta would be playing with fire—a fire that would char her reputation to an ash. To my surprise, Halinka greeted my meddling with simple frankness. She told me that Janta meant nothing to her except as a symbol of the fragility of the wall. I'm inclined to believe her because her account of the party agreed in every detail with Meier Berson's account: they could not have planned such an ornate alibi. Of her encounter with Janta in the Britannia, Halinka says:

Halinka saw Janta when he first came in the door. He was dressed almost exactly as he had been at Gruber's, except that he had a lightweight turtle-neck sweater and a summer jacket on: evidently Janta is positive he looks well in that formula, Halinka says —and furthermore, she says, he does. The headwaiter led him toward Tauber's table, and suddenly Halinka, remembering her pretense to Janta at Gruber's party, ashamed to be found here and Jewish, terrified that Janta might make Stefan jealous by bringing up her escapade, tried to make herself small, looked away, busily talked to Stefan, powdered her face. But when Herr Gruber introduced Janta all the way around the table, the young man shook Halinka's hand with a curt greeting, as if he had never seen her before.

Later Janta asked her to dance. She felt suddenly triumphant: he had not forgotten her. Perhaps *he* was embarrassed to have been found out—his talk of having designed cotton machinery! After they had danced awhile she spoke:

Halinka, throwing her head back: —— I see your work as an engineer really does require fine calculations, as you said: to the nearest three or four thousand zlotys!

Janta, laughing: —— We all have our pretenses, don't we?

Halinka: —— Were you surprised to see me here?

Janta: —— Not at all. Herr Gruber told me to expect it. I was only pleased.

Halinka says Janta's teeth glistened and his eyes flashed—with what suddenly seemed to her (she says) a cheap conceit. She says she said:

—— Let's sit down.

EVENTS MAY 4, 1941. ENTRY MAY 4, 1941. FROM DOLEK BERSON. Berson received payment today for his watch, and he tells me that he was surprised to see who Janta's "little helper" was:

There was a bold knock at the apartment door, and Berson answered. Outside stood a ragged boy, and at once Berson recognized his face: deeply sunken big eyes, a squashed nose, lips seeming to smile—and a pallid scar running diagonally across from right temple to left jaw. So this, Berson thought, remembering the canceled face running away from the caricature of Hitler on that bright anniversary morning long, long ago [ENTRY NOVEMBER 9, 1939] —so *this* was the smuggler's accomplice!

The boy reached into his pocket, with the same deep-digging squirm Berson had seen before, and pulled out four notes, each for a thousand zlotys, and handed them to Berson. Berson thanked the boy.

The boy: —— Could I have a taste of bread for my work?

Berson went to the kitchen and brought back a slice of bread. The boy crammed a corner of it into his mouth and turned and went stealthily down the stairs, looking back with an enigmatic, scar-split stare at Berson.

EVENTS MAY 5, 1941. ENTRY DITTO. FROM MORDECAI APT. This evening Dolek Berson told a group of us of having seen the boy with the scar, and recalled the circumstances under which he had seen him before (though naturally he did not reveal the boy's errand this time, as Symka was there). Mordecai picked him up right away, saying that he had seen this same boy just about two weeks ago, in this way:

Mordecai was working on a new section of wall, which is to exclude the Jewish cemetery from the ghetto. [NOTE. N.L. We do not know yet whether we will be permitted to go out to tend our "farms" in the cemetery.] Mordecai worked steadily and skillfully, now, as if he had been a bricklayer for years. With one convoluted swing of his trowel, he scooped up some mortar, peeled off damp strips of it onto several edges of a brick, gave the deposits a spreading dab, and then inverted the brick and lowered it into place, lining it up with the guide-string with gentle taps of the trowel handle. Fein was working beside him.

Fein: —— Tomorrow there will be a gap in your ranks, fellow brick-lifters. I (he spoke opulently) am going into business.

Mordecai: —— Ladies' underwear?

Fein: —— More interesting. Something close to women's skins, though.

Mordecai: —— What?

Fein: —— Wigs.

Mordecai: —— Wigs!

Fein: —— Certainly. This is May. Summer and the typhus season will be here soon. Hundreds of ladies will lose their hair. What is more hideous than a bald woman? I shall satisfy the vanities of these ladies who are naked on top—at enormous fees. (Fein wagged an admonitory finger at Mordecai.) And now is the time to jump into this business—now that Hasidim are cutting off their beards and excellent hair from the chins of decent men can be had for a song.

Mordecai: —— I suppose you are teasing.

Fein: —— No. Seriously. I am tired of building brick walls around my own kind. My conscience demands that I merely take their money away from them. . . .

At this point, says Mordecai, he heard shouting across the cemetery, and he turned to see what the commotion was. He saw the figure of a small boy, darting erratically among the headstones, evading the lumbering pursuit of two Navy-blues. The boy had a bundle under his arm. As he dashed across a cultivated section among the graves, he stopped suddenly, bent down, pulled a radish, and spurted forward again, beating the dirt of the radish onto his ragged pants as he ran. He came straight for Mordecai's hip-high stretch of wall, and vaulted it with one hand on the wall. Mordecai says he distinctly saw the pallid scar slanting across the whole ageful, cynical, radish-chawing child's face. On the other side of the wall one of the German gendarmes supervising the bricklayers' detail ran toward the boy's path and grabbed the urchin by the upper arm. The scarred face spit out fragments of radish and bent down sideways toward the gendarme's hand. The gendarme cried out in surprise and pain as the boy bit into his knuckles. The German loosed his grip and released the horrible little gamin, who ran crookedly away.

EVENTS APRIL 30, 1941. ‘ENTRY MAY 5, 1941. FROM DO-LEK BERSON. These things emerge only slowly. Berson now reluctantly tells me that on the evening when he was making arrangements with Janta at the Britannia, Stefan told the men at Tauber's table that Berson is an accomplished pianist; they persuaded him to play; Halinka sang songs with him; all the customers in the café listened and applauded; and day before yesterday Berson was approached by a representative of the Britannia and offered a job; Halinka the same. They have both accepted. They start next week. Berson is not proud of this, but he says he will be glad to have a chance to "practice" the piano every night. Also, incidentally, he will eat well.

EVENTS MAY 7, 1941. ENTRY DITTO. FROM DOLEK BERSON. In conversation this evening, the Drifter seemed troubled by the problem of corruption. Even the most honorable men in the ghetto, he says, are finding themselves—are surprised to find themselves—involved in transactions and practices which they would not have dreamed of touching three or four years ago. He would not say what had roused his worry on this subject, but I think it must have been his brief exposure to the black market in selling his "books," toward the worthy (yet corrupt, if you think of it) end of buying Symka an exemption from labor duty. Perhaps he is also concerned about his cousin Meier Berson, who is now notorious as a messenger boy for the German Gruber and for Tauber and others; but I doubt it, because I think Berson wrote Meier off as a washout some time ago.

[INSERT. FROM ENTRY APRIL 14, 1941. N.L. Smuggling is now universally accepted and highly organized. And is there any wonder? Our rations are staples: twenty grams of bread a day, potatoes, groats, a dull vegetable jam sweetened with saccharine, one egg a month; while we hear tales of abundance on the Aryan side: fresh peaches, salmon, artichokes. Last fall quite a few Polish workers were still coming to work in Polish enterprises inside the ghetto, and they smuggled things in; and for a while, as the wall was being built, sections of our boundary, especially Zlota Street, were temporarily defined only by barbed wire, which was easy to traverse. Recently the traffic has had to come and go through tunnels dug from cellars on our edges; through the sewers; through holes in the wall —single bricks removed and replaced; over the wall, on ropes with hooks on them. Especially are the children active; they are ingenious and fearless. Some things come in through the cemetery, where graves, coffins, and hearse-carts allow an ambiguous, death-into-life traffic. (NOTE. EDITOR. Evidently being cut off by the new wall as of ENTRY MAY 5, 1941.) All sorts of things are brought in: sugar, butter, cheese; vodka and wine; even leather and textiles for illegal factories. Jews are allowed to buy only such medicines as purgatives and aspirin; typhus serum is smuggled in. Valuta, gold, jewels go out. Once in a while a whole wagon full of food or goods comes through one of the gates, for bribery can always find its weak spots. Officially the punishment for smuggling is a ten-thousand-zloty fine and a year in jail. Often children are shot.]

I tried to point out to Berson that our ghetto differs from a normal society only in that all the normal pressures are increased a hundredfold; consequently the end products of pressure are also manifest a hundredfold—among them, ingenuity for survival, the willingness to do anything for oneself and one's own, selfishness, corruption. This hydraulic press of a ghetto squeezes things out of us that our thin hides would normally contain, and that we would prefer not to see issue from us. By the same token, I told Berson I thought he could look about, now or in the future, and see nobility just as exaggerated and generosity and selflessness grown just as enormous as he now sees corruption to be.

Berson: —— Where? Where?

I admit I was rather vague. I told him to look sharply.

Nevertheless, I believe it. I could not live if I did not believe it.

EVENTS JUNE 22, 1941. ENTRY JUNE 26, 1941. FROM DO-
LEK BERSON. Berson sat reading the *Gazeta Zydowska* in his living room the other day. Symka was sewing by a window.

Symka: —— What time is it?

Berson's hand went automatically to his watch pocket, and then he remembered:

—— I don't know.

—— You don't know?

—— I haven't my watch with me.

—— Where is it?

—— In the bedroom, I guess.

Symka, putting the back of her hand to her forehead: —— I have a terrible headache.

Berson, reading the paper, mumbled an acknowledgment.

Symka, after a few moments, insisting: —— Dolek, I feel awful.

Dolek, still reading, absently: —— I'm sorry.

Berson had not finished when he heard Symka sobbing. He stood up and went to her.

Dolek: —— Why, Symka! What is it?

Symka: —— How little you know me!

She stood up and slipped away, weeping, to the bedroom. Berson followed her as far as the door and then, seeing her crying face down on the bed, and supposing her to be suffering from some ineffable, transitory, inconsolable mood, he went back to his reading.

Some minutes later a sound like a scream, but not quite a scream, came from the bedroom. Berson ran in. Symka lay on her back, her eyes wide with fear, and gasped:

—— Something is happening to me!

EVENTS JUNE 23, 1941. ENTRY DITTO. N.L. Symka Berson has typhus. She came down with it yesterday late in the afternoon. At least, we assume it is typhus: we will not know for sure until the spots appear. She is very sick. This is one of the first cases on Sienna Street, and all the people in No. 17 seem terribly shocked, for they seem to have believed that by keeping clean they could avoid the disease; they had persuaded themselves that typhus was really a lower-class disease, which would take lodgings only in crowded streets like Nowolipki, Nowolipie, Gensia, Nalewki, and Pawia.

EVENTS JUNE 29, 1941. ENTRY JULY 1, 1941. FROM STEFAN MAZUR. I have an account of Berson's retort from Stefan Mazur. I wish I had been there to see it. This is a little thing, but it makes me proud of Berson. Of course it is hard to say whether he was motivated by principle or by sheer exasperation: he was worried about Symka. Still and all, a nice piece of work.

It seems that the proprietor of the Britannia makes a practice of allowing his entertainers—at present, Berson and Halinka Apt—to bring one guest an evening: considering the food the café serves, this is quite a favor. That night Berson had asked Fein—and it is quite characteristic of Berson that he would have kept contact with the jovial, round-faced workman whom he met during the short time when he was working on the wall; whereas so far as I know, Mordecai Apt, who worked with Fein right up until Fein quit to make wigs, has never taken the trouble to see Fein outside working hours.

Stefan says that Fein was making quite a sensation in the café. Fein was being funny. Indeed, he was out of place in the elegant atmosphere, and it was not so much his wit as his roly-poly clumsiness and crude way of shouting above the orchestra's noise that

made him amusing. Besides the very laughter of his audience—
Halinka, Berson, and Stefan—made them laugh the more: they
had arrived at that rare stage of nonsense which is self-perpetuat-
ing. Halinka shed tears from laughing. Fein, realizing that he was
funny, but not realizing why, was beginning to force his humor,
was repeating stories, and was trying too hard. He had had great
success with his version of the ambush at Nalewki Street, when the
Polish hooligans had been caught in a shower of bricks, and now
he was telling about a day when Hartmann let the bung out of
a water-cart so that the water spilled all over Kurtz. [NOTE.
N.L. This must have been just before Hartmann openly broke
with the Communists.]

Fein, broadly: —— Kurtz is talking to me, you know, and
Hartmann pushes the cart up and aims it, you know, right at
Kurtz's back, and then Hartmann slips around and *zip*, out comes
the bung, and Kurtz is talking along and then his leg is wet, you
know, and a look comes over his face, as if he's thinking, *Something's wet around here*, then he's surprised. *My God! It's me!*
Then he jumps out of the way and turns. . . . I thought I knew
some language! . . .

Stefan says that Berson had been joining in the hilarity, but
when, at this juncture, the proprietor came up to the table and
told Halinka and Berson that they were to go on after the orchestra finished the piece it was playing, Berson turned to Halinka and
said:

—— I don't feel much like it tonight.

[INSERT. FROM ENTRY JUNE 28, 1941. N.L. This was Symka's fifth day. The pink-purple spots have appeared, on her shoulders, all over her trunk, and down her arms and legs—even on the
soles of her feet; yet not on her face. Her fever remains alarmingly
high. She has been delirious part of the time; when she is calm, she
complains of a persistent, unbearable headache. She must be approaching a crisis. . . .]

Halinka and Berson left the table and pushed past the thin
brown curtain hanging in the door beside the orchestra stand.
After the music ended, Halinka came out with Berson, unannounced. Halinka was dressed in a new silk print the café has
given her. Berson sat at the piano and together the two performed
some songs. Most of the people at the tables went right on talking.
[NOTE. N.L. Berson has told me several times how much this

annoys him.] On Halinka's behalf, Stefan says he glared at some of the talkers, and during one of the songs Fein, seeing the transported glow on Stefan's face as he listened, nudged him hard and said:

—— You can't eat her!

Halinka was singing a song with words by Heine when a loud, harsh voice came from a table very close to Stefan's, at the edge of the floor, where six men were sitting:

—— Stop that racket!

Halinka broke off her singing, but Berson continued to play. The voice shouted:

—— Stop that damned noise!

Stefan stood up. He saw at once that the men were valuta traders, and that one of them had two gold coins balanced on the middle fingers of his hands, and was jingling them together to test them. Stefan ran around the floor and up behind Berson at the piano, and he muttered:

—— Be careful. There may be someone important at that table.

Berson nevertheless went on playing. As Stefan stood by in great anxiety, Berson turned to Halinka, who had turned pale as paper, and said:

—— Next verse, Halinka.

Halinka began to sing again in a wavering voice. The whole café was listening now. One of the men at the table got up and walked toward the orchestra stand. As he approached, Berson stopped playing, leaving Halinka dangling in mid-phrase, and stepped to the front of the low platform. He took a position next to Halinka, and he said to the man, with a cold and cutting authority:

—— Sit down.

The man opened his mouth to speak, and Stefan says he hated to imagine what would come out, but Berson rushed in before he could say anything. This time Berson spoke with scornful patience, as if he were addressing a stupid child:

—— In case you don't know it, Frailin Apt was singing a song by Heinrich Heine. In case you didn't know it, Heine was a Jewish poet whom even the Germans admire. Your profit can wait just a few moments for Heine, can't it?

Stefan says the impasse was magnificent. At last the man

165

shrugged and went back to the table. Berson resumed his seat at the piano and said:

—— Begin that verse again, Halinka.

Halinka's spirits, like those of everyone in the café, had been suddenly lifted by Berson's few words, and now she sang boldly. This time the whole crowd, even the six men, listened to Heine's limpid lines.

EVENTS JULY 6, 1941. ENTRY DITTO. FROM DOLEK BERSON. Berson has come to work for the *Judenrat!* Purely speculative: is this an indirect result of the incident of the Heine song? Having made the move, Berson is now unsure whether he should have done it. His account of his interview with Sokolczyk this morning is full of rather humorous misgivings:

Berson says he was filled with anticipatory pleasure as he waited in the Chairman's office. Sokolczyk has a corner office on the second floor of this building, with a carpet on the floor and a glass-topped desk. On the desk are elegantly framed Baum-Forbert photographs of the Chairman's three grandchildren; as well as a repoussé silver writing stand, a stainless blotter, and a brightly polished copper humidor. Berson says that for the first time in several years he was conscious of being shabbily dressed: his shoes were cracked and unpolished, his trousers were baggy, the top button was missing from his jacket, the collar of his shirt was frayed, and his necktie was stringy and drab. All these things had been true for months and months: it took the effulgent humidor to remind him.

—— Well, well, Berson!

Ruddy, white-haired, cheerful, quick, the Chairman strode into his office. Chairman Sokolczyk has the look, Berson remarks, of a businessman in a period of splendid profits. He reminded Berson of his father. He is always well dressed: Felix Mandeltort once said that he had the impression that although Sokolczyk's grey beard is quite opaque, the Chairman always wears under it a starched dickey and a tie with a pearl stickpin. The Chairman sat down at his desk, beamed, pushed forward the humidor, and said:

—— Cigar?

Caught by surprise, flattered, somehow carried back and back to the atmosphere of his own home long ago—and forgetting that he has not eaten adequately for weeks—Berson accepted a cigar. Absent-mindedly he tried at first to light it without clipping it; he realized his error when the Chairman offered him some dainty cigar shears. While this was happening, the Chairman was saying:

—— I was delighted to hear that you had made an appointment to see me. I don't think I've seen you since way back in October, 1939—that day we accidentally collared you and made a jailbird of you.

The Chairman laughed, in the manner of a gay fellow recalling Old Times. Berson fumbling with the cigar, said with gratitude:

—— I didn't think you noticed me that day!

—— Of course I did. How could I miss that name? Your family has a distinguished record, now don't deny it! I knew your father slightly. My, what a noble face he had! . . . You look a little like him, Berson, I can see that you do.

With his cigar finally lit, Berson sat back, puffing out a luxurious, azure gauze that hung on the air about his shoulders and head. Berson says he had not realized how much he had missed pure comfort—the club-like, inner-group, waited-upon, softly felt comfort of his boyhood home. Only dimly he realized it this morning, he says: at the moment he felt, more than anything else, a friendliness and kinship with this gracious man, the Chairman.

Sokolczyk, with a look of heartfelt concern: —— How do you find life these days?

Berson, exhaling casually: —— Oh, my wife and I make out very nicely, thank you. (Berson admits that upon saying this, he squirmed ever so slightly in his chair: an image had flickered in his mind of Symka, sleeping in the pale dawn, her cheeks drawn and yellowish with fever, her crown almost bare from pyrexia-baldness.)

Sokolczyk: —— Good! Good! I'm sure you do. (The Chairman leaned forward in his seat.) And what can I do for you?

Berson said he wanted to ask about the possibility of getting a job with the *Judenrat*. I can imagine that he spoke diffidently and in a rather roundabout way: he hates to ask for favors. But the moment the Chairman caught the drift of his request, he cried:

—— Welcome, welcome! We certainly have room for such as you. As a matter of fact, just yesterday I was talking with Fostel, in the Taxation and Revenue Department, and he was telling me that he needs a shrewd young man.

Berson tried to say: *But.* . . . But he had come into the *Judenrat* with the idea of working in one of the self-help departments. But he thought the Jews in the ghetto were bearing all the burden of taxation they could. But what was there about the atmosphere of this office—what had there been about the atmosphere of his father's office, that was so pleasant, and yet . . . ? Berson puffed and puffed on the sweet Havana.

—— It is trying work, making ends meet around here. We can use a man with your background. In fact (the Chairman spoke softly, in a confidentially muted tone), you may not realize it, but I've had my eye on you, Berson. I've been hoping you'd come to us. One of these days a fairly big job is going to open up that will be an immense alleviation to the Jews here in Warsaw. Immense! And I've been looking for a young man. . . .

[NOTE. N.L. Help! Who among us in the *Judenrat* has not heard this vague and glittering promise from the Chairman, on a day when he was in an expansive mood, or when he wanted something?]

Berson, finally getting out the single word: —— But . . .

Sokolczyk, standing up in a signal of adjournment: —— Come to work day after tomorrow. I'll speak to Fostel. And *thank* you for coming to us.

Berson stood up. His head swam. He moved around as quickly as he could to the back of the chair in which he had been smoking, and steadied himself. The smoke from his cigar now seemed sickening.

Sokolczyk: —— We are honored to have a Berson among us. Thank you again. . . .

Berson, who wanted only to get out of the office: —— You're welcome. . . . Glad. . . .

Berson walked unsteadily and hastily out through the anteroom, along the corridor, down the stairs, and to the men's bathroom, where, to his enormous regret, he vomited the precious little breakfast he ate this morning.

6

Events July 11, 1941. Entry ditto. From Lazar Slonim. Spent the evening at the Bersons'. Slonim was there. Agate-eyed fellow. Yanking away at his forelock, he told of this conversation in which Berson figured:

Rapaport and Slonim took their bowls of soup to a stretch of one of the long plank tables that was empty and sat down. Slonim says he admires old Rapaport for establishing, as the Socialists' casual meeting place, a Hechalutz soup kitchen: drinking from the Zionists' pot and planning their downfall at the same time!

Rapaport gulped his hot soup systematically and with noises, both of ingestion and appreciation, that did not go well with his imposing and dignified appearance—nor with his famous stomach trouble, for that matter. He did not speak until he was finished. Then, while Slonim, who had scarcely begun, blew on each spoonful and sipped it slowly, the old Socialist said in an undertone:

—— Well, Slonim, one good result of the wall around us is that the Hasidim are coming out of uniform: you've probably noticed, they're shedding their black robes and snipping off their beards and side-curls. How I like that! It's like the demobilization of a hostile army! They're frightened. They're trying to hide themselves among the rest of us Jews! I heard of one religious Jew the other day who had his wife cut up his kaftan and make it into a dress, with lace ruffles and a colored lining, and then smuggled it outside and sold it on the black market. There's godliness-in-hardtimes for you! Another good thing: the intellectuals and professionals are all becoming workers—tailors, glazers, carpenters, bricklayers, fur-cleaners. There go the parasites!

Slonim says he knew that Rapaport knew that Slonim was himself an intellectual-turned-bricklayer, and he wondered whether this remark from the old man was simply absent-minded tactlessness or was a more deliberate prod.

Rapaport, continuing: —— I even heard of a journalist who has turned barber: a turncoat intellectual cutting off the beards of turncoat Hasidim! (With a sudden snapping sound, Rapaport laughed loudly and humorlessly. Then, again in his quiet, somber tone:) That's delightful! (Now Rapaport's manner changed.) . . .

Some unfinished business, Slonim. Have you taken another try at that baker on whom you had a failure?

Slonim: —— Menkes? No.

—— Does Menkes understand he will be practically alone?

—— He prefers it that way.

—— Now. But let him wait until our troubles really begin. Don't you think you'd better try again?

—— No, I don't. I think it would be a waste of time.

—— Very well, Slonim. That's your decision. Very well. I accept it. (Slonim says that Rapaport seemed to be controlling himself just a little more visibly than necessary.) Then what about Berson? I remember you told me some time ago that he was somehow or other almost ready to be approached—growing up, I think you said.

One thing you have to grant this aging revolutionary, Slonim says, is a memory. During the reorganization of these recent months Rapaport must have discussed a thousand candidates with various Bundists, and he remembers Berson, "growing up." Slonim says that this discussion of Berson had taken place six months before, and had been purely speculative on Slonim's part—perhaps as much to make Rapaport think he was working as anything else.

Slonim: —— I have decided that I was wrong about Berson. Potentially he is a remarkable man, and would bring to any organization many useful talents. But he's not quite right for Socialism.

—— How can that be? There is a place for any man in the movement.

—— I think perhaps you are wrong about that. Socialism demands a discipline of which some men are incapable. If it were simply the discipline of the Idea, a subservience to the best welfare of the greatest number of people, in everything a man did, that would be one thing—Berson would bend himself to that discipline. No, what I mean is the discipline of tactics. The discipline of the zigzag. We zig when the Stalinists zag. The Zionists zaggle, we ziggle. We are for the brotherhood of the workers of the Zigworld: watch out for the Zags! Some men simply aren't flexible enough to accept this discipline.

Rapaport, his eyes shrewd: — And do I take it that Berson is such a man—and that you, Slonim, are beginning to think that perhaps you are such a man?

Slonim: —— If so, it would be for different reasons. Berson is not subtle. He would not see the humor of your journalist barber shaving beards. He would say: Isn't that pathetic! On both sides, pathetic! . . . Berson has a great capacity for sympathy and compassion—which ought to be the basis of every good Socialist's personality, I suppose; but he's an emotional, not an intellectual man. His compassion makes no political distinctions. He can't discriminate, and for this reason he has made and will continue to make political mistakes that are, from our point of view, inexcusable. Out of human kindness he joined first the police and now the *Judenrat*, for the love of God! . . . My case is the contrary. I am too complex intellectually. I am too cold. I understand fine points that are better never seen. I understand, among other things, that I have a keener mind than you have.

Rapaport's cheeks became instantly drawn, his eyes hateful. Slonim says he immediately realized that that remark had been a foolish one: worse than foolish, cruel.

There was no more conversation. Rapaport's face was as shut as a shopfront bearing a sign: Closed for the Afternoon.

At the cashier's desk, on the way out, Slonim fell into the line of people waiting to pay ahead of Rapaport. He realized suddenly that there were many things he wanted to say to the older man, explanations, clarifications—and that he might never have a chance to say them. At the desk, as he approached it, Slonim says he saw "the little mouse of an Apt girl," Rachel, taking in the payments of one zloty twenty groszy.

Rachel, cheerfully: —— Hello, Pan Slonim! Did you enjoy your soup?

Slonim, his ordinary manner unruffled: —— Nectar! Though thin as nectar goes. (He handed Rachel a five-zloty note.) How long have you been working here?

Rachel, proudly: —— This is my second day. (Then, apparently having seen Rapaport and Slonim sitting together at the table, she asked:) Are you two gentlemen together?

Rapaport, with calm finality: —— No, we are not together.

The old lion held forward a five-zloty note of his own.

7

EVENTS JULY 3, 1941. ENTRY DITTO. FROM RUTKA MA-
ZUR. Symka Berson is out of danger, but young Schlome Mazur
has fallen sick. Typhus is everywhere. There is so much of it that
one can almost believe that this *is* why they built the wall. Rutka
says the Mazurs expected Schlome to get typhus. They had been
watching him all through the two-week incubation period. Froi
Mazur, who seems to be employed by the Angel of Cleanliness,
found lice on him. It happened this way:

The Mazurs, except for Schlome, who was still at the Yeshiva,
were sitting around talking about whether or not Reb Yechiel
Mazur should take the position of janitor in Sienna 17. The post
had fallen open because the man who had succeeded the Pole,
Kucharski, had recently come down with typhus.

Froi Mazur: —— I think you should take it, Yechiel.

Reb Yechiel: —— But it's so undignified.

Froi Mazur: —— It wasn't beneath Reb Yosel Schar's dig-
nity. He took such a post in Sienna 23. That's where Reb Felix
Mandeltort lives. He went to Reb Felix for help in getting the post.
Why should he be so eager?

Stefan: —— It's absurd. There are many better opportunities
to make money—in the *Judenrat*, for instance.

Froi Mazur: —— Perhaps it is a question of self-respect,
Stefan. Perhaps there are some people who wouldn't want to work
in the *Judenrat*. Perhaps that was what decided Reb Yosel Schar.

Stefan: —— Schar! Schar! That old goatskin!

Froi Mazur: —— Stefan! What has got into you lately?

Rutka: —— We can get David Apt to help you with the hard
work, Father.

Reb Yechiel, timidly: —— It is necessary in such cases to get
the approval of everyone in the courtyard. I have enemies.

Rutka: —— I can organize that. Enemies!

Froi Mazur: —— Then what's to prevent it, Yechiel?

Reb Yechiel: —— All of you crowd me so! Give me time to
think!

[NOTE. N.L. Rutka and Froi Mazur had not used with
Reb Yechiel what might have been a most appealing argument

with another man: janitors are respectable in the ghetto these days. Inside the wall, within the general hardship, the social scale still operates. Only the standards are not what they formerly were.

Those who managed to bring wealth into the ghetto with them, and who have conserved what they brought, still enjoy the respect and resentment their privileged position gave them before. Some who arrived wealthy have squandered their substance, and are now sunk down into the working classes; some poor but opportunistic men have seen amazing chances in the ghetto, and are now going upward, rung by rung. A man's address is still more or less a key to his social standing. Manners and education still make a certain amount of difference: an impoverished family of high breeding and training sneers self-consolingly at vulgar *arrivistes*; but at the same time, the new rich chuckle vindictively over the descent of others whom they themselves have swindled and bilked, or merely jostled aside. Energy and enterprise are rewarded with surprising rapidity, and the scythe swings fast, too, to cut down those who let themselves grow apathetic and unvigilant. Unexpected jobs turn out to be the rewarding ones. For instance: janitorships.

All through the Little Ghetto, janitorships are being assumed by lawyers, engineers, professors, and other declassed professionals, as well as a few former businessmen, and these janitors are making their way to the top of the social scale. The position of janitor carries with it certain privileges and benefits: janitors wear special yellow brassards; they carry passes exempting them from labor duty; they receive two hundred zlotys a month in salary; they are excused from certain taxes; they receive extra rations; but above all, they have a steady extra income, which may come to as much as four or five hundred zlotys a month—from tips. Tips for delivering messages, for doing odd jobs, for keeping their mouths shut, above all for letting people into the courtyard after the courtyard gates are closed in the evenings.]

A knock came at the door.

Froi Mazur, rising: —— Keep them out, whoever they are, until I am ready.

Rutka went to the door and opened it a few inches. Out on the landing, stiff and solemn, like a messenger with bad news, stood Schlome.

Rutka: —— Wait till Mother comes. (Then, sociably:) You're early tonight.

Schlome: —— I was tired. It's very exhausting, reading history.

Rutka: —— Why so?

Schlome: —— Oh, I don't know; you keep thinking what might have been.

Froi Mazur came to the door with a pair of tweezers and a saucer of alcohol, and out on the landing, before she would admit Schlome to the apartment, she inspected him from head to foot. Ever since typhus had come to epidemic proportions, she had been doing this regularly, not only with Schlome, but with all members of the family and indeed with guests, whenever they came. The young ones had argued in vain that it would be a fool of a louse who would wait outside anyone's clothing to be found by Froi Mazur; she continued the practice. This time she found four lice on Schlome.

Froi Mazur, scolding: —— That Yeshiva must be filthy! You young scholars think you can live off in another world, just reading and dreaming. If you don't sweep that place out and disinfect it, you *will* be in another world. Now go and take your clothes off and search them carefully. Here, take the alcohol with you. Disgraceful!

Later Schlome told the family that when he had undressed he had found three lice on his body. He said he had been so tired that he had ridden home that night in a ricksha—the vehicle of the rich. That must have been where he picked up the parasites.

Events July, 1941. Entry July 22, 1941. N.L. The shoulder of the summer has lifted the sun almost as high as it can this summer. It is hot. Death has become commonplace. In the poorer sections of the ghetto, corpses of typhus victims are put out into the street at night and the tumbrels of Rotblat's Funeral Service pick them up the next day and cart them to mass graves in the Jewish cemetery. In the early mornings the corpses lie naked in the streets, covered only by pieces of newspaper pinned down with bricks. One cannot say that the bereaved have grown callous: funerals are expensive, clothes can be sold. Everyone in the ghetto has become more provident than before. Well may he! Prices are soaring. Skilled workers get only fifteen or twenty zlotys a day. A half-kilo of bread costs twelve. A few vegetables are coming in from the Jewish collective farm at Grochow, and the authorities still allow us to till the miserable gardens in the cemetery, but

174

there is not nearly enough food for the population. Jews have been brought in from the towns near Warsaw, and even, more recently, from Germany and Czechoslovakia (how our guests from Germany try to lord it over us!): the ghetto is extremely crowded. Typhus finds an easy harvest among our enfeebled mob.

In the first half of 1941, according to the Vital Statistics Department of the *Judenrat*, there were 15,749 cases of typhus in the ghetto. The worst streets are Gensia, Nalewki, Nowolipki, Nowolipie, Pawia, and the most horrible conditions are in the former synagogues, schools, libraries, and stores which have been made into dormitories for refugee Jews who have been driven into Warsaw from outlying towns. On the whole the situation is not quite so bad in the so-called Little Ghetto, the southern section where the wealthier Jews live. [NOTE. EDITOR. Sienna Street was in the Little Ghetto.] The two hospitals on Leszno have closed their doors. The children's hospital on Sliska is turning patients away. Dr. Breithorn and some of his colleagues have organized lectures for "block doctors"—for anyone with the slightest medical training, even dentists; nurses and orderlies are being given pre-medical training. The motto of these spontaneous medical students is: *Science is my hope and salvation.*

Lice are on everything. They are on newspapers, on the money you get in change, on chairs, on shop counters, on friends. People grow cautious; they fear the slightest touch of elbow to elbow in the crowded streets; they shut themselves in at home and find lice crawling up their own clean walls. A doctor has invented a louse-killing belt, but where can you buy one?

EVENTS JULY 18–23, 1941. ENTRY JULY 23, 1941. FROM RACHEL APT. Rachel has been nursing Schlome, as she did Symka. I imagine that she is tender and just right.

For the first four days, it was impossible to get a doctor to look at Schlome, for special visits were out of the question. Symka is more or less recovered, but Dr. Breithorn has still been coming to visit her from time to time, and the night when Schlome first became sick, Froi Mazur sent Rutka up to the Bersons' to find out when the next visit would be: it was not to be until the twenty-second, yesterday. (Pan Apt is also sick in bed, Rachel tells me—not typhus, some stomach trouble or something rather mysterious: Rachel doesn't seem to know exactly what it is. Dr. Breithorn was

to call on him also yesterday.) Froi Mazur waited on the staircase
and stopped Dr. Breithorn on his way up to see Symka: that is the
way to call a doctor these days. Schlome was already showing spots
by the time the doctor saw him.

Meanwhile, before the doctor came, Rachel spent most of her
time down at the Mazurs'. Indeed, for the first forty-eight hours
she stayed in the Mazurs' apartment, with only an occasional nap
on the sofa, and she tended the delicate boy, forcing broth or cool
water between his cracked lips or bathing his feverish face, which
varied alarmingly, she says, from a hot red to a gelid white. She
also says she talked a lot with Froi Mazur. Ever since the night
when she took courage from Froi Mazur's flashing eyes to talk
back to Professor Benlevi [ENTRY APRIL 22, 1941], she says she has
gone back to Froi Mazur again and again for refreshment and
balance.

Late the second night of Schlome's illness, when all the world
seemed to be asleep except for the homely girl and the quiet, motherly woman, Rachel said:

—— I had an awful thing happen to me when I was tending
Symka. It was the ninth or tenth day, when she was in that second crisis she had. She had been so feverish for a couple of days
that she had just tossed around and moaned and seemed to be out
of her head. But once that afternoon, all of a sudden, she opened
her eyes, and they seemed perfectly clear, and she looked at me
and knew me and she said, as if she hated me: *You want me to die,
don't you?*

Froi Mazur: —— Poor girl!

Rachel does not know whether Froi Mazur meant Symka or
herself.

Rachel: —— I was terrified. Why should she say such a thing
to me?

Froi Mazur: —— Probably she was jealous of you, my dear.

Rachel: —— Jealous! Whatever about?

[NOTE. N.L. Froi Mazur has a remarkable intuition. And
yet, as Rachel asks—whatever about?]

Rachel says she might have forgotten this exchange, but for
another time when Symka's name came up, a couple of days later
(yesterday). Rachel and Mordecai were having supper—a thin
soup and some bread—at the Mazurs'. Halinka was at the Britannia and Pan Apt did not seem to want anyone around the apart-

ment. NOTE. N.L. I wonder just what his "stomach trouble" is. Rachel is very peculiar about this.] During the meal Rachel announced:

—— Symka is losing her hair. Even her eyebrows.

Stefan, teasing: —— You don't have to sound so happy about it, Rachel.

Rachel says she blushed, and she felt as if her own blush mocked her more than Stefan's remark had.

Mordecai: —— Say! I know just the man for Symka. Fein. He's in the wig business. I wonder if Dolek has thought of going to Fein.

Stefan: —— Wonderful! What color do you suppose Symka will order?

Mordecai: —— I'll wager she tries to make herself a redhead.

Stefan: —— Do you suppose she'll order a Vandyke for you-know-where?

Froi Mazur: —— Stefan! Mordecai! You should be ashamed of yourselves.

Rachel says that something strange has come into her relationship with Symka. She wonders humbly whether this could be because poor, wasted Symka now is ugly too.

EVENTS JULY 25, 1941. ENTRY JULY 27, 1941. FROM RUTKA MAZUR. Rutka says that while she was taking her turn in the constant watch at Schlome's bedside day before yesterday, she seemed to see her brother for the first time in her life. It was early afternoon. Schlome had scarcely moved for many hours: his face had an almost incandescent pallor, and his eyes were sunk into such deep hollows that it would have been difficult, in the room's dimness, to tell whether he was staring or sleeping. His religious earlocks, though damp and stringy, still seemed a reminder of his separateness, his being set aside for a spirit-life. [NOTE. N.L. Reb Yechiel Mazur has shaved his beard, but Schlome refused to lose his earlocks.]

Rutka says she remembered a scene in the first weeks of the ghetto. A meeting of the courtyard's young people's club was being held in Berson's apartment. Schlome was the secretary, and he was taking notes on what seemed to the members an important matter. Schlome, in his black gown and with his black side-curls, holding a black pen and making notations with black ink in a black

177

notebook, seemed not to have the right to smile, but at one point, Rutka recalls, his wan face broke into a sunny smile.

The club Rutka had started in Sienna 17 had found a function, beyond the holding of parties: it had become a sort of labor exchange. For at that time even the well-to-do young men and women of Sienna Street, "the golden youth," were on the prowl for employment. Rutka had appointed herself a kind of agent for the other young people in the courtyard. She had visited the *Judenrat's* Labor Department every day, had made tours of the principal workshops, and had walked along the various thoroughfares inspecting the help-wanted notices which occasionally appeared on hoardings and notice boards. Together she and Schlome had kept records of available jobs that might be suitable for their friends in the courtyard. In this way work had already been found for several of them. At this particular meeting, work for Schlome himself was being discussed. Rutka was reviewing their index cards.

Rutka: —— At Rotblat's Funeral Parlor there are three places open for young men who would like to apprentice themselves as embalmers.

This was the remark that made Schlome smile. He was not at all offended.

Schlome: —— Something warmer, if possible.

Rutka: —— Sausage-stuffer wanted at Smocza 23.

Rachel, suddenly speaking up: —— Did we come here to make fun of Schlome?

Rutka: —— He's my brother. He understands me.

Rachel, with blazing eyes: —— Brother or no brother, let's get on with our work.

[NOTE. N.L. This was at the time when Rachel and Rutka had not yet come to pleasant terms with each other; nevertheless, I am surprised at Rachel's vehemence in defending Schlome.]

Regina Orlewska, the teacher, hastily but quietly interposing a suggestion, on a note of tact: —— I know just the thing for Schlome. Our house school and others need books, and there is no way of getting them. Perhaps we could raise some money to pay Schlome to copy off some textbooks for us by hand. I know where I can borrow the originals.

Then Schlome shook his head, and his two side-curls waved like tassels on a purse, and he said in his deep, serious voice:

—— Money would not be required.

. . . Now watching by Schlome's bedside, Rutka thought how unmaterial Schlome's world was. Money will never be required in the realm where he dwells. Sometimes the family has had to remind him to eat. His has been the inner world of the great books, the Torah, the Talmud, the *Tree of Life*, the *Book of Splendor*, the *Guide of the Perplexed*. He has sat for hours on end, day after day, at the crude trestle tables of Yeshivas, and spread before him on the sleeve-polished wood has been his printed world. Rutka says she has always, since childhood, teased young Schlome for being a book-boy. *But*, he has often said gravely, *we are the Book People*. And now, in his calmness and resignation, Rutka seemed to recognize him for the first time. She had seen Symka twisting in the grip of the disease, fighting it, groaning, making faces. Schlome lay quietly, his face a placid page.

EVENTS JULY 29, 1941. ENTRY AUGUST 2, 1941. FROM FROI MAZUR. Froi Mazur opened her heart to me tonight, and I was very much touched. With others I was at the Mazurs' for supper, and she drew me aside for a time and talked to me. She can still talk only of Schlome, of course, and she began by saying that the reason she wanted to talk with me was because I was the kind of man she had wanted Schlome to become. Thus she did me great honor. Later she told me this:

Froi Mazur said it was dark in the room when it happened, but that she *felt* it. She stood up and turned on the light. Something had changed: a rhythm had crept out of the room and away. She looked down at the pale face on the pale sheet and knew that her son had just died.

She tells me what her thoughts were: Schlome, she thought, had always been the weakest one. When he had been an infant, it had taken the greatest pains to keep food in him: feeding him was as hard as painting a watercolor, each move had to be exactly right the first time. At Tarbuth school, Schlome had cried more than any other child: the teacher told the mother that once. Stefan and Rutka had teased Schlome tirelessly, like animals brutalizing a runted sib, and the mother thought how she had felt protecting the child from his own brother and sister: full of such heavy pity that she ached—her love for her youngest one had actually given her a hurtful sensation. Standing beside the bed, she thought of the time when her child—only twelve years old then—had come to her and gravely announced that he wanted to study to be a rabbi: an announcement that should have made her sing with joy; but somehow, for a boy only twelve! . . .

Froi Mazur says that she bent down, lifted the edge of her skirt, and with a violent jerk tore the fabric right through the hem and up about a foot—the formal gesture of grief. She was not yet torn herself. With eyes still dry, she went and wakened her husband, who, she knew, had never thought too much of his weakling third child, even though the boy was religious. But Reb Yechiel began to rock and weep at once, and it was only then, Froi Mazur says, that she collapsed and began to sob. . . .

EVENTS JULY 30, 1941. ENTRY DITTO. N.L. They buried Schlome today in paper clothes. This was that he might go to his grave decently—and yet leave behind his real clothes for someone who may need them badly. The wooden coffin, on a Rotblat handcart pushed by two men from the funeral parlor, went first in the procession. The mother and father sat side by side in a double ricksha. Rabbi Goldflamm and all of us younger people rode on bicycles behind. [NOTE. N.L. I saw the other day an advertisement in the *Gazeta Zydowska* for the arrangement of bicycle funerals by one of the parlors. *Aesthetic and practical in all respects*, the ad said.] We had to present passes to get through the gate to the cemetery. The grave was cut rawly into somebody's carefully tended beet patch. [INSERT. EVENTS JULY 30, 1941. FROM RACHEL APT. Rachel, who says she had had no opportunity to develop strong feeling for Schlome, watched Froi Mazur's face: Rachel recalled the maternal look she had seen on that face directed toward Schlome the night of the Seder ceremony (ENTRY AUGUST 16, 1940), when she herself had taken strength from that motherly look; now Rachel was amazed by the look of submission, so soft and feminine.] Berson stepped forward with a serious face and helped the Mazur men and the Rotblat hirelings to lower the coffin: it got stuck for a while on a slant, but the men tugged on the slings and freed it. On the way out of the cemetery, Reb Yechiel Mazur bent down three or four times and picked some weeds, until he had quite a handful—brome, fescue, and devilgrass. Finally he said:

—— And they of the city shall flourish like the grass of the earth.

EVENTS JULY 30, 1941. ENTRY JULY 31, 1941. N.L. In that moment when the tipped coffin became lodged in the grave-hole, Berson's face was covered with such horror—such unselfconscious, undisguised repugnance and shuddering fascination—as I have never seen in him or, I think, in anyone else. It could not have been just the thought of the fragile young theologian's corpse caught slanting head downward, because Berson must have realized, as we all did, that the accident was capable of correction. The Rotblat men were right there with their tools. The diggers, who must be undernourished and weakened like all the rest of us, had evidently tried to give themselves a minimum of work by making the grave a tight fit with the standard-sized coffin. We of the audience realized, when the coffin became stuck, that if the pallbearers could not wrench it loose, the Rotblat men would be able to prize it free with their spades and crowbars. This last was not necessary, as it soon turned out. But in the moment when the sad box was caught awry, Berson's face assumed the expression I have described —and I wondered why.

It is idle—and useless—to try to imagine what thoughts run through another's head, but I cannot help speculating as to what was behind that grimace of Berson's. Of one thing I am fairly sure. This death was the first that had come close to him. He had seen bodies in the street: everyone had. He had heard the terrible, mounting figures; I know, because I had discussed them with him: February, 1,023; March, 1,668; April, 2,655; May, 3,821; June, 4,290. But statistics are themselves dead: here was a boy Berson knew, and here was the prostration in grief of a family Berson loves. I'm sure he must have felt this close gesture of death reaching in his own direction; I did, and I'm not nearly so intimate with the Mazurs as he is. I think this closeness brought home to him, as nothing had previously, the realization of what a narrow margin had spared Symka. (She is a scarecrow, pathetically emaciated—I saw her yesterday: she wears an artful black wig from Fein's shop, but the very fact that the wig is so normal, so glistening and healthy, makes it grotesque on her wasted head.) By the same token, Berson must have had a sudden realization of what bereavement would mean to him, what the loss of Symka would mean; he must have had a glimpse at loneliness. But something more important, I imagine, was in that look on his face: an understanding of the real meaning of the ghetto and of our life in it. It was as if

Meaning had been discovered crouching in the grave, supporting the coffin askew.

As for Froi Mazur's face, it had an expression so spiritual, so beautiful in its simple defiance and fortitude, that one almost rejoiced. . . .

8

EVENTS JUNE 26, 1941. ENTRY DITTO. FROM RACHEL APT. Rachel has come to me perplexed about something that happened this morning:

Rachel and her father were sitting in their living room; the apartment door was open. When Pan Apt heard footsteps descending from above, he went out on the landing, and Rachel listened to the following exchange:

Pan Apt: —— I know you are a busy man, doctor. I was waiting for you. I will take only a moment of your time. . . . I have heard that some Russian anti-typhus serum was captured by the Germans, and that some of it has made its way . . .

Dr. Breithorn, interrupting as if he knew what Pan Apt was going to take a long roundabout speech to say: —— Yes, some serum has been smuggled in.

Pan Apt: —— I am worried to distraction about my children. Four children. I was wondering . . .

Dr. Breithorn: —— For my part, Pan Apt, I am worried beyond distraction by my patients in the two Leszno hopsitals. Nine hundred patients. In the corridors, in the lecture hall, in the waiting rooms. Where do you think the serum should be used?

Pan Apt, in a pleading whine: —— Enough only for four or five.

Dr. Breithorn: —— Or five? If you were forced to take an inoculation yourself, you would reluctantly submit to it?

Pan Apt: —— I can pay.

Dr. Breithorn, in a very tired voice: —— I know. You can pay well. . . . All right, have your young people here on Thursday morning at nine o'clock, when I am to come back to Froi Berson.

Pan Apt: —— Thank you, doctor, thank you. Before you go

doctor, there is one other thing. This is for myself, and I realize it might be expensive. . . .

At this point Rachel heard the outer door close. She wonders: what was this expensive other thing?

EVENTS JULY 7, 1941. ENTRY JULY 8, 1941. FROM DOLEK BERSON. Berson says that Mauritzi Apt came to his doorway again yesterday with that benevolent, charitable air that surely signaled the asking of a favor. Not a bribe this time, however! Pan Apt seemed unwilling to enter the apartment.

Pan Apt: —— Couldn't we talk downstairs? I don't want to disturb your poor, sick wife.

Berson, believing he knew Pan Apt's real reason for hesitating: —— There's no more danger here than downstairs, Pan Apt. Come in.

Slowly, seeming to suck himself inward, as if to reduce his contaminable surface area, Pan Apt entered the apartment. He sat in a chair, after inspecting it quickly for crawlers. Then he said there were several things he wanted to discuss with Berson, and paused, as though he had intended by this remark rather to postpone the discussion than to introduce it. Finally he said:

—— I have not even told my children what I am about to tell you.

At that very moment, one of his children, Rachel, appeared in the doorway of the short hall leading to the bedroom where Symka lay sick.

Pan Apt, almost shouting, his face alarmed: —— What are you doing up here?

Rachel: —— Nursing Symka. Somebody has to do it. Dolek here is hopeless!

Pan Apt, quite forgetting himself: —— I thought I told you not to come up here.

Rachel, ignoring her father: —— Dolek, where will I find a clean face-cloth?

Berson: —— Top shelf of the hall closet—I think.

Rachel left, closing the hall door behind her.

Pan Apt: —— That is part of it! They never obey me. Even David, still a child, disobeys me all the time. I love them too much, everything I do seems to be wrong in their eyes. . . . If only a man's motives and his behavior could be kept separate! I know that my motives are all good, and yet people don't understand me, because some of the things I do out of those motives seem—how shall I say it?—seem ruthless. But I've learned by bitter experience, Berson, by *bitter* experience, that the only way to get something is to find out how it can be gotten and then get it and ignore the consequences.

Pan Apt toyed with a vest button, as if he wondered whether he should have come here at all. Then he went on:

—— My children have turned against me. Mordecai will scarcely speak to me. You've seen how this girl behaves: I have never understood Rachel. Halinka is like her mother, but even she has grown away from me and argues with me all the time. The child David is under Rachel's wing: he runs to her and avoids me. My own have no use for me. Everything I have done has been for them, my whole life for these last years has been for them, and they don't want me.

Berson says he knew that there was nothing he could say; Pan Apt seemed only to require room to move about in. He was like a dog squirming its body round and round settling in a soft place.

—— I remember once (his eyes narrowed as if to screen out present time), at the other house, the big house, years ago, we were all in the living room during that pleasant hour just before the children went to bed. Froi Apt was reading to them, and Morde-cai—I guess he was seven or eight—unexpectedly got up from her and came across the room to me and kissed me and then went back to her, without saying a word. It was one of those surprises children give you. It was nothing to him, just a passing impulse. I've always remembered it. . . . He was about seven. . . . Maybe only six. . . .

Pan Apt seemed for a while to have forgotten what he had come to say or do. Then, with a kind of shudder, he said:

—— Berson, I have decided to go to the Aryan side. I have friends there. My children don't need me or want me here in the ghetto. . . .

Berson says he thought Pan Apt was going to weep. Berson said:

—— It's very dangerous.

—— My friends with whom I work will make arrangements. There will be no trouble. And on the outside, I have from many

years back Polish friends. Oh, I will live well—much better than
here, perhaps. . . . But there is one thing I need. I am told it is
essential that I learn Catholic ritual: that is the one test the authorities apply if someone falls in their hands who is suspected.
. . . I thought perhaps the Jablonskis . . .

Berson, suddenly resenting being put in the position of agent
for this kind of commerce: —— You'll have to ask them yourself.
And you'd better hurry, too. This sickness of Symka's has frightened them, and they're to move in a couple of days to the converts'
courtyard in All Saints' Church. They're there now. They ought to
be back in an hour. . . .

Pan Apt, musing: —— I could go to All Saints' for my lessons.
Yes, that would be fitting. (Then:) Wouldn't you speak to them
for me? (Again Berson noticed the tone of charity in Pan Apt's
voice.) I understand they are devout. I wouldn't wish to offend
their scruples.

Berson, giving in, as he always does: —— I'll say something
to them.

EVENTS JULY 21, 1941. ENTRY DITTO. FROM RACHEL APT.
Pan Apt is in bed with some mysterious "stomach trouble." Rachel
says that Dr. Breithorn said something about her father this morning so bitter, so sneering, that she is terribly upset—without knowing what she is upset about. [NOTE. N.L. Breithorn was sour
to begin with, and things have happened to him such that one can
scarcely reproach him for throwing a plain-looking girl off balance.
He has been banned from the panel of the State Sick Fund, and
the decree—of last summer, before the ghetto was closed—forbidding Jewish doctors to treat gentile patients, while it did not affect
his practice much, did attack his self-esteem dreadfully, I understand. In the decree Jewish doctors were referred to, not as physi-
cians, but as *Krankenbehändler*—"handlers of the sick," as grooms
are handlers of horses.] I gather that Rachel now knows of her
father's intention to leave the ghetto, but she says she does not
know what keeps her father in bed and Breithorn visiting him
these days; I believe this. Today, when Breithorn called on Schlome
Mazur, he found Rachel at the Mazurs' nursing the boy, and he
said to her:

—— You're the Apt girl, aren't you?—ah, yes, the one who
refused to come the day I brought the smuggled serum for your

family: that was pigheaded of you. Well (Rachel says he sounded bored and cold), I suppose I should congratulate you.

—— On what?

—— On your father's recovery—not (and here came the terrible bitterness) from this disease transmitted by lice, but from that other one which is transmitted by parents. . . .

[NOTE. N.L. Jewishness? How "recovered"?]

EVENTS AUGUST 8, 1941. ENTRY DITTO. N.L. Rachel was terribly despondent today, almost sick. She says it is not her father's imminent departure that depresses her, though I believe it is something to do with him. She still says she does not know what was the matter with him; but somehow I doubt her word this time. I think she knows and will not tell. I see this in her manner. I wish to help her, but I cannot, without knowing what troubles her.

[NOTE. EDITOR. Levinson was not to learn what this was until ✿ CONVERSATION, MAY 9-10, 1943.]

EVENTS AUGUST 15, 1941. ENTRY AUGUST 16, 1941. FROM RABBI GOLDFLAMM. Yesterday our rabbi had the following conversation with Mauritzi Apt:

Goldflamm: —— But it is not possible, Pan Apt, to "Aryanize." You are trying to abdicate something which simply cannot be renounced.

The rabbi had discovered Pan Apt's plan by accident. In a discussion of housing, the night before, in connection with the possibility that Sienna Street may be separated from the ghetto, Berson had spoken of an idea for a joint apartment for a number of friends, and in an accounting of heads, Berson had carelessly said:

—— After Pan Apt leaves the ghetto. . . .

Rabbi Goldflamm had picked up that casual clause and evidently Berson, thinking that mystification would be worse in the long run than frankness, considering Rabbi Goldflamm's penchant for gossip, told the rabbi of Pan Apt's intentions. In his blunt, forthright way, the Rabbi had gone straight to Pan Apt, on the subsequent day, to try to dissuade him from the project. Rachel was present at the interview; the rabbi says that she was in the living room when he arrived, and as soon as the topic of the escape was entered upon, she subsided into a pouting, restless silence.

Pan Apt: —— I beg your pardon, it is possible. Everything is arranged. Day after tomorrow I am already a Pole. Identity card, certificate of police registration, labor card. (As he listed these items, Pan Apt laid the index finger of his right hand in succession against the thumb, forefinger, and middle finger of his left hand, in the manner of a lecturer presenting points one, two, three—the conclusive, authenticating, irrefutable arguments.) They were not cheap, I'll grant you that the price of becoming an Aryan has gone up with everything else. Eighteen thousand zlotys, one half in American dollars, for the papers alone. But foolproof, Rabbi, completely foolproof. The method of escape is also absolutely without risk. I would sell you insurance on it at a very low rate.

Goldflamm: —— I'm not talking about the mechanics of escape. . . . What sets us apart from the rest of the world, as you well know, is not this wall around us, but our religion—and you cannot shake that.

Pan Apt: —— I can't shake off something I've never worn. I'm a practical man, Rabbi, I understand the usefulness of mysticism and ethics for some people, but for me—I apply ethics when necessary and suspend them when necessary. My daughter here can testify: I've never had any use for religion, have I, Rachel? (Rabbi Goldflamm says that Rachel shook her head almost imperceptibly, but that in that economical motion of the homely head there was a negative loaded with such feeling—with such pity, scorn, and love—that even Rabbi Goldflamm, who is not given to subtlety in his understanding of personal relationships, says he saw the overtones.) The closest I've come to religion is in having Yechiel Mazur downstairs for a friend. That old codger fills his head full of more benedictions and rites and shibboleths than I can even imagine. But it gives him something to do with himself. I can't refuse him such entertainment.

Goldflamm: —— No, Pan Apt, you still misunderstand me. Who should know better than I that you are not "religious," in the outward sense? But it is not necessary to be Reb Yechiel Mazur. The Jewish faith is in you, it shows.

Pan Apt: —— I have made the acquaintance of an ex-Communist, recently, a man named Edek Hartmann. Until I was told of his apostasy, I never would have seen the leftovers of his religion in him. Quite the contrary.

Goldflamm: —— Ah, there's a difference. And the difference

187

is this: the Jewish faith is ancient. Through centuries and generations it has come down to you. You are a product of its traditions: traditions of humility, of the Torah, of family bonds, of hard work, of love of music and art, of poverty and frugality—traditions, above all, of being persecuted. Especially here in Poland. You may not realize it, but the way you hold your head when you walk in the streets has our past in it; your face is accidentally not easy to distinguish from a Polish face, but every time you speak or laugh or nod or lift an eyebrow or express any emotion, our heritage is in that movement of the muscles of your face, our way of doing things.

Pan Apt: —— Again I beg your pardon. I have corrected those characteristics. For weeks I have watched myself in a mirror, you understand.

Goldflamm (who himself admits that he was becoming rhetorical): —— The sign of the Covenant is on your body.

Pan Apt: —— Very few things are irrevocable in this world.

Goldflamm: —— It is in the jokes on your tongue.

Pan Apt: —— I am not a humorous man. (But he said this with a laugh, as if, to the contrary, he was quite funny.)

Goldflamm: —— It is in your heart. It's an inheritance in your fingertips and in the nerve behind your eyeball and in the drumstick of your ear and in the membranes of your nostrils— even if the Germans do not see anything Semitic about the outside of your nose. The heritage is in your heart, it is a glorious heritage, you should be proud of it.

Pan Apt (there were tiny drops of perspiration on his forehead): —— Nevertheless, at six thirty in the morning, day after tomorrow, I go out.

EVENTS AUGUST 17, 1941. ENTRY DITTO. FROM RACHEL APT. Mauritzi Apt left us today. Rachel says that her father's farewell kiss was a disappointment to her. She hardly knows what she expected: not the hurried smack on the cheek she got, at any rate. She says she did not expect so much as Halinka—she has never had that from him; and yet in the goodbye kiss she received more, somehow, than Halinka, who was also kissed on the cheek, but with even greater absent-mindedness (Rachel thinks) than she herself had been. Her father had tears in his eyes, but Rachel says they seemed to have been planned. Rachel was so mixed up in her feelings, she tells me—so full of contempt and tenderness, of hate and love, of gladness to be rid of her father and terror at his departure—that she was dry-eyed and more irritable than sad.

One of the thousands of details Pan Apt had seen to—really, Rachel thought, he has an incredible mind!—was an arrangement for Halinka, Mordecai, and herself to watch his easy departure through the ghetto gates from a fine balcony seat, in the window of an apartment on the north side of Chlodna Street, looking down on the barrier. But Rachel decided not to go: she told her father she could visualize everything very clearly from his description of the process: he would go, in the working clothes he now wore, to the corner of Wronia and Chlodna, and when the labor battalion that is these days digging up the Karolkowa Street sewer, outside the ghetto, came past, he would fall into line and simply march with them to the gate; the Kapo of the battalion had been bribed; the guards at the Chlodna Street gate had been bribed; Meier Berson would be on hand as a casual pedestrian to see that there were no slips; and Pan Apt's possessions would be delivered to him at a prearranged address by a Polish smuggler named Janta.

Pan Apt, his eyes sparkling mischievously: —— You should see him, my girls! He has curly hair and he wears a turtle-necked sweater up to his ears! A manly one!

Halinka, flirtatiously [NOTE. N.L. Was she too brazen to blush?]: —— Oooh, I'd like to meet him.

After the quick kiss, Pan Apt patted Rachel on the shoulder and told her to take care of little David. And that was all. That was the farewell. Rachel watched him go out of the apartment door with Halinka and Mordecai—they had decided to go to the "balcony"—and then Rachel pushed the door shut and leaned against it. David ran into her arms and looked up at her face, to see whether he ought to cry. Rachel looked down at her brother and said:

—— Whatever happens, Dovidl, always remember, always, always, that your father was a wonderful man.

Rachel says she is very desirous that her baby brother should be able to believe that.

EVENTS SEPTEMBER 23, 1941. ENTRY DITTO. FROM RACHEL APT. Today was Rosh-ha-Shanah. A number of us gathered in the Mazurs' apartment to hear New Year services conducted by Reb Ycchiel Mazur. Rachel tells me that during the prayers she thought about her father and about her brother David. (She says she has never been able to keep her mind on business during ceremonies: they affect her as do concerts: she thinks of other things.) She wondered how her father was getting along. He had said he would not send messages, because he did not want to get his children into trouble (or, just possibly, himself!). With a sudden wrench, Rachel missed her father; her filtering memory had been at work. He had been, at least, solicitous. . . . With but a twist of mood and mind, she then began to worry about her brother. Her father's very last words to her had been: *Take care of little David.* Yet she reflected that she is too busy with her work at the soup kitchen and with her Hashomer chores to watch out properly for David. Halinka and Mordecai are both working. Regina Orlewska's school has been disbanded during the typhus epidemic, and Regina has taken work for CENTOS, the children's welfare organization. Thus there is nothing to keep David busy except assisting Reb Yechiel Mazur in his duties as janitor—and that, in truth, she decided, keeps the boy too busy. Sweeping down the staircases is heavy work, and on his meager diet David is growing thin and slipping into an ever deeper lassitude. What could she do?

Reb Yechiel, crying out with no irony or bitterness: —— Blessed art Thou, O Lord our God, King of the universe, who hast chosen us from all peoples and exalted us above all tongues, and sanctified us by Thy commandments. And Thou hast given us in love, O Lord our God, this day of memorial, a day of blowing the Shofar. . . .

And at the proper times, in another room—offstage, as it were—Berson used his versatile little concertina to produce the sounds of the noble ram's horn: the mournful triads, the *Tekiah*, the *Teruah*, and the *Shebarim*, the Shofar's shouts and wails and sighs and the joyous going-up of God on the day of remembrance.

EVENTS SEPTEMBER 25, 1941. ENTRY DITTO. FROM RA-CHEL APT. Rachel has put David into the Rukner Children's Home. Since her father entrusted the boy to her wardship, she considered it her right to make this hard decision. She had elaborated all the reasons for this move during the Rosh-ha-Shanah service the other day [ENTRY SEPTEMBER 23, 1941], but it seems she had not entirely visualized what it would be like to lose her brother. she has not really lost him: she can visit him, of course: but she has lost his proximity. And tonight she is a sad young girl.

Rachel had heard of the marvelous work of the Rukner Home from Regina: of how "Colonel" Rukner (he was once, in truth, a corporal), in his Polish Army medical corps uniform, begs, borrows, steals, and wheedles extra rations for his children; of the excellent religious and general teaching his several "mothers" give; of the games his children play; above all, of the atmosphere in the Home of optimism and love all around the children.

Yesterday Rachel went to Rukner. At first he would not hear of taking David: he objected that the child has living relatives, that the Home is already too full, and that he prefers to take younger children. Then Rachel, as an ironic memorial to her father, offered the Home a fairly substantial donation in kind— for Pan Apt left behind plenty of the stock of his store, divided equally among the four children. And so I see that Rachel has some of her father in her, at that. When the Mauritzi Apt Memorial Gift actually appeared, sparkling and valuable, upon the "Colonel's" desk, he abruptly discovered that he had room for just one more boy in his Home.

9

Events July 23, 1941. Entry September 3, 1941. From Rutka Mazur. [Note. Editor. The events described in this entry took place on the fifth day of Schlome's sickness; while the entry itself was not made for several weeks.] . . . Rutka was keeping watch with Schlome. A gentle knock at the door of Schlome's room was followed by its opening, and Reb Yechiel Mazur, in his person as janitor, handed Rutka a note; in his person as parent, he stood waiting to see what it was all about. Rutka carried the note to the window and tilted it deliberately away from her father. When she had finished reading, she said:

—— I have to go out for a few minutes. Wait with Schlome, Father: I'll get Rachel to come.

Rutka ran upstairs, but David, resting after sweeping the staircase for Reb Yechiel, told her that Rachel was out.

Rutka: —— Then would you sit with Schlome for a while for me, David? Be an angel! I've been called out on an errand.

David: —— So was Rachel. A note came, and she ran out.

Rutka: —— Something different.

David, who agreed to take Rutka's place in the vigil and followed her down to Schlome's room, was evidently frightened by the scholar's waxen face. David sat stiffly in a corner of the room, staring at the sick figure. It was arranged that if anything happened, he should call Reb Yechiel Mazur at the janitor's lodge.

Rutka hurried out into the street. She says her heart was pounding, for she imagined that the note summoned her to get her orders for the courier trip outside the ghetto that Zilberzweig had spoken about. She almost ran to the "workroom"—the cellar room where she had printed Zilberzweig's editorial on the hectograph; the note had commanded her to be there at two thirty, and it was already almost three. When she reached the room, she tapped on the door, and it was opened from inside.

Some mistake: Rachel inside.

Rutka, impatiently: —— What are you doing here?

Rachel: —— I was to do some work here.

Rutka: —— So was I. I wonder what it means. . . . I didn't even know you were doing confidential work. [Note. N.L. I deduce that this "workshop" is used only for secret Hashomer affairs.]

Rachel: —— Oh, I've been active for quite a while now. I was approached by one of the leaders in the soup kitchen where you got me the job.

Rutka says she could scarcely hide her disappointment: this was obviously not to be what she had hoped. Rachel talked on:

—— They put me into peripheral work first, and they seemed to be convinced that I really wanted to work hard, so they let me in on some more realistic things. (Rutka says she certainly was not interested in Rachel's neophyte days, and she wanted to ask if anyone else had been here in the "workroom": perhaps her own contact had come and gone; but Rachel babbled on:) I still work at the kitchen and get my meals there. Why don't you come sometimes? I even met the mighty Zilberzweig there the other day. Incidentally, some of us were having an argument—do you happen to know his first name?

Rutka, the words she knew so terribly well pouring off her tongue: —— Some call him Hillel, but Hil is correct.

Rutka wanted to fly into Rachel's arms and cry, out of joy and fear, but Rachel, showing only by the redness of her cheeks that she was involved in anything unusual, said mechanically, speaking obviously memorized words:

—— You are to go, after you have completed preparations, to the city of Wilno, and ask of the caretaker at Newka 34, in that place, for Chaim. Chaim will have something for you to bring back to Warsaw.

Rachel pulled her blouse up from inside her skirt, reached under it, and drew out an envelope. Handing Rutka the envelope and tucking her blouse in again, she said:

—— Here are your papers. They are complete except for photographs. Have passport pictures taken at the studio on the fourth floor at Chlodna 27—eight copies. Attach the necessary ones to these papers and take the extra ones to Wilno, in case it becomes necessary to change papers there. Leave in about two weeks. When you are ready to leave, let me know and we (and upon that "we," for the first time, Rachel smiled) will make arrangements for your departure from the ghetto.

EVENTS AUGUST 2, 1941. ENTRY SEPTEMBER 3, 1941. FROM RUTKA MAZUR. . . . and Rutka told also of the circumstances of her decision:

During the intermission, in the wooden lobby of the Femina Theater, the crowd moved in a thoughtful, clockwise wheel. Echoes of the sweet tones of the Nightingale's voice were in many of the heads, and some people actually began to hum strains from the queer, antique French songs she had sung; but these hummers, shamed by their immediate failure to recapture the magic they had just experienced, broke off their attempts almost at once. Rutka and Mordecai shuffled along, holding hands lightly. Rutka says she felt exalted.

Rutka: —— Isn't she superb?

Mordecai nodded, but without real enthusiasm.

Rutka: —— Did you see how proud *he* was? (She referred to the conductor, the former choir-master of the Tlomatzkie Street synagogue, director now of the thin and ragged-toned twenty-man "symphony," and father of the Nightingale; who had, she says, wagged his head and waved his arms with a great and justifiable pride.) Did you notice the way he conducted? As if he were boxing. As if he were being attacked by the whole orchestra and were trying to defend himself and his daughter from them.

But Mordecai did not smile.

Rutka: —— What's the matter?

Mordecai: —— I was just thinking. (Rutka waited, and soon he added:) I was just thinking that I wish I could be as willing to follow my father as that girl is hers. (Mordecai turned his eyes toward Rutka's, and she looked at him with pity: he looked so tired, his eyesockets were so deep and black!) I hate mine.

Rutka, compassionately: —— That doesn't do any good.

Mordecai: —— I know. But it's true. All he ever thought about was himself—and his "beloved children." (This last phrase Mordecai uttered, Rutka says, in a spiteful mimicry of his father's voice.) He never loved his children. He only saw us as a reflection of himself.

Rutka, suddenly impatient, for she was annoyed that Mordecai had snapped her pleasant mood: —— Let's talk about something else.

Mordecai: —— So what should we talk about? Olive trees?

A retort was on its way to Rutka's tongue when a jarring bell, announcing the second half of the concert, cut off her speech. The couple returned to their seats in silence. The orchestra was carrying on its preliminary gossiping. The conductor and his daughter returned. Rutka was dismayed that Mordecai had settled his own outrage upon this father and child: it was going to spoil the concert for her, she says she thought.

The Nightingale sang a group of songs and arias by Mozart, and before she knew it, Rutka was carried away on the eider-down music. For a while she says she thought of her dead brother Schlome—but dead souls travel quickly, and Schlome was already far from her: beyond the area of sharp grief, out in the huge sky of memory. . . . Then regret dissolved into anticipation, and she began daydreaming about her forthcoming trip as a courier. She sat very still, but she was excited. She saw herself in comfortable perils—comfortable because by a flick of her imagination she could get herself out of them, to the wonderment of imagined audiences. She forgot Mordecai's anger. Soon he was sweetly felt beside her.

The people clapped. The concert was all over. On the way up the disenchanted aisle, Rutka felt Mordecai's hand slip between her arm and her waist.

Mordecai, murmuring: —— I'm sorry I was . . . as I was. (Then, in a lively, clear-faced way—Rutka thought, seeing the difference in his eyes: What that music did for us!—he added:) I tell you what! Let's try something new: let's ride home on a Kohn-Heller.

Rutka, squealing like a child offered a ride on a merry-go-round at a country festival: —— Oh! Could we?

[NOTE. N.L. The "Kohn-Hellers," which appeared on the streets of the ghetto not long ago, are high, square, horse-drawn trolleys. The body of these vehicles appears unsuited for motion: it is more like a small, square house, with glass windows, and with a flat roof which overhangs about six inches all around; this edifice rests top-heavily upon automobile-tired wheels. These vehicles are painted yellow above and blue below, and they bear the Star of David. They are named for two Lodz Jews who thought up the idea and obtained the concession.] Rutka and Mordecai had never ridden on a Kohn-Heller. They waited on the corner by the theater until they could squeeze into one of the crazy carts, pulled by two emaciated bays. A conductor in a dark blue uniform squirmed and elbowed through the standing crowd—a tall, skinny man whose Adam's apple took a long plunge deep down under his loose collar, like some mechanical cash-registering device, each time he thanked a passenger for a fare.

Rutka, giggling, still in her country-fair frame of mind: —— Isn't this good?

Mordecai, shrugging, as a man accustomed to modern transportation: —— Like a streetcar.

Rutka, in a whisper: —— When we get home, you must look carefully for lice.

Mordecai, as if, in her mere solicitude, she had spoken some poetic endearment: —— Thank you.

Rutka felt Mordecai press against her. She saw, and responded to the pathetic ardor in his eyes.

Rutka: —— I have a secret.

Mordecai: —— What is it?

Rutka says she leaned forward, put her cheek against Mordecai's, and whispered:
—— I'll marry you tomorrow.

EVENTS AUGUST 5, 1941. ENTRY DITTO. N.L. Rutka and
Mordecai were married today. [NOTE. EDITOR. The marriage
took place, not the day after, but three days after, Rutka's promise;
evidently arrangements intervened. This entry, unlike the previous
ones, was made at the time of the events.] I was amazed. Rutka
told me only yesterday. Rabbi Goldflamm, Rachel, Berson, and I
were the only ones who knew. The secrecy was because of Schlome's
recent death: Rutka did not think it would be fair to tell her
parents yet. Rabbi Goldflamm agreed to perform the ceremony
without a *minyan* [NOTE. EDITOR. The traditional quorum of
ten bystanders.] in his own room. Mordecai, in a paroxysm of embarrassment, asked Berson if he and Rutka might use the Bersons'
spare room to consummate the marriage. [INSERT. FROM ENTRY
JULY 7, 1941. N.L. The Jablonskis have moved out of the Bersons' apartment and into the converts' community centered in the
Church of All Saints. This pleases everybody, including me. . . .]
Rutka told Rachel of her sudden decision to marry Mordecai, because she thought someone in Mordecai's family should know. I
guess I was told in order that the marriage might be registered
officially at the *Judenrat*. Berson and Rachel were the two marriage
witnesses. The ceremony, with so few present, seemed to me barren and forbidding, but for the glowing faces of the young couple.
They will live with their respective families until they can properly
break the secret.

EVENTS AUGUST 8, 1941. ENTRY SEPTEMBER 2, 1941.
FROM RACHEL APT. Rachel says that Rutka's departure moved
her more than her own father's. On the surface, that may have
been true. Rachel says she was jealous of Rutka's courage: not
once had Rutka confessed the fears she must have felt about her
errand outside the ghetto. Her announcement to Rachel of her
preparedness, delivered in a whisper on the staircase at Sienna 17
one night, was lighthearted:
—— Tell Hil that I'm all ready. (And then, with a leer, as
if a delightful assignation were being arranged:) Any time he's
ready!

Rachel had made the final arrangements—or rather, had run the errands in connection with them—with faint spirit. She imagined all sorts of hazards that waited for Rutka in the outside world. She pictured these dangers, not as something remote and impersonal, but as actually happening to herself, Rachel—and as being the fault of another self, the Rachel who had looked out for the arrangements back in the ghetto. On a railroad train, a grating voice: *Your travel permit, please. . . . Look here! The signature has been left off here! What's the meaning of this?* On a strange and darkling street corner: *All right, your labor card next. . . . Attention! This has expired: the date is too old. Come with me, miss.* Rachel says she never saw Rutka in these scrapes: she saw herself, a Rachel with a "safe" face, a Rachel who sometimes earned her way out of the difficulties by a suggestion of flirtation in her face. And at the end of each imagined scene, Rachel checked over again in her mind all the preparations she had completed on Rutka's behalf and all she had still to take; and finally, with the familiar sinking sensation the conscious thought of her face had so often brought her, she would realize again that she herself would never be able to leave the ghetto and experience the dangers which Rutka seemed to be anticipating so lightly.

Rachel wept when the time came to say goodbye to Rutka, and she says she thought: I wasn't able to cry for my own father. As they parted:

Rutka, uttering the traveler's prayer somewhat satirically, as if it were a needless precaution: —— May the will come from Thee, Adonai, my God, that Thou walk me in peace, and march me in peace, and support me in peace. . . .

Rachel, through tears: —— Go to Tomasz Kucharski, our old janitor, you can trust him. I put his address in the memorandum with your new passes. . . . Oh, Rutka, be careful!

Rutka, smiling: —— I'll be back in no time. Don't be so dramatic!

EVENTS AUGUST 8–SEPTEMBER 2, 1941. ENTRY SEPTEMBER 2, 1941. FROM RACHEL APT. Rachel says she lived the twenty-six days while Rutka was away as if she had an icebox for a body. She was cold in summer; her hands were cold, her feet were cold. She was terrified all the time. Already on the fourth or fifth day she became convinced that Rutka was lost. . . .

EVENTS SEPTEMBER 2, 1941. ENTRY DITTO. FROM RUTKA MAZUR. Rutka sat in a straight chair at one end of the Mazurs' living room and told us at least part of her story:

She said that the moment she got outside the ghetto gates, she felt lost, because all the time she had been preparing to leave, she had only imagined the frightening process of getting past the guards at the wall; beyond that she had no concrete plans at all. She had been told simply to go to Wilno; she says she had no idea how to do it. She was taken out with a labor battalion at the Solna Street gate. She walked in a daze to the Saxon Garden and there, alone for a minute on one of the paths, she took her armband off.

She says that all she could think of to do was to go to Kucharski, whose address Rachel had given her. Kucharski has another job as janitor, Rutka says, and he looks and sounds exactly the same as he used to here—the same old green sweater with the holes in the elbows, the same flow of talk. She says he was wonderful to her. He pretended not to be the least surprised to see her, and he took her to his rooms and gave her hot tea and bread with marmalade [NOTE. N.L. Imagine!] without even asking if she was hungry. He told Rutka that Pan Apt was well, but that he has been having a hard time: his Polish friends turned out not to be so friendly as formerly, he had lived with the janitor for a few days, sleeping on the floor, and has finally settled, rather uncertainly, with a Polish carpenter and his family, who do not know that he is Jewish, but are charging him outrageous rent. That was all Kucharski said about Rachel's father.

Rutka explained to Kucharski her problem: to get to Wilno. Even that, she says, did not seem to surprise him; he asked no questions. He told Rutka he had a friend who could help her get on the train, and he went with her to the Wilno Station. Kucharski's friend was a porter, a straight old man with enormous dark eyebrows and a white mustache that drooped down on either side of his chin; he looked like Pilsudski. He made Rutka buy a *Nowy Kurjer*—said she might find a newspaper useful. He bought her ticket for her. He led her right up to the ticket taker at the gate onto the train platform, and when they reached the gate, he began asking the ticket taker a lot of loud questions about arrivals and departures, and the ticket taker punched Rutka's ticket without asking for her travel permit or even looking at her.

On the train Rutka felt completely alone. How grateful she was to the old porter for making her get a newspaper! She put herself off in a corner and held up the paper and began to read. When the conductor and inspector came through the car, she just poked her ticket and permit out from behind the paper, as if she were too engrossed to look up. The conductor pushed his face in over the newspaper, but all he asked was whether she had any baggage.

—— No baggage. (Keeping her head down.)

The officials went on. Rutka remained frightened. She seemed unable to move. She sat bolt upright "reading" for hours—for eight or nine hours, on the same inside pages. She says she thinks she can even now recite the entire contents of those columns: *On the Russian front, in the direction of Orel, grenadier forces of the 53rd Linz Regiment.* . . . Her arms became heavy as iron. She grew hot and then she felt cold. Everyone around her was talking and laughing. She was amazed at the audacity of some of the passengers. In the afternoon there was one voice especially, the croaking voice of a workman who boarded the train at Bialystok and who had taken the seat opposite Rutka, that kept making remarks about the Germans, and people all around laughed. Toward evening, Rutka heard the voice say:

—— Any interesting news?

The laughter among Rutka's neighbors seemed sharp. The question was repeated:

—— Any interesting news today?

This time the laughs were louder. Suddenly Rutka realized that the voice was addressing her, because she had been "reading" so long. She became panicky: she wanted to get up and run into the next coach, but she knew that such behavior would only give her away. She lowered the paper—all the faces were looking at her: a whole ring of white blobs: her eyes could not focus, somehow. She had not had anything to eat since early morning—Kucharski's bread; she was giddy and her heart was going almost as fast as the wheel-clicks on the tracks. She just managed to say:

—— Rather dull today.

This remark, on top of her having concentrated on the paper all day long, struck everyone as very funny, and the laughter lasted a long time. Rutka says she felt all right then: the passengers were not against her. Nevertheless, she retired again to her little room with walls of newsprint.

The train arrived at Wilno late at night. Rutka was again without ideas as to what she should do. She was afraid that if she asked her way of a railroad official or a policeman, she would be found out. In the crowd fighting its way along the platform, she saw the elderly workman who had been doing all the talking in the car, so she got through the mob to him and asked him where Newka Street was. He said:

—— Come with me, dear, I'll show you.

Rutka did not know whether to trust him, but she followed him—what else could she have done? He talked a blue streak as they walked—about a guitar his brother had bought and a bad case of spotted fever his granddaughter had had and a gallstone, as hard as slate and as big as a man's head, that he had found in a cow he had slaughtered the week before. At last he stopped under a lamppost and pointed up to a street sign on the wall of the corner house. It was Newka. The man said in his croak:

—— You see, my dear, I did what I said I would do.

Rutka says she was on the verge of tears. The man asked:

—— What number?

Rutka did not want to tell him, because she was afraid she might get the Hashomer people there in trouble, but her rough friend insisted. Not to make an issue, she told him, and he led her right to the number. He wore a cloth cap, and he tipped it and said:

—— Goodbye, my dear. Be more careless, my dear. Next time, don't read the newspaper *all* the way.

Rutka says she found her contact at once, and was taken to the place where she was to stay. [NOTE. N.L. Rutka says that at the present time she does not feel free to discuss her business of the next few days. Patience, Levinson. . . .]

By the time Rutka was to return to Warsaw, she was more relaxed: she says she had learned not to be afraid of freedom. She says she was to carry back to Warsaw a small, rectangular bundle wrapped in brown paper. She put the parcel under her dress, in her bosom, and she says that when she bunched her light overcoat in front, the package seemed well hidden to her. Her friends sent her to the train with a Pole who was going part way to Warsaw, and as long as she was with him, she felt safe. He got off at

Malkinia and a big farm woman with a couple of baskets, who boarded the train there, sat beside her. The sturdy woman talked with other passengers, several of whom seemed to know her. She had a ruddy, pockmarked face, and she was very outgoing and gay. She asked one of the men near her if there had been any rumors about inspections at the Warsaw station that day, and he replied:

—— Nothing special today.

The farm woman ignored Rutka until just a few minutes before Warsaw, when she turned to her and said in a whisper:

—— Are you just a beginner, darling?

Rutka asked her what she meant by that. The big woman said:

—— A pretty girl your age doesn't have square teats, dear. Give it to me, whatever it is. I'll get it through the station for you.

Rutka says she trusted her neighbor completely. She was just a big scoundrel of a woman from a farm. Apparently she thought Rutka was an inexperienced Polish girl trying to smuggle something into Warsaw. At any rate, Rutka reached under her coat and dress and got the packet and handed it to the woman. The woman took the cloth off one of her baskets—it was filled with groats—and she plunged the parcel down into the grain and quickly rounded the top off into a perfect shallow cone. The thing that surprised Rutka was that she did not hide anything from the other passengers.

When the train stopped, Rutka and the woman walked straight up the platform. The goods inspector—he knew the farm woman, called her not only by her first name but even used the diminutive—lifted the cloth on her basket and put it right down again. And then Rutka and her companion walked out into the city. The woman took Rutka to a cellar shop on Targowa Street and gave her the parcel and showed her how to strap it into the small of her back. With her coat hanging free, Rutka says nothing showed at all. She walked to the Vistula and strolled there quite a while—practicing walking as naturally as she could with the parcel pushing her in the kidneys; but also savoring being outside. From what Rutka says, the birches in Luna Park must be lovely this year: she says they make the sound of soft brooms cleaning the breeze. She put her armband back on. She had no trouble at the gate: they seem glad to have Jews come inside the wall.

EVENTS SEPTEMBER 2–7, 1941. ENTRY SEPTEMBER 7, 1941.
N.L. . . . Now we know. Any of us who had any doubts knows now. The report brought back by Rutka Mazur was passed around to us at the *Judenrat* by Zilberzweig, and it is not necessary to know any more. The nature of the mass killings in Bialystok and Wilno, the thoroughness, the technique employed—these leave no doubt as to our future. And yet the impossible is happening: people are rejecting this certainty. Influential people. I heard one man very high in the *Judenrat* say: *The Hashomer crowd is exaggerating these things in order to rouse us to their particular political program.* I am a historian, an archivist, I have studied the Mazur documents: there is internal evidence of their authenticity and of their modesty and understatement. I have heard others say: *All right, suppose these killings did take place. They were in the zone that was formerly Russian. The victims were very likely actual Communists, or suspected of being Communists. We have no such hazard here.* Another formula one hears is this: *We all know that the Germans insist upon collective responsibility. How do we know what provocations the people in Bialystok and Wilno gave the Germans?* Others simply shrug and say: *Those were local happenings.* As if one could not see all the other awful tiles being prepared for the grand mosaic! The worst of all the reactions to the Mazur documents, in my opinion, also emanated from the *Judenrat*, one of whose officials in a formal meeting—this is a matter of record, in Mandeltort's minutes—said: *The ghetto populace has enough to depress it without our stirring up apprehensions with such material as this.* When I heard that, it was all I could do to keep from singing out loud a lullabye my mother used when I was a child to put me to sleep:

> *Sleep my little bird,*
> *Shut your little eyes,*
> *Ayleh lu lu lu.*

So we know: we delude ourselves. We know: we refuse to understand. It is really incredible.

In sophisticated circles in the ghetto, the Mazur girl has become more or less a heroine. I understand from Rachel, who has talked with her quite a bit about the trip, that she doesn't comprehend exactly what she has done: she regards her errand as a

PART TWO

kind of Lag B'Omer outing. [NOTE. EDITOR. Lag B'Omer is a festive holiday, observed mostly by children and young people, celebrating the Jewish heroes, Bar Kokhba and Akiba. In Eastern Europe, Jewish schools used to be closed for the day, and the pupils would go on picnics.] Indeed, her account of her travels to us the other day [ENTRY SEPTEMBER 2, 1941], shows that her heroism consisted mostly of the fact that her "safe" face allowed her to be included in the general Polish feeling that Poland belongs to the Poles. But the Hashomer leaders, who are outrageously smug about this report, and the Bund leaders, who are polite and depreciatory about it, and the *Judenrat* leaders, who are, as I have indicated, soporific about it, are all agreed on the one really unimportant element in the whole thing—namely, they feel that Rutka Mazur has personally done something remarkable.

Poor girl! Now she will be forced into the uncomfortable postures of a public figure. And worse: now the public will admire her instead of the facts. . . .

10

EVENTS LATE SEPTEMBER, 1941. ENTRY SEPTEMBER 26, 1941. N.L. Noach Levinson: family man. I have to contemplate this idea. I have to think about it. It is conceivable that I could be very happy. Yet again, my independence. . . .

Berson proposed the idea to me today in my office. Felix Mandeltort sat by listening to it all, grey and trembling. [NOTE. N.L. And what has reduced Felix to this bad state he is in but worry about *his* family? There are many ramifications to this delightful prospect.]

For some weeks we have been hearing rumors that the Germans intended to cut down the size of the ghetto, and that one of the streets that would be eliminated was to be Sienna. A few days ago representatives of the Gestapo made it understood to the house committee of Sienna Street that if the various courtyards along the street could collect seven pounds of gold, as a sort of ransom, the street would not be excised. The gold was collected: carrings, watches, wedding rings: seven pounds of gold and who can say

203

what weight of sentiment, memory, tears, and love? And now we hear new rumors. The ransom may have been paid to the wrong authorities. The street may go anyhow.

It is Berson's idea that if the various families on his staircase try separately to find new quarters (supposing that Sienna *is* eliminated), they will have to pry themselves into uncomfortable crannies here and there—while if they band together. . . . In short, he urges that a big "family" be formed: the Mazurs, the Apts, the Bersons, Rabbi Goldflamm, and N.L.

I am not an emotional man. I am famously "cold." But this morning, when Berson told me that they all wanted me . . .

EVENTS SEPTEMBER 28, 1941. ENTRY DITTO. N.L. Rachel is looking for a new apartment for all. I am not sure that anything suitable can be found. The crowding is appalling. Is this bad of me?—I am terrified that they may *not* separate Sienna Street from the ghetto, and thus crowd us even further.

EVENTS SEPTEMBER, 1941. ENTRY SEPTEMBER 20, 1941. N.L. We now estimate that half a million Jews are inside the wall. That is, within an area of one thousand acres, one hundred city blocks. During this year, some seventy thousand refugees have come to us from the small towns around Warsaw, particularly those on the other side of the Vistula; forty-four thousand have come from farther away, many of them from Czechoslovakia and Germany. It is said that the average tenancy is now fourteen people per room. Of course, this average includes the huge and horrible "Transfer Points"—the converted public buildings where refugees are settled, in theory temporarily, but for the most part permanently. At Nalewki 35, 1,882 Jews reside; at Krochmalna 17, 1,029; at Bagno 3, 1,016. The filth among these refugees is desperate. Villagers' earthiness has become city-dwellers' dirtiness. Typhus rages ever more furiously: if the death rate reported so far in September continues, we will have more than seven thousand burials this month. We pray for colder weather (and when it comes, we will pray for warmer weather). Our crowded streets seem infested rather than inhabited: the swollen, scurvied children in the cellars of Komitetowa Street! And yet in these crowded streets there is a sound of laughter. There is hard work. We are permitted, now, to work as tailors, shoemakers, brushmakers, cabinet-makers, carpenters, weavers, knitters, bookbinders, glovemakers, light engineers, glass-blowers, spinners, button-makers, hatmakers, electricians, candlers, soap-makers, paper-makers. Swientojerska is the street of furs and brushes, Gensia of textiles, Franciszkanska of leather, Walowa of junk, crockery, and peddling, Nalewki of stores; in Gensuvka, a small square off Gensia, personal belongings are for sale. Each street has the smell of its trade, the smell of overcrowding, the smell of sickness and death. And all this is wedged into the area between the Main Railroad Station, Saxon Garden, and the Danzig Station. I think of the spacious, green-splashed southeastern part of the city, with its parks, its walks by the Vistula, its famous homes, and its new apartments. We used to walk freely there. And now they are even going to tighten our wall. . . .

EVENTS OCTOBER 1, 1941. ENTRY DITTO. N.L. The Germans always seem to time these things with our religious holidays in mind: they seem to calculate how they can discomfort our bodies and spirits simultaneously. Last evening, just at the hour of the Kol Nidre prayers ushering in the Day of Atonement, they posted a decree announcing that Sienna, parts of Gensia and Muranowska, and certain specific houses on the borders of the ghetto will from October 5 be excluded from the Jewish area. My own feelings are mixed.

EVENTS OCTOBER 3, 1941. ENTRY DITTO. N.L. Today I had a glimpse of family life, and I see that it is not entirely mutual love, protection, and unity. It is also argument, cliques, backbiting, personalities. Perhaps this is because we are not consanguineous—though the disagreement today was not entirely along blood lines: Stefan attacked Rachel while his true sister Rutka defended her.

There seems to be a feeling on the part of one faction that Rachel, who has found us a place to live, could have done better. Stefan started it:

—— Why did she have to stick us off on Nowolipie Street? We'll be like herring in a vender's stall. It wouldn't have taken much arranging to get onto Chlodna. That's going to be the new Sienna Street: watch and see if it isn't. Everybody who *is* anybody will be on Chlodna.

Mordecai: —— Nobody told *me* about this "family" idea.

Halinka: —— Rachel didn't ask any of us: she just went ahead and signed up for the Nowolipie apartment.

Rutka: —— We ought to be grateful to Rachel that we have a place to go to.

I was tempted to speak angrily, but I kept my nose out of it, thank God. Rachel behaved very well, I must say. She sat silent, though it was easy to see that she was hurt and annoyed. How much time are we going to devote to absurd petty disagreements, while our world crumbles about our heads?

EVENTS OCTOBER 5, 1941. ENTRY DITTO. N.L. Well, we have moved. My family has moved. How does that sound? When I crawled out of the hole in the wall that I have called home for these years, I was confronted with my worldly goods: one suitcase full of personal things, four big boxes of papers, three carts full of books. My wealth is in words on paper, it seems. And now I am among my beloved friends, who wanted me to be with them. Noach Levinson: family man. Still I have to cogitate that phrase. I am rather nervous about this new closeness.

The living room of this apartment is small and dark, and, crowded as it is with the heterogeneous furnishings of three families and three tastes, every inch of its walls populated by Mauritzi Apt's paintings, Berson's piano taking up far too much space, it seems to bespeak new wealth: individual objects are rich-looking, but the combined mass is in execrable taste. And yet, by the standards of Nowolipie Street, there is a melancholy magnificence about this cluttered room which seems to make the "family" an object of awe among our neighbors. They take every opportunity they can to peek in at the door. We are a zoo.

11

EVENTS DECEMBER 22, 1941. ENTRY DECEMBER 23, 1941. N.L. Winter has come with vindictive anger, and the Germans are stealing our furs. Haensch, the new Commissioner for Jewish Affairs, has issued an order that all furs shall be turned in to collection centers designated by the *Judenrat*, on or before January 1,

1942, on pain of death. This winter seems colder than any we have ever known. There is no coal in our furnaces and no fat on our frames. Plumbing is frozen. Toilets do not flush. Filth piles up in courtyards—and this is all very well during the refrigerated months, but what about next spring and summer? We sit in coats and gloves to chat at night. On special occasions we burn furniture for warmth. Whole trees are disappearing from the streets—first branches, then trunks and all! And this is the time the Germans take to steal our women's furs. . . .

EVENTS DECEMBER 24, 1941. ENTRY DITTO. FROM RA-CHEL APT. Rachel has described for me the consultation that took place this morning.

The women of the family laid out their inventory of furs in neat rows on the living-room floor:

Froi Mazur—a black caracul coat, now rather worn, with a caracul handbag-muff to match, and a brown fox jacket, waist-length;

Symka Berson—an overcoat, fairly good-looking, of some indistinguishable, straight-haired fur, badger or dog, died black, and astrakhan lapels and cuffs on a suit;

Rutka Mazur—a very practical and warm cloth coat lined with lambskin, and a fox jacket exactly like her mother's, and mole-skin gloves;

Rachel Apt—nothing but a stringy neckpiece, evidently of young foxes' skins but now so threadbare as to seem made of mouse fur; and

Halinka Apt—a sealskin coat, a short mink shoulder-cape, a white fox jacket, a squirrel jacket, a rough sheepskin jacket, an astrakhan hat and gloves, a white fox muff, a pair of fur-lined boots, and three pairs of various fur gloves.

Froi Mazur, chuckling: —— I can see the valiant stormtroops advancing on Moscow in those! Halinka, dear, you have enough for a whole regiment yourself. . . . But seriously, what should we do?

The question, at least its statement thus in the first person plural, was Rutka's. The women had reacted in differing ways to Haensch's order. Rachel, who, since she owns nothing but that sad little neckpiece, might be considered to have the least vested interest in fur clothing, had saluted the order with smiles. This was the first concrete evidence the Jews of Warsaw had had, she had said, that the Germans were suffering shortages or hardships of any kind. Some of the others in the apartment had not been so delighted. None of them was especially impressed by the threat of death in the decree: by now that threat, both from natural and from savagely unnatural causes, and in connection with the most trivial aspects of life, has become so familiar as to inspire only feeble precautions—like those occasioned by the threats of sore throats or tired feet. Nevertheless, to avoid harassment, sore throats, tired feet, humiliation, expense, and death, it is necessary to make certain decisions and act upon them. It was Rutka who had urged the others to get out their furs and try to settle on a collective decision as to what to do.

Symka: —— I think we ought to turn them in.

[NOTE. N.L. Symka is terribly thin. Ever since her sickness, she has been mild and dispirited, though she continuously makes what is obviously an inner effort to be her old gay, feminine, lively self. Now only the effort shows: the result is not winsomeness, as before, but only a hollow-eyed debility. She used to pretend to be helpless; now she really is. The poverty of her resources appears whenever there is a problem to be settled, like this one.]

Halinka: —— Each person can decide for herself. I have already decided for myself. You can all do what you wish. I'm going to hide my mink and sell the other things on the Aryan side.

Rutka (who has been displaying a slightly exaggerated sense of her public responsibility ever since her trip to Wilno): —— Everybody has been asking me what I plan to do about my furs. I think this handing in of furs can be a very important symbolical act. The cold weather in Russia seems to have the Germans worried: we—even we Jews—can add to their torment. I know what I think we all ought to do—what I'm going to do. I'm going to mutilate my furs in such a way that it doesn't show and hand them in. I've heard of a method.

Rachel, enthusiastically: —— That's what I'm going to do!

Halinka, pointing at Rachel's pathetic neckpiece: —— And how are you going to mutilate *that* monkey-tail?

Rachel, with a dignity worn as thin and wretched as the fur at which Halinka had just pointed: —— We didn't drag these furs out to compare them.

Froi Mazur: —— No, we didn't. (Froi Mazur has assumed the part of mother in the new household, and she treats all the young people to precisely the same impartial love and firm cheerfulness as she formerly gave her own children.) But I think Halinka's right—this is a decision we'd better make individually. It's a shame, since the Germans hold us responsible all together for the things each one of us does, that we can't act all together all the time—but that's not easy for us, is it, Rutka?

Rutka, inflexible in her determination that others should follow her leadership: —— I still think we all ought to do the same thing.

Halinka: —— Didn't you hear Mother Mazur? *That's not easy for us.*

Rachel: —— I'm afraid she's right, Rutka.

EVENTS DECEMBER 31, 1941. ENTRY JANUARY 1, 1942. N.L. Regina Orlewska blew out the candles and drew back the blackout cloth. It was warm in Regina's room: she had hoarded fuel for this night. It was the last hour of the old year, and outdoors there was magic: snow was falling, but there was a full moon above the overcast and its glow filtered through the cloudbank to give pale life to the dancing white mites outside the window.

Berson was playing the concertina. He had made a little formal speech:

—— Here in our confinement, on this last night of the year 1941, Common Era, I wish to play German music. This is not to mock you or torture you, but to delight you and to comfort you— to remind you. As you know, there is a decree of the "G.G." forbidding Jews to play Aryan music. In defiance of German madness I shall invoke German genius. Listen!

Berson squeezed miracles from the little octagonal push-box. He was very clever in extracting from the simple device all sorts of complexities and subtleties of sound, so that we in the room felt one minute as if we were being shaken by a whole orchestra and a host of singers pouring out Wagner's diapasons, and the next as if a Bach prelude were tinkling out of a harpsichord. *Eine kleine Nachtmusik,* the *Eroica* funeral march, the mysteries of *Orfeo* and the *Zauberflöte,* the *Ode to Joy* and Wolfram's *Evening Star,* the light laughter of Zerlina and the doomful tones of the

Commandant; delicate lieder by Schubert; the cosmic groaning of Mahler, broad Brahms, and the cantering gaiety of Beethoven's Eighth—for hours on end the magnificent procession went on.

Rachel sat alone, noticeably alone. All the other guests at the party in Regina's apartment were paired—except Berson, who was busy. Mordecai and Rutka were crowded into one end of the couch, and at the other end poor Symka leaned back with her head on my shoulder. (Thus does Noach Levinson, family man, use the office of kindly brother; very pleasant.) Stefan, on cushions on the floor beside Halinka, held her hand until the lights went out, and then he seemed to become more operative. Wladislaw Jablonski had a Catholic girl he had discovered in the converts' courtyard, named Marya, on his lap. Dr. Breithorn was paying morose court to Regina. And Rachel sat alone. In a straight chair.

I saw Rachel's hands go over her face. She seemed to be weeping. [INSERT. FROM ENTRY JANUARY 2, 1942. FROM RACHEL APT. Rachel tells me that she did cry at the party the other night. She began thinking about the furs, and especially about her own threadbare neckpiece. Her father had given it to her, when she was sixteen, to wear to her first dance. She was to be escorted that night—she could remember lying on the Chinese rug in front of a coal fire twinkling in the living-room grate, imagining what the dance would be like—she was to be escorted, by arrangement, by Marek Zelechowski, an eighteen-year-old who had always been beyond the farthest horizon of her dreams: a tall, black-haired rapier of a boy, a friend of a friend of Halinka's. In the flames of the coal fire, that night before the dance, Rachel saw herself, whirling in a waltz. She was careful in her fantasy not to imagine too much: once in the leaping red she saw a tall, black-haired boy bend down and kiss a girl's hand, but no, she decided, that was not Rachel's hand, that must be some other girl's hand. But that was Rachel waltzing! That was Rachel, far outstripping the awkward, jouncing steps of her dancing-school days. . . .

The evening came; Zelechowski took her, with her fox draped carelessly around her shoulders, to the dance—in a taxi along with Halinka and her escort, and he talked with Halinka all the way. At the party Rachel suffered an agony of embarrassment: her dancing was atrocious, her tongue was paralyzed. The end of the dance came as a blessed relief; but outdoors, waiting for a cab, Zelechowski and several other young men who were full of champagne and mischief surrounded her, and Zelechowski snatched the fox neck-piece off Rachel's shoulders, held the slender fur to his backsides as a tail, jumped about, scratched himself, and made as if to climb a lamppost. (The monkey-tail, Halinka had called the neckpiece ever since.) Rachel remembered the nightmare when she had finally fallen asleep in the dawn: Rachel dancing superbly, wildly, with a sweet and powerful partner . . . and her skirt on fire and her partner something . . . not a man. . . . She had awakened with a scream. . . .]

I felt sorry for Rachel. Berson was playing Schubert songs. I went over to Rachel and touched her on the shoulder. She started and looked up. I leaned down and whispered:

—— You look uncomfortable. There's room for one more on the sofa. Come sit with us.

On the sofa, between Symka on the one side and Rachel on the other, pressed tightly there, I suddenly felt drowsy, contented, and warmed with song. *Du bist die Ruh'. Der Lindenbaum. Ungeduld.* . . . I slept.

. . . The room was silent. The snow had stopped falling. The interior was haunted by the dimmest reflection of muffled moonlight. Waking, I sensed that Rachel beside me was calm now, for her head, too, was on my shoulder. I heard Berson's voice:

—— It seems to me that this past year was the last good one. The New Year will be the end. I feel it.

Halinka, as gentle as I have ever heard her: —— You're tired, little Dolek. Thank you for playing so wonderfully.

Others: —— Thank you. . . . Thank you, little Dolek. . . . Thank you. . . .

The voices were subdued. Dr. Breithorn blew his nose with the bravura of a veteran trombonist. I wondered whether he had been crying.

Berson: —— It's time to go.

Everyone but Regina bundled up. The girls were all wearing their furs: this was the last night it would be permitted. Rachel had her monkey-tail. The party looked elegant when all were ready to leave; Halinka, in a long dress and wearing her white fox jacket and muff, looked absolutely "prewar," as Stefan said. Outdoors, in the sharp, silent night, a sudden reaction of exuberance seized the group. We swung along the lightening streets, the black-and-white streets, through the valley of white snow and black windows, strangely foliaged with Hebrew shop inscriptions in white paper strips pasted on black signboards; and we had our arms around each other's waists and we were singing softly:

A golden peacock came flying for a foreign land,
And she lost her golden feather in burning shame. . . .

Suddenly in the gay line Halinka fell, and Stefan after her. On the way down Halinka screamed. Both jumped to their feet and recoiled from the thing over which they had stumbled. It was a naked corpse that had been covered and hidden by a drift of the swirling snow. Rutka, evidently pushed by curiosity, stepped forward to see it—and at once she muttered in a shuddering, horrified voice:

—— Oh God! Look at it. It's laughing.

In her fall, Halinka had knocked the loose snow from the corpse's face. The head seemed to be raised up, lying on a chill, white pillow of snow. And it was true: in the haze-thinned moonlight, the face was grinning. The eyes were wide open. All stared at the mirthful dead mask, and we quaked, until Dr. Breithorn, clearing his throat, said cheerlessly:

—— It's nothing, friends, this often happens. Risus sardonicus, we doctors call it: the laugh sardonic. A contraction of certain muscles around the mouth, cheeks, and eyes in rigor mortis. Don't be distressed.

Berson: —— A happy smile for the New Year.

The celebrants walked home in silence. When Reb Yechiel Mazur came to the gate in response to our ringing, in an overcoat and overshoes on top of his pajamas, he muttered, through his chattering teeth:

—— Children! Children! It's foolish to stay out so late.

EVENTS JANUARY 14, 1942. ENTRY DITTO. FROM RACHEL APT. On New Year's morning, the Nowy Kurjer carried a tiny notice to the effect that the deadline for Jews and Jewesses to turn in all furs at the Judenrat collection centers would be January 10, instead of January 1, as previously announced; later the Gazeta Zydowska proclaimed another postponement, until January 16. This morning, two days before what now appears to be the final deadline, Rutka and Rachel got out Rutka's lambskin coat and fox jacket and Rachel's monkey-tail, and with razors borrowed from

Mordecai and Berson, they removed the linings of all three pieces and laid out the bare hides on the floor, fur-side down. Working with utmost care, they then cut parallel slits, every two or three inches, almost all the way through the leather from the inside, to the very roots of the hair on the outside but not quite through— also making sure never to cut the threads used to piece the skins together. Then they cut similar parallel slits going the other way, perpendicular to the first ones. When they were done, the hides were cross-hatched into *potential* tiny squares. Next, handling the skins as if they were gossamer, they stitched the linings back into place.

When the fur pieces were reassembled, they looked from the outside exactly as they had before the girls had started. The utter uselessness of the skins would not become apparent until they were being pieced into the lining of some German officer's greatcoat at some factory in some other city. How the girls admired their workmanship!

Rachel says that she and Rutka could not wait until the last day for the pleasure of turning in their furs: they took them at once to the nearest collection center, which happened, in their case, to be on Grzybowska, near the *Judenrat* itself. At the table in the collecting office, which was a former bookshop, an official of the *Judenrat* and a German noncom received the furs, which the girls put down gingerly.

The *Judenrat* man, in German: —— Sensible girls, beating the last-minute rush.

Rutka: —— Certainly. Why get caught in a crowd?

The official made out a yellow slip for each piece, and assessed the girls two zlotys per slip.

Rutka, in Yiddish to Rachel: —— A two-zloty tax for the privilege of giving away our furs.

The *Judenrat* man, also in Yiddish, beaming pleasantly: —— That's right. That's right, sister.

Rutka, to Rachel: —— It's worth it, I guess, isn't it?

Rachel: —— Seems to me very reasonable—for *this* privilege.

Out in the street, off to the right, there could be heard shouts, which seemed to be German military commands: *Left FACE! Forward MARCH! Left, right, left, right, left, right. . . .* The sound approached the collection center. Rachel's heart sank. She says she felt drawn toward the door, and Rutka, too, edged forward.

213

The German noncom stood up and stamped around to the doorway and took a position right in front of the girls, and the *Judenrat* man glided behind him. Over the German's shoulder, Rachel saw:

Fischel Schpunt, goosestepping alone up the center of the snow-packed street, dressed in a shabby woman's overcoat that was much too small for him, and wearing a squirrel hat with a desiccated, stringy feather in it, and carrying, at shoulder arms, a broomstick with a squirrel muff at the top of it. Schpunt's legs shot way up, stiff, and each time his feet clomped down, his cheeks and dewlaps shook, and he bellowed: *Links, Rechts, Links, Rechts.* . . . Directly in front of the collection center he shouted: *HALT! Eins! Zwei!* And in response to his own commands, he stamped to a halt, faced left toward the German noncom and the *Judenrat* man, snapped the broomstick, one-two-three, to parade rest, and presented arms. Then, commanding himself further, he advanced upon the collection center, and at last dumped the coat, hat, and muff on the table. The noncom was doubled over with laughter, and the *Judenrat* man was howling. But as once before, Rachel says she did not think that Schpunt was funny. His joke was somehow too childish: he had pranked himself like a small boy after a rummage in an attic. And his face was hectically purple. Rachel says she does not know whether this was because of hatred or cold.

12

Events February, 1942.   Entry February 19, 1942.   N.L. I reproach myself that I did not forestall this calamity of Felix Mandeltort's. Surely I saw it coming. How often did he rehearse his troubles to me? How many times did I remark, to my friends and his, on his ghastly appearance? He had become drawn, greenish, and dull-eyed; his elegance was altogether vanished. But more particularly I had witnessed again and again his transactions. Should I have discouraged them? On the one hand, I knew how much he needed money; on the other, I knew that he felt he was tricking, harassing, and resisting the Germans by these deeds, and helping Jews. He asked for praise: could I discourage him?

Still, I think I might have done something.

[INSERT. FROM ENTRY APRIL 7, 1940. N.L. My closest colleague here in the *Judenrat* is of course Felix Mandeltort, with whom I share an office. I know Felix's faults very well; watching a man work day in and day out is the easiest way to learn his faults. Yet I like Felix, and I think he is essentially a fine man. Felix is between fifty and fifty-five years old. He wears formal clothes and has a formal bearing, but I notice that he has the desire for attention that such conventional-seeming men so often do. He makes himself seen and heard. He is, I am sorry to say, a snob. He is uncomfortable with people he considers his inferiors, and of course makes them uncomfortable. He would be glad to think he was a cynical, practical, hard man: I remember the way he used to try to impress Mauritzi Apt along those lines. Actually he is softhearted, impractical, and sloppy. His desk is a frightful sight. . . . FROM ENTRY JUNE 2, 1941. N.L. Spent last evening with Felix at his apartment. It is amazing to see Felix *en famille*. His formality disappears. He is jovial, warm, and good-tempered. He has a fat, dumpy little wife, whom he adores, obviously, though one seldom sees him with her at receptions or public functions—perhaps she is not quite stylish enough to accord with Felix's official front. He has two charming daughters—fresh, witty, and almost pretty. They are, more or less, eighteen and twenty. It is easy to see that here is where Felix's life lies: his Secretaryship of the *Judenrat*, important as that may seem, is but sleepwalking compared to his wakefulness when he is with these three women. . . . FROM ENTRY DECEMBER 12, 1939. N.L. The Secretary, F. Mandeltort, is a professional social worker who has developed, over the years, the manner of the philanthropists from whom he has had to raise money to carry on his work. As early as 1918, he worked in Kiev in an organization that took care of refugees from the Ukrainian pogroms. He has lived in Warsaw since the early 'twenties, and has worked for the Joint Distribution Committee, for co-operative loan societies, and for YIVO. Year before last he became a functionary of the *Kehilla*, the Community Council, when it was still a religious body. What a grand manner he has! . . . FROM ENTRY AUGUST 21, 1941. FROM FELIX MANDELTORT. Felix is apparently very hard-pressed for money. He had never saved very much, and this was because he always had to live in a certain style. He really is very worried about getting enough money to support his family —in that same style; which means black market; which means great expense. . . . ENTRY DECEMBER 7, 1941. N.L. Berson, Mandeltort, and I were rejoicing over the news that America is in the war today when Felix said very importantly: *I have a cousin in Chicago.* He said this as if the kinship put him somewhere just behind the American front lines. He said he would write his cousin. I asked by what route the letter would go, and Felix said: *We'll find some way. Seriously. My cousin is rich. It might help.* And so now we Jews of Eastern Europe can stop worrying. Felix's cousin will take care of everything. . . . FROM ENTRY OCTOBER 5, 1942. N.L. Felix, who lived at Sienna 23 and was very proud of his address, is quite seriously crushed by having to move out. He cannot afford to buy his way into Chlodna Street. . . . FROM ENTRY JANUARY 10, 1942. N.L. Felix looked badly today. . . .]

EVENTS FEBRUARY 12, 1942. ENTRY FEBRUARY 19, 1942. N.L. Berson swears he did not know what was in the parcel, and there is nothing to do but believe him. He says that Halinka gave it to him as he was starting for work here on the morning of the twelfth. I remember his turning it over to Felix:

Berson came into our office with a rather large package wrapped in heavy brown paper under his arm. He put it on Mandeltort's desk, saying:

—— From Panna Halinka Apt. She told me to say it is for the Welfare Drive. She said you would know all about it.

Mandeltort, with unexpected testiness: —— Yes, yes, I know about it.

These little bursts of uncalled-for temper had become more and more frequent. Mandeltort took the package and threw it on the floor behind his desk, then said:

—— How would you and your family like some horsemeat, Berson?

Berson: —— Are you teasing me? Personally I could eat one horse. How many have you?

Mandeltort, humorlessly and hurriedly: —— One. . . . I can make arrangements for you to have one live horse, if you can get ten thousand zlotys to me by four this afternoon.

I think Felix was just as surprised as I was to see Berson reach into his pocket, without a moment's hesitation, pull out a fat roll of bills, and peel off ten thousand-zloty notes. He gave them to Felix. I whistled.

Berson, humorless in his turn: —— When do I take delivery?
Mandeltort: —— In about a month. It may not be very fat,
it's a Kohn-Heller horse, been pulling a trolley. At least it will be
alive, so that you will know that what there is of it is fresh. Keep
in touch with me or (here Felix paused, and looked sidelong at
me)—or just see your cousin Meier. He'll take care of it.

[NOTE. N.L. This was the first I knew of *that* affiliation.]

EVENTS FEBRUARY 19, 1942. ENTRY DITTO. N.L. This
morning I went into Berson's office and without comment dropped
today's *Nowy Kurjer* on his desk, opened to the second page. I had
ringed the item in red pencil. Berson read it:

*At five o'clock yesterday afternoon the Jew Felix Mandel-
tort, Secretary of the Judenrat of the Jewish living-quarter, was arrested at a house on Miodowa Street, outside the Jewish living-
quarter. He was taken to Pawiak Prison. He was charged with the
crime of smuggling furs from the Jewish living-quarter to the
Aryan section of the city. At the time of his arrest he was in possession of a white fox fur jacket and muff, both bearing the label
of Apfelbaum's Fur Store. Condition good. Estimated real value
fourteen thousand zlotys. Authorities stated that Jew Mandeltort
would be fined ten thousand zlotys and jailed for a year. The case
will be tried in the* Sondergericht *next Wednesday.*

Berson stared out the window. I asked him what he was thinking. He said he was thinking how lovely Halinka had looked in her
white fox jacket on New Year's Eve.

EVENTS FEBRUARY, 1942. ENTRY FEBRUARY 22, 1942.
FROM DOLEK BERSON. With respect to the Mandeltort case, Berson is not upset about the things he should worry about to be consistent with his character, as I think I know it—though of course
there is an inner logic in his very inconsistency. I should have imagined that he would feel terribly because he had handed Felix the
very piece of fur that tripped Felix up; that brought about Felix's
downfall. But not Berson. I should also have imagined that he
would be fearful, both for his own reputation and the *Judenrat*'s,
lest it be discovered (indeed, lest it be wrested with rubber hose
and fingernail pliers from Mandeltort) that he, Berson, had handed
the contraband to the distinguished smuggler. Not Berson. No, he

is worried because Halinka Apt is not going to get her money. Even though he still maintains he had no idea what was in the package, he is very depressed that he did the business somehow badly for Halinka. He even speaks rather petulantly about Felix, as if poor Felix had swindled the girl. He was also very concerned, incidentally, at the thought that his own ten thousand zlotys for horseflesh might have gone into the wastebasket, and he shot round to his cousin Meier's to check up; he was relieved to find that that transaction will go through (and so was I, I must admit, since I have been invited to partake of the beast, when it is delivered). I was astounded at his having ten thousand zlotys in his pocket that day, and more, too. I've been to the *Judenrat* employees' soup kitchen many a day when he couldn't scrape up the sixty groszys for a bowl of soup. And here he is worrying about Panna Apt's black-market money. A curious sense of values—or rather, of loyalties, I suppose. Berson has no reason, really, to regret this thing that has happened to Felix, as I do. A year in the Pawiak. A week, such as the one Berson and I had when the Germans first threatened to put us in a ghetto, was entertaining, but a year. . . .

13

EVENTS MARCH, 1942. ENTRY MARCH 26, 1942. N.L. Rachel is suspended, as so many of us are here, between two worlds: private and public: the world within herself and the world within the wall. She is not able to let go of the one, and the other has not quite got hold of her. Thus she is irresolute, vacillating, moody, cautious, and taciturn. Yet I think she is striving for a balance. . . .

EVENTS MARCH 16, 1942. ENTRY DITTO. FROM RACHEL APT. Talked with Rachel today just after she paid young David a visit at the Rukner Home. The boy has been there nearly six months now. I have noted how depressed Rachel was to "lose" him at first [ENTRY SEPTEMBER 25, 1941]. Now she thanks God that she had the inspiration to put David in the Home. She says that he thrives; that he is a blossom among parched rocks. He has gained weight, and the merry, mischievous look he used to have in prewar days has returned. During her visit to him today he smiled and giggled constantly.

David: —— We're going to have a garden this spring in the place where one of the bombed houses was on Gensia Street. The TOPORAL lady gave us the choice between flowers and vegetables, and some of the others had a hard time making up their minds, but I said I wanted to grow peas—because they put out both flowers and vegetables!

In an obscure way, Rachel seems to regret having lost an object of pity in David: it must have been sweet and comforting to ache for her poor, skinny, little old man of a brother—now this self-indulgence is impossible. David is better off than she: he is a child, permitted to live once again a child's life. In place of her former pity, Rachel now urges pride. Peas! How much cleverer than the other children he is!

Events March 24, 1942. Entry ditto. From Rachel Apt. Rachel is still upset tonight, and I have an idea that part of what bothers her is that Zilberzweig's business this morning was private, and not some exciting Hashomer project. Of course Rachel would not say that, even if she recognized it: she centers her misery on the thing itself.

Rachel says that when she came in from an errand this morning, she found on the vestibule table a sealed envelope, addressed to her. Inside was a note:

—— *Come when you can to workshop number three. Hil.*

"Workshop number three" appears to be Zilberzweig's own two-room apartment on Pawia Street. When Rachel arrived there, the leader, in a frayed tan wool dressing-gown, was talking to a man Rachel had never seen; she waited a few minutes while the two murmured by the door, until the stranger left.

Zilberzweig invited Rachel inside, offered her a seat, and said cordially:

—— I summoned you because I have a message for you from your father. One of our couriers brought it in. She says she was directed to your father by a janitor named Kucharski, to whom Rutka Mazur had sent her. What do you know about this Kucharski? Is he reliable?

—— Yes, I . . . I think so. He was very helpful to Rutka when she went to Wilno. Why?

—— No particular reason. It's just that we have to be careful. As I understand it, he was janitor at your courtyard in the beginning, is that right?

—— That's right. (Rachel says she wondered: Why does he palaver this way? Why doesn't he tell me the message?)

—— Was he extremely talkative then?

—— He was quite a gossip. Like an old lady. But never malicious and usually truthful.

—— The truth can hurt, you know, especially in our business.

Rachel says she now burst out irritably:

—— What did my father say?

Zilberzweig, drawing a hand across his forehead, as if to wipe away the delicate scar-lines of worry there: —— I'm sorry. The message was this: *Please send three or four small diamonds.*

Rachel says she flushed; she felt angry and humiliated.

Rachel: —— Was that all?

Zilberzweig: —— You must assume that if he was able to send the message, he was well. You must assume that if he is your father, he loves you. I admire him for the economy of his message. . . . My dear girl!

For Rachel had begun to weep, with the silent, eye-brimming stare of a girl who has lost a fight to suppress a sudden misery. [NOTE. N.L. And I am positive, at least, that some of Rachel's continuing unhappiness tonight comes from her embarrassment at having broken down before Zilberzweig.]

EVENTS MARCH 26, 1942. ENTRY DITTO. FROM RACHEL APT. When the urgent message came this morning, inviting Rachel to assist Zilberzweig at *a most important conference with leaders of other Jewish organizations,* as Zilberzweig's secretary, Rachel says she was tortured by the thought that Zilberzweig had invited her more or less out of pity—because she had appeared so crushed by that interview about her father, and Zilberzweig had been embarrassed and sorry for her, and wanted now to cheer her up. This may be true. If so, the two worlds overlap: Rachel is now drawn out into the public world because of her deep involvement in her private world. . . . On the other hand, there is the possibility that Zilberzweig invited Rachel simply because he thinks her a bright girl. . . .

The delegates were crowded into Pan Zilberzweig's room, and

some of them had to sit on the floor. Rachel says that Zilberzweig whispered the names and identities of the representatives at the conference to her, not to entertain her, but because he wanted a record of all that would be said. Rachel was nervous; Zilberzweig had told her that writing would not be permitted at such a meeting as this and that she would have to remember everything and write it down afterward.

—— Rapaport and Slonim of the Bund, Kurtz and Budko of the Communists, Lakh and . . . (delegates, she says, of Left Poale-Zion, Dror, Akiba, Misrachi, the general Zionists, and two rabbis of the Orthodoxy. The Revisionists were not present).

There were only three women on hand; Rachel says she felt great self-esteem. She recognized one of the Poale-Zion delegates as the stranger who had been talking with Zilberzweig when she had gone to get her father's message; perhaps they had been making arrangements for this meeting. Her father! What would he think of her if he could see her now, sitting in a room with two live Socialists and two Communists? He would have apoplexy; vindictively (her father had to pay *something* for those four diamonds!), Rachel imagined her father walking into the room, seeing her in such company, turning purple, and keeling over—she would fetch a rag with cold water and bring him to consciousness and he would soon see that it was all right, everything was quite comfortable here.

Zilberzweig, loudly: —— We have called this meeting in order to determine whether we can undertake a common course of action—whether we can begin now to work, not as divergent political units, but as organized Jewry. I need not recite to you the danger signals we have been receiving—the Mazur Report from Bialystok and Wilno, the ugly rumors from Lublin, the brutalities in Lodz, Radom, Lwow, and Krakow, and now especially the report some of us have heard that we here in Warsaw may be treated to something unpleasant in the very near future. You have all heard of this last; you all have your intelligence services. The experience in other cities has shown the *Judenrats* there to have been ineffectual in the extreme. Only by banding together can we do anything to defend our people against these outrages. As political parties, we all have our ultimate aims—and more power to them!—but to achieve them separately, we must survive together. . . . I'd like to hear from some others on this question. . . .

Several men spoke, each in his own terms and using his own clichés (Kurtz spoke of an *anti-Fascist bloc*, one of the rabbis of *the community of the Law*); but the meeting did not sharpen into focus until Rapaport stood up. The white-haired Socialist said:

—— In principle, we are one hundred per cent with you. We very much desire the destruction of the Nazis. It is just a question of the best methods. In that connection, Chaver Delegate of Hashomer Hatsair, I am reminded of an occasion as far back as October, 1939, when you and I spoke to a rally in front of the Community Building concerning the very first threat to put us in a ghetto, and, as I remember it, I was the one who urged resistance then, and you, speaking for Hashomer, urged moderation and patience. Yes, the record of the Bund is clear and consistent. However, on the point of mechanical liaison now between all Jewish organizations, I regret to state that the Bund cannot participate. The Bund is a Socialist party, not a Jewish party, primarily. We seek the brotherhood of all working men—Jewish, Polish, Czech, French, and yes, German and Russian, too. We will continue to work, along with our Polish comrades, for the defeat of Hitler, the arch-enemy of the working class. I regret that we cannot join with other enemies of the working class—even Jewish ones—to achieve that end.

The meeting became a hubbub. Several speakers tried to argue with Rapaport, until at last he put an end to persuasion, by saying, in what Rachel thought was a pathetic appeal:

—— Gentlemen! This is not a personal decision taken by me alone. My party has decided. The decision is not presently revocable.

The Socialists were thereupon asked to leave the meeting, and the other organizations tried to agree on the formation of a liaison group. But the mood of the meeting was depressed, its business was done in a desultory fashion.

After the adjournment, Zilberzweig agreed with Rachel that there was no need for minutes of the meeting. What was there to write, Rachel says, but one sentence?—

—— Among ourselves we could not agree to agree.

EVENTS MARCH, 1942. ENTRY MARCH 26, 1942. N.L. . . . And yet, is a "balance" possible? Will not the two worlds always tug her back and forth, in starts and spasms?

14

Events March 29, 1942. Entry ditto. N.L. A "family" scene this evening:

Reb Yechiel Mazur: —— What do you think, Rabbi? Should we eat this animal if Dolek gets it?

Rabbi Goldflamm answered rather pompously—but with what seemed to me to be an unconsciously humorous rationalization. Somehow Reb Yechiel demands a little pomposity in a rabbi; besides, several members of the "family" were sitting around, listening critically: the question called for an agile answer.

The rabbi: —— By the strict application of our dietary laws, the horse is unclean. As you know, we are permitted the flesh of animals that have cleft hooves and chew their cud. Neither applies to our horse. But the basis of these laws is health and common sense. First, we can say that health and common sense urge that if we have been meat-eaters in the past, any meat (if it is itself healthy) should be good for us, since we have been so long without meat. Second, we can say that the animals who have cleft hooves and chew cud are the herbivorous and peace-loving animals: our horse is certainly that. Third, the only exceptions to the rule that cud-chewing and cleft feet go together in animals are the pig, which only has the cleft hoof, and the camel, which only chews. The pig was presumably ruled out from our diet because he is actually and demonstrably unclean in his choice of victuals, in his habits, and especially in his susceptibility to trichinae; none of these things would apply to our horse. The camel was probably eliminated because in the desert, where these rules had their origin, he was too useful to be spared; we are assured by the Kohn-Heller organization, I gather, that our horse is beyond usefulness. It is my opinion (the rabbi pulled at his beard) that our horse should be eaten. However (he held up his hand), it must be killed by ritual slaughter. Because the animal is itself normally "unclean" does not mean that we should, having made an exception for the best of reasons, deliberately eat double-*terefah*. The purpose of kosher slaughter is to take health precautions: they are especially indicated, I should say, in the case of our horse. This is not a young horse.

Berson: —— If you'll forgive my making a comment, Rabbi, I've noticed two things about your discourse: you have referred to this animal throughout as *our horse*, and you're swallowing a great deal—your mouth seems to be watering.

Reb Yechiel Mazur was the only person in the room who was not amused—even Rabbi Goldflamm forced out a little bark of a laugh at Berson's remark. Reb Yechiel was already a step farther along: he was worrying about the fact that kosher slaughter is illegal. [Note. Editor. Kosher slaughter, which requires draining of blood from the meat and examination of organs and entrails for signs of disease, had been banned by decree on October 26, 1939—for humanitarian reasons!]

Reb Yechiel Mazur: —— Do you know a certified Shohet who can do a kosher killing for us, Rabbi?

Goldflamm: —— A very fine one. Benkewitz by name. You should see him take the sinew from the hind leg!

Reb Yechiel Mazur, to Berson: —— When does our horse arrive?

Berson: —— Thursday night, if it lives that long.

Froi Mazur: —— Good! Then I can cook it on Friday and we can share it on the Sabbath with some friends.

Events April 2, 1942. Entry April 3, 1942. From Dolek Berson; N.L. Very late last night, Berson and his cousin Meier stood waiting together in a cavernous doorway on Kozhla Street, the little winding alley where the animal market used to be and where one of the Kohn-Heller stables is now located. Berson says he supposed that Meier's extreme affability in connection with this Kohn-Heller nag showed he expected to be invited to assist at the feast; but this time, Berson tells me, he had decided he simply would not ask his cousin. Assuredly Meier had already pocketed a fair slice of Berson's ten thousand zlotys. Let that be enough this time! Meier is said to be working for Gruber in setting up a button factory here in the ghetto. . . .

At last, in the dimmest glow of a less-than-quarter moon, Berson saw something coming along the street. It moved silently and took form. Yes, it was a man and a horse. Meier stepped out onto

the pavement, exchanged whispers with the man, and hissed softly
to Dolek, who then joined the other two.

Meier, in a whisper: —— Take it away while it still can walk!

Berson grasped the rope halter and set off alone for the address on Karmelitzka Street that Rabbi Goldflamm had given him.
The horse's hooves were wrapped in burlap. It breathed heavily.
Once it snorted. Berson met no one in the night-streets. On Karmelitzka he looked for a certain narrow passageway between two
houses, and when he found it, he led the horse in there. Someone
moved up from a sunken areaway and murmured:

—— This way, bring it down here.

Reluctantly, one jouncing step downward at a time, the big
animal descended into the areaway. A double door opened: lights
within were hastily dimmed. Berson led his animal inside; the
doors were shut; the carbide lamps were uncovered. There in the
sudden brightness in the cellar, its ears touching the ceiling, stood
a gaunt, bony, drab, brown horse, with moistily blinking eyes and
dribbling nostrils, as if, on its silent walk, it had been thinking mortal thoughts and weeping horse tears of self-pity.

Benkewitz the Shohet was a mean-looking little man with a
cat's face and a scraggly, inadequate beard. He sniffed when he saw
the horse, as if to suggest that this meager creature was scarcely
worth his talents. Rabbi Goldflamm, Reb Yechiel Mazur, Mordecai Apt, and N.L. had come to witness the slaughter; we and Berson stood in a crescent around Benkewitz the Shohet, allowing him
light for his preparations. First the Shohet handed Rabbi Goldflamm his *Kabbalah*, the certificate of his expertness in both the
theoretical and practical aspects of slaughter, for inspection. Then
he opened a beautiful, velvet-lined container, something like a
violin case, and took out a long, brightly polished steel knife and
a big, round whetting iron. With dazzling speed and with clank-
ings and scrapings in primitive rhythms, he sharpened the knife.
Next he took a small silicon-carbide whet and more gently repeated
the honing. Finally, with a tiny, nearly smooth steel rod, scarcely
touching the razor-edge, he endowed the blade with a most merciful final sharpness. Peering down close to the knife, near one of
the lamps, Benkewitz examined the knife's keenness; he ran his
finger along the sides three times, his nail three times.

The Shohet put on a white tunic, like a doctor's, washed his hands, then turned toward the horse, with the big knife in his hand.

Benkewitz: —— Stand back, please. I'm a little out of practice.

I could hardly follow what happened next. I had one glimpse of a powerful wrist—a disproportionate wrist for such a small man —holding the sparkling blade in readiness under the horse's sad but calm face. A flash. The horse sagged slowly down, dead before it could be surprised, its esophagus, windpipe, and great veins all severed in one astounding, old-fashioned, up-curving stroke-and-pull. The Shohet seemed to swarm over the carcass, and in a matter of minutes, the horse had been flayed, its blood on the cellar floor had been sprinkled with earth, and its gleaming viscera had been taken out onto the Shohet's cutting table. The Shohet used a number of knives and scalpels from his velvet-lined case. He washed his hands several times. Not a drop of blood got onto his white tunic. First he inspected the lungs; then, in order, the windpipe, esophagus, heart, brains, stomach, and intestines. Finally he said:

—— This horse was healthy. Indeed, it probably had to be healthy to reach such a fine old age.

Next the Shohet proceeded to butchery and the removal of veins and prohibited fat. He divided the carcass into cuts. There was fair meat at the crest, withers, haunches, and stifles; but the Shohet wasted nothing, not even from the most bony sections, the hocks, the cannons, the pasterns, and the shanks. As he finished each piece, he dropped it into one of several barrels of water that stood along one wall of the cellar. When the Shohet came to the removal of the hamstring from the hindquarter, the most difficult excision of all, Rabbi Goldflamm nudged Berson and nodded his bearded head.

Goldflamm, ecstatically: —— What did I tell you? He's a genius!

I saw Berson go pale. He says he felt faint, and he staggered outdoors to get some fresh air. When he returned, some time later, the meat was all salted and stood dripping on the slanting, perforated blood-boards. The Shohet was cleaning his winking knives; the witnesses were gossiping. It was nearly two in the morning when the Shohet gave the meat its final rinsing and said:

—— Kosher, gentlemen; and a pleasure. May you have the power and the will to chew it!

We made big parcels of the meat and bones and carried them home.

EVENTS APRIL 4, 1942. ENTRY APRIL 5, 1942. N.L. Froi Mazur, holding her sides, was the last to stop laughing.

—— Oh, oh, oh! This is like before the war!

She wiped her laughing-tears away. She could afford to be mirthful. The meal had been beyond everyone's imaginings. The day before yesterday, Froi Mazur had pounded and chopped and worked and soaked the toughness out of the meat and had cooked the tiny shreds of it into a great *cholent*, with potatoes, turnips, carrots, and yes, even onions—hoarded, scraped together, bought for fortunes, somehow assembled by the whole family's efforts. Some bayleaves that Froi Mazur had brought from Lodz, a small cupful of wine from the bottle that Menkes had shyly offered, some flour he had also brought, salt wheedled from the Shohet by the quick-witted rabbi—all had gone into the big pot. Froi Mazur had boiled the stew for a long time, and late in the afternoon it had filled the apartment with a painfully delicious promissory aroma. The *cholent* had matured overnight and had simmered all yesterday morning. When the company had assembled, Pavel's bottle went around to all—besides the "family," which today included little David Apt, the guests were Regina Orlewska, Lazar Slonim, Benlevi, the Jablonskis, and Pavel Menkes—and each one of us became a little drunk on a thimbleful of wine and the prospect of a feast. Reb Yechiel Mazur seemed quite tipsy as he said:

—— I know hundreds of benedictions for all sorts of occasions —for the sniffing of fragrant barks, for hearing thunder, for seeing a rainbow, for listening to a wise man lecture on the Law, for seeing kings and their courts, for encountering strangely-formed men, giants, dwarfs, and crooked persons—outlandish things—but I've never heard of a benediction for smelling the fragrance of horse-meat stew on an extremely empty stomach, and I've never been so eager to pronounce one!

On that note of rabbinical levity, the occasion had begun— and it became gayer and gayer, and by three fifteen on that Sabbath afternoon, eighteen people had eaten a horse and laughed very much. Even Rabbi Goldflamm and Reb Yechiel Mazur had violated, without any visible signs of struggle, the prohibition of the Talmud: *A man shall not eat to the fill in time of hunger.*

Berson, announcing yet another story: —— From before the ghetto. . . . Maybe you've heard it, about the Jew and his chicken.

Stefan: —— Oh, yes, that's an old one.

Berson, doubtfully: —— Well, if it's old . . .

Menkes: —— Tell it, tell it.

Berson: —— Well, this Jew had a chicken and he *nebich* had nothing to feed it, so he took it under his arm to get something. On Gensia Street he met a Navy-blue, and the Navy-blue says: *Where are you going, Jew?* And the Jew says: *To the poultry store, to buy my chicken some food.* And the policeman says: *What food?* The Jew says: *Millet.* So the Navy-blue says: *Millet? Poles are starving and you, you Jew, you feed your chicken good millet!* So the Navy-blue beats up the Jew. A little later, on Franciszkanska, an S.S. man meets the Jew and he says: *Where are you going, you guttersnipe?* So the Jew says: *To the store, to buy my chicken something to eat.* The S.S. man says: *What are you going to get him?* By this time the Jew is wise about millet; he says: *A little groats.* The S.S. man roars: *Groats! Even Germans are going hungry and you stuff your Jewish chicken on groats.* So he gives the Jew a beating. On Bonifraterska a *Wehrmacht* sergeant meets the Jew, and he says: *Where do you think you're going?* So the Jew says: *To buy my chicken some food.* The German says: *Ach, so! And what kind will you buy?* The German looks very threatening. *Listen,* the Jew says, *I'll give him a couple of zlotys and let him shop around and get anything he wants. It's up to him.*

Again everyone rocked and hugged himself, laughing. Then Stefan told a story in questionable taste, and to offset it Rabbi Goldflamm told a story that was in perfect taste but was not funny, and Berson tried to tell a political story but lost the point entirely. The mood of hilarity tapered off. Everyone was marvelously sated. Suddenly Rutka, in a new frame of mind, spoke to me:

Rutka: —— Have you been hearing rumors, Noach?

N.L.: —— I have heard some whispering.

Rutka: —— It sounds bad.

N.L.: —— They speak of a manhunt. They say an S.D. unit has arrived.

Froi Mazur, with a shudder: —— A manhunt?

N.L., drily (my parlor courage): —— Just what the word says. The only question: which men?

228

Menkes: —— Just more nonsense to get us stirred up.

N.L., lending the rumor weight by repetition: —— One hears talk of a manhunt, that's all I know.

Reb Yechiel Mazur: —— Let's not speak of such things on the Sabbath.

Rutka: —— Reticence won't prevent anything, Papa.

Thus fearful thoughts and conversation stole into our afternoon. I myself, when the subject changed, thought of a "snatcher" I saw on Grzybowska Street the other day: one of the famished urchins who patrol the streets looking for pedestrians carrying bread or other food, and who sneak up behind these fortunates and grab the parcels right out of their arms and run off eating. The one I saw was so crazed by hunger that after snatching a loaf from a woman he fell right down in the street, gnawing the bread, while the woman shrieked and kicked him. . . . My thoughts on a full stomach.

We became depressed, all of us, and I think the reason was only this: our feast was behind us. . . .

15

EVENTS APRIL 17, 1942. ENTRY APRIL 18, 1942. N.L. We were sitting around eating supper—tincture of horse-bone broth; even now, sipping this almost tasteless liquid, we nourish ourselves with the memory of that great meal Froi Mazur gave us —when Stefan came in, breathing like a spent sheepdog. Even with normal respiration, I think he would have been incoherent:

Stefan: —— I can't stay. . . . Just a second. . . . Tonight! We think it begins tonight. . . . Tell everybody. . . . We all have been called for extra duty tonight, all the Jewish police. . . . Stay inside. . . . We don't know exactly. . . .

And out he went, still puffing and babbling.

This harum-scarum visit opened up the situation. Berson and I, with all the employees of the *Judenrat*, had been dismissed from work a half-hour early, and had been directed by the office-boy who circulated the dismissal to go straight home; disturbed by this unusual order, but not quite understanding it, we had compacted between us to say nothing of it to the family. But now Stefan's inarticulate signals made me turn to Froi Mazur and say:

—— Do you remember the rumors we were discussing the other day?

It was not necessary to say more. All understood. Froi Mazur packed a basket with some food and water, and it was arranged that she, Reb Yechiel Mazur, and the four girls, Symka, Rutka, Rachel, and Halinka, would go down in the cellar and hide. The younger men would stay in the apartment. But when the time came for the cellar party to go downstairs, Rutka announced that she was not going to join it. She and Mordecai were going out for a walk, she said. It was Berson who took hold of the moment.

Berson: —— Where are you going?

Mordecai: —— To buy my chicken some food.

Berson: —— You heard what Stefan told us. You can't go out.

Mordecai, bristling: —— Oh, can't we?

Berson: —— I won't let you. I feel that you shouldn't.

Rutka: —— Thank you, you are too kind. . . . Nevertheless, try to stop us!

Rachel, interrupting, almost exuberantly: —— Let them go, Dolek. They must know what they are doing.

Berson: —— Please take care!

EVENTS APRIL 17, 1942. ENTRY APRIL 18, 1942. N.L. Berson was jumpy and irritable all evening. With Stefan on duty and Mordecai out with Rutka, he and I were alone in the apartment. I too was nervous, of course, but he seemed to feel angry with himself that he had not *forcibly* prevented Rutka and Mordecai from going out. In my present debilitated state, I can sustain anxiety only so long; then for some reason I yawn and become sleepy. So I went to bed, leaving Berson fidgeting in the living room. Still Rutka and Mordecai had not returned. I went to sleep and slept through the whole thing. Even the shots in near-by streets did not rouse me. Only when Menkes came in roaring and blubbering. . . .

FROM ✿ CONVERSATION. [NOTE. EDITOR. The following passage is excerpted from Levinson's notes on the conversations of May 9–10, 1943, already briefly alluded to.] FROM MORDECAI APT.

. . . Questioned Mordecai Apt about night of manhunt in April last year, about his foolhardy excursion with Rutka. At first all he would say was that he and Rutka had gone out on *an urgent errand.* Then after some thought he told me the whole story, thus:

Rutka and Mordecai walked slowly through the empty streets of the ghetto. They were, he said, like absent-minded sweethearts. They held hands and staggered with emotion. They were oblivious of everything but each other—though, since into oblivion there may intrude from time to time grey, partly illuminated shapes and reminders, they hugged the sides of the streets and secreted themselves occasionally in doorways. Mordecai says his chest burned.

Mordecai: —— Rutka! Rutka! I am consumed.

Rutka (even in passion more methodical than Mordecai): —— Where shall we go?

They had already been walking for some time. Mordecai had no idea either where they were or where they should go. He drew her into the cavern of a shop front and kissed her and groaned in an access of desire. She pulled away from him.

Rutka, sharply: —— What was that? [NOTE. N.L. Evidently she had heard a shot in the distance.]

Mordecai: —— I heard nothing. I have no ears.

Rutka, as they began walking again: —— It sounded like . . . nothing.

—— Like what?

—— Nothing.

—— Tell me.

—— It was nothing—imagination.

Soon Mordecai was in a tremendous fury as they strolled. He ground his teeth and cursed his wife; he said she had deliberately tried to provoke him by not finishing her thought, to tantalize him.

Rutka: —— You seem to have forgotten your errand.

Mordecai wavered and wilted and breathed an anguished apology. Frustration had made him unreasonable, he says: what kind of marriage was this?—twelve people in three rooms, stumbling over each other, bickering, hungry, short-tempered, what sort of home for a new marriage was this?

Mordecai: —— I want to be let out of the cage I'm in.

Rutka, laughing: —— My tiger!

Mordecai was vaguely aware of a gap between buildings by the street—a place where a house had been bombed out. Without a word he steered Rutka into the area. He felt as if he were in a private place. He kissed her. He drew her deeper into the recess. Underfoot, a mound of some kind. . . . Down, down. Now down, flatly near to her, he felt the mounting and pounding of his affection. Rutka, Rutka, Rutka. A corner of his receding awareness said to him: This is not quite right, this is a pile of refuse we are on, we should . . . but then the door to that corner of his mind was quite closed. Rutka, Rutka, Rutka.

Rutka, in a low, low voice: —— My tiger! . . .

. . . They lay in the litter, in love. He was almost asleep, almost unconscious, unknotted, free. She laughed, in that same low voice, and called him a splendid man.

Mordecai: —— And you, you consume me. I'm a cinder, lying in cinders.

—— I didn't know you realized what we're on.

—— I didn't realize until too late. I'm sorry, my Rutka.

—— It's a nice simple bed.

—— At least we are together in it.

—— Shhh.

Rutka suddenly put a finger on Mordecai's lips, and though he knew she was silencing him, he kissed the finger and his chest burned.

A man's footsteps, running headlong in the street. Past the mouth of the cavern. Somehow, a real haste in those driving feet, terror. Yet Mordecai says he felt no fear. Later in the night they heard the shots; still they told each other that they were not afraid.

16

EVENTS NIGHT APRIL 17–18, 1942. ENTRY APRIL 18, 1942. N.L. I wish I knew what happened between Berson and Menkes here last night. Berson looks as if he had seen the Angel of Vengeance. Considering the number of bakers who were killed, Menkes is lucky to be only in jail—though of course he may be shot there. I curse my lassitude: I was awakened by Menkes' bellowing in the apartment last night, but I rolled over and went back to sleep.

EVENTS NIGHT APRIL 17–18, 1942. ENTRY APRIL 19, 1942.
N.L. Berson said tonight:
—— If Pavel is shot, I will consider that I killed him.

EVENTS NIGHT APRIL 17–18, 1942. ENTRY APRIL 20, 1942.
N.L. Poor Berson! What a paralyzing dilemma that must have
been! I have persuaded him to tell me what happened:

Berson sat up in the living room, helpless and angry with
himself, waiting for Rutka and Mordecai to come back in—as if
waiting would do any good. I had gone to bed. He heard shooting
in the streets, and he was very nervous. At last the staircase door
below creaked and slammed. Footsteps running up the stairs. But
God!—only one pair. Berson jumped up and went to the apartment
door, and opened it. Menkes rushed up and in.

Menkes' face was greenish and covered with perspiration, and
the big baker trembled all over. He gasped:
—— Hide me! Hide me!
—— Quiet yourself. Nothing can happen to you here.

Menkes flung himself into an easy chair; he sat straight, his
chest heaving.
—— They're killing all the bakers. One of the apprentices
from Dant's bakery ran to my shop . . .
—— And you didn't want to believe the warnings. *Just nonsense to stir us* . . .
—— What good are you? What are you doing about anything,
since you know so much?
—— I don't know anything. . . . Tell me.
—— This boy, this apprentice, he told me how old Dant was
simply hauled out into the street, and the Germans ordered Dant
to run away, and he began running, and they shot him down from
behind. Then they told the apprentice to run, and he started,
thinking he would get it any moment, but they held back, so he
ran faster and faster, but there wasn't any shot, finally just the
sound of the Germans laughing at him. He told me he ran to the
Feiwicz Bakery, to hide, but it was empty and he found Feiwicz
in a mess of blood in the courtyard. So he ran to Haleazar, and
he had been killed, and the boy kept hearing shots all over the
ghetto. So then he came to me. And he'd been there a few minutes
when a Jewish policeman named Marbekssohn ran by my place:
he said Lazar Slonim had asked him to warn me—why Slonim, I

can't imagine. He said he'd heard that the Gestapo had a list of thirty-two bakers, he didn't know whether I was on it or not, about fifteen had already been killed. [NOTE. N.L. This warning of Slonim's *is* curious, considering Menkes' rejection of the Bund proposals. One remembers Slonim's words: *Most of the bakers will be joining.* A forlorn company that night! I should think Slonim's warning would only make Menkes feel he was right not to have joined. Though perhaps Slonim was afraid that by merely having approached Menkes, he might have endangered him.] I didn't wait to hear any more.

——I don't blame you. Anyhow, you're safe here, for the time being.

Finally Menkes stopped trembling. The two men speculated as to why the bakers had been honored in this way. [NOTE. N.L. They did not realize then that printers and others were also being hunted.] Suddenly they heard the staircase door squeal open and slam. Heavy boots began climbing the steps, slowly. Menkes stood up, in a new round of shaking. Berson pointed to the kitchen and Menkes ran there and closed the door.

It was Stefan. He came in from the stairway. The young policeman threw his official hat on the floor, sat down heavily, and took his head in his hands.

Stefan: —— If I ever have to witness that sort of work again, I'll resign. . . . I'll . . . I'll kill myself.

Berson, quietly: —— Pavel Menkes is here. I'm going to hide him.

Stefan, standing up, protested with a systematic calmness:

—— That is a mistake, Berson.

—— Shhh! He may be able to hear you.

—— I don't care. (Nevertheless, Stefan lowered his voice.) It's still a mistake.

—— He's a friend. I have to do it.

—— What comes first, your friend or your family? Listen! The Germans are in earnest tonight. They don't mind killing people. The days of mere pranks and humiliations are over. I've seen this thing, Dolek, I tell you they mean business tonight. They ask a question of a janitor in a courtyard where there's a bakery, and if the janitor stops to think, *bim,* he's dead. They mean business.

Berson says that he was already so gripped by indecision that he could not think clearly.

Stefan, pressing: —— Take your choice. It's Menkes or all of us. They'll track him. God, I heard dogs barking tonight. . . . And then they'll kill Symka and Halinka and Rachel and . . . all of us. Collective. You know their minds. It would be your doing.

—— We could hide him here tonight, and move him tomorrow.

—— Tonight is the night when the killing is being done. Look! I was at the Abramowicz Bakery: the old lady begins wailing and rocking back and forth, so what do they do? They shoot everybody on the staircase. They don't like wailing. . . . They're out on an assignment, tonight, I can tell you.

—— We can't turn him out.

—— I'll do what has to be done.

Stefan picked up his hat.

—— Wait!

—— What?

—— Isn't there (Berson says his mind absolutely refused to function) anything we can do?

—— It's not on you. I'm the one who is going to do it.

And Stefan left; the heavy boots ran down the stairs. Berson hesitated, then went to the kitchen door.

Menkes: —— Who was it?

Berson: —— Stefan Mazur. He . . . he forgot something.

—— What were you talking about?

—— He was telling me about the manhunt.

—— I thought I heard my name.

—— No, Pavel. I didn't tell him you're here. I don't trust that boy.

Berson says that of all the various shames he feels about this thing, he is most ashamed of this lie, which came quickly to his tongue. He was still brain-tied. Should he tell Menkes to run away? No, because Stefan was calling someone to come here; there would be a collective punishment. Should he tell Menkes what was going to happen? Should he try to explain why? Should he give Menkes a chance to kill himself?

Menkes seemed satisfied. He said:

—— I'm sorry about Haleazar. He was a good baker.

And they began talking (Berson says his tongue did all the work, as if by reflex; his mind did not participate) and after some time a party came for Menkes. Mercifully, those who came were

Jewish policemen. They said they had orders to take Menkes to the Pawiak.

Berson says that Menkes did not look at him once as he was being taken away.

EVENTS NIGHT APRIL 17–18, 1942. ENTRY APRIL 18, 1942. N.L. Apparently Rutka and Mordecai did not come in until early morning.

EVENTS NIGHT APRIL 17–18, 1942. ENTRY APRIL 21, 1942. N.L. The pattern of the manhunt now seems evident: information must have fallen into the Germans' hands, either accidentally or through informers: they were after underground people. The Jewish police who led the S.S. men and Gestapo to the victims had specific lists and addresses. Mostly bakers and printers. A man from the barbers' union. A binder. These were people involved in printing and distributing underground papers, I would guess; and those involved in illicit flour mills; and some others. Perhaps Menkes would not have been taken, but for Stefan's tale-bearing; perhaps this accounts for the fact that he was taken to the Pawiak, and not shot. Not shot that night, anyhow.

EVENTS APRIL 21, 1942. ENTRY APRIL 22, 1942. N.L. Menkes has been freed. He is in bad condition. His hands. Berson looks twenty years younger; Menkes has said something to him. . . .

EVENTS APRIL 21, 1942. ENTRY APRIL 24, 1942. FROM PAVEL MENKES. I have this from Menkes:

As dawn of the fourth day suffused the tiny window-square, Menkes, sitting like a sack on the stone floor of Cell 19, leaning against the wall, reviewed what had happened to him during the previous three days, trying to understand it. There were seventeen prisoners in the former solitary-confinement cell; they were so crowded that not all could lie down at once. One of them was Felix Mandeltort! [NOTE. N.L. Menkes says that Felix keeps remarkably well, under the circumstances; his spirit is good, and indeed he sustained Menkes.] Menkes thought back over his three long daymares:

The registration at the Pawiak, the polite questions by the

somnolent registrar, as if Menkes were matriculating in some institution of higher learning, but his watch and the photograph of his mother taken away. . . . The long questioning next morning in the prison chapel—mostly about the bakers' systems of getting flour, and a repeated question as to whether he had contributed money to the underground. . . . The first trip to Gestapo headquarters on Aleja Szucha: Cubicle 5B2: the long wait with the terrible noises—screams, laughter, snoring in the next cubicle, a gramophone playing cheerfully down the hall; then the session of polite questions, astounding questions, personal questions, questions about friends, from which Pavel had the feeling he was learning more than the inquisitor did from his answers: a wonderful, unexpected luncheon of German Army food, with even a square of candy; then more questions—repeated questions—the first blows—the feather at the back of the throat bringing up the now-understood luncheon—repeated questions—repeated questions—then pain and dreadful pain and pain and repeated questions and pain. . . . And each evening, on return to Pawiak, Mandeltort, waiting:

—— *Nu*, Pavel?

—— I have nothing to tell them.

—— Good boy, Pavel.

And the other prisoners, giving pieces of their shirts for bandages; they were kind.

Some of the questions! Does Berson have contact with Slonim? What happened to Berson's police record in the *Judenrat* file? What are the sleeping arrangements in the Berson-Mazur-Apt apartment?

I don't know. I don't know. I don't know. I don't know. I don't know. I don't know. . . .

Later (it was still only about five in the morning) Menkes and Felix were talking together.

Menkes: —— What hurts me most of all is the feeling that Berson told the young Mazur boy to turn me in. From the kitchen, I couldn't hear what they were saying, but after the Mazur boy left, Berson seemed tightened up. My good friend, Berson. I cannot imagine such a thing, but there it is.

Mandeltort: —— I believe in Berson. (Felix's voice is rather thin and senescent, Menkes says.) You may be surprised to hear that I believe in anything. . . .

—— Why should I be?

—— After what I did.

—— You're not ashamed of what you did, you're ashamed because they caught you.

—— I believe in Berson. I don't know him very well, but Noach Levinson has told me a great deal about him, and I have seen him several times. I've had a strange feeling about him, all along. I've had a feeling that he is indestructible. He will outlast us all.

—— How can a man without a sense of humor be indestructible?

—— That's shrewd, Menkes. It's true, Berson would have a much easier time if he were quicker to understand the ironies and incongruities in people. But you are hard on him; he has *some* humor. The reason I think he is durable is that he is incorruptible. Without even realizing it. I know, he deals on the black market, he joined the Jewish police, he fixed bribes for Apt; and he worries absurdly about those things—he has a whole useless mechanism of conscience that hampers him just as much as lack of humor. But he is free of true corruption. Our life here in the ghetto is nothing but hard choices, and true corruption, in my opinion, comes when a man begins to base every choice on self-interest. Corruption isn't just episodic bribery, venality, smuggling, black-market deals. Corruption shows up in every choice.

—— Berson chose to turn me in. At least he sat there and let it happen.

—— You don't know what the alternative choice may have been. I think I can guess. . . . From what Levinson tells me, Berson's community used to consist of Berson and Froi Berson. It then grew to include you and Levinson and Slonim and Rachel Apt, and perhaps that teacher, whatever her name is. [NOTE. N.L. Regina Orlewska.] Then after they moved up from Sienna Street, his community became what he calls the "family," the Mazurs, the Apts, the Bersons, Levinson, the rabbi, plus you. That's where it stands now.

—— You mean, he weighed me against all of them?

—— Something like that, though choices are never that simple. He must have been thinking of the way the Germans force collective responsibility on us. . . . Most of us, in time of trouble, narrow our communities down—that's where I failed, I let my community shrink to family size, I even cut out Levinson—and then I got into this. Berson is widening his community. Levinson calls him a "drifter"—

—— I know. That's very just.

—— and everywhere Berson drifts he takes in something. I think his community will spread right out to the walls around us. And he'll outlast us all. He'll make a lot of mistakes: he's laughable in some ways. But in the choices . . .

—— I hope you're right. I hope you're right about why he turned me in. . . .

It was about six o'clock that morning when the awful clanking came at the cell door: the key in the lock: seventeen heads turning together. The Lithuanian guard put his head inside. He pronounced Menkes' name, in his thick speech shushing the s.

Menkes stood up, working his hurt hands up the wall behind him as he rose. Mandeltort scrambled up, too, and reaching upward to Menkes' big shoulder, said:

—— Remember.

Menkes, as if persuading himself: —— I'll be back at the usual time.

Menkes stepped carefully toward the door among the prostrate and sitting prisoners, steadying himself occasionally by reaching out to the wall with one arm. At the door he looked back at Mandeltort. The straight, grey man nodded. Menkes turned and followed the guard along the dark-doored block, down the metal stairs, on the familiar path to the truck for Aleja Szucha—but this time, in the downstairs block, the Lithuanian turned right instead of left, toward the Dzielna rather than the Pawia Street door of the prison. There he whispered to the German doorkeep, who unlocked the iron door and motioned Menkes out. There was no truck outside. There was no guard. Menkes stood waiting for some time uncomprehending. When realization came, he says, it seemed to strike him a bodily blow: he jumped and ran away.

He went directly to Berson's apartment. Berson was still in bed; Symka called him. Berson came out with a puffy face and touseled hair. Menkes says he saw Berson blanch and check his pace when he recognized his caller, especially when he got a look at Menkes' hands.

—— God, Pavel! What happened?

—— They let me go. I just wanted to tell you, I had a talk this morning with Mandeltort in the jail. I think he made me understand. I wanted to tell you, Dolek: I'm not angry. I just wanted to say: . . .

But Menkes fainted before he could speak any more.

THE WALL   PART III

1

Events May 26, 1942. Entry May 27, 1942. From Dolek Berson. Spring has come this year like a flight of small birds, on erratic separate wings, swiftly. Suddenly, on the upper floors of a number of apartments on the east side of the ghetto, it is possible to smell the drifting fragrance of the lilacs in the Saxon Garden, beyond the wall. The warmth of the sun, granted to us Jews in equal portion with Poles and Germans, raises our spirits.

Yesterday, says Berson, he walked along Karmelitzka to the tree. There is a linden tree on Karmelitzka Street—one of the few trees left in the whole ghetto—and in this quick spring, each of its heart-shaped leaves has been shaken out from a folded bud, like a lady's fan, it almost seems, in a single gesture of wind and branch. The yellowish flowers have a clean fragrance, less lush than the lilacs'. Many people come to this tree, simply to look at it and be near it: the soft, consoling season seems to be dressed in its brave green. An enterprising old man named Krimstyk has built a circular bench around the tree's trunk, and he charges two zlotys an hour to those who wish to sit under the lime shade. The bench is always full, from six in the morning until the very moment of curfew at night. Women come there to sew and gossip. Pious men come there to say prayers, so that the errant souls whispering in the branches, hiding from God, waiting for deliverance through the mediation of good Jews, will at last be set free.

Berson, to the ragged proprietor of the bench, holding out two zlotys: —— Well, Fraind Krimstyk, have you place for just one more?

Krimstyk: —— *Sholem aleichem*, Fraind Berson. Just three minutes, Fraind Berson. (Then, pushing his bearded face close up to Berson's, putting a reassuring hand on Berson's sleeve, and using the confidential tone reserved for old customers—for, in truth, Berson says he had begun to make a habit of sitting under the tree an hour each morning, and has watched the entire sudden

241

season there in the twigs overhead—the old man said:) I'll slip you in on the street side in just three minutes.

The street side is considered to be the best—the box seats for springtime are there: up through the pattern between the outer leaves one sees the endless, wall-less sky, and straight ahead, Jews in their warm-weather mood, the whole passing show of people suddenly more friendly and talkative than they were but a few short days ago, walking slowly now with their shabby coats unbuttoned and hope showing on their faces. You can see the window boxes across the way, with radish leaves already pushing up. Trundle-carts go by with all sorts of wares—though no one ever seems to buy: brown onions, muddy turnips, aromatic herring. The young girls pass in this year's ghetto fashion—the jackets without collars they call *French blazers*, full skirts, and home-made high heels of wood or cork. It is very pleasant on the street side.

Krimstyk has no watch. His measurement of the hours is considered to be fairly accurate, and is in any case law under the linden tree. When Berson had waited a very short time, Krimstyk went up to a grey-haired woman with a shawl over her head, sitting full in the center of the street side, and said:

—— Time's up!

The woman, looking up with flashing eyes: —— I just came. I've been here only a few minutes.

Krimstyk, shaking his beard as if it were very heavy: —— Sorry. Time goes *nebich* fast here.

The woman: —— It's an outrage. Two zlotys!

An elderly man, sitting on the bench next to the woman, speaking to no one in particular, but quite loudly: —— Oi, help! Some people always think they're being cheated.

Another bench-sitter, farther along: —— Some people are never satisfied.

The woman: —— And some people . . .

Standing up, she abruptly broke off her sentence, as if the people she had in mind were beyond the scope of her vocabulary. She spat in the open street and walked off with the haughtiness of a lady of means, to whom two zlotys were not worth the spittle she had deposited by the ragged old tree. Krimstyk motioned Berson to her seat.

The old man who had first spoken, shaking his head: —— No

wonder they put us in a ghetto. We should be ashamed to behave that way. She'd been here two hours, at least.

Berson, smiling: —— I don't blame her. It's nice here in the woods.

The old man grinned at Berson's hyperbole, and nodded.

Berson sat back and looked up at the heart-shaped leaves, which were barely stirring in the leisurely air. Somewhere on the street, or in an apartment beside it, a girl's voice was singing a haunting ghetto song: *I Believe in the Coming of the Messiah.* Two men on the bench were arguing about getting back to Nature. *Pfui, Palestine!* one of them said. *Too crowded already. I think I'll go to Australia: a whole continent to irrigate and plenty of land. And animals. Show me a jumper like the kangaroo in your Palestine.* The other man said scornfully: *So kangaroos can jump! Is it to watch jumping that you want an end to the war?* A vender shouted praise of the rags he was selling as if they were rare textiles from Kashmir, Shanghai, Edinburgh. There was laughter under the tree and in the street.

A group of students walked by in the street, carrying satchels and boxes. Berson saw Rachel Apt among them, and he shouted: —— Rochele, Rochele! Where are you going? [NOTE. N.L. So far as I can remember, this is the first time I have heard Berson use the diminutive for Rachel.]

Rachel broke away from the group and ran to the tree. Her wide cheeks, tapering away with such disastrous haste to her reticent little chin, were flushed.

—— We're going to decorate a "children's corner." Come along with us! Come, Dolek!

For a moment Berson resisted the idea of breaking his contemplative hour, but Rachel's excitement eventually reached him. He stood up and called to the landlord of the bench: —— I'm leaving, Fraind Krimstyk.

The old man who had been sitting next to Berson: —— Hey, Krimstyk! Here's our young man leaving. For one person, two hours aren't worth two zlotys, another throws time away. Huh, Krimstyk?

Krimstyk, waving off the portion of this remark that seemed to characterize Berson as a wastrel: —— Don't worry. I've seen him stay overtime, too.

Rachel and Berson hurried to catch up with the students. As they half-ran:

Rachel: —— What were you doing on the old people's bench, anyway?

The old people's bench. Berson says he looked back. Why, it was true! All those pleasant, unhurried, leaf-loving people were white- or grey-haired. Berson wondered: What *had* he been doing in such company? Did he belong there? It had been so comfortable passing the springtime there, but—

The two had caught up to the students now. These young people walked rapidly, swinging their arms high. Their eyes were bright; they joked with each other. This was a class from the *Judenrat* School of Design, Rachel told Berson; and in addition a number of Hashomer girls who had been recruited through a "mother" at the Rukner Home. Rachel took Berson up to the leader of the group, a teacher. The teacher, an effeminate, middle-aged man, greeted Berson with an appropriate courtesy, then asked politely:

—— Are you interested in young people, Pan Berson?

Berson thought that one over: Interested in young people! Suddenly Berson wondered, he says, what his age really was. Had this last winter cut seams into his face? Had frost caught in his hair? Did he belong on the bench under the tree? For a few days —while Menkes had been in jail—he had felt old, he remembered that: his joints had been stiff, he had had premonitions of death, so remorseful had he been. Then Menkes had come out of jail almost apologizing to him, actually almost grateful. And since then spring had come quickly, and Berson had felt ageless.

Rachel, answering in his stead, since he seemed to be hesitating: —— Of course he is! He's one himself.

Berson says he thanked Rachel for that reply.

The group went to an open place, where a house had been bombed out, on Krochmalna Street. Already the gap had been transformed into a playground. Members of TOPORAL had planted some feeble greenery in marked-off borders and plots, and workmen for CENTOS had built swings, seesaws, dirt-boxes, and a kind of maypole with ropes. Now the students attacked the walls of the buildings on the three sides of the "corner": they cleaned off the bricks with stiff brushes and then, working from a design they had brought with them, they painted a parade of garish and

comical animals around the walls. Berson and Rachel were put to
work with others painting the seesaws and swings with a cheap
grey paint the *Judenrat* had procured from the Germans. Berson
says the seesaws conjured up a very specific image in his mind, for
the first snapshot he had ever seen of himself had been taken on
the Tarbuth school playground—a pudgy eight-year-old boy, leaning on a seesaw in an elaborately casual pose, with a fake-modest
smirk on his face: the picture had been given him in later years,
and had shocked him a little, for this was as others had seen him,
not as he had seen himself in careful restraint in a mirror, and this
picture was of a smug, fat, spoiled boy. Berson says he now swung
his paintbrush angrily, mortified by that memory, but soon, absorbed in the work, listening to the inconsequential chatter of the
students, he felt forgetful and free. Rachel was gay as she worked,
and she sang, not quite having mastered the tune:

> Buy some cigarets!
> Buy some saccharine!
> Everything is cheaper today.
> Life only costs one groszy, one coin,
> Life only costs a groszy.

Interested in young people? As he worked in the sunlight,
Berson felt something like strength flowing through his arms. Of
course he is! He's one himself!

EVENTS JUNE 4, 1942. ENTRY JUNE 5, 1942. FROM DOLEK
BERSON. The question of his real age, not reckoned in years since
his birth, but calculated in state of mind, has stayed with Berson
ever since Rachel teased him about sitting under "the old people's
tree." He says he has spent much of his time with people younger
than himself, trying clumsily to be their age, not his own. Yesterday morning, it being Sunday, he sat with a group of them on the
"beach" on the roof at Chlodna 20. Lolling under the hot sun on
folding chairs in swimming trunks (*Bathing Suits Mandatory*, the
sign downstairs from the "beach" says), the young people gossiped,
speaking with equal interest of the opening of a new play at the
Femina, and of the marriage of the son of the commandant of the
ghetto police, and of a meeting of the literary club the next evening at which, it was said, ghetto love poems would be read. Ber-

son pretended, with lively questions and exclamations, to be interested in all this, and he was pleased to be accepted naturally by the group.

Halinka, at one point: —— Dolek, be a sweetheart and get me a limeade.

Berson: —— Delighted. (And he was, he says—who had a better right to try to be a sweetheart?) Any other orders?

—— I'd love one.

—— Thanks, Dolek.

—— Please.

On the way to the "bar," in the pentshed at one end of the roof, to get the drinks, Berson thought of Symka. He had tried to persuade her to come to the "beach," arguing that the sun would be good for her, but she had protested, half-jokingly, that she couldn't sit around with the golden youth in nothing but her bones. Berson says he remembered the first time he had ever seen Symka in a bathing suit: at the Baltic, on a beach near Riga, on a vacation trip long before their marriage—she had been there with a party of students; he had been alone, in the same hotel in the same town by "coincidence," for that had been at the beginning of his love for Symka, when he had been following her everywhere. She had certainly been one of the golden youth then, with her glistening skin and her musical laugh. And he remembered now how his breath had been taken away the first time he had seen her in her bathing suit on the rocks at the seaside. The memory—and its corollary of contrast—made Berson feel out of sorts. But when he went out on the bright roof again, and into the cordial sunlight and laughter, he forgot his melancholy. He passed the drinks, stepping carefully over the girls' legs and balancing with pursed lips the cheap glasses, anxious not to spill a drop.

Stefan Mazur: —— We're playing a game, Berson!

And the handsome boy explained the pastime—a guessing game involving the initials of famous people and questions about them. Apparently Rachel was outstanding in the game, quicker than any of the men and quicker, too, than Regina, from whom, as a teacher, everyone expected universal knowledge. Berson says he was bemused by the warmth of the day and by the undertone of sensuousness in the young people's byplay. He decided, on the basis of the slightest telegraphy between their eyes, that Stefan

and Halinka were in love. He found this, he says, mildly annoying.
[NOTE. N.L. Halinka is an *annoying* girl.]

Suddenly—Rachel was *It* again; her character was a philosopher of the eighteenth century, beginning with *H*— suddenly the
"bartender," a young man actually wearing a white coat, to fit
into the pretense of seaside luxury, came out onto the "beach"
clearing his throat ostentatiously, as if to convey some sort of
warning. Not far behind him walked a half-dozen German soldiers
—two officers and four enlisted men. In the moment of seeing
them, Berson says, he realized how much he had forgotten, how
far he had abandoned himself—ever since Menkes' release—to the
mood of springtime and forgetfulness. Halinka gave a squeal and
drew a towel up over her bosom, as if it might have invited this
whole brutishly uniformed squad to violate her. Berson saw Rachel
begin to tremble.

One of the officers, rubbing his hands: —— Splendid! Splendid! (Turning to one of the enlisted men:) Have them bring the
things up.

The enlisted man turned and hurried inside and downstairs.

Stefan, who knows all the German insignia, muttering in self-
consciously casual Yiddish: —— Signal troops. Something new.

The major who had given the order, coming forward smiling
to the group of sunbathers: —— This is marvelous. No! No! (This
to two or three who jumped to their feet, and to others who sat
up straight, waving them down:) As you were! Please! Don't be
nervous. It was marvelous just as you were. (Those who had stood
settled down uneasily. Sounds of climbing, and of the portage of
heavy objects, could be heard from the stairwell.) Please relax,
and stay just as you are. (Moving off to one side, the major beckoned to his companion, a captain.) Marburger, see here! (The
major sighted the group through a sort of frame that he made
with his thumbs, horizontal, and forefingers, perpendicular.) An
ironic touch, Marburger! That extensive panorama of the Aryan
city beyond, and especially the church towers. This is wonder-
beautiful! Just what we needed.

A group of ragged Jews emerged now from the pentshed. The
first few of them were carrying round metal containers and a heavy,
metal tripod. Then came four carrying a large motion-picture camera. The German enlisted men quickly mounted the camera on

247

the tripod, loaded a roll of film, and moved the camera to the place where the major had stood making his finger-frame. The major, meanwhile, was saying to the people in their bathing suits:

—— I want you to be perfectly natural, just as you were before we came up. What was in those glasses? Here! Waiter! (He snapped his fingers at the Jew in the white coat.) Fill the glasses! Be ready to pass them when I give you the signal. Excuse me, young lady (and he bent down over Rachel), please loosen your shoulderstraps, you know . . . as much sun as possible. And here, a handsome young man, I need a young man! You, please. (He beckoned with a finger to Berson.) Please sit in this deckchair, facing the camera. Good! Now! A pretty girl. If you please (indicating Halinka), would you kindly sit on the gentleman's lap? That's right, an arm around the shoulders. Spendid. Splendid.

Berson admits to me that he felt Halinka's warm black bathing suit against his bare chest and her bare arm around his bare shoulders as an unsettling surprise. Out of evident fear, she hugged him tightly and squirmed in his lap. He says he blushed. He did not know what to do with his left hand. At last he put it, as casually as he could, on Halinka's waist. He could feel the reverberations of her heart.

The major: —— Excellent. Excellent. All right, Marburger. Roll! (The steady whirring of the camera began.) Now talk to each other, my friends. Be natural. Smile. Very good. That's fine. Be natural. . . .

Regina, in Yiddish, smiling mechanically: —— What do we say? What do we say to this?

One of the other girls: —— At least it's not what I expected. I was terrified when the pigs first came out.

The major: —— Excellent. Very good. Eh, Marburger?

Stefan, without malice: —— And you, Berson. Are you having a good time?

Halinka, squeezing Berson's shoulders playfully: —— Are you, are you?

Berson nodded and grinned dumbly.

The major: —— Oh, very good. (Then he snapped his fingers.) Now, waiter, the refreshments!

The bartender, with a terrified expression, passed the drinks. The camera whirred and whirred. Halinka hugged Berson tight. Berson's flesh crawled with desire, embarrassment, horror. He looked at Rachel, and saw that she had ignored the major's invitation to loosen her shoulderstraps. She sat stiffly with her arms folded over her bosom. And on her face, directed at Berson, was a blazing look of hatred and contempt.

2

EVENTS JUNE 5, 1942. ENTRY DITTO. N.L. A crowd of nearly a hundred people was jammed into the apartment of one of the officers of the literary club—a fairly large apartment, fortunately, on Chlodna Street. I arrived late (indeed I did!); I understand that a few love poems had been read, as I have noted that the young gossips on the "beach" had advertised they would be: among others, Mordecai Apt had recited one of his, apparently a simple, lyrical, conventional statement that was fairly well received. I am told that everyone had had a good laugh over the satirical *Who Says You Can Love Only in Palaces?* Evidently the people had enjoyed the slight and sentimental verses they had heard, but they also had seemed to want something more serious, something they could get their teeth into. Finally our host, Minton, a tall, thin man, read some Kacenelenson (this was shortly after my arrival on the scene), and next I was called upon, and I recited *Campo di Fiori*, by Czeslaw Milosz.

Berson says that I looked as stiff as a broom before the audience, with my arms pushed down straight into my coat pockets, my neck too small for my collar, my thick lenses seeming to put all of me behind glass. He says I was evidently nervous, that I even looked frightened [NOTE. N.L. *Looked* frightened!], but that the trembling of my voice enriched what I said. Berson was kind enough to say that I was like some inspired cantor dealing with the most moving of liturgies:

> *In Rome, on Campo di Fiori,*
> *Baskets of olives and lemons:*
> *The pavement dewy with red wine*
> *And flaked with petals of flowers:*
> *The pink fruit of the seas*

Flung by venders on counters:
Bunches of grapes—how many?—
Couched on the softness of peaches.
Here on this very square
They burned Giordano Bruno.
The torchman set fire to the faggots
In front of the crowd of the curious.
And before the flames had died down,
Tosspots returned to the taverns.
Baskets of olives and lemons! . . .

and the slow, devastating, roundabout course of the poem brought it gradually to its sections about Warsaw, about the ghetto, about that very room and those very people. Baskets of olives and lemons! The ironic images drove home, and soon many were weeping. I finished the poem, and no one clapped. Here and there noses were blown, and two or three figures swayed silently back and forth, like mourners.

[FROM DOLEK BERSON.] Berson says the poem filled him with a feeling he had not had much lately—a feeling of immense pride. He was proud of the man who wrote the bitter-sweet lines; he was proud of the Jewish martyrs they celebrated; he was proud of the living Jews, pressed around him in the room and in the ghetto, whom the verses also implicitly honored. The offense of these people was existing: they stood guilty of the crime of being alive. How could they be so humble, so patient, so oblivious, so full of humor, so forgiving, so tenacious?—in the face of their now obvious and implacable fate, how could they be so tenacious?

The people around Berson were jostling him: the meeting was breaking up. He shuffled about in a kind of daze at first, he says, and then began looking for friends. He saw Rutka, Mordecai, and Rachel, not far off, moving toward the door; the girls were congratulating Mordecai. Berson hurried and pushed and came up behind Rachel. He put a salutatory hand on her shoulder. She looked around, and when she saw who it was, her homely little face grew even uglier—she gave him the same look of contempt and distaste he had seen on the "beach" during the filming.

Rachel: —— I could have killed you yesterday morning, when they were taking that movie: smirking and squeezing Halinka that way! Don't you know that they're going to show that picture all over Germany: *This is the luxury the Jews live in—this is the way they cavort . . . ?*

Berson says he told himself: I am not as young as I thought I was. I am not as young and fiery as this girl.

Berson, ignoring the attack altogether: —— Wasn't Noach superb?

Rachel, wholly altered, suddenly gentle: —— Yes, he has great dignity.

[NOTE. N.L. Berson was kind to report this exchange, just as he was unkind to report that I had looked *like a broom*.]

EVENTS JUNE 5, 1942. ENTRY JUNE 6, 1942. N.L. They said that my reading of those florid lines was affecting, and I think it must have been. I can write these words in all modesty, for it was not so much my talent as my terror that made the recital of *Campo di Fiori* moving, if it was. Here is what had happened:

On the way to the literary club meeting, which was to be held in Minton's apartment in Chlodna, I was walking alone up Zelazna Street, on the east side of the street, mumbling over to myself the words of a poem by Tuwim, which, at that time, I intended to recite at the meeting: I always become very nervous over any public appearance, and I was certain that I would suffer a sudden amnesiac attack in the midst of my turn: even worse, I was terrified lest I might drop a line from my reading *and not notice the loss*, with the result that my recital would make absolutely no sense. I was walking along, therefore, totally engrossed, very likely with my lips moving around the words of the poem, when suddenly I heard a stinging, soft-edged sound of something flying down the street, and immediately afterward the clap of the engine from which this something originated: it had been a bullet, I concluded: the revolver or rifle or machine pistol or whatever-it-was from which the bullet came must have been several blocks to the northward, in the direction toward which I was walking, and the missile must have traveled right down the center of the street-valley. I had scarcely had time to register the sounds I had heard, much less carry out the retrospective analysis I have just set down, when I found myself alone in the street: every other pedestrian had dodged, with a musteline swiftness, into the recess of a shop entry. Then a part of a pilaster on the building on my left, about eight feet above my

251

head, perhaps less, seemed to explode, and afterward I heard the erratic, fluttering whine of a ricochet. By now poetry had vanished from my mind, and my deductive processes had been stimulated to an extraordinary degree (Oi, misery, I wish I could think quickly all the time!), and I knew at once that I, as the only available target in the open street, had been very personally shot at. I jumped into a doorway. I then heard two shots up the street, followed by a piercing scream (I think a woman's, though somehow at death sex goes out of a voice); a pause; one more shot, much nearer, preceded by and almost covered by a scream of anticipatory and then realized terror; footsteps running—and then I saw a young German soldier hurrying down the middle of the street: he paused a few paces south of my recess, turned left, raised an automatic pistol and fired a single shot into the group of seven or eight huddled into one rather large shop entranceway. One of the men there, silently, with an amazingly understated expression on his face, as if he had merely been taken with a slight pressure of gas on the stomach, folded his hands over that part, and then fell down, I suppose dead or dying. The soldier, meanwhile—he was a very young boy, with a face of such cliché freshness that when I came to recite the poem, later, and reached the phrase *softness of peaches*, I thought of him, fearfully, and stumbled slightly in my declamation—took from his pocket a paper-backed notebook, wrote something down, placed the pistol he had been using in a holster, took another out from another holster, and ran on. Apparently he turned a corner, for the next shot was quite a bit later and greatly muffled. All of the people in the doorways on Zelazna were willing, evidently, to postpone whatever business they were doing for quite a long time, until it seemed certain that the young man's course would not double back on Zelazna. Then, as if at a signal, all began moving again at the same time, with a slightly quickened pace.

When I reached Minton's apartment, the meeting had already begun. I certainly was not going to spoil it by announcing what had just happened. But I did decide to change my plans and recite *Campo di Fiore*, instead of the Tuwim. I had just read *Campo di Fiore* the day before, in an underground pamphlet which had been given me for the files, and although I am not usually interested in such inflammatory, swollen poems, this one for some reason interested me, and I read it over several times. I had made no conscious effort to memorize it, but now—and if there

was anything truly remarkable about my recitation, this was it—
every word of it came back to me; the page was before me. . . .

EVENTS EARLY JUNE. ENTRY JUNE 11, 1942. N.L. . . . and
since that day, the young man has been at his work (or play:
there was something sporting about that notation in the little
book: a scoring) almost every day. And each day he varies his performance: today he counts loudly, and shoots every eighteenth
Jew he sees, tomorrow he is interested only in shooting women,
and so on. He is said to be very tender with children; he has told
some that he has five children of his own. These daily exercises
have put a definite end to the pronounced ease and complacency
that had prevailed in the ghetto ever since the so-called manhunt
in April. This performance, though solo, better fulfills the sense of
that word: manhunt. The young hunter is popularly called Frankenstein: the common confusion between the student of the Shelley
novel and the monster that the student created; but from what I
saw of this youngster, he hardly fits the label:

> Bunches of grapes—how many?—
> Couched on softness of peaches. . . .

3

EVENTS JULY 9, 1942. ENTRY JULY 10, 1942. N.L. Last
evening after soup, Rabbi Goldflamm said:
—— I must tell you, my dear "family," that I have made up
my mind to something.
It was still light: Froi Mazur had just cleared away the bowls.
Everyone listened, because the rabbi spoke portentously, and there
was a suggestion of moisture in his eyes. He said:
—— I have decided to bury my Torah in the cemetery. One
moment, if you please. . . .
And he stood up and went into the room where he kept his
things and came back carrying his beloved Torah: a parchment
scroll, about eighteen inches high, wound around two exquisitely
carved ivory handles, with the Five Books handwritten in a firm,

clear Hebrew script and illuminated at the chapter endings with dainty, cabalistic symbols. He sat down again. Rolling the scroll and watching abstractedly the procession of sacred words, he said:

—— Mind you, it is not that I feel that this Torah is dead. It will never die. It is simply that I want to give it a dignified residence among Jews who are going to stay put. I wouldn't like to have any accidents happening to this Torah of mine. If anything happened to me . . . (The rabbi pulled out a handkerchief and blew his nose. Reb Yechiel and Froi Mazur were both crying silently. Most of us younger people kept our eyes fixed on the floor.) If anything happened to me, who would watch out for it?

Rachel, gently: —— Nothing is going to happen to you, Rebbe.

The rabbi nodded with his eyes closed, as if agreeing not with Rachel, but with an unspoken thought in everyone's mind.

—— Yes (opening his eyes, which were dry now), I know, you have always thought me a talkative old fool, running around with the rumors. And I don't blame you. I love news. I suppose I like the idea that I know more than anyone else. Who doesn't? (He broke off for a moment, stopped rolling the handles of the Torah, and read out loud, mumbling, a few words from Leviticus. Then he said:) The scribe who copied this Torah had a good hand. . . . Rumors! Ai, I know how many ridiculous pieces of "authentic information" I have passed along to all of you, and to others. Sometimes I am ashamed. Sometimes I just laugh at myself. But, you see, I have become a kind of scholar of rumors. Eliazar Goldflamm, Doctor of Idle Talk. I think I know more about rumors than most of you. I understand them. They are like old friends. And that is the point: now, in the last few days, the texture of the rumors has somehow changed. It seems to me that even the crows that circle around over the ghetto understand that: have you heard them lately? Their cries are not such buffoonery as before. They are serious, they are trying to raise an alarm. You listen to them: *Caw! Caw! Caw!*

The rabbi threw back his head and gave out these crow-screams with an almost frighteningly realistic mimicry—and indeed, the sounds as he imitated them did contain some kind of awful hint, a black-winged warning.

—— All right (in his natural voice), so we hear that Herr

Himmler came to pay us a quiet visit last week, *nu*, so what? We heard that he visited us last February. Same rumor. But a different feeling to the goods now. . . . (The rabbi rubbed a thumb and forefinger together, like a tailor trying a cloth.) All right, so we hear about the factory for making soap out of Jews in Lublin, we laugh and say, "I'll be washing you!"—*Nu*, so what, there were supposed to be sausage plants with Jewish meat in Tarnopol in March. Same kind of foolishness. But I don't know, somehow—

The rabbi completed his idea simply by rubbing his thumb and forefinger again.

[NOTE. N.L. The tangible, verifiable happenings, which had changed the texture of every rumor, Rabbi Goldflamm left unmentioned, evidently taking for granted that they would be in all our minds: the arrival in the ghetto of my friend Frankenstein, the hundred and ten prisoners shot the other day in the Gensia Street Jail for minor offenses, the random raids in apartments and irresponsible shootings on those raids, the abductions for forced labor and sudden roundups in the street, the Polish petty criminals brought into the ghetto and shot and left dead.]

Goldflamm: —— So. . . . I am an old loose-tongue, Doctor of Idle Talk. Well (and now tears returned to the rabbi's eyes), *nu*, I have decided to bury my Torah. Will you help me, Dolek, with the arrangements?

Berson: —— What I can.

—— Will you help me, Noach?

N.L.: —— Of course.

EVENTS JULY, 1942. ENTRY JULY 12, 1942. N.L. I have changed somewhat my opinion of Rabbi Goldflamm. Up to a few weeks ago, I thought him a pompous fool. His whole elastic body seemed only to be a vehicle for his *very* elastic tongue. But I now see that he has a definite integrity and backbone, and in a quiet way he has braced us all. When most of the religious Jews shaved their beards off, when Reb Yechiel Mazur, among others, came out in his bare face, the rabbi refused to surrender, and he still wears a fine, curly, black beard. I remember that the day Schpunt volunteered himself as rabbi of the congregation in Sapir's Hat and Gloves and was made to do that dance, I thought that Goldflamm's failure to put himself forward was cowardice. I now think I was wrong. It was inflexibility: his determination to have no traffic whatsoever with Germans. In almost three years, I think Rabbi Goldflamm has not once spoken to a German. He is a chatterbox; but I think he is stronger than he seems.

EVENTS JULY 15, 1942. ENTRY DITTO. N.L. This day broke grey and dank: Warsaw had put on its iron hat. We set out just at dawn.

Berson had discovered that the only way to get into the cemetery, since the recent stringent prohibition against funerals, was to pose as Rotblat employees, obtain fake working papers from the funeral establishment, and push handcarts of street-corpses through to one of the mass graves. The rabbi was so determined to go on with the burial of his Torah that he agreed to this procedure. Berson and I between us arranged the papers, and it was agreed that we would do the work today. It was on this errand that we walked out in the first mournful light of day.

At the Rotblat offices, we were received by a superintendent, who gave us the black brassards and black-banded black hats of the Burial Society, and who told us that the convoy would start in about fifteen or twenty minutes: the carts were being loaded out back, he said, *if we cared to help.* This conditional clause, as uttered by the superintendent, was clearly a suggestion, verging on command—the price of our false papers would be a little early-morning labor.

The superintendent led us three amateurs along a corridor and out a door into a death-smelling courtyard backed by a tall, wooden fence. In the center of the courtyard, in the dim first light of day, we could see a pile of naked bodies. We were led close to the pile, which was about three meters high and five or six meters across. The bodies were entangled with each other, like huge maggots suddenly stilled at their work of cleaning the putrescence from some great earth-wound. Men, women, children: every age, it seemed, except the age of beauty, whenever that might be. Limbs, mops of hair, an isolated hand emerging in a seeming gesture of entreaty, male and female privacies in casual proximity, eyes staring, one man's hand accidentally cupped behind another man's ear in a strange, posthumous, co-operative effort to catch some mysterious whisper. Berson told me afterward that he was reminded of a drawing by William Blake he had seen at Bonn, of goyish "condemned souls" on their way to the Christian Gehenna

256

—except that these bodies in the courtyard did not have the over-bearing muscularity of Blake's nudes: these were but poor Jewish souls, with their ribs and hip bones protruding.

Along the fenced side of the courtyard were ranged, three deep, about thirty pushcarts, and twice as many men were lifting corpses from the pile and loading them onto the carts. To this work we three applied ourselves. The corpses were surprisingly free of smell: they were evidently a fresh crop, gathered from the streets just last night. . . . Typhus, tuberculosis, hunger cachexy. I remembered the expression on Berson's face the day young Schlome Mazur's coffin got stuck aslant in the grave; now his face showed nothing at all as he walked across the courtyard carrying corpses. [INSERT. FROM ENTRY JULY 17, 1942. FROM DOLEK BERSON. Questioned Berson about his feelings in the Rotblat courtyard the other morning. He said he was quite unmoved by either the sight of, or contact with, the bodies there. They were the abstraction, Death, with which he is now quite familiar. The abstraction does not touch him: he says he even feels that he is somehow protected from It. Those bodies were disgusting pieces of luggage, some heavy and difficult to manage, others very light and a relative pleasure to carry—that was all.] Similarly, I saw by Rabbi Gold-flamm's face that even that tenderhearted man has become insu-lated from any feeling about dead bodies. The rabbi worked with an evident impatience: he had something important to do.

Finally the procession of handcarts started out. There were a few coffins on carts at the rear—the wealthy dead. The superin-tendent, in what he evidently considered a gesture of mercy, as-signed the rabbi, Berson, and me to a single pushcart of quicklime that was also to go to the cemetery. At the ghetto gate through to the burial ground, the whole convoy stopped, and a German gen-darme and a Navy-blue came down the line checking passes hur-riedly: *their* faces, I noticed, and their haste in the inspection of papers, showed that they were deeply disturbed by the cold crowd of passengers on these carts. How they disliked the job of raising the unfastened coffin-lids and poking inside with bayonets to make sure that no live Jews were being smuggled out! I think that we three felt superior to these queasy brutalizers; I, at any rate, felt that our fiber had grown tough—and I felt confidence in the rabbi and in Berson, and a common strength shared with all the shabby men pushing these carts. They, these Jewish workmen, were indifferent to the Abstraction: in fact, it seemed to me that they were only one step from being immortal.

The line of pushcarts moved again. It threaded its way through the cemetery to a huge, continuous ditch-grave, partly filled and still being extended, about two meters wide and three deep, into which the Rotblat men began to unload the bodies. There was no German or Polish supervision. Rabbi Goldflamm borrowed a spade from one of the Rotblat men and the three of us went off to look for Schlome Mazur's grave. We found the general section where the delicate Yeshiva student lies, but, there being no headstone, we were not sure which was the boy's exact mound.

Goldflamm: —— It's too bad Yechiel didn't come. He would have known. . . . Let's not tell him we couldn't find it.

Rabbi Goldflamm picked a suitable place—where two mounds were so close together that a new grave could not be put between them; and he dug a hole about a foot deep and with a short prayer buried, for safekeeping till eternity, the Book of the Law.

4

EVENTS JULY 17, 1942. ENTRY JULY 18, 1942. N.L. Berson moves slowly, but at least he does not stand still, he moves. Or, is moved. Is pushed, by friends and circumstances. Now he is about to enlist in the underground; thus one can say that he has drifted very far from the positions he used to take on resisting the Germans. [E.G., ENTRIES NOVEMBER 9, 1939, AUGUST 16, 1940.] Again I call his motion drifting. I begin to wonder whether this is just, since his motion, at least in this important matter of resistance, has been in a fairly straight line. Menkes, with much more opportunity to go in the same direction, has stood still. And yet Berson certainly did not take the initiative in this latest step. He was pushed. . . .

EVENTS JULY 6, 1942. ENTRY JULY 18, 1942. FROM RUTKA MAZUR. Zilberzweig called together the Hashomer Hatsair "circle" to which Rutka and Rachel both belong—they are secretive about the size and membership of the group—to discuss drawing in new members. This was the day before yesterday, July 16. The circle discussed Menkes (who has since turned down its invitation to join) and Mordecai Apt (who, as Rutka's husband, could not very well turn the invitation down). Then Rachel proposed Dolek Berson.

Rutka: —— Rachel, you're as inconstant as the weather! I thought you despised Berson. You said, just the other day, after that moving-picture affair, that you thought he was "stupid and insensitive and a rotten Jew." Those were your words, I remember.

Rachel: —— Perhaps I was wrong.

Zilberzweig: —— But doesn't this Berson work at the *Judenrat?*

Rachel: —— He is in the *Judenrat* but he is not part of it.

[NOTE. N.L. This was an interesting distinction on Rachel's part—and I hope she would say the same of me. No longer can one blind oneself to the fact that working for the *Judenrat* is opprobrious. It is considered equivalent to working for the Germans. We in the *Judenrat* have become very unpopular.

I have evolved a comfortable set of excuses for myself here in the *Judenrat.* I believe that tending the *Judenrat* archive and keeping these notes of my own can be considered valid work. Why should I care what people think of me?

Berson, now, is different. Reputation is rather important to him—though he would never admit it; he covers up his concern about it by discussions about whether various things the *Judenrat* does are abstractly right or wrong. On a day when he wants to justify his working for the *Judenrat,* he praises the work of TOZ, the medical society, or CENTOS, the children's agency; on another day, when he feels rather guilty, he lashes out at this or that official who is, he says, nothing but a German tool. I remember his talking about the *Judenrat* budgets one day, and it was as if he were carrying on a bitter debate with himself (as indeed I believe he inwardly was): How could one justify the expenditure of 415,000 zlotys on the construction of the ghetto wall? And yet, was it not a matter of pride that 250,000 zlotys a month were going to the hospitals and various sanitary projects? For shame!—to spend 2,800,000 zlotys on labor battalions working for the Germans! Taxes on eating! Taxes on receiving letters! Taxes on being put six feet under the ground when dead! And yet, in six months, expenditures of 24,541,800 zlotys for many good causes, against receipts of only 16,979,000 zlotys. Yes, there had to be taxes.

Thus, though only a clerk and practically invisible in our bureaucracy, Berson has reflected the dilemmas of authority seen in the bigger men here in the *Judenrat*. Selfish ends *versus* the public good. Seductions (and subsequent disappointments) of power. The demeaning, and at the very same time the ennobling, effects of minor authority. I have seen Berson, in his unimportant ways, fighting out these conflicts within himself: his application directly to Sokolczyk to be removed from the Taxation and Revenue Department; his wanderings, then, through Supply, Vital Statistics, Auditing, Housing, and finally to Health and Social Welfare; his clashes with superiors, particularly with Fostel of Taxation and Revenue; his insufferable but fortunately temporary grand manner during the period when he was dispensing Joint Distribution Committee funds in Health and Social Welfare. At every step of the way, I have seen him trying to persuade himself that what he was doing was for the Jews. He has not had an easy time of it, and his rationalizations grow more and more complicated, more and more forced.]

Rutka says that the discussion of Berson by the Hashomer circle lasted quite some time. Rachel became testy and sharp in his defense. Finally Zilberzweig asked Rutka what she thought.

Rutka: —— I have nothing against Berson. I only thought Rachel did.

And so it was decided that Berson should be invited.

EVENTS JULY 16, 1942. ENTRY DITTO. FROM DOLEK BERSON. This morning Symka Berson, while attempting to dust the living room—actually, Froi Mazur has been having to dust up after Symka for some time now, so feeble has Symka been—called in a pinched voice for Dolek, who was of course at work, and fainted. Froi Mazur put her to bed. Symka seemed to be all right later in the day, and she insisted upon getting up and dressing herself in time for Dolek's return from the *Judenrat*. She fainted again, however, just before supper, and this time she remained unconscious for quite a long time, putting forth an extremely weak pulse. Berson decided to take her to the hospital. Reb Yechiel Mazur has a pushcart, belonging to the courtyard, in his janitor's shop, and Berson carried Symka downstairs and, putting her in the pushcart on some pillows arranged by Rachel, he trundled her out the courtyard gate and along the street—oppressed all the way, he tells me, by the fresh remembrance of his last connection with push-carts, the day we buried the Torah. At the hospital, which is now on Stawki Street, Berson, after tipping the hospital gateman to keep an eye on the pillows in the pushcart, picked up Symka and carried her inside to the receiving desk, where, holding his wife in his arms, he asked for Dr. Breithorn. He was told to wait, and he sat on a bench, still holding Symka as if she were a hurt child: she looked up at him with wide eyes in which a lambent light played, at odds with the sickly pallor of her cheeks. Dr. Breithorn came out in a few minutes, and agreed, after some argument, to accept Symka for observation, even though the hospital was severely over-crowded.

Breithorn: —— It means that some nameless patient loses a bed. That's the way it happens—the names replace the nameless.

In spite of the tip, the pillows were gone from the pushcart when Berson emerged from the hospital.

EVENTS JULY 17, 1942. ENTRY JULY 18, 1942. N.L. I say Berson was "pushed." Well, Rutka and Rachel talked to him about Hashomer yesterday—the day after Symka's collapse. He decided to join, and is there any wonder? How much can a man take before he grows angry? Yes, anger was what Berson lacked before. It is terrible to see a kindly man inflamed.

5

EVENTS JULY 21–23, 1942. ENTRY JULY 23, 1942. N.L. I participated in the entire event. I have come directly from Sokol-czyk's office. They are removing the Chairman's body now. My head swims, and I feel too confused to write a coherent account of what has taken place, but I must try. The time element: I have the feelings of a man who has just learned that he has cancer—only, somehow, *everybody* has this sickness, we all suffer from a contagion that operates far more quickly than mere cancer. How can I write a factual summary of such occurrences? And yet it is my duty. I am supposed to be the Archivist. Up till now all the things that I have written in this notebook—in all the dozens of fillers I have stored away in my safe—have been the slightest kind of personal, diaristic notes for some polite Jewish history I intended in a quiet year to write. Now there will be no time for thought and comment: now only the febrile, hand-tremorous act of recording. To begin, then:

Day before yesterday, July 21, 1942, at 11 a.m., four *Sicherheitsdienst* cars and a truck drove up in front of the Community Building, and altogether eighteen *S.D.* and *S.S.* personnel came clattering into the building. Three of these Germans, officers, walked straight into Chairman Sokolczyk's office, without knocking, and commanded him to call a meeting of the *Judenrat* at once. Luckily for the remainder, only eleven of the twenty-four members of the Council were present in the building. The *S.S.* men, with no explanation whatsoever, and without waiting for other councilors to be summoned, herded those who were on hand into the truck and drove them to the Pawiak. I was not among those arrested. I had gone into the conference room to record the minutes of the meeting that was supposed to take place, and when the presiding *S.S.* officer announced the arrest of all Council members present, he made certain, with his Germanic attention to minor detail, that a check be made of all present, to see whether each man was actually a councilor: I was thus excluded. Chairman Sokolczyk was also told to stay in his office. During the afternoon, while the arrested members of the *Judenrat* sat locked up in the Pawiak, flying squads of German police—evidently men from the so-called *Einsatz Reinhardt*, of which we have heard so many rumors—ranged through the ghetto and in random fashion entered apartments, looked for relatively well-dressed Jews, shot some without discussion, and hurried away. I estimate that between seventy-five and a hundred upper-class Jews were killed in this way. Late in the afternoon, again without explanation, the Germans released the arrested *Judenrat* officers and sent them home.

That day was T'isha B'Ab. [NOTE. EDITOR. The Jewish holiday commemorating the destruction of the Temple in Jerusalem.]

Early yesterday morning a number of us were gathered in the *Judenrat* building discussing the happenings of the day before: we noted that whereas everything that had occurred in the ghetto previously had had a kind of logic about it (we had learned, for instance, that the April manhunt had come about as a result of the discovery, at one of the bakeries, of a list of some fifty men, mostly bakers and printers, who had contributed to a specific underground drive: yes, it required only a single deductive process to arrive at the "manhunt")—the events of this T'isha B'Ab, by contrast, had been quite mad. No explanations, no orders, no pattern, no consistency. When the Council members arrested this morning were released, Felix Mandeltort was let out with them—no reason given. I was overjoyed to see him, though he seems to have aged ten years. He does not know why he was released: probably it was just a mistake: his sentence for smuggling still had four years and seven months to run! Quite mad. We were still talking about these things, when, at about nine o'clock, several passenger cars and two trucks containing Ukrainian militiamen pulled up in front of the *Judenrat*. (We learned later that Germans and Junaks—Ukrainians, Lithuanians, and Latvians—had already been posted in a cordon around the entire ghetto, one man every thirty paces.) At first we expected a repetition of the previous day's merry games; but soon a certain difference was notable: the Uks surrounded the entire building—throughout which there had fallen, incidentally, a most uncharacteristic stillness—and somewhat more than a dozen S.S. men marched to the Chairman's office on the first floor and commanded Sokolczyk to call a meeting of the Council. The Chairman's secretary, Froi Bronstein, ran from office to office, summoning the members. I was again asked to attend, even though Felix was on hand to act as Secretary; because of having been rejected the previous day, I felt fairly safe, no matter what. Felix and I walked down the corridor together and into the Chairman's office. The Chairman is (was: I almost forgot: was) a remarkable man. He had not seen Felix since before the arrest last February. He showed absolutely no surprise at seeing him now. The Chairman must have sensed immediately that the Germans might not have realized what they had done in releasing Mandeltort, and he said, in his inflexibly suave manner:

—— Good morning, Felix! I don't believe you have had the pleasure of meeting S.S. *Untersturmführer* Mundt and these other officers. . . . Gentlemen, this is Secretary Mandeltort, one of my most useful men. You remember the fur collections last winter, when the Army (what tact and nerve!—as if there were no other army in the world but Hitler's, and as if he, Sokolczyk, shared allegiance to that Only Army) was rather cold in Russia? Well, Mandeltort here was my best collector.

Sokolczyk always put forward his subordinates in this way: they may have despised the very things for which he praised them, but they were deeply grateful to be recommended to the Germans —it was the finest life insurance in the world. Here was Mandeltort: twenty-four hours before, a convict (for smuggling furs!—ah, there was the ironic twist in the Chairman's praise); and now, in the eyes of those present, somehow the man who had singlehandedly warmed up the freezing soldiers of the Only Army. Outsiders may have had contempt for the Chairman: we his subordinates in the *Judenrat* often laughed at him, but in a curious way we were devoted to him.

Jewish policemen had been hastily collecting chairs in the conference room, and S.S. enlisted men had been driving (they behaved like cattle-herders) all *Judenrat* employees not invited to the meeting to a far upstairs corner of the building, as if the underlings should not hear even a whispering echo of what was to be said in the conference room. Berson was among those swept upstairs in this way. At last we moved into the long room where the Council usually meets. The Germans sat along one side of the table, we Jews along the other side. Among the Germans *there was but one man with whom we were accustomed to deal*: we had to presume that all the others were from the *Einsatz Reinhardt*. There was utter silence all through the usually dinful building: my heart beat hard: outside the window one of the German drivers, in a scout-car, had his radio on full blast, playing the *Merry Widow Waltz*. (The tune has come back to me, again and again, throughout these last two days. Will I ever be free from it?)

Mundt started talking, and I must say, he was explicit.

—— An order has been issued (as if from Him on high!) for the resettlement in the East of all Jews in the Warsaw ghetto. (Suddenly Mundt's dry manner broke and with a queer petulance he said:) You know very well there are too many Jews here! (Dry again:) I am entrusting part of the responsibility for the execution of this order to the *Judenrat*. (Very dry:) If the *Judenrat* proves incapable, all its members will be executed.

Then, reading from a typewritten order, Mundt dictated the regulations for the resettlement: who would go and who be exempted, and in what manner. The heart of the order was in Instruction Number Two, which made my hands and feet go clammy:

—— The *Judenrat* is responsible for producing the Jews designated daily for resettlement. In order to accomplish that task, the *Judenrat* is to use the Jewish Order Service. The *Judenrat* is to see to it that 6,000 Jews are delivered daily, not later than at 4 p.m., to the *Umschlagplatz*, beginning July 22, 1942. The *Umschlagplatz* for the duration of the evacuation is the Jewish Hospital at Stawki Street. On July 22, 1942, 6,000 Jews are to be delivered directly to the loading station at the *Transferstelle*. For the time being, the *Judenrat* may draw the daily quota of Jews from the general population. Later on, the *Judenrat* will receive definite instructions as to the parts of streets or housing blocks to be emptied.

Instruction Number Eight, which had the repetitive insistence of certain prayers, and which was delivered by S.S. *Untersturmführer* Mundt in the sonorous manner of a rabbi—I swear it! —gave us all fair notice as to how this resettlement will be carried out:

—— Every Jew who does not nor has so far the right to belong to Point 2, Groups a. to e. [NOTE. N.L. Groups exempt from resettlement.], and who leaves the Jewish quarter after the start of the resettlement, will be shot. Every Jew who undertakes a move which may circumvent or disturb the carrying out of the resettlement orders will be shot. Every Jew who assists a move which may circumvent or disturb the carrying out of the resettlement orders will be shot. All Jews not belonging to exempt categories enumerated under Point 2, Groups a. to h., who will be found in Warsaw after the conclusion of the resettlement will be shot. The *Judenrat* is warned that should its instructions and orders not be carried out freely, a proper number of hostages will be taken and shot.

When Mundt finished dictating (Felix and I had both been writing all this down: the Germans have never handed us written orders), we were all silent for a moment; music drifted in the window. Then, clearing his throat, Sokolczyk said in a formal manner:

—— I have a question under Point 2, Group c., I believe it was.

Mundt: —— Please.

Sokolczyk: —— I wondered whether employees of Jewish self-help organizations would be exempted along with *Judenrat* employees, as equivalent to them, you might say.

Mundt agreed that they would, asked the Chairman to specify the organizations, and dictated a protocol to the Instructions. That was all. Mundt and his cortege left.

At first we sat stunned. Then bedlam broke out in the building. The sequestered underlings rushed forward to hear what had happened. Everyone jabbered and remonstrated and argued and wailed and pleaded—of course to no purpose. Felix and I, thank God, had to retire to type up the orders so that posters might be prepared; we were at least busy. My fingers were like lead plugs on the typewriter keys: I made many mistakes. When we were done, Felix and I went together to the Chairman's office. He had cleared everyone out and had closed the door, and he was sitting alone at his desk staring at the photographs of his grandchildren. Finally he said, absent-mindedly:

—— Yes, yes. What is it?

He read the order through without comment. Always, up to this time, instructions to the ghetto populace had been signed: *M. Sokolczyk, Obermann des Judenrats bei der Jüdischen Kultur-Gemeinde in Warschau* [NOTE. EDITOR. Chairman of the *Judenrat* at the Jewish Community Building, Warsaw.]; and I—who had been working on the second half of the order—had again used this form. The only change Sokolczyk made in the entire typed copy for the poster was to cross out his name and the words *Obermann des*. This time he wanted the load shifted from himself to the *Judenrat* in general. Perhaps I should have seen a prediction in that simple act of editing: I didn't: it simply seemed uncharacteristically modest of Sokolczyk at the time.

The posters were set up. For a few minutes, at one of the notice-boards, I watched the people come up, read, and go shocked away; but I could not stand it for long. The first day's quota was easily attained. The Jewish police rounded up the thousands of three-quarters-dead inmates of the notorious "Death Points," the charity refuges for homeless people, into which poverty-stricken Jews from the provinces had poured and which got their somber name during the typhus epidemic last year; emptied the jails, particularly the Gensia Street Prison, where those convicted of petty infractions of rules had been confined; drove beggars in off the streets; and took out certain incurables from the hospital.

The second day's roundup was progressing satisfactorily to-day, when, late this afternoon, *Untersturmführer* Mundt and one other officer returned to the *Judenrat* and went directly into Sokolczyk's office. They were there only about five minutes. Some ten minutes after they left, I went to the Chairman's office, walked through Froi Bronstein's office on the way, nodded to her, knocked on his door, and walked in (I had been encouraged by the Chairman to be thus informal). He was alone at the desk in what seemed to me a peculiar attitude for this vigorous man, a lazy slouch. I went closer. He was dead in his chair, with his eyes open, staring (by chance?) at the photographs of his grandchildren. I ran for others. Dr. Breithorn came in eventually and pronounced the Chairman dead of potassium-cyanide poisoning. A half-finished glass of water and a small vial were on the Chairman's desk blotter.

Just before sitting down to write this account, I talked with the Chairman's secretary, Froi Bronstein. She is one of those marvelous, faithful, adoring secretaries, a ministering angel in the master's office but in her anteroom a tigress protecting her cub. She was too loyal to "Dr." Sokolczyk (she always gave him that honorary title, though so far as I know he never earned a doctorate) to exhibit outwardly more than the slightest emotion over his death, though I am certain the better part of her died with him. She told me that after the two Germans left his office, he stepped out to her alcove and said, in no perceptible excitement:

—— A glass of water, please, Froi Bronstein.

Froi Bronstein says she poured one from the carafe she always kept for the "Doctor," and then asked him:

—— Anything new?

Then, according to the way she told it, he lifted his eyebrows twice quickly—a mannerism he had—and he said:

—— During our conversation just now, Mundt characterized Jews as parasites. I remarked to him, Froi Bronstein (and as she told this, the adoring woman, for the first time admitting tears to her eyes, said that she had had a distinct feeling that the "Doctor" was telling her what he *wished* he had said to the S.S. man), *Herr Untersturmführer*, I said, I want you to realize what the Jews have done here in Eastern Europe. When we first came here, at the invitation of King Kazimir, Poland was nothing but a forest, a wilderness. Look now at the cities, the factories, the museums, the concert halls, the libraries! See what Jewish initiative has done.

Every day you hear the names of the builders: the Rathvans, the Poznanskis, the Gepners, the Bersons, the Blochs, the Ettingons— great names here! But (and the secretary says he shouted this furiously) *we built on a damned volcano!* We should have built in the wilderness that is properly ours, in Palestine. We should have!

The Chairman shot his eyebrows up, Froi Bronstein says, turned with the glass of water in his hand, and went into his office.

It is with reluctance that I note here an inaccuracy in this speech of the Chairman's, one which indicates a kind of fuzzy-mindedness he had along with his nobility: it was not King Kazimir, of course, who invited the Jews to Poland, but King Wladislaw Herman. It is true that under Kazimir's reforms the lot of the Jews in Poland was markedly alleviated.

Chairman Sokolczyk left no message, letter, or communication of any kind—at least that we have found so far. There is only one clue as to what happened. On the pad on his desk, among the crowd of nervously scribbled emblems and patterns, was the figure 6,000—the number of Jews to have been delivered daily, according to yesterday's order. This figure had been crossed out, and under it was written another number: 10,000.

6

EVENTS JULY 22, 1942. ENTRY JULY 24, 1942. FROM DOLEK BERSON. As yet I cannot say what my own reactions are: I am befuddled. Today I got Berson to tell me how he first saw this unseeable thing, and his story helped me. Curious how comforting another's discomfort can be. The only fearful thing is to be alone.

Berson went home for the noon hour on the twenty-second. Having accepted the Hashomer invitation, he had already thrown himself, with his typical fervor, into the rudimentary work that had been assigned him: he was in the kindergarten of the underground, and he enjoyed it.

At just about twelve thirty, Berson, sitting in the living room, became aware of an unusual commotion outdoors. A few minutes before there had been quiet all about; then, in isolated, quickly successive sounds—a door slammed, a shout from an open window across the courtyard, a gramophone record started up and then suddenly stopped with a screech of the needle pushed across the grooves, a window hurriedly closed, a scream in the streets, more shouts, distant wailing—the racket grew, until at last a whole conglomerate of new noises made a great, eerie, supra-ghetto buzz. Berson got up, went to the window, and looked out. He saw agitation in the streets: everyone seemed to be hurrying. He went into the kitchen and said to Froi Mazur, the only other member of the "family" in the apartment at the time:

—— Something is happening. I'll go out and see what it is.

Berson ran downstairs and out into the street. Outside the disturbance seemed directionless, aimless, and even meaningless. The usually idle street-populace was in a hurry, but every which way: they were not running away from anything, nor toward anything. Berson met a man in a black suit with a collarless shirt which was carefully fastened at the neck with a brass stud.

Berson: —— What is happening?

The man: —— We're going on a trip.

This reply was delivered in a shout and accompanied by what seemed to be a grin of real happiness, though it may only have been a grimace; the man ran on. Berson confronted a woman who ran along clutching a brown shawl over her head.

—— What's happening?

—— Oi, misery!

The woman lifted her eyes to heaven and wagged her head back and forth mournfully; that was all; she hastened away.

Berson, mystified and frustrated, says he suddenly remembered the way he had felt when, many years before, his father had assigned him to the sales force of the glove factory and one after another of the sure fire customers had given Berson evasive answers: *Business is terrible. . . . I can't move the gloves I have in stock. . . . Maybe next autumn. . . .* Berson felt the same bafflement now as he had experienced then; once again his self-pity was mixed with an unclear pity for those whom he approached: they seemed, both then and now, to be in the grip of some external circumstance that forced them to answer equivocally.

Seeing a Jewish policeman, Berson went up to him and grabbed him by the coat (as, he immediately remembered, he had once desperately grabbed a potential customer and tried to *shake* an order out of him) and asked:

—— What's happening?

The policeman, reaching for his truncheon: —— Let go of me or I'll bash your head in.

Berson thought then of the *Judenrat*, and he began running toward Grzybowska Street. As he ran, he says he wondered whether Symka in the hospital could hear the buzz of this elusive excitement hovering over the ghetto: he saw her in his imagination, lying on one of the twelve iron beds in the ward, which also housed more than forty people on straw ticks on the floor—her face pale and drawn (*Just a general exhaustion-and-undernourishment syndrome*, Dr. Breithorn had said. *I have a few vitamin concentrates left—but if they don't work* . . . ; the doctor had shrugged), but her eyes intelligent, yet, and beautiful, and those eyes, he now imagined, inquiring of the passing nurses as to the rumor in the air —was it real or just something in her ears? *We're going on a trip*, a nurse might say, smiling. *Oi, misery!* another might say. *I'll bash your head in*, another might perfectly well say. Berson felt so sorry for Symka alone in the multitude of the sick that he almost turned around to run northward to the hospital, in order to comfort her. *The sound, dear girl, is only in your ears—and mine.* . . . But then Berson saw a knot of people fighting to get near one of the street hoardings where public notices were regularly posted, and he ran toward it. The people looked like a litter of black-coated animals fighting to get at maternal sources of supply. Berson plunged in and by main strength was able to get close enough to read the beginning of a new poster:

1. *On the order of the German authorities, all Jewish inhabitants of Warsaw will*—

A head swung into Berson's line of vision. All Jewish inhabitants of Warsaw will *what*? Be declared British citizens? Be given a feast of *lox* and *gribbenes* and *gefillte fish* and *tzimmes*? Berson, his hopes suddenly wildly high, bobbed his head and pushed.

—— *be resettled in the East.*

So that was the cause of the murmur in the air! Berson says he decided at once: He would not go. East or west, he would not go. He would refuse to go anywhere. His heart jumped when he read the next sentence:

2. *The following categories are exempt from resettlement:* . . .

Dancing, dodging, craning, shoving, he read the list. [NOTE. N.L. The categories are: Jews employed by German enterprises;

270

Judenrat and its employees; Jewish police; personnel of Jewish hospitals and sanitary columns; Jews on forced labor, or fit for it; immediate families—i.e., wives and children—of above types; hospitalized sick who could get special permits from *Judenrat* doctors.] Berson says his first thought was for himself: that as a *Judenrat* employee, he was safe. His second thought, glass-clear and decisive, was that because of this poster, which was signed by the *Judenrat*, he could no longer tolerate working there: he would resign. His third thought was for Symka: after his resignation from the *Judenrat*, she would no longer be protected as the wife of a man in an exempt category: perhaps she could be exempted under the sick clause, if Dr. Breithorn would help. . . . [NOTE. N.L. The sick category, 2h., reads as follows: *All Jews who on the first day of resettlement find themselves in one of the Jewish hospitals and are not fit to be released; the unfitness for release must be stated by a physician designated by the* Judenrat.]

Berson burrowed out from the crowd and started for the hospital. He ran at first, but then, tiring, slowed to a breathless, hard-working walk. Going along Smocza, he saw an elderly man dart out of a house, running awkwardly because he was buttoning his trousers, and heading straight for Berson. The old man asked, in a bewildered way:

—— What is happening?

Berson: —— It's the end.

At once Berson realized that in his impatient despair he, too, had given an evasive answer, and he turned toward the old man, who was already rushing away, and shouted:

—— Wait! Wait! All the Jews of Warsaw will—

But the old man ran on, unhearing.

Berson himself now hurried northward. At the intersection of Smocza with Mila, a crowd of people completely blocked the street. Berson was in no state of mind to brook any more frustration: he offered his right shoulder to the mob and forced his way into it. He was filled with a brutish intolerance of delay: he drove forward. It was only when there were no more people directly in front of him that he was stopped—by a sight:

Coming out from Mila Street, and turning northward on Smocza, was as wretched a parade of Jewry as Berson had ever in his life seen, even in his *Lumpenproletariat* days. Beggars, rag-pickers, *schnorrers*, corpse-gatherers, grave-diggers, garbage-looters

—Berson had seen all such in the ghetto, but those were prince-
lings and velvet-wearers compared with this array of outcasts. Looking along Mila, Berson could see that the Mila "Death Point," one
of the so-called "way stations" for homeless refugees, was being
emptied. Ragged, dejected, empty-faced, these barely living men
and women limped and staggered along, mostly in together-lean-
ing duets and trios, their mouths working as if in painful concert,
though in fact they were silent. At the end of the procession there
were carts into which those who fell down were loaded, log-like.

Resettlement, Berson thought bitterly—as though these feeble
beings had ever been settled anywhere!

Then Berson saw something that startled him: the parade of
poverty-stricken Jews was being constrained to move by Jewish
policemen, and midway along the column Berson could see Stefan
Mazur, his face contorted with something that was not quite rage
and yet was beyond rage; Stefan was beating the miserable marchers
with his wooden club, cursing them, occasionally shoving them:
the handsome young man seemed possessed by some bestial, sadis-
tic Other Self whom Berson had never met (though now Berson
says he remembered the haste with which Stefan had hurried
away, that night in April, to inform on Pavel Menkes). For a
moment Berson considered running out and remonstrating with
Stefan, but then he thought how queer he would look in the eyes
of the crowd, and besides, he began to feel within himself an emotion akin to the dreadful one on Stefan's face and in the boy's
ferocious actions: hatred: hatred for these miserable Jewish speci-
mens. What right had they to be so mean? How dared they be
such vivid reminders of human inequality? What right had they to
advertise the depths to which Jews could be driven? Quickly Berson's hatred surged over the threshold into the place of compassion
and became mixed up with compassion and at last was wholly
converted into compassion: and he wept. All morning, ever since
first hearing the rapid crescendo of the rumors of alarm, he had
wanted to cry; for weeks, months, years, he had wanted to cry; and
now he did, with great racking sobs.

EVENTS JULY 22, 1942. ENTRY JULY 25, 1942. FROM DO-
LEK BERSON. Continuing Berson's account:

By the time the end of the procession from the Mila "Death
Point" had moved up Smocza Street, Berson had recovered him-

272

self, and he walked slowly along behind it. The line turned right on Stawki Street. The refugees were being led, apparently, to the *Transferstelle*, so the parade would take its course past the hospital, on Stawki. Berson accommodated his pace to the mournful march of the refugees; he was empty, now, he says, empty, empty.

In front of the hospital, there was a new confusion. A large crowd of porters, ricksha-pullers, handcartmen, and hospital attendants was milling about in front of the building, carrying and stacking and loading hospital equipment: to get past, the ranks of the refugees were driven across the street and had to trickle through a narrow bottleneck there. In sight of the hospital and more mindful of Symka than he had been, suddenly frightened by the thought that the hospital was being closed for resettlement as the Mila "Death Point" had evidently been, Berson began fighting his way forward again. For a few uncomfortable moments he was among the refugees: but going through them was as easy as going through a farmer's field—they offered no more resistance, it seemed, than stalks of grain. Then he was in the agitated mob before the hospital—a more resistant mass. A man in a white coat shouted right in Berson's face (as Berson pressed toward the hospital doors): *Eliahu, have you the bedpans there?* A man with a ricksha was haggling over a price with a Jewish nurse. *But,* she said, on the verge of tears, *we're doing this work for all the Jews.* The ricksha-puller, evidently maintaining at this inappropriate moment the habit of bitter gibes he must always have used in bargaining, said: *Nu, so it's for the Jews, does that make my work cheaper? You don't like the Jews? Is that it?* Berson elbowed and jostled his way in through the front door of the hospital. There was no one at the reception desk. Berson ran along a hallway until he met a nurse, a hard-faced, elderly woman.

Berson: —— Have you seen Dr. Breithorn?

The nurse, with a precision for which Berson was grateful: —— He is among the patients, on the rounds. On Corridor Thirteen, I believe, by this time.

Berson thanked her and walked quickly back along the hallway to a staircase, which he ascended. He had no idea where Corridor Thirteen was. He began putting his head into wards and laboratories. People were running up and down the halls, carrying things. After some time, he stopped another nurse, a young woman, and asked her where Corridor Thirteen was.

—— We have no Corridor Thirteen. Twelve is the highest number.

The young nurse hurried away on some urgent errand. Berson ran up another flight of stairs and explored three hallways on the floor above. At last, in a ward that seemed somehow familiar to Berson, he saw Dr. Breithorn, on his knees beside a palliasse in the middle of the floor, and he ran up to him. Panting, leaning over the doctor, he said:

—— Have you read the notices?

Berson saw that Dr. Breithorn was listening through his stethoscope to the heartbeat of a fragile woman: a purse-thin breast was shoved askew by the metal ear-horn.

—— Dolek! Dolek!

Berson turned and saw Symka in her proper bed, down the ward—her ward! He held up a hand to indicate that she should wait a minute. The doctor took his stethoscope out from his ears and let it hang on his neck. Berson said:

—— Doctor, have you heard about the resettlement?

Dr. Breithorn, looking up disgustedly: —— No, we're just turning the hospital inside out for an airing.

—— Could you give me a certificate for Froi Berson? To exempt her?

The doctor stood up slowly. Slowly and without evident anger, he said:

—— Berson, you are the next-to-last person to ask me for a personal favor today. The next one I am going to kill. With this. (He took a large, cheap, folding jackknife from his pocket, an incongruously crude piece of machinery for a doctor to be carrying. He held it, unopened, a few centimeters from the end of Berson's nose. Then, as coolly as before:) Now get out. . . .

—— But under Paragraph 2, Article h., on the poster—

Dr. Breithorn, speaking now as to a friend, but with an odd, dispirited air: —— Listen, I have been given twenty-four hours in which to evacuate this entire hospital to another building. I am trying to keep two thousand people alive. I haven't time for Article h. Do you want my advice? Hire one of the rickshas in front of this building and take your wife home. She will die—perhaps not right away: it depends on courage more than medicines. It would be best to have her near you. Forget Article h. And forget that you ever knew me.

274

With a terrible look of self-hate, the doctor turned away and then crouched down by the next palliasse.

Berson went to Symka's bed, showing nothing (he thinks) on his face, and, wrapping a threadbare blanket about her, he picked her up and walked out of the ward with her in his arms. Her light body was an easy load.

—— Where are we going, Dolek?

—— Home, dear.

—— Am I better, then?

—— Yes, dear. Much better.

EVENTS JULY 23, 1942. ENTRY JULY 25, 1942. FROM DO-LEK BERSON. Berson has gone through with his resignation from the *Judenrat*. I argued against it. I told him it was a reflex, not something he had thought out. But his mind was firm and set.

I cannot call Berson any more the Drifter.

EVENTS JULY 23, 1942. ENTRY JULY 25, 1942. FROM DO-LEK BERSON. Berson convened the "family"—which, under the regulation that defines a family as consisting only of the wife and children of the principal, is no longer entitled to consider itself as such, but nevertheless still does—in order to survey its hazard.

Stefan Mazur, in the police, and N.L., in the *Judenrat*, are exempt from the resettlement. Mordecai Apt, in the bricklayers' battalion, has already received an *Ausweis*, a precious work certificate that protects him. Rutka, as Mordecai's wife, is safe. That leaves the senior Mazurs, the Bersons, the rabbi, Rachel, and Halinka still vulnerable. Froi Mazur and Symka would be all right if their husbands could get into an exempt category. On the twenty-third, therefore, the second day of the resettlement, the two husbands, the two Apt girls, and the rabbi went job-hunting.

We fixed the rabbi up with precisely Berson's job in the *Judenrat*, as a clerk in the Health and Welfare Department. Berson could have his job back, or another like it, if he wanted; but no, he has decided.

Halinka had no trouble. She had heard from a girl she knew at the Britannia that anyone with a sewing machine could get a job easily, and she talked Froi Mazur into letting her "borrow" the small machine Froi Mazur brought from Lodz. Halinka hired a ricksha and took the machine with her to the Toebbens plant on Prosta. She was admitted at once and put directly to work as a seamstress. [NOTE. N.L. That is something I should like to see with my own eyes!]

Berson told Reb Yechiel Mazur and Rachel that he thought it would be easy for all three of them to get work at the button plant Gruber has set up, through his cousin Meier, who was certain to be in favor there. [NOTE. N.L. We know that Meier helped Gruber with arrangements; ENTRY APRIL 3, 1942.] And so the three went together to the shabby buildings on Muranowska that Gruber has bought for his shops. In the streets, there prevailed the same agitation as had been evident, uninterruptedly, since the news of the resettlement made its first, noisy capture of the ghetto: people were still moving about with apparent aimlessness, some carrying household goods, others gathering in argumentative knots, and still others running full tilt and wide-eyed, as if the Angel of Death were skittering his wings along the pavements behind them. In front of each factory workshop and office that had official sanction, a large crowd was gathered—and this was true at the Gruber shops, when Berson, Reb Yechiel Mazur, and Rachel reached it.

Muranowska Street was half filled with the crowd. The three doors of the shops were tightly closed; two of them, in fact, were boarded over, nailed tight, fort-like. A Jewish policeman stood guard at the third. From time to time he opened the door and whispered to a man inside, and occasionally the latter would stick his head out and murmur something to the policeman, who would then admit a single applicant. Some time later this person would emerge, usually with an expression of intoxicated relief and shameless exuberance. Personal fates were being decided by that slowly opening and closing door, and by the confidential mumbling between the policeman and the grim doorkeeper. The crowd around the policeman was dense and intractable: men who had been given a hard negative six, eight, and ten times would not move away, but would ask again and again. Consequently, it took nearly an hour for Berson and his two companions to make their way, with many a purposeful nudge and rude word, to the neighborhood of the policeman's weary ear. When at last they were close, Berson said:

—— Message for Meier Berson. Tell him, D. B. Berson and two others are here.

The policeman opened the door. The doorkeeper's head came

276

out. The policeman repeated Berson's words. The doorkeeper's expression did not change: he withdrew his head; the door closed. Berson looked at his friends and smiled and nodded in a confident and (he says) slightly patronizing way. Nothing happened for a long time. Finally the door opened. Not the doorkeeper, but an elated, successful applicant came bouncing out, whispered to a waiting woman, and, bobbing his head down like a diving loon, made his way out under the surface of the crowd, as it were; his wife ducked and swam underneath and after him. The door closed again. The three waited a long time. Finally Reb Yechiel Mazur said:

—— Do you think we should send word in again?

—— Meier will answer, don't worry.

But an excessive time seemed to pass—it was, in fact, only a few minutes, but the minutes were doom-laden and they dragged under their burden—and Berson asked the policeman:

—— How long should it take to get an answer?

The policeman, shrugging: —— It depends.

This sounded somehow reassuring, and Berson, Rachel, and Reb Yechiel Mazur exchanged smiles. . . .

The door opened. The doorkeeper put his head out. Berson leaned forward and heard:

—— Pan Meier Berson to D. B. Berson: Pan Meier Berson is very sorry, he cannot handle the request.

Berson: —— No! That can't be! Please be so good as to check up on that answer. I'm certain there is a mistake.

The doorkeeper, still addressing the policeman and not even looking at Berson: —— There is no mistake. I spoke to Pan Meier Berson personally. I thought (as if regretting wasted zeal) it might be something special.

Berson felt dazed—and he says he also felt Rachel's hand take his.

Rachel: —— It's all right, Dolek. We'll find something. (When the three had pushed out to a less dense section of the crowd, she said:) You know, I had a feeling, that day we ate the horsemeat *cholent*, that Cousin Meier should have been invited.

Berson: —— Do you suppose that could be the reason?

Reb Yechiel Mazur, irritable, in the first uncharitable utterance Berson had ever heard from the saintly man: —— What other reason?

277

All day the three friends hurried from factory to factory—to Toebbens, Hallmann, Roerich, Schultz, Schilling, Oksaka, Avia. At some places there was not even a possibility of getting near the gate or door; at others, they were told, as everyone without connections was: *Full up, full up!* At one workshop, Berson was nearly admitted, but when he said he had two friends, all three were turned away. It was then—already well into the afternoon—that Reb Yechiel Mazur said:

—— We must try separately. Three is too many.

Rachel: —— That's right, Dolek. It's every dog for himself now. And (she smiled) when the dogs get hungry for dogmeat, please don't eat me!

And they split up.

When the whole "family" had gathered at the apartment just before curfew, at ten that night, Berson said he had finally landed a job as a carpenter at Reisinger's joining factory on Swientojerska Street; Reb Yechiel Mazur said that his old friend Felix Mandeltort had helped him get a place in a tiny shop where they make artificial flowers; as for Rachel, she was still without work— but she seemed strangely happy. She confessed, at last, that she had not even tried to find anything: she had gone to see little David, at the Rukner Home, and she had had a marvelous time in a game of blindman's buff.

7

EVENTS JULY 22–28, 1942. ENTRY JULY 29, 1942. N.L. . . . To a degree I have mastered the hysteria which gripped me last week. I am even ashamed of it. I would forget all about it, were it not for the rule I set myself long ago that I should never destroy anything from this record: the principal value of these jottings for later use will be as a guide to reactions of the moment, and I cannot help it if they remind me and embarrass me.

The most important thing I have to record now is the number of Jews evacuated to date. As archivist, I am handed these figures daily by Zweinarcz, a young fellow who used to be a clerk in Felix's secretariat but who now seems to be coming forward as a favorite of the new Chairman, Engineer Grossmann. Zweinarcz gets these figures at about noon each day from a German officer who drops in to see Grossmann, and somewhat later Zweinarcz puts his head in my office and hands me a small slip of paper with nothing written on it but a penciled number. I am not specially horrified by this act, because the numbers, staggering as they are, do not depress me nearly so much as the sight of a single face of a deportee. In fact, the numbers have given me a perverse satisfaction—in that the Germans are not getting the ten thousand per day they demanded.

For the first week, then: July 22—6,289; July 23—7,815; July 24—7,444; July 25—7,530; July 26—6,691; July 27—6,424; July 28 —5,241. Total—47,434.

Since the evacuation is principally in the hands of the Jewish police, it has been conducted without too much brutality, though we understand that a number of the obviously infirm have been taken over by the Junaks, shot, and buried in the mass graves in our own cemetery. This itself is in a way comforting, as it tends · to confirm the German allegation that they are taking our people to the East to work: they dump beforehand those who obviously cannot work, as excess baggage. In these first days, a substantial number of Jews, especially poor people, who consider the conditions in work camps on the Russian front cannot be worse than conditions as they have experienced them here, have been voluntarily reporting for resettlement. We have no idea how many the Germans intend to take. I am told that at the already famous meeting yesterday in which the underground elements finally formed a joint committee, the conservatives were saying that they had information (where from, God knows) that the Germans plan to take only seventy thousand. If that is true, the resettlement action will be over in a few days now: they already had nearly fifty thousand, as of yesterday.

(In passing: The episode at the meeting yesterday of the premature handshake between Hashomer and Bund, between Zionism and Socialism, in the persons of Zilberzweig and Rapaport, is all over the place, and is the joke of the *Judenrat*. Zilberzweig must feel a fool. All the same, it must have been a moving act at the time. We at the *Judenrat* can laugh. *Nobody* wants to shake hands with us.)

Another consequence of the fact that the Jewish police are

279

executing the resettlement is that influence and connections play
a large part in whether or not one is taken away. During the panicky rush for *Ausweise*, on the first two or three days, the crowds
besieging certain factories had definite complexions. For instance,
the Schultz factory is in the building of a Hasidic manufacturer
who is now active in Schultz affairs; consequently there were many
religious Jews, and especially Yeshiva students, trying to get—
and getting—employment there. At the larger of the two Toebbens
plants in the Leszno-Prosta area, one of the Zionist leaders apparently has some influence, so the Zionists flocked there. A Socialist
has some money capitalistically invested in the Hoffmann works
on Nowolipki, so the Bund ran there. And so on. Many enterprises
were started up overnight, centering on two or three sewing machines and a couple of bolts of cloth; and the inevitable swindlers
have been in evidence, issuing *Ausweise* from nonexistent shops
and enterprises. A large number of religious Jews of the poorer
class, who are too honest to pay bribes and who have no useful
connections, have been deported.

The resettlement is keeping office hours, so to speak. The
action lasts from eight in the morning until six in the evening.
During those hours, the streets are absolutely deserted—one would
never guess that the ghetto wall encloses hundreds of thousands
of people: the place is dead—or playing dead. But early in the
morning, from dawn until eight, and in the evenings, from six
until curfew, the streets are abnormally crowded. People are out
taking the air, almost as if nothing were happening—shopping for
food, gossiping, looking for relatives and friends to see whether
they have been resettled.

The evacuation is being done on a house-to-house basis. A
squad of ghetto police, perhaps two dozen men, under command
of a *Sicherheitspolizei* officer, blocks off all entrances and exits to
a building or courtyard. All residents and tenants are then ordered
out into the courtyard or street, and are rooted out by searching
Jewish policemen (some of whom, it is regrettable to report, have
been playing the roles of Gestapo operatives, and have swaggered,
been domineering, and sometimes have acted downright cruelly).
Outside, the commander of the squad, usually the *Sicherheitspolizei* man, examines the residents' documents, sending those whose
Ausweise are valid to the right, the rest to the left. The former are
released, the latter taken to the Stawki Street hospital buildings,

and from there they are taken in time to the near-by *Umschlag-platz*, at the loading platforms of the Danzig Station sidings. Since some incautious people with valid *Ausweise* have been picked up and taken off, nobody that I know of has yet ventured near the *Umschlagplatz*. We have no idea what happens there, or beyond there, except that there is a constant shunting of trains, which we can hear from a distance.

Odd, speaking of what one hears: I hear shooting today. There has been very little shooting up till now. Today, however, it is quite frequent. . . .

EVENTS JULY 28, 1942. ENTRY JULY 29, 1942. FROM RACHEL APT. I heard this afternoon that it was Rachel who precipitated the Zilberzweig-Rapaport handshake. My God, I am proud!

Zilberzweig took her to the meeting, again, as a kind of auxiliary memory. Here is what happened, as she told it to me tonight:

Rachel says she had a weird, inner-mind sensation that this had happened before—that she had sat in exactly the same seat in the same room and had heard the same men say the same things in the same tone to the same dead consequence. The unsettling thing about the sensation, which she had had at other times under other circumstances in her life, was that *this time the sensation had some substance*. She had, in fact, sat in the same chair in Hil Zilberzweig's room, back in April, surrounded for the most part by the same men (Zilberzweig, Rapaport, Kurtz, and leaders of Left Poale-Zion, Dror, Akiba, Misrachi, the General Zionists, and rabbis from the Agudah Rabbinical Council; and on this occasion three members of the underground press, the Director of the Lublin Yeshiva, and a Revisionist additionally on hand) and bathed in the same atmosphere, conscious of the same urgency (only greater) and of the same formal politeness expressed in the same phrases (*If I may remind the honorable representative of the Bund . . . In that connection, Chaver Delegate of Hashomer Hatsair . . .*) and oppressed by the same feeling of frustration (only much greater). Rachel says she was deeply disturbed by this sense of repetition and by her feeling of inevitability—that the earlier themes would have to be gone over again, as in a recapitulation in a primitive sonata, *da capo al fine*, note for note. The feeling grew in her, until she felt a little mad—as if she did not know whether she was in April or July, despite the inescapable July-ness of some of the words spoken this time: one man reported that the German unit which is carrying out the resettlement is none other than the dread *Vernichtungskommando* of Lublin and Tarnow, the *Schutzstaffel und Sicherheitspolizei Distrikt Lublin Einsatz Reinhardt*, and that this notorious outfit is billeted amongst us, at Zelazna 103—inconceivable in April; and yet the April-ness of some of the sentiments made Rachel doubt whether she had really heard that report, or was hearing these other July things: all inmates of the ghetto with foreign passports now incarcerated in the Pawiak, the converts' churches shut down—essence of July-ness there; and yet the Akiba man saying, *The Germans would not dare!* . . . and the Misrachi man saying, *They only want seventy thousand, my source is unimpeachable*—April words; the curfew had just been extended in July by Commissioner Haensch, from nine till ten at night, an event that jibed with the April-mindedness of the optimists: around and around and around, until one's head grew dizzy, Rachel says, and April-July time squashed itself into a repetitive, obsessive rhythm: we must unite, we cannot, we must, we cannot, we must, we cannot. . . .

At last, almost literally rocking back and forth in this rhythm, Rachel pounded her hand on the table and stood up.

—— I have no right to speak here, I am an assistant delegate, as they call me. Nevertheless . . .

Rachel says she saw the eyes in the room turned toward her, and she hated them all. (For a moment, she recollected the loving maternal eyes of Froi Mazur turned on her the night she challenged Benlevi; she felt the same courage now, she says.) She began shouting angrily. She abused the eyes and the minds behind the eyes, she cursed them and spat upon them verbally. *The so-called underground*, she cried, dragging out and weighing down the "so-called," so as to make the phrase utterly contemptuous. She used recollected phrases, images that had recently been at the front of her mind (*We are treated like dogs*, she said once, *yet we would be glad to eat dogmeat: we would devour one another!*); she felt herself burn inwardly, as if consumptively; she recited some of the things she had seen and heard in the past week, and though these were events in which all her listeners had shared, she said she thinks she tore some of the quilting from the surface of events.

She referred several times to the children in the Rukner Home, and she believes her most telling anecdotes were those which silhouetted the innocence and blithesomeness of the children against the week's general degradation. [INSERT. FROM ENTRY JULY 26, 1942. FROM RACHEL APT. It develops that Rachel's game of blindman's buff the other day was not so light-headed as it seemed at the time: she now has a job at the Rukner Home, as one of that institution's "mothers." She has an *Ausweis*. She will be with her dear brother David much of the time. She will simulate motherhood. What could be better?] One can guess that as Rachel spoke, her ugly little face worked and writhed. She called for no program. She had none. And when at last she sat down, she says she felt confused and embarrassed, as if she had allowed herself to enjoy the sound of her own voice too much and too long; she says somebody should have told her not to rattle the top of her teakettle that way. Now she burned outwardly; she felt her face glow. But she tells me that *in the very moment of her shame, she nevertheless felt, for the first time in her life, pretty.*

In a proprietary manner, as if he owned Rachel, or had single-handedly produced her, Zilberzweig stood up and asked:

—— Gentlemen! Need anything more be said?

Zilberzweig sat down at once. Then Rapaport, standing slowly, said:

—— No. Enough has been said. We of the Bund wish to do all we can in co-operation with other elements in the ghetto. . . .

Without waiting for Rapaport to speak any further, Zilberzweig stood up again, leaned forward across the table that separated him from the Socialist, and reached out a hand. Rapaport took it, and the Zionist and the Socialist stood shaking hands for a long, long time, with an almost imperceptible up-and-down motion, gripping so hard that the knuckles of both their hands went white. The two men differed sharply in appearance, Rachel says: Zilberzweig rather fat and sleek, his thin hair combed back with oily neatness, his face inscrutable but his whole manner expressive of a powerful, suppressed emotion; Rapaport like an eagle, his vast white eyebrows working, tears in his eyes, his mouth open—his emotions altogether legible. But no matter how different, the two men were one! Everyone in the room was utterly overcome by the warm, brotherly gesture of these two implacables.

283

Bravo! someone shouted. Everyone stood up and moved around, congratulating and saluting. Zilberzweig kissed Rachel on both cheeks, and Rachel burst into tears.

Rapaport, loudly, stilling the celebration with a single, warning word: —— However! (When the others had quieted themselves:) However, I should make myself clear. You may have misunderstood. I should be sorry if there were a misunderstanding. I intended an expression of sympathy and common interest. You all know that the Bund intends to fight the Germans with all its resources. But I should make myself clear: The Bund will not be able to join formally with other organizations. That is still our position. Our position is essentially unchanged. We shall work with the Polish Socialist Party. We expect assistance from our Polish comrades. In a very few days I expect to visit our Polish Central Committee and receive word as to help from them. I hope there was not a misunderstanding. I trust . . .

Looking around, but obviously seeing nothing, since his eyes were full of tears, the old man sat down with jarring suddenness. The meeting was deathly still.

Then for a few minutes the group became inanely confused. Useless proposals were put forward, more in embarrassment than in seriousness, Rachel thought. One delegate made a substantial offer of money to bribe Haensch—*for what that may be worth,* the delegate said. The representative of another organization proposed the establishment of new workshops, to give more Jews work, in case the usefulness of Jews to the German war effort might be persuasive. Still another man proposed that a courier be sent to Switzerland to meet with the representative of international Jewry there and urge him, perhaps, to prevail upon the government of Great Britain immediately to recognize all Jews everywhere as citizens of Palestine. . . .

At last Zilberzweig rose again. It was obvious that he was badly mortified over his premature gesture of welcome, and irritated by it—yet also moved by its consequences.

—— We are sorry to hear this reiteration from our friend of the Bund. It is time nevertheless to move ahead, with or without. . . . For some time we of Hashomer have had in preparation a table of organization. . . .

And in a matter of minutes the Jewish National Committee, embracing Hashomer, Left and Right Poale-Zion, Hechalutz, Dror,

Gordonia, the General Zionists, and the Communist P.P.R., but not the Bund, had been called into being.

Zilberzweig: —— And now, as a symbol of our intention to pool our resources unstintingly, Hashomer wishes to offer its entire arsenal to the Jewish National Committee. (He smiled a twisted, ironic, defiant smile.) Our armament consists of one automatic pistol, and here it is.

With that, the prosperous-looking conspirator reached into his coat pocket, pulled out a German Army Luger, and dropped it with a clatter on the table. It lay there, black, cold, darkly luminous, reflecting the blue, hard light of July that streamed in the window.

8

EVENTS JULY 24–29, 1942. ENTRY JULY 29, 1942. FROM DOLEK BERSON. Berson's talent for keeping in touch with all sorts of people now pays off. Fein, the jovial, round-faced workman whom Berson first met in the bricklayers' battalion, whom he took to the Britannia the night of the Heine incident, and from whom he later bought Symka's wig, is working at Reisinger's now as a carpenter, and has appointed himself Berson's tutor in the mysteries of carpentry. Fein told Berson, the very first day the latter went to work:

—— You must learn, you know. You must learn to make these window sashes well. It's not enough to have an *Ausweis* in your pocket. Soon, when they want more Jewish bones for soap, they'll start sniffing around to find those who cannot really work, and they'll take out the piano-players like you, Berson.

Fein began with the care of tools:

—— You wash your hands, don't you? You pick your teeth, don't you? These things are just extra fingers and teeth—you have to take care of them as if they were part of you.

His next point, and his constant preachment in the first days, was precision:

—— It takes less work to measure four times than it does to saw once, and it's a funny thing: if you intend to cut too much off a piece of wood, you might as well save yourself work and throw it away in the first place. Check your measurements!

It turned out, quite soon, that this admonition of Fein's was not simply the fruit of an idiosyncratic love of exactness. On the fourth or fifth morning, Fein whispered to Berson that beginning on August 3, everyone in the shop was going to begin adding a half-centimeter [NOTE. EDITOR. About one fifth of an inch.] to the sash measurements (certain crosspieces would require a lesser addition): the finished sashes would *look* exactly right, the inspections in the plant were delegated to a Jew, who was "fixed," the error would not be discovered until thousands of glassless window sashes had been shipped to another city (Lwow; this had been checked) to be glazed—or, quite possibly, since the difference in the tiny quarter-panes would not be much, until they came to be set up in sills manufactured at another series of shops, as windows in temporary barracks on a cold, cold steppe, where they would be found quite unsuitable. Fein emphasized that it was imperative that every workman be precise in his miscalculations, because one man who cut one piece of wood to the proper German specification without making the addition might expose the entire, painfully organized sabotage. Fein could now be heard shouting gaily—as he had been shouting for days, while he taught his intellectual apprentices:

—— Check your measurements!

The descents of the German licensee, Reisinger, upon his shop were dreaded. He came two or three times a day, at irregular hours. A man who worked by a window commanding a view of Reisinger's only approach, across a courtyard from another staircase where the office was situated, warned the others of the German's approach by hissing the catchword, *Six!* The pleasant atmosphere in the shop would then be suddenly broken off, and the twenty-odd carpenters would apply themselves, in sullen concentration, to their work. Reisinger cares about only two things—cleanliness and filling his quota. He goes into a frenzy if the shop's lumber supply is not kept in precisely squared stacks; the sight of sawdust on the floor makes him shout and threaten; the carpenters have to wash the walls of the shop twice a week, and they are forced to sweep all day every day. His profit and indeed his existence depend upon the delivery of a daily quota of sashes, and every afternoon at about three he becomes terribly nervous lest his workers fail him.

Reisinger is apparently a heavy, bald-headed, unimaginative man, who knows nothing about carpentry but who wears a brown carpenter's apron around the office and shop, perhaps to impress his superiors, in case of visits from them.

This morning, Fein was holding forth to Berson and one or two others about the resettlement.

—— Listen. I've been resettled in the East before. How old do you think I am?

Berson: —— Forty.

Fein: —— You are wrong, my duckling. I'm fifty-one. In 1915 I was twenty-four years old, and I liked to move around then the way I do now—only then I was also stupid. I went to Russia. I resettled myself. So what happens? They arrest me because I'm a Jew. Oh, sure, they tell me my papers are not correct, but I can see the real reason in his eyes: this big fat Russian policeman covered with tinfoil and brass! So then I say *pfui* on the Russians, I come back and join the Hungarian Army to fight the Russians, because Germany and the Central Powers announce that one of their war aims is to stop the Tsar from persecuting Jews. Help! How things get turned around!

Fein talked almost incessantly, and Berson had become accustomed to working along and listening at the same time. At this point, Berson was beveling crosspieces.

Fein: —— You see? Last time it was the Russians hated the Jews, and the Germans protected them. Now, the other way around. Maybe that mixes you up? Me: not at all! To me it means only one thing: never trust a *goy* who says he wants to help the Jews. He'll be reaching in your pocket the very next day. So, resettlement! Let them move me around, they'll still hate me! It will serve them right.

—— Six!

At the suddenly hissed warning signal, Berson, absorbed in what Fein had been saying, turned, fumbled, and dropped the wooden block bevel-plane with which he was working, then reached for it so quickly while it was still falling that (just as Herr Reisinger entered the shop), stumbling in some waste ends of lumber and losing his balance, he fell forward across a set of about a dozen delicate, beveled lengths of wood, lying across two sawhorses ready to be cut up for crosspieces. These broke with an explosive crackling sound. In a few seconds Reisinger was standing over Berson, who was still groping about on his hands and knees, picking up the beveled splinters. The German poured abuse on Berson for wasting semi-finished lumber—and said, among other things, that he would take Berson's *Ausweis* away from him: a threadbare threat that he has apparently worn out with use. The proprietor roared in rich, multisyllabic, spit-sprayed German:

—— Clumsy Jewish doltish underdevelopedbrain: you'll never make a carpenter!

Fein, stepping forward: —— It was my fault. I pushed him.

Reisinger, turning on Fein: —— You *what?*

Since Reisinger had obviously heard Fein's statement, this question was a sign of the slightest hesitation, an indecision— nearly covered by the red-faced roar—as to what to believe and how harsh to be. Fein moved brashly in.

—— I pushed him. (Fein shrugged.) We were having an argument. I said the Germans opposed the Tsar's anti-Jewish policy in the last war, he said Germans would never have been so stupid as to do that. One thing led to another. You know how Jews are. One minute talking quietly, next minute, *bam!*

Fein gave this explanation with a mixture of respectfulness and loutish, foolish lightheartedness. Reisinger could not possibly have helped realizing that he was being ridiculed: the whole shop was stilled, Berson says, and every Jew in it stood tense and delighted.

—— Get back to work!

Reisinger shouted this at the shop in general, standing on his tiptoes to give the command. Then, shaking his head in a disgust that was sufficiently grand to restore his self-esteem, he stalked out of the room.

EVENTS AUGUST 4, 1942. ENTRY DITTO. FROM DOLEK BERSON. This morning Fein told Berson about an organization which calls itself the Wall Men. This consists, according to Fein, of about eighteen or twenty men who are, to use his expression, *in business together*. Fein says the Wall Men can do anything. If you want *blintzes* and caviar, the Wall Men can get them for you. If you want to kill a Gestapo officer, the Wall Men will do it—for a price. If you want to rescue your mother from the *Umschlagplatz*, they can arrange it. Fein apparently belongs to this organization. He would not identify its leaders for Berson, though he hinted at far-reaching connections in both the outer world and the underworld. Fein swears that the Wall Men refuse to deal with the Germans; they are, he says, dedicated to circumventing the Germans and helping the Jews. Profits in this setup are more or less accidental; one might say that they come as a pleasant surprise.

[NOTE. N.L. Berson says he believes Fein on this peculiar integrity of the Wall Men. This is purely intuitive. He *senses* that Fein is dependable. Never having met Fein, I must take Berson's word for this. It seems that Fein is one of those people whose joviality lies embedded in fatty tissue. He is, by his own testimony (ENTRY APRIL 20, 1940) a restless and mobile man. Berson says he was the seventh of a family of twelve children, and he has the easy gregariousness of one brought up in a huge family. Uneducated, but a quick mind. And this trait of unbending good faith.]

Fein's account of the Wall Men, which he said he was giving Berson in case Berson should ever need anything, was interrupted by the warning signal from the shop lookout—and this time the signal was uttered with unusual vehemence and haste.

The carpenters fell suddenly silent: now only the voice of the saw, plane-scrapings, and a hammer's *top top top top top.* . . .

The door burst open and Reisinger, in his workman's smock, holding his gold-rimmed glasses in one hand, entered. His face was pale and he was talking a blue streak to the men behind him: *Sicherheitspolizei* officers. [NOTE. N.L. This is something new: Germans rather than Jewish police.]

—— They assured me that there would be no selection here. Look! Look! My certificate of necessity! (He fumbled in a waistcoat pocket and brought out a piece of paper.) We are making sashes for the *Wehrmacht*—barrack windows. These are all trained carpenters: look at them! (Every man in the shop was bent over his bench. Reisinger led the officers to a stack of finished sashes at one end of the shop.) Look at this workmanship! Look at those joints! See how the beveled joints fit! (The sashes were, indeed, little masterpieces, Berson says he thought: beautiful to look at, and every single one of them a half-centimeter wrong on each outside dimension.)

Reisinger was now bringing the officers toward the first row of benches, where Fein and Berson worked. In a pleading tone, the husky proprietor said:

—— Look at these artisans! Here (stopping at Berson)—one

of my best men. See that precision! (*Stupid Jewish doltish under-developedbrain that will never make a carpenter*, Berson says he thought, and he trembled with the comedy and terror of the situation, but nevertheless was also flattered, he wryly admits.) Let me explain to you the process.

One of the officers: —— Never mind. (Then to one of his companions:) Come here a moment, Herzenreden.

The two *Sicherheitspolizei* men went to the end of the shop, beside the stack of outsized sashes, and muttered to each other there. Soon the superior officer turned to Reisinger, who was standing trembling, with spittle at the corners of his mouth. The officer spoke loudly, like a schoolmaster dealing with a rapscallion boy:

—— Very well. We'll let you off easily. Give us five Jews.

Berson saw a tiny shudder seize Fein. His own hands were shaking.

Reisinger, relieved and beaming, wiping his mouth with the back of his hand, turned and walked from bench to bench, indicating by taps on shoulders the five men to be resettled. When he came to Berson, Berson looked up and stared at the German full in the eye. He saw a moment's weighing of one-of-my-best against stupid-Jewish-doltish . . . then Reisinger moved on. He did not even hesitate at Fein. He tapped the next man beyond. . . .

When the Germans and their haul and Reisinger had left, Fein looked up at Berson and said:

—— Congratulations, my fellow artisan, at having such a protector as Hans Reisinger. *One of my best men!* Ha! (Then, with a hard, furious expression, yet with the irrepressible twinkle still in his eye, Fein cursed Reisinger, who could still be seen out in the courtyard talking pompously now with the German officers:) Go use the ocean for a toilet seat!

9

EVENTS AUGUST 1, 1942. ENTRY AUGUST 3, 1942. FROM LAZAR SLONIM. Slonim has some sort of cruel streak in him. I remember how sincere his regret seemed to be at his remark in the soup kitchen on the inferiority of Rapaport's brain compared with his own [ENTRY JUNE 11, 1941]. Yet with what delight did he tell us last night that Rapaport has failed in his effort to get help from the Polish Socialists!

The news of Rapaport's failure went quickly around today. There is a tendency to laugh at the old fellow, because of his having alleged, the day of the famous handshake [ENTRY JULY 29, 1942], that the reason the Bund could not join other Jewish organizations was that it was planning to fight the Germans shoulder to shoulder with its Polish Socialist comrades. It seems the shoulders do not like each other's touch too much. But I do not join in the laughter. I think this must be very hard for Rapaport, who always has striven for co-operation with the Polish Socialists. I got Felix Mandeltort to persuade his friend to tell me what happened:

Rapaport made his exit from the ghetto through the New Court Building, on Leszno Street. This strategic building, incidentally, with entrances on both the ghetto and Aryan sides, is a center of official (and illegal) transactions between the Jewish quarter and the outside world. With papers to spare and a doorguard primed, Rapaport had no trouble getting through: he went out under legitimations of an official of the *Judenrat*. [NOTE. N.L. How were these arranged, I wonder?] He was dressed in a neat black suit; with his tidy mane and huge, pointed eyebrows, his lined face and his piercing eyes, he must have looked responsible, official. Outside, he walked north and east, diagonally toward the Vistula, up Dluga Street. About half a mile northeast of the ghetto area, he cut to the banks of the river, where he paid a zloty to a man in a flat-bottomed boat to take him across to Praga. He walked to a narrow alley off Florjanska Street and knocked on a plank door to one side of a poor-looking courtyard there.

A disheveled, twisted-seeming Pole opened the door and said in a pleasant voice:

—— Ah, Comrade Henryk! Come in! And how are things in the Jewish quarter?

—— Hello, Comrade Boleslav. (And he gave a meaningless answer, he says, to the Polish comrade's meaningless question:) Not too bad. (Then:) Has the meeting begun? It took me longer to get here than I expected.

—— No, we haven't begun yet. The Chairman asked me to tell you to wait here.

Comrade Boleslav indicated the single straight chair in the

barren anteroom, the walls of which were papered with yellowed sheets of the *Nowy Kurjer*.

Rapaport, making himself as comfortable as he could in the chair, stretching his legs out jauntily and putting one over the other: —— You mean, until the meeting begins?

Comrade Boleslav: —— The Chairman meant during the meeting.

Rapaport, standing up again quickly, the easy swagger gone out of his manner: —— But I thought I was to have an opportunity of explaining to the Central Committee . . .

Comrade Boleslav, running a hand through his hair: —— The Chairman was quite explicit. He said here.

Rapaport says that Comrade Boleslav's voice was not harsh; to the contrary, he spoke gently. Rapaport says he has known this Boleslav *from the earliest days*.

Rapaport: —— But you understand, Comrade Boleslav, I have come at considerable personal risk. It is not easy to arrange to come. . . .

Comrade Boleslav, his hand still going through his black bush of hair: —— Your problem is on the agenda of the Central Committee. The Central Committee will discuss it. (He repeated then pointedly:) The Chairman was explicit.

Rapaport sat down heavily. Comrade Boleslav excused himself and backed through a door with a limping walk he evidently has, and closed the door behind him. Rapaport heard Comrade Boleslav's uneven footsteps cross a room; another door opened and closed. Then there was quiet inside: in the far distance, out of doors, Rapaport could hear the shunting of trains. . . .

Rapaport says that during the meeting he entertained bitter thoughts about his former friend, Comrade Boleslav Kwasniewski.

[FROM ✿ CONVERSATIONS. INSERT INTO EVENTS AUGUST 1, 1942. FROM LEVINSON'S RECORD OF THE CONVERSATIONS OF MAY 9–10, 1943. . . . For instance, says Rapaport, do you remember my telling you about the day the Polish Central Committee turned me down? —— I remember it. —— Do you remember my description of the crippled Polish comrade, Boleslav? —— I do. —— Do you remember my saying I was bitter about him? —— I do. —— *Nu:*

A scene came back to Rapaport as he waited that day: a rough, improvised camp in a strip of woods near a road in western

Galicia in 1935: he remembered unrolling his blanket to spread it out for the night, and finding the chocolate gone. . . . He and Comrade Boleslav Kwasniewski and a taciturn, moody pit-miner named Winkler were working together as a flying squad of agitators, showing up successively at trouble spot after trouble spot. He remembered how much he had liked Comrade Boleslav. This young Pole had hurt his back when some scaffolding had buckled under him a couple of years before, yet he was far from immobilized, he could limp thirty miles a day, and was always cheerful, gentle, mild, kindly, and understanding. A marvelous companion. An honest eye and a steady hand. Never argued, always wanted to help. Rapaport himself had been more mercurial in those days, and had depended upon Comrade Boleslav to cheer him when he was discouraged and quiet him when he grew imprudently angry. Boleslav had not worked much since his accident and was terribly poor; Rapaport, who had saved some money, had bought, among the provender for this trip, three large bars of bitter Swiss chocolate, and each evening, when the men had finished their work for the day, had walked to some isolated country place, had supped on bread, cheese, and milk, and were talking or singing songs, Rapaport took out a chocolate bar and cut a little mouthful for Winkler, Boleslav, and himself. This was a pleasant diurnal sensation: the stars emerging, crickets exclaiming—the hard, puckering square in the mouth. Then one evening—when less than one bar had so far been consumed—he unrolled the blanket and found the rest of the chocolate gone. He knew that the chocolate could not have fallen out of the roll; he had had a special way of folding it in. Rapaport suspected stupid Winkler; cheerfully that night Boleslav had asked: *No ration this evening, Henryk?* . . . Several months later, in Krakow—Rapaport had forgotten all about the episode on the road—a meeting of a strike committee was being held, and Rapaport was arguing against raising a strike fund from non-striking plants, on the ground that many of the workers, especially the Catholics, were growing rather resentful of the so-numerous strikes at that time; whereupon gentle little Boleslav had turned to him and said, with a sudden flicker of a sneer: *What do you expect the strikers to live on—Jewish chocolate?* Boleslav had asked this with such intensity that Rapaport had immediately absolved poor, slow-minded Winkler from the suspicion he had previously held. . . .

And then, at the meeting on a back street in Praga nearly

seven years later, the hand running through the hair (that was a new mannerism; Boleslav never had used to do that) and: *The Chairman was quite explicit. . . .*]

The meeting was over. The inner door had opened; footsteps across the next room—two pairs; Comrade Boleslav and the Chairman standing finally in the news-encased room. Rapaport says the Chairman is an overpoweringly big man, with excessive hands and jaw; and with the mild, loose manner of such giants.

The Chairman, with a measure of cordiality: —— Rapaport! It's good to see you.

Rapaport: —— It has been several months.

The Chairman, protesting, as if it were Rapaport's fault: —— Months! Years, man!

Rapaport: —— Have you any news for me?

The Chairman, his manner becoming deprecatory: —— A terrible agenda today. We had one of the worst agendas I have ever seen. (He cleared his throat.) I regret to say that we did not reach the Jewish matter on the agenda.

Rapaport says he looked at Comrade Boleslav [From ✡ conversation. Insert. . . . The gentle, appealing tone: *No ration this evening, Henryk?* . . .], then back at the Chairman, and he burst out:

—— In other words . . .

The Chairman, raising his great, simian hand with surprising swiftness, and trying to placate: —— There are no *other words*, Comrade Henryk. Our agenda . . .

Rapaport, insisting: —— In other words, you, too, are against us.

The Chairman, with a heartbreaking look of sympathy, regret, and pity: —— My dear Comrade!

Rapaport turned and went out the door.

10

Events July 27, 1942. Entry ditto. From Rachel Apt. Rachel says her blood froze. She stood at the open window, watching. She had just been thinking, as she had washed and put away the pans from the noonday broth, how lucky little David was to be in this sheltered place, the Rukner Home. Games, lessons, handicrafts, story-telling, lullabies. Animal pictures, hobbyhorses, blocks. It was an atmosphere of healthy, normal, growing children, and the only sadnesses were the tear-spattering, transitory squalls of the very young. Here, so far as Rachel had been able to see, there was not even a whisper of the events in the rest of the ghetto . . . unless, perhaps, on the long walks they took each morning. . . .

She says she had been pleased with little David's behavior. He is one of the biggest children, yet he is never a bully. He has, in fact, taken some of the younger ones under his wing—a big-eared sprite, Nechemiah, who seems incapable of doing anything for himself; Benjamin, a boy who under other circumstances would have been awfully fat, who even here is soft-textured, clumsy, and the goat of many a tease; and Gershon, thin and hard as a nail, for which he is nicknamed. These three follow David everywhere, worship him, slave for him; and he in turn protects them. These children, and others, have apparently given their hearts to Rachel, and have taken hers in exchange. Rachel proudly reports to me that "Colonel" Rukner, the benign and tireless superintendent, has told her that the children, especially the smaller boys, have never accepted a "mother" so immediately and so warmly. As she had dried the pans, this afternoon, Rachel had sung happily:

> Play me a non-Aryan dance:
> A waltz non-Aryan,
> Non-barbarian . . .

and once she had whirled across the kitchen floor with a saucepan, as if dancing with it. She had stacked away the last tin bowls on the high shelf in the pantry, standing on tiptoe to do it; had untied her apron and hung it on its hook on the back of the kitchen door; had smoothed her uniform; and had walked out, happy and expectant, to help with the supervision of afternoon games. The children would be up from their naps by this time, she had decided, and out in the decorated courtyard. She had walked through the refectory to the library and there—at the first window giving out onto the courtyard—she had seen it:

The children were in the sunny part of the courtyard; none of the other four "mothers" was with them, for some reason. At one end, against the wall, stood David, looking imperious, chesty, mil-

295

itary; he held a short stick in his right hand and tapped it, in the manner of an impatient officer with a riding crop, against the side of his leg. His three followers were ranged, most of the time, beside him. Soft Benjamin, pulling at a nonexistent beard and grotesquely dignified, was apparently playing the part of a Jewish official. All the other children were in a line up the middle of the courtyard, facing David, and gathered into mock-tearful groups, moving slowly forward. From time to time Nechemiah and Gershon the Nail ran down the line, slapping and viciously shoving the docile children there. David, with an unutterably cruel and delighted face, was shouting:

—— Right . . . left . . . left . . . right. . . . Send that bunch to the *Umschlagplatz*, Nechemiah. . . . Get me some more Jews! . . . Left . . . left . . . right. . . .

Rachel ran through the library, into the hall, and outdoors. She cried:

—— Children! Children!

The "selection" dissolved and the children crowded around Rachel. David hung back. Those nearest Rachel shouted to her about their new game. They had learned it from a new boy, Zwi, whose mother and father had been resettled just two days before. A little girl, Aneta, barely four years old, waited gravely to get Rachel's ear, then said, with tremendous pride—as if nothing finer could happen to anyone:

—— Dovidl chose me for the *Umschagpatz!*

Rachel, pulling as many of the squirming children as her arms could encompass to her aching breast: —— My darlings, my darlings!

But the children were not keyed to tragic feelings. They pushed away from Rachel. Gershon the Nail shouted:

—— Dovidl! Dovidl! Let's play that again. That was fun!

EVENTS AUGUST 3, 1942. ENTRY DITTO. FROM STEFAN MAZUR. It was not altogether by chance that Stefan got the warning to Rachel. Stefan and his companions in the Jewish police station on Ogrodowa Street spend their time waiting for assignments in what they call the Ready Room. This is a large room on the second floor of the station, and it combines the features of office and lounge. There are coat hooks along two walls, with the initials of policemen burnt with a poker into small wooden signs above the hooks: here the men hang their "uniforms"—belts, hats, truncheons—while they are off duty. Benches are pushed against all four walls. There are some large filing cases and a desk for the duty policeman in one corner. In the center of the room, a round table covered with green cloth is surrounded by a number of ancient, crackly, inappropriate rattan-and-reed chairs.

Now, the convenience of this Ready Room is that it is next to the office of the district commandant, and the convenience of the district commandant is that he has enough voice for three men. As orders are telephoned to him usually a day in advance, and as he has the habit of shouting them back for confirmation, it is often possible for Stefan and his companions to learn ahead of time what has to be done. The young policemen lounging and joking in the Ready Room have a habit of keeping one ear tuned to the commandant's shouts.

Thus it was that Stefan, while waiting to be sent out on a call this morning, heard the commandant use in passing a word that sounded like *Rukner*. Stefan was not certain of this, as a friend of his named Vilshinsky was at the time telling a story; it was an insubstantial clue, but it was enough for Stefan. A quarter of an hour later, he was sent out with a man named Fakel on call. He persuaded Fakel to go around by way of Krochmalna Street, and he ran into the Rukner Home, found Rachel, and hastily whispered to her all that he knew — that he *thought* he had heard the commandant say a word that *sounded* like *Rukner* in a telephone conversation at headquarters; he had no idea what it meant if that was what he had heard. [FROM RACHEL APT.] This was enough for Rachel, too. She took David up to his dormitory, changed him from his uniform to his own clothes, out of his locker—they were too small for him; his wrists and ankles were partly covered sticks —then went for her own street dress, and, speaking only to one of the other mothers (she lied: she said that Froi Mazur was dying), she took David out of the orphanage and to the apartment on Nowolipie Street.

[FROM STEFAN MAZUR.] At four o'clock this afternoon, Stefan learned that he had heard correctly the word pronounced by his district commandant. Along with his entire Company, he was assigned under the command of an *S.D.* detachment to go to Krochmalna Street and the Rukner Home. Stefan, in the so-called "inner patrol," was present when the senior *Sicherheitsdienst* officer told "Colonel" Rukner to prepare the children for evacuation. Rukner, without abandoning for a moment his benign expression, went out in the courtyard, clapped his hands, and said to the children, who at his signal had quickly formed a quiet circle around him:

—— I have good news for you. We are going on a picnic. Go at once to your dormitories, put on clean uniforms, and come back here in fifteen minutes.

The crowd of children went off squealing and laughing.

At the end of the fifteen minutes, Stefan was ordered to help search the buildings. On a stairway he met a mother bringing down the last few children. Grabbing her sleeve, he asked in a hasty whisper:

—— Rachel Apt?

—— Gone, praise God. She took her brother.

Stefan ran on up the stairs. In the dormitories he found perfect order—the beds made, lockers neat, toys stacked away on shelves. He made a thorough search; no one was hidden; he descended to the courtyard. There he saw that the children were formed into ranks. They wore clean grey uniforms, and new cloth shoes with wooden soles; the girls had crisp, white aprons. "Colonel" Rukner was wearing his bare Polish medical corps uniform; his tunic was freshly laundered, his trousers were stuffed into brightly polished knee-boots; he wore a legionnaire's Maciejówka cap.

When the search was completed, the senior German officer nodded to Rukner.

Rukner: —— Now, my pioneers! Let us march smartly! Ready! Forward!

And as the ranks started up, with an out-of-step *clipper-clopper* noise of the wooden soles on the cobbles, the "Colonel" began a song, which the bigger boys, at the head of the procession, took up lustily. One of the boys was carrying a violin in a felt case. The "mothers," whose *Ausweise* had been honored, waved goodbye to the children from the doorway. The children, who thought they would see the "mothers" that evening as usual, scarcely bothered to wave back. The Jewish police walked alongside the children's parade in an escorting cordon.

The procession had quite a long way to go: from the "small

ghetto" across the Chlodna Street bridge and the entire length of the "large ghetto." The "Colonel" picked up a big-eyed little girl who was having trouble keeping up, and carried her in his arms. The parade was going along Gensia, toward Zamenhofa, when a man whom Stefan recognized as a *Judenrat* messenger came running up to the *Sicherheitsdienst* group, at the head of the column, and handed them a message. The march was halted. The senior officer took a note from the envelope the messenger had given him, and read it. Then he turned to "Colonel" Rukner and said:

—— At the request of Engineer Grossman of the *Judenrat*, you are personally excused from the deportation. We will take the children from here.

Rukner: —— Oh, no. Where my children go, I also go. (He turned, not permitting argument.) Come, children. Ready! March!

As Stefan walked along, not far from the "Colonel," he heard one of the older boys, a big-eared, funny-faced child, speak up to Rukner:

—— *Tate-niu*, little father! Where's Dovidl?

—— He couldn't come, Nechemiah.

—— That's too bad. He would have had a good time with us today, wouldn't he, *Tate-niu*?

—— Yes, Nechemiah, but we can't all have the luck, you know.

EVENTS AUGUST 4, 1942. ENTRY DITTO. FROM RACHEL APT. Berson suggested to Rachel that she try Fein and the Wall Men. She did. This was the interview, as she describes it:

At first Fein spent some time talking about the Wall Men. She says he is boyishly proud of the group.

—— Here. (Reaching into a drawer for a little canvas-backed booklet, and holding it up.) Here is the tidiest job we have done yet. Uruguayan passport for a gentleman who is—shall we say?—weary of his Polish citizenship. See! Absolutely genuine article, properly authenticated, can be investigated with the Uruguayan authorities perfectly safely. (Fein riffled through the pages of the passport, and he had the air of a proud craftsman displaying his work, a watchmaker pointing out the precision of an instrument he has just made.) Our friend will turn up one of these years as a distinguished citizen of Montevideo. . . . (The flipping pages came to rest for a moment at the photograph of the prospective traveler.) Doesn't he *look* like a Latin-American gentleman? (Fein smiled ironically.) Especially suitable for Sephardic Jews. . . .

It was Benlevi. The "Latin American" staring out with the stately boredom of a pontiff was old Benlevi. The booklet lay open at the photograph only a second or two, but in that time Rachel recalled, with renewed mortification, her brief talk (if it could have been called that) with Benlevi, when she had been trying to organize the secret school in the Sienna Street courtyard; and she also remembered again the evening when she had taken courage from the flashing eyes of Froi Mazur to rebuke the famous old man. That had been the first time she had ever spoken out a conviction boldly. She tells me she thought: How far I have come since then! They think in Hashomer that I'm some kind of orator. And it all started when this pompous old pre-Uruguayan had said, so contemptuously, *Foolish girl!* Well, she could look him straight in the eye now.

Fein: —— Of course, in order to assume the duties and prerogatives of Uruguayan citizenship, it will be necessary for our friend here (Fein tapped the closed passport on the knuckles of his left hand.) to intern himself with all the neutral foreigners in the Pawiak, and then. . . . One can only guess. He is on his own. But at least he has an authentic document.

Authentic document. Rachel says she was reminded that she is moving about the streets these days, in the hours before and after the daily resettlement action, on nothing but an *Ausweis* from the liquidated Rukner Home. But, she says, she feels quite safe. She feels that Hashomer will shelter her; the "family" will protect her. And—possibly this is where her sense of security is really grounded—she will do all she can for them.

Fein acknowledged at last that preliminaries were over. (Rachel says he evidently enjoys to the utmost play-acting as a grand businessman.)

—— You said you had some proposition to discuss.

Rachel, speaking now in a direct and concise way [NOTE. N.L. Possibly she enjoys doing business herself; for I have noticed before that she is her father's daughter, though she may think she is not.]: —— Yes. I want to insure my younger brother, David —he's nine years old—I want to make sure that he will not be resettled. How do we know where these resettled people are being taken? I'd like to get David to the Aryan side, if that is possible. My father is there, but I don't know where he is living now, and I have an idea it might be best not to put the boy with him in any case. They might endanger each other. My father looks Aryan [NOTE. N.L. How carelessly we fall into using the Nazis' phrases!], but David is unmistakably Semitic. I think my father would be afraid to risk his life by living with such a giveaway. And so what I wanted to ask you is: can you find a hiding place for a very Jewish little boy who isn't ready to take care of himself?

Fein: —— That I don't know. That is a problem our organization has so far not dealt with. I'll have to talk with the others— and I'll let you know. But I think we'll find a way. You see (Fein's expression was almost a gloat.), what we like best is new problems!

And Rachel says she thought: Well, if this entertains Fein and his friends, that's all right—so long as the task is done.

11

EVENTS JULY 29, 1942. ENTRY JULY 30, 1942. FROM DO-LEK BERSON. Symka Berson has grown weaker. Berson carries her out into the living room in the evenings with a blanket wrapped around her, and puts her in the deep, soft chair for which, in preparation for the party on their fateful fifth wedding aninversary, Symka encased the pillows in bright green satin [ENTRY NOVEMBER 4, 1939]; the satin seems unchanged, nearly as fresh as the day it was bought—only the hands and heads that touch the pillows seem to have been buffed and frayed with age. Berson props his wife up with these pillows, and then he gets her her handmirror, so that she can satisfy herself that her wig is on straight. (Her hair has never come back in properly; she still wears the wig. Poor vain creature, she even insists on wearing it to bed at night.)

What with factory rations and occasional help from Pavel Menkes in the form of a stale loaf, we have enough food to survive on. But Symka is not interested in eating for survival. She keeps asking for something sweet. Berson has recalled to us several times, as a kind of apology, that she had a sugartooth before the war: she loved Menkes' sweet buns and often used to tease Berson to bring her rock candy. Symka's requests for sweet food have constantly reminded the rest of us that we are not getting anything sweet, and finally, at breakfast one day last week, Mordecai said irritably:

—— For God's sake, Dolek, can't you keep her quiet?

This was the first time I had heard anyone refer to Symka before her face as if she were not there. It has happened several times since then.

Last evening most of the "family" was sitting in the living room listening to Berson play the concertina. This instrument has become more and more a focal point of the family life: the tones of the famous Bechstein piano are too grating in the small room, and besides, the instrument is out of key and piano-tuners are not to be found in the ghetto these days. The concertina's small tone, melancholy or brilliant depending upon the need, is just right for all, and since Berson loves to play, many evenings are passed in recital. All around the courtyard, people can be seen leaning out of windows listening to the nasal strains.

Last evening, Berson was playing the sweeping melodies of Schubert's C Major Symphony when Stefan came in, his work for the day over. The music broke off. Stefan seemed to be in unusually high spirits. He kissed his mother, then he went to Halinka and kissed her. These open demonstrations between Stefan and Halinka have become common since the resettlement began, with the result that without ever discussing the matter openly, we have all arrived at certain conclusions, I think. Accordingly Symka's sudden remark, which seemed to come out of her perfectly naturally as if it followed from something that was being *said*, rather startled us:

—— At *our* wedding, we had a canopy with real gold thread in it.

Berson: —— Yes, dear.

Stefan sat down. Berson pulled a few random chords from the instrument.

Stefan, half in admiration and half in dismay: —— Those Ger-. mans! I guess the resettlement is lagging, so they've put up posters today saying that anyone who reports voluntarily to the *Umschlagplatz* gets three kilograms of bread and one kilogram of marmalade.

Berson: —— No, thanks, they can't bribe *me!*

And with a fanfare he began playing again.

In the middle of last night, Berson tells me, he woke up. Someone was moving about. Since six sleep in the bedroom together, Berson thought nothing of the rustling and was about to go back to sleep when, putting out a hand for that touch which even now, against the tiny staircase of a fleshless spine, is, he says, reassuring—when he found that Symka was not in bed.

Berson, whispering: —— Symka!

The rustling stopped a moment, then continued. Berson jumped up and went to a corner of the room, where he found Symka fully dressed, except for her shoes, which she had evidently been unable to find.

—— My dear girl, what are you doing?

—— I'm going to the *Umschlagplatz*. I want the marmalade.

Berson had to use force (but very little) to keep Symka from leaving.

12

EVENTS JULY 29–AUGUST 5, 1942. ENTRY AUGUST 5, 1942. N.L. I have here recorded, in the past few days, without recapitulating and so without facing the *tendency* of the deportations, a number of separate episodes that clearly pointed that tendency—the executions in the Pawiak, the reappearance of "Frankenstein," the use of whips in the Ceglana-Twarda resettlement actions, the account of brutality in the *Umschlagplatz* from the man who escaped through the railroad yard, and especially the free and easy use of pistols during house searches to dispose of any hiding, ill, argumentative, or appellant Jews: cases cited from Ceglana, Solna, Orla Streets. It is now time for me to face up to a recapitulation and to the curve of facts:

There has been a crescendo of violence in the resettlement. It makes us wonder: where are these people being taken, and for what?

I see, in looking back over these notes, that I registered, a week ago today, a mystification over hearing widespread shooting for the first time. It now appears to me that that day, July 29, marked the beginning of a second phase in the resettlement action.

Up to that time, Jewish police had been managing the selections; since then, the work has been increasingly handled by Germans, Ukrainians, Lithuanians, and Latvians, with the Jewish *Ordnungsdienst* men acting more and more as sentinels, messengers, searchers, servants, and onlookers. Before the twenty-ninth, there had been little shooting; since then, there have been many, many deaths. In the first phase, refugees, beggars, incurables, prisoners, and the unemployed were evacuated; in the second, the Germans began entering factories and taking perfectly sound workers. Some smaller shops were entirely evacuated. Before July 29, the selections were for the most part house-to-house affairs; in recent days, entire blocks have been cut off, by barbed wire and human cordons, and searched.

The deportations have also become increasingly haphazard and unpredictable. Wives and children of men with valid *Ausweise* are supposed to be spared, but I have heard of several cases of workers returning home from their shops at night to find their entire families gone. *Ausweise* themselves are sometimes not respected. A Jewish policeman witnessed the accosting of one of our ZITOS workers in the street by a German, and when the man produced his *Judenrat* social-service *Ausweis*, the German said:

—— If you were really working, you wouldn't have time to loiter about in the streets.

And he took the ZITOS man off.

According to the regulations, each deportee is supposed to be permitted to take along fifteen kilograms of baggage, but people taken thus in the streets, and even some taken in selections, have been dragged away without any belongings whatsoever.

A result of the increasing violence and uncertainty is that the Jews have become more and more stubborn about the deportations. At first many Jews reported voluntarily. Now almost none. You have to give old Rapaport credit: he got out a superb broadside, called *Storm*, the other day, warning the ghetto inhabitants that deportations might mean death, and urging them not to go to the *Umschlagplatz* voluntarily. The Germans, evidently sensing the growing resistance (passive though it has been) pulled their bread-and-marmalade stunt on July 29, 30, and 31, and again on August 2, 3, and 4. They actually kept their promise and handed out the food to those who reported.

Well, they didn't stop at 70,000, as our optimists wanted us to

believe they would. The figures: July 29—5,722; July 30—6,651;
July 31—6,894; August 1—6,265; August 2—6,325; August 3—6,357;
August 4—6,728. Total for the week, 44,942. Grand total to date,
92,376.

Now we know that the "candidates for resettlement" are
loaded into boxcars at the Danzig Station sidings. One hundred
Jews per car, approximately.

Destination—unknown.

EVENTS AUGUST 5–8, 1942. ENTRY AUGUST 8, 1942. N.L.
FROM M. SCHORR. . . . A discovery that changes everything.
That changes nothing, really. Except that it kills hope, and that is
nearly everything.

It is ironical that this discovery, which may be of the greatest
value to the Jews here, should have been made by one of those
men so hated by the entire Jewish community—a Jewish policeman. In general I feel rather sorry for the Jewish police. Originally
most of them enlisted with a sincere conviction that the "Order
Service" might fulfill the sense of that phrase: might bring order
and might be of service; even Berson signed up with this conviction. In spite of themselves, and often without knowing what was
happening to them, the Jewish police have been driven into becoming executors of German cruelty. Many would have withdrawn,
as Berson did, but they felt that their position protected their families. I have seen a couple of them in agonies over this dilemma.
In these two cases (Dickstein, Brotles) the decision to stay at a
hated job in order to protect beloved relatives has had two tragic
reversals in effect: it has made them openly hate their relatives and
it has made them love their jobs, or at least seem to, so that they
have become brutal, Gestapo-like policemen. Two years ago, Dickstein and Brotles were both gentle, respected, intelligent lawyers.
Now they are monsters.

Anyhow, it was a policeman named Schorr who made the discovery to which I have referred. He came running to the *Judenrat*,
when he was sure of his facts, and I was given the job of questioning him. Schorr told me he had been assigned to the *Umschlagplatz*, as an underling to the Junaks who do the policing there. His
job was to assist in loading Jews into the boxcars on the Danzig
Station sidings. He became interested in the cars. They were mostly
steel-framed, wooden-walled vans of German, Czech, and French

manufacture, and they had various markings on them. Schorr says that he found that reading the numbers on the cars kept his mind off unpleasant thoughts, and soon he had a habit of scanning these numbers rather systematically. Schorr was a journalist before the war: he says he never had the slightest mathematical inclination that he was aware of. At any rate, one day he memorized the serial markings on three German-type cars full of Jews, the doors of which he himself sealed, intending to watch for the cars' return. He thought he might be able to tell by the number of days or weeks the cars were gone approximately how far into Russia the deportees are being taken; it would, he realized, give only the barest approximation.

The transport with the three cars whose numbers he had memorized left at about ten o'clock on the morning of August 5. *All three cars were back the same afternoon, empty.*

Schorr thought he had made some mistake. He thought perhaps the cars had been shunted to another siding, without his having noticed it, and had never left the yards (though he had sealed those three cars, and he had not seen any cars evacuated on the sidings during the day). He had read the markings on the new empties that afternoon by sheer chance—or rather, by force of habit, obsessively. He was not willing to believe his own eyes.

Accordingly, next morning, as he sealed Jews into a newly made-up train, he noted that two of the same three cars were in the train. As the train started up, he asked a Junak the time. (The Junaks, it seems, all have nice wristwatches; one wonders how procured.) It was 9:37 a.m. Schorr saw the train all the way out of the yards.

The two cars came back into the yards on a load of empties which halted on Siding Seven at 3:43 p.m.

Schorr timed four cars the next day. All left on the same train at 10:03 a.m. Three came back in at 4:07 p.m. The fourth came in on another train at 4:19.

It then occurred to Schorr that the serial markings might be repeated on all cars of various given types. He therefore procured a piece of chalk from his headquarters next day, and as he locked each door in a transport of fourteen cars, he marked a small x beside the lock; it must have seemed, to anyone who saw him, a perfectly normal, rather conscientious thing to be doing. The transport left at 9:42 a.m. Eleven of his fourteen x's were back at 3:51 that afternoon.

So. Though it takes a through train at least twenty hours to the Russian border on the Bialystok-Minsk line, and a load of miserable Jews could hardly be considered "through" cargo, so would take *much* longer, it actually requires only three hours for our Jews to be "resettled in the East"—to go to "labor duty on the Russian front." It takes three hours for the trains to come back again. Six hours altogether. Our Jews are being "resettled" somewhere just outside Warsaw. What is this?

13

EVENTS AUGUST 7, 1942. ENTRY DITTO. N.L. Our conclusions concerning Halinka and Stefan were justified. I wish her luck.

EVENTS JULY 28, 1942. ENTRY AUGUST 9, 1942. FROM STEFAN MAZUR. Already by the end of the first week of the resettlement, the atmosphere in the Ready Room of the Ogrodowa Street police station had changed, Stefan says. Formerly there had always been a card game going at the round, green-clothed table at the center of the room; the circle of rattan chairs had been a trading post for jokes; songs could often be heard from a group on one of the benches. There had been excitement in the Ready Room, something doing every minute.

Now the room was sad, quiet, heavy. There was a real sense of waiting: time went along slowly. No cards, few songs, dull anecdotes. An air of weariness and insensibility. Only when the commandant's loud voice shouted into the telephone in the next room was there a kind of alertness in the Ready Room.

Stefan sat, that morning, in one of the rattan chairs, with his feet on the edge of the table; he stared at them. Vilshinsky, a blunt-minded, tough-nerved young man who has for some time been Stefan's friend—he is nearly as handsome as Stefan, it seems, but not nearly so quick and keen; he plays a lieutenant's role to Stefan's intellectual captaincy—Vilshinsky now said:

—— What's your trouble? You look awful.

Stefan, with rheumy cow-eyes, sad and still staring: —— I'm getting married.

—— Halinka?

Stefan nodded.

Vilshinsky: —— What! You don't have to be so gloomy about it! Hey, Fakel! Ausbach! Fellows! Here's Mazur about to get it regularly from one of the prettiest girls in the ghetto, and look at him! Cheer up, policeman!

Others gathered around and listlessly, with a coarseness that no longer had the customary verve to it, tried to make sport of Stefan's news. [NOTE. N.L. News which Stefan withheld from his own "family," incidentally, until day before yesterday.] What ruined the boys' half-hearted fun was that the butt of their jokes (who had used to be so quick to anger or laughter, according to his mood) now sat paying scarcely any attention.

Vilshinsky, identifying the bride for his friends: —— The Apt beauty. The singer.

Fakel: —— The one who used to be at the Britannia?

Vilshinsky: —— That's the one! And Mazur crying about getting next to her!

Fakel (a very short man, Stefan says, with a pockmarked face): —— Maybe Mazur's little soldier won't come to attention for him any more. Maybe it has been frightened.

Vilshinsky: —— Maybe it has been resettled in the East.

Stefan, stirring in his chair: —— No, really. I don't feel very humorous about this today. I'm pleased to be getting married. I love my bride. That's all. There's nothing more to say. (Then, contradicting his own last statement:) I don't know why I feel this way.

Fakel, with a kindhearted cheerfulness: —— I know what you need. You need a gay wedding. Listen! You've been looking forward for a long time to getting married, it was supposed to be one of the big things . . . and now, with this (Stefan says it was a big *this*—the resettlement, the sounds of shots in the distance, the misery of life inside the wall.), I don't wonder you're depressed.

Stefan, speaking sarcastically, as if it would be easier to fly to the moon: —— Yes, I will have a gay wedding.

Fakel: —— Seriously, I mean it. It can be done. I know a group who can arrange a real old-fashioned wedding. They can arrange anything. They call themselves the Wall Men. . . .

Vilshinsky, quoting with a sly grin from the Jewish policemen's manual: —— *Smuggling will be put down with the utmost
vigilance.* . . .

Fakel, answering Vilshinsky's dig with an answering grin: ——
Never mind that. This is a useful bunch. They'll get you a beautiful canopy, Stefan, and wine glasses for two hundred people, and
smoked salmon and *kreplach*, and a marriage broker, and kosher
wine, and schnapps, and a rabbi—

Stefan, sitting up a little straighter now: —— A rabbi I have.

Fakel: —— They could even get you a bride.

Stefan: —— A bride I have.

Vilshinsky: —— The way you used to boast, you may need an
extra one before the first night is over.

Fakel: —— Listen, we'll get in touch with them. There's a
fellow named Fein at Reisinger's joining factory—

Stefan: —— Fein! Used to make wigs?

Fakel: —— That's the one.

Stefan: —— This is going to be easy.

Already, Stefan says, he was expansive.

Events August 8, 1942. Entry ditto. N.L. Halinka
was married today. I will have no more trouble from that quarter.

[Note. Editor. In fairness it can be said that Levinson
clarifies this cryptic entry in ✿ conversations, May 9–10, 1943.]

Events August 8, 1942. Entry August 9, 1942. From
Rachel Apt. Preferring not to see the wedding through my own
eyes, I watched Rachel's. I thought I saw much there. Today she
has told me what was going on behind those eyes of hers:

There were about fifty guests in the tiny apartment. Rachel
stood to one side of the splendid canopy, and David was in front
of her; she stood with her hands on David's shoulders. She says
she was lost in a pleasant pensiveness. Reb Yechiel Mazur's ceremonial voice droned the Hundredth Psalm: . . . *and into his
courts with praise.* . . . Rachel says she had what she calls "the
family feeling" very strongly; it was a kind of undiscriminating
love she felt. She saw Rutka, on the other side of the canopy, with
tears in her eyes: tears for her handsome brother Stefan, the
groom—the appropriate, trite, wedding mood; and Rachel thought
how unselfish Rutka had been: not once, not even in the most par-

enthetical remark, had Rutka expressed the wish that her own wedding could have been as grand and open as Stefan's was to be. And Rachel saw her brother, Mordecai, hard-looking, impassive. . . . Froi Mazur, gazing at her son Stefan with that look of pride and unstinting, sacrificial motherliness which Rachel had once seen her bestow on Schlome. . . . The rabbi, rather flustered-looking, his attention divided, apparently, between the lint on his long-disused black suit and Reb Yechiel's sonorities (. . . *hast sanctioned unto us such as are wedded by the rite of the canopy and the sacred covenant of wedlock* . . .). . . . Berson, staring with his big, kindhearted eyes at the couple under the canopy. . . . N.L., squirrel wearing glasses—what historical process was conducting itself behind the lenses? [NOTE. N.L. Rachel talks about me in this way with such a sweetness that I cannot be offended. A squirrel now.]

Then, suddenly, taking Rachel's breath and bringing stealthy tears to her eyes, Stefan, the exquisite, curly-haired bridegroom, turned to his lovely Halinka—the two together seemed to Rachel magically beautiful—and pronounced the crucial words:

—— Behold! Thou art consecrated unto me by this coin in accordance with the Law of Moses and of Israel.

And Stefan pressed gently into the bride's hand, in lieu of a ring, a coin, admissible by ancient custom—not a Polish coin, certainly not a German coin, but (this was Stefan's own idea) a French coin, out of a collection he gathered as a boy and still keeps in a black tin box with a tiny round key: an almost worthless piece of alloy with a hole in it, a ten-centime piece, mintage of 1923, but with these values: on one side, the symbolical cap of freedom; on the reverse, the words, in other times so hackneyed, now in the ghetto so rich in meaning: *LIBERTÉ, ÉGALITÉ, FRATERNITÉ.* Rabbi Goldflamm began reading the marriage contract. Berson had moved away and softly now played the tragic music that seems to go with weddings. Froi Mazur gave herself over to weeping. Shots could be heard in the street. . . .

Rachel looked at the bride, her sister, and felt for her (she says) an unqualified, pure love. Suddenly she remembered, with still a vestige of both gratitude and resentment, the day of Mordecai's "coffin": it had been when they were children: usually Mordecai and Halinka had paired together and either played tricks on Rachel or begged Rachel to read to them or somehow entertain them, but that morning—Mordecai was then about twelve, Rachel ten, and Halinka nine—Halinka had out of some momentary caprice teamed up with Rachel, and during a hiding game the two girls had seen the hinged cover of the north windowseat in the living room move slightly, and with a telepathically shared impulse, both of them had rushed across the living room and pounced on the seat; onto the long, harsh-textured *petit-point* cushion on the windowseat, with the pattern of knights on horseback and gigantic lilies. Mordecai had been hiding in the big musty-smelling box of the windowseat, where the rolled-up reed porch-shades were kept in wintertime, and now he had been captured there. Halinka had squealed:

—— Mordecai's in his coffin! Mordecai's in his coffin!

Then, with the drumming of Mordecai's fists and toes on the windowseat beneath them, Halinka had leaned over, her eyes sparkling, and kissed Rachel, and with a giggle had said:

—— You're *nebich* a wonderful sister, Rochele!

Pity and admiration in one breath!

. . . Rabbi Goldflamm sang out the seven benedictions, the bride and groom sipped the glass of wine, and Stefan, turning, threw the glass to the floor, where it crashed into many pieces.

Rachel saw Fein bend over and pick up a piece of the stem of the glass, which had skipped across the open circle of floor in front of him and stopped at his feet. He twirled the little cylinder of glass between his thumb and forefinger with a mock-bitter expression, as if to say: *We get the best and they throw it on the floor.* Rachel looked at the pretty canopy, held up by spear-like iron rods, that Fein and his group had produced; she thought of the astounding delicacies they had brought that morning; she felt David sighing with boredom under her light hands, and she wondered whether, as Berson had said, Fein's Wall Men could do *anything.* . . .

Reb Yechiel: —— Praise Him with the blast of the horn: praise Him with the harp and the lyre. Praise Him with the timbrel and the dance: praise Him with stringed instruments and the pipe. Praise Him with the clear-toned cymbal; praise Him with the loud-sounding cymbals. Let everything that hath breath praise the Lord: praise ye the Lord.

Then the married couple stepped out from under the canopy, and there began exchanges of *Mazl-tov*, feasting, laughter, and

311

praising of the Lord with the sweet-toned concertina. Outside in the streets more shots could be heard.

Rachel waited her turn, embraced Halinka, and, still thinking of the day of Mordecai's "coffin," said:

—— *Mazl-tov*, Halinka. You're a . . . a wonderful sister, Halinka.

No place for pity on a wedding day!

14

EVENTS AUGUST 11, 1942. ENTRY DITTO. FROM WLADIS-LAW JABLONSKI. The "family"—all save Stefan, who was out on duty—sat around the living room, listening to the story that Wladislaw Jablonski, the son of the convert whom Berson housed for a time, told us. The tall, thin boy, with his stringy neck, sat bolt upright on the piano stool, and he talked all in a flood. He twisted his hands, and he looked mostly at his former host, Berson.

—— In the confusion when they first herded all of us Catholics into the church, I slipped out through the private chapel to the sacristy. I had been given the job, several times, of cleaning the sacred vessels and the altar candlesticks, and I knew that the closet off the sacristy, where the altar covers and vestments were kept, had deep, deep shelves at one end, and that the shelves were mostly hidden from view by the priests' and altar boys' and choir's vestments, on hangers on a bar running across the closet. I had picked that out to be my hiding place, in case. . . . I went into the closet and closed the closet door and sliced through behind the vestments and climbed way back onto the top shelf and covered myself over with a piece of altar cloth, or whatever it was. I could barely hear the noises in the church. Once somebody opened the sacristy door for a moment but closed it soon again — a careless search, if it was a search. After a while it grew quiet. I stayed in the closet for what seemed like days, though I guess it was only about five hours. The selection had begun, as I said, at about four o'clock. It was just getting dark when I finally came out of the closet. From the sacristy I could hear noises in the streets, so I knew it was not

yet curfew hour. They hadn't left any sentries at the church. . . .
I came straight here. . . . You are the only people I know.

The "family" was silent.

Wladislaw, confusedly: —— It was pleasant at All Saints'.
The courtyard was like something in a monastery in Italy. I used
to imagine I was in Italy. Everybody around me seemed to be pretending that he wasn't Jewish. We had a beautiful acacia tree
there. It was very quiet in our vegetable garden. (The embarrassed, tumbling sentences stopped. Then Wladislaw said:) You
are the only Jews I know.

[INSERT. FROM ENTRY AUGUST 18, 1942. FROM WLADISLAW
JABLONSKI. Young Jablonski's story, or rather the mortified anguish with which he told it, made me feel very sorry for him. I
have talked with him now, and I am more than ever sorry for him.
He is an ungainly, simpering, spindly boy, but is there any wonder?
In appearance, he is definitely Semitic. The decision that he should
attempt to pass as a Pole was taken by his father, while the boy was
still an infant; he had no choice in the matter. Yet in everything
he did where Jews were involved, he was reproached for his "es-
capism." He told me of an occasion when our own Stefan, one day
while Jablonski was still at the Sienna courtyard, sneeringly said:

—— You needn't be so proud, Jablonski. Don't forget that
your Christ was just a Jew like the rest of us.

Wladislaw tells me that for several weeks he has had the intention of taking back his father's Jewish name and faith. But he
has not done it. He has gone on posing as a Pole. I can see that he
feels terribly guilty that it took a deportation action and a real
scare to make him act; and now he is by no means accepted "back"
by our young people, Mordecai and Stefan in particular. Not once
has he mentioned his lost father.]

Berson, turning toward the others: —— What do you think?

Rachel: —— We have to take him in. Where else can he go?

Mordecai, looking at the floor: —— If it were discovered that
we were harboring someone improperly . . . (Obviously he did
not want young Jablonski to move in. Something special was bothering Mordecai, and at last he blurted out emotionally:) I won't
let anything happen that threatens my—my baby.

[NOTE. N.L. Thus do we learn things in our peculiarly
close-mouthed family. Thus obliquely and accidentally did we

learn that Rutka is pregnant. Of course this is the only secret in life that human beings cannot keep indefinitely: it gets out within a fixed period. To be sure, Rutka is only two months along, but this does seem an incongruous way for such a valuable and beloved secret to come tumbling out. When Mordecai uttered these words, we sat amazed. Before the Jablonski boy, we did not wish to make an immediate fuss; that came later. But Froi Mazur began to cry and Rachel got an exultant sparkle in her eye, and young Jablonski could not help seeing that there was a definite flurry of emotion in the room. Later we had a session of excited questions and congratulations (Rutka says she and Mordecai had been trying for this for over three months, and she had begun to think that the times had made her barren); and still later, we were all overwhelmed, I think, by the thought of the confidence and optimism that this new, small life means in these days. At the time of this revelation on Mordecai's part, Wladislaw thought—and one cannot blame him—that it was his own story that had moved us so, and he began again to talk, as if to consolidate the advantage he imagined he had gained.]

—— I never agreed with my father. I always thought we should be Jewish. Look at my face, anyhow! He was a very positive man. . . . (Wladislaw looked around and saw us all stirred up; he said sententiously:) Wasn't it strange that they took the Jews who didn't want to be Jews?

Rachel, to Wladislaw, impatiently, for she was trying to fix her mind on this new thing Mordecai had told us: —— Be still, Wladislaw! Of course we'll take you in.

15

EVENTS AUGUST 5, 1942. ENTRY AUGUST 12, 1942. FROM LAZAR SLONIM. Rapaport called on Slonim, rather than summoning Slonim to him. In spite of this gesture, one can imagine the tension there must have been between these two men, at least at the beginning of their conversation. Slonim himself acknowledges that there were long pauses in their colloquy, as if each speech were a move in a game of chess.

Rapaport: —— I wouldn't blame you for feeling discouraged. You must have thought we were never going to use you for anything but delivering *Storm* and the news bulletins. . . . Or perhaps you were satisfied to be an errand boy?

Slonim, after a long wait, mumbling wearily: —— Is this necessary?

Rapaport seemed to be considering whether he should go on at all. At last he said:

—— I've never told you, have I, that I was saving you for something really important? Something so important you may choose to go back to paper deliveries?

—— *Nu?* (A pawn, exploring.)

—— I'm going to ask you to risk your life for Jewry.

Slonim, laughing: —— Really, don't you think that's a comical thing to say—at this stage?

Rapaport, his face showing no sense of comedy, and after pondering again: —— You see these postcards? They have been brought to me by our comrades. They purport to be from the relatives of these comrades. Here!

Rapaport tossed into Slonim's hands three German form-postcards from a stack that he held in his hand. Slonim read them:

The work here is quite hard, but we eat well. Better than the ghetto. Join me. Ask for Julag XIV.

[Signed]   Moishe Katzen

Strongly urge you apply for transfer to this camp (near Pinsk). We are draining swamps to make small airfield. Love.

[Signed]   Samson Perl

Here we get two hot meals a day! My back is bothering me, but I am much happier here. Come.

[Signed]   Nachum Freund

Rapaport: —— They're all the same. Notice: all postmarked from various places in Russia. Each one twenty words. Quite credible. The people who get these are absolutely convinced that they are authentic. The handwritings are precisely those of their relatives. Our Chaver Hirschel Freund, who received the one from Nachum Freund that you just read, says that his brother always had trouble with his back when he did heavy work. These cards are

315

being passed around and discussed. They are having an effect: even some of our best comrades are wavering and want to report for deportation. Slonim, I want you to go to the Aryan side and somehow trace the deportees to their *final* destination, even if it means going deep into Russia. If our people are being taken to such work camps, where conditions are not bad, we must know it. If they are not, we must know that, too, and we must know where they *are* going, and what happens to them when they get there. . . . So that is the kind of thing I have been saving for you. Will you go?

Slonim: —— Of course.

Rapaport, without a word of comment or thanks or praise: —— We will arrange some kind of papers to help you get outside the wall. If you learn anything, bring us back a report, or if that is impossible, send us a message using the following code words. . . .

Whether or not there was hostility between the two men when the interview began, Slonim says that at the end of it, *he admitted to himself that there was method and even a certain talent in Rapaport's leadership.*

Events August 7–8, 1942. Entry August 12, 1942. From Lazar Slonim. The Polish railroad worker, moving his index finger, which was striated in the skin-marks with remnants of the grime of his work, along a narrow double stripe on the route-map, said:

—— In block seventeen, as you can see, there is a main-line junction. Here the line for Danzig and the one for Bialystok meet. If your trains are going east to Russia, they go straight on; if north and west, they swing to the left.

One can imagine Slonim bending down nearsightedly over the map, his cowlick hanging straight down, almost perpendicular to his forehead. He said:

—— Block seventeen. Then that is where I must make my first observation.

—— Correct. From there, it depends.

The two men were in a small room in an apartment on the Aryan side. A cotton blackout curtain hung untidily over the only window; light came from a small carbide lamp, holding down one edge of the map. The walls had been painted yellow years ago. There were big mottled, fanning, damp spots on them, with paint upcurling at the edges; these looked, Slonim says, like gigantic lichens. The railroad worker, to whom Slonim had been directed by Polish Socialists, had a hard, square face, and the folds of skin under his eyebrows hung heavily over his eyes. He now said:

—— To get to block seventeen, you'll have to cross the Vistula and pick up the tracks on the other side. Then simply follow them till you reach the fork. Not too far from the river. . . .

Slonim was aware of an opened tin of sardines and a large chunk of bread on a plate on a crude plank chest by the window. These, he supposed, were to be Comrade Jan's supper, but he could not help feeling angry with the railroad worker for not having at least hidden them. Ever since he had come into the room, Slonim had smelled the heavy fragrance of the sardine oil. He found it hard to concentrate on Comrade Jan's directions.

—— If the trains go straight ahead toward Russia, you'll just have to walk the tracks. If the trains turn left, you may find it easiest to get a boat and travel northward down the Vistula: the tracks follow the river as far as the confluence with the Bug. You can check along the way. Beyond the Bug, go overland (The grease-patterned finger traveled along the tracks on the map.) and follow the line. There is a junction with the Bialystok-Bydgoszcz line about fifty kilometers beyond the Bug—the other side of Ciechanów. . . .

The dry, emotionless directions went on; the smell of the fish oil seemed to grow stronger in the room. Slonim thought of the last time he had eaten sardines: 1939, actually three years before. How smooth the flesh! The little melting bones!

Comrade Jan, continuing in a matter-of-fact way: —— It would seem unlikely to me that trains for Russia would go up the Danzig line; it is possible, however, that they might route them by back lines so as to keep the main east-west lines free for military trains. . . .

Slonim was obsessed with the sardine tin. For a moment an appeal—*My God, Comrade, I'm starving to death!*—was on the tip of his tongue; but pride before a Pole pushed it back. Instead he became inwardly angry: he wanted to argue with the phlegmatic, well-stuffed, self-assured animal; but all that Comrade Jan said was unassailable, even kind and helpful. Slonim swallowed his anger, but it was not so satisfactory a meal as the soft fish would have been; it roiled his guts. How could a man be so insensitive, selfish, and cruel as to leave food lying around under these circumstances?

—— I have heard a rumor—you see, my work is at the Aleje Jerozolimskie yards and I wouldn't know much about the trains you want to follow—but I've heard a rumor that they make a round trip of only half a day. That would be only about fifty kilometers and back, if that much. You may not have to go too far. Though this is only a vague report, I must warn you, from one of our workers. . . .

Slonim could stand the smell of the sardines no longer. He stood up and said tersely:

—— Thank you for the help. I must go now.

—— Go? But where do you intend to spend the night?

Slonim had no intentions: he had no idea where he would spend the night. He would have to go back to his first contact, and beg a bed on a floor, probably. He lied:

—— Comrade Wolo is expecting me.

The Pole stood up. On his face was the same rather stupid, unfeeling expression as he had worn all along.

—— But Comrade Wolo told me that I could put you up. Look, I've made up my bed for you, and for myself borrowed a bedroll from a friend of mine. You're going to need a good rest.

Slonim looked where Comrade Jan pointed. He was right: on the floor at the head of the bed lay a Polish Army bedroll.

—— Besides, I fixed something special for you. I thought perhaps . . . with your rationing in the ghetto . . .

Comrade Jan went to the wooden chest and picked up the loaf and the sardines and carried them to the table.

Slonim, pulling at his cowlick: —— No. No, that is your supper.

—— I have had my supper. I eat at our workers' kitchen. I got these for you. Baltic sardines! Sit down, sit down!

Slonim sat down, staring at the sardine tin. With a big clasp knife the Pole cut off a thick slice of bread, lifted a dripping sardine out onto the slice, and offered it to Slonim. Slonim's hand trembled as he took it.

—— I don't want to deprive you. . . . Are you sure . . . ?

The Pole, neither pleasantly nor unpleasantly: —— Eat. Also this. (He went again to the chest, lifted the cover, and took out an unopened bottle of amber liquor. He said, unsmiling:) Huntsman's vodka.

Slonim still held the slab of bread and the fragrant sardine, and he felt the dampness of soaked-through oil on the under side. He waited for the Pole to open the bottle and pour some of the vodka into two tin cups. The Pole pushed one cup toward Slonim and lifted the other.

—— Solidarity!

But the Pole spoke the word as a formula. They drank. Slonim coughed.

The Pole, again: —— Eat!

Slonim, still holding the bread and sardine: —— And you?

The Pole cut himself a thin slice of bread and put half a sardine on it. He took a bite and with a smothered, chewing sound, said once more:

—— Eat!

Slonim ate. He finished the whole chunk of bread and all the sardines and drank some vodka and quickly became drunk. He tried to tell Comrade Jan about conditions in the ghetto, but he began crying, and Comrade Jan pointed to the bed, and Slonim went over to it, fell on it, and went right to sleep.

Next morning Comrade Jan gave Slonim some railroad working clothes Slonim's own shabby suit was too obviously that of an impoverished intellectual), fed him a cup of *ersatz* coffee, let him have another half-loaf of bread from the chest, and started him out at about six thirty. Slonim walked across the city, went over the Vistula in a hired punt, found the tracks, and went parallel to them until he located a signal stone with the number 17 on it and, not much farther along, the switches of the junction. There was a wooden signal bridge a few hundred meters before the junction. Slonim arrived there at about eight thirty; he expected the morning trains at about ten. He did not dare loiter near the switches, so he wandered away and strolled up and down the streets parallel to the tracks until he heard a train crossing the Vistula railroad bridge. He hurried to the bridge over the tracks; from it, he could see the switches. The train came slowly. It was a freight train. As the first cars went under the wooden bridge, Slonim heard muffled cries and, in one car, a sound like the echo of a song: *I Believe in the Coming of the Messiah*. The train's bulk soon obliterated the view of the switch. The engine approached the switch. Then it shuddered slightly and went straight on. Eastward. Toward Russia.

Slonim left the city on the Bialystok highway. He followed the road until he was in open country, then he cut across the fields northward until he came to the tracks; he hiked then along the rail line. For a time he walked on the ties, but they were too close together for his pace and too far apart to be taken two at a time; they demanded a halting, limping, irregular pace. So he walked in the cinders beside the track-bed. Cinders got into his shoes and galled his feet. Mostly the undergrowth beside the tracks—reeds and briers—was too thick for progress there. There were few trains on the line, but whenever one came, he hid, until it was past, in the reeds or in a ditch beside a field from which he could see the train without being seen himself. He saw no other train that could have been a transport of Jews. Once when a passenger train approached, he threw himself down in shallow water, and afterward he was muddy; his clothes dried quickly in the summer sun, and he dusted out most of the caked dirt. He grew thirsty. Whenever he came near to a village or town, he left the tracks and entered the town by road; once there, he made his way to the railroad station, to be sure there was no spur or that there were no trains on sidings; he quitted each populated place by road again and skirted back to the tracks when he could, unobserved, in the country. He walked all day. In the afternoon he saw two freight trains going toward Warsaw—possibly empty deportation trains. After dark he sat on an embankment and ate about a quarter of his bread and rested awhile. Then he trudged on. He felt stiff and tired. He walked until about midnight and then sat down on the tracks to rest again.

All afternoon and evening, Slonim had been thinking about running away. Some Jews paid enormous sums of money in bribes to get out of the ghetto; he had come out, marching in a labor battalion, scot-free. It would be easy, in one of these villages, to ingratiate himself with a peasant—half of the hundred zlotys he had in his pocket would be ample ingratiation in many of the hovels he had seen! And then he would simply wait. The question of responsibility? Well, what did he owe the Bund? The Bund had kept him down, had worked him like a clerk and parcel-wrapper, and had given him nothing in all the years—unless one counted the ambush of the Polish hooligans that time—until this exit. He had been snubbed, laughed at, argued with, and left out; he had never been respected, listened to, or followed. The word "Chaver," comrade, itself seemed a mockery when applied to him: "Subordinate," "Student," "Boy"—something like those words would have been more suitable. He thought of his colleagues. Colleagues, indeed! Henryk, Herman, Velvel, Mosze, Zwi, Hannah; the conspiratorial first names, but the surly, surname attitude. Old Rapaport. Rapaport. That fcline head; the noble white eyebrows; the scorn in the resonant voice. And yet: Rapaport. Slonim thought of Rapaport's vanity, his procrastinations, his insistence on authority. But he thought, too, he says, of an incident in the ghetto not long before:

Rapaport had been hiding with Chaver Velvel. The Bund Executive Committee had decided that Rapaport should move from apartment to apartment, staying with various comrades, because if he settled down anywhere permanently, the Germans would surely catch up with him and ship him off. Slonim had gone that day to Velvel's to hand in some dues-money he had collected. Rapaport and Velvel were talking about Sokolczyk's suicide, then only a few days old, when Slonim entered. Rapaport said the *Judenrat* Chairman could have helped the Jews much more by leaving some sort of message warning that the *Judenrat* was nothing but a German agency and that compromise was no longer possible. Slonim remembered that he had argued this point: he thought the unlabeled deed said the same thing, and more effectively than an emotional message could have done. The argument had shifted (as Slonim's arguments often did, he admitted to himself) to more personal grounds: soon Slonim was challenging, not Rapaport's ideas, but Rapaport himself. Then suddenly the old leader had said: *Slonim, resentment is such a waste of energy. Especially in a young man.* And with that he had turned away, breaking off the conversation altogether, and had begun talking about something entirely different with Velvel. . . .

At about noon the next day, Slonim, still walking automatically northeastward, and still debating his idea of running away, saw that he was approaching a town. Two Jewish transport trains (he had been able to hear shouts and wails from inside both of them) had gone past in quick succession about fifteen minutes before. Upon seeing the small station and signal apparatus ahead of him along the line, Slonim swung away from the tracks and worked out into the fields beside them. He found a cart track that seemed to go toward the town; it later ran into a larger road, which took him into the place. Slonim found the station—the town was called Malkinia—and saw that just beyond the freight house a side track turned off southward and swung out away from Malkinia into some woods. On a siding at the station, an open car of coal was being unloaded in baskets by a gang of Polish workmen. Slonim walked up to one of them and asked:

—— Where does the spur go?

A bowlegged little man who was wearing as a jacket a burlap bag, with holes for his head and arms, and who had sacking bound around his legs over his trousers, and who was dusted from head to foot with black, said with a short laugh:

—— To the glue factory. Where have you been, brother?

Slonim: —— I'm a line-worker. I've never been here before.

Another worker, who, though barechested, seemed clothed in coal dust: —— If the wind was right, you'd know where the spur went!

All the workmen laughed, but Slonim thought their laughter had very little heart in it.

—— Seriously, where does it go?

The burlap man: —— It's the line to Sokolów. First stop is Treblinka. The Jew-camp.

Slonim, laughing, almost exactly reproducing the character of the burlap man's hard chuckle: —— Oh. So that's where they're sending the Jews from Warsaw! Good for them, too! Filthy swine. It's a good thing the Germans are doing the job. Saves us the work. (He spat.)

The burlap man: —— Truth, brother!

There was laughter all around again.

As Slonim turned away—he intended to walk back to the freight station, dodge away behind it, get out of town to the southward, and then . . . and then, either cut out across country eastward for a day or two to find a soft-hearted farmer (it wouldn't be sensible to try to find a sanctuary near Malkinia where, when the wind was right—), or else . . . it was not precisely clear what the other intention was—as Slonim turned away from the coal car on the siding, he thought again, for some reason, of Rapaport: the kindly eyes, the so obvious desire to be approved; the fame of the things he did as a young man; the stubbornness. Rapaport. A fail-

ure, most of the young Bundists liked to say. They laughed at him.
Finished ten years ago and still hanging on by his fingernails. Old
Rapaport. He won arguments by falling back on the authority of
his position. Vain, talkative, senile, finished. And yet . . . and yet:
Resentment is such a waste of energy. Especially . . .

[NOTE. N.L. Slonim now says, looking back on this struggle
within himself, on whether or not to run away, that it is curious
that his conflict was so narrow: it was a matter between Rapaport
and himself, a question of mere personalities. The greater issues he
never considered. He never asked himself whether this mission on
which he was embarked could have an important outcome for the
Bund, or for the Jews of Warsaw; he never stopped to wonder
what is happening to us all; he never even dealt with his errand in
the terms that once would have been so natural to him—as a romantic exploit. No, he says, he was concerned only with justifying
himself.]

Slonim found himself—hardly knowing how he had come
there, still revolving his uncertainties in his mind—at the edge of
the thicket into which the rail spur curved away from the main
line. He was lightheaded with lack of sleep, stiffness, hunger, pain
in his feet, and want of resolution. Bewildered, he plunged into the
dark forest. . . .

EVENTS AUGUST 11, 1942. ENTRY AUGUST 12, 1942. FROM
RACHEL APT. Yesterday Rachel, Rutka, Berson, and Mordecai
Apt, our Hashomer contingent, received summons by urgent message to report to Zilberzweig's "Workshop Three" in the evening.
This they did, and found there about twenty-five other young
people. When they arrived, Zilberzweig handed them a copy of the
new edition of the Socialist broadside, *Storm*, which had been
published just yesterday afternoon. Rachel's face was at the center
of a cluster of reading faces, and she had a good view of the words,
but she says they seemed to jump and jerk before her eyes; she
could scarcely credit the snatches as she saw them:

. . . *Treblinka B, more recently constructed, lies beyond
these woods on some sandy hills. Area roughly 5,000 hectares . . .
newly-built sideline spur from Malkinia-Sokolów line terminates
at the entrance to an enclosure (capacity, about three thousand
people standing) . . . while south of the enclosure one finds the*

Lumpensortierungsplatz (*clothes-sorting-place*) *with warehouse sheds . . . path runs through a green fence intertwined with barbed wire enclosing the general camp area, continues about 200 meters, swings around the incompleted, windowless walls of a new building, which is being constructed, incidentally, of bricks taken all the way from Warsaw, until it debouches before a building of unusual design . . . three blank-walled rooms, about two meters high, area 25 square meters, with a narrow corridor fronting all three . . . pipes with valves . . . outside, curious scoops reminding one of ship ventilators . . . power room at one end . . . hermetic seals around the doors and at the scoops and valves . . . floors with terra-cotta inlay which moisture renders very slippery. . . .*

. . . was especially struck by the irony of the classification signs in the first enclosure—Tailors, Hatmakers, Carpenters, Roadbuilders, and so on—tending to make the Jews believe they were to be sorted for labor farther east . . . kindly speech by a gentle-looking S.S. officer: . . . After the bath and disinfection, this property will be returned to you in accordance with your receipts *. . . along the path naked, carrying a small piece of soap and his documents . . . about 15 minutes . . . are carried by the Jewish auxiliary, led by Kapos whose identification is a yellow patch at the knee, to the cemetery . . . and this duty, according to the escaped Kapo interviewed by our courier in a hut a few kilometers south of Malkinia, is trying in the extreme . . . covered over by bulldozers, the exhausts of whose Diesel motors provide the constant music of Treblinka. . . .*

When Rachel finished the broadside, she sat silent. She says her heart was beating very fast. She wanted to leave the room, to think, to be moving; the presence of her silent companions held her still.

Zilberzweig, after a while: —— Nu?

One of the young Hashomer zealots: —— Who is this Slonim?

Zilberzweig: —— He's a Socialist, he has been to some of the National Committee meetings with Rapaport. Isn't he a friend of yours, Chaverte Rachel?

Rachel: —— He's a friend of Chaver Dolek here.

Berson: —— I know him.

PART THREE

Another of the Hashomer young people: —— What does he look like?

Berson: —— Oh, he's rather frightened-looking, short, he walks like a piece of machinery, you expect him to clank. His hair falls down over his face. Quite untidy.

[NOTE. N.L. Again this fascination with heroes! As if the report were not sufficient in itself.]

Zilberzweig: —— Well, people, do you believe what you have read?

Rachel, staring: —— It's true. It must be. The report is so circumstantial, so detailed. No young Jew, even if he clanks when he walks, could imagine such things.

—— And you others, what do you think?

—— I agree. The picture is complete.

—— No doubt.

—— I believe it.

—— I certainly believe it. . . .

Zilberzweig: —— Good. I have talked now with all our Hashomer circles. We are practically unanimous in accepting this report, even though it comes from the Bund. Now you must tell everyone you meet what you know. Force them to believe it. And then work in the light of your knowledge.

A young man: —— But now what *can* we do?

Rachel heard Zilberzweig make the first confession of uncertainty and helplessness she had ever observed in him. He simply turned this question inside out and returned it:

—— Now do what you can.

EVENTS AUGUST 12, 1942. ENTRY DITTO. FROM RACHEL APT. Zilberzweig has sent by courier and also by post the following message, for the representatives of Jewry in Berne and Istanbul:

—— *Cousin Israel is sick and is going to live with Uncle Mavetski. Any help you can send must hurry. Hil.*

[NOTE. EDITOR. *Mavet* is Hebrew for death.]

THE WALL PART IV

1

Events August 5–12, 1942. Entry August 12, 1942. N.L. An appalling week. Quite apart from the news Slonim brought us, this has been the worst week we have had in the resettlement.

August 5—6,783; August 6—11,454; August 7—10,826; August 8—7,655; August 9—8,212; August 10—3,679; August 11—8,177. Total for the week: 56,786. Grand total to date: 149,162.

But personally appalling for me, too. The Germans are liquidating the Small Ghetto. This means, among other things, that the *Judenrat* was obliged to move, this week, from the building the *Kehilla* had occupied for many years, Grzybowska 26–28, in the Small Ghetto, to the building that recently has housed the Jewish Post Office, Zamenhofa 19, in the Large Ghetto. Our new locale is said to have been a palace of the last of the Polish kings, Stanislaw August; it was restored in the eighteenth century, they say, and served later as a military prison. These accounts may or may not have historicity, but they are, in any case, no comfort to this particular historian. The Germans allowed us to bring typewriters and office equipment from the Grzybowska building, but *so far I have not been permitted to bring my archive.*

I am going to fight tooth and nail for permission to move the archive, and if I fail, I shall kill myself. Or report for evacuation. Indeed, what's the difference? I can hardly bear to think of those documents, manuscripts, *Judenrat* records, financial accounts, diaries, unpublished novels and poems, unacted plays, unfinished essays, unresolved histories—my aggrandizement of three years; my pleading, stealing, hoarding; those bitter nights in the tunnel—all left behind! Above all, we must keep a record. Else how will the world ever know? It may not care, when it knows: if there is apathy right here in the ghetto in Warsaw (and there *is*: my God! the debates this week as to whether the Slonim account is "true," "accurate," "exaggerated," "a calculated attempt by the Socialists to create panic," and even, so help me, "totally imaginary—a sick fantasy"!)—if there is apathy and incredulity right here, what must there be, what will there not be forever and ever, at the untouched ends of the earth, in Melbourne, in Rio de Janeiro, in Shanghai, in Chicago?

I must work fast. The Small Ghetto has been emptied by decree. *The* Judenrat *announces that all Jews living in the southern part of the Jewish Quarter (that is, south of Chlodna Street) are to leave the premises they occupy.* . . . That wonderfully calm language of the *Judenrat* pronunciamentos, as if such a move did not mean, for many Jews, the loss of Home, the end of the Past! What scenes this week!—Jews by the thousands carrying and dragging their goods over the Chlodna Street bridge; hopeless wanderers. Already most of them know the content of Slonim's sad report, for that news has swept across the area within our wall like fire through dry grass. . . .

EVENTS AUGUST 12–16, 1942. ENTRY AUGUST 16, 1942. N.L. Even before the *Judenrat* was moved, I had become monomaniacal on the subject of preserving records. I am a pessimist, and I think we are all doomed. For that reason, I feel that it is terribly important to leave as much as possible in the way of paper record of our ordeal. That will be our only estate. We will leave no children. The Germans cart away our furniture and all our personal possessions as soon as they lock us into the trains. There is nothing to leave behind but history. I have been making a great nuisance of myself. Not only do I ask everyone for his diaries, his letters, his books—whatever he has on paper; I also take notes myself on anything and everything. While two friends of mine are having a conversation that seems to me interesting or significant, I flip my notebook open and begin jotting down what they say right in front of them. I have enlisted all my friends as scavengers of documents: for instance, I received the Farbszmul letter in the following manner:

[FROM YECHIEL MAZUR.] Reb Yechiel Mazur and Rabbi Goldflamm now both work for the W*ertverfassungstelle*—the German organization which evacuates furniture from the homes of Jews already deported. The furniture is sorted and taken to various storage places—to warehouses on Nalewki and Stawki, if it is rich and elegant, so that it may be shipped to Germany for the personal use of high Nazis; to the former Jewish library on Tlomatzkie Street, if it is less fancy, also to go to Germany, for bombed-out civilians; to the Tlomatzkie Street synagogue, if it is cheap and threadbare, to be sold to Poles. Reb Yechiel Mazur says that there are miracles of skill and antiquity in the Nalewki warehouse: one wonders exactly what a Nazi official would do with an engraved, silver-handled, twelfth-century circumcision knife.

[NOTE. N.L. The artificial-flower factory in which Reb Yechiel Mazur found work at the beginning of the resettlement was wiped out and most of its workers resettled early in August. Reb Yechiel Mazur managed to save himself by bribery. I was able to place him and the rabbi with the *Wertverfassungstelle*, and the rabbi had himself transferred, through *Judenrat* channels, in order to be with his friend.]

Day before yesterday morning, the two saintly, elderly men entered a vacant apartment. These two are in a squad with some healthy, young toughs, and so, though they bustle and make a great fuss whenever they have to carry something past a German overseer, they are spared from carrying the heaviest objects and they manage, I gather, to putter quite a bit when they are alone together in an apartment, as they were on this occasion.

Reb Yechiel, looking around: —— People of good taste.

Goldflamm: —— Evidently. But I've found, Yechiel, that it is inconvenient to think too much about *people*.

Reb Yechiel: —— Look at this chess set! See the color of the ivory! Think how many generations of fingers must have handled these pieces!

Goldflamm: —— Yechiel! See here! This rosewood box!

Reb Yechiel took the box from the rabbi's hand, and he raised it to his nose and sniffed it, with his eyes closed. Then he said:

—— Blessed art Thou, O Lord our God, King of the universe, who createst fragrant woods.

Idly Reb Yechiel opened the box. Inside he found a piece of paper. He unfolded it, and, moving to the rabbi's side, held it up, and the two men read together:

To whosoever discovers this:
I have a fateful feeling that we will be taken soon for re-settlement, and I have seldom been deceived in my premonitions. This box was given to me by my husband, Israel Farbszmul, when

we were young. We had been married, I can say, exactly two years and three months. I had just given birth to what was to have been our first child—stillborn. My husband had bought this box to be a present at birth. I was never able to have children after that experience, and I came to regard this box with a kind of superstition. It symbolized my issue. My children. I have always kept in this box everything I valued most, my most precious jewels. It has contained my sorrows. I leave it behind now because I know my husband and I will never return. His branch of the Farbszmul family ends with us, as we have no children. Therefore I leave this box, representing those children; in it I leave the memory of the Farbszmuls. If you be a German who takes this box into your home, you must know that you have taken Jewishness into your home, you have adopted the Farbszmuls, forever and ever. You will consider this a curse. I consider this a very great blessing, for you, though possibly not for the Farbszmuls.

"Hear, O Israel: the Lord, our God, the Lord is One!"

[Signed] *Rega Farbszmul*

Reb Yechiel Mazur says he picked up the box and smelled it again.

Goldflamm: —— We should give that letter to Noach Levinson. He said he wanted any scrap of writing we found for the archive.

Reb Yechiel: —— No, Eliazar. This is not for the archive. I think we had better make sure that this box gets to the Nalewki warehouse—with the letter in it.

Goldflamm: —— At least we could copy it for Levinson.

And so, with the rabbi standing as a sentinel at the door of the apartment, Reb Yechiel Mazur hastily copied off the letter for me. Then he folded the original and put it back in the box, and the two men began carrying things down to the carts waiting below. They put the box in the handcart for the Nalewki warehouse—goods destined for the homes of high-ranking Nazis.

EVENTS AUGUST 12–19, 1942. ENTRY AUGUST 19, 1942. N.L. I have had a partial success. First I persuaded Engineer Grossmann, the new Chairman of the *Judenrat*, to ask Haensch to allow us to bring certain records up from the old *Judenrat* building—census sheets, tax records, accounting, and so on. Haensch agreed. I was assigned ten men with handcarts. Under cover of the authorized removals, I brought out about three quarters of my historical archive. (I must also confess that I found some blank notebook paper in the storerooms that fits my loose-leaf folder; I "captured" this paper for my own use.) As for the remaining material, I will have to get it piecemeal and by guile. I will do it, no matter what the risks.

It appears now that the Germans intend to get rid of all of us; it will just be a matter of time, as I see it, though our optimists —and how stubborn they are!—still maintain that part of the population will be spared. The deportations slacked off this last week: a total of 31,396 for the week, compared with 56,786 in the preceding week. The optimists say: *See! They are letting up. Only thirty thousand this week!* It seems to me a big "only." The grand total so far is 180,558: enough Jews to populate a fine city.

No, we are all going. We will exist only on paper.

Now, there is but one question. In what manner will we go? Proudly? Or cravenly?

EVENTS AUGUST 21, 1942. ENTRY DITTO. N.L. I feel that I have won an important victory, and a rather sarcastic one, too.

Not only have I succeeded in removing the balance of my archive from Grzybowska 26 to the new *Judenrat*; I have also been able indirectly to legitimize the gathering of further documents. I have received authorization, from both Engineer Grossmann and Commissioner Haensch, to form a "purely religious" society, which will be permitted to hold meetings of not more than twelve persons each Saturday—and which I shall use as a small document-hunting club. The whimsical feature of this accomplishment lies in the title of our organization:

The Society for the Pleasures of the Sabbath.

The other day I wrote that there were two alternative ways for us to meet death: proudly or cravenly. My little society gives me an idea that there is a third possibility, somewhere between those two. No matter how prideful or how fearful we may be, we are a people who can do things—can even prepare for death—with an ironical air.

2

EVENTS AUGUST 23, 1942. ENTRY AUGUST 24, 1942. FROM DOLEK BERSON. Berson lay awake, he says. *Loyalty*, he says he was thinking, had formerly been an abstract, rather pompous word. It had been something the Gymnasium demanded of its basket-ball players. There had always been that factor of requirement about it: one's father demanded it, one's school demanded it, one's employer demanded it, one's cause demanded it, one's country demanded it. But now, Berson thought, he had begun to learn a deeper meaning of the word: a meaning with reciprocity to it. In the ghetto, since the news that Slonim brought back of Treblinka, the word had developed a very special definition in his mind:

Loyalty—that selective faithfulness which chooses the friends whom one would wish to help survive, and of whom, in turn, one would expect help in surviving oneself.

Using this definition, Berson began to catalogue those toward whom he felt, and on whose part he assumed, loyalty. Symka, of course. Her capacity to help him survive would be less than her will to help, but he could depend on the latter. Rachel, definitely; next only to Symka. Reb Yechiel and Froi Mazur. She more than he: Berson says he feels that Froi Mazur has granted him a measure of motherliness, without restraint or condition, whereas he feels something reserved, something almost selfish, about the saintly-seeming husband. Levinson. [NOTE. N.L. Thank you.] Rutka: dependable, solid, lively, not very imaginative, pregnant— yes, loyal. Mordecai: shallow, boastful, rather sour, but trustworthy up to a point. Stefan: doubtful, a self-interested young man, with erratic and unpredictable spurts of consideration for others; very doubtful. Halinka: sweet to Berson, but quite incapable of loyalty in this narrow sense; no. Rabbi Goldflamm: yes, unqualifiedly. Pavel Menkes: a gruff man, who tries to isolate himself—yet, one could say, loyal. [NOTE. N.L. Forced to close his bakery by the liquidation of the Small Ghetto, Menkes has now succeeded in getting permission to reopen the Feiwicz Bakery on Wolynska Street, which has been shut down ever since Feiwicz was killed in the manhunt last April.] Meier Berson: no, not loyal, the tie of blood is meaningless. Wladislaw Jablonski: opportunistic; no. David Apt: in a special category: helpless; yes. Zilberzweig: possessed of a doctrinaire, organizational loyalty. Slonim: in spite of his contrary tendency, yes, loyal. Regina Orlewska [NOTE. N.L. Orlewska has joined the "family" since her apartment was cut off with the rest of the Small Ghetto.]: yes, loyal.

Next Berson arranged these friends in concentric orbits of loyalty—and he tells me he was himself surprised at where he put some of them:

Inner orbit: Symka, Rachel, Froi Mazur. [NOTE. N.L. For being left out of this group, I find only one consolation: they are all women. Interesting fact.]

Second orbit: Rutka, the rabbi, Pavel Menkes, Noach Levinson. [NOTE. N.L. Sigh of relief.]

Third orbit: Reb Yechiel Mazur, Slonim, Mordecai, Zilberzweig, Regina Orlewska, David.

Outside: Stefan, Halinka, Meier, Wladislaw, all others.

And next Berson tried to assign a definite limit of sacrifice for each orbit. For the inner, the limit would be death. . . .

But now (having, in his imagination, more or less immolated himself for his beloved friends) Berson became sidetracked in his thinking. This tendency to classify, narrow down, be definite, he reflected—that was something new in him. He remembered how much he had hated in his student days biology, trigonometry, physics, anything exact; he had preferred history, political science, the study of man, translations of Byron and Pushkin, the inflated style of Benlevi. He wondered whether it was the growing uncertainty of life that drove him into exactitude, a love of neatness, a quest for the dependables. Yet others, he knew, were growing more and more romantic and vague-minded under these circumstances. . . .

Berson heard someone enter the apartment. A careful, tiptoeing tread made its way across the living room, evidently circling to avoid the sleeping forms of Rabbi Goldflamm, Wladislaw Jablonski, and N.L. on the living room floor, and approached the door of the room where Berson sleeps (along with Symka, the senior Mazurs, Rutka, and Mordecai). The door creaked. A form leaned into the room. A whisper, seeming loud as a scream to Berson in his wakefulness:

—— Dolek! Dolek!

Berson got up quickly from his creaking bed (it was too hot for covers) and went to the door. He whispered:
—— What is it?
—— Come in the kitchen. I want to tell you something.

It seemed to be Stefan. Berson followed the form in a curving path back across the living room and into the kitchen. Berson closed the door behind him. The form struck flint and lit up a carbide lamp: yes, it was Stefan, who turned (his face was pallid and moronic-looking as a result of fear) and said:
—— My district commandant tipped me off tonight that there would be an action in this block. He didn't say when; he only said, definitely not tomorrow, tomorrow's schedule is full: after tomorrow.

Berson, inanely, still blinking in the light and scratching himself through his pajama tunic: —— Well, we must make preparations.

Stefan: —— The commandant goes to Zelazna 103 to *Einsatz Reinhardt* headquarters every day: they show him their schedules. The only thing he could say for sure was: not tomorrow.

Berson: —— Wait a minute. I think we should tell Rachel and Noach. I'll get them.

[NOTE. N.L. Thus, though I am only in the second circle of Berson's private hell, he summons me, *in extremis*, as it were. Perhaps he simply wanted a record kept of this occasion!]

Berson says he stepped into the living room, where he was obliged to pause till his eyes adjusted themselves to the darkness, and then he went stealthily into the tiny bedroom, barely more than a closet, where Rachel, Halinka, Stefan, Regina, and David sleep. Berson knows that the cot in which Rachel and David sleep is nearest the door; he bent over it until he could make out which shape was which, and he put down a hand to waken Rachel. He was so startled by the softness and warmth he touched that he quickly pulled back his hand. After a moment he put it out again and found Rachel's shoulder and shook it gently. She woke up with a jump and asked with a vehemence that indicated she had sensed the gender of the hand that had been on her:
—— Who is that?

Berson, whispering that most useless and customary answer in the dark: —— It's me. . . . Come in the kitchen a minute. Stefan has something to tell us.

Rachel rose and followed Berson, who roused N.L. on the way back through the living room. In the kitchen, the four of us stood and conferred. Rachel's loosened hair hung around her shoulders, and there was a puffy, softened, sleepy look about her odd little face. When Stefan had gone over his news, we began discussing what to do.

Stefan: —— Halinka and I will be all right. I can take her to our headquarters and keep her there for a couple of days. Others in our company have done that. It's accepted practice.

[NOTE. N.L. Stefan had looked out for his own—a fact not too surprising to me; but that Berson should have looked out for *his* own, as it now became apparent he had, was more noteworthy. I commend him!]

Berson: —— I have discovered a hiding place for some of the "family." There is room for about five or six.

Rachel: —— Where is it?

Berson has since told me that he now had one thought: Stefan is outside all three of my orbits of loyalty, and is therefore not to be trusted in a matter of life and death; and he said to Rachel:

—— I'll show you when the time comes.

Rachel: —— Let's see. We are fourteen in the family. You said you had room for—

—— At most a half-dozen. All right, we will take [NOTE. N.L. I now realize that Berson worked from his innermost orbit outward in making these selections.] Symka. You, Rachel. Froi Mazur. (He paused.) That's three.

Rachel: —— Four with you.

Berson: —— Noach, I suppose you are safe, with *Judenrat* papers.

N.L.: —— I am as safe as a Jew can be, I guess.

Berson: —— All right. Rutka, the rabbi. That's about all there would be room for.

Rachel, shocked at the omission: —— We'd *have* to take David.

Berson, realizing, as he has since told me, that there are tangents in the geometry of loyalty: —— Of course. (And on the same basis:) I guess we'd have to take Reb Yechiel Mazur and Mordecai.

Rachel: —— Who is left out?

N.L.: —— Orlewska and the Jablonski boy.

334

Rachel: —— We'd have to take Regina; Regina would be helpless.

Berson: —— I refuse to take Wladislaw. If he wouldn't look out for his own father, I don't see why we should look out for him. He seems to have a talent for hiding, anyhow. Perhaps he has thought of a place of his own.

Rachel, who had been keeping track on her fingers: —— That's ten.

Berson: —— In space for five.

Rachel: —— Can it be done?

Berson: —— We can try.

EVENTS AUGUST 24, 1942. ENTRY AUGUST 27, 1942. FROM RACHEL APT. Early the morning after Stefan's warning, at the very moment when curfew was lifted, Rachel hurried out. The streets, empty when she first stepped out, filled rapidly, as if some huge, subterranean man-faucet had been turned on and was spewing humanity out through every aperture into the streets. Rachel hastened, half running, to Fein's apartment on Chlodna Street. One of the men living with Fein, a thin fellow, an ascetic-looking pirate, opened the door and stood buttoning his shirt.

Rachel: —— Is Herr Fein at home?

—— Fein is very much at home—in bed. He's always the last one to get up. I'll see if the lazy guttersnipe is awake.

Rachel waited on the landing. Soon Fein shuffled out, in a long nightshirt, blinking and yawning. When he saw that his caller was a girl, he became somewhat more alert, and half-hid himself behind the door.

Rachel: —— I came to ask you whether you had had any results on the plan to get my young brother out of the ghetto.

Fein, with a seriousness that in his somnolence was quite comical: —— We are working on it. Definitely. We have two plans. I am very hopeful.

—— Would there be any possibility of completing one of the plans today?

—— Today! (Fein laughed, and the laugh transformed itself into a yawn.) No, my dear, either plan will take six or eight weeks. There are many steps. Don't be impatient. . . .

EVENTS AUGUST 24, 1942. ENTRY AUGUST 27, 1942. FROM DOLEK BERSON. Berson might be late for work; he knew that. It

335

was a chance he would have to take. Other risks were greater. Setting out a few minutes earlier than usual, the morning after Stefan's warning, he stopped in at the low, one and a half storey building next to the apartment house on Nowolipie where the "family" lives and asked the watchman if he might see the proprietor. He was led into a large, dirty room, with a peculiar, mixed odor of oil, of new cloth, and of the distant sea. There were three huge tables in the room; the floor was strewn with scraps of striped ticking; against one wall were two tremendous bins, one of which contained human hair and the other, dried seaweed. A stack of about a dozen new mattresses was at one side. Berson particularly noticed that there was nothing but a kind of ladder to the second floor above. When the proprietor—a sloppy, heavyset Jew wearing an undershirt, trousers, and bedroom slippers whose uppers were tramped flat at the heel—came down the ladder, Berson, pretending to be unemployed, asked for a job. The request was greeted with a whining complaint that the proprietor already had too many workers, too little room, and too little work.

Berson: —— Wouldn't you have room for some workers upstairs?

The proprietor, chanting miserably: —— Upstairs! Upstairs I have scarcely room for a desk and shelves to keep the ticking. I can't even sleep in my own factory. Upstairs! No, go on, I can't keep you alive. Every day twenty people come in here asking for work, *Ausweise*, their lives. I'm not the Angel of Death. It's not my choice. Get out! You waste my time. Get out!

Berson says he did not even bother to look crestfallen as he left. He was, in truth, delighted. He was convinced that no one in the mattress factory ever went above the second floor to the attic. That was decisive knowledge.

3

Events August 25, 1942. Entry August 26, 1942. N.L. I feel better. I have faced a fifty-fifty chance of dying, and although I was terrified by the ordeal, I know now that it is possible to face this terror and neither go mad nor collapse—two possibilities that had frightened me, in anticipation, almost more than the thought of death itself. It is curious that my innate timidity, making me shamefully servile in the face of any authority, even that which I hate, did not show itself in this moment of judgment. I was even rather bold.

At about ten o'clock yesterday morning, I was sitting at my desk at the *Judenrat* more or less daydreaming. As a matter of fact, I was thinking about the "family," wondering whether they were safe. I recalled the way they had tiptoed out of the apartment, in groups of three or four, in the middle of the night before; and how despite all their efforts to get out without waking Wladislaw, the boy had suddenly jumped up from the living room floor, leaping in one instant from sound asleep into vociferous wakefulness. He demanded in a loud voice to know what was going on, and of course, in order to avoid having the whole scheme given away by his trumpeting, the others ended by taking him along. I had lain alone the rest of the night, trying to guess where they had hidden themselves. Provident Berson! I had got away to the office before anything happened at the apartment, and now I sat at my desk, feeling love and sorrow for my dear friends—at the very moment when I myself could have used just those feelings from others. For we at the *Judenrat* were about to suffer our own selection.

It was in the midst of my reverie that a sudden racket broke out in the courtyard of our building. This noise was soon dominated by a bellowing German voice in one of the corridors:

—— *Alle Juden 'raus. 'Raus, 'raus! Hinunter! Alle Juden hinunter!* All Jews out. Out, out! Downstairs! All Jews downstairs!

Felix Mandeltort at his desk and I at mine both jumped to our feet, and with a quickly exchanged glance we each saw that the other knew what was happening. We walked out of our office and down into the courtyard. There we found a disordered scene. At one side of the courtyard, against the north wing of the building, a portable desk had been set up. There a group of S.D. officers and men was centered; a commanding officer was spreading out papers. In the rest of the courtyard, Jews were milling frantically, seeking relatives and friends, asking frightened questions, talking excitedly. A large number of Jews not connected with the *Judenrat* had been brought in from neighboring buildings. A gang of Ukrainian and Lithuanian cadets was trying, with a great hubbub and occasional roughness, to drive this agitated mass into a line, starting at the desk, running across the courtyard, and doubling back around one side.

Beside the desk and with the Germans stood Engineer Grossmann, our Chairman, and behind him were the Chief of the Jewish Police and the Chairman's secretary. I could see that these high officials were being besieged by influence-seekers, and were waving them off impatiently. Schpunt was standing beside the dignitaries. Schpunt is not so much official as officious these days: he goes around to all the selections, as a kind of jester at the Germans' feast of death, maintaining a prattle of abuse of both Jews and Germans. The Germans, who are greatly amused by him, tolerate and even encourage this behavior on his part.

Gradually the tumult in the courtyard abated.

Directly in front of Felix and me in the line were a man and wife, arguing. They were not *Judenrat* people; they were quite poor, to judge by their clothing. He wore a greasy black cap, a heavy, patched, dirty shirt, and shiny cloth trousers; she had on a torn and spot-stained black dress. They had become abusive toward each other in this their peril. The husband accused the wife of slatternly habits; she said he was lazy. He said he had never loved her—that the marriage broker had cheated him in the first place and never since then had he loved her. She accused him of having kept his earnings from her and the children, and then he said she had made "*nebich* animals" of the children. An unnatural hatred blazed between the two; it seemed that the sudden confrontation with death had made these poor people turn on each other and say things to each other that they had always buried, that they had never said before, and that may even have been untrue now. The woman seemed to sustain a physical blow every time the man said he had never loved her; he perceived this, and said it again and again.

The selection commenced. At the desk the officer began to pronounce the simple reprieves and sentences: *right* or *left*, according to the evidence of working cards, appearances, the officer's judgment, the moment's sheer whim, or Chairman Grossmann's opinion. Indeed, so far as the *Judenrat* personnel was concerned, it can be said that this selection was conducted by Engineer Grossmann, for it was his intervention, or the lack of it, that decided who should be sent to the left and who to the right.

The couple in front of us continued their bitter reproaches to each other, hissing now in undertones: they seemed to want to destroy each other before the inexorable German destroyed them both. Ahead of them, in the line, was a big workman carrying a suitcase. And ahead of him stood a young woman, holding a long disused compact, powdering her face, applying rouge and lipstick, combing her stringy hair, in hopes, evidently, that she might make herself appear attractive and above all *healthy* to the German: healthy enough to be a worker and survive. Felix seemed to stand rather apathetically beside me.

—— Right . . . left . . . left . . . left. . . .

I thought once more of the "family." I wondered whether any of us would ever see each other again. I quieted my fears and for a few moments felt rather comfortable imagining their mourning me, in case they survived and I did not.

—— Left . . . left . . . death . . . death. . . .

Some of the Jews tried to argue, some to beg; many were crying, men as well as women. I suppose everyone knew about Treblinka by this time. Each person tried, I dare say, to persuade himself that Treblinka does not exist; but each had to admit the possibility that it does. If any Jews who had been sent to the *left* caused delays, Junaks stepped in and bodily lifted them to the group headed for the *Umschlagplatz*. Some who were doomed bit, clawed, and fought back. Others were dull and passive.

—— Left. . . .

Now it was the turn of the girl who had primped herself. She had no papers to offer. Her name was checked on the tenants' list of the near-by apartment from which she had been brought. The commanding officer looked up at her and smiled. In automatic response to the smile, in an awkward gesture that seemed to arise from a vague memory of a feeling as long disused as the girl's battered compact, she put a hand to her hair and preened it around the back. A cracked voice—I saw that it came from the grotesque mouth of Fischel Schpunt—said, in what evidently seemed to the Germans a comical Yiddish-twisted German:

—— Oi, she's for a party dressed already.

The officer's smile, benign, almost urbane, widened, and the other Germans laughed.

—— Left.

The girl walked without a moment's hesitation to the group designated for the *Umschlagplatz*.

The man with the suitcase stepped forward. He offered some papers. They seemed to be valid. The officer said:

—— Right. (Then he asked:) What's in the suitcase?

—— Personal possessions. The regulations permit fifteen kilograms to be taken, in case of resettlement. I thought perhaps . . .

—— Correct. Fifteen kilograms are permitted. . . . Mittendorf, examine the suitcase.

—— But you said I could go to the right.

The officer merely looked up at the workman, as if to say: *Speak when spoken to.* The noncom addressed as Mittendorf took the suitcase from the workman, let it down on the cobblestones, flopped it onto one side, dropped on one knee, and opened the suitcase. Clothing seemed to be crammed into it. The noncom pulled the top pieces out. Underneath there was something larger. The noncom tore out the contents of the suitcase. Mainly there was a bundle, from which the noncom peeled off layers of shirting and articles of clothing. Inside was a baby. It was perhaps a year old. It was alive. Its mouth had been bound with strips of cloth. Its thin, old-looking face was bluish, but it struggled in the hands of the noncom, who seemed not to know how to hold the squirming body. The workman stood looking at the ground.

The German officer, expressing neither surprise nor anger:

—— For the little stranger, left.

The noncom, Mittendorf, carried the baby to the group for the *Umschlagplatz* and put the infant in the arms of the girl who had prettied herself. The workman stood still, watching. The officer said to him:

—— For you, right.

Slowly the workman walked to the group on the right, of those who were spared.

Now the man and wife who had just discovered that they had never loved each other came forward. The man presented papers; the woman had none. The officer held out the papers for the husband to take back, and said the man could go to the right. Then he looked at the woman and with a jerk of his head sent her to the left. The woman turned away from her husband without even looking at him and went to the group for the *Umschlagplatz*. The husband looked after her for a moment, then, with an unearthly sob, went after her and, showing no affection or surrender, stood beside her in the group designated for death.

Felix stepped forward. Grossmann condemned him. Felix went left. Felix!

It was my turn. My boldness, to which I have referred, consisted in the fact that when I approached the Germans' desk, I ignored the Germans entirely; I looked Engineer Grossmann squarely in the eye. I have never been close to him, as I think I was to Sokolczyk: it has always been necessary for me to make appointments to see Grossmann, whereas I was on a walk-in basis with his predecessor. I have sometimes had the feeling that Grossmann has actually disliked me. He is a "practical" man, one of those "realists" who like to fancy that they never let sentiment carry any weight with them, and I believe he considers me to be highly emotional and therefore highly suspect. He regards emotionalism and radicalism as synonymous: anyone who weeps easily is probably a Communist and certainly a Socialist. I regard myself as inwardly sensitive and perhaps even sentimental but on the surface fairly dry (actually the Drifter used to accuse me of being enigmatical— he blamed it partly on my eye-glasses); but these judgments as between men are usually founded upon inadequate evidence, and Engineer Grossmann judges me, I suppose, on the basis of a couple of displays of temper in *Judenrat* conferences.

At any rate, I came up to Grossmann, with my life wholly in his hands, thinking these thoughts, and I stared at him as coldly and scornfully as I could. I had seen him, a few moments before, press his lips together and shrug as Felix Mandeltort came up to the desk, and in the instant when the German harshly said, *Left!* I saw a momentary flicker of torment in Grossmann's eye. Indeed, what a horrible responsibility, to have to send some of his colleagues and subordinates to Treblinka! When I saw that blink of misery, I had an idea that I might be able to save myself by outcountenancing Grossmann. I tried to make my look at him say: *I hate you. You are practically a Nazi. Even if you send me to my death, I don't care, because I know that you will die a thousand deaths of guilt and regret and self-reproach. I hate you. Everyone hates you.* That is what my eyes said, and I think his eyes received that message; anyhow they soon dropped and looked then toward the German.

Grossmann: —— This man keeps all my records. I can't function without him.

And the German sent me to the right.

Of course I cannot say whether my boldness had any influence upon this outcome. The Chairman might have said the same thing had I avoided his eye altogether. But at least my defiance made me feel better.

I stood in the group at the right, not daring to look across at those on the other side, for fear that now my eyes might meet those of my old friend Felix Mandeltort.

4

EVENTS AUGUST 25, 1942. ENTRY AUGUST 26, 1942. FROM DOLEK BERSON. Berson says he could scarcely breathe. One beam pressed against his chest, one against his thighs; between, emptiness. He had a frightening inclination to cough, which he fought back with utmost difficulty: a cough might be enough to give away the hiding place and all its eleven occupants. This was odd; he hadn't coughed, or even wanted to cough, since he had had a cold last winter. Perhaps the pressure on his chest, perhaps the dust on the beams, perhaps just being in hiding. . . .

There it was!

In the distance, muffled yet unmistakable, Berson heard the famous shouts:

—— Alle Juden, 'raus! Hinunter. Juden hinunter!

The precaution had been justified; Berson thanked God. And he thanked God, too, that the selection had come on this day and not the next or the next after that. [NOTE. N.L. That the selection on Nowolipie should have come on the same day as the one at the Judenrat, on Zamenhofa, was not too startlingly coincidental, considering the fact that several—as many as ten or twelve —may be conducted at scattered points on any given day.] It was hard to know how long one could stand this cramped position, this strain, this hunger, this smell of living, unbathed, anxious bodies, this small, dark place. The eleven people were absolutely silent. Berson's heart beat so hard when he heard the distant shouting that it almost seemed the pounding must be audible to others, as it was, in thumping, rushing sounds, in his own ears. He could make out rapid pulsations in Froi Mazur's neck, in his line of dim vision to the right. Eleven hearts must have been going hard all around.

Again the shouting in the distance:

—— 'Raus, 'raus! Juden hinunter!

Scuffling and agitation downstairs in the mattress factory, too; then the sound of sewing machines and orderly industry. More shouting in the distance.

Berson says he was suddenly really afraid for the first time in his life: he felt a surge of panic, which he tried to put down, but it rose in wave after wave. He needed to cough, he wanted to cry out, he wanted to get up from this dark, imprisoning place of refuge and crawl out to the daylight. Death would be better than this enclosed fear of death, it seemed. He shut his eyes and clenched his teeth and closed his moist fists. Then, as he heard, far away, clamorous sounds, the noises of an excited crowd, shouts in German, his fear drained away to a certain extent, and he thought: I am afraid because I am responsible for all these, my "family": I brought them here: if they are discovered, something terrible will happen, and it will be my fault. The thought of the others itself helped to quiet his fear. He opened his eyes. The eleven were absolutely silent, with a rigid, awful stillness. And Berson says he thought: if we are this quiet, if I can keep from coughing, we will never be found. And then, as the last of his panic ebbed away, he felt suddenly almost exultant. If we survive, he says he thought, I will have done it: I will have saved them all!

The noises in the distance died down gradually; downstairs the sounds of work continued. As nearly as Berson could make out, the first selection was taking place in the "family's" own courtyard. Undoubtedly the whole block was shut off. The selections would move down the street: this building next (that would be the test!), then buildings further on toward Smocza. Berson tried to visualize the scene of the selection: he saw Germans standing, a line, groups being formed right and left. He pictured a Jew from the "family's" staircase, a noisy old fool named Mundlak, coming before the officers, an officer saying . . .

What did the officer say? Which way? Berson says his imagination suddenly failed. Again, for a moment, Berson says he felt a rush of intense fear, but this time it was gone quickly.

Now the remote sounds had died down altogether: evidently the actual business of selection was being conducted. Berson could

343

hear the breathing of his friends. He says he thought back over the events of the night before:

Two accidents had happened: one did not matter, the other might prove to have been serious. The family had gone to bed as usual, except that Stefan and Halinka were both out—at a police party, someone explained; actually, at Stefan's headquarters, according to plan [ENTRY AUGUST 24, 1942]. At about three o'clock, Berson, who had kept himself awake all night, for fear of sleeping through until dawn, wakened Symka, Rachel, and David. They tiptoed out to the landing and downstairs, one by one, without waking Wladislaw in the living room. [NOTE. N.L. Or me, either. I was only roused, as Wladislaw was, by Mordecai's fall, later.]

Berson had decided to get the family across to the hiding place in relays of three: then if any single relay were caught in transit, the others might have a chance of surviving. When the first three were outside and downstairs, Berson followed. He led them then to the staircase at the end of the courtyard in the direction of Smocza Street, and took them to the second storey. There a staircase window looked out on a low hip roof: the roof of a former bicycle and ricksha repair shop, now a small factory for the manufacture of Army mattresses. The window was less than four feet from the gutter of the tile roof, and its sill was about a foot higher.

Berson jumped across onto the roof, went around on hands and knees to the side of the roof away from the street, and returned in a few minutes slowly trailing on the clay tiles a stout plank about six feet long. This he put across to the window sill as a bridge.

At first Symka refused to cross: she whispered to Rachel that she would rather die. Rachel sent David across to tell Berson, and Berson returned by the plank to the window. There he pleaded in whispers with Symka, warning her that she was endangering the lives of all, and finally she agreed to wriggle across the plank on her belly, if Rachel would hold her feet and if Berson would be ready to take her hands. Berson crossed to the roof again. It took Symka a long time to get up the courage to start out, but once she had started, the actual transition did not take long.

Rachel crawled across. Berson drew the plank onto the roof and led the three around to the rear hip, where there was a box-like trap, about two feet square. Berson took the sloping lid off and let himself down inside: his head and shoulders were still above the edge when his feet touched. He whispered a warning to the others to step only on beams inside, otherwise they would go down through lathing and ceiling to the storeroom below. The three followed Berson one at a time through the trap into a tiny half-attic. He guided them, by tugging and shoving, to a section of the attic where the beams were covered by loose planks like the one he had taken for a bridge. The three lay on these planks.

Berson went back, then, for Regina, Froi Mazur, and Rutka; and after they had reached the attic, by the same method, Berson fetched the rabbi, Reb Yechiel Mazur, and Mordecai. Whenever no one was crossing the bridge, Berson drew the plank aside, either onto the roof or into the stairway; and with each coming and going he replaced the cover on the trap.

The first mistake happened when Berson was getting the three men. Mordecai stumbled over his own shoes, knocking, in a half-fall, into one of the iron beds, which gave out a noisy clank. This wakened Wladislaw. [NOTE. N.L. And me. I would just as soon not have been wakened. I did not sleep all the rest of the night.] Wladislaw made such a saucy outcry that Berson decided to take him. Berson tells me he was upset by this, not because he feels vindictive toward Wladislaw, but because there was barely enough planking in the attic for four or five to lie on, and barely room in the whole tiny space for seven or eight people. Discomfort to one might prove dangerous to all. At any rate, the men got across safely to the roof; whereupon the second accident happened.

Berson, by this time perspiring heavily, weary, trembling, doubtless flustered by the recruitment of Wladislaw, fumbled the plank as he pulled it across, and it dropped with a loud clatter into the alleyway between the apartment and the shop. The fall attracted no attention at the time, and it would be easy for the hiders to get back eventually on another board from the attic, but the fallen plank might be noticed during the selection. Why would such a plank be lying askew in an alleyway? . . .

Berson says that as he lay in the dark attic he also thought farther back, to the many nights when he had been out, catlike, exploring his courtyard, its roofs, its cellars, its arcaways, its alleys, looking for a satisfactory hiding place. He remembered his excitement when he had found the roof opposite the staircase window: he had thought that in a pinch one or two people might be able

345

to lie out on the far side of such a roof, unseen for a precious, if short, time. Exploring it, the night after he discovered it, he had found the trap into what appeared to be a false attic. He had later discovered, within, another trapdoor from this small space to the floor below, but it would not budge: it seemed to be locked, and the depth of the dust on it suggested it had been kept closed a long time. And his visit to the mattress factory in pretended quest of a job had satisfied him, so far as it was possible to be satisfied, that the half-attic would be the safest hiding place he could find. . . .

Now, looking at the others—mere shadows in this shadowy place; the pounding in Froi Mazur's neck had diminished, she was calmer—Dolek was filled with pity, a pity he felt partly for himself. That eleven human beings could be lowered to such animal behavior was something almost beyond understanding. This had, in truth, been an animal performance: his own stealthy night-prowlings, the discovery of the lair, the selection of the pack, the going to ground. Suddenly, out of the dim past, came a phrase from the days when Berson considered himself not only a man, but even perhaps an intellectual man: Benlevi's phrase, at Bonn: *The citizen's sense of personal dignity.* . . . What richness (lying there in a dark attic, smelling Wladislaw Jablonski on one side and barely seeing Froi Mazur's trembling throat on the other) in that single word: *Citizen!*

God, there it was!

—— *'Raus, alle 'raus.* (Directly below.)

Someone moved in the attic. A plank creaked. Berson heard a faint *shhh.*

There were scrambling and scuffling below; curses; pounding; footsteps. Then the noise all seemed to move outside the building. A few seconds later, anew, the whining voice of the proprietor and a deeper voice. Steps apparently on the ladder up from the ground floor. Suddenly, shockingly close, the voice of the proprietor, in German:

—— There's no one here. See, only my desk and these shelves. All right, look for yourself: bolts of cloth, that's all. (There were thumping sounds, as if things were being thrown on the floor. The high insistent whine said:) Nothing here.

A deep voice: —— *Da herüber?*

—— Nothing up there. You can see, the door is nailed shut. Nobody has been up there for years.

A grunt.

The whine, less loudly: —— Listen, let my shop off! I'll make it worth your while.

A grunt. More thumping.

The voice, almost seeming to howl in pain: —— Fifty thousand zlotys.

—— Impossible.

—— Sixty thousand. (An incantation of misery.)

—— I am not the commanding officer. Anyway, he is powerless, he has orders. Impossible.

Sounds on the ladder. The high-pitched voice, retreating: —— Which is the commander?

A gruff, indistinguishable answer. Footsteps below. Silence.

Above the pulsating neck beside him, Berson saw a face dimly swim into focus: Froi Mazur's face, smiling in a wild and animalistic joy, suitable to the occasion, but weeping, too. Berson's chest and throat were bursting with relief and exultation.

5

Events August 25, 1942. Entry August 26, 1942. N.L. Back in the *Judenrat* building, after the selection, we hurried about from office to office discussing the affair, and I found a considerable resentment against the Chairman for having let Mandeltort go. Since Felix was caught smuggling, we have all felt rather sorry for him. No one has taken him very seriously. He has been calm and happy, in a queer way, and negligible. In terms of what Felix has been able to contribute to *Judenrat* labors recently, Grossmann may have been correct in letting him go to the *Umschlagplatz*. And yet, as I say, several of us found that we were resentful over this one decision—as we were not resentful at similar decisions in the cases of Szmertskopf, Horowicz, Banagar, and Weinstein, for example. Perhaps this is because we all envy Mandeltort, to some extent. He was formerly a rather stiff and snobbish, but on the

whole a kindly, intelligent, conventional man. More than anything
in the world he loved his family—his dowdy, dumpy, humorous
wife and his two nice little girls. I shall never forget the first evening I spent in Felix's home, when I saw this formal man unbent
and gay. [ENTRY JUNE 2, 1941.] This love destroyed Felix. He
put it before everything: before his job, before the Jews, before his
personal integrity, before common sense: and he began to deal on
the black market and to smuggle in the hopes that he might build
up an unshakable security for his family. He was caught and sent
to jail. His wife and one daughter died during his confinement,
both of t.b., I believe, and the other daughter was deported early
in the resettlement. Thus Felix had lost everything; he had been
destroyed. I wrote above that all of us who knew him in the *Judenrat* envy him. We are all being destroyed: we know this. We all
wish that like Felix we had something outside ourselves (in his
case: family) for the sake of which we would be glad to be destroyed. I have my archive. To me it is almost what Felix's family
was to him. And yet, at the selection yesterday, I gave no thought
to the archive. *Afterward* I was greatly agitated about it, as I began to think what might have happened to it had I been shipped
away. I have now hidden my notebooks. I must take further precautions; perhaps I shall bury my papers. At any rate, in the moment of judgment yesterday, I thought about myself, mostly, and
I believe that Felix thought about nothing except his family,
even though its members have been taken from him. Thus he
was enviable; we all envied him—and resented the decision to
deport him.

At all accounts, we went in to Grossmann in a delegation this
morning, and asked permission to rescue Mandeltort. Grossmann
grudgingly acquiesced. Since the *Judenrat* messenger we sent with
a letter in the hopes of freeing Hymanski last week was swallowed
up in the *Umschlagplatz* and not only failed to save Hymanski but
was carried off himself, we decided to try something else today.
We decided to risk a broad interpretation of the article of the original resettlement order which exempted sick Jews needing hospitalization who could be vouched for by a *Judenrat* doctor. Our interpretation was to be "broad" because it ignored the limitation in the
original order—*on the first day of the deportation*—and because
there was now no "*Judenrat* doctor" left. Dr. Emmanuel has been
deported. Dr. Breithorn committed suicide last week. [NOTE.

348

N.L.   Incidentally, our Vital Statistics Department calculates that there are 40 per cent less suicides this year than there were in 1939. It seems that people want to live this year.] [NOTE. EDITOR. In this curious but characteristic way, with a crisp statistical note, Levinson dismisses a man he must have known quite well, and whose death he must have regretted deeply.]

I agreed to serve as "doctor" in the rescue party. Three of us went to the pathetic "hospital"—i.e., charnel house—on Gensia Street, and commandeered white smocks, two nurses, and the ambulance (just about the last gasoline-operated vehicle allowed us Jews in the ghetto), and we drove to the *Umschlagplatz*. My two colleagues, carrying a folded stretcher, the two nurses, and I all went to the Stawki Street entrance of the *Umschlagplatz* and in a high-handed manner showed the sentry *Judenrat* credentials and told him we had come, under Article 2h of the resettlement order, to pick up an authenticated patient for hospitalization. We sounded so sure of our ground that he let us through. We decided not to report to authorities within, but simply to try to find Felix and get him out past the same sentry.

We went out first into the yard behind the building that used to be the Stawki Street hospital. This yard, which is about thirty meters wide and fifty meters long, is entirely surrounded by a high brick wall and the backs of the former hospital buildings, except for a gap of about eight meters, at the southwest corner, which is cut off by a wire fence. The yard was filled with Jews waiting to be carried off in the boxcars, and beside the short wire fence scores of Jews stood shouting appeals to whatever German, Junak, or even Jewish policeman they could see on the outside. Many stretched out papers in hands thrust through the fence, crying out that they had valid legitimations. But apart from this suppliant group, most of the people inside the yard seemed despondent and resigned. We wandered through the crowd looking for Felix. I saw a small pot of potatoes being cooked over a wood fire between two stacks of bricks; the group to whom this meal belonged stood as sullen pickets around the fire. Against one wall several people sat picking lice from their clothes, as if typhus and even discomfort were still things to be avoided. A number of Junaks were circulating about, buying watches and other valuable things for pitiful sums of money; one was bartering slices of bread for rings, precious stones, and watches. I started when I saw the girl who had made up her face in our selection, still holding the workman's baby, rocking it back and forth and clucking and singing to it as sweetly as if it were her own infant; as she stood looking down into the child's face, a large vein stood out in the middle of her forehead; her face was flushed and there was a line on each cheek where tears had run down through her unsuccessful powder, but she looked rather happy now. On the whole the people in the yard were quiet. We were unable to find Felix, so we went indoors.

We discovered Felix on the third floor of the hospital building. The conditions in this building were beyond description. The hospital toilets are apparently locked. The deportees have relieved themselves wherever they could. In the halls and rooms were people in all states and degrees of humanity and inhumanity. I saw two men, evidently Hasids, but clean-shaven now, having quite a merry theological discussion, hurling quips and quodlibets at each other's head: *But don't forget,* said one as we passed, *that a disciple of Pinhas the Black Melammed of Koretz cried out once: 'What a boon that God prohibited pride! If He had bidden us be proud, how could I possibly obey His bidding?'* Right next to these bliss-ridden Hasids there lay an insane, naked old man on the floor. A group of young people were singing songs of Palestine: songs of arable lands and hard work in the sun. A Jewish boy was selling candies for sums of money that in the old days would have bought glorious pieces of furniture and nicely bound books: who had use for money now? One little man, stripped to the waist, was flexing his muscles before a Junak and wrestling furiously with some waterpipes against a wall, to show how strong he was and what a mistake it would be to deport him. A young man, who must have belonged to some underground group, shouted: *Fools! You are being taken to death!* A woman spat on him and said contemptuously: *Troublemaker!* Many of the deportees rushed at us and begged with wild eyes for water. I can only say that I was far more terrified by this scene than I was yesterday by the selection. The *Umschlagplatz* is Gehenna. It is beyond life.

Felix was crouching on the floor with his feet under his haunches, in a hopeless, apathetic state—no longer the figure of an enviable man.

[INSERT. FROM ENTRY AUGUST 31, 1942. FROM FELIX MANDELTORT. Felix was sufficiently recovered today to tell me more about his experience at the *Umschlagplatz.* I asked him how he happened to be sitting in that remote room on the third floor when we found him, and he told me this:

That first afternoon Felix stood out in the yard, merely observing. He says he had a curious sensation of being a witness. He was near the group of shouting people by the wire fence, but he himself was making no effort to save himself. From the other side of the yard, someone suddenly screamed:

—— The cars!

Others took up the alarm:

—— The cars! The cars!

The crowd tightened and swayed. People looked this way and that. At first Felix was curious, he says, then he became infected with the general tenseness. A woman screamed piercingly. At that the crowd broke for the hospital building. Involuntarily Felix ran, too. Like a mob panicked by a fire—only, trying to get into a building rather than out from one—the crowd pressed toward two small doorways. Women were knocked down and trampled. A man tripped over a pot boiling on a fire and howled with the real pain of his scalds. Finally Felix got through one of the doors. It appeared that the crowd was trying to get as far up into the building as possible. Felix followed, gripped by a force he could not comprehend, a crowd-fever. He ran up four flights of stairs, until the mob was pressed so tight on the stairway that he could go no further; he turned back then with others to the third floor, ran along a corridor and into a room at the end of it. The room became packed. The corridors and this room smelled sickeningly of excrement. People fainted. There was a constant noise of shouting and frantic chattering.

Shots could be heard soon on the ground floor, and louder shouting. Then Felix realized the meaning of the rush: a trainload of Jews was about to be taken away, and these people wanted to survive one day longer. Felix says he began to shake; his teeth rattled. A rabbi, in phylacteries and prayer shawl, came down the corridor to the door of the crowded room and said, in a stately voice: *Why do you mourn and tremble, Jews? We are going to the Messiah. Be glad! Be glad!* Then he moved to another doorway. The noises below lasted a long time, and finally, at about ten minutes before four (NOTE. N.L. Felix still has his wristwatch; he did not sell it or barter it—a sign, perhaps, that he had not entirely given up hope; as he told this he held the watch up for me to see.),

351

Junaks appeared at the door of the room where Felix was, and with shouts and by force, with pistol shots which now maimed and now only frightened, with fist and toe, with whip and stick, the Junaks drove about half the Jews from the room—and then for no reason left the rest, Felix among them. Thus spared, Felix felt absurdly safe in the room, and he was still there when we found him. . . .]

I touched Felix on the shoulder and said, quickly and quietly:

—— Felix, we have come to rescue you. You are to pretend you are sick.

He looked up at me, and I thought he failed to recognize me, so dull were his eyes. He said in a loud voice:

—— I'm not sick.

I told him to be still and do what I said. He stood up slowly and showed that he had recognized me after all, by saying:

—— Noach, I have no wish to go back. Leave me alone.

My two "stretcher-bearers" and I exchanged glances and agreed, with a nod but without a word, to use force. While I argued in whispers with Felix, they opened out their stretcher and then jumped on Felix from behind. Together we forced him down and strapped him into the stretcher. He began shouting, fortunately in big, sob-like, wordless cries. He appeared and sounded, in truth, sick to death. We carried him out that way, against his will, back to "life." The sentry did not even question us. And now, tonight, as I write these words, I am attacked by doubts as to the mercy and wisdom of our mission.

6

EVENTS LATE AUGUST, 1942. ENTRY SEPTEMBER 2, 1942. N.L. The "family" is broken up—and in more senses than one. It is physically scattered. Worse, there is hatred where before there was only the tension that is normal when people live cheek by whisker. Specifically, Stefan hates two people: Berson and himself.

EVENTS LATE AUGUST, 1942. ENTRY AUGUST 31, 1942. N.L. A subsequence of the selection at the Nowolipie courtyard was that we all had to move out. The building was pretty well cleared that day, and the Germans ordered it closed, as they have many buildings—and, in some cases, whole streets. Thus they drive the survivors into an ever smaller, ever more compressed ghetto.

The conglomerate furniture, Pan Apt's paintings, much of our personal gear—all is left behind. Berson's beloved Bechstein piano is left behind, and now he has only his concertina. And left behind, oi misery! is what Rachel used to call "the family feeling." Having shared it, can I live without it?

I am sleeping at the *Judenrat*. Quite a few of us are doing that now; there seems to be an opinion that that is the only safe place in the ghetto. I have Felix's company, but so far it has been forlorn company: he is just beginning to come round from his experience at the *Umschlagplatz*. I can't tell yet how angry he is with me for having saved him.

Pavel Menkes has been prevailed upon—but only after the most intensive persuasion by Berson—to take the Apts (Rachel, David, Mordecai, and Rutka) into the bakery for safekeeping. Menkes seems to be feeling the increased importance of his position: I suppose the bakers are quite the safest of all the Jews in the ghetto. Menkes is rather haughty, now; well dressed, short-tempered.

In place of some who were deported, I have now managed to get work in the *Judenrat* for both Reb Yechiel and Froi Mazur. Rabbi Goldflamm, who is masquerading as laity these days, has had himself transferred into the *Judenrat* bureaus again, in order to stay with his friend Mazur. Reb Yechiel and Goldflamm are both in the Labor Department, and Froi Mazur is in the now ironic Health and Social Welfare Department, which still goes on. We have arranged for these three, and for Berson and his failing Symka, to move into the kitchen of the apartment in which lives (with several other people) Murin of the Auditing Department here. Murin's wife, Bluma, is a sturdy and capable woman, and Berson says she has been the soul of tender care with Symka.

Stefan and Halinka have removed to the billets now assigned to the Jewish police on Ostrowska Street.

Regina Orlewska has gone to live (we hope she lives) with another former teacher, a Frailin Goldensztein.

We have no idea what has become of Wladislaw Jablonski, but I have a feeling he has not been deported. The instinct for survival runs strong in that young man.

If we of the "family" are to have any gathering place, henceforth, I think it will be the bakery. We tend as if by accident to find each other there in the evenings, before curfew. Menkes, the high and mighty, dislikes this very much. But let him wait and see: he will catch some of "the family feeling," and he will be glad to have us.

EVENTS AUGUST 29, 1942. ENTRY AUGUST 30, 1942. N.L. A startling and embarrassing scene last evening:

Menkes, Berson, Rachel, Rutka, small David, and N.L. were sitting on the benches in the oven room of the bakery talking together. We were having quite a good time: sometimes I feel that we do not maintain a high enough standard of lugubriousness these days. In the midst of some laughter, in came Stefan like a bolt. He was in uniform, and I think we must all have turned a rather anti-official glower in his direction. He nevertheless looked unusually pleased with himself, and he said at once, holding up some papers:

—— See what I have got for the family!

Berson, squinting: —— What are they?

Stefan: —— Ausweise, legitimate Ausweise! Four of them— for whoever needs them in the "family."

Berson, bluntly: —— But we don't need them.

Stefan, with a note of triumph: —— You don't need them— but others in the "family" do.

Berson, with contradictory sharpness: —— I think not.

Stefan: —— What about my father?

Berson: —— We got a job for him at the Judenrat. Through Noach here. [NOTE. N.L. I felt like saying: Don't drag me into this. The atmosphere was unpleasant.] Just yesterday. Your father and your mother, too.

Stefan, his handsome face blushing: —— What about Rachel?

Berson: —— Menkes is going to legitimize her under the bakery here.

[NOTE. N.L. Help! This was the first Menkes had heard of this intention on his own part, I am certain. Something contrary was in Berson. He and Stefan were now snarling at each other. They were mutually stimulating—like two dogs who, at a mere sniff of a suggestion of hostility, begin to bristle, and seeing the bristling, begin to growl, and hearing the growling, begin to snarl. . . .]

Berson, rubbing it in: —— I am safely back with Reisinger. Mordecai is still with the bricklayers. . . .

Suddenly Stefan began trembling. His face grew redder and redder. He shouted:

—— You think you're too good for black-market working cards!

Berson, switching suddenly to a placating tone (but still a maddening one): —— Not at all, Stefan. It just happens that we all have work. You might have had the sense to consult with us before going off on your own this way.

Stefan: —— No! No! You think you're too good for me. You think you can get along without me. Here! Take them! (He held out the certificates.) Burn them in your oven. They only cost a few hundred thousand zlotys. [INSERT. FROM ENTRY SEPTEMBER 2, 1942. N.L. I have learned that Stefan paid fifty thousand zlotys for these *Ausweise*, so his "few hundred thousand zlotys" was an exaggeration by quite a bit. Still, fifty thousand is not to be sneezed at—as an intellectual concept: as money, of course, it is meaningless.] Burn them! They're good enough to save other people's lives, but they're not good enough for Berson. Take them!

But Berson sat still on the bench, and said condescendingly:

—— Calm down, boy.

—— Take them! Take them!

And as he shouted these words, Stefan threw the cards at Berson. He threw them hard, as if he wanted them to slap Berson in the face. But as a final frustration to Stefan, the invisible, playful hands of the air caught the cards, and the scorned *Ausweise* fluttered off, spinning in all directions. Stefan turned and left the shop with a tense, staggering gait.

EVENTS AUGUST 29, 1942. ENTRY AUGUST 31, 1942. N.L. At first I was inclined to blame Berson. He certainly went much too far—that business about Rachel going to work for Menkes! It was unlike him to be so resourcefully sharp. And yet, thinking about it, I cannot blame him too much. I cannot blame anyone for bad temper these days: we are all neighbors to rage. Besides, young Stefan's whole attitude in presenting the papers (one of which, to Berson's shame, may come in very handy—for Regina Orlewska) was that this was something he had done without Berson and in spite of Berson. . . .

EVENTS AUGUST 29, 1942. ENTRY AUGUST 31, 1942. FROM
RACHEL APT. Rachel now tells me that *she* may have been responsible for the clash the other night. She has been talking with
Halinka, who recounted to her (backwards chronologically) the
steps in Stefan's procurement of the *Ausweise*:

Stefan got the papers from Hartmann, the skinny ex-Communist whom Stefan had met while working for The Thirteen, and
who has now become one of the most prominent black-marketeers
in the ghetto. When Stefan first asked Hartmann for four *Ausweise*, Hartmann asked how much Stefan wanted to pay: a certificate for the Toebbens or Gruber factories would be rather expensive, while papers for smaller places (such as Reisinger's, where
Berson works, I suppose) would cost much less—but would also
afford less protection, since such smaller shops might be altogether
liquidated any day. Stefan said price was no consideration, he
wanted four of the best—Toebbens, Schultz, Gruber, the best.
Hartmann told Stefan to come back the next evening, and to bring
sixty thousand zlotys or their equivalent. Halinka says Stefan asked
her for some jewels—at the time he said only that he wanted them
for the safety of the "family"—and he must have taken some of
the cash he has saved up from various "official situations"; and he
returned to Hartmann the next evening with ample riches. Hartmann said that for an old friend like Stefan he would set a "wholesale" price on the work certificates (he showed them to Stefan:
they were real *Ausweise*, properly authenticated, dead Jews' papers, not mere forgeries); he would give Stefan the lot for fifty
thousand zlotys. There was some haggling over the valuation of
jewels, and finally Stefan got his papers; he felt he had been given
a bargain. He went directly to the bakery on Wolynska Street, in
a high mood of anticipation. . . .

Halinka says that the morning before he went to Hartmann,
Stefan had seemed full of affection toward the family. Warmly
and nostalgically, he had talked about the many happy evenings
they had all had together. He worried about how the various ones
would get by now that the group was scattered. Halinka says she
had seldom seen Stefan so kindly-minded. Yet this was all a reaction, she thinks. . . .

The previous evening, Stefan had come back from his session
with Rachel, having listened to her story of how the eleven had
hidden in the half-attic of the mattress factory, Halinka says, tight-

lipped and disgusted. At first he would not say what was the matter with him, but then, as he in turn retailed the story of the hiding place to her, she could see, from the bitter way he quoted Rachel, what the trouble was. It was *Dolek put the plank across* and *Dolek took us by threes* and *Dolek had even checked up on the trapdoor from below* and *Dolek this* and *Dolek that*—until, as a last straw, *Dolek really saved us all*. Not one word of acknowledgment that without the warning—Stefan's own warning—there would have been no such thing as saving the "family." Yet Halinka says Stefan stifled his hurt feelings and his anger; he put them away. He told Halinka that it was enough to know within himself that he had saved the family. He would make no protest; he would not demand gratitude. . . .

And so Rachel now feels badly. And I blame Stefan less.

EVENTS AUGUST 20–25, 1942.   ENTRY SEPTEMBER 2.   FROM HALINKA APT VIA RACHEL APT.   *Very* interesting. Perhaps this is what really accounts for Stefan's rage the other night; perhaps, after all, he was more furious with himself than with Berson. According to Halinka, this happened before the family hid itself:

One evening, Stefan and Halinka went to a party at the rooms of Stefan's friend Vilshinsky. That night Stefan seemed depressed, and at one point he went into a bedroom, and Vilshinsky and Halinka went and found him there later, sitting on the edge of a bed with his head in his hands. The good-looking, empty-headed host, Vilshinsky, asked Stefan what his trouble was.

Stefan, swaying from side to side: —— I can't stand it. I can't stand it any longer. Tomorrow I resign.

Vilshinsky regarded his suffering companion blankly and said, absolutely without understanding:

—— Oh, don't take things so seriously.

Stefan looked up at Halinka, wordlessly, but with an obvious appeal to her comprehension. Then he lowered his face into his hands again, and rubbed his eyes, as if to push back the crowd of images recollected from his duties during recent days.

Halinka (who now says she is sorry she was so stupid as to say this): —— What about me?

Stefan, not uncovering his face, moaning through his hands: —— Ai, Halinka, I love you: you know that I love you. And I will watch out for you as well as I can. But don't ask me to go on in

357

this job. (Now Stefan's face came up. It was flushed and his eyes were wide open and anguished.) I can't stand it! I can't stand it! (Then, quickly:) Tomorrow I quit.

Vilshinsky: —— Come on, Stefan, stop the dramatics. Come out in the living room with the others and let's play some cards. . . .

Next morning Stefan, while standing by in the Ready Room for the first call, sat alone in a corner in one of the creaking rattan chairs, rehearsing the speech he would make, and twice he actually went to the door of the commandant's office, but the first time the commandant began telephoning just as he got there, and the second time, as Stefan loitered on the landing outside the closed door of the office waiting for the last, decisive ounce of courage to accumulate within him, Fakel came along up the stairs and said:

—— Hello, Stefan! You waiting to ask the commandant for a promotion? You'll never get it! *Say*, did you hear the joke about the Ukrainian and the Polish whore? No? Come in the Ready Room and I'll tell you.

Stefan went back to hear the joke, which was remarkable for its pungency but not for its humor—though Stefan forced out a dutiful and customary guffaw—and by the time Fakel's story was over and Ausbach had told the one it brought to his mind, the first call had come. Stefan's next chance to catch the commandant was in mid-afternoon, and somehow Stefan found one thing and another to do—in particular there was some blood on his armband from carrying down from an apartment the body of an elderly Jew who had claimed to a Junak that he was too sick to go to selection and had been shot in his bed; Stefan was very thorough in cleaning this blood off his brassard—and before he knew it the second call had been handed into the Ready Room, and as it turned out, there simply was no chance that day to see the commandant. That night Stefan improved his speech, Halinka says, in the sense that he found a wording that would not alienate· the commandant so much as the previous wording and might even leave the way open to a return to the *Ordnungsdienst* if circumstances required it, but again various duties as well as the busybodied intervention of Fakel, Ausbach, and Vilshinsky, with their gossip, jokes, and rumors, prevented Stefan from seeing the commandant before first call, and that day the Company did not get back in until evening, and the next day again Stefan, who by now had his speech of resignation in perfect form, was unable to snatch even a minute to see the commandant, and the same thing happened the next day and the day after that. And the day after *that*, when Stefan was called in for a personal talk with the commandant, who wanted advice on how to strengthen morale in the company, Stefan considered that another time would be more tactful. . . .

7

EVENTS SEPTEMBER 1, 1942. ENTRY SEPTEMBER 3, 1942. N.L. Rapaport now lives in hiding in the bakery and can almost be considered a new member of our "family." And who is responsible for this? Slonim! Since his hike to Treblinka and back, Slonim has been a changed man. He is now, at last, romantically fulfilled. At the time of his trip and report, he says he had no idea of the romantic import of what he was doing. By now he has made up for lost time, and has become—in everyone's mind, not just his own—a legend already. Naturally this has had an impact on him. One of the most obvious effects has been that he has suddenly become Rapaport's champion, even in the heart of the Bund. I have recorded some of the background of this change of heart [ENTRIES AUGUST 12, 1942]; but until I heard Slonim urging Rapaport upon the reluctant Menkes, night before last, I could not have imagined how enthusiastic Slonim has become for the old man whom he once despised so much.

EVENTS AUGUST 28, 1942. ENTRY SEPTEMBER 3, 1942. FROM LAZAR SLONIM. The deportations having hit the Bund hard, the surviving members of the Executive Committee were meeting to discuss reorganization.

Rapaport: —— Let's see. What have our most serious losses been? Chaverte Hannah. Chaver Zwi. Chaver Herman. We will miss Zwi Lipszuc. I've never seen such a man with machinery. I remember once—it was not long before the Semperit strike—he and I were traveling by automobile—a French car, a Renault, and we ran into some flooded roads along the Warta on the way up to Inowroclaw. The car just stopped dead once in water up to the hubs, in a small village, and Zwi . . .

Chaver Velvel: —— Yes, Chaver Henryk, let's take that up later. Just now the Executive Committee . . .

Rapaport, looking at his hands: —— I wanted you to realize what the loss of Chaver Zwi means to the Bund.

Velvel: —— Of course, Chaver Henryk. We feel it deeply. But it's late. We have to get on with the reorganization. As I was saying . . . (The young man—he has a shiny, shaved head, Slonim says—turned to the other members of the Committee and resumed:) We have had thirty-seven deportations reported by the Fives. The difficulty, from our point of view, is that the losses have been unevenly distributed through the Fives. One—Chaverte Hannah's—was completely wiped out. Another lost four. Several have lost two. . . .

[INSERT. FROM ENTRY SEPTEMBER 4, 1942. FROM HENRYK RAPAPORT. Slonim asked Rapaport yesterday to complete his reminiscence of Zwi Lipszuc, and he did so readily; and Slonim has passed the brief anecdote on to me; Rapaport says he was thinking about Lipszuc while Velvel pressed his business at the meeting:

Zwi, when the car became mired and stalled in the pool in the road, climbed out astride the hood of the shovel-nosed Renault—Zwi, with one eye good for nothing because of a cataract, sitting on the hood, waving the wrench and saying, *The trouble with this car is that the French sacrifice everything for grace and suavity; this car is very suave.* . . . The lake-like puddle of yellowish, muddy water, above the running boards; the whole village sitting on its high doorsteps, laughing at the breakdown and especially amused when one village wit pointed out that this was a Jewish automobile. And yet how that same wit had jumped and run when Zwi roared at him, from his saddle on the hood, shaking the wrench threateningly: *Get us two horses, you stupid fool!* And the horses had been produced, hitched, and whipped forward, the Renault had been towed out, and Zwi had not wetted a toe; he had just sat on the hood giving orders. The trouble had been nothing but water in the manifold. . . .]

Velvel: —— And another thing. I think we owe it to Chaver Henryk here to escort him to the Aryan side. I need not speak to this group of what Henryk Rapaport's leadership has meant to all of us in the past. He is too important to be risked in the ghetto during these deportations. Chaver Mosze can make arrangements for Chaver Henryk to be hidden in Zoliborz. . . . I should like to propose this formally.

Slonim says that Rapaport looked bewildered: What was this? What was this? Evidently still thinking of one-eyed Zwi, apparently not quite certain exactly what had been said, obviously not knowing how to interpret what he had heard, Rapaport looked around at the faces of the Committee. No one would look at him.

Mosze: —— I can make arrangements.

Sarah: —— I believe Velvel is right, it is a duty we have.

Rapaport, quietly: —— My place is here. My place is where the Bund ranks are getting thinned out.

Velvel: —— Your safety is very important to us.

Rapaport: —— Isn't it rather late in the game to discard Rapaport?

Velvel, with apparently sincere feeling: —— No, no, we want to save you, Chaver Henryk.

Rapaport: —— From what? From what fate worse than safety?

Mosze: —— I second Chaver Velvel's suggestion. And I'm afraid it has to be put in the form of an order from the Executive Committee.

The order was drafted and passed. Slonim says he was the only one who voted against it.

EVENTS AUGUST 28–SEPTEMBER 1, 1942. ENTRY SEPTEMBER 3, 1942. FROM LAZAR SLONIM. When Chaver Velvel gave Rapaport asylum, it was understood that the arrangement would be temporary—until the hiding place in the Warsaw suburbs could be prepared by Mosze. The old leader sat in a kind of perpetual night—in a room with blackout curtains drawn, its egress into the living room of the apartment entirely hidden from the view of anyone in the living room by a tremendous, ugly, mirrored cabinet: a searcher, and even a fairly thorough one, might never know that Rapaport's room existed. There was a secondary exit from the room in the form of a small hole cut in the floor of a closet off the room. This hole gave down into the kitchen of an apartment on the next floor below, occupied by the family of a Bundist. Rapaport seemed perfectly happy. He sat most of the day

361

at a small table playing patience by the light of a carbide lamp. On the day when Chaver Velvel announced that preparations for his escape from the ghetto were completed, and that it would be carried out the next morning, Rapaport seemed especially light-hearted—and Slonim says with a grin that Chaver Velvel was puzzled by this, but that he, Slonim, was not. There were sounds of cheerful singing from the room all day long:

But he is better off, better off,
Who gouges out someone's eyes!

That day was the first day of September.

The next afternoon Slonim, sly fellow, went around to Velvel's apartment and pretended to be amazed at what he was told: Early in the morning, when Velvel had pulled the cabinet away from the living-room wall and went into the hideaway to get the old leader, he had found the room empty. The linoleum false floor over the closet hole had been displaced. Velvel said the family downstairs had reported having heard a slight noise in the night, but what with the cabinet upstairs having been pushed back and forth at all hours, day and night, and in consideration of the strict injunction Chaver Velvel had given them to mind their own business and not be curious as to *whatever* noises might be heard in the room above their kitchen, they had felt it prudent simply to turn over and go back to sleep. Chaver Velvel could not help remarking on the agility and resourcefulness of old Rapaport, who, said Velvel, must have hung by his hands from the edge of the closet hole and dropped himself into the kitchen below with a cat's flexibility.

EVENTS SEPTEMBER 1, 1942. ENTRY SEPTEMBER 3, 1942. FROM LAZAR SLONIM. Actually, I gather, the only difficult part of the whole transaction was persuading Menkes to take Rapaport in. Slonim was eloquent; Berson and I also applied some pressure. Menkes finally gave in, rather sullenly. He said, among other things:

—— Anyhow, I have no privacy any more. It has got so a man can't be alone with his own thoughts any more.

[NOTE. N.L. And thank goodness, I say!]

Rapaport came to the bakery in the middle of the night. I

wish I had been there to see the arrival. Menkes was churlish about being wakened out of a deep sleep—where, at any rate, he apparently feels that he can be alone. Either Slonim had warned Rapaport of Menkes' reluctance to take him in, or else the old rogue sensed it; he set out at once, Slonim says, to charm Menkes. He began by recalling every word of Slonim's reports on Menkes back when the Bund was trying to recruit all the bakers, and these reports now made Menkes laugh and Slonim blush: they were marvelously true, and were delivered precisely in Slonim's acid manner; Rapaport tugged on a nonexistent cowlick as he quoted Slonim. Menkes ended by getting a bench from the oven-room, and the three sat talking till the small hours.

And now it is quite nice having this famous old man among us. I remember having written in this record several times of Felix Mandeltort's snobbishness. We are all snobs. I, too. How we all show off in front of this Socialist, knowing that he has a great reputation!

8

EVENTS AUGUST 28, 1942. ENTRY DITTO. FROM RACHEL APT. . . . And naturally Rachel's only hope is that the thing can be pulled off before it is too late. It is hard to hide a small boy: how can you keep a small boy from wiggling and jumping and making a noise? Rachel describes Fein's visit thus:

At the door, on seeing her, Fein uttered a quaint benediction —in praise of God for letting him find the girl he was looking for. The formal part of the benediction sounded odd, Rachel says, on this rough man's thick lips, as if he were trying to say something in a foreign language and could barely get around the words.

It was evening, not long after the end of the working day, and Reb Yechiel and Froi Mazur had stopped by at the bakery for a visit; they were talking with Rachel and David. Menkes was out delivering bread. Others of the family had yet to arrive for the evening chat. Rachel introduced Fein to the Mazurs.

Fein, abruptly: —— I have completed the business you brought me.

Rachel's face took on a look, she supposes, of surprise and delight. She said:

—— Run in the other room, Dovidl. I want to talk with the man.

David, with finality, as if he did not intend even to discuss Rachel's command: —— No.

Rachel: —— David! (And she waited.)

David, in the tone of an adult who has been asked if he would not prefer another chair: —— Thank you, I'm comfortable here.

Froi Mazur, rising, stretching out an inviting hand: —— Come with me, David.

David, whining: —— Every time anything interesting happens, you send me into the other room, like a baby.

But Rachel had turned to Fein, with a look of expectancy and hope, and David went out sulkily with Froi Mazur. Reb Yechiel Mazur sat where he was.

Rachel: —— Tell me.

Fein: —— You know, Berson is a man with a big mind. (As Fein said this, he bunched all the fingers of his left hand together in a point and tapped them against his own temple.) I guess you know we work at neighboring benches in Reisinger's carpentry shop. It is easier there for me than for him—I look like a carpenter and he looks (and Fein repeated the gesture at his temple) like a headworker. And yet he helps me, you know. He talks to me. I remember once he took me to the nightclub where he worked and gave me a big meal: how he laughed that night! What I mean is, there has never been any reason for him to be civil to me—and yet *he treats me as if I had a brain.* You see? What should I do— treat him like a carpenter?

Rachel laughed.

Fein: —— All the time Berson used to talk about some girl who wasn't his wife, and I used to say to myself, *Hmmm, something fancy going on in the Berson house.* And then—who is this girl? You see? It's you, Frailin Apt. [Note. N.L. Should I be surprised that Rachel told me this with an immodest giggle?] So when you come to me about the little brother, you are already my friend's favorite subject of conversation. I *have* to do the job. You see?

Rachel, impatiently: —— So?

Fein: —— So we will take care of your boy on the Aryan side.

Reb Yechiel Mazur, finally catching the drift of Fein's errand:
—— Rachel! Good girl!

Fein: —— Not only that. I give you your choice of merchandise. Two kinds of goods. First kind: we can place your young fellow with some Catholic nuns in a convent outside Warsaw, very gentle, sweet women—they are saints, I can tell you that, I have talked with them personally, and they are real saints; already they are sheltering a number of Jewish children; wonderful women! —and if you don't mind having your young man dress like a magpie for some years in a woman's clothes—as a novice, you see?— and if you don't mind having him surrounded entirely by women and learning the Catholic claptrap (in fact, they would probably want to keep his soul permanently; I hear they are rather possessive, these women)—if you don't mind any of that, this would be a very good solution. In my estimation, absolutely foolproof. (I don't know what they do when his voice changes, but you don't have to worry about that for a while. That's their problem, in more ways than one.) That's the first plan—no danger. The second piece of goods—nothing but danger. Here the idea is to include your young man in a group of children being taken by an underground route—and a very roundabout one, I'm afraid—to Palestine. From Warsaw to Palestine—*on foot*. Many inspections. Great hardships. A very difficult trip. You see? The Jews (said Fein, speaking as if he were not one) are peculiar: they call this ordeal *tiul*, a walk. Just out for a walk. The groups go from Warsaw south to Czechoslovakia, and across Slovakia to Hungary, and beyond that, I don't like to stretch my imagination. Istanbul, I understand. I am told there are very reliable men and women handling this. In Prague there is a woman, they say she is magnificent, docs everything right in the middle of the Germans' eyeballs. . . . *Nu?*

Rachel says she was trembling, and was on the verge of tears. She said:

—— I'll have to ask him which he chooses, but I am sure he will want—the walk. When could he leave?

—— It will take some time—perhaps even weeks—to arrange everything.

—— Let me get the boy.

As Rachel left the room, she was dimly aware of Reb Yechiel Mazur's standing up and saying in a low voice to Fein:

—— I understand you people can get things done. There is something I would like to ask you. . . .

When Rachel returned, she heard Fein say, perfectly openly and in a normal conversational tone:

—— Oh yes, without hesitation, I would recommend prussic acid. Its effect is very rapid: just a little giddiness, headache, palpitations, and that is all. Strychnine is very violent: hideous convulsions. No, prussic acid is much the best.

Reb Yechiel Mazur: —— Very well, then.

Fein: —— Prussic acid has the odor of peachblossoms.

—— All right.

—— For how many?

—— For two.

—— Good. I will deliver it next week.

—— We live with Reb Jakov Murin of *Judenrat* Auditing.

—— Ach, we know where *he* lives.

Rachel cleared her throat and said to David:

—— Thank this man for being very kind to us.

David, whining: —— I can't listen to him, but I have to thank him. What kind of a *shlimazl* are you trying to make of me?

Rachel: —— But Dovidl! Listen! Let me tell you what he said. . . .

9

EVENTS SEPTEMBER 5–12, 1942. ENTRY SEPTEMBER 14, 1942, N.L. We are calling this horrible experience "the Kettle." The Germans' purpose seems to have been to disrupt our order completely—moving us from our homes, invalidating our previous system of working cards, and thereby shaking out all those who had managed before those days improperly to evade deportation. They shut us up in a manageable area—the "Kettle"—and combed through our helpless crowd. According to the best estimate I can make, we numbered about 120,000 when the "Kettle" was put on the stove, so to speak. The German figures on deportation for the six days are 47,791 Jews taken. On one day, September 8, they took 13,596—the worst day we have had. It may be that this was the worst day in all of Jewish history—up to now, at any rate. There are today perhaps 70,000 of us left here in the ghetto, where once half a million Jews were crowded together.

Our first warning of the "Kettle" came when the Germans put up posters. . . .

EVENTS SEPTEMBER 4, 1942. ENTRY DITTO. N.L. Berson and I were walking in the streets together when we first saw the poster.

N.L., after I had read only a few words: —— The noose is tightening.

The poster commanded that by ten o'clock tomorrow morning all Jews remaining within the Large Ghetto are to gather *for registration purposes* in the area bounded by the streets Smocza, Gensia, Zamenhofa, Szczenliwa, and Parysowski Square. They are directed to bring food for two days and drinking utensils, and to leave their apartments unlocked. Anyone found outside the designated area—six city blocks by two, to contain more than a hundred thousand Jews—will be shot.

Berson, with earnest expression: —— Soon we must choose: either die fighting or die like sheep in a shambles.

I think he is right, but how could we ever make such a choice?

EVENTS SEPTEMBER 4, 1942. ENTRY DITTO. FROM DOLEK BERSON. I have been restless this evening—can I be blamed?— and I went over to the bakery to talk with Berson. Earlier Rabbi Goldflamm had dropped in, and Berson says:

Berson finds himself inquisitive toward Rabbi Goldflamm. The rabbi had come to the bakery to ask Berson's opinion of a preposterous rumor he had heard. Berson has noticed recently that the rabbi maintains an extraordinary serenity, and he says he wonders how the rabbi does it. Since the beginning of the deportations, Berson has observed in the members of the "family" all sorts of accentuations—of excitability, temper, nervousness, illness, untrustworthiness; and, in some of them, of humor, physical agility, sound judgment, and other desirable qualities: qualities which had previously been either dormant or latent, and which had just recently come into view under the squeeze of events. He says he has noticed in himself a general quickening of all his faculties. He says he feels that he is more mature, more dependable, and more available (in the sense that a friendly man is available and a cold and self-centered one is not) than he has ever been; he feels as if he has suddenly found himself. He fancies that he sees in himself that special warmth of spirit that is commonly observed in cripples or in those who have suffered deeply and mastered their suffering: with the difference that he has reached this state in a period of only a few weeks. Berson is humble about these sensations he has had; he says he doubts them and interrogates them constantly, fearful lest they be illusory or mere conceit. But he thinks they have substance; they insist. However, one quality to which he has not attained, he says, is serenity. During the frequent crises in our life, his hands tremble, his heart pounds, he stammers, his memory sometimes fails him; he is by no means serene. Hence his curiosity about Rabbi Goldflamm's serenity.

If there is any change in Rabbi Goldflamm, it is that he talks a little less. Not that he has become taciturn: far from it. Nor can it be said that he has stopped babbling foolishly: much of his talk is still quite silly. But in the period when most men have become progressively agitated, the rabbi has somehow managed to become more and more calm and steady.

Like all of the rabbi's rumors, the one he wanted Berson to hear this evening was circumstantial. It was to the effect that President Roosevelt had sent a cable two days before to Commissioner Haensch, declaring that the United States had opened its immigration quotas without limit for Jews, and that the Germans were to regard the Jews in the Warsaw ghetto as prisoners of war and were to make arrangements to exchange them for German soldier-prisoners by way of Istanbul.

The rabbi wanted to know what Berson thought of this.

Berson said that in the first place he doubted whether President Roosevelt would be in direct cable communication with the Germans, and that in the second place, it would be surprising if he addressed such a message to an underling like Haensch, rather than to Himmler or Hitler, and in the third place—

Goldflamm, refusing to surrender the substance of his rumor: —— You understand, I may have been misled on certain details.

Berson: —— The report doesn't seem to jibe with the order that was posted today.

Goldflamm: —— I wondered. I thought perhaps they were gathering us together to announce the change in our status and to take us to a prisoner-of-war camp.

Now Berson's curiosity about the rabbi came out. He asked:
—— How can you go on believing such hopeful things?

Goldflamm: —— Nu, they could happen, couldn't they?

Berson: —— How do you keep so hopeful?

Goldflamm: —— I pray. I have certain habits of prayer.

Berson, almost angrily: —— Don't you ever get excited?

Goldflamm: —— I'm afraid to die, if that's what you mean.
Like anyone else. A man who says he is not afraid to die is a
liar and is more afraid than a man who admits his fear. But in one
respect I am never disturbed. I am not worried about *how* I must
die. That is what bothers most of our people. They are shaking
all over because they think they will die a humiliating death. To
me, it makes no difference whether I am to die at the hands of
Nazis or of microbes. In some respects I prefer Nazis. I understand it will take me only about fifteen minutes to die at Treblinka: death by typhus may last three weeks and is very uncomfortable, they say. If I must go to Treblinka, I intend to die as
decently and quietly as I would hope to die of typhus. It is nonsense
to feel humiliated by the Nazis, because we all know that our
faith will survive their persecutions: we are better and stronger
than they are, *and they already know it*—therefore we can regard
our death as humiliating to them. What faith was ever wiped out
by torture or arms or gags or faggots? Dolek, I am calm because
I know that any system that is based upon love and respect will
outlive any system that is based upon hatred and contempt. That
is all there is to it. I am not worried. . . . Now, about President
Roosevelt. . . .

[NOTE. N.L. This is all very well, but I should like to ask
Rabbi Goldflamm exactly how his benign system will remain so
vigorous when all its practitioners are dead.]

EVENTS SEPTEMBER 4, 1942. ENTRY DITTO. N.L. . . .
but we did not talk about the rabbi for long, because of the
urgency of this technical problem.

Berson has become, among other things, a specialist in hiding
things, and now, on the eve of this "registration," he and Rachel
have some very precious things to hide. Berson's specialty started
several weeks ago, back at the Nowolipic apartment, more as a
hobby than anything else. Later, Hashomer gave him some papers
for safekeeping. Berson, who is extremely dexterous (how fleetly

his fingers tattoo the keys of his concertina!), hid the papers by boring a half-inch hole up from the bottom of the leg of a table, with a brace and bit, and by rolling the papers tightly and putting them in the hole, and then whittling a perfectly fitting plug. Once in his mind, the methods of hiding things fascinated him. He began devising all sorts of secret cubbies and caches and sconces. He made a beautiful double bottom in a drawer, drawing upon his experience at Reisinger's for skill; he recessed some jewels in one of the bass-note valves of his concertina, so that now sometimes a nice melody will have a gap in it, like the smile of a man who has lost a lower tooth.

The problem Berson had this evening was a new one: it was to hide two large and dear objects: Symka and David.

We all felt certain that the "registration" was to be a ruse. Rapaport (who has now been taken wholeheartedly into the group; Menkes likes him) suggested that even if there is an actual registration, this will weed out all those without proper working cards and all those—Symka, alas, is in this category—too feeble to work. As a child, David would certainly be taken. Menkes' new bakery, on Wolynska Street, is within the "registration" area. If Symka and David could be concealed for a few days, they would at least have survived this emergency, and it is enough, now, to measure one's life span, not by birthdays, from year to year, but by predicaments, from week to week.

At first Berson was troubled by the proposition. When he hid the family [EVENTS AUGUST 25, 1942], he had found a ready-made refuge for them. Now he had only one night to work and he was in unfamiliar terrain. Nevertheless, he began an examination of Menkes' shop.

—— Let's see, assuming that I am an S.D. man and that I have some sense—if those two things together are possible—where do I search? I look in the flour bins (and Berson did). . . . In the mixing tubs. . . .

And he carefully scrutinized all the bread shelves, boxes for gear, water barrels, and closets. He opened the oven door and looked into the deep, bricked space; it was cold at this time. Then he opened the fire-door of the furnace beneath the oven. The fire-door is a hinged, metal cover, with sliding vents, about three quarters of a meter across. The furnace itself is an arched brick cavern, about two meters square and averaging one meter in

height. There is no grating. The baker builds his fires directly on
the brick floor: some dying charcoals glowed there now. The roof
of the furnace arch slopes upward toward the back, and the opening of the flue is at the uppermost and inmost end. Berson examined this cavern for some time. Then he asked Menkes:

—— How thick are the walls of the furnace?

—— This one, I don't know.

—— In general?

—— In general, about three bricks thick, to hold the heat.

—— What is beyond the oven?

—— The back wall of my shop, and beyond that, the courtyard.

—— For absolute safety, this is where we must work.

And Berson described his already decided plan: it would be
possible, he thought, to excavate a small tunnel with just enough
diameter for a human body, from the floor at the back of the
furnace, downward through the brick and about three feet deep in
the dirt beneath, then turn the tunnel back at a sharp angle and
extend it out from under the furnace and there make a rounded
place like a rabbit's burrow, big enough for two. Berson believed
it would be quite safe to hide Symka and David in his hole and
then *light the furnace fire*, the heat and smoke from which would
be conducted upward, and would be kept from the lair by the
insulation of the brick and dirt and by the turn in the tunnel. And
with a piece of waterpipe driven down from the edge of the courtyard into the hole for ventilation, the convective action of the fire
in the furnace would keep drawing cool, fresh air in through the
pipe. What German was vindictive enough to go through fire to
hunt for Jews? Symka and David could be given loaves of bread,
water, and a pan and a large spoon—these last to be used as a
gong and gong-stick, if the heat should become unbearable or if
any accident should take place in the cavern, in which case the
furnace fire could quickly be doused. Undoubtedly Menkes would
go right on baking bread—as he is most anxious to do, since this
industry is his greatest protection against deportation—and he
could tend the situation.

Symka and David both agreed to hide in such a hole, if it
could be dug. Four of us—Berson, Menkes, Rapaport, and N.L.—
dampened the remaining coals in the furnace and went right to
work. We disposed of the refuse of our digging in Menkes' ashcans

and, after dark, in the courtyard (being careful to hide the fresh dirt under other trash). Rapaport worked with an extraordinary vigor and he was, I noticed, in a curious temper, an almost sprightly mood: he joked and sang songs with Berson as we worked. Late in the night, when the work was nearly done, Rapaport, who had been digging beyond the turn in the tunnel, stuck his head out into the lamplit furnace, and said, in mock-serious tones, his voice reverberating under the arch:

—— I should like to apply for tenancy in this worm-hole. (Then, with a sudden gravity:) If I enlarge the hole myself, may I stay in it? I know that as a man . . . I think of the future. . . . Believe me, I am not simply afraid. . . .

Berson and Menkes, who were gathering dirt in the furnace, looked at each other.

Menkes: —— Nu?

Berson, shrugging: —— Why not?

The exchange between the two men was gruff and casual, but underneath it lay an unspoken but clearly understood sentence: *The ghetto needs this old man more than it needs us young ones.*

Rapaport, resuming his airy way: —— After all, I have been in the underground for nearly half a century but I have never gone under the ground.

With my head and shoulders now in the furnace, I looked at the old, joking man and saw that tears had welled up in his eyes under cover of his humor: Rapaport, too, must have understood the tacit sentence that had traveled between Berson and Menkes.

EVENTS SEPTEMBER 4, 1942. ENTRY DITTO. N.L. I am still at the bakery. I have been writing, it seems, for several hours. the others are talking yet. Who wishes to sleep?

EVENTS SEPTEMBER 5, 1942. ENTRY DITTO. N.L.; AND FROM RACHEL APT. Early this morning—the so-called registration was to begin at ten o'clock—members of the "family" began gathering at the bakery. It was the one address they all know within the registration area. Menkes warned them that during the actual registration (or whatever it would be) he could not shelter them in his bakery; he planned to continue making bread. If any of the "family" could get to the bakery undetected by night, supposing that this affair went on more than one day, then he would give them scraps of bread on which to live—he did not want the family to feel that he was abandoning them. He was, after all, to hide three. [NOTE. N.L. So! Menkes *has* caught some of "the family feeling."] On the other hand, he wanted it clearly understood that the bakery was not to be regarded as a haven. [NOTE. N.L. Yet Menkes is still careful Menkes!]

Reb Yechiel and Froi Mazur came to the shop at about nine o'clock, and when Rachel went up to kiss them—she had not seen them for a few days—she noticed at once a change in them, she says. They held their heads high; they smiled sweetly and vaguely. They seemed somehow not to be paying attention to the bustle and tremor of the ones around them: they gestured slowly, they smiled, they answered startling statements with commonplaces.

Rachel, her eyes sparkling with excitement: —— We have dug a tunnel to hide David and Symka and Herr Rapaport.

Froi Mazur, nodding, as if Rachel and the others had done the three some minor, trite favor: —— That was thoughtful of you.

The elderly couple sat on one of the benches and folded their hands in their laps. They sat still as stone, while all about them the other members of the family, even the strongest, like Berson and Menkes and Mordecai Apt, seemed seized with a timorous quivering. Rachel wondered about this stolidity, which was particularly noticeable in Reb Yechiel Mazur, who had been, in previous exigencies, a jumper, a mumbler, a dancer, a worrier; now he was as quiet as a monument. At first Rachel says she thought the Mazurs might be dazed with sickness. Then, in a few minutes, she remembered the rag of conversation she had caught in passage between Reb Yechiel Mazur and Fein, the week before [ENTRY AUGUST 28, 1942]. *Prussic acid has the odor,* Fein had said, *of peachblossoms.* Rachel had heard Berson's account of having quizzed Rabbi Goldflamm about serenity. She decided she must tell Berson: Here was a way to achieve it: be in control of one's own fate: have about oneself a tiny glass bottle containing a fluid with the odor of peachblossoms.

EVENTS SEPTEMBER 5, 1942. ENTRY DITTO. N.L. Menkes got down on his hands and knees, opened the furnace door, and put his head inside. Berson, bending down beside him, could hear him say in a harsh whisper:

—— Are you settled?

As from the bowels of the world, the answer came, in Rapaport's hollowed voice:
—— All settled.
—— Then we will light up.
Menkes, withdrawing his head, touched a match to the paper under the kindling. Menkes and Berson remained bent down for a long time, listening. Berson was sweating so freely that it seemed *he* was in the furnace. The fire grew from a tiny crackle of kindling to a hot-throated roar; still the two listened for the sound of the spoon beating on the pan. Finally, Berson says, he thought he heard a fragile sound beyond the deep oratory of the fire, but it was such an improbable sound that he turned to Menkes and said:
—— Did you hear that?
—— I thought I heard somebody laughing—Symka or David.
—— It was David! That was what I heard! (And Menkes stood up with a radiant face, and he lifted his eyes and let escape, almost as a sigh, a cryptic benediction:) Blessed art Thou. . . .

EVENTS SEPTEMBER 5, 1942. ENTRY DITTO. N.L. The members of the "family" exchanged embraces. For some reason Rutka, and only Rutka, wept. [NOTE. N.L. Pregnancy? Hope of life and despair of life?] The elder Mazurs were still iron-calm. Berson had suggested that the "family" should break up into pairs, and we went out mostly that way: Reb Yechiel and Froi Mazur, Mordecai and Rutka, Berson and Rachel; the rabbi went alone, and so did N.L. Stefan and Halinka had not joined the rest of us.

EVENTS SEPTEMBER 5, 1942. ENTRY DITTO. N.L. For me, anticlimax. Welcome anticlimax! I walk to the *Judenrat* building and find that all department heads have automatically been cleared.
But for the others. I fear—judging by the sounds of turmoil and anguish in the streets—not an anticlimax.

EVENTS SEPTEMBER 5–8, 1942. ENTRY SEPTEMBER 8, 1942. N.L. This thing is being conducted on two planes: on the official, organizational plane, and on the human plane.
On the official plane, the Germans have invented a devilish scheme: they make us select among ourselves. They have disallowed the previous system of *Ausweise*, and have now issued to

374

each enterprise and organization a certain series of numbers; as many Jews can be legitimized by each organization as it has numbers, no more, and the task of selecting *which* Jews is left to the Jews themselves: out come all our fratricidal impulses. This system fairly effectively eliminates the possibility of black-market credentials, and removes from each factory and from the *Judenrat* any discretion as to the number of Jews it will admit to its ranks. For instance, the *Judenrat* has now been allowed 2,800 numbers, where before we had 5,000 workers. The old battle between department heads for zlotys in the annual budget is now waged—with what bitterness!—for lives in the budget of numbers. Fortunately, by prodigious arguing and outrageous lying, I have procured enough numbers for all my staff.

After this damned "registration," the Germans have notified us they will impose a further control upon us by billeting Jews with the establishment for which they work. All *Judenrat* employees will be billeted together, mostly on Gensia; all the police are to be on two blocks (Ostrowska-Wolynska); all the workers for Toebbens are housed around the factories on Prosta-Walitzow and Leszno. Thus we are to be fragmented into a number of separate, easily policed small ghettos, each surrounded by barbed wire with sentry posts at the gates (according to the Germans' advance notice to us at the *Judenrat*).

On the human plane, this "registration" is the most pitiful process I have seen yet. So many thousands in the streets. . . . And my friends, subject to these random, wandering selections. . . .

EVENTS SEPTEMBER 5–10, 1942. ENTRY SEPTEMBER 11, 1942. FROM DOLEK BERSON. Berson says that he and Rachel were the last to leave the bakery, and behind them they heard Menkes bar and double-bar his stout door. In the street was a confused mob of people, drifting this way and that. For a time Berson and Rachel let themselves be pushed and carried by the crowd, now half a block toward Zamenhofa Street, now back a few yards toward Lubetzkiego, purposelessly. At the sound of a shot down the street to the eastward, part of the mob recoiled and with a violent surge broke through into Ostrowska Street, which was itself crowded, and there the meaningless undulations began again.

375

Nothing seemed to be happening. Berson and Rachel exchanged only brief mutterings. Berson says he was impatient with Rachel. He felt as if he were in the grip of a bad dream; he had the sensation of struggling to wake up and being unable to. The crowd pushed and pulled.

It was late afternoon before Berson recovered from his dazed, dreamlike state. Suddenly once he looked down and saw and felt Rachel beating on his chest with her fists, crying:

—— Do something! Do something!

He took her by the hand and threaded her through the crowd. They came to a place where the mob was, if possible, thicker than elsewhere. Berson lifted Rachel up above the heads of the people to see what she could see. She told him that a huge selection was taking place at the street corner. Berson eased her down and said:

—— Why should we go to them? Let them come and get us!

Most of the houses and courtyards were barricaded or guarded, but Berson and Rachel found one into which the mob had broken, and they went inside and climbed a staircase and with many others jumped from a second-storey window into the next courtyard and broke through a fence behind that into still another and climbed high in a building and got out onto some roofs (by this time the sky was darkling) and crossed the roofs until they found a skylight, which they broke (now there were fewer people, perhaps a score; the group had scattered on the roofs), and they let themselves down into an empty apartment house and went into one of them and threw themselves on the beds and lay there through the night, hearing shots and screams all night near by and naturally not sleeping, and stayed there half the next day until curiosity and fear made them go out and down the stairs of the apartment to the street level, but when they saw, in the courtyard, a pile of perhaps thirty bloody Jewish corpses, newly executed, they drew back and climbed again into the same apartment, this time taking the precaution, however, of observing and preparing three different escape routes—downstairs into some cellars and out an areaway; up through the skylight; and, as a third choice, out into the courtyard past the corpses and directly to the street—and during the second night they had occasion to be thankful for this foresight, because at a late hour they heard footsteps and the shouts of German hunters and, escaping by the skylight, they spent the hot night shivering on the roofs, listening to shots and screams below, and in the soft dawn they returned yet once more to the same apartment, on the theory that the chances of its being searched again immediately were slight. . . .

And thus, in what seemed a scarcely punctuated continuity of terror, movement, vigilance, hunger, filth, and bare survival, returning again and again to the same apartment, Berson and Rachel passed six days without facing the peripatetic selections. At the end of six days it was over. A few of the former tenants of the apartment came home and said it was over. The Germans and Junaks had left the "registration area." Berson and Rachel went through hushed and dreary streets to Pavel's shop.

FROM ✡ CONVERSATIONS, MAY 8–10, 1943. EVENTS SEPTEMBER 5–10, 1942. FROM DOLEK BERSON. Berson sat in a round tin tub in the back room of Pavel's shop, bathing himself. The water, brought by Pavel in buckets from one of the few remaining waterpoints, and heated in the bakery oven, was a precious commodity; the bath (Berson's first all-over bath in more than six weeks) was a great luxury. The tub was small: Berson sat in about thirty centimeters of water, with his knees drawn up. He was thinking back over the "Kettle." Particularly he thought about Rachel. Berson was satisfied with his own role in the hazardous events: among the twenty or so in his and Rachel's group, he had been the most resilient and thorough (it had been he who had found the skylight; he who had insisted upon establishing three escape routes from the apartment; he, on the third night, who had fetched two loaves from Menkes; he, on the fourth day, who had barricaded the staircase below the apartment so that the group hiding there would at least gain time in case of further searches). He had been a kind of colonel, and this had been a pleasant surprise to him, he says. But the greatest surprise had been Rachel. In any dangerous juncture, she had been the one to whom everyone looked to see what state of mind was appropriate. She had set the pitch of the entire group's feelings. If there was danger of panic, she drove sense and steadiness into her companions. If they became apathetic and morose, she lifted them to a proper level of apprehension. If a single man or woman began to feel self-pitiful, she was ready with comfort. The force of her sympathy was enormous: she could do more with a look than anyone else with a lecture. She had been singlehandedly cohesive, and once, more or less jokingly, Berson

377

had called her "Little Mother." He had said, in some hard situation:

—— What do you think, *Mutterl*?

And Rachel, with her not very pretty face turned to him, had given him a look so deep, so warm, so kind, that he would never forget it.

EVENTS SEPTEMBER 10, 1942. ENTRY DITTO. N.L. Separately, by twos for the most part, as we had gone out, we of the "family" returned to Menkes' shop. Mordecai and Rutka, who got back first, eventually told us that they had met up with some Hashomer people who had prepared a hiding place outside the registration area, and they had stayed there. Reb Yechiel and Froi Mazur came in about an hour later: Reb Yechiel Mazur had gone to the *Judenrat* and Felix and I had made sure that the couple obtained their *Judenrat* numbers, and they had passed safely through three selections; they had slept in the open streets. Berson and Rachel came in next; they . . . [NOTE. EDITOR. Their experiences have already been set forth here.] I was next; I had been comfortable at the *Judenrat* the whole time. Symka, David, and Rapaport had got through all right in their refuge, though after a couple of days the time must have gone terribly slowly. Symka seems very weak. Rapaport is pale, but he looks cheerful and passably well. David is even lively. Menkes had remained in the bakery, making bread; he had gone through nearly a score of inspections, without difficulty; he had even been given new validations for his papers. Out of the blue, who should show up but Wladislaw Jablonski? He followed Mordecai and Rutka here. He smells to the rooftops: he spent the last three days of the "Kettle" in a sewer culvert. Rabbi Goldflamm did not return. We have sat up late into the night waiting for him, but it is obvious that he is not going to come.

One by one, about an hour ago, the members of the "family" began to speak of the rabbi, and in our recollections we inferentially agreed that he has been taken away. We laughed together over some of the bizarre and wishful rumors the rabbi has believed and circulated. Berson told, for the benefit of those who had not heard of it before, about his conversation with Rabbi Goldflamm the day before the "Kettle," and of the rabbi's attitude toward death; this was comforting. Froi Mazur told some anecdotes of the rabbi's generosity, and we all began to forget our impression

378

that he was a rather foolish man. Finally Reb Yechiel Mazur pronounced, with eerie effect and great feeling, the words of the burial ritual, when the coffin is lowered:

—— May he come to his place in peace!

10

EVENTS SEPTEMBER 5, 1942. ENTRY SEPTEMBER 12, 1942. FROM SYMKA BERSON. Ever since Menkes struck flint and lit the fire, and we waited and waited, and then the two men stood up saying they had heard laughter from beyond the furnace, I have been haunted by that idea; and now, by easy stages, I have heard from Symka what happened:

It was pitch-black in the hole. The three had just settled down. Rapaport held the big, wooden mixing spoon in his right hand; his left arm encircled Symka's frail body. She lay with her head on Rapaport's shoulder. The boy, curled up on the other side of Rapaport, was whimpering a little. Rapaport had entrusted the pan to David. Rugs and blankets sheltered the three from the damp earth.

A distant sound, echoing as if from another place and time, came down the tunnel. It was a clanking and squeaking sound— a metallic door being opened. Then a ghostly, reverberating whisper (which we had heard from the other end):

—— Are you settled?

Symka says she shuddered as Rapaport answered. The second whisper from above:

—— Then we will light up.

The young boy began to cry.

Rapaport, nudging David: —— Listen! I will tell you a story. Listen! It is about a grasshopper and an ant.

David's thin whine stopped. A tiny crackling sound could be heard coming down the tunnel.

Rapaport: —— Once there was an ant, who was carrying home to his family a very large breadcrumb, about six times his own size. He was walking backwards, dragging the breadcrumb, and I can tell you he was proud of himself. But all of a sudden he heard a deep and loud voice, above him, saying, *Tsk tsk-tsk! You are a tiny fellow to be carrying such a load. Let me help you.* The ant looked up and saw a big, friendly-looking grasshopper, and he said in his squeaky voice, *Thank you. You are very kind.* The grasshopper roared, *Allow me*; and he picked up the breadcrumb and, in one enormous gulp, ate it. *That was a cruel, unfriendly act,* the poor little ant said. The grasshopper turned on the ant and shouted, *Hold your tongue and feelers! I see you're a strong little ant. I have work for you—and you had better do it, too, or I'll eat you as quickly as I did the breadcrumb.* It appeared that the grasshopper wanted to travel, and he gave the ant the task of carrying his belongings, which were wrapped in part of a birch leaf and made a bundle even larger than the breadcrumb. The grasshopper would take a big hop and while the ant was painfully dragging the leaf-case across to where the grasshopper had landed, the grasshopper would snooze. When the ant arrived, he would get up, yawn, stretch his leapers, and hop several more ant-kilometers away. The poor ant got no rest and was very worried about his family.

Rapaport paused. The crackling coming down the tunnel had grown very loud; it seemed as if the fire were approaching closer and closer. But the dark hole was still cool, and now it was lit up by a flickering, dim, reddish, reflected light.

—— One day the ant came up to the grasshopper and saw that he had landed after the last hop right next to a puddle. It was a small puddle, and the ant knew that the grasshopper could hop across a puddle ten times larger, but he said, *I'll wager a year of my servitude that you can't jump across that puddle.* The grasshopper laughed so hard that he rolled over on his back, and then he got up and, scarcely bending his leapers, he whipped himself across the puddle and far beyond it. When the ant caught up, he put the leaf-case down and shook his head and said, *I didn't think you could do it.* The next morning the grasshopper and the ant had breakfast beside a low wall. The ant had seen the grasshopper jump three times as high as this wall, but he said, *I'll wager two years of my servitude that you can't hop over that wall*; whereupon the grasshopper said, *What a foolish ant! You didn't think I could jump over that puddle yesterday.* And he snapped his leapers and went up four times as high as the wall and over. The ant got over the wall as over a mountain range, and when he came down to the grasshopper, he said in grudging admiration, *Oi, you are a remarkable jumper, I must admit.*

Now a steady roar could be heard in the tunnel. Rapaport spoke louder.

—— The next day the travelers came to a narrow stream, and the ant said, *I'll wager four years of my servitude you can't hop across that stream.* The grasshopper said in sarcastic mimicry, *I'm a remarkable jumper,* and without a moment's hesitation he bounded across the stream with many meters to spare. The ant crossed on a twig and came up to the grasshopper, saying *You are the most talented of all grasshoppers.* The same thing happened the next day at a narrow country road. This time the ant wagered eight years of slavery. *You notice,* he said, *that I am betting double or quits each time.* The grasshopper said, *Ha ha! Do you think the most talented of all grasshoppers cannot hop over this mud-track, this footpath?* And he whisked across the road easily. So they traversed a great distance, and the wagers grew more frequent and the ant's admiration after each successful jump grew more and more extravagant until, on the bet which bound the ant in service for eight thousand one hundred and ninety-two years, after the grasshopper had made the leap without accident, the ant, on catching up, said, *I am sure there is nothing you cannot do.*

It was pleasantly warm in the burrow now. Fresh air was drawing in through the ventilation pipe. The steady roar went on.

—— The day after that, the grasshopper and the ant came to the edge of the sea, and the ant said quietly, *I will wager you double or quits—sixteen thousand three hundred and eighty-four years of servitude or not one minute more—that you can't jump across that sea.* The grasshopper stood up. There was a wild look in his eye. He shouted, *There is nothing I cannot do!* And, bending his leapers double, with pearls of sweat on his green forehead, he gave a mighty jump—into the sea, where he drowned. The ant just smiled a little ant-smile, picked up the grasshopper's belongings, and started for home.

It was then that David uttered a high, piercing, happy laugh, and said:

—— It's nice in here. Tell me another story.

11

EVENTS SEPTEMBER 14–19, 1942. ENTRY SEPTEMBER 19, 1942. N.L. In my opinion, this idea first occurred to me on the day when we buried the rabbi's Torah in the cemetery [ENTRY JULY 15, 1942]; and it was fastened in my mind by my reaction, the day I faced the selection [ENTRY AUGUST 26, 1942], when I suddenly thought of what might have happened to my archive had I been deported. I decided, six days ago, to take Berson into my confidence, and he and I chose some others. . . .

EVENTS SEPTEMBER 14, 1942. ENTRY SEPTEMBER 19, 1942. N.L. First I had to persuade Berson to come back to work for the *Judenrat*, and because of his stubbornness, that was not easy—until, at last, I told him my plan.

N.L. —— You'll have to admit, Dolek, that circumstances have changed since you resigned.

Berson: —— Very much. I admit it. And yet I feel that the essential circumstance has not changed—that is, the *Judenrat* really works against the Jews.

—— You would be in my department. I can assure you (and with this I knew I was on the verge of spilling my plan, though beforehand I had intended to hold it back for a few days) that from now on my department will work only for the Jews: for future generations of Jews.

—— The *Judenrat* is a single agency: it acts on behalf of the Germans. How can you escape that fact? I can find some other place to hide: I would rather hide in the hole under Menkes' stove.

N.L., now speaking in that awful pompous manner I always assume when I am trying to be confidential: —— Dolek, I have told no one what I am about to tell you. I need your help. I need you not for your qualities as a historian—I'm afraid you'd make a poor historian, you're too much of an enthusiast—but for your strong arms. Do you remember when we dug the tunnel of the library?

—— Of course.

—— I need you now for work like that—only this is far more important work.

—— After the ghetto (From force of habit, Berson still uses that optimistic phrase.), I think I'll become a miner.

—— I intend, Dolek, to bury my entire archive, so that when we are all gone away, others may at some time dig up these records and know something about us.

Unable to attack this plan in general, yet not flexible enough to embrace it at once, Berson caviled:

—— But if we are all destroyed, how are your "others" going to know where to go grubbing for the records?

—— We shall send out letters and couriers. We'll send messages to Palestine. We shall find ways.

Berson's mind is like a still: ideas have to ferment there awhile. He stood looking a bit dazed and witless for a while. Then he said quietly:

—— Naturally I will help you.

EVENTS SEPTEMBER 14–17, ENTRY SEPTEMBER 17, 1942. FROM DOLEK BERSON. Berson tells me that later he was struck by his own self-deception in his exchange with me about returning to the *Judenrat*. He had allowed himself to be quite righteous about the *Judenrat*—while all the time he was working, at Reisinger's, for whom else but the Germans? This insight into his own hypocrisy, he says, struck him only when he thought about my plan. The tremendous force of the idea behind the intention to bury the archive—its hopefulness: its meliorism: the belief implicit in it that man can learn from man's tragedies—this excited Berson and retrieved him, he says, from the fear and despondency that had begun to descend on him as a reaction to the dreadful "Kettle."

Indeed, a new, cautious hopefulness colored everything Berson did in the ensuing days, he says—and helped, too, to give him the drive to do all that he felt he had to do. He plunged with much energy into Hashomer work. Like all the underground, Hashomer Hatsair has been terribly disrupted by the "Kettle" and by the geographic dislocations of the ghetto. The carefully worked-out systems of communications between groups and sections of the ghetto have been broken up. Members have been deported or have gone into hiding. Rutka had got back in touch with Zilberzweig, and she sent both Berson and Rachel to him. Zilberzweig gave them a list of Hashomer workers to try to find and re-form into groups. This is dangerous work, as it means moving around, unauthorized,

383

from factory area to factory area. Berson also finds the work tremendously rewarding, however, because each discovery of a worker is an unforgettable experience: each one is delighted and relieved to be restored to the security of the Hashomer band. This repeated excitement, of which Berson is the agent, atones for the repeated disappointment when he learns that other Hashomer workers have been taken off. Rachel has gone out with Berson on a number of these errands. The work is done at night. Rachel says that Berson's talent for hiding things translates itself, during these nocturnal excursions, into a genius for finding secret and safe routes from place to place—across roofs, through cellars, in and out of windows.

Daytimes, meanwhile, I have put Berson to work sorting the archive. There is no question of sorting papers to be kept from papers not to be kept: I have but one criterion for the suitability of a piece of writing for preservation: legibility. Berson's sorting is simply a very rough cataloguing process—the diaries together, the poems together, the plays, the essays, the account books, the newspaper clippings, and so on—for in smuggling the collection from the old *Judenrat* building, I had lost much of the order of the original archive. Berson says he cannot help pausing and browsing through papers as he works, and increasingly he has been infected with my zeal for the task. What makes it exciting for him, he says, is his conclusion that the people here are not all so small and despicable as he had thought. Meanness, wanton cruelty, self-interest, lust, covetousness, thievishness, murderousness—all the persistent qualities interdicted in the Mosaic law and in every system of ethics and jurisprudence ever devised—these Berson has seen aplenty in the leaves of the archive; but he has also seen, he says, in separate revelations of motive and impulse and actual deed, that man can be on the whole an agreeable and indestructible creature —and that his staying quality was to be found, in the last analysis, in his tendency, under stress, to band together with his fellows. Familial man: mere hatred (even his own most scientific malice) can never wholly destroy him. So, at any rate, Berson says he has felt as he has glimpsed at the handwritten papers and tossed them to one side and to the other.

[NOTE. N.L. Each one of us is different. I have at the moment a pessimistic reaction to the papers in the archive. My fellows seem to me to be shortsighted, stupid, incapable of unanimity, and really not satisfied to wait for destruction: they seem bent upon self-destruction, in their systematic unwillingness to face facts. Not I, of course: I am a rather sensible and level-headed fellow at all times. So I tell myself. *Nu*, I am getting very little good news these days—why shouldn't I tell myself something acceptable?]

EVENTS SEPTEMBER 19, 1942. ENTRY SEPTEMBER 20, 1942. N.L. We have begun to bury the archive in the courtyards of Swientojerska 34 and Nowolipki 68. We are packing the papers and books as carefully as we can in large metal strong-boxes and filing cabinets, which I wangled from the Supply Department. I believe these boxes should be capable of withstanding dampness and corrosion for a few seasons. How long, O Lord? . . .

In anticipation, beforehand, I expected to get the same thrill from this act of preservation as I had from the rescue of books from the Grosser Library in December, 1940. I was disappointed. This was only hard work. There was an element of risk in this work, but mostly it was merely exhausting. Our tools were inadequate: some coal shovels, which do not have a stiff enough biting edge to go into Warsaw's hard-packed, sandy foundation soil; some metal rods, therefore, to loosen the dirt; and potato bags and reed baskets to carry the waste away. We hid the new dirt in neighboring cellars, and that proved to be almost as hard work as hiding the precious archive.

I was horrified to discover how weak I have become. When our squad of half a dozen men dug that tunnel through to the library in 1940, I became very stiff from the work, I remember, but I was able to carry on fairly steadily. This time I was forced to pause every few minutes and sit down, and I had to force myself back to work after each rest with a very considerable output of willpower. And watching the friends I had enlisted at work, watching the difference between the strong men and the weak, I made a most important observation:

Those men will survive the physical hardships of ghetto life who manage, each day, to expend a few less calories than they take in.

I may call this Levinson's Law of Survival. It seems a simple rule, but how few observe it! In our work, the weak men were reckless. They would work with deep concentration at first—too long; they would rest imperfectly, talking and moving about; and they would go back at their work with tense and violent motions;

385

and they also spent energy in complaint, apprehension, and anger. The strong men were not lazier (they got much more done, in the long run, than the weak); but instinctively they began slowly, rested soon and completely, worked again in leisurely and indifferent fashion, and kept an even rhythm of effort and recovery, as well as an even temper. Berson is still strong, and this instinct for the conservation of energy and emotion is clearly evident in him. Levinson's Law has a cumulative effect. The man who saves two calories of intake over outgo in one day will have the resources, next day, to save five calories rather than two; and the day after that it will be ten; and so on, until he has become noticeably stronger than he was and than his fellows are. The converse is of course true in case of over-expenditure of energy: one loses more and more from day to day. The fittest men in circumstances like ours will always be those who make a daily profit of energy *by instinct*, who are incapable of wasting energy by exertions of body and excesses of spirit. But I think the men who accomplish a profit, not by instinct, but by calculation, conscious thrift, budgeting, control, and even niggardliness, will be close behind. I intend, now that my aim of burying the archive is being accomplished, to be a miser of energy. . . .

EVENTS SEPTEMBER 20, 1942. ENTRY DITTO. N.L. In these days of intense and generally more cheerful feelings, Berson has grown somewhat sentimental. His most convenient object of emotion, and the one which has arisen directly from his thoughts as he has sorted the archive, has been the "family." The experiences he has shared with its members seem so precious, he says, that the thought of being separated from any of them is almost unbearable. Berson still cannot believe that Rabbi Goldflamm was taken: he keeps imagining that he will encounter that mournful, rumor-swollen face in the streets.

This evening, at the bakery, Berson, Mordecai, and N.L. sat talking together. Menkes was in his batter-room mixing dough for tomorrow morning's baking, and David was helping. Rachel was out. Mordecai was telling of the haunting labor he had been put to in the bricklayers' battalion: he was working on a section of wall where he had worked before—on Zamenhofa, between Nowolipki and Nowolipie—but the first time he had been building the wall, now he was tearing it down. The ghetto having been re-

duced, there was no further need for that stretch of wall. Mordecai said the work reminded him of a trick German slow-motion
moving picture he had seen years before—a woman gracefully
floating through the air from a divingboard and swallowed slowly
by the water beneath it, a splash rising and falling languorously,
then the splash going up and down again, and the woman's feet
emerging from the water and her body coming up lazily and crazily
upside down and soaring feet-first back to the divingboard. In demolishing the wall he had built, Mordecai felt that he was carrying
out the second half of a similarly unnatural act. The work gave
him an especially peculiar sensation, he said, because he had often
dreamt of demolishing the wall in fierce joy—taking down the wall
to free the Jews. But now there was already another wall within
this wall. Mordecai said that he felt nothing now, beyond the act-
in-reverse sensation, except mild surprise that the bricks were so
easy to pry away from the mortar.

—— I thought I built better than that. . . . Or perhaps the
Germans gave us rottenly calcined lime.

It was obvious at this point that Berson was overwhelmed by
a piteous fellow-feeling: tears came into his eyes. He exclaimed:

—— Mordecai! I hope we have a chance all together to break
down the inner walls. . . . But in case we don't, in case we are all
separated, I want you to carry with you a memento of me and
mine, and you, too, Noach; and I want to carry one from each of
you. Think! We are brothers! Here!

And from a pocket of his wallet he took a now useless key to
the Sienna Street apartment and a tiny locket his mother had
owned, and he gave the key to Mordecai and the locket to me.
And Mordecai and I looked for tokens. Mordecai gave Berson a
small snapshot of Rutka and to me he gave a wolf's tooth he has
carried for luck for years. I am a feeble one for bits of property: I
gave Mordecai a piece of broken comb, and, having nothing else
suitable about me, I offered Berson a ten-zloty note.

N.L.: —— Will that do?

Berson: —— A million zlotys couldn't buy these ten!

And Berson put both the snapshot and the bill in the place
in the wallet where he had carried his mother's locket.

12

When the Mazurs and Berson arrived home
from work at the *Judenrat* and found out about Symka, Reb
Yechiel Mazur immediately told Berson and his wife what had happened that morning between Stefan and himself; now I have the
story from Reb Yechiel. Stefan arrived at the Murin apartment,
where the Mazurs and Bersons have been staying, at breakfast
time, before anyone had left for the day.

Berson: —— What brings you here so early in the morning?

Stefan, offhandedly: —— Oh, I came to see your new quarters.
(He looked around.) Not precisely the Brühl Palace.

This was a fair judgment. The bed that the Mazurs and the
Bersons have been sharing together is the bare floor of a tiny
kitchen in the apartment of the Murins on Gensia Street. Murin
is the chief of the Auditing Department at the *Judenrat*, and his
cheerful wife, Bluma, has apparently taken the newcomers as wards,
rather than merely as guests; especially she has been helpful with
Symka. The floor of this kitchen was covered long ago with a linoleum of a brightly checked pattern; in several places the composition has worn away, and the dirty and damp fabric underneath
has a pungent, stale odor. An iron coal stove sits against one wall,
chilly and dead now; the cupboards contain a few dusty dishes and
pots and pans; the plaster has come away from a part of one wall,
and the lathing shows starkly and unhealthily in the open place.
Beside the kitchen table there has recently been an overstuffed
chair, evidently borrowed from another room for Symka to use:
she sat in it this morning, when Stefan came, and she seemed but
a wraith on cushions.

Dolek, repeating in agreement: —— Not exactly the Brühl
Palace.

Reb Yechiel Mazur says he thought his son looked badly; the
boy has lost a lot of weight. [NOTE. N.L. Understandably, Reb
Yechiel feels terribly distressed about what has happened, and he
looks for explanations. The senior Mazurs questioned Stefan about
Halinka, and about his work, and about his living arrangements.

Stefan answered stiffly, as if he were not disposed to talk about himself. Finally he turned to Reb Yechiel Mazur and said:

—— Could I talk with you, Father?

Reb Yechiel, to his wife and Dolek: —— Why don't you two go on to work? I'll be along in a few minutes.

Berson arranged Symka's pillows and asked if she was comfortable.

Symka, with a toss of her head—a vestigial gesture from her beguiling days, slow, feeble, and pathetic now: —— Fine, my dear.

Berson, gently: —— Bluma says she will come in to see you this morning.

Symka, again: —— Fine, my dear.

Berson and Froi Mazur left. Stefan backed into the corner of the room farthest from Symka, and his father followed him.

Reb Yechiel Mazur: —— What is it, son?

Stefan, whispering, so that Symka would not hear: —— They have given us a new order. Each policeman has to bring four people to the *Umschlagplatz* each day. Or else he and his family have to go.

—— Poor boy!

—— I love Halinka. I love her more than myself. . . . I thought, by staying in the police . . .

Reb Yechiel Mazur, with what must have been uncharacteristic vehemence: —— They are *devils!*

Stefan, still whispering: —— I was wondering whether you would go with me to the *Umschlagplatz*, Father.

Reb Yechiel Mazur says he took this in for a moment, feeling a flush mounting on his face. He perfectly freely confesses that he then spoke these hateful, bitter words:

—— Why do you choose me and not your mother?

Stefan, his face pale and his eyes starting: —— I meant both of you, to make two for me.

Reb Yechiel Mazur, raising his voice: —— And you were too cowardly to speak of this to your mother. You had to ask me.

Stefan, whispering urgently: —— You will be taken anyhow. They will get you one of these days. You can save Halinka and me by going a few days sooner.

Reb Yechiel Mazur, more loudly than before: —— You call yourself my son!

The father drew back his hand and slapped Stefan hard on the cheek.

Symka, as if sleepily: —— What is it? What is it?

Stefan, one hand over the cheek his father had struck, began moving toward the door of the kitchen, and he said, loudly now: —— They'll get you one of these days! They'll take you anyhow. I thought you would want to help me.

And the boy turned and ran from the apartment.

Symka, fearfully: —— What was it? What did he want?

Reb Yechiel Mazur, in an amazing bit of self-revelation, says that upon Symka's question, he made a *startlingly sudden recovery of his kindly manner*, and said: —— It was nothing, dear. Don't be disturbed.

—— Why did you hit him?

But Reb Yechiel Mazur had put on his visored black cap and was leaving the room.

EVENTS SEPTEMBER 12, 1942. ENTRY DITTO. FROM BLUMA MURIN. At about ten o'clock this morning, Bluma Murin was sitting in the kitchen reading the Sholem Aleichem stories about the village of Kasrilevke aloud to Symka. [NOTE. N.L. As wife of a *Judenrat* official, Froi Murin is exempt from deportation.] She says she herself would laugh over the pages, but Symka just sat nodding. She says that as she was reading, a young Jewish policeman, a handsome young man with curly hair, came in: she understood he was the Mazurs' son. When he came in, Symka looked at him and asked with a troubled face, and as if no time had elapsed since she had last seen the young man: —— Why did your father hit you?

The young policeman did not answer, Froi Murin says. He walked across the room directly to Symka's chair, pulled the pillows out from behind her, bent over, put one arm under her back and one under her legs, and lifted her out of the chair.

Symka, in a fragile, feminine, out-of-place tone, suitable to a more amorous situation: —— What are you doing? Stop it!

Stefan, his face very close to Symka's: —— Don't be alarmed.

He moved toward the door. Froi Murin says all this had happened so fast that she had scarcely had time to understand the situation. She now stood up and exclaimed: —— What are you doing?

The young man did not respond. Symka said in a tiny, hardly audible voice:

—— Help me, Bluma!

Stefan raised a knee to support Symka as he fumbled for the doorknob with his left hand. He opened the door and started out. Bluma says she rushed forward in a hen-like flurry, shouting:

—— What are you doing? She is legitimized! Put her down! Where are you going?

On the landing, the young policeman turned back toward Froi Murin with his lips drawn in the snarl of a creature threatened with the loss of food. He said viciously:

—— Get back, or you will go, too.

With a horrified feeling, Bluma drew back into the doorway and watched the young man carry Symka down the stairs.

[NOTE. N.L. Bluma Murin says she has always considered herself a phlegmatic woman. She comes of a heritage rare among the Jews of Warsaw—a peasant background: her father was a smallholder who owned eleven hectares of damp and unrewarding land near Przasnysz, some ninety kilometers north of Warsaw. She grew up stocky, chesty, broad-cheeked, and cheerful; and some years ago she married a harassed, small-boned man who is physically by no means her equal, but who, by his shrewdness and nimble footwork, gets the best of her as often as she does of him, I gather. All through the deportations, she says, she has managed to take things as they came, on the whole stolidly and without too much fear. This situation struck her in a new way, apparently.]

Bluma Murin was alone in the apartment. She did not know what to do. She says she liked the Bersons—patrician people who were perfectly willing to sleep on a kitchen floor; nursing the enfeebled Symka had given Bluma pleasant occupation. Now she was suddenly very frightened—it seemed, she says, as if tending this half-dead girl had been her reason for living. Dolek Berson would know best what to do. Even her husband would have some good ideas. This was a man's situation. She felt that she must make her way to the *Judenrat*, even though she knew that it is strictly forbidden to move in the streets during the day. It might be too late to do anything if she waited for her husband and Dolek Berson to come home from work in the evening. She walked nervously in the kitchen. For a while she wept. She felt very confused. Finally she took a shawl from a peg beside the door, covered her head, and went out and down the stairs. At the archway out to Gensia Street, she looked both ways, east and west. She saw not a single person in the street. She says that this emptiness, where there had once been almost intolerable commerce, terrified her unreasonably, so that she was unable for a few seconds even to move—and then she fled back up to the apartment, where she stayed all day, weeping and overcome with fright.

EVENTS SEPTEMBER 12, 1942. ENTRY DITTO. FROM DOLEK BERSON. In the evening, back at the Murin apartment, when Berson and the Mazurs had heard Bluma Murin's story and Reb Yechiel Mazur had told of his interview with his son, Reb Yechiel said:

—— You'd better go and talk to Stefan.

Berson: —— What good would that do?

Instead Berson came to the bakery and talked with Menkes, Rachel, and me about Symka. He is not angry or bitter. Symka has been sick for so long.

EVENTS SEPTEMBER 13, 1942. ENTRY SEPTEMBER 14, 1942. FROM WLADISLAW JABLONSKI. Yesterday was Rosh-ha-Shanah, the first day of a new Jewish year. How relentless the calendar is! While we had all been assembled at the bakery, the night before, talking about Stefan and Symka, Reb Yechiel Mazur had expressed the wish that he could get to the banks of the Vistula the following day, in order to pronounce, at the side of a body of water moving toward the sea, the customary New Year's prayer for the washing away of sins. Wladislaw Jablonski, overhearing, said jokingly that he could lead Reb Yechiel Mazur to a passable place for saying this prayer: the culvert of the sewer where he had hidden during the last days of the "registration." Reb Yechiel took the joke seriously: he said he thought that would be all right—the sewer ran into the Vistula, and the Vistula into the sea. He really wanted to go; he became insistent. Wladislaw agreed at last to take him.

Early yesterday morning, before it was time to go to work, Wladislaw led Reb Yechiel Mazur to an apartment house on Mila Street, and took him down to the cellar under one of the staircases, and there he lit a carbide lamp and took a shovel into a coal bin and moved some of the coal within to one side. A barrelhead was exposed. Wladislaw took the barrelhead away from the wall, and this uncovered the mouth of a small tunnel. Through this tunnel, which sloped downward about four meters, Wladislaw, holding the lamp, led Reb Yechiel Mazur. The smell there was evil. The two came to the big concrete pipe of the sewer. A hole had been chiseled through from the tunnel. The sewer pipe was about a meter high. Wladislaw, who wanted to stay in the tunnel, let Reb Yechiel Mazur wriggle past and the older man went down into the tube. A foul, watery stream, apparently not much more than ankle-deep, ran along the drainage-way. Reb Yechiel Mazur crouched all doubled over, with a foot on each side of the pipe above the stream. Wladislaw, the Jewish boy who had been brought up to be a Catholic, held the light down through the jagged, chiseled hole, as the voice of Reb Yechiel Mazur echoed and echoed in the arched conduit:

—— . . . And Thou wilt cast all their sins into the depths of the sea. Oh, mayest Thou cast all the sins of Thy people, the house of Israel, into a place where they shall be no more remembered or visited, or ever again come to mind. Thou wilt show faithfulness to Jacob, and lovingkindness to Abraham, as Thou hast sworn unto our fathers from the days of old.

Reb Yechiel Mazur raised his head, sighed, and said he was ready to go back. Wladislaw says that in the light of the carbide lamp the elderly man's face, bent down over the stream, during the prayer, had had a look of repugnance, as if the noisome waters of this ghetto stream did in fact contain all the sins of Israel, the sins Reb Yechiel Mazur had seen and felt, the sins, above all, of his own curly-haired son.

EVENTS SEPTEMBER 21, 1942. ENTRY SEPTEMBER 23, 1942. FROM HALINKA APT. . . . So Stefan's rationalization, that he was protecting Halinka, had proved illusory. It is my opinion that this thing happened to Stefan *by his own volition*, but it is not possible to substantiate this opinion by anything that Halinka says. It is just my opinion. Here is what she says:

Halinka's first impression was of an unusual blowing of whistles. She looked down from the apartment window to Ostrowska Street, four storeys below, and she saw formations of Jewish police marching in from Lubetzkiego Street and being halted and dismissed; the ranks broke and the men ran to the various apartment entrances. For a few moments, Halinka was elated: a miracle! The Germans were apparently giving the Jewish police a holiday on the Day of Atonement.

This impression, however, did not last very long. Soon Halinka heard policemen pouring into the staircase below. Their shouts were not festive: they were clearly frightened. The whistling continued. Stefan's friend Vilshinsky was the first to come clattering into the apartment, and his usual jovial, stupid expression had deserted him. He shouted to his wife in a raucous way:

—— Zivia! Zivia! We have to go below. It's a selection!

Zivia Vilshinska asked incredulously, as if such a thing were impossible:

—— For us?

Vilshinsky, still shouting: —— Dress up! Look as well as you can.

Halinka heard these commands and herself responded to them at once, as something she could comprehend: she ran into the room where she and Stefan slept, and there she tore off the dress she was wearing and kicked off her shoes, took a key from a string around her neck, lifted a tin lockbox from under a bed, opened it, and took out a pair of silk stockings. She was pulling these on when Stefan came in, pale and rather dazed-looking. He sat on the edge of a bed; his teeth chattered for a second or two, as if he were having a chill, and then he said:

—— I didn't know this would happen.

Halinka, adjusting her stocking seams down the backs of her legs [Note. N.L. Why does she remember, and why does she feel that she has to tell me, a detail like *that?*]: —— Get ready! Brush your hair.

But Stefan still sat on the bed. Halinka went to a cupboard and took out a flowered silk print she had used to wear as a singer at the Britannia. She pulled it on over her head.

Stefan, as if defending himself against an unspoken accusation: —— There was really nothing else I could do.

Swiftly Halinka arranged her hair and made up her face. She turned to Stefan, with a forced smile. She says her dress hung loosely from her thin body. Stefan looked at her, she says, and began weeping. Others were rushing about the apartment, tidying themselves, gathering up a few belongings, speaking abnormally loudly in their haste.

Vilshinski: —— Time's nearly up. They gave us fifteen minutes. Come *on*, Zivia!

Halinka put a hand on Stefan's shoulder and said:

—— You'll have to put a better face on it. You mustn't look beaten, Stefan—not down there!

Events September 22, 1942.   Entry September 24, 1942. Continuing Halinka Apt's account.   . . . Halinka and Stefan stood among four hundred and twenty policemen and their families who had been selected for Treblinka in the hospital courtyard at the *Umschlagplatz*. There was in the crowd a very strong mob spirit of resentment at what seemed a betrayal. The habit of months of authority, the attitude of men who for a long time had had the power of life and death over their fellows, the assurance that had come from the impression that they were safe forever— these had not yet left the condemned policemen. They sneered at the Ukrainians who escorted them, and at each other. They were surly toward their own families. They shook their fists at the German guards at the *Umschlagplatz*, and the Germans, seeing resistant Jews in large numbers for the first time, became nervous and unusually harsh.

Vilshinski came up to Stefan in the yard. He growled:

—— That damned selection was unfair. Pure chance. Listen: they let Ausbach and Fakel stay. What kind of work have they been doing lately? They haven't the strength you and I have, their attitude has been terrible. . . .

Stefan: —— It's our own fault! We should have got out months ago. I told you that: you were the one who laughed at me, Vilshinski!

Vilshinski: —— Look here: let's get all the men together from our Company. Let's try to get a message through to the commandant, telling him the selection was unfair.

Stefan: —— Nonsense! You're as good as dead.

Vilshinski looked at Stefan for a moment with an outraged expression, then rushed off.

At the center of the yard stood an ambiguously costumed man: over his *Ordnungsdienst* uniform he had thrown a tasseled prayer shawl. Loudly he was pronouncing some Yom Kippur prayers. A crowd of devout policemen was around him, and they chanted the responses as he spoke the prayer *Al-het*:

395

The crowd: —— . . . For all these, O God of forgiveness, forgive us, pardon us, grant us remission.

The officiant policeman: —— For the sin we have done before Thee by denying and lying, and for the sin we have done before Thee by taking of bribes; for the sin we have done before Thee by scoffing, and for the sin we have done before Thee by slander; for the sin we have done before Thee in business, and for the sin we have done before Thee in eating and drinking; for the sin we have done before Thee by usury and interest, and for the sin we have done before Thee by the stretched forth neck of pride. . . .

The prayer was suddenly drowned by an unearthly howl, coming, it seemed, from all directions. It was the mournful, clamorous wail of Warsaw's air-raid sirens.

The mob of the police and their families was suddenly gripped by a unanimity, a singleness of mind, so strongly shared that it could not have been arrived at by days of discussion and planning: the mob decided to exult. The Russians were coming to bomb the Germans in Warsaw. This fact, announced by the sirens' horrible wail, made the mob cheer. The arrested policemen sent up huzzahs and the crowd turned its collective, grinning face toward the fence of the hospital yard. Outside the fence the German and Ukrainian guards stood doubly frightened—by the advertisement of the bombs to come, and by the laughing, jeering pack of Jews on the other side of the slender wires of the fence. As time passed, as finally the distant roar of planes could be heard, the attitudes on either side of the fence became more and more intensified and rigid: on the one side, laughter and jibes, on the other, taut, pallid fear. The mob pressed against the wire. The guards cocked their rifles and held them at the ready.

Halinka says that during all this Stefan stood relaxed and apathetic: he was in the mob but he was somehow separated from it.

The first bomb broke the equilibrium between the two sides of the fence. A bomb landed not far from the *Umschlagplatz*, to the south. [NOTE. N.L. Probably the one that hit and wrecked Dzielna 3, the former Scala Theater.] At its detonation, two of the twenty-odd guards screamed, turned, and ran for cover. The break in spirit communicated itself to a dozen more of the Ger-

PART FOUR

mans and Junaks, who ran away at once, looking around for shelter. The mob reacted to these defections with animal shrieks. Three more guards, looking about for authority or some other support, and finding none, scuttered away; then two more; then the last half-dozen all together.

Hands clutched at the unlocked latch of the wire gate; it flew open. The Jews nearest the gate poured out. Bombs were falling, and the mob cheered louder than ever. Stefan and Halinka were about five or six meters from the gate, and Halinka says she had to take Stefan's hand to start him moving. Around the gate in the yard, the mob was packed tight; outside the Jews who had gone through fanned out, running. Halinka tugged at Stefan and they got out. They were running toward the walled passageway to Zamenhofa Street, about fifty meters from the fence, when, suddenly, Stefan's hand jerked out from Halinka's. She looked around. Stefan was standing dumbly, being shaken by the runners who bumped into him. Halinka cried out to him, but he did not seem to see or hear her. Some shots were fired. Halinka turned and ran.

This was two days ago. Stefan has still not showed up. There can be but one assumption.

EVENTS SEPTEMBER 22, 1942. ENTRY SEPTEMBER 24, 1942. FROM DOLEK BERSON. Berson has told me how he sat at the kitchen table in the Murin apartment and listened to Halinka's story. Halinka sat in Symka's armchair, and Berson could not help seeing a contrast there. Berson says he was in a whirlpool of feeling. He felt sorry for Stefan and he hated Stefan; he felt embarrassed by Halinka's visit; he felt guilty that he felt so glad over the death, or the dooming to death, whichever it was, of a fellow Jew, Stefan; he pitied Halinka, he resented her reminding him of Symka's emaciation—and so his feelings went, around and around. Then suddenly, in something Halinka said, Berson was overwhelmed, as he says he had not had a chance to be, in the last few busy days, by his loss in Symka.

Halinka: —— Stefan was always so moody. One day he was on top of the world, and the next, you'd think he had invented all the torments of the ghetto. I always wanted to help him, but I never knew how.

Symka, Berson thought, admitting her to his mind abruptly,

397

had never inflicted moroseness on him. There had been times, in recent months, when she had wept, in sheer physical pain and in fear of natural death; but even then she had faced the reasons for her misery, she had never blamed dark and frontless storms of the soul, she had never used it as a weapon of reproach toward him. All at once Berson was engulfed by a terrible feeling of lost opportunities. How many hours on how many days had he allowed Symka simply to sit silently with her thoughts in that armchair now decorated by Halinka, when he might have delighted her by playing his concertina or reading a book out loud, or might have told her about his childhood (how little she had ever learned about him!), or might have discussed his Hashomer work or a worry about Menkes or about Rachel, or might have dreamt with her of a wonderful menu for some future day, or might merely have held her hand and sat silent *with* her, rather than apart from her? He remembered then a scene:

It was in the Sienna Street apartment, before the war, in 1937 or 1938. It was late afternoon. Berson was having a pleasant talk with Lazar Slonim, and they were in their Western European intellectual phase: Warsaw's Jewry was far from them then. They were discussing Kant, particularly Kant's views on permanent peace —Kant as the unique philosopher of the League of Nations, and the irony that this should have been a German; when Symka came in. She walked right across the living room to Berson and looked down at him and said cryptically, *He told me it would be impossible—ever.* Berson knew that the "he" of Symka's wretched statement was her gynecologist, and that the impossibility of which she spoke was of her ever having a child; this was a desperately unhappy message. Whether enmeshed in the conversation with Slonim, or unable at once to take in the implications of what Symka had said, or hoping to divert Symka—for what reason Berson cannot remember, but he does remember that he said disastrously wrong words: *That's too bad, dear. Sit down and talk with us: Slonim has been reading Kant.* But Symka turned and ran into the bedroom. Berson went on talking with Slonim. . . .

Halinka: —— Where do you think I should stay? Can I stay here?

Berson recalled himself. He says he was weeping, and Halinka, evidently thinking the tears were spent in sympathy for her, seemed very grateful. Berson said:

—— No, Halinka. Your being here would remind the Mazurs
of their boy, that would be hard. Let's go to Pavel. You would be
with Rachel at the bakery. Let's try Pavel.

13

EVENTS SEPTEMBER 26–27, 1942. ENTRY SEPTEMBER 28,
1942. FROM DOLEK BERSON. Anyone would be silly who denied
the part that *accident* plays in our mortality here. And yet I am
becoming more and more convinced that mostly those die who
have no more wish to live. There comes a time when both hope
and ingenuity go out of a man, and he disappears. . . . In short, I
am trying to weigh the effect upon Reb Yechiel Mazur of his interview with Stefan, the morning Stefan took Symka. I have a feeling
that that interview was in fact an act of patricide, though at the
time it seemed just short of that. Ever since then, at any rate, one
has seen Yechiel Mazur flag—one has seen him grow dry and brown
and weak and sad and nearly dead. And now:

Day before yesterday in the evening Reb Yechiel Mazur did
not come home. He had not stopped by for Froi Mazur at her office in the Health and Social Welfare Department at the usual
time, and, after waiting a quarter of an hour, she went up to
the Special Personnel room of the Labor Department, where he
worked, and someone there said that he had been sent on an errand to the brushmaking factory on Swientojerska Street at about
four o'clock; he should surely have returned by six fifteen, which it
then was. Froi Mazur went home and waited with Berson. Reb
Yechiel Mazur did not come. Froi Mazur sat with perfect control and conversed with Berson on impersonal subjects. At ten
o'clock, which she considered her bedtime, she remarked that
Yechiel had probably had some work at the brushmakers' plant
that had kept him overnight, and she prepared herself for sleep and
lay down in her blanket on the kitchen floor. The next morning
Reb Yechiel did not return to the *Judenrat* from the brushmakers'.
At noon Berson persuaded me to send to the brushmakers' to inquire about Reb Yechiel, and word came back that Reb Yechiel
Mazur had not been there at all. It was necessary to deduce that

he had been taken alone in the empty streets and had been deported, in spite of his excellent papers. When this deduction was
tactfully unfolded before Froi Mazur, she said quietly that she did
not think anything had happened to her husband, and that she
would prefer to wait until later before reaching any conclusions.
Berson tried to persuade me to send someone to the *Umschlagplatz* to check up, but I said there was no use throwing a five-
zloty piece into a pond to see if the ripples on its surface were of
the type made by another five-zloty piece: the second coin would
only be lost, too. That evening Froi Mazur was unshakably pleasant and insistent that nothing had happened to her husband. She
went to bed at ten as usual. For some time Berson was insomniac.
He heard Froi Mazur breathing in a half-snore—obviously asleep.
But much later, after he had finally gone off into a shallow doze,
Berson was wakened by the sound of sobbing. The sound was stifled, evidently by bedclothes.

14

EVENTS EARLY OCTOBER, 1942. ENTRY OCTOBER 8, 1942.
N.L. Ever since the loss of Stefan, I have been wondering what
would become of Halinka. I believe she was quite devoted to
young Mazur: at any rate, I have never had reason to doubt that
she was. But she is so utterly feminine, so soft and dependent, such
a man's woman, that I have had no doubt that she would very
soon make an arrangement of some kind—preferably one that
would not interfere with her deep and dramatic mourning of
Stefan. So now that she has done just that, I am not surprised at
the fact: I am amazed at her choice. I expected her to fall into a
readily available situation: with Berson, for instance, or Menkes,
and I have even imagined . . . but all sorts of wild thoughts pass
through one's head in these disturbed days.

The solution she has found, however! Rachel saw it coming.
A week ago. . . .

EVENTS OCTOBER 2, 1942. ENTRY DITTO. FROM RACHEL
APT. Halinka is bored. She throws herself about tragically, moan-

ing after Stefan. But really the trouble is that she is bored with hiding at the bakery, Rachel says. She is used to high life among the police. A trivial girl.

EVENTS OCTOBER 3, 1942. ENTRY DITTO. FROM RACHEL APT. Rachel was right about Halinka. Today, when Rachel suggested that Halinka might like to do some Hashomer work, the pretty sister jumped at the chance for some entertainment. When Rachel warned that the work might be dangerous, Halinka said she would rather die in peril than die (how *precisely* right Rachel was!) of boredom.

So Rachel took Halinka around to a Hashomer recruitment meeting. After the meeting Rachel introduced her sister to Zilberzweig. He seemed very cordial, Rachel says.

EVENTS OCTOBER 8, 1942. ENTRY DITTO. FROM RACHEL APT. Cordial! I see, on looking back, that in ENTRY OCTOBER 3, I wrote that Zilberzweig greeted Rachel's new candidate cordially. It appears that Zilberzweig took a personal interest in the candidate. He found her work (suitable work for a light-framed girl) as a checking clerk in the Bonner factory, on Mila, where a Hashomer man has some influence. He whisked her through her peripheral training in a matter of hours, where it might take a plain girl several weeks. He put her to work, unusually quickly for a neophyte, on personal errands for himself. Apparently Halinka's temperament is cut just right for Zilberzweig: the two laugh constantly when they are together. Halinka began calling the Hashomer leader Hil within two or three days—whereas Rachel, who has worked closely with Zilberzweig for many months, still addresses him formally.

Last night Zilberzweig invited Halinka to come and stay at his apartment. She has accepted and will move this evening. Zilberzweig told Rachel that he had invited Halinka because he understood that conditions were exceedingly crowded at the bakery, but of course he did not say why it had not occurred to him to ask Rachel, whom he knows very well, rather than Halinka, with whom he is barely acquainted. Halinka's report of Zilberzweig's reason for the invitation is slightly different. She says Hil is lonely. There are, it happens, eleven people, mostly Hashomer workers, living in the apartment with him; but he is lonely. And she is sorry for him.

He works so desperately hard and he is so lonely. He has told her —and she is delighted to tell all comers—that he is lonely for the company of someone lighthearted like Halinka, someone with whom he can both work and play.

[NOTE. N.L. What should I think of this? These informal household arrangements are so prevalent now that one cannot with any humor make a scandal of this one. It is hard to say what moral sanctions we respect any more. We expect death at any moment. We love life very much. We want to cram as much as possible into our remaining hours. Appetites are exaggerated. Flirtation is hurried. Courtship is telescoped. In conversation, even, we come quickly to the point. We live as if by telegraphy. . . . And yet something about this liaison makes me uneasy. (I do not mean a selfish, childish something; I do not mean an irrational, unfounded jealousy.) What makes me uncomfortable here is a kind of disappointment in Zilberzweig, a feeling that he is cheapening himself. He has no right to be a man: he is the leader of Hashomer. Hundreds of our young people look to him. The underground organizations are preparing themselves—for what, it is hard to say: he *has* to dedicate himself to these preparations, he cannot relax now. What is really disappointing, I suppose, is that the events we have lived through have not magnified Zilberzweig. He is no greater than he was: Zilberzweig is still Zilberzweig. I remember Rutka's remark when she was describing to me her hectographing of Zilberzweig's editorial on the German attack against Russia (ENTRY JUNE 24, 1941), to the effect that she felt something sensuous about this man; she felt his temptation to caress her. I suppose I am after all too demanding. And in one way I have to admire Zilberzweig. He is forty-four years old, and one is obliged to say that this tennis ball is losing some of its fuzz and bounce. All the same, he is the one who now lies with Halinka, and not one of our handsome young men, our Bersons and Menkeses.

Next: what of the effect of this affair upon Rachel? For months she has been working with complete selflessness for Hashomer and personally for Zilberzweig. All of a sudden, within a few days, her shallow sister is trusted just as much as she is, Halinka is given work precisely like Rachel's; to say nothing of Halinka's more basic inroad. How can Rachel help feeling put out? Yet she has shown nothing. Rachel is a woman of admirable control. She is our Little Mother.]

15

Events October 1, 1942. Entry October 3, 1942. From Lazar Slonim. Slonim says that the Executive Committee of the Bund was meeting in Velvel's room at Zamenhofa 44. They were discussing a difficult point. The Bund needed funds, as always; its members needed to keep alive. Recently there has sprung up in the ghetto a refreshed trade in goods looted from the apartments of evacuated Jews. The Bund fought the looting from the very beginning, in broadsides and in education through the Fives. But the looting, and barter across the wall associated with it, has now become tremendously lucrative, and the Executive Committee was trying to decide whether to change its point of view.

Velvel, who was presiding: —— Chavairim, it seems to me difficult to face the practical issue here. (Velvel always speaks, Slonim says, in rigid party clichés.) We would be hindered in the activation of our comrades if we undertook a program of planned looting, or even suddenly tolerated individual looting, because that would be so inconsistent with our recent preachments. We attack the Communists for their inconsistencies. How can we . . .

There came a rapid knock at the door. The door opened a little. Comrade Mosze, who had been standing watch outside, put his head in the gap. He was grinning and he said he had a surprise for all. He pushed the door wide open, and the members within could see Rapaport standing in the doorway. Rapaport looked rather foolish and sheepish. His clothes were dirty.

—— Comrade Henryk!

It was Velvel who was the first to shout, and he stood up and ran to the door and embraced the old man. Meanwhile the others had begun to exclaim and laugh, and everyone rushed to Rapaport and greeted him warmly. Slonim says this scene gave him as much satisfaction as anything he can remember: he says he thought he was going to weep for the first time since his childhood, but his tear ducts disappointed him; they did not give. [Note. N.L. What a shrewd and arid fellow Slonim is!]

Comrade Mosze: —— We thought you were dead.

Rapaport, with a twinkle: —— Not dead. Disobedient.

Comrade Velvel: —— Come in, we need your opinion.

Slonim: —— We have missed you, Comrade, and we censure you—with gratitude—for defying our order to leave the ghetto. Tell us where you have been.

Rapaport, not betraying by the slightest flicker of a lash his complicity with Slonim: —— I have been in a hole in the ground. Very cozy. But after the meeting. . . . (Rapaport, who had seated himself in the chair formerly occupied by Velvel, straightened himself, with a thrust of the shoulders that the older Bundists recognized as Rapaport's calling-to-order gesture. Evidently he simply assumed that he would preside again.) And now, Chavairim, let us get along. What is the business, Velvel?

Velvel meekly presented the quandary about looting. Rapaport said promptly:

—— Friends, let's look at it this way: What would the Jews in the cattle cars on the way to Treblinka prefer—to have the goods they have left behind stolen by Germans officially, or stolen by Jews informally?

The matter was decided. No more had to be said. Then Rapaport, with what Slonim says is still the old man's great quality, brushed aside all trivia and bluntly jumped to the heart of things:

—— And now, Chavairim, what are we doing to get ready to fight the Germans?

16

EVENTS EARLY OCTOBER, 1942. ENTRY OCTOBER 3, 1942. N.L. . . . The deportations seem to have come to some sort of pause, or perhaps (extravagant hope!) to an end. I have the figures given Zweinarcz by the Germans up through September 21. From July 22, when the "resettlement" began, until that date, a total of 265,954 had been verifiably deported. This figure does not represent by any means the total, since the numbers Zweinarcz received for August 28–31 and for September 5 were illegible, and neither he nor I were ever able to check them. One can assume a minimum of 15,000 deported in the five illegible days. Besides, in the same period, the German figures show 11,580 Jews not deported, but "Sent to the Jewish Burying Ground, Warsaw." These were the elderly and infirm Jews killed, especially early in the action, to give the impression that those who could not work were being liquidated before the "resettlement." All together, counting the more sporadic deportations since September 21, it is safe to say that more than 300,000 Jews have been liquidated in a period of about two and a half months. Assuming that there were 350,000 here when the action began, we can imagine that there are about 50,000 of us left. Since at its peak, before the typhus epidemic of the summer of 1941, the ghetto contained about half a million Jews, it can be seen that we have been reduced by disease, starvation, and deportation to one tenth of our original number. This leads our more religious optimists to say with assurance that the deportations are at last at an end. They cite the authority of the prophet Isaiah. They say that the entire deportation was prophesied:

—— For, behold, the Lord, the Lord of hosts, doth take away [from the Warsaw ghetto] the stay and the staff, the whole stay of bread, and the whole stay of water, the mighty man, and the man of war, the judge, and the prophet, and the prudent, and the ancient, the captain of fifty, and the honorable man, and the counselor, and the cunning artificer, and the eloquent orator. . . . In that day the Lord will take away the bravery of their tinkling ornaments about their feet, and their cauls, and their round tires like the moon, the chains, and the bracelets, and the mufflers, the bonnets, and the ornaments of the legs, and the headbands, and the tablets, and the earrings, the rings, and nose jewels, the changeable suits of apparel, and the mantles, and the wimples, and the crisping pins, the glasses, and the fine linen, and the hoods, and the veils. And it shall come to pass, that instead of sweet smell there shall be a stink; and instead of a girdle a rent; and instead of well set hair baldness. . . .

And now that only one in ten is left here, these people point to Isaiah VI, 11–13:

—— Then said I, Lord, how long? And he answered, Until the [ghetto] be wasted without inhabitant, and the houses without man, and the [ghetto] be utterly desolate and the Lord have removed men far away, and there be a great forsaking in the midst of the [ghetto]. *But yet in it shall be a tenth.* . . .

This phrase is widely quoted among our hopefuls. Personally I think the prophet was talking about something more important than the Warsaw ghetto. Though one would like to think. . . .

405

17

Events October 12, 1942. Entry October 13, 1942. From Rachel Apt. With what simple, unaffected sadness did Rachel tell this story! This happened last night:

Fein: —— You may go with us as far as the wall, if you insist.

Rachel: —— Naturally. That much at least I must do.

Rachel says that three huge men stood behind Fein. Their feet were wrapped in burlap, and as they shuffled on the brick floor of the baking room, the cloth made a queer, whispering sound. In the light of a single candle the four men were scarcely to be seen: they were dressed all in black, and their faces, too, were blacked. Only their brilliant eyes and teeth and the pale, mobile softness of their tongues were visible, floating, it seemed, as disembodied winged organs. The men seemed, indeed, quite unreal. They had come, without warning, at two o'clock in the morning, to take David to the Aryan side.

Fein: —— Please impress upon the child that he must be absolutely silent.

Rachel, in a trembling voice: —— He's nearly grown up. He'll be quiet. Won't you, Dovidl?

David, in an excited whisper: —— Will I have a black face, too?

Fein, threateningly: —— Say, boy, will you be quiet in the streets? We'll all be killed if you aren't.

David, in a very soft whisper, as if Danger had already sneaked into the room: —— I'll be quiet.

Fein charred a piece of cork over the candle flame, and with it blackened first David's face, then Rachel's. One of the men put forward some burlap to muffle the boy's feet, and Rachel tied up her own in some of Menkes' flour sacking. When all were ready, Fein spoke to his helpers, and one by one the three big men glided from the room. Then Fein took Rachel's hand and told her to hold David's and not to lose it in the streets under any circumstances, even if they were forced to run and if one of them stumbled or collided with something. Fein's voice was brusque, almost cruel; he had always seemed so soft and jovial before.

Suddenly the workman and the girl and the small boy were in the street—in what seemed absolute blackness outside the door of the bakery; the night was overcast and a damp fog muffled whatever glow might have come down on the blacked-out city from the stars above—and Rachel realized that in the excitement she had not said goodbye to David. Now she would not be able to whisper even a word to him. She squeezed his hand; he responded, as they moved forward very slowly. Fein was evidently feeling his way along the faces of the buildings. He would move perhaps ten or fifteen meters, then stand still a few moments. Rachel has no idea how long they stole through the streets this way. Once they heard a scream in the distance, and Rachel, whose skin crept at the sound, felt Fein's hand tighten on her own; almost automatically, she transmitted this reassurance to David. She could not imagine what streets they were following: they took several turns.

Rachel wondered whether her brother would ever reach Palestine. She thought not. Surely there were too many hazards. She needed a prodigy of imagination even to picture Palestine now, sneaking through a fog-curtained, chilly street in Warsaw: for one moment Rachel conjured the picture—her own picture of Palestine, as she has always seen it, she says, since she was about ten, when her fat little Uncle Gershon came back from a visit in that country, just before his death, and talked with her father about the neglected business opportunities there: she saw a bare hill of sand, with a line of untended, dying olive trees going over it and on and on into the desert, and a shepherdless flock of sheep moving over the hill looking for grass, and at the foot of the hill a white, modern building, all horizontal balconies and windows, with some men leaning against the front wall dozing in the sun, and a lake of precious, black petroleum in front of the building, and none of the men even bothering to go and get any of it, and a symphony orchestra playing for its own amusement on one of the balconies of the modern building. Rachel says she knew, even when her Uncle Gershon told about Palestine, that it was not like that (her late Uncle Gershon was evidently rather glum: she says he could describe a sunny spring day in Saxon Garden, and it would sound like a November snow-squall in a Prypets swamp); still, that was her picture. And now she tried to put David on that

407

bright, unexploited landscape, but her imagination refused her the extra effort. The picture vanished altogether. Rachel's whole being was drawn, for a moment, to the palm of her hand against her brother's palm.

Fein stopped. He stood still a long time. Rachel sensed that they were near the place of action. By now her eyes were adjusted somewhat to the very dark night, and although in the fog she could not see any housetops, she had a *feeling* that they were standing close to a section of the ghetto wall. She wanted to embrace her brother, but Fein held her right hand and she had been adjured not to let go of David's with her left. Suddenly she thought she saw—she did see—three forms, three darknesses just darker than the night. They passed very close by. They were carrying something. Fein moved forward with them. They stopped very close to a wall. Fein reached across Rachel and took David's hand from hers: her heart was heavy: was *that* the farewell? Rachel saw one of the shapes moving upward, evidently on a ladder. She heard something soft, like a heavy quilt or a mattress, thrown over the top of the wall; two or three of the pieces of glass embedded in the top of the wall broke underneath this pad, whatever it was. The shape came down again. Fein, still holding Rachel's hand, moved a few steps toward the place where the ladder apparently was. Rachel felt Fein pull her right hand forward and David's small hand was put into hers. She shook her brother's hand. For some reason, she says, she thought of the day when she had caught David running the mock selection at the Rukner Home; with an effort she put this repulsive memory out of her mind and she thought of him the day their father had left the ghetto, David with his small head on her breast, looking up into her eyes to see whether he should cry: her boy, her baby boy! She felt Fein's hand on hers again, and David's pulled away. A form climbed the ladder. Then another—it must be David, she thought. She put her left hand out and touched an upright of the ladder: it was entirely wrapped in cloth. While her hand was still touching it, the ladder jerked away upward. Fein's hand drew her back, and they turned and began walking.

EVENTS OCTOBER, 1942. ENTRY OCTOBER 15, 1942. N.L. I think it can be said that Rachel has gained a kind of *position*, especially in her Hashomer circles. One hears her talked about. I remember that as far back as Passover, 1941, I wrote of having heard "the Apt girl," meaning Rachel, discussed frequently, and I commented then that *something about Rachel causes her to be remembered and talked about* [ENTRY APRIL 21, 1941]. I have never tried to analyze this quality in her, and I think I would not want to. For she seems to me wholly natural, absolutely without cunning—and I like to think of her this way. Perhaps if I looked too closely . . .

One thing is certain: she is completely unaware of her reputation and influence.

EVENTS OCTOBER 16, 1942. ENTRY DITTO. FROM RACHEL APT. Fein came to the bakery this afternoon just after working hours, Rachel says.

Fein, with his old grin back on his face, the harshness of his commands three nights ago quite gone: —— I imagine that you miss your brother.

Rachel: —— I do. He was almost like a son to me.

Fein: —— My colleagues tell me that he is a cool number. They say he behaves like a grown man. In some cases he is more calm than they are.

Rachel: —— My Dovidl!

Fein: —— I thought perhaps you'd like to see him once more before he goes "walking."

Rachel, standing up, as if she were ready to run to this opportunity: —— Is it possible?

Fein: —— Only from a very great distance. But you will see him. And he will be looking from a window for you. In about twenty minutes. Shall we go?

Rachel: —— *Shall* we! Wait a moment.

Rachel ran and put on her best dress and combed her hair; she put no make-up on, but her color was high and she was as pretty as she could ever be.

Fein, when she came out into the baking room again: —— Ah, there is a sight to please the young man. Come along!

On the way, Rachel asked:

—— What street-end was it where you put him over the wall? I couldn't tell in such darkness.

Fein, with a severe expression: —— Shhh. Let's not discuss it in public. (Gradually his stern face relented, and he turned to her

409

and whispered with a boyishly proud smile:) Niska at Pokorna. We did it well, didn't we?

This time Fein took Rachel along Gensia and Franciszkanska, then turned northward on Bonifraterska. As they walked he told a casual and interminable story about an experience he had had when he had been working in the masonry battalion with Rapaport and Berson. Suddenly, in a matter-of-fact parenthesis, continuing in exactly his narrative tone though somewhat more quietly, he said:

—— And if you were to look at the building on the opposite corner, outside the wall, the light grey stone building with the heavy cornices, on the fourth floor, second window from the left, you should see what we are looking for. It would be extremely unwise to make any gesture whatsoever. Be casual. Talk to me.

Fein was not looking across at the building. Rachel counted floors, then windows.

—— I can't see anything.

Fein, in a louder voice: ——. . . And then I pushed this handcart full of bricks along in front of the water-cart—understand?—and as I was getting closer to the mortar trough—

Rachel, with a voice that came from deep down: —— Oh, God! I can see him.

—— and there was a big, sloppy pile of mortar mixed in the bin. . . .

—— I can see him!

All she could see was a small, blurred shape in the dark cavern of the window Fein had designated. Suddenly, as she looked, the shape came forward and defined itself: a boy's figure with the arms lifted, the hands and face pressed eagerly against the glass.

—— Oh, God! Oh, God! He sees me!

—— . . . This mortar, you understand, had been mixed from unslaked lime, and it was still steaming when . . .

A larger blur came forward in the inner darkness behind the boy. Hands took hold of the boy's shoulders. The boy's figure seemed to writhe briefly, as if struggling. Then it moved back and itself became a blur again. The blur stood still.

Rachel: —— Shma Yisroel. . . . Hear, O Israel . . .

—— . . . and as the Junak fell over backwards, I dumped my cart of bricks so the noise would cover his fall—don't linger, dear girl—and it was some time before . . .

—— I want to go back.

—— We cannot chance it, Frailin Apt. As I was saying, this Junak . . .

When Fein and Rachel returned to the bakery, she found Berson there. [NOTE. N.L. Berson is moving into the bakery and Froi Mazur will go to live with Mordecai and Rutka. That armchair in the kitchen at the Murin apartment finally made Berson unbearably depressed.] She thanked Fein and on an impulse kissed the rough workman—but also paid him the agreed fee. Then she hurried to Berson on the bench where he sat in the oven-room, and she exclaimed:

—— I have seen Dovidl! He looked very well.

[NOTE. FROM DOLEK BERSON. Berson says Rachel spoke as if she had actually seen the bloom on the boy's cheeks.]

18

EVENTS OCTOBER 18, 1942. ENTRY OCTOBER 20, 1942. FROM DOLEK BERSON. Berson now tells me that he knew in advance that the assassinations were to take place, though of course he did not know when or where. He knew that a Hashomer man was to carry them out: a very young fellow named Yitzhok Katz. Berson says that he himself might have been selected for the task, but how can one imagine this gentle, musical fellow as an executioner? Berson had heard the whole question of the killings thrashed out at a Hashomer meeting. Was it proper for Jews to execute Jews for collaborating with Germans—or should Jews kill only Germans? Back and forth. Berson says that he himself was of the faction that wanted to stick to Germans. He argued that collaboration would in the long run supply its own punishment. This was his reasoning:

There are several ways a man can behave who works in the *Judenrat*. He can have absolute integrity, as (he tells me he said at this meeting) N.L. has: N.L. is a dedicated Jew (he said) and his life as an official is a duplicity, which N.L. sustains for a worthwhile purpose—his archive. Or he can compromise, as Felix Mandeltort did, during his smuggling phase, and then waver between living down the compromise and compounding it. Or he can go crazy, or pretend he has gone crazy, as Fischel Schpunt has done, or has pretended to do. Or he can out-German the Germans, as Mashkrov and Zweinarcz—the first two men marked for assassination—did: they tried to be hard, cruel, consistent, and wholly egoistic. At the beginning, Berson argued, such men would be quite free of the fear of death. Entirely given over to the desire for power, and gradually achieving it, they would be, indeed, rather happy and complacent. [NOTE. N.L. I believe this does describe the state of mind of Mashkrov and Zweinarcz in recent months. Under our former chairman, Sokolczyk, these two were nobodies—an assistant district commandant in the *Ordnungsdienst*, and a clerk in the *Judenrat* secretariat, subordinate to Mandeltort. After Sokolczyk's suicide, I watched them climb and climb, aided by Engineer Grossmann's favoritism and impelled by their own self-centered lusts. And all the way up the ladder they were very happy men: what hearty laughter one could hear from those two! Then they reached the top: Mashkrov as Police Chief and Zweinarcz as the Jew in charge of the deportations, and their power was final: that is, they had the power of life and death over all of us. Indeed, they were more powerful than Engineer Grossmann himself; hence their election to death before the Chairman.] There would come a point, Berson argues, when these power-driven men would find out the meaning of their power: when they would discover how much they were hated by the Jews and despised by the Germans. They would, at last, punish themselves, in agony of soul.

But Berson was argued down. He is too reasonable. There are some sturdy and violent young men in Hashomer, who perhaps had sooner or later to be blooded.

[NOTE. N.L. What really interests me about this argument of Berson's is the possibility that this was a complicated way of justifying himself, before his Hashomer colleagues, and even before the court of his own conscience, for working in the *Judenrat* himself. He attaches integrity to N.L.; he works for N.L.; *ergo*, he has integrity, and should not be taken for a proto-Mashkrov or a fledgling Zweinarcz.]

EVENTS OCTOBER 18, 1942. ENTRY OCTOBER 20, 1942. FROM DOLEK BERSON; and N.L. Both Berson and I found that for us the most noteworthy aspect of these killings lay, not in themselves, but in Felix Mandeltort's reaction to them.

At about ten fifteen on the morning of October 18, I sent Berson on an errand to the third floor of the *Judenrat* building, to the Real Property Section, to look up some figures for me. Felix Mandeltort's office is now on the third floor, and on the way to the Real Property Section, Berson put his head into Mandeltort's room simply to pass in a greeting. As it happens, the Office of Resettlement Affairs—Zweinarcz's bureau—is on the same floor, not far from the secretariat.

Berson: —— *Sholem aleichem.*

Mandeltort: —— *Aleichem sholem.* What's new?

—— Nothing. Just wanted to ask after your liver.

—— There's nothing wrong with my stomach and liver that a heavier load of work would not cure.

—— I'm glad to hear it. Anything I can do for you this morning?

—— Get rid of Hitler.

That was all. Berson went on down the corridor, thinking that Mandeltort seemed somewhat less grey and haggard than he had a few days before. The slacking off in the deportations has been good for everyone, like the arrival of a long-awaited spring. Berson turned into the Real Property Section and asked a girl there for the records he wanted to examine. She found them for him and assigned him an empty desk at which to work. He had been reading and taking notes for about twenty minutes when—very close by, it seemed—there were three loud bangs.

Berson jumped up, along with practically everybody in the section, and ran out into the corridor. There was already a crowd at the north end of the hallway, and Berson ran up there with the others. The crowd was standing outside the door of Zweinarcz's office. By stretching on tiptoe, Berson could see a number of men bending down over Zweinarcz's desk, and Felix Mandeltort standing beside them, with a pistol in his hand, his face strangely puzzled and hurt-looking. Pushing and bluffing, Berson made his way into the office and went up to Mandeltort. Felix looked at Berson with a baffled, dull expression, and said:

—— It was a Jew who did it. He threw this on the floor.

Felix held up the pistol, and then, as if suddenly realizing how disgusting the instrument in his hand was, he turned and took

413

it to Zweinarcz's desk and set it down there. Zweinarcz lay slumped forward onto the desk, bleeding onto it and already dead. . . .

Brokenly, gradually, back in his own office behind a closed door, Mandeltort told Berson and me what had happened. Felix said he had gone in to see Zweinarcz about a report on the last week of the deportations that he was preparing for the next meeting of the *Judenrat*. He said he had lately had a strange sensation in calling upon Zweinarcz:

—— I brought him into the secretariat. He was nothing to me. They told me he was a bright boy. Oi, how bright! Recently when I've gone into his office, I've looked into his eyes to see if his eyes said, *You will be taken soon, Mandeltort: a personal project of mine.*

Felix says he was talking with Zweinarcz when a young Jew came in unannounced, and asked which one was Zweinarcz. Felix had indicated by a nod which one was.

Zweinarcz: —— Do you have an appointment? I am busy just now. Please see my secretary.

To this the boy answered, Felix says, with a formal statement, to the effect that a tribunal of the Jewish National Committee had sat in trial of Zweinarcz and had found him guilty of collaborating with the Germans, to the detriment of the Warsaw Jews and to the shame of Jewry everywhere. Zweinarcz, sensing that the boy was dangerous to him, reached for the button that would summon his secretary. The boy responded to this gesture by pulling the pistol from his coat pocket and firing three shots, which found and killed their target. The boy ran away.

Mandeltort: —— He was a fine-looking Jewish boy.

Felix could not get over this fact, and as he retold the story that day to others in the *Judenrat*, we heard the refrain keep returning:

—— It was a Jewish boy that did it.

[INSERT. FROM ENTRY OCTOBER 22, 1942. N.L. It is common knowledge that the assassin was a young Hashomer fellow named Yitzhok Katz. Berson had no hesitation in telling me this. No one is doing anything to punish Katz. His act was popular; it is never described as a crime.

Yitzhok Katz is, I am told by Berson and Rutka, a chunky, strong, vigorous, hard-eyed boy. He is twenty-two years old. He was born and brought up in the proletarian Polish quarter of Warsaw, where, as a Jew, he had to take care of himself. His father died when he was a child; his mother sold fish in one of those big street-tubs with crude scales and a big umbrella slanting up overhead. Young Katz earned a few groszy by delivering bread on his way to school. He went to the Jewish Gymnasium on Nalewki Street, and early showed a remarkable combination of scholastic brilliance and athletic skill. He joined Hashomer Hatsair when he was only about fourteen, and he became an outstanding member of the cyclists' section of the sport union. He ran away from home to go to a Zionist summer camp when he was sixteen, because he did not dare tell his mother that both boys and girls attended the camp. Later he worked as a clerk in a cosmetic store on Gensia while studying to be an electrician. He is energetic, nationalistic, headstrong, autocratic, and conceited.]

All day Felix was upset by what he had seen; he appeared grey and haggard again. He wanted to talk with Berson and me in the evening, and we had him around to the bakery.

Mandeltort: —— I can understand why they hated Zweinarcz, but was it necessary to kill him?

Berson: —— You say "they" as if the Jews were nothing to do with you.

Mandeltort, blushing: —— I meant the underground.

N.L.: —— At this stage there can hardly be a distinction between "Jews" and "underground," either.

Mandeltort, after thinking a long time: —— I guess I see what you mean. But it seems such a waste for Jews to kill Jews.

Berson: —— How many Jews did Zweinarcz kill?

Mandeltort: —— Oh!

There was a note of shocked surprise in this ejaculation, as if Felix had never thought of this before.

EVENTS OCTOBER 19, 1942. ENTRY OCTOBER 20, 1942. N.L. Late in the afternoon on October 19, the news rushed through the *Judenrat* building that Mashkrov's body had been found in a ricksha in Zamenhofa Street not far from the *Umschlagplatz*. Within five minutes of the arrival of this report, Mandeltort showed up in my office. Berson was there discussing the news with me. Felix was very pale and was shaking.

[INSERT. FROM ENTRY OCTOBER 22, 1942. N.L. I have been trying to puzzle out why Felix was so disturbed by the *Judenrat*

415

assassinations. In ENTRY AUGUST 26, 1942, I registered my uneasy question as to whether we had been wise or merciful to rescue Felix from the *Umschlagplatz*. He seemed then to want to die. In losing his family he had lost his real life already. For some time after the rescue, Felix remained apathetic and morose; but in recent weeks he seemed more interested in his work. Curiously, the days of the "Kettle" seemed literally to wake him up. He began to talk with me about what the Jews ought to do to defend themselves; he began to ask me about the underground; he took interest in my archive. I was much encouraged. Then the Zweinarcz assassination seemed to throw him back into an almost imbecilic nervousness. I imagine that the following things in connection with the Zweinarcz killing might have bothered him:

That he was seen, by the first *Judenrat* workers who rushed to Zwienarcz's office, holding the pistol, and that he might have been considered, therefore, the murderer. (On the first day there was, in fact, some talk to that effect.)

That the killing was done by a Jew.

That the killer saw him, Mandeltort, in friendly conversation with the victim and might, therefore, consider him also a collaborator with the Germans.

That the victim was in charge of deportations, and that he himself was working on a report on deportations, and that therefore, in a way, he *was* a collaborator.

However, Felix's attitude after the Mashkrov assassination was different. He was still terribly nervous, but he had a better look in his eyes. I could see the moment he came down to us after the news reached us that day that he had somehow straightened himself out.]

Mandeltort, to Berson: —— I have made a decision, I want to do some work with the underground. I am not afraid for myself. Can you put me in touch with a proper person?

Berson, too hastily: —— Is this conviction or insurance? Do you think "they" are going after all the department heads, Felix?

N.L.: —— That's unfair, Berson. Give him the benefit of the doubt.

Mandeltort, forcing a wan smile: —— I admit, my timing is unfortunate.

Berson, growing effusive in regret over his cruel remark: —— I'm sure the Zionists will be glad to have you, Felix.

19

Events October 20–24, 1942. Entry October 24, 1942.
N.L. If it is possible to be stunned by joy, then I think Rachel
has been so stunned. She is really quite stupid in her happiness
and surprise. I don't think she realizes yet how much she is going
to miss Berson: I realize it only because I notice how she has
suddenly turned to me. But I think she is going to do a superior
job. As for myself, I can understand that all this is in theory tremendous, but up to now I can only visualize the thing in personal
terms: in terms of what it has done to Rachel and to Berson. I
dimly know that history has been made in the past five days, but
all I can see clearly through these thick glasses of mine is that
Rachel is elated and Berson is gone. Things have moved so fast
in these days that I have not had a chance to shake down my
reactions. In the first place, the actual formation. . . .

Events October 20, 1942. Entry ditto. N.L. Last
night Rapaport indicated to a member of the National Committee
[Note. N.L. I must check which member: this is big.] that the
Bund has decided it is now ready to join forces with other parties
in a resistance movement. This morning the so-called Jewish Co-
ordinating Committee was formed. This consists of the compo-
nents of the Jewish National Committee—Hechalutz, the P.P.R.,
Hashomer Hatsair, Dror, Gordonia, Left and Right Poale-Zion,
and the General Zionists—plus the Bund. At its first meeting the
Co-ordinating Committee drew up plans for its military arm,
which will be called the *Zydowska Organizacja Bojowa*, the Jewish
Fighter Organization. It was decided that the Z.O.B. will be com-
prised of self-contained Fighter Groups from the various parties
and factions; each party will form as many Groups as it can. Each
Group is to have a definite number of fighters, and is to be sub-
divided into Sections and Battalions. Certain fighters acceptable to
the various parties will serve as Couriers between the Groups, and
a few especially trusted men will be Reserve Couriers, who will
know the names, headquarters, and command posts of all Group
Commanders, and will tie the entire network together under the
Central Command, which will be designated in a few days. Pro-

curement of arms from the Aryan side will be up to each party
and its Fighter Groups.

My God! That we can even think in these terms!

EVENTS OCTOBER 20, 1942. ENTRY DITTO. FROM DOLEK
BERSON. For the first time, I have the feeling of being outside
Jewish affairs. I have thought I was preserving a certain objectivity,
so that I could blend all points of view. But if the price of objectivity is to be this *exclusion*, I think it is too high. Tonight when
I knew that Rachel, Rutka, and Berson were going off to a Hashomer circle meeting, I could hardly tolerate waiting for their return
to find out what had happened. And when they came in, and Rachel was as if intoxicated! Well, I drank in this stiff, short account
from Berson:

Zilberzwcig called the meeting to order and, in an atmosphere
of high excitement, told the Hashomer workers of the decisions
taken by the National and Co-ordinating Committees this morning. As a result of the assassinations, carried out by Hashomer's
Katz, the morale in the Hashomer organization is extremely good,
and Berson says that news of the formation of the Z.O.B. was
received in a competitive spirit: there was a feeling that Hashomer
ought to have the strongest and best-trained Groups, and that it
should have general command of the whole Z.O.B. At once, Zilberzweig called for a canvass of the membership, to see who was fit
and willing to enlist in the Z.O.B., and after discussion and reck-
oning, it appeared that Hashomer will probably be able to provide
four Groups.

When the question of commanders for these Groups came up,
Zilberzweig warned that the greatest care must be taken in their
selection: upon them, he emphasized, the honor and prestige of
the movement would rest.

Zilberzweig, his manner agitated and emotional: —— I wish
to say that I feel that these leaders must be from among our
younger members. I believe that you will agree with me that I
. . . speaking personally . . . much as I should like . . . that
is to say, my dear friends, I am too old. You will excuse me.

[NOTE. FROM DOLEK BERSON. Berson says he was moved
by these fumbling words of Zilberzweig's. He felt what a wrench it
must be for the man who had stood so long at the center of the
movement to realize that in this final crisis he would be, in effect,

useless; he could be an administrator but surely not a captain
among fighters. Zilberzweig had for several years been in the anom-
alous position of the leader of a youth movement himself in his
middle age; that paradox: the partly bald "young firebrand." There
was something petulant about this clumsy declaration of senescence
on Zilberzweig's part, and the petulance itself was what made it so
moving. His speech was as embarrassing as the spectacle of an
operatic prima donna, her voice gone, singing a farewell recital:
one had a feeling that perhaps this would not be absolutely final,
as the billboards advertised; perhaps there would be subsequent
"absolutely final" farewells. After the meeting Berson heard hints
from some of the younger Halutzim that Zilberzweig is simply a
coward and cannot face commanding a Fighter Group: this Berson says he doubts and argued against. There was a certain amount
of whispering that Zilberzweig had not been too old to take command of Halinka Apt. There was, undeniably, something not quite
in proper taste, something too self-conscious, something embarrassing about Zilberzweig's pointed effacement of himself: and yet it
was precisely this wrong note that made the act so moving.]

A discussion followed as to candidates for command. Yitzhok
Katz, whose cool work in the assassinations of Zweinarcz and Mashkrov had made him a hero among his colleagues, was the first to
be proposed. The names of several other candidates were brought
up. Berson says it was a young man whose name he does not know,
whom he barely remembers having seen at Hashomer meetings,
who proposed that Rachel Apt be given one group.

The mere idea of putting a girl in command of a unit of
fighters was so dramatic that for a few moments there was a pause,
while a sensation ran around. Berson was sitting a couple of seats
from Rachel. He looked at her. She was blushing and shaking her
head in disbelief and humility.

[NOTE. N.L. There is absolutely no doubt that Rachel was
taken by surprise. All of us have been. It is a safe bet that the idea
of her name coming up had not occurred to Rachel, as it is also a
safe bet it *had* occurred to several others in the room. Indeed, is
not this selflessness the very reason why Rachel was named? By
a stranger. That seems to me significant. It was enough to have
looked at Rachel and to have heard her voice a few times to be
willing to fight under her. One other thing which is worth writing
down: there are no criticisms of this choice to be heard. There is

not even any questioning whether it was wise to pick a girl. None of our "family" is jealous. No one teases her. So has Rachel, with her odd face, won us.]

The four who were chosen: Yitzhok Katz, almost unanimously; Rachel, by a very high plurality; and two young fellows named Jankiel Montefiore and Aron Weiss.

On the way from the meeting, Berson says he said:

—— Congratulations, Little Mother!

Rachel, flashing him a look of over-modesty: —— Don't be ironic.

Berson, for his part rather gruff: —— I'm not. I'm very proud.

EVENTS OCTOBER 21, 1942. ENTRY OCTOBER 22, 1942. FROM DOLEK BERSON. Yesterday Zilberzweig called Berson to his apartment. Zilberzweig seemed to be having quite a few appointments and conferences, and Berson had to wait a long time in the living room, which had the air of a doctor's anteroom: those who were waiting pretended, like patients, to be calm, but they betrayed, by the way they twisted in the chairs and gripped themselves, or by the unreading way they turned the pages of books borrowed from the bookcase at one side of the room, that they were apprehensive, and that, like waiting patients, they wondered what was going to happen to them.

At last Berson's turn came. He was summoned into a bedroom by Yitzhok Katz. In the room, besides Zilberzweig, were the four Group Commanders chosen the day before. Zilberzweig introduced Berson to Katz, Montefiore, and Weiss, and said:

—— You know Rachel Apt, I believe.

Berson, who says that this time there *was* a shade of irony in his voice (he felt on the defensive): —— I know the Little Mother.

Montefiore: —— The Little Mother. That's good.

Berson, anxious to show that he was at ease: —— That was an exciting meeting yesterday.

Zilberzweig: —— It was. And now, Berson . . .

Zilberzweig was brisk, businesslike, and very much in charge. He told Berson that throughout the Z.O.B. conspiratorial first names would be used. The Hashomer Group Commanders should be referred to as Yitzhok, Aron, Jankiel, and Rachel.

Zilberzweig, with a trace of a smile on his lips: —— Despite the difference in our ages, you will address me as Hil.

Now came the point. Zilberzweig said that Berson had been chosen, partly because he had a "safe face," but mainly because he was considered to have a steady nerve and good sense, to go to the Aryan side to help procure arms for the Z.O.B. Groups. It would be dangerous but highly important work.

Berson looked at once at Rachel. Was this her doing?

Rachel read his thought and said, smiling:

—— Don't blame me. It wasn't my idea. Personally I considered you too vague.

Riposte, Berson thought: in return for his "Little Mother" remark. Proud girl!

Zilberzweig outlined Berson's duties and named some outside contacts. He told Berson that, "for the time being," he should report to Zilberzweig. Zilberzweig said he had been persuaded to work with the Hashomer Fighter Groups in an advisory capacity, that this was, however, a temporary arrangement, and that Berson would be given the name of someone else to whom to report in due course. The absolutely final concert, Berson says he thought.

Berson: —— When do you want me to go?

It was young Yitzhok who answered. Berson says this seems to be a hard boy, utterly sure of himself.

—— We hope to get you out within two days. There is no time to squander any more.

EVENTS OCTOBER 21, 1942. ENTRY OCTOBER 22, 1942. N.L. In one way, sending Berson outside will be wasting a known talent of his: his bent for hiding things. What he has begun to do with that hole under the furnace of Menkes' oven! Now we will have to finish the work on his design. It will be the best bunker in the ghetto: like a suite at the Europejski Hotel!

EVENTS OCTOBER 23, 1942. ENTRY DITTO. FROM RACHEL APT. Rachel has told me of this scene between herself and Berson in the bakery early this morning:

Rachel and Berson sat together on a bench in the oven-room. Berson was waiting for his "escort," with his final orders.

Rachel: —— I'm sorry about what I said in front of the Commanders about your being too vague. What I really meant was that I was against your going to the Aryan side because I

421

didn't think I'd be a very good Group Commander without you near by.

Berson: —— My advice has never been much use.

Rachel: —— I will be lonely. Think of the ones who are gone: Dovidl, Froi Mazur, Symka, my father, Reb Yechiel Mazur, Schlome, the rabbi, Stefan, your cousin Meier. [NOTE. N.L. taken in the "Kettle," we have learned.] We are dwindling, Dolek.

—— Pavel is here. Noach is here. Rutka. . . .

—— I know, but . . .

—— I am proud of you, Rochele! Here we are at the decisive point, and you are an important person.

Rachel, bitterly: —— What can we do? A few Jews: what can we really do?

Berson: —— Without arms, not much.

—— With arms, how much? Be honest.

—— It is nearly time for me to go.

—— Take care.

—— You have helped me, Rochele. Very much. Especially since Symka was taken.

—— Please! Formal speeches!

—— Little Mother.

—— Why do you tease me?

—— I don't tease you. . . . I'll try to find your father on the outside.

—— I wonder if he is still alive. . . . Dolek, what can we do, really? It is pitiful.

Menkes, coming into the oven-room: —— Your friend has come, Berson.

Berson: —— Take care of the prosperous baker here while I am gone, Rachel.

With these words, and shaking her hand formally, Berson left her.

[FROM PAVEL MENKES.] Menkes took Berson into the outer room of the bakery, where the young man who had asked for Berson was waiting. This fellow gave Berson some papers and told him that he would cross over to the Aryan side as a member of the masonry labor battalion, which is at this time going outside the present ghetto boundaries to demolish the old ghetto wall along Zelazna Street at about Krochmalna. This battalion of *Platzuf-kazhes* [NOTE. EDITOR. Designation for workers who each day got outside the ghetto.] is constantly under guard, the young fellow said, but Berson would doubtless find an opportunity to slip away. The Smocza-Gensia ghetto gate, where the battalion leaves the Large Ghetto, would probably be the most dangerous place; if he got by there, he would be all right. Did he remember the names and addresses of his contacts?

Berson paused, evidently to recite these over to himself. Then he said he did remember them.

—— Let's go.

EVENTS OCTOBER 23, 1942. ENTRY DITTO. FROM MORDE-CAI APT. Mordecai tells me that most of the members of the masonry battalion were gathered in the *Judenrat* building courtyard when Berson came in with a young stranger. Seeing Mordecai, Berson approached him, and the stranger just melted away.

Mordecai, quietly: —— I expected you.

Berson, with a suspicious air: —— What made you expect me?

—— Rutka told me to.

—— How did she know?

—— You are valuable now. (Mordecai says he whispered this with a rather sarcastic inflection.) People are looking out for you.

A whistle blew. The battalion formed into columns of four. Berson stayed beside Mordecai. Jewish *Werkschutz* were in charge. The columns began marching. Along the way, Mordecai says he was mostly quiet, but once he spoke, quickly and low:

—— We will arrange a time for you to slip away.

Berson: —— Who is "we"?

Mordecai: —— You ask too many questions.

The battalion approached the Smocza-Gensia gate. Mordecai says Berson looked calm. He himself felt inwardly nervous, and he says his apprehension was increased when he saw Fischel Schpunt standing near the gate. The ugly little man is still the sport of the Germans. He seems to many Jews to have become truly mad in the weeks of the deportations. He has stood by at selections, meddling and joking. Some think he is actually working for the Germans. No Jew considers him amusing any more: yet his slightest grimace can throw the Germans into paroxysms of laughter.

The sentries began checking the bricklayers' papers. Schpunt moved closer to the sentry box at the gate; he began to make mild fun of the Jewish workmen. Mordecai was in front of Berson in the line, which was now in single file. Just as Mordecai handed his papers to the inspecting sentry, Schpunt said in German that he felt unusually well that morning. And he began to dance, a grotesque, bullfrog's dance. [NOTE. N.L. One thinks of Schpunt's dance outside the secret prayerhouse, that day so long ago.] The Germans began to shout their laughter. The inspecting sentry took Berson's papers and handed them back without looking at them at all: he was watching Schpunt and gargling uproariously. Suddenly Schpunt stopped:

—— Ai, now I don't feel good any more. My little *fisnoga* hurt.

The Germans laughed at his Yiddish word, without understanding it [NOTE. EDITOR. It is a buffoonish word for feet.], and then the inspecting sentry applied himself more carefully to his work again.

Mordecai said it was not until much later, after Berson had slipped away from the gang of *Platzufkazhes* under cover of an "accident," in which two men (one a Junak) were hurt, that he was suddenly struck by an idea: Schpunt was a decoy. Schpunt was taking the sentry's attention away from Berson's papers. Even Schpunt is in on the preparations. Schpunt is not so crazy. People *are* looking out for Berson. Mordecai is very much impressed. He says he had been making a big joke when he called Berson "valuable," and now it turns out that this is perhaps true.

THE WALL   PART V

1

Events November 4, 1942. Entry ditto. N.L. The most unexpected eventuality in the history of our ghettodom has come about. I, Noach Levinson, have become a soldier of Israel. I, who without my glasses cannot see a four-storey house unless it touches the end of my nose, have joined the Z.O.B. This means, I discover, that I have just begun to live. The dedication of those young people in the Z.O.B. has made my old bones juvenescent. The young fighters gather in closets and talk with hollow eyes and lips flaking from dryness—about revenge. They should make good soldiers, because they have no fear of death: they assume death, death is their axiom. I joined Rachel Apt's group. I remember that I once wrote in this record [ENTRY APRIL 20, 1941] that if I ever got into deep trouble, I felt I would want to take that trouble to "the Apt girl." That declaration has now come home. The trouble in which I found myself was a realization of the axiom I just wrote about—a realization that death in the ghetto is neither accidental nor evitable. Until recently I have persuaded myself that by one means or another—by staring down the judge at a selection, by hiding in an attic, by holding an official position, by hoarding calories, by some act of postponement—I could survive until the end of the war and a change in our affairs. About a week ago I surrendered that persuasion. I am now convinced that we are all to die. All, that is, but the barest handful—like those miraculous few who, when a ship has foundered far at sea, sometimes survive through a prodigy of endurance, riding out storms on random flotsam, snatching at perched seagulls, and licking fortuitous raindrops from their cupped hands. Naturally I shall continue to use every means I can find to delay my fate as long and ingeniously as possible, in the hope, at a maximum, that I may find myself among the handful on the ultimate raft, but principally, now, in the hope that I may contribute my share, no matter how trifling, to the defeat of Anti-Humanity. I arrive late. I realize that. But consider how late we have all arrived! The Z.O.B. was formed only last month, when nine tenths of our population had been destroyed. Even the organized revolutionaries arrived at their slightly earlier convictions, in most cases, for secondary reasons: the zealots of Hechalutz at least partly because they hoped to emigrate to Palestine, the Communists at least partly because they had been instructed as to the need for a Soviet victory; and so on. Now at last the secondary considerations have disappeared, and within our wall we are finally unanimous in adhering to the primary consideration—namely, mankind must destroy Anti-Humanity before it becomes extinct itself.

We have had to bury some differences to arrive at this unanimity, but we have now done so. The Communist is my comrade. The once-contemptible smuggler now smuggles for me. The Zionist dreams of freedom for me, it matters not where:—either in Jerusalem or on the Aleje Jerozolimskie, Warsaw. For we have reduced all our various politics to a single maxim:

The fact that a man is a man is more important than the fact that he believes what he believes.

Nothing is quite that simple: I know it. But when circumstances grow unbearably complex, it is natural that we should grope about for a very simple credo. And so, after all, we tell ourselves, man's real quiddity is that he is a human being, not that he is a Zionist, a Communist, a Socialist, a Jew, a Pole, or, for that matter, a Nazi. But (and here is why we prepare to kill) any man who cannot recognize this basic maxim is an agent of Anti-Humanity, and his purpose, whether conscious or not, is the wiping out of mankind. We must kill him first, for the sake of all the others.

All this I have learned, really, from the Apt girl. She conveyed these ideas to me in far simpler words than those I have used here (I have come to a simple belief but I am still incapable of simple articulation; I am a damnable dryasdust archivist) and even without words, in acts and gestures. I look at her unprofitable, soft-skinned face and her sparkling eyes—and I believe in the simple, one-sentence politics of Humanity. She leaps across a room with an overhanded windmill-gesture and then crashes to the floor, in an attempt to teach *me* how to throw a hand-grenade and take cover—and I understand why we must kill (if not precisely how, for though I am Pro-Humanity, I am still Anti-

Athletics). She takes apart and analyzes a revolver before my eyes, fondling the weapon—and I believe paradoxically in the sanctity of man's life.

Perhaps I am merely living out my Jewish fate; or perhaps I am just full of self-pity and self-idealization. I think not. I think this is not so specific and negligible a case. I think we are indeed involved in the struggle of Humanity against Anti-Humanity. Here, we are outnumbered. We are a little hysterical. We may all die. But we will win.

2

EVENTS NOVEMBER 5, 1942. ENTRY DITTO. N.L. Berson has been gone two weeks today. What better could I say of him than that we are as much aware of him in his absence as we were when he was here? The completion of the bunker—his bunker; the sudden emergence of Menkes from long years of isolation— his influence; Zilberzweig's messages—about him and from him; the strange strengthening now of our "family feeling" among the few of us who remain in the ghetto and who miss him—these and other things make us think and speak often of Berson. I remember once, just about a month ago, Berson talked with me about separation and loss. Rapaport had just left the bakery and gone back to his Bund associates. Menkes, young David, and Berson were in the oven-room together.

Menkes: —— I miss Rapaport. He kept things going around here.

David: —— He could tell good stories.

These two spoke of Rapaport, Berson said, as if he were dead, and for practical purposes, from their point of view (he kept things going; a story-teller), perhaps he might as well be dead. Berson told me he wondered whether his own sense of loss was as selfish as this: these two mourned the lack of entertainment since Rapaport had left. Would he mourn Symka only until he found substitutes for the amusements she had once given him, and for her former ministrations? Did he regret, in having lost her, no more than the segment of his own life so exclusively devoted to her? Did he regret his own resulting loneliness, rather than her death? How long would he remember her? What would remind him of her? And who would remember him, when he was taken away, and for how long a time? Or, he amended dourly, for how short a time?

Berson need not have worried, for the length of time we remember a dead friend depends entirely upon how alive he was before he died. One who lived in a daze, three quarters dead all his life long, is not long remembered. One who was vital and devoured the days eagerly—he is with us hauntingly. Thus Berson (not dead now, but removed beyond this wall, which seems to be the frontier of our mortality) is very much in our midst.

EVENTS NOVEMBER 3, 1942. ENTRY DITTO. N.L. The bunker, which was finished today, is something superb. I think we could live there forever.

Work on the bunker began when Berson decided to expand the burrow in which Symka, David, and Rapaport hid during the "Kettle." At first this expansion was simply a rather haphazard enlargement of the tunnel and hole; but later, when we began to hear that bunkers are being made in attics and cellars all through the Large Ghetto, Berson sat down and laid out a careful plan.

The bunker has two rooms. The "front room," which is entered through the tunnel down from Menkes' furnace, is about three meters cubed. Against its walls are four four-tiered sleeping shelves. The ceiling is shored with timbers and beams; the floor is actually planked (the wood came piecemeal from abandoned apartments). There is a small stove in the front room, which is vented into the flue of the bakery. Recessed closet-like into the walls at one corner are food- and fuel-storage shelves: Berson has arranged things so that the occupants of the bunker can light and tend the furnace of Menkes' oven *from within*. A commodious tunnel goes through to the "back room," where there are, again, four sets of bunks, a toilet connected with the sewers, a well six meters deep, and a secondary escape route—a winding tunnel into the basement of the building next to the bakery. Berson indicated on his plan the intention of tapping electricity, gas and running water from the bakery, but this will have to wait for his return. There are several ventilation ducts which can be opened or closed with dampers, according to the need.

Really, if they had enough food, thirty-five to forty people could live in Berson's caves for several months.

This afternoon, during our little celebration for the opening of the bunker, Rachel told me that one day before Berson left the ghetto, he showed her his renderings of the plan for the bunker, and he said that working on the bunker reminded him of the forts he and his friends used to build when they were boys. He said he had never been the commander in gang warfare, but he had always been the one who could build the forts. He said he built one once with two rooms—just like this one, only smaller. He said he had been very proud of it.

Rachel, telling me of this: —— It's strange how even in our most lighthearted moments we are being prepared for our destinies. The same thing has happened to me, Noach: I was always chosen to be "It" when we played hiding games, and often when we picked up teams I had to choose one side; even when boys were playing. And now I'm "It" again. I used to think it was because I was so ugly. Do you think, Noach . . . ?

N.L.: —— No, I don't think, Rachel. . . .

EVENTS NOVEMBER 5, 1942. ENTRY DITTO. FROM RACHEL APT. Pavel Menkes has asked Rachel if he could join Hashomer and enlist in her Fighter Group! Our careful Pavel has decided to commit himself.

When I asked Menkes why he had taken this step, he said, without a moment's hesitation, that it was because of Berson's influence. I asked him whether Berson had explicitly persuaded him to join the underground. He said, no, that Berson had never talked about it; he said it was simply a matter of his having observed Berson.

EVENTS NOVEMBER 7, 1942. ENTRY DITTO. FROM RACHEL APT. Far from having withdrawn from Hashomer affairs, Zilberzweig appears to be more active than ever. Tonight, in the course of a kind of tour of Hashomer circles that he is conducting these days, he met at the bakery with Rachel, Rutka, Menkes, and Mordecai Apt. The meeting took place in the evening, after dark, between the end of the working day and the curfew hour, in order that Rutka, who is now four months pregnant, and begins to be noticeably so, might safely attend.

429

As soon as the five sat down together, Zilberzweig launched into his business, in his abrupt way. He told the others that he had had a message from Berson. He said as an intended joke that he had become a doddering old liaison between the active young people. Berson, he reported, had sent his message in three parts, and in various ways all three concerned those present.

First of all, Berson had sent word that he was making excellent progress in establishing his contacts and that he had, in fact, found two sources of arms and ammunition; that he now needed only one thing: a large fund of money. Zilberzweig said he was now going to entrust to these four the task of raising at least part of such a fund. He would leave the method largely up to them, but he strongly recommended the technique already in fashion in the Z.O.B.: the so-called "X." This "X," said Zilberzweig, could stand for expropriation. It is, in effect, an assessment by the Z.O.B. upon the rich. The method of collection might be regarded by some, especially by the rich, as being somewhat crude, for it consists in the invasion of an apartment by two or more members of the Z.O.B., wearing masks and carrying revolvers, and of a straightforward demand for cash or jewels. It might seem to resemble banditry, Zilberzweig said with a twisted-up grin, but it is definitely on a higher plane. The request for money, in an "X," is couched in noble terms, he explained—not in terms of philanthropy, for by the act of giving to the Z.O.B., the wealthy also protect themselves, but in terms of pride in Jewishness, of common resistance against tyranny, and of a just sharing of the burden. Besides, the size of the "assessment" is varied according to the record of the assessee. It is amazing, he said, how eager to co-operate most of the wealthy Jews were—particularly those who had collaborated to some degree with the Germans—the moment they were confronted with the nobility of the idea and with the muzzles of pistols. Zilberzweig then took from his pocket three weapons: a Luger and two childrens' cap pistols. Holding one of the latter in his hand, he said:

—— These are persuasive things. It's curious: no one stops to ask what kind of ammunition is in a gun that is being pointed at him.

Zilberzweig handed all three weapons to Rachel, and he said he hoped to be able to send Berson one million zlotys. Pavel Menkes gave out a low whistle of surprise.

Berson's second request, Zilberzweig said, was for a helper. Zilberzweig turned now to Mordecai, and he said that he had been giving Berson's application for aid a lot of thought, and he had concluded, subject to Mordecai's approval, that Rutka would be the perfect courier. A pregnant woman: what more innocent figure could there be? No one would ever imagine the truth. Besides, Rutka might be safer and more comfortable outside: surely it was not convenient to have to hide herself in the ghetto.

Mordecai: —— It's up to Rutka. This would be a heavy strain.

Rutka, putting her hand in Mordecai's: —— I will go—so long as it is understood that I may come back in the ghetto to have my baby. I would want to be with my people then.

Zilberzweig, promptly, with contractual firmness: —— Understood.

Mordecai, with the helpless, ignorant, outsider's solicitude of a husband addressing a pregnant wife: —— The work wouldn't be too much?

Rutka, obviously glad of the prospect of doing some work: —— I've been on the Aryan side before. After all, my trip to Wilno.

The third matter Berson had reported upon, Zilberzweig said, speaking now to Rachel and Mordecai, was that Berson had unearthed (and this word was almost literally apposite) their father. Pan Apt is safe but abject. He has never received a little finger's support from any of his former Polish friends, and he has slipped from room to cellar to hovel to vagabondage; when Berson found him, he was living in a stable in Praga, sleeping in a horse's stall, half tolerated by the proprietor of the establishment and by the horse: it is apparently a precarious tenancy, and may last only a few more days. Pan Apt has concluded that his only hope now lies in a paradox: to flee the Germans by going into Germany. He has heard that it is quite easy for Poles to get work as domestic servants in Germany, and he feels that with his safe face, his tough constitution, and his optimism, he can make out all right. [NOTE. N.L. It is common knowledge among us that although Germans are responsible for what we are going through now, they are not so quick as Poles to spot Jews by appearances. It is easier to fool Germans than Poles.] Berson wrote that Pan Apt sounded to him like an entrepreneur about to buy into a new business.

Rachel, sad-humorously: —— He has had plenty of opportunity to learn the domestic servants' trade by observation—in his own home.

Berson had written that Pan Apt needed some money, and asked that his children send him a jewel or two, by the next courier, if any were left.

Rutka, again taking Mordecai's hand: —— A bitter request from the former owner of the Apt Jewelry Store. I remember (narrowing her eyes) the magic of that window.

Rachel tells me that she could not help weeping. She says she does not know whether she was crying in pity for her father, or because Berson had been thinking of her in searching him out. Zilberzweig spoke heartily, to cover the distressing moments while Rachel mastered her tears, of the clarity and conciseness of Berson's report.

Zilberzweig: —— He has the style of an ambassador.

Finally, hurriedly, Zilberzweig conveyed to Menkes, his newest recruit, one last instruction: the Z.O.B. was beginning to lay up a supply of bread-rusks and grain for storage in bunkers, and he would be expected to contribute. Gone was Menkes' old, deep caution, as he said:

—— Naturally. I can begin hiding it here, in Berson's bunker.

Zilberzweig: —— I hear Berson is also an architect.

Rachel, her tears dried now: —— Tel Aviv has nothing on us.

And for a moment, she says, with Palestinian architecture on her tongue, she imagined part of her picture of the Holy Land— the white, modernistic building beside the petroleum lake, and in front of it, the idle, sun-soaked men dozing easily on their haunches listening to the orchestra on the balcony playing the anthem *Hatikva*, which means: Hope.

3

EVENTS NOVEMBER 5, 1942. ENTRY DITTO. N.L. On a pick-up round, this morning, one of the delivery boys in the *Judenrat* building told me that a package had just arrived for Secretary Mandeltort by registered mail from Berlin. Hearing this report six months ago, I would have been mildly dismayed by the poverty of the office boys' gossip; today, I got up and went directly up to the third floor, to Felix's office. When I reached it, there were already several people around the Secretary's desk, including the Chairman, Engineer Grossmann, himself.

Felix, as I entered the office: —— There are fifty-four.

N.L., to one of the men near the desk: —— Fifty-four what?

This man: —— Certificates for emigration to Palestine.

Felix, seeing me press forward: —— Look, Noach! Approved by the British. Validated in Berlin. (The Secretary's face was glowing.) Fifty-four lives.

N.L.: —— But how many are in the names of people who are still alive?

Felix: —— That's different. Let's go through them and see.

And so Mandeltort began reading off the names, one by one, and the people around his desk would say, *Deported*, or, *Alive*, as the case might be. There were about twenty names that no one recognized; we checked them later as best we could against the records of the Vital Statistics and Labor Departments, and we also asked around the *Judenrat* building; and finally we narrowed down the unaccounted list to seven. By this time it had been established that of the fifty-four certificates issued, only twelve were in the names of people who were still living and could be found. Engineer Grossmann went this afternoon to Commissioner Haensch at the Brühl Palace and asked whether it would be possible to substitute new names for those of men and women definitely deported, and to the surprise of everyone, Haensch said he would authorize the departure of twenty-one Jews to Palestine, and if substitutions would be necessary, in order to fill that quota, he would approve them. Engineer Grossmann immediately called a meeting of the *Judenrat* in order to select the nine "personalities" to be given the extra certificates. The certificates were offered first to the department heads of the *Judenrat*, and they were accepted promptly by Fostel of Taxation and Revenue, Kohn of Sanitation, Murin of Auditing, and Zadkin of Supply. It was then the turn of the secretariat, and Engineer Grossmann said:

—— Mandeltort?

Felix, shaking his head: —— No, thank you.

It can be imagined that this refusal made us all catch our breaths. Engineer Grossmann addressed Mandeltort as if the Secretary's had been a rather naughty reply:

433

—— After all, the package of certificates was addressed to you in the first place.

But I could see that Felix had his mind made up. He looked straight at the Chairman, and said:

—— No. I think I will stay here in Warsaw.

EVENTS NOVEMBER 7, 1942. ENTRY DITTO. N.L. . . . At any rate, the whole question of the Palestinian certificates is now academic, since Haensch has told us that action on them must be postponed a few days: we know what that means. The only substantial residue of the hope-lifting, hope-dashing episode is our new respect for Felix Mandeltort, engendered by his quiet announcement that he preferred to stay here in Warsaw.

After that first day, I had to laugh at my alacrity in rushing up to Felix's office simply because an office messenger had told me of the arrival of a registered parcel from Berlin. Actually, of course, that reaction had a perfectly sound foundation. I must have had at the back of my mind the report given at the meeting of surviving *Judenrat* department heads, only a few days ago, by the chief of the Postal Department, comparing traffic in the Post Office on the single day of July 21, the day before the deportations began, with that on October 20, the day, it happens, when the Z.O.B. was formed. On July 21, according to my notes on that report, 2,446 food packages arrived in the ghetto Post Office; on October 20, eight arrived. The figures on cables, money orders, foreign postcards, registered letters, and ordinary letters reflected in the same way the disruption of our contact with the outside world as a result of the deportations. It was as if the wall around us had grown immensely higher. Altogether, 11,813 pieces arrived on July 21; by October 20, when the wall had gone up skyward, only 688 arrived. And very few of the latter, of course, could be delivered. Was it any wonder, then, that I jumped up in a silly way and ran upstairs when that sallow messenger told me about a registered parcel that had come to my friend straight from the adders' nest?

How Felix's face shone as he leafed through the certificates! One would have thought he had dreamt all his life of the hill of Zion. I have not seen such beatitude here for months. My reminder that not all the certified persons were alive seemed to strike him as being in rather bad taste. He really had been transported by

434

those certificates. Then, over the next few hours, as it became clear how few had survived long enough to make use of those ironic documents, and especially when it turned out that, as usual, the officials of the *Judenrat* were going to divide the windfallen fruits among themselves, I saw Felix hardening up to his decision. And when he delivered it, he did it with grace and humility, not making it a better-than-thou drama, but only uttering the choice as for himself.

Until this decision—and I include his determination to join the underground—I have regarded most of Felix's choices either as expiation for, or as confirmation of, his weakness in getting involved in smuggling; or, for that matter, in getting involved in the *Judenrat* to begin with. This was bigger than that. Felix is calm again, and he is less pompous and more natural than he has ever been in public. He acts as if his late family were standing around him, just back of him, near enough to whisper in his ear, all the time. I have recorded the deep impression the Zweinarcz murder made on him; that must have been part of this same, final process. Felix is now a man who knows himself. He knows what it means to be a Jew in Warsaw at the present time. He is, in short, perfectly awake. He is steady and even seems fortunate compared with some of our anxious people. For the first time since I made his acquaintance, his first name, which is Latin for "happy," fits him.

4

Events November 9, 1942. Entry February 12, 1943. From Dolek Berson. Berson says he walked confidently into the lobby of the Bristol Hotel and to a pay telephone and asked for the number 11–47–32. He was dressed in a double-breasted blue overcoat over a new but rather cheap-looking dark grey suit, and was wearing a silver-grey necktie with an imitation pearl stickpin. He looked like a somewhat pretentious middle-class Pole; he resembled many others in the hotel and in the streets who were dressed in the same unobtrusive yet aspiring way.

A faint voice spoke on the other end of Berson's wire.

Berson: —— Pan Gribbenes? Can you hear me? (Berson

spoke in Polish.) Pan Gribbenes! Here speaks Dolek Jawardnik. [NOTE. N.L. Berson's "Aryan" name.] Can you hear me clearly? The faint voice: —— Yes. Go ahead, Pan Jawardnik.

Berson says he pictured in his mind the man at the other end —a Jew he had never met, a Socialist, member of the Z.O.B., with a fictitious and facetious name, sitting at the telephone in one of the offices of the Leszczynski factory on Ogrodowa Street in the ghetto, pretending that this was a routine business call on a factory matter; perhaps a German was sitting at an adjacent desk. It was impossible to know whether the wire was tapped, but in general it was probably safest to work from a public telephone. Berson pictured the man on the other end as being rather small and dried up. His voice sounded—so much of it as could be heard beyond the crackling and whispering of the delicately curved Swedish telephone—fastidious, tenor, and somewhat timid; though obviously Gribbenes was a courageous man. Berson had talked with him twice a day now for about ten days; he was beginning to feel that he knew Gribbenes pretty well: the insistence, the careful reminders, the veiled encouragements. One of the contacts outside had told Berson that Gribbenes was a Socialist; Berson supposed he must be a friend of Rapaport's.

—— Good news for you, Pan Gribbenes.

—— What was that?

—— I say: I have good news for you, for a change. (Berson spoke now in code.) We can make delivery on four cartons of chromium-plated bolts.

—— Did you say four cartons of chromium bolts?

—— Correct.

—— How many units?

—— There are six packages in each carton.

—— That is very good. When can we expect delivery?

—— Tomorrow afternoon, probably late afternoon. The usual arrangements. Kindly make advance payments against future deliveries as soon as possible. You will appreciate, Pan Gribbenes, that we need operating cash.

—— When can you send the nuts for these bolts?

—— That is difficult.

—— The bolts are no good to us without nuts.

—— You will get them, Pan Gribbenes. Be patient. Just keep your advance payments coming, and you will get them.

—— Very well, Pan Jawardnik. You know that we are depending on you.

—— You can trust me. It is a pleasure to do business with you.

—— You have been very co-operative. I know I speak for our German superintendent when I say we appreciate your prompt deliveries. Goodbye.

—— Goodbye, Pan Gribbenes.

Berson hung up the phone. He looked at the watch Zilberzweig had lent him. Ten forty. He had about three quarters of an hour before his appointment with Kucharski. He looked around the lobby. A German functionary, in a bowler hat, angry with a porter: Berson felt a perverse satisfaction in the Polish porter's discomfiture, a satisfaction and also a companionship. . . . A well-dressed woman, sitting on a lobby sofa, with an annoyed expression, as if she had been kept waiting much too long, her legs crossed (under the silk stockings the flesh firm, round, and healthy), one foot twitching up and down. . . . Three or four Polish businessmen — or men, at any rate, like Berson, in the dull, grey uniforms of Polish businessmen: what *were* their various concerns? . . . A newsboy, threading through the lobby, murmuring prudently of victories in Russia, selling no papers. . . .

On an impulse, Berson took off his overcoat and walked to the sofa on which the well-dressed woman was waiting, and he sat down at its other end. He was bathed at once in a sweet, haunting odor—of a perfume Symka had worn on special evenings! How incongruous! Berson leaned back in the sofa. The impatient foot bobbed up and down over there at the other end. Berson felt the strange sense of well-being he had always experienced whenever he had gone into luxurious surroundings. He remembered having been taken occasionally as a young boy by his father to an expensive restaurant, and having felt at home, as if he belonged in that setting, and as if he were, for a short and magical while, adult. Now, too, Berson says he enjoyed a strange fantasy: he was well dressed, well fed, and safe; he was Polish, he was almost German; there was nothing different about him. For a moment he thought of speaking to the woman at the other end of the sofa. He yawned. He was drowsy. There was a fragrance of Symka and a whispering of expensive trade in the air. Under his feet the carpet was thick. The sofa was soft. . . .

Berson caught his toppling skull with a jerk in mid-fall, and

437

he straightened up on the sofa and looked around to see if anyone had been watching his stupid, humiliating, sleepy-headed performance: he had struggled to keep his eyes open, his head had sagged forward in a half-moment's nap. The well-dressed woman had apparently not seen this: her foot ducked and circled. Then a German officer walked across the lobby toward the woman, and Berson's heart tripped and he knew he was not even slightly German and not the least bit Polish; he was an anxious Jew and he stood up quickly and walked out of the hotel.

There was snow on the ground, and underfoot it was hard-packed and crisply frozen. Even his steps might give him away: they sounded like the chewing of matzos. Berson walked quickly along, and he was filled with outrage.

He reached the apartment on Gurnoslonska Street a few minutes early, so he walked on and around a couple of blocks and back again, in order to make his entry precisely the appointed time; for, of the instructions given Berson by his first contact, that which was most urgently stressed of all was: in this business, never be early and never be late: you don't want to run into anyone except the man you are supposed to meet.

As Berson climbed the stairs to Tomasz Kucharski's apartment, he was still weighed down by the sense of shame, resentment, and degradation the brief experience in the hotel lobby had given him. But when old Kucharski opened the door of his rooms and greeted Berson—*Well, Berson, come in, come in!*—as cordially as if Berson were a son, his taut nerves slackened. The old man was bluff and friendly—and just seeing that face, being reminded of the days on Sienna Street when Kucharski had been the gossipy janitor, made Berson feel comfortable and reminiscent, he says. Kucharski had changed. He was no longer a janitor, either professionally or in countenance. He no longer wore his ancient green sweater with the holes at the elbows. He was, indeed, rather well outfitted, and his apartment, though not large, was far above what a janitor could acquire on his earnings or his savings. It was quite gaudy. Old Tomasz was more polished, too; somehow he had suddenly become a kind of *ersatz* gentleman: what he lacked, like *ersatz* coffee, was taste. Berson had not failed to notice that the old man now addressed him by his last name. In the ghetto, where Kucharski had been outwardly servile, the form had been, in the Polish style, Pan Berson. Now it was simply Berson, with a hint of condescension in the saying. Having closed the door, Kucharski said:

—— I have another little treasure for you, Berson. It's a gem —as light as a seashell.

The old man produced, from a drawer, an Italian revolver, a Beretta. Berson admired the fragile-looking little machine.

Berson: —— How much?

Kucharski, clearing his throat: —— Eight thousand zlotys.

—— Old Tomasz, you're like a mistress—the expenses go up as the pleasure diminishes. That's twice as much as the last one!

—— It's Italian.

—— Can an Italian revolver kill two people at a time?

—— Here (Kucharski spoke curtly, reaching out his hand, the gentlemanliness all rubbed off), if you don't like it, give it back. I have plenty of chances to sell it.

Berson says he thought: how cool you are—you who used to collect our garbage.

Berson: —— Seven thousand zlotys, for an old friend.

Kucharski, whining: —— It cost me sixty-eight hundred. I have to make *some* profit for my risk.

Berson felt suddenly exasperated: his cowardly retreat from the comfortable sofa in the hotel lobby still stung. He burst out (and immediately regretted it):

—— You're against us, too, really, aren't you?

—— I am only against mixing sentiment and business, Berson. You, as a Jew, should understand that.

How pleasant it was in the ghetto, Berson says he thought.

—— Very well. Eight thousand zlotys. (Berson took a pad of money from his wallet and told off that sum to the Pole. He put the pistol in his pocket and stood up.) I'll come back on Friday morning at the same time.

—— I hope I will have something for you then. . . . Did you find Pan Apt?

The old man seemed (now that he had the money in his pocket) placatory: he seemed to remember old times, to be putting out a hand to be shaken. *Pan* Apt. A thin wisp of the smoke of servility. Berson felt more annoyed than ever.

—— I found him. (And Berson turned to leave.)

439

Kucharski, rebuffed: —— He became tiresome to me: he was forever coming around trying to borrow money from me.

And what a sense of power it must have given you, Berson says he thought, to refuse to lend ten zlotys to Mauritzi Apt, the famous jeweler!

Berson: —— Friday.

Berson left. He had lunch alone in an inexpensive restaurant. After a fortnight, he still felt ambivalent toward restaurants: to be able to walk in and order even a frugal meal gave him an anachronistic thrill, and yet, to think of his friends inside—Rachel, Noach, Pavel, and the others—scraping along on rusks and groats, gave him, at the same time, a pang. Berson is honest enough to admit that in spite of these mixed feelings, he was gaining weight rapidly: he had put on about ten kilos in two weeks.

After lunch Berson says he went to see a Polish "maker" on Miodowa to arrange the smuggling of the cases he had discussed with Gribbenes; they were to be taken through Pfeiffer's leather factory on Okopowa near Gliniana, on the edge of the ghetto. This business quickly done, he went across the Vistula to Praga (the river was frozen and snow-covered, and people were crossing by paths on the ice, but Berson, feeling audacious, used one of the bridges) and to the stable where Pan Apt was staying. He found the stubborn little man currying the horses.

Pan Apt: —— I can't stand inactivity.

Berson: —— I have a present for you.

Pan Apt, with pathetic eagerness: —— Did my children remember me?

Berson: —— I haven't seen them. It was brought by messenger.

Berson handed Pan Apt a small paper parcel. With trembling fingers Pan Apt opened the package and spread out its wrappings on the palm of his left hand. Within were six stones, each individually folded into a piece of tissue paper; he undid them, one after another. Then he looked up with tears in his eyes.

Pan Apt: —— I wonder if they knew that they were sending me the six best stones I left behind. This little ruby, how well I remember it!

Berson: —— Mordecai knew, you can be sure of that.

Pan Apt, forgetting already Berson's denial that he had seen the children: —— Tell me, is my Halinka as pretty as ever?

Berson says he thought: Pan Apt is reduced to combing

horses in a shabby stable, he sleeps in dung, and still he dreams of the beauty of his little princess.

Berson: —— She's lovely. And your Rachel has become a leader in the underground.

Pan Apt: —— I always thought she would be a troublemaker.

They talked of Pan Apt's plans. The hardy little man said that he would be going to Germany to work as a servant in a few days. He said with a cocky smile:

—— Tell them not to worry about me. I'll probably wind up as managing director of I. G. Farben.

How could anyone possibly worry, Berson thought, about such a rubber-fibered man? . . .

At supper that night, in the apartment for transient couriers, maintained by two Aryan-looking Jewish girls, known to Berson as Marysia and Lodzia, Berson told the girls that he felt uneasy about old Kucharski as a contact.

—— He has become too prosperous too quickly. His eyes are bloodshot. There is something wrong. I can't put my finger on it. (Berson frankly says that he has inside him a small pocket of pride, and this prevented him from admitting to these girls, especially to the one called Marysia, that old Kucharski had once been his janitor and had scrubbed Berson's doorstep on his hands and knees. [NOTE. N.L. I understand that this Marysia was formerly a nurse in the Jewish hospital. Last summer, deciding that there was nothing left to do inside the wall but die, she left the ghetto. Later she joined the underground. She has a safe but rather formidable face. It became her task, along with Lodzia, who was sent to her later, to provide quarters for couriers and fugitives from the ghetto. The two girls set themselves up in an apartment on Mlynarska, posing as prostitutes. Their great feat was the building of a false wall, for which, with the help of two Polish Socialist workmen, and under the pretext to officials that they needed a bathroom in their apartment, they acquired and carried in all the materials themselves. Behind this false wall they kept underground papers, cash, false documents, and, on occasions, Jewish colleagues.]

While the three were still discussing Kucharski, there came a knock at the apartment door. Swiftly Berson ducked behind a bookcase that stood ajar from the wall, and through a low hole in the wall went into the apartment's dark haven. The girls quickly

441

pushed the bookcase back against the opening. Berson heard one of them go to the door. And in the distance he heard a frightened feminine voice say:

—— Is Marysia here?

It was Rutka's voice.

EVENTS NOVEMBER 12, 1942. ENTRY FEBRUARY 12, 1942. FROM DOLEK BERSON. Berson walked and walked, in the suburb of Zoliborz, and frowned as he moved. If he could only remember! All he could recall was how much he had hated chemistry: the sulphurous smell of experiments; his miscalculations, resulting in muddy, putty-like messes where magical, fiery reactions were supposed to take place; and that professor—what had been his name? —with the beard and the eyes of a goat. Pan Pan, the students had called him behind his back: the Polish word for "mister," plus the name of the goat-god. Pan Pan. There was one day of experimentation Berson wanted to bring into focus. He could see, at the edge of his memory, the long tables of the laboratory, the little dishes, the minute drams of salt-like powder, drops of some liquid, the beautiful miniature flashes in front of each studious face. What had the experiment been? What had the substance been?

Berson wondered what the new "contact," to whose apartment he was now on his way, would be like. This one, a woman, had been recommended by the tall, mild Pole, Tadek, who looked strangely like an Oriental. Berson felt quite smug. He had done well. To date, seventy-three bolts (pistols) and six hundred twenty nuts (rounds of ammunition). He had been congratulated, through a courier, by the Jewish Co-ordinating Committee, and had had personal messages from both Zilberzweig and Rapaport. He had, above all, widened the ring: he had moved from old "contacts" to new ones, and he felt that he had been a sound judge of trustworthiness or the lack of it: so much of this work was in the realm of human understanding—one had to be a kind of radio receiver, with the capacity of tuning in on the exact wave length of each person one met, and one's judgment of the quality of transmission was decisive: it meant one's own life or death, and others'. But still, good as Berson felt he was at the job, the gathering of small arms was a terribly slow and discouraging process. Every once in a while Berson saw a company of German soldiers marching through the streets of Warsaw—all those rifles, and, behind them, all those howitzers, tanks, divebombers! And Berson, risking his life for the purchase of twenty bullets here, a Czech revolver there. . . . There must be some faster way! What *had* that substance been in the experiment with its tiny explosions?

Berson turned down a side street. He began watching for the number, 139. Suburban houses, stucco and wood, this one with a well-clipped hedge, the next yard blowzy, the next strewn with pleasant children's leavings, a kennel beside the next house; each place showing in some way a pathetic protest its residents had made against having been driven into the urban stamping machine. And now a precise, finical, English sort of cottage, with clean organdy curtains, like pretty, bated window-lips: number 139. Berson walked up the short cement path to the door and rang the bell. A housewife, as prim as the setting, with an apron starched like the curtains and a fussy dimity blouse, a woman of about forty, answered the ring. This is the wrong house, Berson says he thought; a blunder.

—— Is Pani Jadwiga Kowalska here?

—— That is I.

Not a mistake; only a surprise. What a figurine to be in this business!

—— I think Tadek Wolinski spoke to you about me. Jawardnik is the name.

—— Oh yes, come in. I was just boiling some tea. Would you have some?

The delicate woman led Berson into her living room, then, excusing herself, went off to the kitchen. Here the furniture was oppressively well cared for: the slip covers were spotless, the legs of chairs and the table tops were fastidiously oiled, and even the sprigs of ivy coming from the half-dozen tubes of a fragile epergne were daintily symmetrical. Berson could not help thinking of the filth of the abandoned apartment where he and Rachel hid during the "Kettle." Soon the sweet little lady came back. She sat and, pouring the tea, began to ask Berson questions about the ghetto. She seemed particularly interested in Jewish writers and artists. She knew names. One of those she asked about was Noach Levinson. Berson *says* he said:

—— Oh, yes, he's still alive. He's one of the great men of the ghetto.

443

[NOTE. N.L. My friend Berson is sly. I think him capable of inventing things like this out of sheer roguishness. Would that what he said were true!]

Pani Kowalska asked questions but seemed disinterested in answers; she got off onto older, dead Jewish writers—Bialik, Peretz, Sholem Aleichem. She had a facility of information and an apparent understanding which, together with her sweetened tea, made Berson giddily happy. He talked, for the first time in months, like a University intellectual, casually tossing out snatches of learning, trading brilliancies, half listening to his adversary, and only half listened to. He was released. He and the subtle little lady talked for a quick hour.

Suddenly, out of the depths of Berson's stirred-up mind, it came: potassium! The substance was a potassium derivative. This memory excited Berson; he said to Pani Kowalska:

—— You know why I have come to you. We need help.

Pani Kowalska, speaking of conspiracy with the same feminine tintinnabulation as she had used when talking of *Three Gifts* and *Thou Shalt Not Covet*: —— Yes, I know how to help. I think I know how to help.

Berson: —— But my first request may surprise you. I should like to ask you to get for me a University textbook on chemistry.

—— I think I can manage that. Advanced or elementary?

—— We had better begin at the beginning.

5

EVENTS DECEMBER 2–9, 1942. ENTRY DECEMBER 10, 1942. N.L.; AND FROM RACHEL APT. A desperate and comical little rivalry has sprung up between Menkes and Rachel. It is a rivalry for proprietorship of the bunker. Since the bunker is more or less under the bakery, Menkes considers it his. Rachel, whose Fighter Group is to use it as headquarters and even, in case of action, as camp and fort, understandably has felt that she should be mistress and colonel there. (Berson, before he left, considered the bunker *his*, since he designed it.) The rivalry has never been so pronounced as to come into the open. It shows itself only in small,

444

polite ways. When a leader of the Z.O.B. comes to inspect the bunker, both of them push forward to conduct the tour. Each occasionally lets slip, when discussing the bunker, the first person singular inflection of the possessive pronoun—and at once deferentially amends it to the plural.

We have all noticed that Menkes was most strikingly affected by the construction of the bunker. Evidently it made our plight real and tangible to him for the first time. His joining the underground almost exactly coincided with the completion of the bunker. For a long time, one had seen this over-cautious man struggling with himself. The main trouble has been that the remaining bakers have developed a tremendous prestige and importance among us, since they are the only ones who can purvey to us the staff of life; and Menkes, in his careful isolation, began to wonder whether he was worthy of such prestige. Evidently "observing Berson," as he puts it, made him feel that he was not. So he joined Hashomer.

And then the bunker seemed to make Pavel childishly proud and fierce as a lion—at least outwardly. He gave himself over entirely to underground life. He hoarded his own surplus bread, which he cut up and toasted into rusks, for the Z.O.B. He was obliged to produce his daily quota of loaves for public distribution on a rigid allowance of flour and other ingredients; in order to have loaves to spare for the Z.O.B., he diluted the flour for the public loaves with chaff, ground peas, crushed groats—anything ingestible, short of sawdust, that he could get his hands on. Hashomer helped him by organizing the smuggling of base grains and fillers. But those loaves which Menkes baked for his fighting friends were made of pure white flour: only the best. Every idle minute that Menkes could wrest from his work he spent down in the bunker, reading the mimeographed instructions on guerrilla fighting, based on experiences in Spain, that had been put out by the Communists; disassembling, oiling, and reuniting a revolver; conducting target practice, minus ammunition, and therefore minus reality, yet going through all the motions: cocking, aiming with bent elbow, lowering onto the target, firing, and absorbing the shock of a feigned recoil; above all, refining the bunker itself.

Especially as the date for the "X" approached did Menkes become excited. In discussing what rich Jew should be given, through an "X," the privilege of contributing to the Z.O.B., Rachel, Mordecai, and he had settled on Eugeniusz Tauber. This had been Mordecai's suggestion. Mordecai said he had never been able to forget the snowy day, so long ago, when he had been waiting in line to register for forced labor and the elegant and assertive gentleman in the black overcoat and the caracul hat and the German overshoes, talking of rare first editions and the proper oil to preserve leather bindings, had noticed the Communist, Kurtz, in the line; and Mordecai recalled to the other two how excited he, the son of a wealthy jeweler, had been made that day by the mere sight of a Communist, and how congenial he had felt with Pan Tauber; and now, Mordecai said, his only feeling about Pan Tauber was that his overshoes ought to warm the feet of a Jewish fighter. And so the three had decided on Tauber; they had cleared the choice with Zilberzweig, it had been approved by the Z.O.B. command, and the three had set the night of December 9 for their visit.

As the day for the "X" came closer, Menkes acted and talked more and more like a brave man. In fact, he became so blustery —he was heard muttering in open company that there were some Jews in the ghetto, "like that robber Tauber," who ought to be shot even before any Germans—that Mordecai had spoken to Rachel, asking whether she thought they should quiet the baker; Mordecai was afraid that Menkes would spill the plans for the "X" to potential informers, or that he might ruin the chances for future "X's" by killing Tauber in sheer over-zealousness during the course of theirs.

Rachel, however, said she thought things would turn out all right. She tells me that she felt all along that Menkes' noisy bravery only covered up his old cautiousness, and that really he was afraid.

Last night, Rachel, Mordecai, and Menkes met in the bunker to discuss their last-minute plans for the "X." Menkes was aroused and volubly courageous. It was settled that Mordecai should cover the other occupants of Tauber's apartment, if any, and that Rachel and Menkes should deal with Tauber himself. Rachel suggested that Menkes should keep Tauber covered while she got out their plunder. This idea delighted Menkes, who muttered dangerously:

—— If Tauber so much as blinks an eye, I'll . . . I'll . . .

446

And Menkes raised his empty right hand as if he were aiming a revolver.

Rachel: —— Excellent. And here is your pistol.

At this, Rachel reached into a pocket in her skirt and pulled out one of the toy cap pistols Zilberzweig had given her, and offered it to Menkes.

Menkes: —— But we have enough real pistols now. . . .

Rachel: —— What if something went wrong and we were taken? Would it be fair to the others to lavish three pistols on just an "X"? Think how much work Dolek must have to get each one! I'm going to carry a cap pistol myself, Pavel. Only Mordecai . . .

Slowly (something in Rachel's eye must have said: *You have talked dauntlessly, Pavel—what's the matter now?*) Menkes reached out and took the toy. . . .

At Tauber's exquisite apartment, later in the night, the amateur pirates woke up Tauber and the four people who live with him and led them, fittingly, into Tauber's den, where he keeps most of his marvelous private art collection. [NOTE. N.L. I know that he has, among other things, a twelfth-century Kiddush cup, a Torah taken from Spain when the Jews were expelled in 1492, and several wonderful Ketuboth, illustrated seventeenth-century marriage contracts.] The famous leather-bound books have been carefully tended, Rachel reports, and they glistened in the light of the carbide lamps that Rachel lit. While Mordecai supervised the household, whom he lined up with their faces against a wall and with their hands raised, and while Rachel faced Tauber—ridiculous in a flannel nightshirt and bare feet—and allowed Tauber to bargain her demands down from three hundred thousand zlotys to two hundred thousand, at no time insulting him but with a more crushing restraint pointing out to him his abandonment and betrayal of Jewry, lounging as she talked against a desk with her hands in her skirt pockets and not even brandishing her toy revolver—all this while, Menkes stood in an ecstasy of nervousness, trembling only a little less than the flannel-wrapped vibrator at whom he pointed his cap pistol. Rachel says she was painfully deliberate. Almost languidly she followed Tauber's instructions in opening his lockbox and taking out the decks of cash. She counted the two hundred thousand zlotys twice over; she put the rest back in Tauber's hiding place. Then she went to the coat closet in the hall and came back with a pair of galoshes, which she handed, with a smile, to Mordecai. Menkes shook and shook, and the perspiration poured off his bloodless face.

Quite a bit later, back at the bakery, Menkes' teeth finally stopped chattering, and he asked:

—— Where are you going to keep the money for now, Rachel? In your bunker?

So now it is "your" bunker.

EVENTS JANUARY 1–12, 1943. ENTRY JANUARY 12, 1943. N.L.; AND FROM RACHEL APT. Ever since the New Year, rumors have been moving about. It was said that the deportations would be resumed; that this time the Germans were bent upon total liquidation of the ghetto; that the end was near. The rumors made those who heard them, and those who transacted them, too, wary and short-tempered. Day before yesterday, I was able to report to my Group Commander, Rachel, that orders had been passed in to us at the *Judenrat* which indicated, indeed, an imminent resumption of general evacuations: these were "secondary" orders, with respect to working permits, residence areas, and so on—of the types that had previously preceded the "primary" decrees of deportation actions. Rachel passed on this information to Yitzhok Katz, and he in turn reported to Zilberzweig—who, despite all his protestations of senescence, is still the effective head of Hashomer. Zilberzweig called for a meeting of the Co-ordinating Committee. It was held in Rachel's bunker last night.

The question for discussion was what to do in case the deportations should be resumed. Should the Z.O.B. fight?

First of all, Rapaport asked for an inventory of the arms at the disposal of the Z.O.B. Yitzhok Katz, who has been selected as supreme commander of the Z.O.B., reported that the organization now has 143 revolvers and one machine pistol, together with about seven rounds of ammunition per weapon.

Zilberzweig: —— Considering that we started not long ago with one revolver, and considering that each revolver costs between three and four thousand zlotys, and sometimes much more, the figure Commander Yitzhok has given us is not bad.

Kurtz: —— I agree. It is not bad. It is not good, either. How long would that armament last us in actual combat with one

448

regiment of German troops? We would put our bourgeois tails between our legs and go into our cowardly bunkers. No matter what rumors we hear, we cannot risk action until we are stronger.

Rapaport: —— Kurtz is right. The Armja Krajowa, and the Polish partisan organizations with which the Bund has been in contact, all urge us to delay our action as long as possible. They say that it would be definitely premature for them to assist us now. I imagine (Rapaport added to Kurtz, with a genteel bow, as if a political chasm did not gape between the two men) that the partisan groups with which you have dealt have given the same answer.

Kurtz: —— It is too early to fight. The time will come.

Zilberzweig, as if rather pleasantly changing the subject: —— Above all, we need money at the present time.

Yitzhok Katz then proposed levying on the *Judenrat* a "tax" of, say, five million zlotys. He said:

—— After all, the *Judenrat* has been taxing us for everything we have done for four years—for the privilege of working, for eating, for having typhus, for living in a house, for *not* living in a house, for coming and going and *not* coming and going. We couldn't pick our teeth without paying. So now . . .

Katz shrugged and grinned. This proposal delighted the members of the Committee. Rachel says she felt they had been somehow embarrassed by their own unanimity on the question of postponing fighting; they were annoyed with that necessity and with themselves, and Katz's suggestion allowed them to turn their annoyance away from themselves onto the *Judenrat*. Bitter speeches were made, and the Committee unanimously decided in favor of the five-million-zloty assessment, and adjourned in an atmosphere of self-satisfaction and even smugness.

EVENTS JANUARY 12, 1943. ENTRY DITTO. FROM RACHEL APT. Among Rachel's fighters, it was Menkes who took hardest the news that there would be no fighting for now. Since the "X," he has been less squally, less full of derring-do; he received the order postponing the fighting quietly, with a set jaw, like a child denied a promised entertainment. Two or three days before, Rachel says, Menkes had come to her very worried and apologetic about what he called his "weak behavior" during the "X."

Menkes, on that occasion: —— I could not have imagined

that I could be so frightened. I was not so frightened as that when the Gestapo beat me up last April. Do you think it was because we were robbing a helpless Jew? Or have I grown weaker? Or what?

Rachel: —— One should be frightened. It is right to be frightened.

Menkes: —— But you were so calm and slow! You moved around like a caterpillar.

Rachel: —— I was terrified. I was so frightened that my arms and legs felt heavy, and I had to *think* about each move I made. My tongue was as thick and cold as a sausage. I was slow because I couldn't drag myself any faster. I was afraid you would notice how frightened I was, Pavel.

—— Did you want to run away?

—— I couldn't have run.

—— Is this true? Or are you trying to bring back my courage?

—— How can I prove it to you, Pavel? I was stiff with fear.

Menkes had laughed, and had thrown his arms around Rachel, and had shouted, with a reprise of his lost bluff manner:

—— Good girl!

And now, as Rachel relayed to the Sections and Battalions of her Group the admonition of the Co-ordinating Committee not to fight, in case of new deportations, Menkes sat sullenly in a corner of the bunker, looking at the floor. The discussion was almost over before he spoke up, and then he asked, with a heavy querulousness, whether "they," meaning the Co-ordinating Committee, intended to wait until the Z.O.B. could match the *Wehrmacht* in armament. Rachel said that there would be time enough to fight.

EVENTS JANUARY 18–23, 1943. ENTRY JANUARY 24, 1943. N.L. . . . *Nu*, David has slung his first pebble at Goliath. I'm afraid, though, that it just bounced off that thick skull. . . . No, the analogy is poor. The young Fighter Organization has been badly hurt.

Let me begin a few days back. There was a nice ironic scene in the *Judenrat* on the afternoon of January 12. (I had known that it was coming, from Rachel's account of the Co-ordinating Committee meeting the night before; but my foreknowledge made the affair no less interesting.) A number of us were in Engineer

Grossmann's office discussing an embarrassing problem. Haensch had just told Grossmann that the Germans expected the *Judenrat* to finance the new brick wall on Gensia Street, which will reduce the limits of the Large Ghetto. Our people were haggling with each other as to the exact cost of that wall, the bricks of which come mostly from the old ghetto walls (three hundred thousand, four hundred thousand, what should it be?); they had not even come to the really tricky question of how to raise the money—when three delegates from the Jewish Co-ordinating Committee came in, unannounced, and demanded five million zlotys for the support of the Jewish fighters. The three were Zilberzweig, Slonim, and young Katz. This last boy seemed in this setting to have a rather unpleasant, cruel face. One wonders how he has maintained such physical force and such a robust frame. He commands great respect in the *Judenrat*, because it is well known that he assassinated Zweinarcz and Mashkrov. All he had to do was stare hard at one of the members of the Council to make that member squirm in his chair and give an affirmative answer. Even I felt a bit uneasy, although I know that Katz knows that I am in the Z.O.B. Within a few minutes, the *Judenrat* had agreed to pay this "tax" and had actually made a silly little down payment of sixty thousand zlotys—all there was to be found in the Treasurer's safe at the time. The three delegates left, and the group that had been deliberating about raising money for the Germans began soberly to deliberate about raising money to destroy Germans. I think I sensed that day the approaching end of the effectiveness of the *Judenrat*. Now, after the skirmishes of the last few days, I have a feeling that that particular end has actually come.

At five o'clock on the morning of the eighteenth, Ukrainians, Latvians, and Lithuanians formed the now familiar cordon around the ghetto walls. An S.S. squad paid the *Judenrat* what I understand was a perfunctory visit, delivering the customary orders and making a few random arrests, mostly of underlings. (Murin, Chief of Auditing, who only a few days before had thought he was fixed up with a certificate for Palestine, was taken.) I had slipped off to Rachel's bunker at the first report of the cordon, so I missed the scene in the *Judenrat*. The blockades that morning were in Niska Street, of Jews who worked in the *Wertverfassungstelle*; in the brushmaking factory on Swientojerska Street; and in the factories Breuer on Nalewki and Von Schöne and Czarniowski on

451

Kupietska. The selections in the factories were, I understand, exceptionally brutal.

The Jewish Co-ordinating Committee had decided, in a meeting a few days before the deportations were resumed [SEE ENTRY JANUARY 12, 1942], that the Z.O.B. was not yet ready for action. But an accident, in the first hours of the first day's deportations, called for an emergency decision, which, it turned out, resulted in five days of sporadic but hurtful fighting. Young Katz was taken in a selection. Informally some members of the Z.O.B. decided that their commander-in-chief should be rescued. This was a completely impromptu decision: had it been referred to the authority of the Co-ordinating Committee, the decision would doubtless have been against any reaction. One of the Group Commanders, who knew that a good number of Rachel's fighters would be assembled in her bunker and that it was only a couple of blocks from the likeliest place to intercept the column containing Katz, sent off a courier to Rachel. Pavel Menkes, quite comical in his baker's disarray, brought the message down to us in the bunker, and Rachel called for volunteers. As a relatively new fighter, and one who had been only partially trained, I held back and did not volunteer, though I must say I was acutely embarrassed by the reluctance of my colleagues to step forward. . . .

EVENTS JANUARY 18, 1943. ENTRY JANUARY 24, 1943. FROM RACHEL APT. Menkes worked fretfully that morning. The news of the resumption of deportations had caused some panic, even among members of the Z.O.B. A large number of Rachel's Group, both fighters who had work-numbers and others who did not, gathered to hide in the bunker under the bakery. [NOTE. N.L. I confess that I made my way there rather hastily myself. We did not call what we were doing "hiding": we were "standing by."]

[FROM MORDECAI APT.] Mordecai stayed upstairs in the bakery with Menkes. The baker lit the fire and went through his routine of baking: he kneaded the dough that had been set to rise the night before, in order to "kill" part of its leavenous gas, and he dusted the pans and cleaned his long loaf-shovel and shaped loaves. He slammed things, Mordecai says. He was as testy as an old lady who has been beaten in an argument.

Shortly after nine o'clock, when Menkes had shaped about

half his loaves and had set the small pale lozenges into pans, there came a noise, not so much of knocking as of a panic-stricken battering, on the door of the shop. Menkes, moving with an unnatural slowness, Mordecai says [NOTE. N.L. Evidently Menkes was consciously mimicking the deliberation Rachel had shown in the "X."], went to the door, slipped the bolt-bars, opened the doors, and admitted a fearful Jew Mordccai had never seen before, a tall, thin man.

The man, panting: —— I was sent here to find ten fighters.

Menkes: —— The fighters have all gone home to wait for the arrival of our Jewish tanks and artillery. . . . And I am busy. (He turned to his pans.)

The man, with a rasping, frightened insistence: —— I am Ishmael. Courier for Jankiel's Group. I was sent here to tell you that Yitzhok—you understand, Yitzhok!—has been takcn along with a group of "wild" Jews in the *Ostbahn* blockade. He is being held with them on Mila Street. Any minute now they will take them to the *Umschlagplatz*. We are to set an ambush on Zamenhofa at Niska. Are there fighters here?

Menkes, in a fury of bewilderment: —— First they say we are not to fight, then they order us to fight.

Ishmael: —— Are there fighters, or not?

Menkes: —— Wait here.

The torpid manner Menkes had assumed suddenly scaled off him. He ran out the front door of the shop (the fire was going; he could not go down into the bunker through his furnace) and into the apartment building next door, down into its cellar and in, through the secondary exit, to the bunker. [FROM RACHEL APT; AND N.L.] Appearing there, in his flour-dusted apron and with dough-flecked hands, his eyes wild, carrying a livid patch of flour on his cheek, he was greeted, at first, with a laugh.

Menkes, offended, and quite without humor: —— Ha! ha! ha! It is time to laugh now!

Then Menkes told Rachel what Ishmael the courier had said; the excited fighters pressed around. Rachel asked for volunteers. Six responded at once, among them Menkes and two girls. For a long time none other volunteered.

Rachel, sarcastically: —— The moment we have trained for and wished for has come, and now only six . . .

At last, but slowly, one by one, four others put up their hands.

453

There was a scramble for weapons. Then the ten volunteers and Rachel went up into the bakery.

Rachel says she had never seen this Ishmael, but he recognized her at once. He said he had been directed to beg her not to participate in this skirmish. He said she could come with him, if she wished, to an observation post on Zamenhofa, that belonged to a Dror-Gordonia Group, from which she could probably watch the action.

Rachel asked Menkes to take charge of the group. Menkes clapped her on the shoulder and said brusquely:

—— I'll do better today. You'll see.

The courier gave instructions to the volunteers and they left on the run. Ishmael took Rachel to Zamenhofa Street 58.

EVENTS JANUARY 18, 1943. · ENTRY JANUARY 24, 1943. FROM RACHEL APT. Through a hole in the blanket hanging over the window, Rachel looked out on Zamenhofa Street. She had a view at a northward angle, taking in the block of Zamenhofa between Muranowska and Niska. For a time the street, whose snow was packed down into a dirty ice, was empty and desolate. Then another watcher in the observation post, looking southward down Zamenhofa, muttered:

—— Here they come!

Rachel could hear the forlorn march of the candidates for deportation before she could see them: the scrape of shoes on the dull ice, mixed with the *clip-clop* of wood-shod feet, and moans and cries; and the shouts of the convoy of S.D. men. Rachel heard other watchers exclaim:

—— There's Yitzhok!

—— I see him!

—— How healthy he looks among that riff-raff!

By the time the column of bedraggled fours moved into Rachel's sector of vision, the backs of the marchers were turned toward the observation post, and she was unable to identify Yitzhok; though there was one straight figure she thought might be his. As the head of the column approached Muranowska Street, Menkes and the others of Rachel's group came out from the side street, with hands raised, in a gesture of surrender.

Rachel, reporting to the others: —— Our people are giving themselves up!

454

The fighters in the observation post groaned. Out in the street the S.D. men, assuming that the baker and his companions were simply discouraged Jews volunteering for deportation, drove them into the haphazard line. The line started up again. Rachel saw that Menkes was still wearing his apron; he was still smeared with flour and dough.

Rachel says she wondered what had caused the ambush to walk so docilely into the Germans' hands. She hoped it had not been a craven collapse on Menkes' part: she saw him walking now, jerkily and unevenly, as if giddy. She noticed that he patted his apron pocket—his pistol, he was worried about his pistol. Rachel thought: Ten pistols! Menkes had always been cautious: she remembered Slonim and Berson and N.L. talking of the baker's stubborn independence, his refusal to be dragged into strange and risky associations; even after he had got into the underground, his decisions had been careful ones, slow and calculating. Was it some misguided prudence of his that had made him lead the volunteers—the brave ones! Isaac, Chaim, Moshe, Bela!—into surrender? How could he be so *incautious* as to throw away ten pistols and ten lives?

Suddenly Rachel uttered a meaningless cry. Menkes had raised his arms in a crazy, stiff, swinging motion, and he wheeled around, his mouth wide open, and his shout could be heard even behind the window nearly a block away, and then he reached quickly into his apron pocket and drew out his revolver (not a toy this time) and fired it at the S.D. man who had been marching not far from him. The S.D. man curled and fell. Rachel saw that as Menkes turned to look for another German, he had the stooped, round-shouldered, dodging stance he had taken at Tauber's the night of the "X": he was frightened again! After a moment other shots broke out. Rachel understood what Menkes had done: he had surrendered to the Germans in order to get his fighters among the deportees and let them be right on top of their targets. He had done a good job, and now he was terrified. She could see him looking about, pale and uncertain. The crowd of deportees was scattering down Zamenhofa, and along Muranowska and Mila. Shots echoed. Rachel heard whistles blow in the distance. The scene became utterly confused. The watchers in the room called out to Rachel to describe what she was seeing. For a moment she thought she saw Yitzhok, running away, and she exclaimed:

—— I see him!

—— Whom? Whom?

—— They have done a good job!

She saw Menkes bend over a dead German and take his rifle, his revolver, and his cartridge magazines. There were several men down, both German soldiers and Jews. Some of the deportees just stood around. The volunteers gathered in one spot. They seemed not to know what to do. One of them, with two rifles hanging by their slings from his shoulders, ran away down Zamenhofa. Rachel could imagine Menkes shaking with fear; he was hunched forward, tensely. He seemed no longer to be acting as leader. A short man, also carrying two German rifles—was it Moshe? No! No! Yitzhok! It was Yitzhok!—moved toward Niska Street, beckoning; then all together ran into Niska Street, Menkes among them. Rachel heard the sound of boots on the ice. A large squad of S.S. police ran up Zamenhofa and turned into Niska. Rachel spun away from the peephole and tried to tell the others what she had seen.

EVENTS JANUARY 18–23, 1943. ENTRY JANUARY 24, 1943. N.L. . . . and Yitzhok Katz escaped from the beleaguered house on Niska almost miraculously. All of the others, who had gone in with him, had been killed, including Menkes. (I cannot help thinking what effect the news of the baker's death will have on Berson, when he hears it.) Yitzhok scrambled up into an attic and back into a corner of it, where for a few minutes he had a rather good time; he says he picked off three Germans as they showed themselves at the head of the narrow ladderway into the attic. (I should say here that Katz has a slightly boastful streak, and in this instance he enjoys the perfect narrative opportunity: he alone survived.) The Germans then lobbed a grenade up, which providentially settled and exploded, Yitzhok says, on the opposite side of a brick chimney from him. The Germans apparently assumed it had killed him, for they left.

Later that morning the Germans attacked Zamenhofa Street 58, whence Rachel had observed the ambush; but she had run back, meanwhile, to our bunker. The Germans must have learned about Zamenhofa 58 from informers.

Communications within the Z.O.B. broke down almost completely at once. Some of the couriers, it was later discovered, hid themselves through the entire five days. Some Groups went into action, others refrained (like Rachel's; we stayed in the bunker throughout). This was the confusion: the hectographed Z.O.B. manual, under the heading *"Mobilization,"* calls for "automatic mobilization and activation of Battalions, Sections, and Groups in case of any action involving Z.O.B. units"; but the Co-ordinating Committee had specifically ordered that units should wait for further orders before fighting. Yet fighting, as a result of the ambush to rescue Yitzhok, *was* taking place. Should "automatic mobilization" obtain? Some Groups became active. Rachel decided that hers should not, and I think wisely: she felt that this fighting was not harmonized, and that she would do the ghetto a greater service by keeping the remainder of her Group intact.

Isolated skirmishes took place for three days. In none of them did the Jews inflict serious damage, but they apparently gave the Germans a series of nasty surprises. On the twenty-first the Germans came in with their reprisal. Six hundred S.S. police in full battle dress entered the ghetto with light anti-tank weapons and shelled a number of "offending" houses and apartments point-blank. They also threw grenades into windows and affixed petards to walls. Most of the buildings thus attacked housed perfectly innocent Jews. I do not know how many were killed in this way. Probably not too many. (These terms are relative; I think of the weeks when forty thousand Jews were taken away to be killed. How many is "too many"?) The system of bunkers, both for fighters and for non-fighters, has become quite extensive, and much of the population was below ground. The last shots were fired on the twenty-second.

EVENTS JANUARY 24, 1943. ENTRY DITTO. N.L. A victory, after all! *Mirabile dictu,* the deportations have ceased. Apparently our German friends don't like being shot at.

EVENTS JANUARY 25, 1943. ENTRY DITTO. FROM RACHEL APT. Today at last Rachel had an opportunity to talk with Yitzhok, and to ask him about Menkes. Yitzhok described the sharp battle in the house on Niska Street to which he and Menkes' party had retired, and from which only he had come out alive. (Katz's story is improving with age and use.) He told how Menkes had been killed. The squad had blockaded itself in an empty house. The S.S. police had surrounded the house, and had eventually forced an entrance through a rear cellar door, using tear gas and machine pistols. Yitzhok said he had posted Pavel at a second-storey front window, to observe and snipe if possible. When the Germans broke into the house, Yitzhok had yelled to Menkes and the other lookouts to join the core of the group on the third floor. Menkes had been shot from behind while running upstairs.

Rachel: —— Not exactly a hero's death.

Yitzhok: —— He did what he could.

Rachel: —— Did he seem to be afraid?

Yitzhok: —— He was rather afraid. He seemed rattled—not thinking very clearly. I believe that if he had started up immediately when I called. . . . They tell me that the idea of surrendering to the column before opening fire was his. . . . He was confused in the house; quite muddled. I don't know what his trouble was. . . .

Rachel: —— Poor Pavel! He wanted so much to be brave.

6

EVENTS JANUARY 18, 1943. ENTRY FEBRUARY 12, 1943. FROM DOLEK BERSON. As Berson picked up the telephone in the hotel lobby to make his morning report on the eighteenth, he says he thought: In ten days I will have been on the Aryan side exactly three months. That is nearly enough. I will ask to be allowed to return to the "village." [NOTE. N.L. Couriers' slang for the ghetto.] Three months is enough time to be in an alien town on this kind of work.

The operator asked for the number.

Berson: —— One one—four seven—three two. . . . Correct.

One becomes nervous and careless, Berson says he thought. And very soon, he thought, his chemical experiment, his student's game, would be completed and either successful or a failure. On the other end, the phone rang and rang, and Berson waited for the familiar, high-pitched, fussy voice of Gribbenes. He pursed his lips and listened to the ringing.

No! Something queer! On the other end, a harsh, deep voice:

—— *Na! Hallo! . . . Wer spricht? . . . Hallo! Hallo!*

A German. Gribbenes not answering. Something wrong. Berson hung up without speaking. A man waiting to use the phone looked at him oddly.

Berson, in Polish, with a disgusted expression: —— This damned service. Nothing but wrong number, wrong number every time.

Later, Berson and Rutka were talking together in the "false room," behind the double wall in the girls' apartment. Rutka was lying on a mattress on the floor. She was obviously pregnant now. She complained of pains in her back, and she said that when she walked her pelvic bones seemed to grind together; her skin was extremely dry, and she kept scratching herself.

Berson: —— It might have been a wrong number, but I doubt it. The operator had repeated the number back to me correctly. I certainly wasn't going to take the chance of calling back again. I hate to miss a talk with Gribbenes. It happened once before, another Jew answered and said Gribbenes was sick. . . . But this time: the phone rang so long, and then to have a German answer! I'm sure it was a German. No Jew would have sounded like that.

Rutka: —— Marysia got a rumor in town today that one could hear shooting in the village this morning.

—— Where did she hear that?

—— She didn't say.

Berson, speaking like a hurt boy: —— How *could* they start without letting us know?

Rutka: —— Our dear little pistols!

Berson, questioning himself as much as Rutka: —— What do you suppose it's like?

Rutka: —— It's better here behind a double wall. Even with a sore back.

Rutka had been wonderful, Berson says. She had been outside now about nine weeks. She had acquired nearly thirty weapons. She had worked steadily, and seemed to have just as much energy as Berson, if not more. She had helped Berson with the "experiments," and had, in fact, solved the decisive problem: she had made a contact with a worker in a fertilizer plant who had agreed to supply her with potassium chloride smuggled from his factory; this could be reduced by electrolysis to the potassium chlorate that Berson hoped to be able to use in his instrument.

459

Rutka had also found a source for a moderate number of bottles. She had not only been resourceful; she had also been generally persistent, optimistic, and patient. She had never for a moment questioned Berson's idea; she had scolded him when he himself questioned it. And night after night she had lain on the mattress in the "false room," while Berson sat on pillows at the end of the cubicle, talking with him about members of the "family," and about the appropriate attitudes for life in the "village," and about the future, and about her baby. All Rutka's thinking was naturally colored by her pregnancy. There were many shades and quick changes in her thoughts and utterances; Berson had never been aware of such complexity in a woman, or in a man, either. Rutka wept easily during these conversations, but often she laughed before the tears were dry on her cheeks, and she got out bitter witticisms between fits of crying. Her sadnesses were shallow and transient; her hope and optimism were substantive. And so she was good for Berson, who was inclined to become depressed when he let his mind stray away from the particulars of a courier's life to any sort of generalities.

Berson: —— If there really is fighting going on, I wonder how Rachel is behaving.

Rutka: —— Rachel will be quite happy. Many people look up to Rachel. She doesn't know it, and I imagine she is finding it out, if they are fighting. I imagine she is happier than usual.

—— Oh, Rutka, it's terrible!

—— What's so terrible? Tomorrow we throw our bottle! Dolck! (Rutka sat up on the mattress, and she spoke with an urgency that seemed to sweep aside all the harshness of habitual fears, all thoughts of the "village" and of Jewishness, all dread paradoxes such as the possibility of being happier than usual precisely when death was becoming discriminate and was beginning to choose one's friends and family.) Dolek, do you have nightmares, the way I do, for fear the bottle will simply break and the gasoline splash around and nothing at all will happen? Do you?

Yes, after all, why speculate about unsuccessful telephone connections and rumors not yet confirmed?

Berson: —— Don't worry. It will make a beautiful mess.

EVENTS JANUARY 19, 1943. ENTRY FEBRUARY 13, 1943. FROM DOLEK BERSON. Berson and Rutka reached their rendezvous near the brick factory, on the western outskirts of the city, a few minutes late; it was after six o'clock. Berson was carrying a bulky cylindrical package, wrapped in newspapers. Berson's contact, a Polish Socialist named Franciszek Ankiewicz, was waiting, as he had promised to do, under the wooden shelter of a streetcar stop about three hundred yards from the factory. [NOTE. N.L. Evidently Polish Socialists are willing to help on an individual basis.] This man, a strangely scholarly-looking man for a brick-maker, wearing steel-rimmed glasses, said he thought the coast would be clear; the office-workers had left at five, the kiln-tenders at five thirty.

Ankiewicz: —— Will it make a noise?

Berson: —— We have no idea. Theoretically, no.

Ankiewicz: —— And it won't blow up a kiln?

Berson, smiling this time: —— Theoretically, no.

Ankiewicz asked Berson and Rutka to wait a few minutes in the streetcar shed, while he took one last look around the factory grounds. The workman had told Berson that the shed was a superb place for innocent loitering and for trysts, since several classes of trolleys passed this stop, and no one would be suspicious of people letting cars go past. Berson was restless and distracted, he says. He felt scarcely interested in the test he was about to make. Neither of his calls that day to Gribbenes had gone through. Shooting had been unmistakably audible within the ghetto that morning. Rutka had gone near the walls early in the afternoon; she had seen formations of S.S. police and Lithuanians milling around outside the Smocza-Gensia corner gate, as if preparing some sort of exercise or maneuver, and once a German ambulance had come careering out. She had asked some Poles who were gaping there what was happening, but their answers had been tendentious: *They're hunting mice, don't you know anything?* . . . *The Jewboys are learning a lesson.* . . . *Kosher slaughter, very clean.* . . . One woman had said: *It's frightful.* It had been impossible to learn the extent of the disturbances, or, indeed, whether any of the occasional shooting was on the part of Jews. Berson, hearing Rutka's report, had said he was tempted to go inside, unauthorized. Rutka had argued him out of it; she had told him he couldn't throw away the work of months just because of a few hours' uncertainty.

Ankiewicz returned. He said everything was in order, but—

461

he cleared his throat—he thought he would like to be paid in advance. Rutka took out the agreed sum of money and gave it to him, and she said:

—— Solidarity! (Her voice was perfectly friendly; she let the word itself carry the load of her sarcasm.)

Ankiewicz, himself unemotional, unstung: —— It is very risky.

The brickmaker led them then into the factory grounds, past a dull, square, blue-grey brick office building to the kiln yard. Everywhere there were droppings of blue-grey clay, mixed with cinders and dust. There were half a dozen domed kilns, in two rows of threes, like huge, gloomy beehives. The kilns themselves were made of brown clay bricks. At the far end of the yard were stacks of newly baked blue-grey bricks, rather cheap-looking ones, many of them warped in the baking, or cracked, or clinkered together in pairs. Still, Berson says he thought, there were no bricks so elegant as these in the wall around the Jews.

Ankiewicz: —— Kiln six is empty and cold. That would be best.

And he led Berson and Rutka to the leftmost kiln in the second row. Access to the kiln was through an arched tunnel, nearly two meters high and three meters long, like the entrance to an igloo; on the inner end of this tunnel was a big iron door, with ventilating grills. After looking around the yard, Ankiewicz walked into the tunnel, swung open the door, and backed out again. Crouching, Berson and Rutka could see, beyond the doorway, a bricklined cavern, lit with a ghostly glow from the chimney vent at the summit of the dome.

Rutka: —— Nu, a nice place for a fire.

Berson unwrapped his parcel. Inside was an extremely simple engine: a liter bottle, filled with gasoline and containing, just below the neck, two small capsules wrapped in rags and held in place by a stiff wire that ran up through the neck and was stuck in the cork of the bottle. One of the capsules contained potassium chlorate, and the other sulphuric acid. Ankiewicz stood back several meters; he looked very concerned.

Rutka, with exaggerated nervousness that satirized her own real nervousness: —— I wish there were more preparations. We've just arrived, and the experiment is almost over.

Berson kissed the bottle, grasped it firmly by the neck, swung it back side-arm, and threw it into the arched tunnel and into the kiln. It broke with only the noise of a full bottle breaking in a hollow place. For a moment—a moment that seemed endless to Berson—nothing happened: a spreading pool surrounded the fragments of glass. Then suddenly, among those fragments, a brilliant, actinic light flared up, as the potassium salts and acid performed their swift, spontaneous miracle of oxidation, and instantaneously, with a *whoosh*, the widening pool of gasoline burst into flames, which in the throat of the kiln leaped twice as high as a man.

Rutka, breathlessly, speaking Hebrew—the first time she had not used Polish in the presence of Ankiewicz: —— Blessed art Thou, O Lord our God, King of the universe, who hast made the creation.

[NOTE. FROM RUTKA MAZUR. This is the benediction, Rutka says her devout father had always told her, that is suitable upon standing witness to lightning, or upon having the good fortune to see falling stars, lofty mountains, great deserts, and other wonders.]

Berson, jumping to Rutka, throwing his arms around her: —— It works! It works!

Ankiewicz, himself obviously delighted: —— You'd better hurry. The streetcar shed is a better place for celebrations.

EVENTS JANUARY 24, 1943. ENTRY FEBRUARY 13, 1943. FROM DOLEK BERSON. The courier was a man Berson had never seen before: a small fellow with the look of a scarcely wrapped skeleton that so many survivors of typhus have. He was over-apologetic. When he had first entered the girls' apartment and had identified himself as a courier, Berson had dived at him as if to commit battery, and had grabbed him in a preparatory way by the lapels, and had asked, almost malevolently:

—— What has happened? What was the shooting about?

The courier: —— Beg your pardon. Excuse me, I am not authorized to talk freely. I have this letter for Jawardnik. Excuse me. I'm sorry.

Berson had snatched the letter and had gone to the window to read it. Now he looked up at the courier as he turned from one page to another, and his manner had become soft and condolent. He said gently:

—— It must have been terrible.

Berson says he wondered whose the vigorous, dash-splashed style of this letter could be: someone who seemed to know him, and yet did not.

[INSERT. ENTRY FEBRUARY 15, 1943. FROM DOLEK BERSON. Berson has given me the letter he received from the courier on January 24. He says he kept it (foolishly) partly because of Menkes, and partly because it quickly became for him a kind of luck-charm. Here is part of it:

. . . and so far it is too early to count our losses. We know that they were extremely heavy—though we also know in our hearts that we are the victors—the cowards have for the time being ceased deportations. You, Pan Jawardnik, will take satisfaction from the fact that our losses in weapons were not as severe as those in manpower—we may even come out with a net gain, though that is perhaps wishful—at any rate, in the first ambush, described above, we captured from the Germans nine rifles and four revolvers —the rifles will be excellent for sniping—and besides, when the Germans inflicted casualties, they almost never took the precaution of disarming our fighters—our invariable practice with respect to German casualties—for, you see, we do not forget the good work of our couriers.

Please note the following carefully. In our present state of disruption we are in serious need of arms. We will expect deliveries from your unit at three times the rate you have recently maintained—do not report to us that there are only twenty-four hours in a day—we know that—and do not tell us that you cannot find new contacts—do not palaver in any way—we do not care how you do this thing.

Do it.

Your friend Gribbenes is dead—he was shot behind the right ear. From now on, communicate by telephone with the name and telephone number that will be given you orally by bearer.

Bearer also has for you an Italian revolver, a Beretta, which you sent us. This weapon is faulty—the sear is worn out at its points of touching both with the hammer and with the cylinder-releasing bolt—the gun is useless. Please return it to contact with a tongue-lashing and demand replacement—we must teach these people that fighting Jews are not to be bilked—kindly announce *to this swindler that unless he makes good he will be shot by the Z.O.B., which can now speak of itself as blooded and can deliver threats in earnest.*

You are directed to send in to us as many small metal files as possible, preferably three-square or rattail files of no more than six to ten centimeters in length, or about the size of cigarets. If these are unavailable, send ordinary fingernail files. These are to be carried by our leaders so that in case of deportation, they may be able to escape from the trains.

Among the casualties in the fighting of January 18–22 was one baker, Pavel Menkes. I am requested by acquaintances of yours to tell you that this Menkes died bravely, defending Yitzhok. Be proud of him. His courage in action was especially commended by Yitzhok.

We look forward to resumption of your reports, Jawardnik.

The message was signed, simply, Jewish Fighter Organization.

Berson stood at the window for a long time, thinking about Pavel.

The courier: —— Excuse me, I was supposed to give you this weapon (and he laid the Beretta on top of the bookcase) and you are to telephone Pan Nudnik, at one four—three four—six six. Pan Nudnik. Onc four—three four—six six. An easy number to remember. Excuse me, you have had some bad news, I'm very sorry. Forgive me, I am supposed to make sure that you have memorized the name and number. Did you get them?

Slowly Berson nodded.

—— I'm sorry.

Berson turned, and he says that now he was unashamed of his tears.

—— Tell me one thing. Do you know the Group Commander who is a girl, Rachel? Is she all right?

—— You mean the one they call "Little Mother"?

—— That's the one. (So the nickname was around!)

—— Her unit was not in action after the first ambush. She should be safe. Excuse me, I am not supposed to talk too much. I'm sorry. I must go. Thank you for your hospitality.

EVENTS JANUARY 26, 1943. ENTRY FEBRUARY 13, 1943. FROM DOLEK BERSON. Berson says that for some time he had considered his visits to Under-Colonel Bierczyk of the Armja Krajowa simply "routine." As far back as November the Co-ordinating Committee had received a message from the underground army of the Government-in-Exile in London, praising Jewish preparations but not offering any aid. Berson had been instructed to make a contact with the Armja Krajowa and to keep harassing the contact with weekly visits. Under-Colonel Bierczyk had not reacted too pleasantly to Berson's persistence, and on the last two or three occasions had taken a hectoring attitude toward Berson and, worse, the Jews. The visits might be a necessary chafing of the Armja Krajowa from the Z.O.B. point of view, but they had become acutely embarrassing to Berson, and he had postponed this call for three days: he had intended to go the day the courier came out with the news of the fighting, but word of Menkes' death had upset him, and since then he had allowed other errands to intervene. The result was that today he had two unpleasant, postponed jobs to do: this; and returning the Beretta to old Kucharski.

The first surprise came when Under-Colonel Bierczyk's orderly in the "office"-apartment on Blonska Street told Berson that the colonel had been expecting him for several days and wanted him to walk right in; ordinarily Berson had had to cool his heels a good half-hour before being admitted.

The second surprise came when Under-Colonel Bierczyk stood up to greet him.

—— You are late this week, Jawardnik.

—— We have been busy.

—— So I understand. I hear you Jews can fight, after all, and fight fairly well. We have had full reports. I have been directed to tell you—you may find it hard to credit me, Jawardnik—that the Armja Krajowa is ready to turn over some armament to the Jewish Fighter Organization.

Berson, guardedly (he felt a little dizzy): —— How much?

—— Fifty pistols and fifty grenades.

Unable to shake off at once the antagonism he had been building up for so many days, Berson said:

—— Do you consider that sufficient for our needs?

Under-Colonel Bierczyk, his voice taking on a tone more familiar to Berson, a more abrasive tone, which somehow put Berson quickly at ease: —— We are having the utmost difficulty getting arms ourselves. I can tell you that your own efforts, Jawardnik, have hampered us. I happen to be in the procurement line myself. Several of our suppliers, who used to sell us Polish Army revolvers at three thousand zlotys apiece, have been telling us lately, *Those crazy Jews offer us six and seven thousand, so what can we do?* Fifty pistols represent a lot of money and dangerous work, Pan Jawardnik.

—— We are grateful. We are very grateful. It is hard not to be avaricious when one's companions are being killed.

Under-Colonel Bierczyk evidently did not enjoy the implication, which Berson says he had not intended, that *his* companions were idle, and he answered, dangling an implication of his own:

—— We are waiting to fight when we can be effective.

—— And we are fighting before we are all slaughtered. (Berson says he felt very tired; he ached. Why was it necessary to spar over an act of succor? He asked:) When can I pick up your gift?

The colonel gave instructions, and Berson left, with repeated, profuse thanks: it had occurred to him that he was obliged to be demonstrative, against future possibilities. He put into his effusions what heart he could.

The moment Berson was out in the street again, he became wildly elated, he says. The force of the abstract gift, without the confusing overtones of his defensiveness toward the colonel, struck him all at once. Fifty pistols! A month's work for two couriers! Wait till he told Rutka! By the time Berson reached Gurnoslonska Street and Kucharski's apartment, he was walking on air and felt unusually sure of himself.

Kucharski: —— I have nothing for you today. I have been troubled by a migraine. The right side of my head. I have done very little this week.

Berson: —— This time I have something for you, Tomasz. And I'm afraid it may not help your migraine. (Berson tossed the Beretta onto Kucharski's table.) The Italian revolver you sold us. Useless. The sear is worn out. You will kindly replace the weapon.

—— Replace it? I sold it and you bought it. It's yours to replace.

—— You sold it—but not in good faith.

—— It is for the buyer to examine merchandise before he pays. A Jew should know that.

—— I am sorry, Tomasz, but I have been ordered to tell you

467

that unless you replace this pistol, the Jewish Fighter Organization will kill you. My commanders do not like being cheated.

Kucharski, surprisingly cool: —— You are not in a very good position to deliver threats.

—— The Jewish Fighter Organization will know where to find you. Anything that might happen to me would make no difference —if you are threatening me in return, as I assume you are.

—— No, Pan Berson (the old man was apparently contrite, but apparently not frightened), I would not like to say I had threatened you. You and I have known each other too long for such hard words. Leave the pistol with me. I'll see what can be done.

. . . Half an hour later, Berson burst into the girls' apartment in a kind of paroxysm of triumph. But his high mood was dissipated at once by the look he saw in Rutka's eyes; she was sitting waiting for him.

Rutka, standing up as Dolek entered: —— I am being followed.

—— Who is following you?

—— A man. The same man. I've seen him four times now.

—— Does he look like a *Schmaltzovnik*—or worse? [NOTE. EDITOR. *Schmaltzovniks* were Polish hooligans who made a profession of discovering Jews on the Aryan side and blackmailing them.]

—— A *Schmaltzovnik* would have accosted me by now. This one just follows. (Rutka now turned on Berson with an unexpected tone of reproach.) Oh, Dolek, have you made a slip? Have you talked about me to somebody? Could it have been the man at the brickworks?

—— Why do you think I would give you away, Rutka?

—— You're so careless, Dolek. You just don't think of things. Do you remember that Hashomer newspaper I gave you that time, before you were in the movement—how you left it around and talked with Noach Levinson and everybody else about it? Think, Dolek! What have you done?

Berson says he could not imagine having done anything to give away Rutka, of whom he had grown so fond. He retraced everything he had done in recent days, and questioned Rutka about what she had done. Having Kucharski freshly in his mind, Berson wondered whether the old ex-janitor might be working for

the Germans. That fine apartment; the old green sweater dis-
carded now for new grey worsted. But Kucharski didn't know
that Rutka was on the Aryan side. He might have had Berson followed back to the apartment once, where the trailer might have
picked up Rutka. Was the apartment—the best transient apartment Hashomer had ever had, prepared in three months' hard
work—no longer secure? Maybe Rutka had been noticed the day
she went to the ghetto wall to ask about the shooting. Maybe she
was right: maybe it was the man at the brickworks. Or maybe one
of her contacts. Surely it was nothing Berson had done. Could she
be imagining this peril? Had the load of work, on top of her pregnancy, been too much for her?

—— Have you seen him near here? Has he followed you to
this apartment?

—— He followed me here just a few minutes before you came.

—— Then come with me. I want to see this man.

Rutka, hesitating: —— You'll only expose yourself.

—— If the apartment is under observation, I am endangered,
Marysia and Lodzia are endangered, and all our work is endangered.

—— I don't want to go.

—— Mordecai is endangered.

—— I'm frightened. (Nevertheless, Rutka stood up, put on
her coat and galoshes, and took up her gloves.) We may not see
him. I hope we don't see him.

But they did; at least, Rutka said they did. They had walked
less than a block when Rutka looked around, gasped, and looked
ahead again. She whispered to Berson to look back on the opposite
side of the street; there was a man in a shabby brown overcoat and
a fur hat. Rutka's eyesockets looked hollow and purple. She
seemed frantic. Berson told her to take his arm. Her hand shook.
Berson waited until they reached the next street corner, where it
was not unnatural for him to look around. He saw the man she
described. Berson took two successive turns with Rutka; the man, it
eventually developed, was no longer behind them. Had the man
really been following Rutka? She was so palpably terrified, and so
categorical that that was the man who had been trailing her, that
Berson felt he had no choice but to take her at her word.

Berson sent Rutka early that afternoon to the Z.O.B.'s "Travel
Bureau"—a contact on lower Zelazna who made arrangements for

Jews to get in and out of the ghetto—and Rutka was taken into the "village" that night by way of the sewers. When Rutka left Berson, she still seemed convinced that he had made a slip of some kind. Berson asked her to report to Rachel about the Armja Krajowa gift and to explain all about his incendiary bottle. He wondered what she would really say. He decided to write a full report on Rutka's case and send it in by courier—if, indeed, Rutka's information did not cause him to be recalled at once. Berson and Marysia and Lodzia moved out of the apartment and went to live with a Polish woman named Wanda Szilepska, near Wilson Place in Zoliborz; a woman famous for her kindnesses to Jews. On the phone, next day, Berson told Pan Nudnik, in code words, that this move had been made. The day after that a note was delivered to Berson at Pani Szilepska's. It said, to his great relief and joy:

Congratulations on A.K. results. Please send us bottles and ingredients.

[NOTE. EDITOR. A.K. of course referred to Armja Krajowa.]
The message was signed Gebirtig. Berson knew that this was a false signature. It was the name of the author of a fierce song he and Halinka and the others had sung many an evening when he had been entertaining with his concertina—a song of exultation now for Dolek and his bottles:

Fire, fire brothers!
Our little town
Is burning down. . . .

EVENTS JANUARY, 1943. ENTRY JANUARY 28, 1943. FROM RUTKA MAZUR. In Rachel's bunker last evening I had a long talk with Rutka Mazur about the activities of our people outside. Rutka spoke with great feeling about what a relief it is to be back in the ghetto: that is a clue to the hazards this pregnant girl has sustained on the Aryan side. When convenient, I shall record here in detail her account of life on the outside; for now, I should like simply to put down a few of her observations on Berson. She was unstinting in her praise of him. She says that for a few hours, in her extreme agitation over the discovery that she had been followed, she accused him of having been somehow responsible for her having been discovered. She now regards that accusation as quite unfair and

470

regrettable. She says the whole situation of being stalked was so mad that she herself must have become irrationally suspicious. Partly she turned against Berson, she says, because she had depended on him so much, for advice, for encouragement, and for friendship, and when things went wrong, she felt that the person who had helped keep things right must have let her down.

Berson has become, she says, exact and meticulous in everything he does. He works now at the top of his powers, she says, because [NOTE. N.L. I consider this a penetrating estimate.] he is a man with a highly developed sense of responsibility who, for the first time in his life, has as much responsible work as he can handle. So often we think of conscience as a purely negative, or limiting, factor, something like a governor on a motor, that prevents more than certain amounts of wrong-doing. But conscience can be a motor in itself, impelling prodigies of right-doing—providing the "right" is not simply a visionary, unattainable, and egoistic dream, but is evident, practical, available, and negotiable; all of which it so abundantly is, at last, in Berson's case. Not that he is wholly happy now: how could anyone be in these circumstances? Rutka says he is often rather depressed. Yet he is using himself; he is using nearly all of himself. . . .

7

EVENTS JANUARY 26, 1943. ENTRY DITTO. N.L. It was not properly my business to make any comment, since I had been invited to attend the trial simply as recorder, yet a protest burst almost involuntarily from my lips. The trial seemed to have no order or form; it had no presiding officer, and he who was most insistent or vehement held the floor; above all, it followed no laws save those of hate, requital, and slander. About twenty men, most of them influential in the various parties of the ghetto, and all delegated by units of the Z.O.B., sat around Zilberzweig's living room, which has become a frequent meeting place for the National Committee and the Co-ordinating Committee. The meeting had been going along for more than half an hour when I first let my impatience be heard.

N.L.: —— But this is a trial by prosecutors, not by judges!

Kurtz, the Communist leader, who had been the most vituperative voice up to this point, turning to me with an expectant and polite expression: —— Then let us hear from the attorney for the defense.

[NOTE. N.L. The Communists have recently emerged more actively among us. The news we have heard of the fighting at Stalingrad has given them great character. One must say, at the very least, that they are tireless men.]

N.L.: —— I am not afraid to speak up for Dr. Zadkin. (I was in fact rather agitated, and I have the impression that my upper lip quivered, as when a mouse works his whisker-muscles.)

Kurtz: —— I suppose you know him well. Let's see, you have been a loyal worker in the *Judenrat* for some years, haven't you, Levinson?

N.L.: —— I know him. I have worked in the *Judenrat*. I am not quite clear what you are trying to impute to me.

Kurtz: —— Nothing. Nothing. Just keeping the record straight.

N.L., with what I hope was a trace of humor: —— Fraind Kurtz, I would remind you that *I* am making the record of this session—or rather, trying to.

—— Ah, yes. . . . Then, on Zadkin?

—— Dr. Zadkin is in the Supply Department, with which my archive has had little contact. I speak of Dr. Zadkin's distinguished career. I don't think we have a right to condemn a man to death on the basis of suspicions and insubstantial evidence. I think we have to judge the whole man. I ask you to consider Dr. Zadkin's life. He is one of the most astonishingly versatile men we have, and he has contributed to the good name of Jewish culture in many fields. He has been a constant scholar. He is a Doctor of Philosophy and a Doctor of Laws. He has written distinguished commentaries on the Torah, not to speak of several secular novels and plays of great merit. *The Peripatetic Mountain* was produced with success in Vienna in 1924, I think it was. He has composed excellent orchestral and chamber music. His paintings hang—or used to hang—in museums in Krakow, Katowice, and Lwow, that I know about. He is one of those men who acquire a smattering of everything—only, his smatterings are phenomenal. He played a distinguished part in the Jewish nationalist movement in Silesia. More than any of us, he is a complete man, really a remarkable man.

—— I only point out that he has been versatile also in politics: assimilationist, Polish nationalist, Socialist, Zionist—and who knows what else?

—— Is it wrong for a man to grow and change his mind?

—— When the changes are frequent and violent, a man almost invariably settles down as a Fascist.

—— What *is* a Fascist, Fraind Kurtz?

—— Anyone who does not know the definition of a Fascist by now is himself fledging as a Fascist.

At this point I turned away from my uneasy argument with this iron-minded man:

—— I submit to the gentlemen of this so-called court that the evidence against Dr. Zadkin which we have heard is not enough to justify his execution. We have heard that he has taken money to divert supplies from the ghetto and that he has made tremendous profits from his position, but we have heard no first-hand witnesses on these allegations. We have heard that he has been seen coming out of Gestapo headquarters on Aleja Szucha—but we have not been privileged to hear from anyone who actually saw him. We have heard that he has written reports for Dr. Merta in the Gestapo, but we have not seen any such reports or heard them described in detail. . . .

Kurtz: —— Perhaps you will subside long enough, Levinson, to let us finish presenting the evidence. I quite agree, this trial should be based upon concrete evidence, and not upon sentiment —not upon one's appreciation of a sonata our defendant may or may not have written in 1921. (And then, looking serene and patient, Kurtz took from his pocket and unfolded what appeared to be a carbon copy of a typewritten letter several pages long.) Gentlemen, let me read a few excerpts from this report. It is dated January 24, two days ago. It was acquired from Zadkin's personal file by one of our people. It is, as you have doubtless guessed, addressed to Merta. I quote at random: *Since the end of hostilities, the commanders of the Z.O.B. have been discussing their mistakes in these skirmishes. They feel that their greatest weakness was in communications, that one "Group" did not know what another was doing or planned to do, that consequently all action was opportunistic rather than according to set plan. As a consequence all fighters are being given certain addresses for listening posts in case of communications breakdowns in future actions. I have been unable to*

*get many of these addresses yet, but among them are Gensia 23,
Wolynska 41, Zamenhofa 12. Another weakness, the leaders feel,
was in technique.* They feel their groups were trying to fight
*"battles" rather than conduct simple street raids of a strike-and-
run type. We can look for skirmishes of this more evanescent nature in case of further fighting, I believe. Personally, I feel that the
Z.O.B. leaders do not recognize themselves one of their greatest
weaknesses: I refer to internal political divisions and suspicions.
The Socialist Groups do not trust (and therefore withhold proper
liaison from) Communist Groups; even within the Zionist persuasion, Hashomer deals rather trickily with Dror, and so on. . . .*
(Kurtz looked up from his paper.) I ask you, gentlemen, to consider whether this information jibes with the facts as you know
them—and whether this knowledge in German heads will harm us
or not. . . . Here, Levinson, I understand you are a Hashomer
man; this will interest you: *The Hashomer Groups are particularly
strong. This is at least partly a matter of personalities. Zilberzweig,
while still active from a policy point of view, seems to have less
influence in the military. Here the leaders are Y. Katz, whom I
have previously mentioned as being over-all commander of the
Z.O.B., J. Montefiore, A. Weiss, and R. Apt (this last a woman).*
(Kurtz turned to the last page of the report.) Here is Zadkin's conclusion: *The Fighter Organization is determined. Its discipline is
good. Y. Katz is insistent upon a rigid system of personal responsibility and demands utmost loyalty himself. The units are increasingly well provided with small arms. While these fighters cannot
possibly prevent you from carrying out any plans you may have,
they can make your work painful, expensive, and slow. I therefore
recommend: that if further evacuations are contemplated, they be
carried out by guile, persuasion, cunning, and trickery, and not by
force; by marmalade rather than the hand-grenade. You Germans
have shown yourselves skillful in the employment of your power,
but perhaps you do not sufficiently understand that we Jews are a
sweet-natured and gentle people. Weep before us, and we will go
to the* Umschlagplatz *in droves. Shout and shoot, and we will retire to our bunkers. (Addresses of bunkers will follow in next report.) Respectfully submitted, M. Zadkin, Ph.D., LL.D.* (Kurtz
looked up. He handed the papers to me.) You asked for evidence.

I examined the papers. I shook my head.

N.L.: —— I cannot say that this report was not handed to

Merta, or that it has not done us great harm. I only say that in a court of law this would be inadmissible as evidence. It is typewritten. There is not a word written in any handwriting, which might be identifiable as Dr. Zadkin's. Fraind Kurtz, you might have written this report.

Kurtz: —— You are humorous, Levinson, but I cannot laugh.

N.L.: —— I am obliged to wonder why you withheld this piece of "evidence" from us for so long. Why did you vilify Zadkin's character for half an hour before giving us anything like proof?

Kurtz: —— I thought proof would be unnecessary. I thought that intelligent men like yourselves would understand that the purpose of such a trial as this is not the weighing of any one man but simply the provision of an example before the world. Justice, you see, should be used as a prophylactic. It is preventive, not curative.

[NOTE. N.L. With this, I saw that my entire argument had been absurdly futile. The question, in this light, was not the actual guilt or innocence of Zadkin at all; it was whether his death would provide a good enough, or fearful enough, example for all other Jews. Therefore I suppose my praise of Zadkin's versatility was in fact an argument *in support* of his execution: the bigger the man, the more spectacular the example.]

N.L.: —— Forgive me. Gentlemen, forgive me. I am only the stenographer here. I have no right to take the floor. I will remain silent.

Thus ended the exchange between Kurtz and N.L. The trial continued. The questions I had raised weighed heavily with some of the discussants, I could see, but even a man with a double cataract could see that Kurtz's definition of justice had somewhat frightened a few of our brave men, and in the end, by a vote of fourteen to nine, Dr. Zadkin was sentenced to death as an informer and traitor. The trial and the sentence were to be announced by placard. The last paragraph of my minutes ended thus: *Avigdor Kurtz volunteered to have these placards drawn up, printed, and posted in prominent places.*

EVENTS JANUARY 27, 1943. ENTRY DITTO. N.L. The Chairman of the *Judenrat* sat at his customary seat at one end of the conference table in the council room. As always, he had before him a ruled memorandum pad and four or five freshly sharpened pencils. Chairman Grossmann is an undistinguished-looking man; underneath his nervous austerity—he looks like a hungry bird of prey—he tries to hide the personality of one most anxious to please. His hair, his skin, his eyes, his clothes, and his voice are all grey; only the tones and textures differ. In chairs around the conference table, and standing against the walls of the room, were the chiefs and subheads of *Judenrat* departments.

Engineer Grossmann: —— So far as it concerns me, you may all make your individual beds and lie in them. I speak, you realize, merely as your friend—I hope I am your friend—I have no authorization, no orders. (He paused.) Each man should make up his own mind. Some of you may feel that you will be safest for the time being if you remain under the aegis of this Council: you have your work cards. Others may wish to go into hiding or to join the Fighter Organization. I have been told that some of you have already done this last, though I find it hard to believe. (The Chairman picked up one of the pencils and began to draw on his pad little arrows and staircases.) I only wish to say that after my conversation this morning with Commissioner Haensch, I no longer consider the *Judenrat* a stable or permanent body.

Fostel of the Taxation and Revenue Department, an officious man who always has to be heard: —— Do you base this conviction on anything explicit that Herr Haensch said to you?

The Chairman: —— No, I base it, Pan Fostel, upon what I said to him. My friends, I ask you to believe me, that what I said to Commissioner Haensch was not spoken in an undisciplined moment of despair; I had thought about it very carefully. He came to me this morning to order us to levy a tax of one million zlotys *to pay,* he said, *for damage done to railroad rolling stock by Jews while being resettled.* (The Chairman slapped his pencil down hard on the pad, and looked up.) What would you have said, Pan Fostel? You are an expert on levying moneys. What would you have answered?

Fostel of Taxation and Revenue, clearing his throat: —— Collections have become difficult. The population has diminished. Their resources . . .

Grossmann, interrupting: —— *I* said that the Judenrat is no longer the authority in the ghetto. I said that we have no more real power. We command but we are not obeyed. (Engineer Grossmann waited to let this sink in.) *But what about your Jewish police?* the Commissioner asked me. I laughed in his face. This was the first time I have ever abandoned myself so far with the Commissioner. (Engineer Grossmann looked around with an almost pathetic expectation of approval and applause. But the faces around him were silent and grim.) The Commissioner asked me to tell him what *is* the authority in the ghetto, if not the *Judenrat*. I told him that if there is any authority at all, at present, it lies with the Jewish Fighter Organization. So he asked me to call a meeting of the Jewish Fighter Organization.

At this unanimous guffawing broke out in the council room.

—— Yes, my friends, I laughed for the second time in the Commissioner's face. I pointed out to him that in the eyes of the Z.O.B. it is not considered healthy to exist as a functionary of the *Judenrat*, and I asked him to consider the posters put up this morning. (The Chairman looked sharply around.) Where, by the way, is Dr. Zadkin?

Kohn of Sanitation: —— Do you expect him to be walking about this morning? He was always rather discreet.

Lanker, sub-chief of Vital Statistics: —— I don't like the past tense of that verb.

Kohn: —— One can guess that he is in hiding. One can hope that the present tense is justified.

The Chairman: —— The Commissioner had not seen the posters, so I had one brought in. When he read it, he understood my idea. I told him that we would continue to try to carry out his directives to the best of our abilities, but that he should henceforth not expect results as satisfying as those in the past. I told him that if we failed to carry out some order, he could execute us all, and yet that would not serve to get the *order* executed. He agreed and seemed most sympathetic and said that we should go ahead and collect the million zlotys for the damaged railroad boxcars. Pan Fostel, that is your problem.

Fostel of Taxation and Revenue: —— It's outrageous!

The Chairman, commiseratively: —— I know, *Collections have become difficult. The population* . . .

Fostel: —— No! I don't mean that! Damn the collections! What I mean is, after all we have tried to do for our fellow men, we have now to choose: either hide from the Germans, who want to kill us, or hide from the Jews, who also want to kill us; and probably be killed in both cases; either be Murin [Note. N.L. Murin of Auditing was deported on January 18, see entry January 24.] or be Zadkin. What a choice!

Events January 27, 1943. Entry ditto. N.L. Somewhere in the *Judenrat* building a woman screamed. I was up on the third floor talking with Mandeltort, and it sounded to us as if the scream had come from the ground floor. Felix and I looked at each other questioningly: should we go down and see what had happened, or should we be prudent and stay in Felix's office? Without speaking a word, we decided to compromise (and so, we found, did quite a few of the workers on the third floor): we hurried out to the head of the stairwell and peered over the edge and listened. We heard sounds of scuffling feet and exclamations, but these were not extraordinary sounds; it soon seemed safe to descend.

In the main corridor on the ground floor, a large crowd was gathered around the notice board which is customarily used for the organizational bulletins of the *Judenrat*, and for lost-and-found announcements. In time Felix and I were able to get close enough to see what had caused the woman to scream, and what was causing this sensation. A small cloth bag hung by a drawstring from a nail. The nail held also a piece of paper, on which was written, in a heavy crayon script:

FOUND

This bag contains the spectacles, wallet, identity card, key ring, and watch of Dr. Emil Zadkin. He tried to hide from the Z.O.B. He was found. The Z.O.B. is everywhere.

Events January 30, 1943. Entry February 1, 1943. N.L. It was day before yesterday, only three days after Engineer Grossmann's confession, when I received notice, as did about twenty others in the *Judenrat* (I flatter myself that the method of nomination was entirely chancy), that we were to report next morning for work in a construction battalion. One of the men in the Labor Department told me that this might mean anything from brutal foundation-digging to the lettering of draughtsmen's renderings, but that it might just as well mean deportation. At any rate, this order shook me from the apathetic state in which I had

478

resided ever since Engineer Grossmann's warning that the *Judenrat* had lost its potency. Like everyone else, I have a tendency to refuse to believe in catastrophe until the very last and worst moment. Of course I decided, when I received the notice, to evade it and hide. After burying my most recent acquisitions in the archive, I came here to Rachel's bunker, and she has said I may live here, though the bunker is already crowded. I have begun work on a monograph on the deportations: perhaps we can smuggle it to the outside world, as I have smuggled out directions for the discovery of my archive. It keeps me busy, anyhow. I work by day in the back room of the bakery. Since Menkes' death, Hashomer has put the bakery in the hands of a young apprentice baker who used to be with Haleazar: it was vital to keep the bakery operating, else the bunker might be lost.

So the *Judenrat* crumbles. Felix is staying on, for the moment, but he is into Zionist work and hopes to join the Z.O.B., and I imagine he will have "disappeared" in a few days. The Germans are calling out more and more *Judenrat* workers, as they called me. Also, voluntary defections from the *Judenrat* are increasing; very few continue to hope that a job there will save them.

I suppose it can be said that the *Judenrat* is collapsing because of what the Chairman told Haensch the other day about the *Judenrat's* loss of authority: neither the Germans nor its own employees any longer have faith in the organization. And I suppose it can be further argued that Engineer Grossmann was at least partly motivated, in what he told Haensch, by his own fear as a result of having seen the Zadkin poster. (God knows what he would have told Haensch had that little bag of effects been delivered to the *Judenrat* earlier that morning!) And so perhaps that harum-scarum tribunal, before which I made such a fuss, was the actual instrument of the *Judenrat's* downfall. Is the end of the *Judenrat's* authority a good thing? If so, does then a new light fall upon that "trial"? Would that make the decision on Zadkin's fate, if not more just, at least more justifiable? I was stupid not to see that that might have been the Communists' real purpose in instigating the "trial." But I am unable to answer my own questions. I must leave them as questions. Personally, as I think I have noted before in this record, I find myself placing a higher and higher valuation upon each single human life, the closer I come to the end of my own. It was the destruction of Zadkin balanced against the destruction of an authority that was in any case already moribund. I don't know. Maybe I am only trying to rationalize the position I took in the trial the other day, but I still think I may have been right. Zadkin was such a learned and various man, perhaps a genius; perhaps also a traitor. I don't know.

8

EVENTS FEBRUARY 3, 1943. ENTRY FEBRUARY 4, 1943. FROM RUTKA MAZUR. As soon as he was confronted with this choice, Mordecai went right to Rutka and talked it over with her. In ways, it would be easier for a man to choose between his wife and his own mother than to choose between his wife and his wife's mother; for in the latter case, if he loves his wife, he suffers through her.

Mordecai, describing to Rutka his interview with Niemann, the German who is now in charge of the bricklayers' labor battalion: —— He told me that I was lucky to have twenty-four hours in which to make up my mind. He said that I was lucky to have a choice at all, and he quoted the definition of *families* in the deportation orders from last July—that *only wives and children are members of families.* He said he was a loyal family man himself, and rather sentimental, and so he would give me a choice. He said I was lucky!

Rutka: —— Didn't you tell him about Mother's papers with the *Judenrat?*

Mordecai: —— Of course I did. I went and got them from your mother and showed them to him. He said he was sorry, he had to supervise the rooming arrangements of his battalion in his own way; that I appeared to be living in an illegal family unit; and that papers had nothing to do with the case. Besides, he said, your mother's papers were dated September 7, and that showed she had only got the job in the *Judenrat* in order to avoid the "Kettle"; in which he was right, of course. Then I showed him the document signed by Engineer Grossmann himself, giving your mother permission to live with us, and he said that was a Jewish scrap of paper and absolutely invalid. [NOTE. N.L. Indeed, the *Juden-*

rat is impotent.] Then I reminded him of his own oral authorization for your mother to live with us: you remember I was careful to ask for that when he was first put over us; but he said he hadn't thought the matter through at that time. What can you do in the face of such logic?

Rutka says she was utterly paralyzed by what Mordecai told her. Apparently Niemann, in combing through the records of all his Jewish charges, had come across the fact that Mordecai Apt had living with him two women: his wife and his wife's mother. Niemann had now given Mordecai one day in which to decide which of these two women should go to the *Umschlagplatz*. And Rutka realized that the fact that Mordecai told her about this indicated that he had already decided that her mother would be the one to go. Rutka is honest: she says she knew she *ought* to have taken matters in her own hands and to have reported herself directly to Niemann; yet something prevented her from doing this. She was so used to the idea of bringing a child to life that she could not face throwing away her own life, and its, too. Yet how could she think of throwing her mother's life away? Her mind began to go in circles.

—— Have you tried Noach Levinson?

—— He has quit the *Judenrat*.

—— What about Felix Mandeltort?

—— We can't risk anything official. They'll find out you're pregnant.

Rutka says that she and Mordecai talked and talked of things to do—but did nothing. Mordecai had decided, and Rutka felt as if her head were squeezed by a wood-clamp.

EVENTS FEBRUARY 3, 1943, EVENING. ENTRY FEBRUARY 4, 1943. FROM RUTKA MAZUR. The three were alone in their small room.

Froi Mazur: —— What in the world is the matter with you this evening, Mordecai? I've never seen you so grouchy.

Mordecai: —— I'm all right. Just leave me alone.

Froi Mazur: —— Why don't you and Rutka sing some songs? We need a little music.

Rutka: —— Let's do *Poverty Jumps*.

The two young people tried the song, but it had no vigor, and soon they broke off.

Mordecai: —— I'm not in the mood.

Rutka: —— We need Dolek's concertina.

Froi Mazur: —— All right, children. I'll tell you some old stories. Do you remember the story, Rutka, about Rabbi Nachemia Ben Kuth and his three temptations?

Rutka: —— Tell it, Mother.

Froi Mazur settled back in her chair, with her hands folded, and began:

—— Rabbi Nachemia Ben Kuth was a devout man, and his beard fell nearly to his waist, and he used to sit in his garden praying to the Lord to keep him humble. He was afraid of becoming proud of his humbleness. . . .

Rutka says that her mother's voice was soothing. Rutka had heard the story many times; the telling of it took her back to the low grey sofa in the house in Lodz—Stefan and herself (Schlome was too young) leaning against their mother, one on each side of her, as she told them folk tales. . . . Mordecai yawned. Rutka says that she herself felt a sweet, shameful sleepiness attacking her, and she fought it, thinking it callous. Her mother finished the story, and began another, in a different vein: about the *schlemihl* and the *schlimazl* trying to win fifty groszy by lifting the prize pig at the country fair, both struggling on their knees, the clumsy *schlemihl* rolling the huge sow over onto the hapless *schlimazl's* stomach . . . the long conversation between them . . . at the end the *schlimazl*, pinned still to the ground by the animal, grunting, *Oi woe! You give me all the work and expect fifty per cent of the profits?* Dutifully, Mordecai and Rutka laughed at the familiar outcome. Froi Mazur asked if she should tell yet another story. Rutka said she thought it was bedtime.

Mordecai, in an almost ominous voice, as if he had something very important to say (Rutka says she thought he was going to tell her mother everything): —— Mother Mazur!

—— Yes, Mordecai.

Mordecai hesitated. He stood up. He said, in an impatient tone that was incongruous with his words:

—— Thank you for the stories. . . . Let's go to bed.

At breakfast next morning, Mordecai was pale and irritable. At last he said:

—— Mother Mazur. Rutka. I must talk with you two.

Froi Mazur, quietly: —— I know, my boy. It is I who will go.

Mordecai: —— But . . . but Mother Mazur!

Froi Mazur: —— I know all about it, Mordecai. Yesterday, when you came to the *Judenrat* for my papers, I had a feeling that it was not for a housing permit. I finally got Secretary Mandeltort to find out from Niemann what was happening. I have decided for all of us, children. I am going.

Rutka: —— Mother, you can't. I should volunteer to go. (Rutka says that in the moment of utterance, she knew that her statement was false and shallow. The mood—the *should* instead of *shall*—gave away what she calls her hypocrisy.)

Froi Mazur: —— I am the one to go, my Rutka. (Her voice was exactly as it had been when she had told the folk tales.) You two are young. We Jews can't afford to hang onto the past. You are young. Soon you will have a baby. You will bring it up to love God, I am sure of that. . . .

Mordecai: —— Mother Mazur! Do you mean to say that you knew this last night, when you were trying to get us to sing and when you told us the stories? Mother!

Froi Mazur: —— Besides (and she pronounced these words firmly, as positively her last argument), besides, your father needs me, Rutka.

Rutka, in protest but also, she confesses, in acquiescence: —— Mother! Mother!

Froi Mazur reported at about noon to Niemann's office, and she was taken soon afterward to the *Umschlagplatz*. She carried with her nothing but a pair of slippers, symbolizing readiness for death, and a pair of candles, to make her prayers go straight to God.

9

EVENTS FEBRUARY 4–9, 1943. ENTRY FEBRUARY 14, 1943. FROM DOLEK BERSON. At first Berson considered Wanda Szilepska one of the kindest and gentlest women he had ever known. She was a widow of about fifty. Her face was of a waxy and freckled texture, ageless and soft-looking, and her reddish hair was parted in the middle and drawn back tightly into a braided bun at the back. She seemed delighted when Berson, Marysia, and Lodzia moved into her house. The girls had stayed with her before, while they had been apartment-hunting. Pani Szilepska said she had sheltered, at various times and for differing periods, about thirty Jews altogether, including a number of children, and she would reminisce affectionately about some of "my little kittens," as she called her Jewish guests, whether young or old; in the slang of Warsaw, sheltering Jews was called "keeping cats," and Pani Szilepska's insistent diminutive seemed to reflect her real affection for her guests. She had an anecdotal flair. She would sit all evening before a petit-point frame, working and talking, never looking at her hearers. Seldom did she speak about herself, except insofar as she had figured in adventures with "kittens." Berson did learn from her, however, that she had three grown children, all married and living in Warsaw, and all (this was something Berson says he felt rather than knew) somehow disappointing to their mother. In telling her stories about previous Jewish guests, Pani Szilepska displayed an enormous capacity for pity and sympathy; many of her narratives ended in not-quite-suppressed tears. It must have taken her many pains to procure rations for her guests, but she did, and by a canny use of spices and herbs, she made something exotic, something "specially for you," as she often said, out of each simple dish she prepared. She was a faithful Catholic, and one of the things she insisted upon from her guests was that they should spend an hour or so each day memorizing and reciting Catholic prayers. Pani Szilepska used to say jokingly that Christian prayers were just as important to Jews as Aryan identity cards, but there was no joke about the way she taught the prayers. She uttered them, even when she was repeating lines over and over, with her eyes tremblingly closed, speaking with fierceness and inner joy. She collected "rent" from her guests, but it was only twenty zlotys a week apiece, not nearly enough to pay for their food, but just enough, Berson sensed, so that she could keep them from feeling that they were objects of charity; she was very tactful and solemn about her collections, and one day Marysia recalled to Berson that during the girls' previous stay with Pani Szilepska, the landlady had pretended a serious fuss when Marysia had fallen a couple of days behind in a payment.

The first time Berson saw a hint of sharpness underneath Pani Szilepska's surface sweetness was on the evening of the third day he spent with her. For him, it had been a strenuous, nerve-racking day. He had been supervising the introduction into the ghetto of a box full of the Armja Krajowa revolvers. The weapons had been packed into the beautifully designed false bottom of a wagon carrying potatoes to the Breuer factory; the teamster was dependable; the guards at the gate had been thoroughly "fixed"; nothing could have been expected to go wrong—nevertheless, Berson had been tense all day. Even the phone conversation with Nudnik, late in the afternoon, confirming the receipt of the pistols, had been only a relief: the tremendous lift Berson had felt the first few times he had heard that his deliveries had been safely received now no longer came to him: novelty had been buffed off the experience. Furthermore, he had had an anticlimactic and tedious errand to do after the telephone call: buying some second-hand clothes for an expected courier, haggling over a price with a grasping Polish tailor. Then he had just missed a streetcar, and had had to stand nearly half an hour in the bitter evening wind. He looked forward, at last, to Pani Szilepska's hot supper and to her sentimental entertainments. She met him at the door.

—— If you please, take your shoes off outside. The melting snow on my floorboards . . .

Berson removed his shoes on the doorstep and stepped gingerly inside. To his embarrassment, he saw that the big toe of his right foot was altogether out through a hole in his sock. He wiggled it and looked up at Pani Szilepska with a broad, boyish grin, and he expected exclamations of concern and gentle rebuke and considerate promise from her. Instead he found himself looking into a face of steel.

—— Only one thing I expect from my cats. I expect them to be on time for meals.

Berson was on the point of explaining that he had missed a trolley, when he suspected that somehow Pani Szilepska was not really complaining about his tardiness; something else, something dark and irrepressible, was forcing its way out of her. During supper, only a few minutes later, she was charming toward him. She told stories that evening as if she were stroking fur. But as she spoke, Berson was haunted by the hardness, the deep, uncovered hardness, he had glimpsed in that moment by the front door.

In the following days, Berson saw a number of traits in Pani Szilepska that he liked none too well. For one thing, he noticed the extremely high incidence of personal tragedy in the stories she told about the Jews to whom she had given asylum: their stays with her had ended in accidents, discoveries, arrests; she wept buckets in the telling. Berson also noticed that Pani Szilepska showed almost no curiosity about Jewish culture, and considering the traffic of Jews through her house, about which she constantly boasted, it was extraordinary how little information she had on Jewish ways and accomplishments; Berson compared her in his mind with Pani Jadwiga Kowalska, the prim little Polish lady who had known so much about Jewish writers. One night one of Pani Szilepska's sons came to the house, and while Berson and the girls sat in hiding upstairs (Pani Szilepska had sent them up at the first doorknock), a strident argument went on and on down in the living room—and Berson heard shouts that were not in keeping with the tenderness Pani Szilepska wore in the presence of her Jews. Berson found that Pani Szilepska's attentions to him were in direct ratio to his indulgence of her anecdotes and his reactions to her dramatics: if he pretended great sympathy and pity (for her in her narrative bereavements, not for the tragic ends to which her "kittens" came), she would become marvelously gentle with Berson, but if he felt irritable and distrait as a result of an anxious day's work, and therefore gave her scant audience, she would become edgy, demanding, and childishly morose. And in the latter case, she was apt to tell stories that indirectly touched upon those things which were most dangerous to Berson—*Schmaltzovniks*, informers, the Gestapo, Treblinka, the warnings Poles were getting about sheltering Jews—and thus subtly to demonstrate how powerless Berson really was, and how much at her mercy.

Reluctantly, Berson came to the conclusion that Pani Szilepska gave sanctuary to Jews not out of conviction, not out of real understanding and altruism, but as a self-indulgence. It gave her excitement and a sense of power. Furthermore, the moment Berson arrived at this deduction, he had a distinct feeling that she knew how he felt. For her eyes and ears were nothing if not keen.

One morning Berson went to call on Tomasz Kucharski, to see whether he had replaced the Beretta and whether he had anything new. As Berson climbed the stairs to the former janitor's apartment, he was thinking about his strange hostess: she had seemed so genuinely sweet that morning: she had insisted upon giving Marysia and Lodzia their breakfasts in bed. She had said it should happen to every woman at least once a year. She had been playful with Berson in persuading him to carry up the trays, and though the whole performance might have been directed toward the gratitude the girls would show her, nevertheless it had been pleasant and harmless byplay. Berson was just wondering what tragedy there could have been in Pani Szilepska's life, what had happened to her husband, what was wrong between her and her children, when the door to Kucharski's apartment opened. A strange man stood in the doorway.

Berson: —— Excuse me. I think I have the wrong floor.

He began to back away so that he could look down the staircase to count the flights below. I have grown careless, he says he thought. And he thought: Maybe I *was* responsible for Rutka's being discovered.

The stranger, affably: —— You wanted Pan Kucharski?

Berson felt a rush of relief, which must have showed on his face, for before he could answer, the man went on:

—— He moved out three or four days ago, and we moved in day before yesterday. (Berson hesitated, waiting.) He left no forwarding address. Several people have come to call on him already. I inquired about the address. No forwarding address.

The complaisance the stranger had shown at first gave way to a look of annoyance as Berson still stood on the landing, held tightly by a queer vagueness and indecision. He would not get replacement for the Beretta now; that was too bad. Had Kucharski been frightened by Berson's threat?

The stranger, rather shortly: —— I'm sorry, I can't help you.

And the man closed the door in Berson's face. Berson went at once to the apartment of the only other contact to whom Kucharski had sent him. This man, too, had removed from his apartment; the apartment door was ajar; there was not a stick of furniture inside. Now Berson says he became quite agitated. He had several errands to do that day, but he felt unsteady, and he decided to go home to Pani Szilepska's. Perhaps if he could talk to stolid Marysia . . .

The girls were not at home. Berson went to his room and tried to work on a report. He had a sudden impression that the man who had answered the door at Kucharski's place was the same man who, in the shabby brown overcoat and fur cap, had been following Rutka; then at once he told himself that this must be a trick of imagination—after all, he had only seen the man in

487

the brown overcoat for a few seconds, and from nearly a block away.

There was a gentle knocking at Berson's door, and when he answered, the door opened, and Pani Szilepska came in. She was dressed in a handsome green housecoat with a black velvet collar; her hair was down and free and freshly combed. Her appearance surprised Berson, for when he had entered the house just a few minutes before, she had been dusting downstairs, in a drab smock and with a cloth over her head.

—— Come talk with me. You must be lonely here.

—— Thank you. I'm rather busy just now.

—— That's hardly a kind answer for a guest to give. (Pani Szilepska smiled sweetly.)

Berson says his temper gave way. He wondered if there weren't a few hours in the day when he could be lodger rather than guest. After all, he paid "rent." Trying to control his voice, he said:

—— Forgive me. I have some important work to do.

Suddenly Berson noticed pouring into Pani Szilepska's face, effusing from within almost like a blush, the malignant hardness he had momentarily seen the night he had come home late for supper. She said:

—— Come down and talk with me. (Her voice seemed to have no relationship to the look on her face: the hardness had been repressed from it, and it contained a note almost of winsomeness; the metal was still in her face, however.)

Berson decided he was in no position to press a contest with this woman; he rose and followed her downstairs. Seated in her usual chair beside the long-dead fireplace, with the apparatus of her needlework around her, Pani Szilepska began talking, in quite an amiable mood now, and she spoke, as she never had before to Berson, about herself. She said nothing directly; she dealt with what was on her mind in her customary anecdotal way. And even her anecdotes, now that she herself was at their center, were prolix, unclear, moody, and suggestive. She told a long story of something that had happened when she was nineteen, a story that seemed to be about a music lesson, a skating party on the Vistula, and an accident she had witnessed involving primitive automobiles; but Berson felt that a great deal of the burden of the story was contained in a wholly parenthetical sentence describing the crushing by her brother on the ice that day of an onyx cameo she had

488

owned; his skate had gone right over it. This sentence seemed important to Berson, not because of any cunning psychological interpretation he wished to put on it, but simply because there flitted across her face, as she spoke it, the hard, cold look Berson had come now to respect so much. She told several stories of her later life, and spoke quite pleasantly of her husband and her children, though now and then, like a momentary shadow—the black of a leaf blown across the face of a street lamp—the same coldness passed across her face. The monologue only ended at lunchtime. Berson never found out what was Pani Szilepska's trouble—or whether, indeed, there was any single, predominant key to the indefinite and perplexing sadness that seemed to be grinding at her soul. There was something sweet and warm in her; something too, that was nightmarish. At the end of the session, as Pani Szilepska started for the kitchen, she paused by the sofa where Berson sat, and leaning down and gently touching his arm, she spoke of the great pleasure he had given her by listening to her silly stories. And Berson says he thought: I should be able to purr!

EVENTS FEBRUARY 10, 1943. ENTRY FEBRUARY 14, 1943. FROM DOLEK BERSON. Berson walked from Pani Szilepska's house into Wilson Place, toward the streetcar stop. At the edges of the square the street signs always disturbed him. Wilson Place. Woodrow Wilson, he thought, drawing from his superficial schoolboy lore a sudden rush of emotion: a dream of peace. . . . Poland! And after the emotion, again, a familiar, quite trite, but still bitter bitterness. As Berson stood waiting for the trolley, three men joined him at the stop. They, too, seemed to evoke a vague schoolboy feeling in Berson: they were roughs, they were just like some of the bigger Polish boys at the Gymnasium. When the car came, the trio boarded with Berson and somehow all around him. The car was packed. One of the men had eaten raw garlic, and Berson grew quite giddy in his fumes. The three talked in a kind of code, using monosyllabic bits of slang and understood symbols, and they laughed jarringly. Berson had a sensation of being looked at rather much. He was glad when the car approached his stop. He shouldered his way toward the door, and as the car stopped, he stepped down. He noticed (but only vaguely, since the unpleasant ride was over and he now had his day's work on his mind) that the three men also got off.

Berson cut across to a sidewalk. He had not walked far when he realized that he was being followed, close behind, by more than one set of footsteps. He did not look back. There might not be anything worth looking at; perhaps the footsteps belonged to two or three people he had never seen; or, if they belonged to the three roughs, perhaps it was simply a coincidence that they had an errand along the same street as he.

—— Jew.

The word was unmistakable. Harshly but softly pronounced. Berson walked along, not looking back, trying by great self-control not to show the slightest quickening or slackening of his pace, though he knew that this unhearingness could only serve as a postponement. Very strongly he had the schoolboy feeling.

—— Jewish pig.

Berson walked on. This had been spoken more loudly. Berson knew that even a preoccupied Pole in his position would have heard that remark and would have considered it addressed to him. Ignoring the *Schmaltzovniks* too long would be just as much a giveaway as reacting too soon. One more remark. Berson came to a corner. He turned to the right. So did the steps.

—— Foreskin.

Berson spun around. The three men were grinning. One of them said to the others with a wink:

—— Not deaf after all.

Berson, trying to make it appear that he had heard something insulting, though it had not been quite clear what: —— Were you speaking to me?

The garlic-eater: —— Give, Jew.

Berson, as if incredulously: —— Did you address me as a Jew?

—— I said: Give, Jew.

—— How *dare* you call me a Jew?

To this question Berson summoned all the fury he could, and he was very glad to have moved from the stage of control to that of loss of control; now he could more safely tremble and grow hot. He began shouting at the three men, calling on passers-by to witness the libel, threatening police action, and vilifying the trio as blackmailers who would be sorry they had picked on a Pole. A few passers-by gathered to watch the show. In the presence of witnesses, the three men were more cautious, but they seemed not to be intimidated by Berson's shouting. Berson had often discussed *Schmaltzovniks* with other couriers, and he had heard of enough cases in which the blackmailers, unable to frighten the Jew immediately and confronted by outsiders, had backed down, so that he had long since decided to try a bluff; and now, committed to it, he had to decide what to do in the face of the evident fact that these three had not been sufficiently shaken by it. He said to the men at last:

—— You come with me to the police station!

And Berson shouted that he would get the best lawyers in Warsaw after them.

The three men exchanged looks. One of them shrugged. The garlic-eater said:

—— Let's go. To our friends the police.

One of the others, to Berson: —— If you are right, we spend a night in jail. If we are right . . .

Berson saw a certain reasonableness in this unfinished balance. He knew that it would be fatal, or at best terribly expensive, if he fell into the hands of the police. He and the three men began walking back in the direction from which they had come. They turned through an alleyway. Berson wondered whether the men would drag him into a doorway and pull down his pants to see for themselves, as he had heard that blackmailers often did. But they walked through to the bigger street beyond. Suddenly— thinking, he says, of us his friends within the "village," of the bakery, of Rachel, of his unavenged friend Menkes, of N.L.—Berson said:

—— All right, how much do you want?

The garlic-eater, in a rapture of sarcasm: —— Oi! Such slander! Dirty blackmailers! The best lawyers!

—— How much?

—— To begin with, one thousand zlotys for each of us.

—— I don't have that much.

In an ironic vein, one of the men offered to serve as Berson's bodyguard and stay with him until he sold something and did have three thousand. Then the four of them haggled, as if over the price of a vegetable, until finally Berson drew from his pocket twenty-five hundred zlotys, with which he had intended to pay that day for some ammunition.

—— Here. Cash.

At a nod from the garlic-eater, one of the others took the money.

The garlic-eater: —— Good day. Have a pleasant trolley ride to Wilson Place.

By which remark, Berson understood that he might look for the three again, perhaps on that streetcar, perhaps. . . . *To begin with*, the garlic-eater had said. . . .

Berson called Nudnik on the phone as soon as he could and indicated in code that a replacement should be sent out for him and that he was returning to the ghetto. He walked back streets the rest of that day and returned all the way to Wilson Place on foot after dark. At Pani Szilepska's late that night, he managed to get the girls aside and whisper to them something of what had happened. He told them to leave Pani Szilepska's for good the next day and not to tell her where they were going; he also told them not to try to re-establish contact with Kucharski—neither to go to his old apartment nor to see him if his name should be given again by a contact.

That night Berson slept very little. During half-sleep, the fearfulness of his encounter with the *Schmaltzovniks*, or rather, of the narrowly missed subsequences of that encounter, came to him, as it had not during the exigent ten minutes of the interview itself; and he lay perspiring. Later, to keep his mind off the *Schmaltzovniks*, Berson began thinking about other things—about Pani Szilepska, mainly. He was still curious about her. Snatches of her narratives came to him, trivia from her life: a view of Saxon Garden in the spring, her small son running along laughing, looking behind him, and running into a lamppost—not badly hurt; the first time her husband had lost a job, the problem of his pride; . . . *and the skate went right over it, and it sounded like a chicken bone being broken*. . . . Berson says he felt strangely warm toward Pani Szilepska; and then he was afraid of her.

When morning came, and the girls had already left, as if for a single day's work but actually for good (Berson waved to them casually on their departure, though he knew he would not see his dear and crafty companions soon again, if ever), and when Berson himself was nearly ready to go, he was caught up by both tenderness and curiosity, and on an impulse, of which, he later realized, the risk was insanely great, he said:

—— I'm leaving you today, Pani Szilepska.

—— No! (A look of concern and pain rushed into her face.) Something has happened to you. You are in trouble.

—— Not in trouble. (Berson says he got this off easily.) Just Jewish.

Then, in what seemed to be a kind of cramp of pity and fear, Pani Szilepska rushed forward, slipped her hands around Berson's right arm, pulled herself against him, and, with her face pressed to his shoulder, said:

—— What is there about me? Why does this happen to everyone my life touches? Why? Why?

Berson looked down at her face. It had in it, under the superficial agony and deep in the tear-filled eyes, a look of perplexity; along with the self-pity a look that hinted of delight and even of ecstasy; at the same time, and dominant, that hard, cold look. The face was horrible. Berson tore himself away and rushed out of the house.

That day Halinka Apt was sent outside, and Berson came back inside.

10

EVENTS MARCH, 1943. ENTRY MARCH 14, 1943. N.L. We wait in our bunkers. We make preparations, and we wait.

EVENTS MARCH 14–15, 1943. ENTRY MARCH 15, 1943. N.L.; AND FROM RACHEL APT. Throughout the ghetto the widening network of bunkers contains an ever greater population. Our own phalanstery is seriously crowded. I guess nearly forty-five people sleep in our bunker every night. (Rutka and Mordecai Apt have moved in with us, among many others.) Though Berson gave us an excellent ventilating system, the air quickly becomes foul when it is necessary, as it sometimes is, to close the inlets and outlets. Also, we find that all this proximity puts great strains upon our patience: one person in a vile humor can bring the whole crowd's temper tumbling down.

It has been a delight to have Berson back among us; his stories of the work outside, on top of Rutka's, have helped our morale enormously. He seems much strengthened, both physically and in spirit, by his "vacation." But he speaks, as did Rutka, of the fierce happiness and tranquillity he feels at being back inside the wall.

For a few minutes each evening, the vents are closed and Berson plays on his concertina, ever so softly, for the people in the bunker. The night he returned there was a formal debate as to whether fifteen minutes of air or fifteen minutes of music would be more important to the occupants. They voted overwhelmingly for music. With the vents open, the concertina's narrow notes can escape as far as the street; that was tested. Even with the ducts shut off, Berson has to play quietly. Since his return from the Aryan side, Berson has played mostly classical music and cool music: Bach, Mozart, Haydn, Schubert. The first night he tried some melancholy Hebrew songs, and he had to break off quite soon because of his own weeping. So now he confines himself to neat, orderly, fine-lined, unemotional music.

As Berson played for us last night, I watched Rachel. She lay on her back on a straw-covered wooden bunk: hers is what Berson calls the Bunk of Honor, nearest the floor and nearest the "front door." Her small mouth was pursed; her eyes open. She lay unreactive; unlistening. [INSERT. FROM ENTRY FEBRUARY 15, 1943. FROM RACHEL APT. I have asked Rachel about her thoughts during the music last night. She recalls them: Wladislaw Jablonski. The talkative boy, son of the convert, the Jewish-looking boy who was brought up a Catholic, has become a problem, and she was thinking about him, at first. Wladislaw lives in the bunker. He wants, desperately and volubly, to join the Z.O.B. But Rachel says she has felt that he might be a risky addition. He is a mixed-up boy. He wants to prove to the world that he is a good Jew, and he rails unnaturally and monotonously against his father. He is trying to do everything at once: he is taking Hebrew lessons from N.L.; he is trying to learn Jewish rituals from Rutka and from an older man in the bunker, named Granzelmann; he wants to kill all the Germans at once. Rachel says she has been afraid that if he were admitted to her Fighter Group, he might try to do something excessively heroic that would endanger everybody. . . . From thinking of Wladislaw's conflict with his father, Rachel moved naturally to thoughts of her own father. She says she literally shudders with a kind of embarrassment every time she thinks of her father (now she has a weird picture of him in her mind, with diamond rings on his fingers and sapphire shirt studs, sleeping in manure in a horse-stall; a picture that has not been eradicated by her knowledge that her father has gone into Germany). She does not hate her father; she is sorry for him and on guard against his strain in herself. As for Halinka, who was always the favorite, Rachel reflected that Halinka had just recently begun to question the values their father had praised in her. Her new lover-father, Zilberzweig, was waking her up. . . . An idea for young Jablonski! Some solo work. If he was to be so brave, let him be brave on a project that would involve only one or two other people. The electric mine. The last of the parts was supposed to be smuggled in within a day or two. A wonderful solution. . . . Strange to think of the change in Halinka lately: she was doing serious and dangerous work as a courier on the Aryan side. Zilberzweig had been very good for her, and she had been very bad for Zilberzweig. . . .]

There was a harsh knock on the "front door"—the wooden barrier at the base of the tunnel from the furnace in the bakery. Berson's playing stopped. Not the code knock: a repeated and insistent pounding. Rachel jumped up from the bunk. Others, too, were on their feet. I myself wondered if the playing had been audible from the street. The door swung open and a German soldier, hunched and grey-on-grey with ashes on his uniform, tumbled out into the bunker, stood up, and heiled Hitler with a somehow caricatured salute: his stomach stuck out too far.

I saw at once that the man in the German uniform was Mordecai, and I laughed. But there were others in the bunker who were neither so close nor so quick. There were screams and several people rushed for the second room and the "back door." Then Mordecai said in a loud voice in Yiddish:

—— Friends! Friends! It is only Mordecai. It is only a joke.

Things quieted down. Those who had been frightened laughed eagerly at the practical joke, to cover up their own embarrassment. Mordecai, evidently sensing that his humor had been macabre, began to explain that this was one of a score of uniforms that had been stolen from the Roerich factory, that it had been assigned by the Z.O.B. to Rachel's group, that he was sorry if . . .

I saw Rachel spring quickly across the room. Then I saw Rutka on the floor, lying on her right side, writhing, her thin face

495

distorted, the veins of her neck standing out like those of a runner in the last spasmodic paces of a sprint. Rachel had jumped to her, and now Mordecai followed. Rachel bent down and took Rutka's hand, but was obviously helpless. Someone beside Rutka said she had been knocked down by one of the people who had bolted for the other room. Rutka ground her teeth and muttered, and the tenseness continued; Mordecai, evidently thinking she was dying, knelt beside her and rocked back and forth, wailing and cursing himself. A crowd of strangely apathetic onlookers stood around. Then I saw a queer, exultant expression appear on Rachel's face: she says she suddenly realized what was happening, and she felt a hysterical joy welling up in her chest and throat and it burst out on her face in a wild smile and tears all at once. She put her hand firmly on Mordecai's shoulder and said loudly near his ear:

—— Go in the other room and get out of that uniform. The baby is coming.

Mordecai looked up. His face became more frightened-looking than ever. He went tremblingly into the other room.

The first pain was exceptionally long. When it relaxed, Rutka opened her eyes. For a few moments she seemed to be trying to clear her brain, then she said fearfully:

—— He looked like Mordecai! Has he gone? What happened?

Rachel soothed her, and explained that it had been Mordecai, and told Rutka that it was only a joke. Rutka apparently did not yet understand what had happened to her, but in a few minutes, as the second pain approached, she knew.

Rutka, gripping Rachel's hand: —— Rachel! Rachel!

Rachel: —— I know, dear. Lie on your back.

Rutka turned onto her back and looked up into Rachel's eyes with a frightened, questioning look. Rachel says she supposes Rutka was afraid, as she was herself, because the baby was coming two months early. Rachel said:

—— Here. Hold my hand again.

Now the full anger of the second pain poured into Rutka. She took hold of Rachel's hand with both of hers, and Rachel thought Rutka was going to break her bones. This time Rutka's face became contorted, but, now that there was understanding in her suffering, she was silent and even, it seemed, triumphant. Rachel

496

tells me that for a moment she felt a terrible thrust of uneasiness, an abominable sensation: she thought she wanted Rutka to die; then she became remorseful and frightened, and she thought she could not stand by and witness hours of this agony. As the pain reached a climax, she felt again that she hated Rutka. She began to weep.

The cramp let go and Rutka, with a fierce eagerness, still fresh and strong, said to Rachel:

—— There are clean rags and a cake of soap in my bunk. . . . Pray for me, Rochele. . . .

Rachel says that as she turned to go for the things, she was able, suddenly, to face her own feeling. She realized that because of her ugly face she herself would never know these excruciating transports; she was jealous: that was why she had felt that loathing and discomfort. Knowing this, she was suddenly relieved and even happy. She knew she could be of some help now.

Rutka's labor lasted seven hours. Froi Granzelmann, a comfortable, grey-haired, dumpy woman, took charge; she kept saying she had had seven children, she should know what to do. With the help of some of the men, she made a lying-in couch of straw and blankets and a Polish Army poncho belonging to one of the fighters; and Rutka was lifted onto it. There was no question of privacy. Several curious people stood around watching; the more queasy ones went into the other room. Mostly Rutka fought her agonies obdurately. Once, about four hours along, she shrieked: she had had enough, enough, enough. In the lull after that crisis, I spoke to her: I warned her not to lose herself so far again as to cry out like that.

—— No torment, dear girl, is equal to the lives of all your friends.

[NOTE. N.L. Rachel says she was not surprised to see me so firm with Rutka; but she was surprised at my tenderness.]

Rutka nodded weakly, as reply to me; and was thenceforth almost silent in her pains: even her moans seemed to be controlled. Mordecai could not bear to watch her and yet he could not bear to be in the other room; he shuttled in a frenzy. For a while, in Rutka's fifth hour of labor, with pains coming every three minutes or so, she compounded his anxiety and confusion by cursing him during her cramps and praising him between them.

497

The baby was born just after midnight, in the first hour of the fifteenth day of March. It is a boy. He is small and weak. His name is to be Israel.

EVENTS FEBRUARY–MARCH, 1943. ENTRY MARCH 15, 1943. N.L. Almost surreptitiously, toward the end of February, the Germans resumed the deportations. So closely did they adhere to the pattern recommended in that letter allegedly written by Dr. Zadkin—guile instead of force, *marmalade rather than the handgrenade*, as the letter said—that I blush every time I think of my objections to the Zadkin trial (even though I am *still* unconvinced of the rightness of his execution).

Now the Germans started working on a piecemeal basis, evacuating one factory at a time. They are using every possible means of persuasion, and they conduct a kind of softening-up campaign in each factory beforehand, working through the plant superintendents and foremen, to try to make the workers believe that the productive elements of the factory will be moved to two new manufacturing centers in Trawniki and Poniatow and will continue operations there. Since the various factories are more than ever separate little ghettos, and since intercommunication is exclusively through the underground, the majority of the surviving Jews only hear of an isolated action after it has taken place. It is hard to rouse the whole to a pitch of concern over one of its parts.

The first large plant to be evacuated in this phase was Schultz, at Nowolipie 44 and roundabouts. The Germans got a fair haul there; the workers seemed to believe the Trawniki-Poniatow sales talk. But when the Germans came to deport the workers of Hallmann, a few days ago, they got quite a surprise. That factory was well organized; the Bund had been active there building up counter-propaganda, and when the appeal came to report for resettlement, only twenty-seven workers volunteered out of more than a thousand. The Germans were so unprepared for this, and so furious at it, that they fell back on force to root out the others, but again they were amazed. More than half the workers had disappeared. Some of them had gone into bunkers. Most of them had "gone wild," as we say. They had escaped into hiding in the "wild areas" of the ghetto—the previously evacuated spaces outside of, and between, the factory enclosures. I have a feeling that the

498

Zadkin Procedure, if I am just in attributing the new methods to my late colleague, will not be followed for long. After all, Jews are also capable of guile.

EVENTS MARCH 21, 1943. ENTRY DITTO. N.L. As surely as if he were king of our dingy refuge, the infant dominates the lives of the forty-three people in our bunker. The ventilators are opened when he sleeps; they are closed when he wakes crying and hungry. To help the mother breastfeed him, special foraging, bartering, and smuggling parties have been organized: Rutka eats fairly well. The baby, having been born prematurely, and of an undernourished mother, is precariously tiny. There were two anxious days, his fourth and fifth, when he lay listless and apparently feverish, eating little and spitting up what he ate; then suddenly he mended and was voracious, putting demands upon poor Rutka that she was unable to meet. The baby's every act has an audience: onlookers smile at his marvelously eager feeding; Mordecai tries to discover filial devotion in his gaseous smiles; the women stand by criticizing the way Froi Granzelmann bathes him, with rags dipped in water that has been warmed up in the bakery oven; the men have decided that he is well set up in the manly line; bunkermates discuss his bodily functions as naturally and soberly as if they were seaside folk discussing the comings and goings of wind and tide.

This morning, tiny Israel even captured, as it were, the ceremony of the swearing-in of new members of Rachel's Fighter Group. The candidates were Dolek Berson, who, though he has been working for Z.O.B. all this time, was outside the ghetto when the previous swearings-in took place; Wladislaw Jablonski, delighted to be admitted at last; and a nine-year-old boy named Maksi, whose family have all been deported long since, who has lived "wild" for weeks, and who was brought in to the bunker just the other day by one of our women. A few of the members of Rachel's group felt some time ago the need of some act of fealty —they wanted to symbolize *Kiddush ha Shem*: dying in the name of the Lord—and I worked out an oath adapted from a passage in the First Book of Maccabees. In the back room of the bunker, in the dim light of a single small carbide lamp, this morning, Rachel stood holding forward a revolver in her right hand, and with their right hands Berson, Wladislaw, and small Maksi clasped hers and each other's and the revolver; their arms were like four spokes. In a solemn, trembling voice, Rachel said:

—— Do you swear on this our weapon that if you feel fear, you will withdraw then from the field of battle, in order that we may have no cowards among us, and that for the honor of the Torah you will . . .

From the next room, suddenly, came a penetrating squeal. Israel had wakened.

Berson, unceremoniously: —— My God! The ventilators!

And he broke away in a rush, and went and closed the vents. By the time he had come back, and the four had resumed their stiff tableau, the baby was at Rutka's breast and was silent. Rachel began the oath again. Again she had spoken only part of it when the infant began screaming anew. Several of the witnessing fighters ran into the other room, as if some urgent alarm had been sounded, to see what was the matter.

Berson, in mock devotion: —— Hear, O Israel . . . !

By now the attempt at ritual had become only ridiculous. Rachel shrugged her shoulders and in a womanly way simply embraced the three, first Maksi, then Wladislaw, then Berson, as if to indicate that she, Rachel, captain-general of these Maccabees, gladly took them to her heart and ranks.

N.L., standing by: —— You'd better swear in the baby first: he's a one-man resistance movement.

EVENTS MARCH 17–22, 1943. ENTRY MARCH 23, 1943. FROM MORDECAI APT. Mordecai, the new father, and Wladislaw, the new fighter, have pooled their zeal and planted the mine together. Mordecai says they discussed for many hours the best place to put it. They wanted, above everything, to place it at the most dreadful spot in the ghetto, at the entrance to the *Umschlagplatz*, but they realized that with twenty-four-hour sentries there, both on Zamenhofa Street and just within the *Umschlagplatz* itself, the opportunity for digging and burying the mine there simply would not exist. In any case, they rationalized, it would be a rare occasion when they could blow a mine at the threshold to the *Umschlagplatz* without hurting Jews as well as Germans. They finally settled on Gensia Street, at a spot where the paving blocks had in any case been knocked out of place by a fragment of a German bomb, back during the siege, and where the disturbance of setting the mine and the wires to it under the surface of the street would not be noticed. This place had two advantages: Gensia Street was one of the largest interior thoroughfares of the ghetto, where a whole German unit might be caught on the march; and the bomb-scar was just opposite a house containing an attic strongpoint of Hashomer, a convenient observation point from which the mine could be detonated. The pair worked gradually and happily night after night. From the moment they began work, Wladislaw spoke no more of his father and his shame. The effort, however, did not keep Mordecai from talking about his son and his pride. Thus the generations.

EVENTS MARCH, 1943. ENTRY MARCH 20, 1943. FROM DOLEK BERSON. Berson has become the master of an intricacy such as he himself could not have imagined a few months ago. Communication is the obsession of the Z.O.B., and since it is assumed that in any future action the Germans will control the streets, the Z.O.B. high command decided, at about the time when Berson returned to the ghetto, to perfect communications above and below the streets, and it became the task of Berson, with his bent for hiding things, to co-ordinate all the tunnels and attic-connections and bunkers and bunker accesses and sewer-tappings and upstairs forts and roof-drawbridges and rope ladders and interdicted staircases and inter-cellar passages. He keeps all these things in his head, and he remembers, separately, the Hashomer systems and the Communist nets and the Socialist ant-works and the complexities devised by "wild" people; as well as the channels, if any, connecting these separate entities. The same corner of Berson's mind that is able to memorize the most involute music seems to have no trouble with these details and this whole; indeed, the systems hold a sort of musical-creative fascination for him: he says that some groups build neatly, symmetrically, delicately, like Mozart, and others are undisciplined, roundabout, interminable, grandiose, like Wagner or Mahler.

During the last few days, Berson has been breaking through a few final barriers, so that most of the major systems will be joined together: it will be possible to travel from one street to another, and sometimes for two or three blocks, by hidden routes. So confident is Berson of his knowledge of the communications-works that he can take a worker into a cellar, or into an attic, and set him penetrating at a given place in a given direction, and leave him, certain that the worker will emerge, sooner or later, in another specific cellar or attic of the Z.O.B.

For these reasons Berson himself happened to be working, alone, in the middle of last night, in a third-floor room in a house on Wolynska Street, not far from the bakery (he had reached the room from Rachel's bunker by interior channels), mining through a brick wall with a hammer and cold chisel, keeping within a square he had drawn on the wall, kneeling at his work in a blacked-out room with a three-quarters muffled kerosene lantern for only light. He had been working about an hour when he was startled to hear tappings on the opposite side of the wall—was startled, that is, until he remembered that he had marked off a square on the obverse side of the same wall, and had instructed the Dror Group which had a strongpoint in the next building to cut through this wall at their convenience. Berson says he sensed a kind of childish humor in the sounds the chisel made on the other side of the double-thick wall. It imitated the sounds his own chisel made. It echoed his rhythms.

Evidently neither pounder knew a code; Berson certainly did not. Yet to him this conversation was delightful. Here was a contact between human beings separated by a solid wall on a dark night in a world of peril. One could know, merely by the eager and playful replies, that the man or woman beyond the wall, whatever his or her political tendencies or character or endowments, wanted to establish a rapport. The voices of the cold chisels spoke a desire for compatibility. Berson says (in his far-fetched vein) that he supposes if one listens very carefully one can hear similar tappings faintly on both sides of the wall around our ghetto.

It was nearly three in the morning before the walls were broken through. Berson's chisel went through first. He enlarged the hole to a circle with a diameter of the span of a hand. Suddenly, while he rested, a face appeared pressed into the hole. In the moody, dim light, Berson saw the face and was dreadfully taken aback. It was not a man or a woman at all! A beast. A kind of bulldog. A horrible visage of skinfolds and damp nostrils and popping eyes. Oh God, it was Schpunt.

Berson, quickly, in a voice that even to him seemed fantastically normal and social: —— Thank you for covering my departure from the ghetto last October. I've been wanting to thank you.

Schpunt, in one of his ambiguous tantrums, appearing to be both deeply angry and irresistibly whimsical, and seeming to refer both to the work on this wall and to a more general and philosophical labor: —— If you think that we're finished working, your teakettle has a crack in it.

EVENTS MARCH 20, 1943. ENTRY DITTO. FROM RACHEL APT. The little boy, Maksi, who has become a messenger for us, stood beside Rachel's bunk, and what he said to her with a perfectly straight face was, on this particular evening, almost the last straw:

—— There's a German upstairs to see you.

The atmosphere in the bunker earlier this evening was one of sickliness and ill-will. The baby, who at times has been such a diversion, had been cranky, noisy, and implacable all day long. It had been necessary to keep the ventilators closed and the air had become foul, redolent of infantile urine and adult sweat and the rank breath of hungry people. We had noticed just this morning that the bunker's food reserves—established first by the baker Menkes—are beginning to run low, and though we sent out our most skillful people to forage, all we had acquired by evening was five liters of flour and a large sack of horse-oats. There were complaints and recriminations from a few who seemed to feel that they had contributed more than their share to the original larder of the bunker and who therefore now thought they should be exempted from any further effort. Everyone had a headache this evening. Mostly the people lay in their bunks, afraid of their own fears. Berson said he was too busy to play any music, though it seemed to Rachel, she says, that he was not too busy, only too depressed; he went out. In a wild argument about whether the baby should be circumcised or not, Rutka and Mordecai lost their tempers with each other before all the tenants of the bunker; Mordecai thought circumcision would be folly in the time of an anti-Jewish holocaust, and Rutka said that Mordecai was as supine as his father. Others were drawn into the squabble: I myself said at one point that Spinoza considered circumcision alone sufficient to keep the Jewish nation alive. A woman asked bitterly:

—— What use to keep alive a nation of moles and attic-mice? That's the way we live.

Rachel says she had felt ill all day, and she had had neither the pluck nor the wits to lift the spirits of her bunkermates.

Rachel: —— What kind of a German?

Maksi: —— Civilian.

Rachel: —— What does he want?

Maksi: —— Says he is a courier sent by the Joint from Budapest. He gave me this for you to show his good faith.

Maksi handed Rachel a small rectangular package. She unwrapped it. Inside were several American fifty-dollar bills.

Rachel, in a plaintive voice: —— How do I know that these are genuine?

Maksi, who could hardly be expected to answer that, shrugged. Reb Moshe Granzelmann and I examined the money. There were twenty bills, all fifties. They looked all right. Slowly Rachel got up from her bunk. Her head throbbed, she says. She crawled up to the bakery through the furnace. In the oven-room she found a medium-sized blond man, rather deadbeat-looking, with a stubbled chin, friendly in expression. At first Rachel was suspicious of him. He began by asking whether a dishonest man, or even a Gestapo-man, would have taken the trouble to deliver a thousand American dollars to her. He then gave the code names of Istanbul, Budapest, and Berne representatives of Jewry, which she knew. He explained why he, a German, was working as an underground courier (*Even,* he said, *between Jews—especially between Jews.*); he seemed a plausible anti-Nazi. Finally he repeated back to Rachel some code messages she knew the Z.O.B. had sent to Budapest, the receipt of which had been confirmed by the most trusted couriers—among the messages, one she would never forget:

Uncle Yitzhok [NOTE. N.L. Yitzhok Katz.] *is bringing up little Judah.* [NOTE. N.L. The Maccabean warrior Judah, the Hammer; meaning, of course, the Z.O.B.] *He has acquired lots of little toys for him and Judah is learning to play with them very nicely.*

And so at last Rachel said she trusted the German.

The courier: —— The money is for you. You are to keep it.

Rachel: —— Why for me?

—— I only know that we had a message from Switzerland saying that this was for the one called Little Mother, and they tell

me that is you. There is more (the German smiled) for Uncle
Yitzhok.

Rachel asked the German if he would be returning soon to
Budapest, and he said he would. She asked him then to take with
him directions as to where to find N.L.'s archive. The German
said she could take them herself: he said he was authorized to
escort her to Budapest. It was said that she was needed in Palestine. [NOTE. N.L. I am not sure precisely what this "need"
could be. I think various couriers must have carried to the outside
world some romantic stories about our Rachel, so that representatives of the Joint Distribution Committee decided to try to save
her. The money came from the J.D.C., at any rate. I understand
that money has been sent to others of our leaders here, besides,
as formerly, to organizations.] The courier said he would practically guarantee to get Rachel through as far as Budapest. From
there . . .

—— From there (he screwed his face up into an enigmatic
expression) not my territory.

Rachel says she thought of the vile-smelling bunker below.
She felt hunger. Her dress was dirty. Death was certain, and her
dear friend Dolek had been too grumpy this evening to play the
concertina. She thought of her small brother David "walking"
across Czechoslovakia. She thought of her father sweeping the
floor in some German house (perhaps); and of the bag of oats for
cattle on the food-storage shelf in her bunker. And for a moment
she thought of the symphony orchestra playing on the balcony of
the beautiful modern building on the shore of the petroleum lake.

—— With my face? With my Semitic face? I wouldn't dare
make such a trip with my face.

—— I can only give you facilities, not courage.

—— Nu, then I'll have to stay.

—— I suppose (the deadbeat courier shrugged) that takes
courage of a kind, too.

Rachel, shaking her head and weeping: —— No!

EVENTS MARCH 23, 1943. ENTRY DITTO. N.L. Today
was the eighth day of the child's life. Two straight chairs had been
brought down from the bakery and had been set against the row
of bunks on the west wall of the subterranean "front room." Berson, who was to be the Sandek, sat in one of them. The bunker

was crowded. N.L., as the Quatter, brought the infant in from the other room, to which Rutka had been removed; the baby was by chance gurgling and staring contentedly. I put the baby down on the empty chair as Reb Moshe Granzelmann, the Mohel (He had been chosen because he had circumcised a score of babies, including his own four sons. *He is remarkably tidy in these things,* his wife had said.), pronounced the joyous words:

—— This is the throne of Elijah: may he be remembered for good!

Then the Mohel took up the baby and placed him on the knees of Berson, the Sandek, who was sitting up straight and stiff. Berson said the simple benediction. The Mohel bent down and began his work. After a few moments the baby gave out a piercing scream and then with a red face settled down to steady howling —his passionate acknowledgment of having received the Sign of the Covenant. We had nothing sweet for the infant to suck. Reb Moshe Granzelmann's voice gradually grew in volume and dominated the baby's crying:

—— . . . On this account, O living God, our Portion and our Rock, give command to deliver from destruction the dearly beloved of our flesh. . . . This little child Israel, may he become great. Even as he has entered into the covenant, so may he enter into the Law, the nuptial canopy, and into good deeds.

Berson drank wine from a tin cup and dropped a few drops into the baby's vociferous mouth, whereupon, with a sucking and smacking, and to smiles at every corner of the bunker, it at once stopped crying. I took the cup then to Rutka, who drank the wine, too. Then I went back and fetched the baby, and took it and put it in Rutka's arms.

Rutka, in tears: —— Ai, baby, baby, and now you're a Jew with the rest of us.

11

Events April 18, 1943. Entry ditto. N.L. I have always thought that uncertainty was the most unpleasant state of mind for me. Now I wonder. Perhaps certainty is worse. Tonight we have certainty, and I have a feeling that I shall not sleep on it. Tonight we are positive that we face the culmination of all our preparations in a very few hours. I should discover solace, strength, and defiant calmness in this surety. Instead, I find it only terrifying. I suppose it is the lot of every soldier, on the eve of action, to fear failing in battle more than he fears the battle itself. It will be my soldierly duty beginning tomorrow morning to keep a record of all that happens, but I fear that I will only be able to catch a glimpse here, a wink there. My record will be a stammering and a muttering, not a clear recital. I am terrified lest all *my* preparations, all my training in gathering and processing an archive, will be dissipated in the urgent hours to come, and that my account of our final hours within this wall will be but a mockery of the truth. Thus, fearfully, I approach battle with my armament of paper and pencil.

Hastily, tonight, I must review the events leading up to tonight's certainty. (For the temper in the bunker this evening, I must wait and try to recapture it another day, if there be another day, from someone else—probably from Rachel Apt; she talks to me honestly and she knows now what I want.) To begin with, it was Mordecai who first warned us of the arrival of the new . . .

EVENTS APRIL 16, 1943. ENTRY APRIL 18, 1943. FROM MORDECAI APT. The predominant mood among the Fighter Groups in the period of waiting and readiness has been one of irritability. Mordecai Apt and Wladislaw Jablonski, having planted their electrical land mine, sat much of the time in the observation post on Gensia Street, waiting to push home the plunger and trying to live patiently with each other—a meager life in both respects, it seems. Mordecai says he found Wladislaw's garrulousness annoying, and he was forever impatient to be back in the bunker with his tiny son; yet in the bunker, he constantly found fault with Rutka's ways of tending the child, and with what he considered Froi Granzelmann's meddling, and even with the orderly functioning of the bunker's cooking and washing and sleeping arrangements; as a consequence, he was first urged, and finally commanded, to spend most of his time in the lookout on Gensia. He and Wladislaw tried to play cards together, but they argued over scores and once, very angrily, over a card that was accidentally faced in the deal; so they gave up cards, and lay listlessly on the floor, only occasionally getting up on one knee to look out the peepholes scraped out of the newspapers that had been pasted onto the tiny windowpanes of the attic room. Most of the time the street below was empty. Such unimportant events as the passing of a squad of marching workers or of a couple of S.S. police brought the young men to kneeling attention and entertained them disproportionately much. Every time anyone walked near the mine, Wladislaw pretended to squirt home the plunger, and then, with a wild look, he muttered: *Voom!* This rehearsal of slaughter never tired Wladislaw; it was just as enjoyable to him when a Jewish labor battalion passed over the little vault of dynamite as when Germans did. He described over and over to a revolted Mordecai, with images as awful as those of Hieronymus Bosch, the scene of spattering man-fragments, of legless feet kicking neckless heads in mid-air.

The two were in this sore condition, with their fraternity chafed hurtfully, when, at about three o'clock in the afternoon day before yesterday, Wladislaw, having heard footsteps in the street and having hauled himself to the window, urged Mordecai to take a look. Mordecai raised himself with a groan, expecting another of Wladislaw's massacres. But what he saw this time engaged his attention.

A group of German officers and men—perhaps twenty—some of them in a uniform strange to Mordecai, was walking slowly along Gensia Street. One officer in front, a *Sicherheitsdienst* man, was explaining something, pointing here and there.

Mordecai: —— New Germans.

The knot of men, apparently some sort of staff or headquarters outfit, stopped right in front of the observation post, and several of the Germans stood directly on the bomb scar under which the explosive egg was nested. The conducting officer pointed first one way, then back the other, along the street. Mordecai expected the pumping motion and the wishful *voom* from Wladislaw at any moment; but Wladislaw was silent. Mordecai saw that Wladislaw was looking down the street, off to the left. He did the same.

There came Schpunt. The famous, ugly little man seemed to be in playful spirits: he half-skipped as he walked, and it was easy to see that he expected some sport with the Germans. He marched right up to them and with the motion of a hen raising its head to let water run down its neck, he threw back his outsized dome, and he raised his right arm and cried out a salute. This is the kind of behavior with which Schpunt has customarily thrown Germans into antic laughter. But this time the Germans—these new Germans—did not laugh. One of the officers, evidently the senior, even returned the salute. Mordecai says he saw a slight stiffening in Schpunt, as if Schpunt realized that things were not going quite right. Then Schpunt seemed to be saying something: one of his queer, abusive jokes, no doubt. But no laugh from the Germans. Schpunt broke into his crazy, water-jointed dance—his most dependable grotesquerie. No laugh. The dance seemed to break apart and Schpunt stood still. The German officer had stepped forward from the group: he seemed to be shouting. Schpunt said something with a screwed-up face—evidently one last effort to make the German laugh. The German drew a revolver and shouted again. Schpunt turned and fled, and he ran with a co-ordination and speed of which his bumptious clogging never would have suggested him capable. As the officer turned back to the group, stuffing his pistol away in his holster, there was not even a trace of a smile on any face in the squad.

Mordecai, again: —— New Germans.

Wladislaw was pale.

EVENTS APRIL 18, 1943. ENTRY DITTO. FROM LAZAR SLONIM. The actual tip-off to the Z.O.B. this afternoon was given by Slonim. I was able to corner him after the meeting this evening, and got the story from him, thus:

Slonim was on duty by the telephone in the office of the Avia plant, where he has been working. It was just before three o'clock in the afternoon. Slonim's eyes were rather steadily on the fogged glass door of the manager's private room, at the opposite corner of the office. Three S.S. men were inside with Merck, the German factory manager. They had been there about five minutes.

The door opened. The officers came out and Herr Merck behind them; the manager was wearing his drab grey overcoat and his black homburg hat: going out. The four men moved toward the door, which was near the telephone desk. When Herr Merck came opposite the desk, he said to Slonim:

—— I'm going to the city with these officers, Nudnik. [NOTE. N.L. Slonim gravely explained to me that he had gone to work under this false name, with false papers, because he thought the

Gestapo knew the name of Slonim as an active Bundist's. So *this* was the Nudnik to whom the outside couriers made their reports! Until I told him who Nudnik is, this evening, Berson had had no idea at all that the man with whom he had talked twice a day under those dangerous circumstances was his old, argumentative acquaintance, his University friend, Slonim. Slonim says that Herr Merck must know the facetious quality of his alias—*nudnik* means "pompous bore"—yet the German has never alluded to this: perhaps he feels that drawing attention to it would be tactless!] I may not be back this afternoon. Please see that things go along as usual.

"Nudnik": —— Naturally, Herr Merck.

After the men left, Slonim says he debated with himself whether to go into the shop and tell the workers what had happened: finally he decided against it, since he could not decipher the meaning of Herr Merck's having been taken off; he could not even guess whether it was a good or a bad portent. The abduction had not been carried out with any sharp words, yet Herr Merck had seemed pale. It would not be fair to elate or alarm the workers inside by announcing this unclear event.

[NOTE. N.L. We have seen very little of Slonim ever since last November. His friend among us was Berson, and from the time when Berson went to the Aryan side, Slonim stopped coming around to the bakery to see us. I therefore had to ask him a little about his situation these days, and especially about his relationship, which seemed to be rather curious, rather confidential, with this German, Merck. First, I should say that I observe a definite change in Slonim. I remember very well his bitterness and even spitefulness in earlier days: I remember the way he almost boasted to Berson about having told Rapaport that he, Slonim, was the cleverer man of the two: I remember his bitter, abused feelings, as he described them, during his hike to Treblinka, when he trailed the deportation trains. Now he is no longer bitter. He seems quite sure of himself, quite mellow. Even his motions are not so jerky and tense; he no longer hauls at his forelock as if trying to lead his baulky self on a halter. He gave me to believe, when he talked later about Rapaport, that at least some of Slonim's change can be laid to the fact that Rapaport now leans on Slonim in Bund affairs. Rapaport used to treat Slonim with a fatherly condescension: he had the attitude of a not very clever teacher toward a very clever

pupil. Now Slonim is Rapaport's chief counselor. One can understand that Rapaport was disgusted with the man called Velvel for
trying to remove Rapaport from the ghetto; and Slonim's help in
hiding Rapaport at the bakery was doubtless not forgotten. At any
rate, Slonim was given more and more responsibility in the Bund.
I mention this at length because it has had a curious secondary
effect. The increased responsibility having made Slonim steadier,
cooler, and milder, Slonim has been able, as he would not have
been able in his more acid days, to earn the respect and trust of his
German factory manager, Merck. Merck is apparently a rather
easy-going, kindhearted German who has pretended, at least, that
he was horrified by the official German treatment of Jews. He has
been softhearted in the factory, and has maintained relatively decent (though still not absolutely good) working conditions. He has
also been resourceful toward the Gestapo, the S.S. and S.D., with
the result that his plant has had but one selection, in which less
than a third of his people were taken. It may be that he was taken
off day before yesterday because he was again resisting the S.S. At
any rate, he has come to delegate more and more responsibility in
shop management to Slonim, who serves as Merck's only contact
with the workers. And much of this increased responsibility in
factory business Slonim has calmly abused—he has served as the
contact for the couriers on the Aryan side.]

At five forty-five, the telephone rang. Slonim picked up the
receiver.

—— Nudnik here.

A voice, the voice of Herr Merck, said in German only five
words distinctly pronounced:

—— *Verstecken Sie sich heute abend.*

Then there was a click. Herr Merck had hung up.

Hide yourselves tonight.

Slonim put the receiver down. He rose, put on his coat, and
carried his hat with him into the shop. There, in a loud voice, he
told the workers that Herr Merck was not in the factory; that some
kind of crisis could be expected that night or the next morning;
that the men should make their way to their billets or bunkers a
few minutes before the regular quitting time—in about half an
hour; that each man should decide for himself what he wanted to
do; and that those who were members of the Z.O.B. should await
orders in their mobilization points.

Slonim: —— Leave the factory in your regular marching formations. Please try not to spread rumors.

He turned, biting his lip.

Then Slonim went to Rapaport and told him what had happened.

✿ EVENTS APRIL 18, 1943. FROM CONVERSATIONS MAY 8–10,
1943. FROM HIL ZILBERZWEIG. [NOTE. EDITOR. The following passage is taken from the ✿ CONVERSATIONS and is inserted here
because it seems to express the state of mind of Zilberzweig on the
eve of the battle.]

. . . Zilberzweig spoke of his feelings the night before the
battle; he said he had been a professional Jewish social worker for
most of the years of his life, yet in those few moments of sensibility, just after the messenger came to summon him to the meeting of mobilization, he felt the influence of *tradition* more strongly
than he had ever before. This is how he told it.

Zilberzweig walked to the window of his attic crag. The messenger had left. Dusk had come down, and Zilberzweig could just
see the profiles of the roofs and chimneys across the street, a dim
plateau with here and there squat, forlorn monuments to that
warmth which no longer blazed on Jewish hearths and in Jewish
stoves. Zilberzweig, seeing those chimneys, remembered the last
fireplace fire he had had: a chair looted from a "wild" house back
in February; a straight, severe chair; a merry, crackling, thermal
chair. What bearded elder had used to sit in that chair, looking out
with bulging eyes, munching little three-cornered cakes, speaking,
with fanatic jollity and a full mouth, of the holiday Purim, gloating over the way the tyrant Haman was overcome by Jews, and
going on to say that the new Haman of Germany would also be
destroyed—wait, wait, he would be destroyed; or sitting there with
folded hands reciting the prayer of the Nahman of Bratzlav, *An-
nul wars and the shedding of blood*; or half leaning, on the Seder
night, instructing his beloved with the *Hagadah*? Had there ever
been such a man? The fatted, middle-aged youth leader says he
stood in the dark window and thought: My father would not have
been afraid tonight. My Uncle Agaron would not have been afraid
tonight. How they used to sit and talk! Jewishness—their bread
and their meat. Their harsh beards—Hil had imagined them as
eagle's nests! (Tomorrow, he thought, begins Passover; tomorrow

night the Seder night.) The short prayer his father taught him, from the Talmud, of a person in danger:

—— Do Your will in the heavens above, and give pleasure of spirit to those in awe of You, and whatever is good in Your eyes, do.

Dusk. . . .

EVENTS APRIL 18, 1943. ENTRY DITTO. N.L. The meeting took place at about 9:15 this evening. I looked around the cavern where we met—Yitzhok's bunker. Excitement made the younger men look weirdly happy: their eyes flashed and they seemed to be smiling, though really they were only tense around their mouths. (I remembered the smile on the dead face in the snow, the night of the New Year's party. *It's nothing, friends,* Dr. Breithorn said that night.) Here in this room were the best of the survivors—the fittest of Jewry: Yitzhok, Rachel, Jankiel, Aron; that copper wire of a man, Slonim of the Bund; the great brute, Budko, the Communist; the Group leaders, Anselm, Ganzener, Mischa, Peter, Abraham, Mendel, Benz, Ketzl, Nahum; hard, eager faces. In the background, some older men, looking on, shaking their heads but approving really. Why was Zilberzweig weeping? Kurtz, with a face of leather. Rapaport, so kindly and sad. . . .

Yitzhok: —— A comparison of our forces will clarify what I mean about saving ammunition. We must cherish each bullet as if it were made of gold.

The balance sheet, as Yitzhok presented it, with his sharp lower jaw protruding and his deep cut of a mouth seeming, like everyone's, to smile, was not as awful as I had expected it to be. Yitzhok somehow—by his inflections rather than by the figures he gave—made it seem almost favorable. The Z.O.B., he said, had all together twenty-two Fighter Groups: five from Dror, four each from Hashomer, the Bund, and the Communist P.P.R., and one each from Left Poale-Zion, Socialist-Zionist, Gordonia, Hanoer Hazioni, and Akiba. These Groups varied in strength from twenty-five to forty fighters apiece. The total of armed fighters was about six hundred and fifty.

According to Z.O.B. intelligence, Yitzhok said, the Germans had ready for action the Third Battalion of S.S. Grenadiers of the line, Warsaw Regiment, and a detachment of S.S. Cavalry, Warsaw Regiment, together eight hundred and twenty-one men; First and Third Battalions of the Twenty-second Regiment S.S. Police, two hundred and twenty-four men; three hundred and sixty-three Polish police and three hundred and thirty-five Baltic troops comprising the First Battalion of the Trawniki; from the *Wehrmacht*, a light battery of the Third Battalion of the Eighth Regiment of Artillery, a chemical-warfare detachment of the Rembertow Regiment, and the Fourteenth Battalion of Engineers, Gora-Kalwaria Regiment, all together ninety-eight men; together with technicians, sappers, firemen, and security police numbering one hundred and ninety-four. Making a total of just over two thousand men, with officers and headquarters troops probably twenty-one hundred.

Each Jewish fighter, Yitzhok said, now had a revolver and ten or twelve rounds of ammunition. There were also a few rifles and grenades and a fair supply of home-made bottle incendiaries. There were six hundred and fifty Jewish fighters against twenty-one hundred Germans. Each Jew would have to eliminate at least three Germans with, say, a dozen rounds of ammunition. That meant that for every four bullets spent, one German would have to be removed from action.

Yitzhok, perfectly seriously, apparently intending no irony or humor whatsoever: —— Anyone who has studied the science of warfare knows that such a ratio of mortality to rounds expended is very difficult to achieve.

It was also necessary, he added, to mention a disparity in weapons. The Germans had available some tanks and armored cars, some light field guns, probably thirty-five-millimeter anti-tank guns, and various automatic weapons. The aforementioned chemical-warfare detachment, the Rembertows, he said, probably was equipped with flame-throwers and tear gas.

—— But we (and this time he *did* intend humor; his smile was real), we with our revolvers have a certain mobility.

Finally, Yitzhok said, one had to mention the possibility that the Germans would call upon other units to move up in reserve in case the Jews were successful.

—— We have in reserve only the willing hands of our own people. Many workers outside the Z.O.B. are ready to fight.

Slonim: —— In other words, to sum up, Yitzhok: we are in a hard case.

Yitzhok: —— I wouldn't say that. (He spoke gravely.) No, definitely not. (Suddenly Yitzhok seemed to be furious. He clenched a fist and pounded his own thigh. Loudly he said:) We will punish them. We will teach them that Jews can be rough. (He relented then and said:) Forgive me, I assume your determination. This was intended to be a review of information and procedures. I had no intention of shouting at you.

Slonim: —— I didn't mean to sound pessimistic. I am not frightened by your facts, Yitzhok.

[NOTE. FROM RACHEL APT. Not frightened? Rachel says she felt her vitals tremble. If only she could have the men in this room for her soldiers! How would old Granzelmann fight? What about Maksi, only nine years old? Wladislaw, trying to absolve the guilt he felt on his father's behalf. . . . Mordecai, worried about his infant son. . . . Noach, so nearsighted!]

Yitzhok: —— . . . And now, on operations. You all know your own communications facilities: use them. The defense zones should be clear to you. As to tactics, at the beginning, since we do not know exactly what the Germans intend . . .

EVENTS APRIL 18, 1943. ENTRY DITTO. N.L. Rachel and I entered the bunker through the furnace and the passage descending from it. When we jumped down into the "front room" of the bunker, we heard the baby crying, and old lady Granzelmann came flying at us, waving a broom, squealing:

—— Be careful! Be careful! Tracking all that dirt in here! Can't you see that we're trying to get the bunker clean for Passover? Stay there! Let me brush off your clothes. There. That's better. . . . Did you forget that we have Seder tomorrow night?

Rachel, in a loud, clear voice, stepping away from the fussy woman: —— Now, I want you all to listen to me.

Faces turned toward Rachel from every corner of the bunker. Several people came in from the "back room." Some got out of bunks. Most of the faces were in shadow: they seemed truculent, weary, worn; cheekless and huge-eyed. The baby stopped crying, as if repressed by the atmosphere of the bunker. I saw Rachel look at Berson standing beside his bunk: he had that tight-mouthed look that was nearly a smile: he looked like those others in Yitzhok's bunker: *he* could be depended upon. Rachel herself looked unusually strong: the Little Mother!

—— Listen to me, my bunkermates. I have something to tell you.

Slowly, clearly, and with a restraint that was sufficient to keep emotion out of her choice of words, out of her mode of expression, but that was insufficient to mask it altogether from her voice, so that what she said was deeply affecting, Rachel explained to her fighters what was expected and what she wanted them to do if the expected came. She did not tell them all the things that Yitzhok had said; she did not mention the flame-throwers. But she did make it clear that danger would be available to all. She outlined and explained and repeated all the plans.

When Rachel was finished speaking, there was silence in the bunker for a few moments. Then the Granzelmann woman, the homebody, said:

—— Nu, in that case, we certainly have to finish our sweeping and dusting tonight. Klara! Miriam! Get busy, children.

In time the people in the bunker settled down. Several of the fighters cleaned and oiled their clean and oily pistols. . . .

INSERT. FROM ENTRY APRIL 21, 1943. FROM RACHEL APT. I promised myself to ask Rachel for her impression of the mood of the bunker the night before the battle. Now I have done so. She talked mostly about her own thoughts, thus:

Berson, before he went to bed, went to Rachel's low bunk, knelt beside it, and whispered in a queer, formal, broken way:

—— When the difficulty comes, Rochele, please feel free to call on me. . . . I shall be delighted . . . an honor. . . .

And he drew back into the darkened space.

Rachel lay on her bunk and could not sleep. Her mind was in a whirl of rehearsal and reminiscence. Safety catch, cock, elbow bent, down on the target . . . the passwords, the communications channels, the names of the couriers and reserve couriers, points of rendezvous, zones, places to go in case the bunker should fall, the electric mine—in a high, dark window far across the street the face and hands of a small boy pressed against the glass: Dovidl!—gasoline bottles stored in the cellar at Wolynska 19, the stiff overarm delivery for a grenade or bottle bomb—Rapaport and Zilberzweig standing leaning across the table shaking hands, and tears in old Rapaport's eyes—Froi Mazur's look, penetrating, protective, oh, unbearable!—safety catch, God, remember the safety catch—Pavel Menkes, so frightened—useless to fire from more than five or six meters—the big, mild, gentle, good-minded man kneeling there in the dark and whispering: *Please feel free* . . . —the passwords

516

again, the passwords yet again, the electric mine—the smiling dead face on the pillow of snow. . . .

A long procession of these thoughts, and of hours, passed, Rachel says she thought, despairing: I must sleep, I must sleep. Else what sort of commander will I be?

There were sounds of coughing. Soft involuntary moans. One great cavern of a nose snoring—old lady Granzelmann? Was Berson awake? Somebody whispering—prayers. . . . The safety catch. Names of couriers, names of reserve couriers. . . .

Rachel was waltzing. Elegantly, the dress flowing, clinging, smoke-blue, and she herself as light as smoke. With Dolek Berson . . . with a big . . . with an . . . *that hairy face!* Turning, turning . . . oh, oh, oh, oh. . . . A flame fifty feet long from a nozzle coming in, sweeping in. Look out! The pretty dress! The waltz isn't . . . Look out for the pretty dress!—

Had she screamed? . . . Apparently not; the snore, the normal coughing. Strange: that same dream.

The sound now of Rutka's tender murmur, and now of the infant's mouth at Rutka's breast: that most exquisitely gratified and gratifying sound. It must be about five in the morning. Names of couriers, names of reserve . . . passwords . . . safety. . . . Wait! Wait! What was that?

In the distance, far, far away, Rachel heard the sounds of Diesel engines and a certain type of clanking noise.

THE WALL   PART VI

1

Events April 19–20, 1943. Entry April 21, 1943. N.L. A word here, before I try to summarize the first two days of the battle, about my methods of gathering and collating this material, so that if this record is ever dug up, a reader may be able to judge for himself of my veracity. I have found in my interviews with fighters so far that each political party, and even each Group, is partisan in its accounts, tending to exaggerate certain exploits (its own) and to gloss over others (not its own). Thus, there were five Groups involved in the first fighting at Mila-Zamenhofa; of these, four, all except Rachel's, claimed to me that each of them had separately and alone set fire to the tank that was burned at that intersection. Since all accounts agree that there was but one tank, it is evident that the zeal of some of the narrators exceeded their truthfulness. Though I am a member of Hashomer, I humbly approach this task with broader loyalties—those of a Jew and a human being. Since I am but human, I have one great limitation: I can only be in one place at a time, I can only do a certain amount of work each day. I cannot hope to record everything. Since I am a Jew, I have another: I cannot help feeling that these events have a tremendous importance, so perhaps, even though I try to hobble my emotions, I may sound over-heroic.

Rachel has excused me from all combat duties. During the daytime, I depend to a large extent upon the couriers and reserve couriers for information. Our own courier Maksi, who being a child is largely a-political, has been tremendously observant and helpful. I have accompanied him on numerous errands to various Group Command Posts, so that now I am getting to know the communications routes in our area, at least, quite well. Yitzhok has given me permission to hang around his Central Command Post, and I find that there, simply by overhearing the reports and requests of couriers, I get a remarkably clear picture of the whole action; I buttonhole the couriers for some detail, and in the evenings I move around to various bunkers to fill out my sketches with data from the fighters themselves. I have tried to follow two main precepts: first, accept no hearsay, but verify each important detail with someone who saw the thing happen *with his own eyes*; and second, interview people about events, not on the day when they happened, but on the next day, because on the day itself they are still so preoccupied with fear or elation or other extraneous emotions that they cannot see the event clearly; on the following day the true happening, while still fresh, has come better into focus; and already on the next day after that they have begun to romanticize, improve, and exaggerate. The second day is best. I shall bury these notes every four or five days in my Swientojerska cache.

So much for my historical methods; I am dealing, I can say as few historians before me could, with truly "primary sources"— the participants themselves. Now for the events. First, a bare summary:

Beginning between three and four o'clock in the morning, on April 19, the enemy encircled the ghetto and troops began penetrating into the "wild areas," in small parties which rendezvoused, at various points, in platoon and company strength. Shortly after six o'clock, these forces, accompanied by a tank, entered the ghetto with characteristic arrogance—in closed formations, marching. We do not yet know what their actual intention was. Whatever it was, they had no chance to carry it out. The first reaction by our forces was at the corner of Zamenhofa and Mila, where five Groups (Slonim's—Bund; Mendel's—Dror; Rachel's—Hashomer; Abraham's—Bund; and Benz's—P.P.R.) had been carefully barricaded to cover the intersection, and where, by good fortune, the complacent Germans chose to bivouac, presumably preparatory to an unusually forceful "selection." Here the Germans were caught completely by surprise under a concentric fire of snipers' rifles and under the attack of explosive grenades (some given us by the Armja Krajowa, some manufactured by ourselves). The German troops scattered for whatever cover they could find in doorways, former shops, and ruined buildings, but it was necessary for them to bring up their light tank and, in reserve, two armored cars to cover the first retreat in history of German troops under Jewish fire. Incendiary bottles by the dozen were thrown at the tank, and it eventually caught fire and was temporarily immobilized. In my opinion, actual credit for stopping the tank must go to the Dror

Group under Mendel. (Unfortunately the fire was only external, and later in the day German engineers succeeded in removing the tank under its own power.) Our people are speaking now with an idiotic lack of restraint of our "total annihilation" of the Germans in that first trap. Actually I have been able to verify the specific infliction of only eight casualties by men *who were positive that they themselves wounded Germans.* Berson, for an example, says that he saw one newly wounded man during the first shooting, but he feels fairly certain that he himself did not hit the man— though given any sort of incentive, he would certainly claim him; later, as the tank approached, Berson says he saw three wounded men in the street. I have concluded that our fighters may have wounded between ten and fifteen Germans in that ambush; I cannot be certain that they killed any. Late in the morning, the Germans returned with a flame-thrower. They burned to death seven of Abraham's Group and eventually drove all our units (or caused them prudently to retire) from the intersection. By the time the Germans had captured the intersection, they seemed to have forgotten what they wanted to do with it. They withdrew, leaving the buildings on the corner on fire.

Two other important actions took place that morning. At the intersection of Gensia and Nalewki, two Groups (Ketzl's—Dror, and Mischa's—Bund) had been stationed to try to interdict the entrance to the central ghetto by Germans from a southeasterly direction. The fighting here was more protracted than at the Zamenhofa-Mila crossing; it consisted for the most part of German attacks by small shock patrols and Jewish defense by sniping and limited infiltration, and ended, as the first battle had, in fire: the Germans again used a flame-thrower. The fires along Nalewki Street were extensive and severe. The other notable fight took place in the area around the brushmakers' factory, and was centered in Muranowska Street and Muranowski Square. The Germans had evidently intended to cut the brushmakers' area away from the rest of the ghetto and evacuate all the occupants; in this they certainly failed. We had five groups there: Montefiore's— Hashomer, Anselm's—P.P.R., Peter's—Hanoer Hazioni, Nahum's —Bund, and Ganzener's—Dror. At the brushmakers', where in one skirmish a squad of our fighters appeared in the streets in German uniforms, we succeeded in recovering two machine pistols from wounded Germans. The tank that had appeared at Zamenhofa-

Mila, now recovered for action by the Germans, also figured on Muranowski Square, and was again set on fire externally and stopped. From here the Germans finally retired without use of a flame-thrower.

For the Fighter Groups, the remainder of the day was relatively quiet. The Germans were, however, carrying out blockades, searches, and roundups in undefended billets and houses, and they marched off with a fairly large number of Jewish workers.

For some reason, at about noon, the Germans decided to flood the sewers. We must assume that some Jew, hoping to save his own skin by turning informer, told the Germans that we had been using the sewers for communications and that Jews were also hiding there; otherwise it would be hard to account for the Germans' sudden interest, after all these months, in the underground culverts. For the fact that the sewers are still free we can thank Berson, whose incredibly thorough knowledge of our internal communications enabled him at once to go to a reserve valve and drain the system. [INSERT. FROM ENTRY APRIL 22, 1943. FROM DO-LEK BERSON. There are three parallel and interjoined culverts which carry sewage from the ghetto system to the Vistula. The two "auxiliary culverts," on either side, had been shut off for some time. The Germans now turned off the flood valve of the "main culvert," the median one, outside the ghetto, under Freta Street, near the river, where we could not reach it. It was the right-hand, or more southerly, of the "auxiliary culverts" that Berson opened, thus draining the entire system.] The Germans have apparently never figured out what happened; at any rate, they have not tried to flood the sewers again. Had the sewers not been drained, more than half the Z.O.B. bunkers, to say nothing of many of those less scientifically constructed ones inhabited by "wild" people, would have had filth backed into them.

During the afternoon of the nineteenth, the Germans opened artillery fire from howitzers (D.C.A. 2.28's) placed in Krasinski Square, and most of our people retired from attic strongpoints into cellars and bunkers.

The next day, the morning of the twentieth, the Germans used different tactics. They formed assault groups—nine of them, we believe—of about forty men each, and these groups scattered for the purpose of clearing out areas, one house at a time. In this type of action, our communications system helped us tremendously. Our Groups were able to retire fighting (or not fighting) from an assaulted house to neighboring attics and cellars, let the Germans search an empty house to their hearts' content, and then, when the Germans had moved on, simply return to their original positions. The most important pitched battle of the day took place at the brushmakers' again, to which area the Germans foolishly sent only two assault groups. These squads arrived at the gate to the brushmakers' area at about two in the afternoon, and as they milled about in their preparations an electrical mine previously planted there was detonated and eight men were verifiably put out of action. I believe it is safe to say that one of these was killed. [NOTE. N.L. This was not the mine planted by M. Apt and Jablonski of Rachel's Hashomer Group. I have heard nothing of that one; I must find out whether it has been used.] About thirty Germans then penetrated into the brushmakers' area in scattered parties of threes and fours. They were driven out, partly by splendid fighting of workers organized outside Z.O.B. groups.

Our casualties for the two days were seventeen killed and forty-one wounded. I would estimate that some seven hundred Jews were taken to the *Umschlagplatz* during that period. For the same period I have been able to verify three German deaths, nineteen wounded, and none captured. The score, then, is 758–22. Nevertheless I feel able to write, in my most careful judgment— which is to say, not from my heart as a Jew but only acting as an impersonal eye torn from my earthbound body—that this was victory. From my heart as a Jew I write now: this was the greatest thing that has happened yet in this war. For us, it seems to surpass Stalingrad, of which we have heard tremendous things, and perhaps it does: here, at last, man has shown that he holds within himself the capacity to withstand anything. I exaggerate? Just because this "man" is a Jew? Perhaps. Yes, I suppose the goyish historians who come along later will say that Noach Levinson was just an emotional Jew with the usual Jewish tendency to self-dramatize. (Can I forgive myself this moment of bitterness? I realize that in these few intemperate words I vitiate all the effort to establish my veracity that I made in describing my methods.) All right. I stand guilty as charged. My breast *is* filled with emotion. I write now with tears in my eyes. I am moved because of the loneliness of this fighting figure in the ghetto. He stands alone. What has the conscience of the world ever done for him? Nothing.

What will it ever do for him? Nothing. Why should I not be moved?

Thus the general outlines. I shall now try to describe through others' eyes some isolated . . .

EVENTS APRIL 19, 1943. ENTRY APRIL 21, 1943. FROM RACHEL APT. Zamenhofa Street, from a peephole of the stronghold. A dim light of pre-dawn. Emptiness. Across the way, the house fronts, with doorways boarded over and windows shuttered or papered, looked like the faces of wise and taciturn men, casual masks that hinted (to the acquainted) at interesting activities within the skulls: what subterfuges were behind the foreheads of those faces, in the attic-minds, what plans and early-morning stirrings in the recesses just back of the cornice-hairlines? The street empty. Zamenhofa Street desolate, damp, and empty. Rachel, peeping, says she remembered the look of Zamenhofa Street on a spring morning in the first year of the ghetto: along both sides of the street had been the enfilades of hawkers and venders, women for the most part, sitting beside or behind shabby open suitcases that contained their wares—their so intensely personal wares: ritual candlesticks, threadbare underthings, Kiddush goblets, copies of the *Shulkhan Arukh*, rub-shined old gloves, baby-rattles, used shoelaces taken from worn-out shoes; the women wailing out advertisements of the superiority of their goods—and of course it was natural that they (selling their lives; recollections for sale) should be convinced that their own relics and souvenirs should have value for others.

How much difference a little daylight makes, Rachel says she thought. Now most of the churning of her mind was ended; she was frightened, yes, but in a clear and orderly manner. The rules of fighting were gratefully remembered and did not need constant recital; her own memories, except those called out by what she saw now with her eyes, were driven back into their lair.

Zamenhofa, at the intersection with Mila. Empty. Light just beginning to seep down through the vaporous air. And quiet: the motors and the clanking (northward) had stopped at least half an hour before. This intersection, Yitzhok had said, would be the "tinderbox": surely their forces would go past this intersection. Here, above the four corners, in the attics, lay hidden parts of five Groups; besides Rachel's, two of the Bund, one of Dror, and one of P.P.R. Fifteen people were here with Rachel; the reserves in the bunker; Rutka in the bunker with the baby, poor impatient Rutka; Mordecai and Wladislaw watching their mine on Gensia; Noach with Yitzhok, gathering history; Halinka on the Aryan side; gentle Rapaport with Slonim's Group; Maksi here; Dolek Berson here. Dolek here. On the way here through the cellars, Dolek had whispered:

—— By this time in the morning, Pavel used to have the first batch of loaves out of the oven already.

And drawing up the ladder in this house when the last fighter had climbed past the destroyed section of the staircase, he had turned and whispered, with a dreadfully casual smile:

—— It would have taken half an hour to persuade Symka to climb up *this* thing!

Against the opposite wall of the room, Rachel saw the fifteen glistening bottles, and the half-dozen wooden-handled explosive grenades. Her fighters lay in lumps about her: they could not easily abandon the notion that they should try to sleep—most of them had been at the attempt all night. Berson sat beside her at the window, his cheek against the rifle barrel. Rachel had given him the rifle to fire the first few rounds: no one was to open fire until the annunciatory shot came from Slonim's Group on the northwest corner.

The motors! Yes, they were starting up once more!

Rachel looked out at the street again. She remembered that she had stopped, that spring morning in the first year of the ghetto, in front of a dog-chewed, banged-up black composition suitcase, in which, on a dingy heap of old clothes, lay a brilliant little Czech terra-cotta doll. She had asked the price. *Oi,* the woman had said, drawing her shawl close about her, *You don't want that! Here! Buy something useful.* And she had held up a filthy, frayed, stay-starved corset. Rachel had again asked the price of the doll. *Really,* the old woman had said, *you don't want that. It has brought us* nebich *such bad luck. It's . . . it's not for sale.* And the woman had picked up the doll in her dirty talons and held it to her thin breast, as if she loved it better than anything in the world, and she had said shrilly (but with telltale tears in her eyes), *There's a curse on this doll. Buy the corset. The corset is safe to buy. The doll is not for sale.* Rachel remembered that she had said scornfully: *Then why do you have it on display?*

Berson nudged her and whispered:

—— The tanks have started up again.

—— I hear them. (A slightly exasperated tone, as if to say: You fool, don't you know that I have ears? Then at once Rachel regretted her short temper.)

Now down Zamenhofa from the direction of Dzika came the first formations. S.S. troops. God! what stupid arrogance! In formation, squads of fours, parade-marching, in goosestep. Oh, delightful, delightful!

Rachel, in a harsh whisper: —— They're coming. Now, Jews (in admonishment to her fighters). . . . Now, my dears. . . .

Halting in the intersection itself: they were going to bivouac on the very corner! You unthinking Germans! . . . Berson, slow as a cat, rising up and balancing the gun barrel on the sill, just out of sight, all of him just out of sight.

Rachel peeped out on Zamenhofa Street. Busy springtime street. (*But this worthless little doll is not for sale*—the wandering grey hair tucked by a vague hand behind a dirty ear—*not for sale.* . . .)

Crack!

The signal, from the northwest corner. Berson up. Rachel turned and looked at Berson's face, scrunched up, the right cheek against the stock and the whole left side convulsed to shut one eye. Oh what a funny face, Dolek! A little shift of weight. Now, Jew. Now, my dear. . . .

EVENTS APRIL 19, 1943. ENTRY APRIL 21, 1943. FROM DOLEK BERSON. Berson looked down the back of the barrel. For a few moments he could not engage the gunsights for looking at the incredible view: a tremendous crowd of Germans—two or three hundred men, standing and sitting; lounging at the cross-streets, in the basic attitude of war: waiting; in their first spasm of surprise, for they had been fired at here in the ghetto. Fired at by a Jew! Many of the Germans were looking upward, amazed, at the houses roundabout. And now, rewarding their upturned curiosity, several shots came from the eaves, dormers, and window-parapets of all the houses around the square (some Groups had two or three rifles apiece). A sudden turbulence began among the Germans down there; a scrambling.

Berson shifted his weight slightly. I must shoot, he thought, before the clumps break up too much. Dimly he was aware of Rachel leaning back looking at him. The pointer into the notch. There! That tight man-clump around the heavy boxes with the officer screaming! Steady. Pointer into notch. Press.

Look at them scatter! Oh God! God! I got one, Berson says he thought. A man doubled up on the ground already vomiting; redness spreading across his back. Then Berson saw that the doubled-up man was nowhere near the point at which he had aimed. Look at the Germans running for doorways!

Heavy explosions in the street. Other Groups were throwing explosive grenades.

Berson, as if resourceful: —— Quickly! Grenades.

He looked around. Rachel, beside him, had reacted faster than he: she already had a grenade in her hand and she offered it to him. He took it. There would be a long drop from here: therefore he should allow only a short count, and he must throw overhand, so as not to be exposed in the open window. Dolek yanked the cotter. One. Two. *Throw.* Four. Five. Six. Seven. There!

Berson says he wanted to scream out the taunts that crowded into his throat, but instead he just muttered them and felt his chest bursting. What a scene! What an infliction! He felt Rachel's hand on his arm, pulling him away from the window.

Rachel, hissing at him: —— Let the others have a chance.

Berson moved back on the floor and fidgeted there in an agony of excitement. Michal to the rifle. Diament and Mejlach jumping around like monkeys, with grenades. Grunts and exclamations. Little Maksi asking unanswered questions. Rachel passing grenades; not once asking to look out the window: quiet, firm, swift. Once she said, exultantly:

—— Isn't this good?

Berson heard the sound of a heavy motor, the *pank-pank-pank-pank-pank* of treads on cobblestones. Coming close. He got to his knees and craned, but he couldn't see anything. The tank was apparently coming from the left, down Zamenhofa. Rachel was already crouching with a bottle in each hand. One for Michal. One for Diament. Berson says he had to see. He stood up. The street was empty! Except for three men lying there and some droppings of equipment, altogether deserted. *Pank-pank-pank-pank-pank-pank-pank-pank.* Berson saw a bottle arch out from a window across the street: it was bound to fall too short: yes, a bonfire in the street. *Pank-pank-pank.* Diament bobbed up for a look, and down again. Berson stretched his neck. There! There it was. Moving slowly. Half a dozen bottles curved out, neck-over-belly-over-neck. Miss. Short. Miss. Wait a little! Miss. Too far to throw from here, Diament. Brightness all through the street-valley from the wasted fires.

A hit. Another hit. Oh, the sweet, cheery, twinkling flames! *Pank-pank-pank . . . pank . . . pank. . . .* The tank stopped. There were bravos from under a roof across the way.

Berson leaned out yet further to see if the lid, the kind of sewer cover up on top of the halted, burning tank, would swing open, and just then, with the sound of a malevolent, horrible insect, a bullet sped inward past his face and lodged, *puck*, in the ceiling of the attic room.

Rachel, shouting: —— Get down, Dolek! (Then, with violent urgency, almost screaming, in her first hysteria:) Save yourself, Dolek. Get down!

EVENTS APRIL 19, 1943. ENTRY APRIL 21, 1943. FROM MORDECAI APT. Mordecai and Wladislaw crouched at their lookout wordless with hate for each other. They were alone together. The Group proprietary of this strongpoint was stationed now at the corner of Gensia and Nalewki. Mordecai and Wladislaw watched and waited, tormented by their inactivity and incompatibility. For an hour, early in the morning, Wladislaw had talked and talked, in a nervous eruption of memories, anecdotes, opinions. He was so frightened that everything he had said had been monotone: no narrative points, no paragraphs, no emphases, just talk, talk, talk, talk, talk, overriding Mordecai's pleas for silence; until finally Mordecai, upon whom fear had played an opposite trick—he was nearly dumb, his tongue was dry—had briefly shrieked abuse at Wladislaw. From then on the two had just stooped there in uncomfortable postures looking out at the so-far empty street, at the bomb-scar, feeling resentful toward each other.

Now both became even more tense than they had been. A squad of seven Germans was stalking along Gensia, with the queer and artificial cowering walk of inexperienced troops, as if they were pretending to be alert, or imagining what it would be like to be in danger: they seemed not to have any comprehension of what they were doing.

Wladislaw crawled back toward the plunger box. He was breathing so hard that Mordecai could hear the panting across the room.

Wladislaw: —— Tell me when.

Mordecai: —— My God! Are you going to waste it on seven men? After all this waiting?

Wladislaw, bitterly, slowly moving back to the window: —— You think you know everything!

EVENTS APRIL 19, 1943. ENTRY APRIL 21, 1943. FROM RUTKA MAZUR. Rutka stood over the Granzelmann woman, who was seated on the floor, leaning against one of the bunk-stanchions.

Rutka: —— Hold the baby for me.

Froi Granzelmann, taking the infant in her arms: —— Where are you going?

Rutka, bursting out: —— I can't stand it in here. My friends all fighting. . . .

Froi Granzelmann, again: —— Where are you going?

Rutka looked one way and another. What appalled her was the apathy of these people in the bunker. Half-asleep, some of them, lying in their bunks; and others gossiping: this person seems to be antagonistic at the moment, he is perhaps jealous of that person who was made a section leader by the Apt girl, maybe he thought he should have been picked, he hasn't the capacity for leadership, *nu*, a tailor's helper, after all. . . . And with the explosions audible in the distance! How *could* they pretend to be so remote? And the baby was somehow outrageous that morning: demanding, sulky, selfish; a trammel. Rutka thought proudly: I was one of the first to go out as a courier; I went all the way to Wilno: I went after pistols when I was pregnant: I have my place.

Where? What place? Where going?

Rutka, answering Froi Granzelmann: —— Out to one of the strongpoints.

Froi Granzelmann, solicitously: —— Do you know your way?

Rutka: —— I'll find the way.

Rutka left the bunker by the "back door," into the neighboring cellar. She followed several passages and cuts-through, she went from cellar to cellar, not knowing where she was or what direction she was taking, glad only to be moving after weeks in the bunker. How feeble she was! Testing doorways, standing up after crawling through a passage, climbing over obstructions—she shook and grew lightheaded. Now even the distant noises had stopped. She was in a silent, damp, strange, dim world. She sat on a dusty, toppled, empty keg. As she stared across the cellar room, something seemed to move. Yes, something moved! She was too tired to be afraid: she watched carefully. She tried with the outer edges of her fogging mind to imagine what hostile thing would be moving here.

A rat. A big, fat, complacent, unhurried, landlordly rat walked along beside the far wall of the cellar. Once he stopped and looked at Rutka, then moved slowly on again.

Rutka threw her hands over her face and sobbed.

EVENTS APRIL 19, 1943. ENTRY APRIL 21, 1943. FROM DOLEK BERSON. Of course they had come back; they were bound to come back. Berson had said as much when they first withdrew. *Watch out, they're being coy,* he had said: the only sour note in the fighters' gloating. One could not imagine that the quick, stinging surprise at the street corner represented the final victory of Jewry. One could wish it: one could not really believe it. When the Germans had withdrawn, the members of Rachel's Group had cavorted and kissed each other. From across the street had come sounds of singing.

But of course the Germans had come back. And this time they came differently. They were deployed: a man every forty paces; one sprinting from doorway to doorway, the next not coming for fifteen long seconds; zigzag running in the streets; no bunched targets. From across the way Jewish snipers wasted ammunition; they hit nothing.

Rachel was looking out, her small chin level with the sill, when the first horrible, unexpected probing, sword-like flame spurted up from a window off to the lower left and leapt across the street, thrusting up under the roof timbers of a house over there: it reached in through a window and pulled out a piercing scream, withdrawing after one lick and seeming by some grabbing or sucking process to pull the scream right out of the window into the street-air. It left the timbers and sills on fire.

Rachel drew back, pale, with a hand at her mouth. She went to Berson, catching for breath like someone who had just fallen into icy water.

—— That's the one thing I'm afraid of. Let's get away from here.

Berson looked around at the faces of the fighters. He wanted to go but he did not want to *seem* to want to go; and he saw in the eyes of the others the same ambiguous heroism.

Berson, addressing Diament: —— What do you think?

Diament (a small intellectual fellow), doubtfully: —— We're all right so long as they don't set fire to the building underneath us.

Berson: —— We have only one way to retire. By the ladder.

Rachel now seemed to have composed herself. She said, in her normal, strong voice:

—— They are certain to go after all the buildings on this corner. We will move to the strongpoint at Zamenhofa 53. Bring the grenades and bottles.

Even so, Berson says he thought, we had a victory here earlier this morning.

EVENTS APRIL 19, 1943. ENTRY APRIL 21, 1943. N.L. The small boy came into the command post on the run. His sunken cheeks were full of unusual color; his eyes were those of a child about to open a gift. He stood before Yitzhok, the most elevated of his imaginable heroes.

Maksi, speaking through his panting with the mechanical intelligence of rote: —— Rachel's Forward Group has retired from Mila-Zamenhofa because of the flame-thrower. They have gone to the strongpoint at Zamenhofa 53. No casualties.

The Great Yitzhok: —— Thank you, Maksi. (Then, to the others in the command post:) Rachel is a careful girl.

One of the staff: —— I only hope, not too careful.

The boy stepped back and stood for a few moments watching the men. Yitzhok bent over a stolen German map of the ghetto, mounted on a wooden board, and he moved a pin: Rachel's Group. He and three men talked in mumbles. Maksi stood by hesitant and in doubt. [NOTE. FROM MAKSI. Maksi tells me that, standing there smelling what was on his own feet and feeling the wetness there, he was worried: Rachel had told him many times never to say anything, when he ran messages, except what had been dictated to him; she had taught him how to repeat the messages over and over to himself as he moved through cellars and tunnels and sewers, toward his addressee, so as to keep the words exactly right. Still, he thought someone would want to know the reason for the smell. He says he looked at me, and I did not seem to be an important person, so he decided to speak to me. How perceptive children are!]

Maksi moved forward shyly and tugged at my sleeve, and when I absent-mindedly patted him on the head, he pulled again, harder, and got me away from the others and whispered to me the reason for the smell. . . .

N.L., suddenly not absent-minded: —— Where was this?

Maksi: —— You know: that short stretch of sewer you have to go through between Zamenhofa-Wolynska and here.

—— How deep was it?

—— Well, you can usually go along the culvert with one foot on each side of the stream, you know, and not get wet. But this time it was up to my knees. (Then, almost proudly:) Smell me?

—— I certainly do. (I turned then to the men at the table and said:) From what this courier says, I think the Germans may be flooding the sewers. If they back up, a lot of the bunkers . . .

Yitzhok, in his way cutting through to action at once: ——
Get Berson!

Maksi hurried away.

EVENTS APRIL 19, 1943. ENTRY APRIL 21, 1943. FROM RACHEL APT. Yes, no question, they had gone. The houses all around the Mila-Zamenhofa intersection were apparently on fire; there seemed also to be bad fires in the direction of Nalewki. What could be done? Maksi had come back all excited and had taken Dolek away; he said that Yitzhok wanted Dolek. But not a word to the Group from Yitzhok. Wouldn't one think that Yitzhok would have the consideration, just in common decency, to tell the Groups what was happening in various places? No.

Maksi, in the moments before he hurried off with Berson: —— He just said, *Thank you, Maksi.* . . . Yes, I'm sure that was all. . . . He told one of the other men that you are a very careful person. . . .

What did that mean? Was that good?

Rachel: —— We'd better try to get some rest.

She herself stretched out on the floor and almost immediately fell asleep.

EVENTS APRIL 19, 1943. ENTRY APRIL 21. FROM DOLEK
BERSON. Berson moved forward, stooping in the dark, slimy tunnel, with water and filth up to his chest; once his foot slipped and
he almost fell forward into the awful mixture: he cursed out loud,
and he could hear his bitter damnation roll, like thunder in its
summer sky-tubes, down the sewer, reverberating and trembling
on the stinking air. He says he thought: What a horrible piece of
military history, what a communiqué for Jewry, if, after all these
months of the Jews' careful burrowing, after their digging and
shaping and shoring and building, the Germans were to drive
them above ground by pouring the drinking water of the city reser-
voirs into the channels of urine and ordure! The indiscriminate
totalitarian: diluting purity with foulness: like goosestepping to
Mozart.

This could not happen; it simply must not happen. Berson
moved forward with all his energy. He now had this last stretch of
sewer to penetrate; then three cellars, a tunnel, a bunker, a tunnel,
and two more cellars: there at last would be the cool valve wheel of
the "auxiliary" culvert. He hurried as best he could on the slippery footing. He came to the jagged trap-hole (thank God everyone had been urged to break their sewer exits into the *tops* of the
pipes!); climbed out; ran and crawled and hurried. When he went
dripping through the bunker, the stay-behinds cried:

—— Phew! Get out of here! We have to live here!

—— You damned fighters: you endanger us and now you
track this excrement through here!

—— Stink!

Berson, bowing as he walked through: —— Forgive me. I'm
sorry. I can't help it.

Hurry! . . . Then, at the last barrier, extreme caution. What
if the Germans were guarding the valves? If there was to be a
sentry, there could be nothing to do but make an attempt: sneak
up on him, rush him. Berson moved like a jaguar (*What if he
smells me?* he thought) and listened, but heard nothing, and
moved again. Now out through a coal bin: here he must rush because the remaining crumbs of coal were bound to crunch underfoot: stealth would be useless.

Nobody. Empty. Unguarded.

—— *Shmai Yisroel.* . . .

The perspiring, steady wheel turned under his hands with a

high-pitched, rusty protest, and Berson heard, praising in his heart the One God, Lord God of the Jews, King of the universe, first a trickling and then a rushing of the obnoxious waters beneath.

EVENTS APRIL 19, 1943. ENTRY APRIL 21, 1943. N.L. In the bunker that evening there was Babel: different tongues, because those who had seen action did not seem to be using the same language as those who had not, and it was impossible for those who had thrown grenades to communicate with those who had fired rifles, and Mordecai, who had knelt waiting and frustrated all day long, could not wrest the least sense from what his own sister Rachel was talking about, in connection with the flame-thrower.

The Granzelmann woman, at her own level of excitement: —— Did you know that this year Yom Kippur ushers in Hitler's birthday?

Diament, not having comprehended or even listened: —— Very interesting. . . . Now, this particular bottle was a square bottle. . . .

Rachel: —— What are we waiting for?

The Granzelmann woman: —— For our Berson to finish his bath.

Mejlach: —— Lucky Berson! *I* would go swimming in the sewers for a bath tonight.

At last Berson came in, dressed in the Group's German uniform, which was small for him: his wrists and ankles stuck out. For some reason, all laughed at him.

Reb Moshe Granzelmann: —— Now, children, quiet down. Be seated, please.

The inhabitants of the bunker, tightly packed, sat wherever they could, and the Seder ceremony began. Maksi asked the introductory questions. Reb Moshe Granzelmann sonorously recited the *Hagadah*. Someone had found a real Kiddush cup: the wine was just water sweetened with saccharine, and rusks of leavened bread had to serve for matzos.

In time a deep and hollow voice declaimed the names of the plagues, and in that hushed atmosphere, where under the leveling cadences of the long-shared ritual all tongues and all ears had at last come to an understanding of each other, this catalogue of ancient curses sounded so horrible and so awesome that what had happened that very day appeared, by contrast, to be a mere and tiny accident in the life of the Jewish people; nothing; an uncomfortable few hours for a few Jews.

—— Blood! Frogs! Vermin! (The deep voice, crying.) Murrain! Noxious Beasts! Boils! Hail! Locusts! Darkness! Slaying of the first-born babes!

✿ EVENTS APRIL 20, 1943. FROM CONVERSATIONS OF MAY 9–10, 1943. FROM MORDECAI APT. Mordecai spoke with great shame of his behavior on the second day of the battle:

Mordecai took the exquisite weather, on the second morning, almost as a personal insult from God to him, from a vengeful God to Mordecai, watcher of the forlorn bomb-scar on the cobbles of Gensia Street. It was decidedly the first day of spring. The air was as soft as lamb's wool; the day invited one to go outdoors and walk; it was weather for musing. But Mordecai, stiff from his hunched vigil the day before, still crouched, ached, and watched. With Wladislaw, he had finally reached an emotional truce: both were bored with waiting for their precious opportunity, bored with each other, bored even with their reciprocal boredom and with the tiresome quarrels that had arisen from it. They now shared a resentment against Rachel for having condemned them to this isolated place and this inactivity, when they could be doing, they said angrily, much more important things. They were almost companions in their discontent. Yet still they sullenly watched the spot where their mine was planted, and through the window that Mordecai had recklessly thrown open, the sweet air of spring entered and touched their foreheads. . . .

What was that?

Mordecai: —— Listen!

It certainly seemed to be coming along Gensia Street. Mordecai strained to see what it was: some sort of vehicle. He moved back into the room, stood up, and made himself tall on tiptoe to peer down out of the open window.

Mordecai: —— On the plunger! . . . I think maybe . . .

Wladislaw scrambled on hands and knees to the detonator. Now Mordecai could see it: a big, open truck, full of standing troops: maybe thirty, forty. Not too fast. Yes! Yes!

Mordecai: —— Yes. A truck. Stand by!

Anticipate it, he thought. Allow for Wladislaw's responses. Just before the engine came over the place.

—— Fire!

Mordecai heard Wladislaw drive home the contact. He braced himself.

Nothing happened. The truck bounced on the place where the cobblestones were disarranged and then went on. Mordecai clearly saw the face of one German soldier in the pen of the truck, his head tipped back, laughing at something. Nothing at all happened. The truck drove on down the street. There was silence afterward. The soft spring air moved lazily across the window sill.

Mordecai began to shake, and he looked at Wladislaw, and Wladislaw was shaking, too. This boneheaded, rubber-tongued Wladislaw!

Mordecai, viciously: —— What did you forget to do? What connections did you leave loose, anyway? What did you forget?

Slowly Wladislaw stood up, with his back to one wall. He was a greenish color, and he was shaking all over.

Wladislaw, with spite: —— Maybe it was something *you* forgot?

Mordecai, taking a step toward Wladislaw: —— What did you forget? Was it the terminals on the mine? What did you forget?

Wladislaw, shouting: —— You did it! You did it! (Suddenly he grinned a foolish, evil, humorless grin.)

Mordecai, again: —— What did you forget?

Then Mordecai leaped at Wladislaw and seized him by the throat, throwing him, by the impetus of the attack, against the wall; Wladislaw's head hit the wall hard.

Mordecai, screaming, pounding Wladislaw's head against the wall time and again: —— Tell me! Think! Think! Think! Think! Think!

EVENTS APRIL 20, 1943. ENTRY MAY 12, 1943. FROM HALINKA APT. Halinka has given me an account of the couriers' anxiety on the first two days:

. . . Someone was answering! The ringing had stopped. There had been a click. Why no voice?

Halinka stood at the phone in the hotel lobby. She was pale: she could see herself in a small round mirror on the wall. She had dared to come in and ring Nudnik's number ten times in the two preceding days. No answer at all. She and Marysia and Lodzia and the hunchbacked courier Josef had had two terrible days and nights. By day they could hear the explosions and see the smoke, they heard talk of German troop concentrations and attacks; but they knew nothing. And now somebody had picked up the phone at the other end—one could hear sounds over there; but no voice spoke. Halinka remembered again her first, dizzying shock of discovery. She had been walking along a street east of the ghetto, Wronia Street, on an errand that she considered to be dangerous. She had been dimly aware of the explosions but she had thought them connected with some sort of blasting or demolition. Then, at one of the crossings, she had turned her head and had seen, black, high above the ghetto, the languid smoke. . . .

—— Nudnik here.

Halinka almost fainted. She leaned against the wall and held tight with her right hand to the little table on which the telephone rested.

—— Nudnik here.

—— Nudnik! Speaks Halinka.

—— Greetings, Halinka. I'm sorry we kept you waiting. We are rather busy here. Yitzhok wants to talk to you.

—— Who?

—— Yitzhok. Wait a minute.

Again an interminable wait. For a moment the phone sounded dead. Would that be all? *We are rather busy here*—would that be all the report she would hear? Then a quiet, easy voice spoke:

—— Halinka. Good girl. Let me tell you straight out our news. If the Gestapo is listening, so be it. We'll communicate by letter from now on: this is too uncertain. *Nu*, it has begun, as I guess you know. The first day we beat them. Oh, Halinka, we gave them a good scare! . . .

Halinka stood at the telephone with her face turned to the wall so that no one would see the tears pouring down her face. How could Yitzhok speak in such a calm voice? He described the battles. He spoke of unimaginable episodes as if they were Sabbath pleasures.

—— We haven't forgotten you people outside. Last night they left a dead one on Gensia Street and some of us went out to kick the body, and I gave it one for you and one for Lodzia (tell her!) and one for Marysia. Good hard kicks! One also for Josef. No, no, we haven't forgotten you people.

Yitzhok even gave personal news: the arrival of Rutka's baby; Berson in the sewers, one of the feats; Rachel doing very well, Halinka should be proud of her sister; Levinson with his nose into everything taking notes; and news of Hil . . . a very private message from Hil, tactfully delivered. . . .

—— And now, your work. (Yitzhok still spoke in the same even voice.) Smuggling must at all costs continue, even if you have to find new channels and take greater risks: we are taking risks inside here. Get bandages. We need bandages and food. You have not yet reported fulfillment of our promises to execute the swindlers Urbaniak and Kucharski. Above all, please, ammunition. A few more pistols would help, but above all we need every round of ammunition we can get. And Halinka, pray for us. Pray for us, Halinka. . . .

2

EVENTS APRIL 21, 1943. ENTRY DITTO. N.L. . . . I have been asked by the program committee of YIKOR [NOTE. EDITOR. Jewish Cultural Organization.] to make an address on Peretz at a meeting this coming Sabbath. At first when they asked me, I became quite fidgety and wanted to refuse. I thought such a speech during this battle would be absurd. I pictured speaking in a bunker before men and women who are taking mortal risks these days, even speaking on our great Peretz; and I became terrified. Then I thought to myself: this is nonsense: have I any right to be afraid of a mere speech? I accepted and now I am in a better state of mind about it. I remember my terrible fear of speaking before an audience in the old days. The trembling knees and spasms of the stomach. The fast-beating heart. The perspiring hands. The shortness of breath. The dry mouth. The cold face. The aching nape. The addled brain. Then I thought of my sensations that day when I stood before Engineer Grossmann at the selection, when my life was in the balance. I imagine I had somewhat the same sensations that day, though for the hide of me I cannot now remember them, as I can, for instance, remember my nervousness before the speech I made in the Grosser Library in 1938. I do remember having had somewhat those feelings yesterday when I first stood in a Z.O.B. strongpoint and was handed a grenade to throw (I never got a chance to throw it); yet even yesterday, it was not so bad as before a speech. This is nonsense. I have now thought this business through, and I am determined never to be nervous about anything trivial or personal again. I am calm about the forthcoming speech; it will not trouble me. I have the wisdom and experience, now, to understand what is worth fearing and what is not worth fearing. In the small situations, I shall be iron; in order that in the great ones, I may, some day, be steel. I am delighted to have come to this sense of proportion about nervousness. I even look forward to my lecture. How thrilling it will be for us to take time from our battle to refresh our minds with the wonderful Jewish treasures of Peretz! I am calm. . . .

EVENTS APRIL 21, 1943. ENTRY DITTO. FROM FELIX MAN-DELTORT. Our *mise en scène* is now smoke: we live in a pungent vagueness. We are surrounded by fire, smoke, and the stench of burnt flesh. And stumbling out of this repulsive screen, early this morning, came back into our lives, unexpectedly, Felix Mandeltort.

Since Felix got into things, as we have seen [ENTRY FEBRUARY 1, 1943], rather late, he had no choice as to which Fighter Group he would be permitted to join. Naturally he wanted to join Rachel's, to be with me and others of his friends, but he was put into Peter's—Hanoer Hazioni Group. At the beginning of the present battle this group was stationed in the brushmakers' area, and today Felix has told me of the events there. I will pick up at the point where the summary, derived from couriers, in ENTRY APRIL 20, 1943, leaves off.

On the second afternoon, after the two German assault squads had been driven out of the brushmakers' area, an extraordinary thing happened. Three German officers, carrying machine pistols at the slouch, with Dr. Laus, the German director of the factory, walked erect across the courtyard of the main brush factory, pointing at their coat lapels—where, our fighters saw, they were wearing large white rosettes. Felix says he was with Peter and Anselm (P.P.R.), and that for a few wild moments he feels sure that the two Group Commanders, and all who saw the officers with the rosettes, entertained a delirious thought: the Germans were surrendering to the Jews! One of the German officers was shouting,

Truce! Truce! Peter ran down out of the building and from the doorway hailed them, so that Felix could hear him, asking what the Germans desired. They said they wished to speak to the local commander. Peter cried out that *he* was the Area Command. One of the Germans then proposed, in pompous shouts, a fifteen-minute truce for the removal of dead and wounded. Hereupon Felix became almost pathetic in his account:

—— You can imagine how we felt. We were leaning out of the attic windows, breathing the afternoon air and feeling relaxed for the first time in two days. How we wanted that truce! You understand, it was not only the rest we wanted: we wanted to be able to believe that this warfare had some rules, and we wanted to show that we, at least, could abide by those rules.

But Felix says he then thought of previous German tricks—of marmalade offered at the *Umschlagplatz*, of postcards allegedly sent back from work camps in Russia; still, he wavered. But while Felix remained undecided, and while Peter was in the midst of a sentence, exploring exactly how such a truce might be arranged, a rifle (Felix doesn't know who held it) poked itself from an attic window near where Felix was, and a round was fired at the three Germans. The bullet missed its target. Felix burst out laughing at the recollection of those three Germans running away. Two of the three rosettes dropped to the ground.

Felix: —— Of course, whoever fired that shot was right—both morally and tactically.

This remark—and in general Felix's vacillation on the matter of the truce—finally brought home to me the conflict which is probably the key to his troubled soul (and may be, come to think of it, one key to my speech on Peretz). Felix epitomizes the struggle, seen in so many of our educated men here, between the intellectualism of Western Europe and the emotional and instinctual tradition of Eastern Jewry. The concept of the "rules of warfare," sportsmanship in a deadly struggle, and at a deeper level the philosophical idea that man lives in system—this is Western. How almost English of Felix! The rifle shot: the truth intuitively weighed and judged—that was the product (as Felix also partly is) of centuries of ghetto life. This is a basic conflict of Felix's. We all feel it to some extent. I know I do. Berson is a particularly agonized victim of it, with his background of assimilation at Bonn, his wide reading, his relatively prosperous circumstances—and yet his restlessness, his vagabondage, his deep religious feelings, his final Jewishness. Certainly this conflict accounts for the fact that Felix, who is capable of the finest ethical conduct, could have been caught shamefully smuggling and be sent to jail for it. In the very act of smuggling, which he carried on because of his ghetto-Jew's drive for mere survival, he doubtless had in his head a fine Western European rationalization: he was smuggling "for the right reasons."

I digress!

After the rejection of the truce, the Germans vindictively brought up to point-blank range four cannon (three light howitzers and a large field gun), and pounded the buildings of the area. This made a frightful noise but, as most of the fighters went down into their cellars and bunkers, caused few casualties.

The next day, the third of the battle, our people in the brushmakers' area played a fine game of hide-and-seek with the Germans, dodging from bunker to cellar to attic to cellar to sewer to bunker and back. The Germans must have known that there were, counting wild people, more than three hundred Jews in the area, but they probably captured only about thirty Jews all that day. In the afternoon, the Germans resorted to fire. This time they were systematic. They set fire to the entire outer border of the brushmakers' area, on all sides at once. By nightfall, walled, roofed, and floored by fire, with burning beams crashing all about, the courtyard ovens and the pavement griddles, the Groups in the area had no choice but to try to fight their way out to the Large Ghetto. There was but one break in the wall between the brushmakers' area and the rest of the ghetto, and this was guarded, by night, by about a score of the less enthusiastic of our enemy—police troops and the Baltic vagrants of the Trawniki Regiment. The commanders decided that a rush was the best tactic. Accordingly three Groups (Montefiore's —Hashomer, Nahum's—Bund, and Ganzener's—Dror) charged the gateway, while Peter's—Hanoer Hazioni, covered from the rear, ready to follow with Anselm's—P.P.R., after five minutes. The tactic was successful. The first three Groups got through handily. Then, suddenly, a small searchlight in a tower near the gate went on: the entire ante-courtyard was flooded with light. Further escape appeared impossible. However, a fighter named Margolies ran out into the open and threw a grenade, which, by good fortune, put out the light. Margolies himself was hit by machine-pistol fire and was left behind. Felix is incensed at the abandonment of the man who saved two Groups, but when I asked him why, if this outraged him so, he had not stopped himself to help Margolies, he said his section leader had ordered everyone to go through the gate on the double. The rules. Evidently the section leader should have done something about Margolies. It is so often up to somebody else to do things. . . .

At any rate, the Groups got through with few losses, Felix is back, and we are glad. Our bunker grows ever more crowded. . . .

EVENTS NIGHT APRIL 21–22, 1943. ENTRY APRIL 22, 1943. N.L. Last night I wanted to settle down and prepare my Peretz speech, but something more pleasurable intervened. . . . Now such action as the Z.O.B. takes is in the form of night patrols, which sneak among the ruins and ambush the dangerous but clumsy Germans. Last night Berson devised a new harassment.

A patrol was formed and instructed in our bunker. Because of my speech, I decided not to go along. The members of the patrol, six in number, wrapped their feet in rags. Mejlach was to captain the group. I overheard Berson, as they were preparing to leave, say to Mejlach:

—— If you miss me, don't be alarmed. I'll get back alone.

Also I noticed—and thought it odd—that when the party went out, Berson picked up his concertina and walked out with it under his arm.

About ten minutes later we in the bunker jumped to our feet when we heard, startlingly close at hand, the proud strains of *Hatikva* [NOTE. EDITOR. "Hope," the Jewish national anthem.], played on the concertina. Berson must have been standing in the open street: the music came to us down the air vent which opens onto the gutter-drain on Wolynska Street. He played only six or seven bars, then abruptly the music stopped. We below were terribly concerned, lest Berson had been hurt or taken. But in an extraordinarily short time, only a couple of minutes later, we heard the penetrating, trembling sounds of the concertina again, at a great distance. This time, in a somehow mocking, whining tone that Berson can produce, it played a few bars of the *Horst Wessel* song: with a slightly Jewish accent, it seemed. On hearing this we in the bunker began to smile. We thought we were beginning to understand what Berson was doing. Yes, after a few moments, the music broke off again; and there was another pause of a couple of minutes; and then, very far away, the beginning of a Chopin polonaise. This time the thin sounds came to us through the passage that leads to our bunker from the neighboring cellar and from down in the sewers!

[FROM MEJLACH PINKUS.] The patrol got very little done during the night. They were fascinated. They holed up in the ruins of a building on Ostrowska Street and listened. It was evident that Berson was using his acquaintance with every detail of the ghetto's communications to tease the Germans. And how he must have tantalized them! Occasionally two numbers of his "guerrilla concert," as Rutka called it, would be separated in time by only three or four minutes, but in space by as much as two or three blocks, apparently. Now Mejlach and the hypnotized patrol would hear a passage from a Bach prelude high overhead, to the north—coming evidently from an attic; a few minutes later, from a southerly direction, in the street, it seemed, the first melancholy bars from the Mozart G Minor; then, after a longer pause, to the south again but muffled, as if from somewhere indoors or underground, Mendelssohn's *Spring Song*, played tritely, as if to say to the Germans, *Listen! Here's some music by a Jew that you know all too well—aren't you sick of it?—I am!*; then, only a minute or two later and suddenly off to the west, upstairs again, Wagner, Siegfried's funeral march, pompous but hinting, hinting. Oh, it must have been marvelous! The Germans must have thought there were thirty Jews with concertinas! [NOTE. N.L. We in the bunker heard occasional snatches of the music, but we could not get the full humor and mobility of the entertainment. It is amazing how penetrating the sounds of a concertina are: precisely the right instrument for Berson's game.]

Once, by chance, Berson played for a few moments directly in front of the ruins where Mejlach's patrol lay hidden. The music startled the fighters nearly out of their wits: they had been straining to hear the next number at some distant place, when suddenly, right before them in the street, and very loud, they heard the beginning of *Come Join the Jewish Partisans!* The music broke off and they heard the *fush-fush-fush-fush* of Berson's cloth-bound feet running away. A few seconds later they heard leather-shod feet running, and along the street came some Germans. They heard one cursing: *Damned Jewish pigdog!* Then a shot was fired. Immediately after the shot, from the very direction from which the Germans had come running, was heard, heavily and stolidly played, the beery dumpling-notes of a Bavarian *Schuhplattler*.

Several times, as the "concert" went on, shots were fired. It appeared that Berson was engaging the entire German night force alone.

[N.L.] A pleasant night. I went to sleep feeling as if I really had been to a concert.

EVENTS APRIL 23, 1943. ENTRY DITTO. N.L. I am impressed, suddenly, with the extreme importance of my lecture tomorrow night. And here is why:

Early this evening a strange message came down to us from Yitzhok. All children-couriers were to report at once to his command post. We wondered why. Maksi went.

A few minutes ago we learned what this was all about. We were in our usual evening-mood in the bunker: exhausted, rather depressed, talking desultorily. Three dead from the bunker today. I was trying to encourage Mordecai, who has seemed morose ever since the failure of his mine. [NOTE. EDITOR. It must be remembered that N.L. had not at this time learned the facts of Mordecai's fierce assault upon Wladislaw already presented here under EVENTS APRIL 20, 1943. He learned of this episode only in ✿ CONVERSATIONS OF MAY 9–10.] As usual, there was a relatively cheerful clump of people around Rutka and the baby, which had just had its evening feeding and was performing the ritual of the belch. There came a signal-knock on our "back door." The door was opened, and in came a small boy I had never seen but recognized immediately: he had a scar aslant across his face, running from his right temple down across his nose to his left jaw. I remembered at once Berson's account of the crossed-out caricature of Hitler [EVENTS NOVEMBER 4, 1939] and of this boy's having turned up again as a smuggler's courier when Berson sold his watch [EVENTS MAY 4, 1941]. [AN IMPRESSION FROM BERSON. This boy, with the strange, adult craftiness he has—the same quality as that which has animated some of our most prominent men here in the ghetto, only in them it is hidden from social view— this boy is the very image of survival: who could exterminate him?] He came in and, speaking in a strong voice, with the lilt of memorization, said:

543

—— YIKOR invites all fighters to a lecture on Y. L. Peretz by Levinson in Rachel's bunker tomorrow evening, seven thirty o'clock.

He turned to leave, but I could not help speaking to him.

—— Boy!

He swung around toward me.

N.L.: —— Don't you know that this is Rachel's bunker?

Scarface: —— Yes.

—— Don't you suppose people know what is going to happen in their own bunker?

—— I was told to stop in at all bunkers on Wolynska north and Ostrowska north.

N.L.: —— Who is this Levinson?

The boy looked me straight in the eye, and I'll never know whether he knew me by name or not. I suspect he did.

Scarface: —— Levinson makes no difference. Only Peretz.

Then I realized the shrewdness of Yitzhok in sending this notification out by the children: letting the precious ones among us, our children, our Jewish future, risk life to announce a talk on that most discerning of all writers on Jewishness, Peretz.

I believe I will have a good crowd.

EVENTS APRIL 24, 1943. ENTRY DITTO. N.L. What a preparation for my speech! This morning I was talking with Felix about Peretz, hoping to shake down from the garrets of my skull a few more details, when he told me that he had had, on a bookshelf at his last office, a volume of Peretz's essays, including *Hope and Fear* and *The Day*. I became rather excited and persuaded Felix to go to the *Judenrat* offices with me and see if we could find it. My memory of Peretz, because of my own work on his life, is fairly good—I can quote by the kilometer—but I was most anxious to put my eyes again on certain passages.

So we went.

In recent weeks the building at Zamenhofa 19, the last place where the *Judenrat* lived, has become a defensive honeycomb. The building was in the first place solidly constructed; it contained a labyrinth of attics and a complication of cellars. Several of the latter were recently fortified. In my inquiries in the company of couriers during the first days of this battle, I had learned the way to the building by underground passages, and this morning I had no difficulty in leading Felix there. He and I of course agreed that we would go up into the building only in case there was no activity in the vicinity. When we arrived there, all seemed to be quiet. We sneaked upstairs, taking the precaution to duck out of sight as we passed staircase windows, and skittering along the open corridors at a lively pace. The silence of the halls was ghostly: here there had always been activity—gossiping secretaries, men in confidential whispers backbiting their superiors, superiors in grave undertones deploring the incompetence of their underlings; the usual traffic of large offices, but here everything official and stiff-necked: official gossip, official backbiting, official deploring. But this morning: silence. One almost felt, official silence.

We found the book. It was on Felix's bookshelf. There were still some papers on Felix's desk, held down by glass paperweights, as if he were coming back in tomorrow morning to get on with his work. I had throughout the empty building a sense of this suspended effort. Out to lunch. Back shortly. I also fell victim, however, to my archive-mania. I saw about me many written and printed papers and books that were not in my archive, and forgetting all about my speech, I began to browse, coveting everything, trying to choose a few papers to take for burial. Felix sat down at his desk and fingered through the papers there.

Felix, sighing: —— I never could finish anything.

N.L.: —— Does anybody ever really finish anything?

I became quite absorbed, and Felix sneaked off down the corridor. He said he wanted to sit at the desk of the Chairman of the *Judenrat* for a few minutes, just to see how it felt to be in the seat of authority. I worked. Presently I thought I smelled something strange. Just as I was getting up to investigate this scent, Felix came hurrying into the room, whispering:

—— There's a fire somewhere in the building!

We hurried downstairs (after my browsing, I now left everything, even the Peretz for which we had come, where it was, in Felix's office) and we found, indeed, that the building was thoroughly on fire, at the end toward Mila Street. No Germans were in sight, at least within the building. The stairs were still free, and we were able to get down into the cellars and away. The Germans, then, are quietly and systematically setting fire to buildings. Two problems: what do we do when the bakery is burned down from

545

over our heads? and will not some of the communications channels be cut off, as burnt houses collapse into their cellars?

[INSERT. FROM ENTRY APRIL 27, 1943. FROM A HASHOMER
FIGHTER IN THE STRONGPOINT AT ZAMENHOFA 21, ADJOINING THE
Judenrat OFFICE BUILDING. Evidently there were still quite a few
wild people living in the attics of Zamenhofa 19, because when the
fire ate its way up through the building (Felix will never finish
his work now!) and into the lofts, people began jumping out the
top-storey and dormer windows. One group threw down some mattresses and clothing to break their fall in the street, and some who
jumped onto that pile actually rose and began to run away; but
German snipers caught them. Others were crippled or killed by the
fall.]

N.L., in the underground passages on the way back from the
building: —— *Nu*, Felix, how did it feel to be Chairman?

Felix: —— I wasn't in office long enough to do all I should
like to have done for the Jews.

N.L. (pessimistic today): —— We never have time enough,
do we?

EVENTS APRIL 24, 1943, EVENING. ENTRY APRIL 25. N.L.
This bunker could not have held an additional louse or flea. We
had taken into the cellar next door everything that could be moved.
People sat and knelt on the floors of both rooms, lay two and three
in each bunk, clung to the bunk-stanchions, and some even
crouched in the tunnel up to the bakery. The tunnel to the neighboring cellar was kept clear, so that people in that room could hear
my voice, or as much of it as would bounce through the twisting,
earthen hole. A gamin lay curled up on what used to be our fuel
shelf; two men sat hunched on the food shelf. I have never seen
such faces as those about me: gaunt, somber, acquainted with
danger (some seemed to have come to the lecture straight from
some sort of negotiations with Death); and yet exquisitely eager.
The eyes looked up at me with love, gratitude, and poignant sorrow—emotions that the words of Peretz, not those of Levinson,
called up, of course.

Since there was no suitable place to put down a light in the
packed room, we managed to hang a carbide lamp on a piece of
wire from one of the shoring beams against the ceiling of the "back

room" (I was to speak there so that the people in the cellar beyond the tunnel could hear as much as possible). [As SEEN BY DOLEK BERSON. My face was in shadow, since the lamp was above but somewhat behind my head, and my expression was really invisible to most of the audience (a good thing, too). I stood stiffly, I am told, with my hands thrust deep into my coat pockets. My clothes are too big for me. I understand that I looked like some sort of metal frame or clothes-hanging device, a forlorn figure, quite rigid and cold, but for my voice.] My voice, thank the Lord, was all right. At first it was a little froggy, but soon it cleared and it did what I wanted. It felt deep and strong.

I began my speech with the opening passage of *Three Gifts*:

—— *Ages ago, somewhere on this earth, a Jew died. Is there anything unusual about a Jew dying? Surely, nobody can live forever.*

What I wanted to evoke in my speech, if I possibly could, was a definition of Jewishness that was at once exact and yet broad enough to cover all ages, all loci, and all conditions of Jewry: a definition embracing Herod's slaves and the great modern bankers of Paris and London, covering alike the rag-decked furrier's needle-women of our prewar Lodz and Warsaw slums and the ladies in the mink coats stepping from their limousines in prewar Vienna and Rome, going from the *meshummed* who has explicitly forsaken the religion of his forefathers all the way to the Baal Shem Tov and the Great Maggid, taking in the fate-smeared fighters of the Warsaw ghetto and also the very rich and influential men, about whom we have heard, in America, reaching from the lowest pogrom-insect to Spinoza and Disraeli and Mendelssohn and Einstein and Christ. What I wanted to do was to move our small group of desperate men and women out into the great universe of Jewishness, so that we might take a short vacation from our self-pity and (perhaps) have compassion for the masters of Hollywood and pity the marvelous Einstein and feel sorry for all who are more comfortable and more noticeable than we. Not as superiors, not in condescension; as fellow human beings, in all humility, and pitying those others not for their Jewishness but because of the humanity they share with miserable things like us. I thought this feeling might do us good. Already, in merely describing what I was *trying* to do last night, I see that I have become imprecise. How could I possibly arrive at the definition I set myself? I was careful, at the beginning of this paragraph, to use the word "evoke." For that is what I had to try to do. I wanted to weave a web. And of all the Jews who could help me to do what I wanted, Peretz was the best possible ally.

For those of our people who had never been bookish, I told a little about Peretz the man—Peretz, the voice of Eastern European Jewry; Peretz, the most expressive and most all-embracing writer on Jewishness—born at almost the very center of the nineteenth century, a Hebrew scholar at the age of three, a student of Talmud at six; one who had the audacity to divorce the wife his parents had thrust on him when he was eighteen, according to ancient tradition, and then to marry a girl he loved; lawyer, bureaucrat, poor man; story-teller, essayist, dramatist; eclectic Jew, a man who passed through rigid Orthodoxy, the enlightened Haskala movement, and romantic Hasidism, and kept something of all three, who used and revered and purified both Hebrew and Yiddish, who fought for Jewish culture in all the lands of the Diaspora and yet who also felt the pull of Zion; a small, roly-poly soft-eyed man with a scraggly mustache and mussed-up hair, a magical talker —to whose funeral, when he died, in Warsaw in 1915, one hundred thousand mourners flocked. Then, simply by telling bits of his stories, reciting short passages, calling up his images and parading his characters, I began to try to cast the spell for which I aimed. . . .

—— *Hananya, the penitent, punished for using his learning for a show, being made to forget every word of the Torah he had learned, redeemed at last by the death for him of the poor girl Miriam. . . . A bit of earth of the land of Israel; a bloody pin from the leg of a girl dragged through German streets by a wild horse because she had ventured outside the ghetto; a dirty skullcap from the head of a pious Jew running a gantlet of soldiers—three "really beautiful gifts.". . . The merry prophet Elijah, disguised as a German forester, bestowing seven years of plenty on the porter Tovye. . . . Migrations of the happy melody, the Freilachs, danced by the poor bride in the streets of the town of Berditchev to collect a dowry from onlookers. . . .*

For some time, as I talked—and I flatter only Peretz in saying that I believe I was in his words beginning to express that peculiar sadness-in-joy, that sense of order-in-disorder, that striving for bal-

ance, that loneliness, that wittiness and that bitterness, that subtlety and that broadness, that yearning and those dreams, which
are such large parts of our faith and our way—I had been noticing
that the air in the bunker was getting more and more unwhole-
some. Perhaps mistakenly, we had closed the ventilators. There
were so many breathers in our cave! And on the air, besides the
smell of their starving guts, was the odor of death, the clinging
scent of burnt human flesh, the stink of the ashes of our civiliza-
tion within the wall. And as I spoke, I noticed that the light in the
room was growing dim. After my first frightened reaction to this
discovery (about which more later), I realized that either because
the carbide lamp was running low on fuel or because there was no
longer enough oxygen in the air for it to burn, it was going out. At
once, without referring explicitly to the lamp, I took advantage of
its waning, and the eerie effect it created. I asked, as Peretz once
did, straight out:

—— Then what is Jewishness?

And in the bunker's twilight, I gave Peretz's answer:

—— *Jewishness is that which makes the Jews, in eras of national independence, feel free and enables them to fashion institutions as embodiment of their national creative will. Jewishness is,
in such times, joy, ecstasy, zestful living.*

*Jewishness is that which creates, in troubled eras, institu-
tions for defense, for prevention of danger, for protecting itself and
its members. Jewishness is, in such times, a call to battle and a
challenge to heroism.*

*Jewishness is that which must, in times of dependence and
weakness, retreat into its shell, conserve its resources, endure in silence, and wait for better days. Then Jewishness is hope and pain,
messianic dreams, and other-worldliness. Then it demands real
sacrifice.*

It was now almost dark in the bunker, and I went on:

—— *Nomadic blood. A wandering clan in the desert.*

*Implanted in its blood—honesty and justice. Of these qual-
ities does it fashion its God, a God who accompanies it on all its
wanderings and is therefore not formed of wood or stone, a God
who moves and lives.*

*A sublime concept of the deity, a free and breath-taking
concept of a boundless, limitless universe. . . .*

We were in blackness. We seemed, indeed, to be in a universal place, not limited by a wall, not bounded by fear and stench. I think we all felt free. I hurried to the words that Peretz himself, writing decades before we were put in our ghetto, entitled *Conclusion*:

—— *Now, I am not advocating that we shut ourselves up in a spiritual ghetto. On the contrary, we should get out of such a ghetto. But we should get out as Jews, with our own spiritual treasures. We should interchange, give and take, but not beg.*

Ghetto is impotence. Cultural cross-fertilization is the only possibility for human development. Humanity must be the synthesis, the sum, the quintessence of all national cultural forms and philosophies.

☼ EVENTS APRIL 24, 1943. FROM CONVERSATIONS MAY 9–10, 1943. FROM DOLEK BERSON. . . . When the lecture was finished, there was, for a time, silence in the bunker. [NOTE. N.L. I am never applauded, and I take this as a great compliment. I remember the afternoon I recited *Campo di Fiori* at the literary club meeting—ENTRY JUNE 5, 1942. Several of our poetasters, after sawing their wooden verses, received polite slappings of applause; when I was done (having read someone else's poetry, be it said), there were only silence and tears. So with Peretz.] Then for a time there was confusion. It was still impossible to light the lamp. Somebody struck a flint and lit a twisted taper, but it flickered out. Our visitors were trying to get out of the tunnel all at once. Those near the exit became fractious and tinny, really very objectionable; and Berson says he smiled to himself about some of the high-sounding words I had just quoted to characterize these people. Berson also recollects thinking: It would be awful to contemplate a real panic in a bunker. Finally someone lit a flashlight, and someone else opened the ventilators, and we got a lamp lit, and the hubbub diminished. Some of the visitors, who were too exhausted to go back to their own bunkers, decided to stay with us, and it was necessary for a number of people to sleep on the floor. Berson and Rachel were among them. They lay down side by side on the crowded floor. For a time they participated in the general discussion, which had nothing to do with Peretz or my speech. The optimists and the pessimists were at each other, and though the pessimists were very strong among us, as always, it was amazing to hear how widespread was the conviction held by these Jewish fighters that they would survive the ghetto battle and the war. After a time Rachel and Berson broke away from the general conversation and began speaking softly to each other: certain reminiscences. Gradually the bunker settled itself for the night. The lamp was put out.

Berson was intensely aware of Rachel, he says. She was lying on her side with her face toward him and breathing with such control that he knew she was not the least bit inclined to fall asleep. He felt very tender toward her, and he says that his heart "burned" inside him.

Then Berson felt Rachel's left arm go around him and her hand settle between his shoulder blades. She put her cheek against his, and her body pressed close to his. She was trembling all over. Berson's first feeling was an overwhelming gratitude.

Berson, in an irrepressible, sighing whisper: —— Thank you, Rochele, thank you!

At first Berson felt that both he and Rachel were overflowing with the warmth and compassion that my speech had engendered in them. But very soon, he says, he knew that something far deeper and far more particular had been released in both of them. He hardly dared respond to Rachel's caresses.

Berson scrambled to his feet and, taking a hand of hers, drew her up, too. Then, very slowly and carefully, he began moving and, now and again accidentally kicking a sleeping form and once being cursed for clumsiness, he led her out of the bunker and at last into an unknown cellar—

EVENTS APRIL 24, 1943. ENTRY APRIL 25, 1943. N.L. With regard to my determination not to be nervous during my speech: I was nervous. After all, I was terrified. Awful symptoms. From the moment, just after the visit to our bunker by the boy with the scar, two days ago, when I realized the gravity of the occasion, I began to worry and tremble. I slept poorly the night before. Just before the speech, and during it, I suffered dreadfully: all the old manifestations. I became convinced, about halfway through the speech, that I was going to faint from the foulness of the air. And worse!—when the light first began to go dim, I was certain that my eyesight was taking leave of me. I was going blind. Thank God I realized almost at once —before most of my audience

—what really was happening, so that I was able to go on with good effect to my peroration!

Strange: I do not fear death so much as I feared this speech about the nature of Jewishness.

3

EVENTS APRIL 25, 1943. ENTRY MAY 12, 1943. FROM HA-LINKA APT. Halinka says that the pride of the couriers on the Aryan side grew as the fighting in the ghetto went into its fifth, sixth, seventh days (how was it possible that a few Jews could resist the firepower of trained troops so long?); but along with the pride, the couriers felt a bitter self-blame. Halinka suffered. She felt that she ought to be inside. She hated herself.

The seventh day of the battle was Easter Sunday, and Halinka was idle: she could get no appointments with Poles. Restlessly she went out walking. She felt herself drawn, against her better judgment, as if under hypnosis, to the vicinity of the ghetto. Among the Poles of the city, there was a holiday air. It was a good day, and thousands were out in the streets in their best clothes, going to and from church; many carried flowers. There was no holiday for the troops engaged against the Jews. One could hear the sound of cannon. Halinka walked up Miodowa toward this noise of big guns.

Up from the ghetto, in thick grey billows, rose a dreadful mass of smoke. The fires: they must be awful! Halinka thought of the letter she and the others had received from Hil Zilberzweig, the day before, describing the first five days of action, and what he had said of the peril of fire. [INSERT. ZILBERZWEIG'S LETTER TO THE COURIERS. COPY FROM YITZHOK. IN PART: . . . *In all our months of planning, it seems we hardly gave a thought to fire. The Germans have guessed this (seeing our otherwise undislodgeable fighters leaping from the top-storey windows of burning buildings), or else informers—a great scourge and curse, these informers; they tell where our bunkers are, and which sewers are being used for communications, and under which ruins bottle grenades are cached, and all our poor secrets—perhaps informers told the Ger-*

mans that we are vulnerable to fire. Fire destroys our above-ground strongpoints. This means that daytime sniping and grenade-pitching are becoming more and more difficult. It means that we are more and more being driven underground, and from bunkers the only sort of fighting we can do is in night patrols, and even they become hazardous when fires light up the streets and the Germans can lie hidden waiting to see us pass. Another bad thing: the fires have broken some of the links in our communications, which, as you know, ran here and there above ground, through buildings and along roofs. In repairing these breaks, our friend Berson has been doing superb work, but fire is faster to destroy than human hands are to build. I must tell you about what Berson has done with his concertina on night patrols. This is superb. He goes out. . . .]
Halinka says that as she walked among the happy Poles, she began to think of Berson: the evenings of music they had had together at the Britannia. *Blow, Blow, Evil Winds* and *I Don't Want to Give Up My Coupon* and *Why is the Sky?* and *Who Says You Can Love Only in Palaces?* and *Counterattack* and *Poverty Jumps.* . . . She was nearly to Dluga Street now, and the roar of the howitzers, set up in Krasinski Square, was close and awful. . . . Berson, outwardly so casual and impersonal, but really a stove of a man: that night he made her go on with the Heine song! . . .

A young Polish couple walked just ahead of Halinka. They were giggling, and the girl hugged the boy's arm (the smoke turgid across the sky did not interest them). The girl, Halinka noticed, was wearing a new green coat, proper for the season, and once Halinka got a glimpse of some lily-of-the-valley peeping over her shoulder. The girl looked up at her young man with adoring eyes.

Suddenly something up ahead—a sound—tugged at Halinka's heart. A concertina! Berson! A roar of a round from the guns, and then this thin, tinkling sound. Had she imagined it? It seemed to come from the direction of the ghetto. In mid-morning. Greatly agitated, Halinka hastened her pace and brushed past the young couple. Now she came out into Krasinski Square, along the north side of which ran the ghetto wall. The music was more distinct. She was mad; she felt it. To run out into the square where the guns were set up (their trail spades jammed down under the disturbed paving blocks) and expose herself to full view of the German artillerists! Madness. But that music! Was it real? Was it real? The Germans seemed almost to be lounging at their work; they paid no attention to Halinka or anyone else; quite a few Poles were watching the battery, standing in their best clothes on the sidewalks, smiling, nodding, putting their fingers in their ears and squealing like children at a fireworks when a round was sent off; smoke blackened the sky overhead. The music seemed to be off to the left now, and clearer. Halinka turned and ran toward it: it was coming from the direction of Krasinski Garden. It was quite strong. Halinka ran into the park.

The music was not that of a concertina at all.

Halinka stopped running. She felt very foolish, and she looked around to see whether anyone had been watching her. Then going on, Halinka saw that the music came from a little automatic organ in a merry-go-round. Booths were set up in a circle about the carrousel. There were sounds of high laughter and the little snappings of a shooting gallery. Halinka walked around inside the cheerful carnival. How happy the people were! The white horses bobbed up and down in the merry-go-round, and the music was gay and inviting. Slowly Halinka moved toward the glad round machine. It coasted down; the music dwindled and stopped. Halinka stepped quickly to the booth beside the merry-go-round and handed in a zloty; a girl inside pushed out fifty groszy in change. Halinka skipped up onto the platform and chose a horse with a light blue saddle and golden reins. She mounted sidesaddle and waited. Others clambered onto the platform and selected their mounts; there were children. The young lovers she had passed on Miodowa Street came trotting up, calling out to the guard in his shabby uniform not to start up the motor until they could get aboard.

The guard, in a sour voice, very unbecoming to this holiday contraption: —— Can't wait all day!

The couple jumped up. They took a pair of horses just in front of Halinka. The guard blew a tiny whistle and then threw a heavy brake-lever. With a shudder the platform began to move, and the tootle-organ began again. *The Merry Widow.*

For a few moments, with the music in her ears and the wind in her face, rising and falling and swinging around, Halinka was lost and rapturous. The young lovers ahead of her were holding hands, reaching out between their two horses: one went up as the other swooped down, and they laughed. Everything was a whirl of sweet primary colors. Spring!

Then Halinka, looking across the revolving platform, saw the face of an old man who was flirting with a pretty young girl, and she was shocked back to her own world. The merry-go-round turned, and she was aware again of the horrible grey smoke coming up beyond the brick wall at the edge of the park. The old man was Tomasz Kucharski, the former janitor.

Halinka remembered Yitzhok's words, coming thinned and far-hollow over the telephone that day. [INSERT. FROM EVENTS APRIL 20, 1943. Yitzhok: *You have not yet reported fulfillment of our promises to execute the swindlers Urbaniak and Kucharski. . . .*] At first Halinka was frightened. But she did not think he had seen her. Then at once she wondered how she had let herself slip into a carnival mood. The smoke pushed up sullenly from the ghetto.

Halinka kept her head averted from the old man's direction. Above all she must not let him see her. She remembered: she had not brought her revolver: she despised herself: she was giddy with self-hate. At last the roundel stopped. Halinka hurried off. Then near one of the booths she turned and looked: she saw him, with his hands on the girl, leading her off to one of the amusements under the half-tent on the other side of the carnival. Halinka loitered, trying to look casual but keeping track of the couple. How interminable their tolerance of the gaiety around them (the smoke, the heavy smoke!)! They moved from booth to booth, and the old man leered at the girl, and patted her, and gripped her arm.

It was nearly noon before the couple left the park. Halinka followed. On the street she kept nearly a block behind the pair. Once, after a turn, she was afraid she had lost them, but they had ducked into a store entrance in order to window-shop; she almost bumped into them as they came out. Kucharski took the girl into a restaurant on Teatralny Place. Halinka was afraid she would be noticed waiting for them; she moved back and forth as much as she could. They came out after about an hour, and they walked now down around the old ghetto boundaries and then northward on Zelazna. Just beyond the intersection at Chlodna, Halinka saw Kucharski stop the girl abruptly. Up ahead, at the corner of Ogrodowa, a manhole cover had suddenly seemed to lift itself. Up from the sewer opening came about a dozen Jews. They were horribly filthy. Their hair was matted, their clothes were slimy. They scattered like animals in the streets. The Easter Poles with the celebrant bouquets nodded and smiled and shrugged at this bizarre sight. But Halinka, who had closed up behind old Kucharski in this while, noticed that he seemed suddenly nervous and jerky. Halinka herself felt physically sick.

Kucharski doubled back (Halinka hurried past and eventually turned back herself) and out across Chlodna to Wronia, for apparently he could not bring himself to pass the still open sewer at Ogrodowa and Zelazna. He took the girl to an address on Zytnia Street and went in with her.

How long would an old man want on an Easter Sunday afternoon. . . ? Would there be time to get the pistol?

Halinka did not dare leave. She strolled and hung about and worried. At about seven o'clock, the old man came out alone. He seemed to be drunk. He walked to Wolska Street and waited for a streetcar. Halinka took her courage and waited behind him. She boarded the same crowded streetcar and stood on the end platform, not five feet from the old man. Once his eyes swept across her face, but did not pause, except perhaps for a moment's speculation. . . .

Kucharski rode across the river to Praga. Halinka followed him to Stolarska Street 43. Kucharski did not come out again during two hours that Halinka waited. Stolarska 43. She would have to remember that address.

4

EVENTS APRIL, 1943. ENTRY APRIL 26, 1943. N.L. Rachel and Berson have been like fellow conspirators lately. They are inseparable. I wonder what is between them. [NOTE. EDITOR. It must be remembered, again, that N.L. has not yet had the ✿ CONVERSATIONS, and so is unaware of the episode in the bunker the night of his speech, herein placed under EVENTS APRIL 24.]

EVENTS APRIL 26–27, 1943. ENTRY APRIL 27, 1943. N.L. Rachel and Berson away since yesterday afternoon. I hope nothing has happened to them.

EVENTS APRIL 26–28, 1943. ENTRY APRIL 28, 1943. I now discover that Rachel and Berson *planned* to absent themselves from us. Before they went out day before yesterday, Rachel held a conference with her section and battalion leaders, going over all possible contingencies with them, weaning them, as it were. She said that her brother Mordecai would be in command *in case anything happened to her*. Mordecai, unfortunately, is not a popular deputy. The fighters adored their Little Mother, but they find Mordecai rather surly and overbearing.

EVENTS APRIL 26–28, 1943. ENTRY APRIL 29, 1943. FROM DOLEK BERSON. Since last evening, Rachel and Berson are back with us. And they tell a strange story. At least, Berson tells it; Rachel is taciturn, even for her. It seems that their separation from us was accidental, after all.

Rachel and Berson were out together on the twenty-sixth, Berson tells me, because Rachel wanted to report personally to Yitzhok on the general situation of her Group and asked Berson to convoy her. They did report to Yitzhok and then started on their return trip to our bunker. On the way, at the corner of Mila and Lubetzkiego, at a place where there is a gap in our communications and they would have had to run across the street, there was some fighting going on. They therefore remained in a building on the north side of Mila Street. Hearing sounds of the skirmish for some time, they decided to go up in the building to some point of vantage, from which they could watch for an opportunity to get across the street. They had just begun to sneak up the stairs when a Jewish fighter ran in at the street door in quite a panic, as if someone were close after him, and clattered up the stairs.

Not wishing to be overtaken by the fighter's pursuer, Rachel and Berson jumped up and followed the man upstairs. On the top flight, he looked back at them doubtfully, but Rachel gave that day's Z.O.B. password, and the man led them into an apartment and through a bedroom to a closet, down from the false ceiling of which, at a tapping, a rope ladder was unrolled. The three ascended into a perfectly concealed attic strongpoint belonging, Berson says, to Ketzl's Dror Group.

About eight men were up there, playing cards. Ketzl himself was not there; this was apparently a "reserve stronghold." There were sounds of searching downstairs, and while they lasted, the card-players stayed absolutely still. Finally the pursuers gave up. The card game was resumed. A scout went down from the attic after a few minutes, but he came back up very shortly, saying that a group of Germans had bivouacked in a back room on the second floor: they were apparently Germans of a stubborn turn: they were going to play cat to the mice they had heard running upstairs. For two full days the Germans camped in that second-storey room.

Berson (as he tells the story): —— Perhaps they were waiting for us. Perhaps they were just tired of fighting and wanted a short vacation.

For the entire forty-eight hours while the fighters were trapped in the attic room, the men played cards. Berson joined the game for a time at their invitation, but he says he is a poor gambler (he himself says he seems to have the idea that he can prove he is a daredevil and a sport by accepting every wager that is offered; he has no eye for odds and probabilities; he should be, he says with a twinkle, lucky in love) and he had very soon lost all the money he was carrying except for the ten-zloty note I once gave him for a memento.

During the long wait, Berson says, Rachel was extremely impatient to get back to her Group. She kept wanting to send a scout below, or to go herself. The men were enjoying themselves; they were in no hurry; they laughed at her a little.

At last, on the second afternoon, a reconnaissance discovered that the Germans had decamped—leaving behind them a debris of ration tins and cigaret butts. Rachel and Berson hurried back to their bunker.

EVENTS APRIL 29, 1943. ENTRY DITTO. N.L. At a meeting of Z.O.B. commanders tonight, to which I was invited as recorder, I asked Yitzhok, on a hunch, after Rachel had left, whether she had personally reported to him on April 26. Yitzhok said not! I then discovered from Ketzl that he does not have any "reserve stronghold" on the north side of Mila: he has three strongpoints, all on Niska. Peculiar. Berson might have got Ketzl mixed up with one of the other Z.O.B. commanders, but that business of the non-existent report to Yitzhok is not so easy to explain. For that matter, nor is my hunch. . . .

✿ EVENTS APRIL 26–29, 1943. FROM CONVERSATIONS OF MAY 9–10, 1943. FROM DOLEK BERSON. . . . Next Berson told me that everything he said ten days ago about his and Rachel's "accidental" disappearance, April 26–28, had been pure invention.

I asked him why he had told such a careful and complicated story to me, none of it true.

Berson: —— To protect Rachel.

What really happened, he now says, was that, having discovered the night of my lecture on Peretz that they felt as they did, they now decided that for a few hours before they died (as in the extremity of battle they then expected to do) they wanted to find privacy and each other. They planned the escapade carefully, even to making arrangements in advance with a smuggler to rendezvous with them at a certain place once each evening while they were gone, in order to supply them, not only with necessities, but also with current Polish and German newspapers and even a bottle of wine. (*That* is where all of Berson's money except my ten-zloty note went!) They spent the time in a wild house on Nowolipie Street. They spent it, I gather, well.

I asked Berson why that detailed invention about the attic and the card game.

Berson: —— We settled on that story. We had to have some story. After all, Rachel had deserted her fighters in a way.

—— And what made her do that?

—— You'll have to ask her. I can't speak for Rachel . . . I have only this idea: we all sensed that the end was near, and I believe that Rachel felt that because her face is not too pretty, she had so far in her life missed a tremendous experience—for which she thought she might have a certain talent.

—— In this was she right or wrong?

—— She was right. A very appreciable talent, in my opinion.

—— And did not the matter of Rachel's face trouble you?

—— I love her.

—— I see.

I then asked Berson whether his remark about the imaginary German soldiers who camped on the imaginary second floor [INSERT. FROM ENTRY APRIL 29. Berson: *Perhaps they were just tired of fighting and wanted a short vacation. . . .*] might have had an unconscious application to himself and Rachel.

559

Berson: —— Perhaps in my case it might have applied. In Rachel's case I am almost certain not.

—— Then did Rachel show the restlessness and impatience to be back with her fighters that you imputed to her in the imaginary attic during the imaginary card game?

—— I do not wish to sound immodest . . . but . . . no! She regretted leaving her fighters, but I flatter myself that she did not regret being with me.

—— Possibly you are lucky in love, as you suggested in speaking of your imaginary losses!

My next question may have been an unkind reminder (in these last moments I want to know everything!). I asked Berson whether he did not feel that he was somehow betraying Symka.

Berson, with directness and yet leaving something unsaid and withheld: —— Symka is dead.

Then I asked Berson why he had told me that Rachel reported to Yitzhok on the twenty-sixth, when that was a fact so easy to be checked; the same as to Ketzl's "stronghold."

Berson: —— I'm not a practiced liar.

And that, at least, I feel sure, is the truth.

✡ LATER IN THE SAME CONVERSATION. FROM DOLEK BERSON. I would never, until this moment, have attributed to Berson the slightest poetic streak. But now (I am not saying that his poetry is any good: I only say that it is a stuff I had never seen or imagined in Berson):

Berson: —— The moment we entered the room I knew we had come home. It was just right. The place had not been looted. There was dust on the woodwork but Rachel drove it away with a cloth she found. She was frightened. I thought she was going to be irritable, but instead she whistled and worked as if I were not there. I watched her. Then I felt that she was crying and she ran to me and we embraced standing. I bent over and picked her up in my arms. I can say that what came next was natural, if as you listen you will think with all your mind that everything that happens in nature is a miracle. It was as if a bud had been imprisoned in its scales too long and now came into full flower all at once, almost exploding into a wonder of fragrance and color. I could not suppress her, Noach, and she could not imagine me. We were wild enough for a lifetime. . . .

5

Events April 25–30, 1943. Entry April 30, 1943. N.L. To an extent Felix Mandeltort has resolved his conflict. And in the process he has helped all of us resolve ours.

Ours was a hard one, bred of hard fighting: should we remaining Jews try to keep ourselves alive or should we deliberately die in battle?

I feel sure that our decision in the meeting tonight would have been different had it not been for Felix—had it not been for the fact that Felix has to a degree unified himself. I say "to a degree"—for though his integration is apparent, it is also apparent that a man does not change abruptly overnight; besides, in our endangered condition, we are not always as we seem.

To go back a few days, Felix's disappearance was as much . . .

Events night of April 25–26, 1943. Entry April 26. From Dolek Berson and Rachel Apt. Felix was lost on patrol last night. The battle was a week old yesterday, and all of us had grown exhausted and deeply discouraged. It had become clear to us that the Z.O.B. could neither inflict serious damage upon the Germans nor effectively protect the large mass of working and wild Jews from deportation: we estimate that the Germans had evacuated 25,000 Jews in the first seven days of fighting. We of the Z.O.B. were such a small handful! The exhilaration of the first two or three days, when we had stung and even frightened the enemy, had passed. So had the conviction that if we fought hard enough, we would survive. We were in despair last night, and Mandeltort quite obviously shared the desperation.

The patrol went to the "front"—the place where at any given moment the Germans seemed to be most active: last night it was Niska Street. During the day the Germans had set fire to all the buildings on the north side of the street. Hundreds of Jews had swarmed out from the enflamed houses, and those who had not been picked off by the Germans were now hemmed into the courtyards and buildings on the south side of the street. A thick crowd of these helpless refugees would stagger into a courtyard and perhaps rush up into a staircase of a building. Then some of the people, feeling that there was only danger in numbers, would try to get away from the packed mob—out through some window on knotted blankets, or down into a cellar on a hunt for a passage into the sewers; others would follow them, in spite of their protests; and then there would be a surge, a panic, and the blankets would tear with the weight of the impatient climbers, or the cellar would fill up to the choking point. And wherever the Germans came upon these eddying, unarmed, fear-crazed crowds, they would attack them at leisure with automatic weapons; huge piles of the dead could be found in single staircases or in cellars or in the corners of courtyards. Our patrols were trying to protect these herds from attack: this was one thing the Z.O.B. still felt it could do.

There were eleven in the patrol with Felix. Rachel was in command. Berson, Mordecai Apt, and Rutka were along. [NOTE. N.L. Rutka has gone out on several patrols. On one occasion I took a recess from my work as a historian to serve as caretaker to tiny Israel so that Rutka could go out. What an exciting few hours for me! The baby is not yet old enough to recognize even its own mother, but it did seem to me to be making efforts to establish human contacts: it held my finger with a rather desperate fellow-feeling.] The Group went through from our bunker to Mila by one of Berson's cellar-to-cellar passages; ran across Mila overground; got up onto the roofs of the buildings on Mila and moved around to Lubetzkiego and Niska by way of roofs, attics, and courtyards. In one of the Lubetzkiago courtyards, they sneaked up on two Polish policemen looting the clothes from dead Jews, and shot them. [NOTE. FROM DOLEK BERSON. In this courtyard, Berson says he had very strongly a recollection of the courtyard where the "family" lived on Nowolipie Street on a spring evening: the chatter of weary people, the open place strewn with household goods for which there was no room within, a rug being beaten on a frame, some men repairing a broken table, a girl singing on a doorstep, and over all the fragrance of lilacs and a surprisingly good humor.] The patrol found what it was looking for—milling, havenless crowds—in the courtyards of Niska south, and it established itself in a strongpoint at Number 43.

Mandeltort, as they waited there: —— I am old enough to be the father of all you children.

Berson: —— I doubt it. I feel very old tonight. About seventy years old.

Mandeltort, answering Berson rather sentimentally: —— I hope when I get to be seventy, I can make music like yours, Grandfather Dolek.

Mordecai: —— Do you expect to live to be seventy?

Mandeltort: —— Berson has—why shouldn't I?

The patrol waited in the strongpoint for about an hour. Then Rachel spotted a group of Germans going toward the entrance of the courtyard at Niska 41. Rachel commanded the others to open fire, and the shooting had at once the desired effect: it decoyed the Germans away from the courtyard full of Jews. The Germans spread out, surrounded Niska 43, and eventually attacked; they used grenades and machine pistols. When the Germans stormed the staircase in strength, Rachel gave the order to move up to the roof and get away. Mandeltort and Berson stationed themselves on a landing of the staircase to cover the withdrawal.

Mandeltort, when the Germans were part way up the stairs: —— Go along, Grandfather Dolek.

Berson: —— We can both go now.

Mandeltort: —— Go along.

Berson scrambled up to the attics and out onto the roofs. The patrol waited on the roof of Niska 45 for quite a long time, but although no further shots could be heard from 43, Felix did not appear. The patrol finally left. They were puzzled, because there had been no shots: definitely no shots or grenade explosions; yet Felix had not come.

EVENTS APRIL 26, 1943. ENTRY DITTO. FROM MORDECAI APT. Mordecai thought he saw Felix with the Germans today, but I feel sure Mordecai's imagination has been playing tricks on him. Mordecai is awfully tired. He doesn't get enough sleep: who does? But he also works too hard all day. I am worried about him.

At about three o'clock this afternoon a courier came into our bunker to tell us that a tank had appeared on Mila Street, and that it was shelling house after house and causing casualties and panic among wild people there: we were asked to send a handful of fighters with bottle bombs, grenades, and small arms, to try to stop the tank. Mejlach, Mordecai, Wladislaw, and two or three others went.

Mejlach led the group through underground to Mila Street, where it surfaced. The boys, taking up positions just inside a courtyard, could hear the tank, moving in spurts, firing occasional rounds. Mordecai says that Wladislaw was very agitated and short-tempered: he had objected to being jostled accidentally in the dark in the cellars on the way through, and later, as the patrol stood waiting in the courtyard, he pushed Mejlach aside roughly once when Mejlach civilly asked him to stand back so as to be sure of having cover. He snarled at everything and seemed to be in a generally nasty frame of mind. He was particularly ugly toward Mordecai. Yet his behavior, when the tank drew abreast of the courtyard entrance, was, Mordecai says, heroic in a perverse way.

Wladislaw, to Mordecai, in a queer, childish whine: —— If you're so brave, follow me!

Then, with an incendiary bottle in one hand and an explosive grenade in the other, Wladislaw ran out into the street, leaving all cover behind. He appeared to have decided to throw away his life. He managed to shatter his bottle bomb against the side of the tank and he rolled the explosive grenade into its treads. Before the grenade went off, Wladislaw was killed by a burst of machine-pistol fire from the direction of Zamenhofa Street. Mordecai, incidentally, had not followed him out. He would have been foolish to have done so, as it turned out, for the grenade burst the treads.

The boys stood by, hoping for a chance to recover Wladislaw's body, and it was about half an hour later that a German command car drove slowly along the street, and in its front seat, with the driver, Mordecai says, were two Jews—some woman and Felix. There were Germans in the back seat, he thinks. None of the others in the patrol saw these "Jews." Mordecai seems very stubborn in his belief that he saw Felix.

EVENTS APRIL, 1943. ENTRY APRIL 29, 1943. N.L. We survive. We even fight. When I think of it! Anyone who told me, on the first day of this battle, that we would be alive, to say nothing of resisting, twelve days later, I would have regarded as nonsensically optimistic. Yet here we are.

We live by smuggling and barter, and we are getting some basic lessons in economics. For instance: *First Lesson: Foreign Trade: Sufficient incentive will overcome all obstacles of geography, prejudice, politics, and hazard.* We have developed, at this late hour, a new branch of foreign trade—with Poles who actually smuggle their goods in to us Jews from outside. One whom we call Lantern Head came in last night with a rather large package containing bread, cheese, flints, two flashlights, denatured alcohol, and yesterday's *Nowy Kurjer*. Incentive: 75,000 zlotys, payable in second-hand clothing. How strange it was to read a current newspaper and discover that, after all, the universe stretches out beyond our wall! *Second Lesson: Real Values: Rarity is not the finally controlling factor in the worth of anything: some human appetite is the real determinant.* Diamonds, which are rare enough in the ghetto, have become quite worthless in our domestic trade. One pistol equals one hundred cigarets, ten kilograms of lard, and a half-liter of vodka. One cigaret equals one kilogram of flour. Yet in this crazy appetite-economy we are able to eat a little, smoke a little, shoot a little; and before lying down to try to sleep many of us take stiff swigs of vodka.

The rhythm of our life has changed altogether. All our domestic work is done by night. We can safely keep a stove going at night, as our smoke, vented from Menkes' chimney, is lost in the blackness and general conflagration outside, whereas by day the specific plume might be visible. We therefore cook, bathe ourselves, and wash clothes by night. Water is difficult. The running water supply of the whole ghetto has been shut off for several days, along with all other utilities. We have a well six meters deep in the floor of our "back room," and into this hole seeps a rather muddy fluid, which we are obliged to use.

We are crowded. This bunker was designed for forty people at the outside. We are nearly a hundred and thirty now. . . .

EVENTS NIGHT APRIL 29–30, 1943. ENTRY APRIL 30. N.L. At about two o'clock in the morning, in comes Berson, having been out on a "guerrilla concert"—leading Felix! Felix back again! It seems that Felix always reappears. He came back from jail, he came back from the *Umschlagplatz*, he came back from the brushmakers' battle, and now he comes back from . . . I must get the story in detail.

Felix is very tired, but he seems content. I have never before seen him so placid. He wears a completely different suit of clothes from the one he had on when he "disappeared." His face is bruised and he limps badly: his knee hurts.

Mordecai is perfectly delighted, because our firm doubts had begun to make him doubt himself: Felix *was* in that command car, it seems. . . .

EVENTS NIGHT APRIL 29–30, 1943. ENTRY APRIL 30. FROM DOLEK BERSON. Berson tells how he found Felix last night:

Berson was out with his concertina, playing his game of restless music. His scope in these "guerrilla concerts" is not what it used to be, because so many of his channels of communications have been destroyed. Nevertheless, within an area of about four blocks square, he is still able to serenade-and-run. And still he infuriates the Germans, to judge by their quick-trigger response.

Last night Berson got a scare. He had just broken off a number, a Schubert Lied, *Der Erlkönig*, playing in Smocza Street near Gliniana, when he had a feeling that someone was sneaking up on him. Always the Germans had been clumsy in their pursuit of him, perhaps because of their black anger: they curse him from a distance and fire blindly; Berson had been expecting them to try to trap him by craft; and now he had this feeling. He ran off.

Berson played next in a section of sewer under Ostrowska; he was certain that no one followed him there. But then, when he went up into the street again, on Wolynska, he was once more troubled by sounds he heard within the texture of the crackling and crashing of fires, shots, screams, and the throbbing of motors: near him, sounds of careful moving. Next he ran up into an attic of a building on Lubetzkiego: he stopped abruptly on the way upstairs, and below him he heard, distinctly, muffled steps and heavy breathing. All the same, he ran on up and played a few measures. He broke off and was about to climb out onto the roof when he heard a sharp whisper below and behind him:

—— Grandfather Dolek!

This frightened Berson. Felix Mandeltort had made that melancholy joke, the night he disappeared. Berson had been convinced by the rest of us that Felix had been lost; yet he had heard Mordecai insist and insist that he had seen the Mandeltort profile in that German command car. . . .

Berson, harshly using the gibberish phrase that had come to be the accepted challenge, to inquire whether someone met in the dark was Jewish or not: —— *Amkho?*

—— Yes, Dolek. It's Mandeltort.

Berson showed himself. The young man and the elderly man shook hands, like two relatives meeting each other on an evening stroll.

Berson: —— Where have you been?

Felix, cheerfully: —— To death and back.

Berson: —— How was it over there?

Felix: —— Cold. I like it better here. . . . Show me the way to the bunker. I was lost, and I heard your music. Whew! You are agile for a man of seventy!

EVENTS APRIL 25–26, 1943. ENTRY APRIL 30. FROM FE-LIX MANDELTORT. . . . Felix's disappearance was as much of a surprise to him as to his companions. Felix says he fully intended to follow Berson up to the roofs and away. A few seconds after Berson left, when it was apparent that the younger man was safely out, and allowing himself just enough time to get up and go before the climbing Germans would reach him, he thought, he raised himself up to run. He felt suddenly as if his right leg were in a vise, and he fell down on the stair-landing. Apparently his long crouch had induced a cramp in the muscles of his thigh. Three Germans were over him in a moment. One held forward a revolver, and Felix thought he was finished.

Felix, in Hebrew: —— Hear, O Israel! . . .

Then one of the other Germans restrained the man with the revolver and the three muttered together. They bent over Felix.

One of them, in German: —— What is the matter?

—— I have a cramp.

—— Will you give us information?

—— Whatever you wish.

[NOTE. N.I. Felix declares that at the time he did not know what these men were asking of him, or what he was promising.]

There followed an incredible scene, in which the three Germans became suddenly solicitous, and began to massage, thump, stretch, and bend Felix's leg, until, at length, the cramp was quite gone. The Germans invited Felix to stand up and test his leg; he did; it was fine. The Germans smiled to him agreeably and led him off.

They took him to Zelazna Street 101. He remembered that this was next door to what had formerly been (and might still be) headquarters of the *Einsatz Reinhardt,* the evacuation Kommando. He was led into a well-furnished room, with a couple of desks and electric lights, which dazzled his eyes. A clerk at one of the desks asked him a number of questions, among them:

Clerk: —— Your address?

Felix, ironically: —— Do you mean my residence or my place of employment?

Clerk, unruffled and polite: —— Your bunker.

Felix, lying: —— I had none. I was what we call "wild."

Clerk: —— Understood.

After the questioning, which was something like the process of being admitted to a hospital, Felix was led by a German corporal into a kind of locker room. The corporal, taking a clean towel and a cake of soap from a shelf, told Felix in a kindly voice to undress and take a shower, and he pointed to an adjacent room from the open door of which steam was pouring; he said he would have some clean clothing ready for him afterward. But Felix had heard about the infamous "shower baths." Not for him this German way.

Felix: —— Why don't you just shoot me? I would rather be shot.

The corporal, with a smile: —— There is no shooting here. Come, bathe yourself. You are filthy.

Just then a man came out of the shower chamber, drawing a towel across his back and sighing luxuriously. Felix saw with one look at his nakedness that the man was Jewish. Felix began unsteadily to undress.

The showered Jew, dressing himself in freshly laundered underwear: —— A newcomer?

Felix, suspiciously: —— How long have you been here?

The clean Jew: —— About ten days. Since just after the fighting started.

Felix says he did not feel like asking any more questions; he did not want to test his own credulity, or his mental orientation. The clean Jew began to whistle as he dressed. The corporal had left.

The clean Jew, briskly: —— Hot water, it feels good!

Felix went into the shower and bathed. He washed out his encrusted hair with the fragrant soap and cleaned the ulcerous sores on his legs and was released from his own foul odor. He came out feeling as young as Berson, he says wryly. The corporal had laid out clean clothes—cheap but clean linen, and a grey suit that fitted pretty well.

The astounding procedure (this was crazy: it must have been about three in the morning) was elaborated: Felix was taken to a barber, who shaved him and cut his hair; he was taken into a refectory and fed hot onion soup and bread and cheese (And a Polish waiter said: *Not too much at first, friend.*); he was handed a pack of cigarets. He was led into a sitting room and asked to wait. There were volumes of Schiller, Goethe, and Rilke on a table. Felix picked up the Rilke and sat in an easy chair reading until he fell asleep.

Felix says he does not know how long he slept. When he first woke up, he had the strange and pleasant half-recollections of a man who has been enjoying wish-fulfillment dreams. That politeness all around! Then he saw the strange, clean trouser on his leg; he felt the soft upholstery under him. It was daylight. He had not dreamt. He waited.

At last he was led into an office where a single S.S. officer sat, and without beating about the bush this man straightly told Felix that he could stay alive and live well if he would inform the Germans as to the location of bunkers, communication channels, grenade caches, or anything else of interest he might know. The officer held up his hand and said that Felix would not be asked for specific information until he had seen for one day the "routine."

The officer himself took Felix on a tour of the informers' barracks. He showed him the men's dormitory, where, he said, about thirty "congenial" Jews were now domiciled; he showed him an auditorium in which, he told Felix, lectures, concerts, and moving pictures were put on nightly; he showed him a canteen, where everything that was available to the German Army, from candy to birth-control devices, could be bought by the Jewish guests. He called them guests. He was very deferential. He told Felix that during the afternoon, he would be taken on a "demonstration." He begged Felix to make himself at home, meanwhile. Had he had breakfast? . . .

The "demonstration" consisted of a ride in a command car, along with a Jewish woman informer and three Germans. Yes, the car drove slowly through Mila Street at about three thirty on the afternoon of April 26; Mordecai could have seen it. The woman led the Germans to Mila Street 41, and said that there was a bunker underneath. She particularized as to entrances and even ventilation outlets. [INSERT. FROM ENTRY MAY 2. FROM YITZ-HOK KATZ. The bunker at Mila 41, belonging to Mendel's Dror Group, was in fact attacked on the night of April 26–27, with machine guns, grenades, and "some kind of poison gas." (NOTE. N.L. Is this only tear gas?) It is known that sixteen fighters of Mendel's Group, besides a number of wild people taking shelter in the bunker, were killed.] That was all. The command car drove back to the barrack at Zelazna 10ᴸ.

That evening, after a large supper which included a German Army field ration of meat stew, Felix was called into the office of the S.S. man he had seen in the morning. This officer, a very young and fair-faced man, said that he hoped Mandeltort had had a pleasant day; Mandeltort could now unburden himself.

Felix: —— I have made a decision. From your point of view, the wrong one.

The fair-faced officer, without emotion: —— And from yours.

Felix was led forthwith into a bare, benchless room, where he was beaten. He was taken back to the officer, who asked whether he had changed his mind. He said he had not. The officer said he was a fool and summoned two enlisted Germans, who took Felix into another bare room. Here there were four other Jews. Three more joined them shortly. Later, the eight Jews were taken by truck to the *Umschlagplatz*.

Felix, to the other Jews in the truck on the way to the *Umschlagplatz*: —— Nu, anyhow, we have had a pleasant surprise. At Treblinka, we can tell them we don't need a bath—we've just had one!

EVENTS APRIL 26–27. ENTRY APRIL 30, 1943. FROM FELIX MANDELTORT. From what Felix says, the situation at the *Umschlagplatz* has deteriorated horribly. Not that there was ever any order there (even under our Jewish *Ordnungsdienst*). But now it is apparently a scene of utter demoralization, murder, and putridness. In situations where the Baltic troops might previously have used abusive language or at most whips, they now use their pistols, with aim to kill. The bodies of dead Jews are left lying around, purple, swollen, and gaseously rotting. Felix saw a baby, perhaps eighteen months or two years old, playing, gurgling, and laughing around its mother's new-slain corpse. There is no food at the *Umschlagplatz*. Polish police, reduced to the lowest degree of venality, walk in and out among the dead bodies, carrying buckets, trying to swindle living Jews, who may still have jewels, with dippers full of Vistula water.

Felix, unable at last to catalogue the details of this gruesome place: —— It is the end of the world, Noach, the end of the world.

The group from the informers' barrack, distinguished from all the rest by their cleanliness (the men close-shaven, the women with their hair washed and combed), were thankfully led to a train the first morning after their arrival at the *Umschlagplatz*. Felix says that he saw Fischel Schpunt put into one of the boxcars, and the ugly fellow was limp, witless, and empty-eyed, an entertainer no longer.

[INSERT. FROM ENTRY MAY 3, 1943. FROM A FIGHTER IN MONTEFIORE'S HASHOMER GROUP. I have been able at last to find a man who witnessed the taking of Fischel Schpunt. I have wanted thus at least to signalize the departure of the one who, better than any of the rest of us, exercised that inalienable right which we Jews hold so dear: the right to mock the pompous. As background for what happened when he was taken, I remind myself of Mordecai Apt's account of Schpunt's failure to amuse the "new Germans," just before the battle. (ENTRY APRIL 18, 1943.)

Schpunt, I understand, had changed markedly in the last few days. He had become taciturn, deadly earnest, and somehow weak. With his power to make the Germans laugh taken from him, he was a shorn Samson. He became servile, as he had used to be when he was a disfigured little nobody in the Self-Help Department of the *Judenrat*, before the days of his hilarious glory. He asked Jankiel Montefiore to be allowed to join the children as a courier for the fighters, and it was indeed as a child, an outcast, ugly child, that he spent his last few days.

On the afternoon when he was captured, April 29, Montefiore's Group got into some trouble in a building on Mila Street, and Jankiel sent Schpunt to ask Aron Weiss's Group to come into a near-by building and cover a removal. A member of Montefiore's Group at a lookout post saw Schpunt dash out into the street (as evidently there were no cellar communications from that building), and the queer, brachycephalic little man seemed to get along fine for a time: he dashed erratically back and forth as he ran, and took cover every few yards in a doorway. Then once he sprinted into a doorway, which was across the street from the lookout (my witness), and in this doorway, unfortunately, were crouching five Germans, themselves taking cover. Schpunt ran straight into their arms. At once two of the five Germans dragged their prisoner out into the street and began running with him between them back up toward Zamenhofa, past the window in which my witness was stationed. My witness wanted to try to snipe at the Germans, but he says Montefiore restrained him, fearful of giving away the already precarious position of the entire Group.

Schpunt, screaming so loudly that the whole canyon of the street was filled with his anguish: —— My blood will be on your heads!

This was a heartfelt cry, not put forth for purposes of amusement, but now once more, when Schpunt evidently least expected it, his rufous and contorted face struck the two Germans as being comical, and they looked at each other and broke out laughing.

And so this odd trio staggered down the street, the prisoner screaming invective and his captors roaring with laughter. It was Schpunt's last farce.

Schpunt, as they went along: —— You'll pay for this! You'll live in shame!]

CONTINUING EVENTS APRIL 27, AS ABOVE. FROM FELIX MANDELTORT. The door of the boxcar was sealed. The wheels beneath began to roll.

Felix says that the passengers in the car destined for Treblinka were barely human beings. There were nearly two hundred of them. Most of them had been wild people, and in truth Felix now saw some reason in that appellation. Among all except those eight Jews who had refused to turn informer, and who were kempt, these creatures seemed not to be directed by intelligence; they were animals, and beaten animals at that. They moved very little. If they made any sounds, they were mostly grunts or moans. The car was so crowded that not all could recline at once. One of the eight who had refused to inform prayed loudly, standing; he seemed to be going through the entire order of morning prayers.

The mournful voice of the devout one: —— . . . O my God! guard my tongue from evil and to such as curse me, let my soul be dumb, yea . . .

Felix says that ever since he had had his second interview with the S.S. officer at Zelazna 101, and had insisted that he would not betray his fellows, he had felt unafraid. He was suddenly released from the tension and anxiety he had felt for so very long. He says he felt sure this was not just such a simple thing as atonement for all his previous weaknesses and compromises; he knew that the bath, the hot meals, the squares of chocolate, and the marvelous, dizzying cigarets had all raised his spirits. But one thing he did notice: he had stopped mulling over the past. No longer did the constant sequence of recollected pictures, which had been with him day and night during the past weeks, go through his mind's stereopticon: the day at his desk when the certificates had come from Palestine, the assassination of Zweinarcz, the moment when he was apprehended with Halinka's white fox cape, holding it up for the double-dealing Polish smuggler-informer in that dark cellar in the suburb called Brudno. . . . Those pictures had all gone dark. A phrase he had read in the Rilke in that dreamlike waiting room stuck now in his mind:

The future enters into us, in order to transform itself in us, long before it happens.

Felix thought about the future, couched in himself, foetuslike, and he says his thoughts did not revolve about the enclosures and warehouses and dank, poisonous chambers of Treblinka, though he had, from the Slonim Report and other accounts, clear enough pictures of those things stored away in his head. No, he kept thinking of some kind of future in Warsaw. His thoughts were not selfish: he thought of his companions in the ghetto—but he saw himself among them. He kept thinking about such a future, and wondering. . . .

His head tilted back. For some time he had been studying the ventilators at the top of the car. Along the center of the ceiling of the car, running the whole length of it, was a raised, box-like section, which formed the catwalk above. This rectangular elevation was about two feet wide and stood up from the rest of the roof nearly a foot. In its sides, in pairs at each end of the car, were ventilators, wooden flaps suspended on transom rods. These flaps, when open, *might* give room for a human body to wedge itself through. Each flap was controlled by a short lever, which normally would be swung open and shut by a long pole with a finger on it, like a boat hook. There was no such pole in the car, though there were squeeze-brackets to hold one on the end wall of the car.

Felix called for silence in the car. He then asked for volunteers to form a human pyramid so that he could try the ventilators. He said it might be possible for some of those in the car to escape. The lethargic Jews argued against him.

—— There are guards on top of the cars. Haven't you heard them walking along up there?

—— Who's going to kneel at the bottom of the pyramid? We'd never have the strength.

—— No! No! If one jumps, all will be punished.

At last, after argument, pleading, and even vituperation, Felix persuaded some to try. At the base they placed the dead, as a solid foundation. Twelve men knelt shoulder-to-shoulder on this platform. Once, when the pyramid was nearly completed, the train slowed down and jerked to a stop, and the human structure collapsed. Again, as it was built after the train resumed its motion, a man in the second layer fainted, and all fell. A third time it held. Felix scrambled up the staircase of reluctant backs, jerked the lever down, found the flap to be nearly ten inches high, and, getting first one knee up, then the other foot, he put his legs out through the slot, and wriggling and pushing, deflating his chest by exhaling until there were spots in his eyes, thankful indeed that he had in four years lost sixty pounds, at last he managed to push himself out on the roof. He saw a German guard running forward on the catwalks, several cars back. He gathered his feet under him and jumped out from the train far enough to miss the stone track-bed and landed in some bushes. He twisted his knee and, rolling over, banged his face on the ground, jarring bright lights in his head. He heard a shot but felt nothing. The future, he was thinking exultantly, enters into us. . . .

[NOTE ON EVENTS APRIL 27, 1943. N.L. I shall at some future time (if the future enters into *me* in sufficient measure!) attempt to set down in detail the account of Felix's return to Warsaw. From what little he has told of it, the adventure will make a vivid personal account, but in fact I suspect it is not vitally significant—as I feel the escape from the cars, and what went into it, and what has resulted from it, have been. (NOTE. EDITOR. As it turned out, N.L. apparently never found time to write out this promised account. It is lost to us.)]

EXCERPTS FROM MINUTES OF MEETING OF Z.O.B. COMMANDERS AND CO-ORDINATING COMMITTEE, APRIL 30, 1943, 9 P.M., IN YITZHOK'S BUNKER, ZILBERWEIG PRESIDING. N.L. Zilberzweig called the meeting to order. He said that the topic for discussion was whether it would be better for the Z.O.B. to fight on in the ghetto, or to make attempts to evacuate Groups to the forests outside Warsaw; everyone would have to make his personal decision as to his own life and death, but a common cause called for a collective decision.

Yitzhok: —— There are two ways of dying. One is certain; it is now. The other is after an uncertain delay, of perhaps a few days. We have to analyze the difference between these two. It is not great.

Ganzener: —— In most of the ghettos there has been no resistance at all. Why should we be an example for all Jewry? Perhaps it is better for one Jew to live than to kill five Germans and then die.

Anselm: —— We are destined to be liquidated. Neither fighting here nor fleeing to the forest can save our lives. The only course is to die with honor. I don't know whether we have sufficient means to fight much longer, but we *must* fight with what we have.

Abraham: —— Nonsense! There is no more Jewry, just dregs. There is no more resistance, only tatters. There is no question of honor, we ought to hide and save ourselves.

Yitzhok: —— Here in the ghetto we can at least protect the lives of helpless Jews.

Ganzener: —— How long?

Nahum: —— We cannot pull in two directions. We cannot plan to fight here and plan also to go to the woods. The woods are illusion. There is no time. There is only one reply to the Germans, and that is to fight here in the ghetto as long as we can.

Yitzhok: —— I agree. This debate is not natural. Is a soldier on the front line permitted to argue about life and death, or whether to stay or run? Why do we talk so much about perishing?

Our fighters have their work to do; they have their orders. I say that we cannot give anyone any moral excuse for running away.

Zilberzweig: —— Everyone must have a chance to speak up.

Ganzener: —— You force everyone to speak up. You force a "yes" when you know people want to say "no."

Zilberzweig: —— I force nothing.

Yitzhok: —— In the face of death, with nothing to lose and nothing to preserve, one becomes strong.

Abraham: —— I want you to know that I will abide by your decision, whatever it may be, but I am amazed at your calm. When I see a German, I tremble. I am about finished.

Yitzhok: —— Concretely to the matter at hand: we must make detailed plans. Perhaps we could pull in our Groups to defend a smaller area. Let us begin to think along those lines. . . .

[NOTE. N.L. Up to this point in the discussion, the hard and forceful men, like Yitzhok, Nahum, and Anselm, had dominated. One can see that Yitzhok even assumed that the debate was over. Only Ganzener and Abraham, in a rather defeatist mode, had advocated the woods. It should be noted that Rapaport was not present: perhaps his voice might have given a different tone to the discussion. I myself kept thinking: This is going too fast! These people are speaking in telegrams to express volumes. It is not suitable to speak of death in hasty sentences. This matter should be weighed. . . . Then Mandeltort made his remarkable, oblique, quiet, directionless speech. Everyone at the meeting knew that Mandeltort had refused to turn informer and that he had, at the age of fifty-six, jumped the train to Treblinka in order to come back to us: the purple bruise on his face was his badge of authority. We listened hushed. Felix spoke with a thickness, as if he had something in his mouth; probably his cheek was swollen within.]

Mandeltort: —— Wait! We seem to have decided this matter and yet I cannot remember any precise point at which we decided. I cannot remember a vote. I cannot remember that we have asked the poor helpless Jews whose lives we are supposed to be protecting what *they* thought. . . . It is difficult to speak. It is difficult to choose for oneself. I suppose that living is not the important thing. The question of life and death should be insignificant to us, after what we have seen. It is too early to summarize the experiences of these years, but think how we have allowed the enemy to take us

piecemeal! . . . I don't know. . . . It seems to me that heroic
death does not accord with the traditions of our people. We have
had very few brutes and bullies. . . . In speaking of hiding or of
the forest, one should not think of an act of cowardice: no and no!
I place a certain value upon the lives of the young men here, especially perhaps of those who wish so noisily to die. . . . I have lost
my family and everything I held dear, yet I suppose that subcon-
sciously I want to live. My second daughter was my favorite, she
was a very hard one to please. You see, I am trying to say . . . I
don't know exactly . . . I am very much concerned for an infant
child born recently in the bunker where I now live. Its name is Israel. . . . Please, I waste your time. I only wish to say: Do not
be hasty, young men. . . . I wish to put that infant in your
minds. . . .

[NOTE. N.L. Felix's voice trailed off. We were all silent for
a long time after the speech, and thoughtful. What did Felix mean
exactly by those restless, vague words? I thought I knew, but I am
well acquainted with him. I felt like weeping. Finally:]

Yitzhok: —— I did not mean to be hasty. I thought we
agreed.

Nahum, truculently: —— What is this talk of infants?

[NOTE. N.L. But the tide had turned. Zilberzweig now
gravely said that one point that had not been thoroughly discussed
was the future of our respective Jewish movements and organizations. Fifteen minutes later the meeting voted to send two delegates to the Aryan side to explore the possibilities of moving some
Groups to the forests. There was considerable discussion as to who
should be sent, and finally we settled on Lazar Slonim, who because of the integrity of his trip to Treblinka is trusted by all, and
Dolek Berson, since he is an expert on communications and can
help in inventing a means of escape (and incidentally is a man
whom all factions think they can trust, so impartial was he in ex-
tending and connecting the interior channels for and between the
various political groupings). Thus we learned the real importance
of Felix's integration, and of his return to us.]

EVENTS NIGHT APRIL 30–MAY 1, 1943. 3 A.M. ENTRY
DITTO. N.L. I am very tired. After interviewing Felix and writing until about midnight, I went out to bury a parcel of manuscript at the Swientojcrska cache; then I came back to the bunker.

Slonim and our Berson left from here a few minutes ago—these old acquaintances, who so much enjoy arguing with each other. Berson took his concertina. We have heard him play twice in the sewers. I am terribly tired. There! He is playing again. Now he is so far away that I cannot make out the tune; only certain notes, certain pitches and resonances, come to us all this way. What are you playing for us, Dolek? The music stops.

Come back, Dolek, when your errand is done. Come safely back!

6

EVENTS APRIL 30, 1943. ENTRY MAY 1, 1943. FROM RA-CHEL APT. Rachel says she lifted a finger to her lips to shush her companions.

Rachel, Rutka, and three others were in a second-floor room on Ostrowska Street. They had become separated from a section of Rachel's Group, and they were in a fugitive condition. They had fled across some roofs in the open, had jumped down into this building through a skylight, and had come to rest in this room quite by chance: it was as good and bad as any other room in the ghetto: there were photographs on the walls of six innocent-eyed, candlestick-necked Yeshiva students. What high hopes (Rachel says) in those faces!

At Rachel's signal, her fighters listened. Yes, there were footsteps on the staircase. In a slow, slow cadence, with a sound of erratic stealth, somehow peculiar and unsteady, the feet climbed the stone stairs. Rachel says she imagined a young German boy atop that tread, a new conscript, homesick and fearsick, climbing up the stairs uncertain who was hunter and who quarry in this Jew-maze. Rachel felt superior to those footsteps and their obviously miserable cargo: Rachel decided it would be easy to kill this one. She turned to the others in the room and pointed at herself, indicating that she was volunteering for the work. Rutka put a hand on her arm; Rachel says she dissipated the questioning look on Rutka's face by assuming a grand stare of confidence herself. She would do it.

The steps came ever closer, and one could begin to hear spas-

modic breathing, as if this creature were actually inhaling and exhaling despondency. Rachel got up on one knee and cocked her
revolver, muffling the sound by pressing against the clicking metal
with the palm of her left hand. She was all ready to rush.

Onto the stone landing the hesitant footsteps climbed. They
stopped. Then a huge, terrible sob burst out.

Rachel pushed the door open and with the springy (but under the circumstances, she says, rather ridiculous) leap of a des-
perado, she hurtled out, pistol ready.

At the side of the landing, all bloody, terribly alone, leaning
his forehead against the cool stone wall of the stairwell, and crying his heart out, stood Rapaport.

EVENTS MAY 1, 1943. ENTRY DITTO. N.L.; AND FROM
HENRYK RAPAPORT. They brought Rapaport to our shelter and
put him on a bunk. He was not so badly hurt as he looked. He had
been hiding alone for three days, he said, in a wild house, and had
been wounded while attempting to get back to Slonim's bunker.
He had been hit by a sniper in the flesh of his left shoulder as he
ran across a roof; the bullet had passed through above the bone
and out. Most of the blood on his jacket came from a deep cut
behind his right ear, which he says he suffered when he jumped,
after he was wounded, from a second-storey window into a garbage and rubbish heap in a courtyard; he toppled over in the refuse
and was apparently cut by a broken bottle there. Ignoble wound!
He had lost quite a bit of blood and was weak; but mainly he was
depressed. Terribly, rackingly sad.

He was too weak to go to the meeting last evening, and I was
too busy interviewing Felix yesterday afternoon and last night to
be able to talk with him. But I spent several hours with him today.

Rapaport has reached the worst stage of despair: not only does
he feel that everything around him is at this moment futile and
stupid, he also feels that he has wasted his whole past life. He
talked in circles and curlicues, and in a low mumble which I could
just hear kneeling close to his bunk—for though he had faced his
own hopelessness, he apparently wanted to keep intact a façade for
strangers to see. He spoke to me as an ear, not as a man. I could
see that he needed to evacuate his poisonous and embarrassing sadness, so I did not argue with him or try to cheer him up. I let
him talk.

As I say, he spoke in a disordered way, but his self-indictments boiled down to three: 1) he had failed the Movement in his personal relationships, particularly by alienating young enthusiasts, 2) he had been naïvely idealistic, and 3) he had utterly failed to identify himself with the working people whom he was supposed to represent and lead.

First count: personal relationships. Here Rapaport harped on his inharmony with Lazar Slonim. He said he had almost driven Slonim from the Movement, and that he had been motivated by jealousy, by the knowledge that this was a better man than himself, or at least a more brilliant man. Rapaport said bitterly that he had lacked generosity and warmth of spirit.

Second count: naïve and slavish adherence to ideals. Rapaport said that as a practicing Socialist, he had been hampered by taking some of the party slogans too literally. Brotherhood of the working masses, for instance. He had really believed that when the Jewish workers got into trouble, their brothers, the Polish workers, would almost automatically come to their aid. His disillusionment on this count had taken a terrible toll of his self-confidence, he said. Again he compared himself with Slonim: the latter, he said, being a romantic and a creature of impulse, never wasted his energy on the conflict between ideals and realities, but simply rode into each situation as it came, with high spirits in his chest and a feather in his cap, and if the facts as discovered were ugly, he somehow made capital of that very ugliness; Rapaport said that he himself had been too rigid, too literal-minded, too inflexibly hopeful.

Third count: failure to identify himself with the workers. The discouraged old fellow said he had never been able to speak the workers' language. Not that he was an intellectual; far from it. But from his youngest days he had been a professional Socialist, and he had forgotten, if he had ever known, the real habits and attitudes of a worker. . . . [✿ INSERT. FROM CONVERSATIONS OF MAY 9–10, 1943. FROM HENRYK RAPAPORT. Rapaport told me a story. He said that once in Zolochev, in Galicia, during the disturbances of 1936, he had been presiding over an organizational meeting of some tinsmiths who worked for one Mendel Mendelssohn. The leader among the smiths was a hook-nosed, thin-faced, sour-miened Jew from Katowice, nicknamed Big Ear, from a habit of eavesdropping he apparently had. He had not shaved for two or three days, his clothes were filthy, and he wore two dirty bandages on his fingers, indicating that he must be a careless workman. He was supposed to have kept records of a membership drive since a previous visit by Rapaport, and these records were inaccurate, incomplete, and altogether worthless. Rapaport was giving Big Ear a dressing down, and was thinking that if only he himself could settle down in the Mendelssohn smithy for a month or so, *he* could get this job done in short order. Suddenly Big Ear looked at Rapaport with a shrewd expression, pursing his lips like a man who has put his teeth on edge biting into sour fruit.

Big Ear: —— Ai, Mendelssohn treats me like a servant. Am I supposed to be your servant, too?]

I could think of answers to Rapaport's self-abasements. Indeed, on the first count, I had always thought of him as possibly failing as a Socialist precisely because he was too friendly, warm, unsharpened, and even sentimental. I thought of his telling that quiet fable to Symka and David in the tiny warren that time, under Menkes' furnace, and of Slonim's decision on the way to Treblinka, based really on Slonim's impression of Rapaport's greatheartedness, and of. . . . But it is hard to argue with a man who declares and repeats and insists that he is worthless. So I simply let him talk.

Events May 1, 1943. Entry ditto. N.L. Amazing and wonderful! How Rapaport deceived me! Today is May Day, the workers' holiday across the world, a day for parades, congratulations, signs of solidarity. In the bunker of Nahum's Bund Group there was held, this evening, a May Day celebration. Rapaport insisted upon going; he said it meant very much to him. He seemed strong enough, so we let him get up. We still have communication with Nahum's bunker. Rapaport seemed quite eager to have me accompany him, so I went along. The meeting began at about eight o'clock. In a solemn and moving voice, Velvel called the roll of the Bund's membership in the ghetto. He used a list from last August, so that there were many names to which there could be no response. I was a stranger, but I could imagine what that parade of names—each one calling up the memory of a complete person, his strengths and weaknesses, his stature, his face, his gestures, his loves, his failures, his amicability or his repugnant nature—must have meant to the intimates and comrades gathered together there.

At the end, many were weeping. Yitzhok was present, and he made a short, grateful talk on the contribution of the Bund Fighter Groups to the joint resistance of the Jews in the ghetto, and with a fine, robust tact he made the Socialists feel very proud of themselves, no doubt.

Then Rapaport rose. His left arm was in a sling. There was a bandage around his head. He stood straight. I was wary, having listened all afternoon to his innermost misgivings. But there he stood, firm as a lighthouse, and in a powerful voice, with absolute confidence, he made a speech of such strength and passion that even I, listening as it were on two planes, could not resist him but grinned and felt strong myself at last. How curious! He repeated the very slogans that he had told me, so sourly, he no longer could believe, and he repeated them with what seemed to be a deep and heartfelt conviction. He would have seemed to anyone but me to be a burning idealist. He spoke, like an old soldier, modestly yet manfully, of his own contribution to the Bund, and he said that he knew that everyone present could likewise measure and be satisfied with his own past endeavors.

Rapaport, pointing to his own left shoulder: —— I have recently received what the doctors would call (if we had any doctors!) a flesh-wound. That is accurate. I have a flesh-wound in my shoulder from a German bullet. [NOTE. N.L. He seemed to have forgotten all about his more serious cut, earned by jumping incautiously into jagged slops.] The German hurt my flesh. But I say, Comrades, that he could not wound my soul: he could not drive a bullet through my spirit. Perhaps this German will kill my body. Perhaps he can inflict a flesh-death upon me. But he cannot kill, any more than he can wound, my indomitable will!

It was amazing. Had this old fellow lied to me all afternoon? Was he teasing these his younger companions? Or was he deceiving himself and merely acting now? What he said this afternoon seemed true, but so did what he said this evening, which was opposite. I have always thought of Rapaport as a simple man. No! I now see that the greatest mistake we can make is to try to judge a whole man from the few things we hear him say and see him do. . . .

7

EVENTS MAY 5, 1943. ENTRY MAY 6, 1943. N.L. So we
have lost our bunker. We had known that it could only be a matter of time. Indeed, we had had word yesterday morning that the
Germans were working their way along Wolynska Street toward
us, setting fire to buildings as they came. Evidently they intend to
destroy every single building in the ghetto.

It was 5:45, just before the Germans' quitting hour, when
Maksi, who had been acting as a lookout upstairs in the bakery,
came slithering down the hole from the furnace and reported that
German soldiers were out in the street in front of the bakery.

We took up our weapons (I, my notebook) and stood around
for a few seconds, wondering what we should do. A couple of
women became hysterical. Mordecai jumped to one of the ventilators and closed it, and people near the others shut them.

Then a Yiddish voice came, huge and hollow, down the tunnel from the furnace.

—— The fighting is all over! Yitzhok has approved the terms
of a peace. You can all come up now.

My God, what news! We stood impaled on our joy and doubt.
Several began cheering and weeping.

Rachel, sharply: —— Silence!

I myself believed the voice. I wanted to believe what it said so
much that at first I actually did believe it. The Germans were satisfied. They had had enough. They would spare the few (how
many? ten thousand?) remaining survivors. Then at once the question occurred to me: Whose voice was that? If Yitzhok had actually approved the cessation of fighting, had he sent us a known
courier? The voice was hauntingly familiar to me, yet I could not
see the throat, the jaws, and the mouth that went with it.

N.L., to Felix, who was near me: —— Whose voice?

Felix shrugged.

The voice: —— The fighting has ended. Believe me. Come up
and breathe the fresh air! It is all over! You will be sent to the
metal works belonging to Hänner in Poniatow.

I tried to assign to the voice a note of exultation appropriate
to the news, but I found something lacking. This voice, amplified

583

and rolled into cobwebby globules of sound in the furnace and the tunnel, had in it a trace of strain and even of dissatisfaction. I believed it and I doubted it.

A man near the tunnel, starting for the opening: —— What are we waiting for?

Rachel, shouting strenuously: —— Fighters, with me!

Rachel darted for the back room like a rabbit, and I reacted at once and went after her. The speed with which I responded indicates to me (as I think it over) the extent to which I trust her. I wanted very badly to stay and believe the voice and crawl up the tunnel to the fresh air of which it spoke; but three words from Rachel cleared my brain and told me what should have been obvious to me from the beginning: the voice was that of an informer. I was not the only one who answered her call with immediate action: I saw ahead of me, among others, Mordecai with his baby in his arms.

Rachel made straight for the "back door." By the time I reached the entrance, there was already something of a rush, and I saw the wounded Rapaport standing beside the opening of the tunnel, stopping all those who were not Z.O.B. people and pushing them aside with his unhurt right arm.

Rapaport, roughly: —— Fighters first! Fighters first!

On the way through the tunnel, I remembered the face that went with the voice: it belonged to a wild Jew we had briefly sheltered in the bunker, named Harsch, and I remembered his voice because he had complained about everything—our tight rations, our cloudy water, our cramped space—and now his joyful announcement had itself been a complaint.

Rutka was just ahead of me in the tunnel. We ran through the first cellar and to the left in the second cellar and down what we called Berson's Passage into the sewer. Just after I got beyond the first cellar I heard a commotion there behind me, in the midst of which were some German shouts that did not sound like truce-cries to me. Eventually I noticed in the sewer that there were only three people behind me. The others must have been cut off. I supposed there were eight or ten ahead. Rachel was among them; I had seen her ahead of me in the second cellar. Rutka was among them. We scurried along feeling our way in the darkness. There was an explosion in the sewer far behind us. Mordecai's infant squalled. We emerged at last in the unfortified cellar of Zamenhofa 29.

Rapaport was not with us. Felix was not with us. Neither was the boy Maksi.

Where should we go?

EVENTS MAY 5, 1943. ENTRY MAY 7, 1943. FROM HENRYK RAPAPORT. This time (how can I record it?) Felix will not come back again. At least we can be glad, I suppose, that Felix died after having settled matters within himself, rather than before. Rapaport has told me what happened in the bunker after I left:

Rapaport says that after the first few of us got out through the rear tunnel, the voice came rolling down the front one again. This time the good tidings had vanished:

—— This is a warning! Either surrender peaceably or be killed. You have two minutes to come up.

At once, Rapaport says, many of the timid and credulous began to fight for the opportunity to climb up the front tunnel to the bakery and surrender. He himself abandoned the guardianship of the rear tunnel and went out through it, headed for the sewers and escape, he thought. Felix had just previously gone through. When Rapaport reached the first cellar, he found the way already blocked by Germans. The Germans had at first guarded only the upstairs door to that cellar, evidently believing, or having been told by the informer, who may have believed it, that those who went out through the rear exit would have to go up through the next-door building; then at last the Germans had rushed down into the cellar and had interdicted the route to the sewers. [NOTE. N.L. Thank the Lord for that brief delay!] Rapaport, Felix, and perhaps fifteen others were caught in the first cellar. They were herded upstairs and into the street, where about thirty of those who had climbed up through the bakery were already huddled in a circle.

Felix, whispering importunately to Rapaport: —— Stay with me. Be ready. Stay beside me. Stay with me.

Rapaport says that in surveying the abject, ragged, filthy crowd in the middle of the street, standing within a cordon of abusive, ill-grammared, physically unrobust, and strangely frightened-looking German soldiers, who tensely pointed their bayonets at the mud-wallowed sheep they had trapped, he could not help remembering the fiercely happy fantasies he had had on the first morning of the ghetto battle, when he had imagined, along with all of us, that the Jews might at last enjoy some sort of victory over the

Germans. Victory! What prostrate victors! Maksi was in the crowd in the street, and Rapaport saw a German noncom go up to the boy and spin him around in front of him and put a pistol to the back of the boy's head and messily kill him; and no one among the Jewish "victors" protested; no one so much as growled. Rapaport says that he himself did not move a finger or say a word. Maksi was twelve years old.

Felix, insistently: —— Be ready! Stay with me!

Rapaport now saw some more of his former bunkermates coming from the bakery in a horrid condition, crying, holding their heads, coughing, vomiting, and staggering. One of them kept shrieking something about poison gas, until the noncom who had disposed of Maksi also shot this screamer. There were sounds of muffled explosions. Then after a time a number of Germans came out of the bakery. There were two officers, and with them was a Jew—the informer—dressed in clean clothes, shaven, with his hair combed: a smiling profiteer.

Felix: —— Now! Be ready, Henryk.

And taking Rapaport by the arm, Felix approached the two officers and Harsch. Felix's manner was very humble. Rapaport says he did not know what to expect.

Felix, to the Germans: —— Mandeltort, formerly Secretary of the *Judenrat*. Excuse me, I can tell you where Rachel Apt, Group Commander for Hashomer Hatsair, has hidden. If you want to take her, give us three or four men. I'll show you where to find her.

Rapaport says he was very nervous. His head and shoulder throbbed. He knew that Felix had had the courage once to refuse to inform; but he knew how variable Felix's honor had been in the past. His whispering just now had been extremely disturbed. Rapaport says he himself was confused—both about Felix and within himself: he had not been face to face with Germans for years. Then Rapaport remembered Felix had said: Be ready. Rapaport put both hands in the pockets of his baggy coat. In the right-hand pocket his fingers found a cool, metal, cross-hatched thing, which they gripped.

The German officers were rather pleased. They asked Harsch if he recognized Felix, and the informer was full of importance.

Harsch, in German: —— He is truly Mandeltort, he's telling the truth. And the commander of this bunker was the girl, Rachel. That also is true.

One of the Germans, smiling: —— Pretty?

Harsch, enjoying himself: —— Like a Jewish parrot.

And so the Germans assigned three men to Rapaport and Felix, and told Felix (as if he were a dutiful child) that he would be rewarded if the party caught the girl.

Felix: —— Do you want Herr Harsch to come with us to identify the girl's body?

A good idea. So ordered.

Felix led the group into the cellar of the building next to the bakery. There, by the low hole knocked through the foundations to the second cellar, Felix gathered the three Germans and Harsch and Rapaport all together and whispered to them knowingly.

Felix: —— In the next cellar but one. A toolchest beside a coal bin to the right of our entrance. You will find her in the chest.

One of the German soldiers, evidently trusting nobody, least of all his own officers, who had sent him on this doubtful mission: —— And what if she is not there?

At this slightest evidence of suspicion, Felix's manner suddenly changed. He turned and bent down, as if to go through the hole, and as he bent he fumbled at his jacket. Then, without going into the hole, he turned back, straightened up, put a pistol in Harsch's face, and fired. Rapaport got his own pistol out as quickly as he could. Felix meanwhile shot one of the Germans in the stomach and was turning to another when the third, evidently having seen Felix's original fumbling, shot his rifle from the waist at Felix and Felix fell. By this time Rapaport had already shot the second German and he now also hit the one who had killed Felix before the latter could turn on him. Rapaport bent over Felix a moment and found him dead. Then he went through the hole to the cellar beyond, turned left, scrambled down Berson's Passage to the sewer, and went, by a route he had learned from Maksi, to the Z.O.B. headquarters bunker at Mila 18.

Thus Felix. What can I write? After so many doubts and refusals to succumb, thus Felix.

8

EVENTS MAY 5, 1943. ENTRY MAY 6, 1943. N.L. Where could we go? The cellar of Zamenhofa 29, where we found ourselves, was altogether unprotected. The baby kept crying. We decided at last to stay in the cellar, if we could, until late at night, and then try to make our way through the streets to one of the Z.O.B. strongpoints or bunkers. We were twelve. None of us knew whether the baby could be kept quiet; Rutka held little Israel to her breast much of the time.

[✿ INSERT. FROM CONVERSATIONS OF MAY 9–10, 1943. FROM RUTKA MAZUR. In speaking of her feeling about the baby, Rutka said that as we waited for nightfall in the Zamenhofa cellar the other day, she had, briefly, a powerful feeling of resentment and even hatred toward the infant. Israel had been such a care, such an impediment. Rutka says she thought back to the early days of the ghetto, when she had led a hesitant Rachel into underground work; and now—Rachel was the commander, the beloved Little Mother, while Rutka was a mother indeed and a slave. Then she recalled an incident that had occurred in Rachel's bunker just a few days before:

Rachel had just come in from a patrol: her clothes were dirty, her face was smudged. Rutka says that looking at Rachel she felt a terrible, cutting pang of envy at Rachel's free, swaggering, happy look—while she herself was imprisoned in the stifling bunker with her Eating and Evacuating Machine. The infant was at that very moment trumpeting his appetite. Just as Rutka suffered this pang, Rachel, having given to N.L. (NOTE. N.L. I remember this.) an exultant account of the work of the patrol, turned to Rutka and the infant, and with a sudden tenderness she asked Rutka if she might hold the baby and try to quiet him. Rutka gave Israel to Rachel. Rachel cradled the red-faced, squealing baby in her arms and, swinging back and forth, sang a lullaby in her low, sweet, but unmusical voice:

> *Under baby's crib*
> *Stood a golden kid.*
> *The kid went off to trade,*

Handling raisins and almonds:
Handling raisins and figs. . . .

The song had no effect whatsoever on Israel, who was hungry, not for song, but for supper. In fact, Israel grew redder and louder, and some of the inmates of the bunker began to complain, and Rachel blushed. Finally, with a face of complete despair, Rachel handed the baby back to Rutka, whose envy then melted, she says, into pity.

Rachel, herself obviously envious and bitter: —— I'm afraid I'm of no use. . . .]

Israel finally slept. Time passed very slowly. At last we judged that it was about midnight, and we made our way out into the streets.

The sight that night is one I shall never forget. I felt un-worlded. This was some other planet. Nothing was left of the part of the ghetto where we were, it seemed, but fires and trash. Dunes of fallen brick were silhouetted against weird little separate sunsets of flame-touched smoke. The streets were only valleys in the general rubbish-desert. Where parts of walls or frames or chimneys still stood, they were ragged, tapered, and naturalistic; of a stalagmitic architecture. The scene was eerie and unsettling.

We thought we would try to get to an underground bunker belonging to Abraham's Group on Muranowska, which we knew had been intact at least up until the previous day. Very soon Rachel led us away from the street, where in the reflected light of the fires we could so easily have been spotted, back into the mounds and ravines of rubble. We kept stumbling along the best we could. As long as we moved, the baby, in Mordecai's arms, either slept or was entertained by the joggling orange-and-grey surroundings. At last we decided that we had overshot Muranowska Street; personally, I was completely lost. We paused on the near slope of a hill of bricks for a whispered consultation.

The moment Mordecai sat down, Israel gave out a whimper. Immediately afterward I heard sounds of motion near the crest of our hill of ruin, and glancing up I saw a figure rise for a moment evidently to try to get a look at us. The figure was capped by something rounded, something that glinted in the reflected light. A harsh whisper rolled down to us from up there.

—— *Amkho?*

Were we Jewish? I hastily leaned over to Rachel and whispered that I had seen a helmet. The Germans could give that challenge, too. Instead of answering in plain, therefore, Rachel counter-challenged with that night's password, in Yiddish:

—— Where is Jakov?

The answer should have been: With Moya. [NOTE. N.L. How poignant our signals in the night! Jakov and Moya were a vital and keen-minded couple in the Bund who were deported together last September. Everyone loved them. They worked tirelessly for ZITOS. Thus we memorialized them.] But the man at the summit did not answer properly.

—— Who are you?

Our answer was to begin to move away. But then the voice on the hill spoke openly and with a disarming gentleness of tone:

—— We are Jewish here also. Don't be afraid.

We hesitated. The voice on the hill spoke again: it asked how many we were. We did not dare answer. After a few moments Rachel asked who was speaking. No answer to that. We heard sounds of others moving up to the man at the crest. We prepared our weapons. The man at the top asked if we were Z.O.B. fighters. We did not answer. Then, after another pause, he startled us:

—— Is the girl Rachel Apt still alive?

N.L., answering at once: —— She is alive.

The man on the hill: —— Tell her Fein is also alive.

Then the man withdrew from the crest of the hill. Israel began to cry loudly. Suddenly I heard Rachel's voice, shouting over the infant's noise:

—— Wait! Wait!

The man came back over the crest and spoke precisely in the voice of a customer called back by a dickering merchant after having walked off in disgust at the last price:

—— Nu?

Rachel, less raucously (Rutka had taken Israel to breast to quiet him): —— Rachel is here.

The man came down the hill to us directly. It was the workman Fein. He embraced Rachel. Rachel asked him why he had inquired about her, and he said he had thought he recognized her voice. At once Rachel asked him whether he had ever had news of her brother David. Fein said he had not; no news at all. The scene was macabre in its casualness—questions asked about friends, health, and home. Fein said that he and his companions were out to meet a smuggler.

Mordecai (the practical one among us): —— We lost our bunker tonight. Can you take us?

—— How many?

—— Twelve.

—— And an infant. Oi!

Fein climbed the desolate hill to consult with his friends. They came back down to us. There was an argument, in which the central commodity was our fate. I felt sick to my stomach. The baby began to cry again. Fein and his friends agreed at last to take us in for seventy-five thousand zlotys. Rachel had her dollars, and others had gems, and right there, in the hazardous, otherworldly night, Fein's companions struck flints and lit a spill and examined the merchandise. It proved to be somewhat under value (Rachel offered only one of her fifty-dollar bills); but they accepted us, as more or less cut-rate survivors. Fein led us to their bunker, while the others waited for their supplier.

EVENTS NIGHT OF MAY 5–6, 1943. ENTRY MAY 6, 1943. N.L. Conditions in this bunker are terrible. I have been trying to write all day, and it is very hard: I hear nothing but arguments, recriminations, bitterness.

Life in this bunker must have been splendid when Fein and his friends—the Wall Men—were here alone. It is easily the most magnificent underground establishment I have seen. It was built in a leisurely fashion under a house that was destroyed in the German siege of Warsaw in 1939. Its roof, then, consists of six or seven meters of practically impenetrable debris. It utilizes some of the original cellars of that house, so that the walls of two of the four rooms are of brick. The others are of wood, soundly joined. There are several entrances, but the nearest one from the street level is fantastically clever: it comes through the housing of a disused transformer in another ruined building nearly a block away and cuts through several cellars, each hole and break-through being hidden by one device or another. While utilities were still available, the Wall Men had electric lights, electric fans in their ventilators, a gas range, running water (including a flushing toilet), and a radio set. There were nine householders there, and they had beds with mattresses. On one wall is a big map of the German-

Russian front on which they used to keep a front of pins, according to what they heard on the radio. Actually the Wall Men must have been far more comfortable here than most ghetto inhabitants in their apartments above ground.

Now, however, things are different. There are now, including our party, 164 people in the bunker. The crowding is horrible. Worse, these are mostly "paying guests," like ourselves (at the rate of our entry fee, there is altogether 1,537,000 zlotys' worth of human flesh here), and though many, perhaps even most, of the tenants were once members of the Z.O.B., they no longer have any discipline or sense of co-operation or hope. They argue: they fight over six inches of sleeping room, they scream over a bread-rusk. They only want to live and have.

How well poor Rutka and Mordecai know this!

Last night after Fein brought us into the bunker, there was a bad enough time finding space for twelve additional sleepers. Even though Fein is a proprietor of the bunker, he commands very little respect, and even though he is still round and jovial, he has earned very little affection; his tenants growled and grumbled over the danger and inconvenience they saw in us. Then, when things seemed to be almost quieted down, Israel started mewling. Such a roar of protest as went up from the tenants! In brief, they drove Rutka and Mordecai and their troublesome baby from the bunker altogether.

As Rutka and Mordecai left, Rachel told them to try the Z.O.B. headquarters bunker at Mila 18, and she described one of the entrances.

EVENTS MAY 6, 1943. ENTRY MAY 7, 1943. FROM HENRYK RAPAPORT. I am glad that I did not witness what I am about to describe. Rapaport told me the story.

Rutka and Mordecai did find their way to the Z.O.B. bunker, and they were admitted without question. Apparently Israel was as tired as his parents after so much traveling; he went soundly to sleep and slept right through until morning.

The headquarters bunker was just as crowded as this one is, but apparently the atmosphere was much more orderly. Of course Yitzhok and his staff were in charge. Rapaport says Zilberzweig was there. A number of Group leaders were there, including Jankiel, Benz, Nahum, Anselm, Peter, Ketzl, Mendel, and Ganzener. Abra-

ham, Mischa, and Aron had been killed, I understand. Most of
the occupants of the bunker were fighters. They were still organizing patrols, though the whole Z.O.B. now had very little ammunition left.

The misfortune, I gather, was one of timing. Israel chose the
wrong time to cry. A sentry had just come down to report the
presence of a rather large force of Germans on Mila Street, and
apparently the clatter of preparations, together with the palpable
apprehension, tautness, and irritability in the bunker somehow
upset the baby, and he began screaming. Rutka tried everything. The child was not interested in her breast. Sweetened
water, which one of the fighters offered, did no good. Vodka,
from the bunker commissary, only burned the baby's mouth and
made things worse. Mordecai was no help. He stood over Rutka,
shouting at her.

—— Do something! Well, quiet him. Do something, girl!

Rutka, on her knees, working over the baby, dreadfully mortified: —— I'm trying.

Rapaport says he was embarrassed for Rutka and Mordecai,
but he was also very much afraid that the baby might summon the
Germans and give away, all at once, the very cream of Jewish courage, the best of the last. The Group leaders stood around grimly.
One broke out angrily:

—— Do you want to get us all killed?

Rutka by now had given up all special efforts to still the child
and was merely holding him with his face to her breast and was
rocking back and forth. She was weeping herself.

Rutka: —— I'm trying, I'm trying!

Israel howled. An intolerable contest was now established—
between the will of a single infant and the rage and fear of nearly
a hundred adults. Rapaport says he himself was now drawn despite himself into the mob fury against the intractable baby. A
shot distantly heard in a moment between screams tipped the
balance of the contest. Yitzhok walked to Rutka and spoke to her
in a gentle voice.

—— Give me the baby. Let me try to quiet him.

He took the child and carried it across the room away from
Rutka. Rapaport says he could not see exactly what Yitzhok did:
he only saw that the commander was hunched over slightly, and
suddenly (too suddenly, Rapaport says) the child was silent. Rapa-

593

port saw the faces in a circle around stooping Yitzhok: they contained a mixture of relief and horror. Yitzhok carried the baby back to Rutka. She was still on her knees. She had no idea what had happened, only that Israel had stopped wailing, and that Yitzhok had brought this about. She looked up at him through her tears, and her face was grateful and eased.

Rutka, as she took the baby in her arms: —— Thank you so much! How did you manage?

Rutka did not know until the infant's cheek grew cold against her breast that it was dead. Rapaport saw the realization come into her face. He says that he thinks Mordecai knew all along what had happened: he had been sitting on the floor beating his forehead with his fists. But now, when Rutka gave out a dreadful, suppressed, shuddering cry—a quiet one: even in her grief she somehow kept herself from endangering the others—and Mordecai looked up and saw the realization and the dreadful pain in her face, he lost his head and made a rush at Yitzhok. Anselm, Nahum, Benz, and Peter intercepted him and held him. Gradually he recovered himself and wept quietly.

Rutka sat still with the baby in her arms all day, not crying at all. Late at night, in order to break her awful vigil, which was getting on everyone's nerves, Rapaport suggested that she and Mordecai and he go to Fein's bunker. Mordecai had told Rapaport about it earlier in the day. They left, and as they left, Nahum firmly took the baby's body from Rutka's arms.

And so they are with us. I cannot bear to look at Rutka's face. I think back over what that tiny baby has meant to us in recent weeks. I imagine what Rutka must feel: the hopes and frustrations of her long pregnancy, her care of that fragile being under the circumstances of ghetto and battle: and yet the inevitability of what happened. It was not Yitzhok's fault: it was nobody's fault. I feel nauseated again tonight. I must keep hold of myself.

One horrible, incongruous note that haunts me: as Mordecai and Rutka came into the bunker again, and white-haired Rapaport was with them in place of the infant, one of our rent-paying humorists here cried out:

—— Ai! Look how fast the baby has aged!

I write by the light of two candles. It is so hot tonight that the candles droop and bend. I am tired, tired, tired. Oh, Berson, how will you ever find us? We need you! How can you find us now?

9

EVENTS MAY 1, 1943. ENTRY MAY 12, 1943. FROM DO-LEK BERSON. Berson says that he and Slonim had a very hard time getting out of the ghetto on their mission to arrange for fighters to escape. [SEE EVENTS NIGHT OF APRIL 30–MAY 1.] As well as Berson knew the sewers underneath the area within the wall, he did not know that the Germans had recently blocked the culverts with rubble at a number of sewer openings, both within and outside the wall—at Krasinski Square, and along Leszno and Bonifraterska—so that the pair had to double back and detour around several times. Furthermore, Berson was lost the moment they got out from under the ghetto. He felt that they ought to travel quite far outside, so as to reduce the danger of being caught at the manhole when they would leave the sewer; on the other hand, he did not want to come upon a sudden, steep, downward slope and be spewed into the Vistula: he tried to keep working "upstream," southeastward.

They climbed up from the sewer at what turned out to be the corner of Leszno and Karolkowa. It was nearly three o'clock in the morning, and the streets were empty. The two sneaked along against the walls of the buildings and shop-fronts.

First Slonim took Berson to an apartment on Mokotowska Street, where a Polish Socialist lived, a man named Starszczynski, who recognized Slonim, and who seemed not the least bit surprised to be waked from a sound sleep early in the morning by two Jews reeking with sewer filth and asking for a chance to take a bath and borrow some clothes. He led them into his kitchen, produced a big tin tub full of cold water, a precious cake of soap, and two sets of working men's clothes. Starszczynski asked questions about the situation in the ghetto, and Slonim answered emotionally. The host did not of his own accord offer his guests food, but when Slonim asked for some bread, Starszczynski produced a loaf and also heated up some tea. After the pair had finished eating, Starszczynski drily commanded them to mop up the kitchen floor and dispose of every trace of their filth. Berson worked on the floor, while Slonim took newspapers and made tight packages of his and Berson's soiled clothes. Then they set out again, carrying their parcels, for the house in Praga where Halinka and Lodzia were now supposed to be living. [NOTE. N.L. We had received word in the ghetto just before the battle began that Marysia had left on a mission to Bendzin.]

Berson, as they walked: —— Your Polish friend seemed to think we *choose* to be dirty.

Slonim: —— After all, he gave us these clothes. Don't be hard on him.

Berson says that in the streets, as a grey, damp, warm dawn poured in from the east, he almost collapsed with a sudden, nervous letdown. All the agony and tension and aspiration he had felt within the wall drained out of him, and in its place was something awful, which he had never experienced before: an emotional vacuum: dullness and deep depression: emptiness and nothingness. A few hours before he had been a desperate and filthy Jew, fighting for his own life and for the honor of his people; now he was just a clean man walking along with a bundle of laundry under one arm and a concertina under the other. Slonim was silent. Perhaps Slonim felt similar sensations. Berson did not care about anything. He walked automatically.

The two men came to the small house where the girl couriers were supposed to be. Berson says he did not even feel excited at the prospect of seeing Halinka again. Slonim knocked and they waited. Nobody answered. They knocked and knocked. Still no answer. They tried the door but it was locked. Slonim suggested going back to Starszczynski, and just as they were about to walk away, the door opened behind them. A little old woman stood in the doorway.

Berson: —— Does Lodzia live here?

The old woman beckoned Berson and Slonim inside. When they were in and she had closed the door, she spoke in a thin whine that sounded like a voice on a short-wave broadcast under bad atmospheric conditions; it had some kind of bronchial static in it.

—— You can't stay! We already have nine Jews. It is terrible.

Where there is one Jew you suddenly have nine. I can't stand it. Go away!

Berson, his voice dull and heavy: —— We are not going to stay long. Perhaps we will take your Jews away with us. We want to see the ones named Lodzia and Halinka.

—— I can't help it! We already have nine. You must go away.

Slonim, stepping up to the woman and speaking with polite words but with a distinctly threatening manner: —— Please! Allow us to speak to these girls.

Muttering and crackling, like an old-fashioned crystal receiver, the old woman turned and scurried upstairs. In a few moments Halinka came rushing down and threw herself into Berson's arms. Berson says that as soon as he heard Halinka's steps on the stairs, his awful feeling of emptiness left him; he wept.

He was appalled by the change in Halinka's face in ten weeks: she was suddenly middle-aged and not very pretty; and he saw by her eyes that he himself made a pitiful sight.

EVENTS MAY 2, 1943. ENTRY MAY 12, 1943. FROM HA-LINKA APT. Halinka walked toward Stolarska Street 43. It was Easter Sunday. Halinka says she had speculated all week long: What would the former janitor plan to do on the Sunday after Easter? Devotions? A walk under the blue sky? A beer on Teatralny Square? The merry-go-round with a pretty girl? What would he plan?

Halinka says that as she walked along, she was not so afraid as she had expected to be. She was preoccupied and troubled by an argument she had had with Berson the night before. [INSERT. ENTRY MAY 12, 1943. FROM DOLEK BERSON. Have asked Berson about his argument with Halinka, night of May 1. He says this is the only argument he ever had with Halinka, whom he had always considered a docile, spiritless, flirtatious girl. He now feels that he was wrong in the argument. Halinka told him that evening about her careful preparations to execute Kucharski. Berson said that the whole point of killing the former janitor was by that time lost: the act had been intended as an example to other smugglers and arms dealers, to show them that Jews would not stand for being cheated. Now that the battle in the ghetto was practically over, and now that the channels for smuggling arms on a large scale had been shut off, there was no longer any purpose to be served.

Halinka: —— Is it no longer true that Jews will not allow themselves to be cheated?

When it had become clear to Berson that Halinka insisted upon carrying out the execution, he shifted ground: he "offered" to do the job. The offer was put forward solicitously at first, to spare Halinka the danger; then gradually Berson says his tone became more and more insistent, until the offer had become virtually an order. Halinka kept saying that this was her assignment; she had made all the arrangements; Berson should not interfere. Berson said *he* was the one Kucharski had cheated in the first place. At last, Berson says, the argument lost its intrinsic basis altogether; it became a question as to whose desire, the man's or the woman's, should prevail. Halinka had always been submissive, dependent, pliant. Berson could not understand this unusual obduracy: he felt that somehow in the time she had been outside the wall, Halinka had hardened. The argument ended—as it had begun, and as it had continued to be in the middle—all wrong: Halinka refusing to speak to Berson as they retired for the night. It seemed to be understood, however, that Berson would not interefere. It was not until the following day, after the act, when Berson saw the release in Halinka, that he realized that the punishment of Kucharski was something she had *had* to carry out herself. He had tried to argue against her absolute, compulsive determination to do the thing. It had been like arguing against the ghetto wall.]

Halinka was early: it was before seven in the morning, but she had no intention of missing Kucharski. By now Halinka had had practice in unobtrusive loitering: Lodzia had given her instruction in this art. There were enough people in the street, so that by keeping moving, in different directions at varying paces, using all eight sidewalks of an intersection, she was able to keep her eye on the entrance-arch of Stolarska 43 most of the time and still keep from arousing suspicion.

Kucharski came out at about eight thirty. Halinka walked directly to him and accosted him.

Halinka: —— Pan Kucharski, do you remember me?

At first the aging man apparently mistook Halinka for one of his dalliances, and he became gallant. Then, recognizing her, he recovered quickly from his politeness and said:

—— Ah, yes, the daughter of the jeweler.

—— Apt.

—— As you say: Apt.

—— I would like to talk with you. Alone. Indoors.

—— I'm sorry, I'm busy.

—— Too busy for Jews, Pan Kucharski?

—— I have only to cry out, as you know. . . .

—— You have only to cry out and you will cry no more, Pan Kucharski. Why do you think I have my hand in my purse?

—— What is it you want?

—— Alone. Indoors. If you please.

—— I don't dare take a Jewess to my apartment. My landlord is very strict.

—— I think your apartment would be best.

—— Take my arm.

—— Thank you, Pan Kucharski. You are so courteous!

But as they walked back toward the apartment house, Halinka kept her distance from the Pole. She saw that he was trembling, and he fell suddenly into a friendly, reminiscent vein, in which he insanely used the first person plural pronoun.

—— I remember, Panna Apt, when we set up the illegal school in our courtyard, and there were no books, so the books were copied by hand! What was the name of the delicate Mazur boy?— Schlome! He was our scribe, wasn't he? Ha! Ha! Ha! To think that the Germans believed they could prevent us from teaching the children. I remember how excited and pleased that sister of yours was about the school. She was a dear thing, for one so ugly. How is she? . . . This way, Panna Apt. The second entryway. I hope the landlord doesn't . . . Those games we had for the children in the courtyard! I remember one day when you put them all in a circle, and they clapped and crowed like roosters and quacked like ducks and so on. . . . Up here, my dear. I'm a poor man, I live on the fourth floor. . . . You were so sweet with them. You really loved them, didn't you?

On the landing at the top of the first flight, Halinka stopped and took her revolver from her purse.

—— This is far enough.

Kucharski turned. When he saw the revolver, his face went white and his chin shook.

—— What have I done?

—— Your crime is pretense and hypocrisy.

—— But what have I done?

599

—— Do I have to say any more?

—— Perhaps (the old man's chin shook so that his teeth chattered and his words were chewed), perhaps you mean the Beretta that Berson . . . But I can gladly replace . . . I can get five. . . .

Halinka pulled the trigger and the old man slumped down. She ran quickly away. She heard shouting and hurried footsteps as she left the courtyard, but in the streets no one chased her.

EVENTS MAY 5, 1943. ENTRY MAY 12, 1943. FROM DOLEK BERSON. Berson says that after the nightmare of leading Slonim out of the ghetto through the sewers, he had no intention of taking the responsibility for guiding a large number of fighters out to freedom—especially since any plan of escape would involve a rendezvous with outside helpers at a certain, fixed manhole on the Aryan side, and he had shown that he had no knowledge of the sewers under the city outside the wall. It would be necessary, therefore, to find a guide capable of leading the way. Berson discussed the problem with Slonim. Slonim said he thought he might be able to find someone. Slonim said he had noticed something interesting: now that the Jews could be said to have been defeated, the Polish Socialists were suddenly very agreeable to him. He could not say whether they felt guilty, or felt relieved, or felt bereaved; whatever the reason, they were now rather eager to help. He thought he could find a man to help with the sewers.

Indeed, promptly, on the night of May 5, Slonim introduced Berson to a Polish Socialist named Kreszewski, a repairman in the city waterworks.

Kreszewski looked as if he had grown up in a sewer. Not that he was dirty: he was, in fact, very clean, quite fussy. But he was tiny—only a little above a meter and a half tall [NOTE. EDITOR. About five feet.], so that he would barely have to stoop in the main culverts; and his skin had a waxy pallor, as if it had not had much friction with weather. His eyes and ears were big, and his two upper front teeth were enormous; one could imagine that there had been a slight burrowing and gnawing tendency among his forebears. And he was an absolute genius on the sewers; he could say exactly when, to the month and year, any given segment had been dug up and repaired: he even knew the average flow of drainage, in centimeters of depth, at any given place. Berson says he wondered why this little troglodyte was a Socialist. Perhaps, rankling under the certainty that within a capitalist bureaucracy he would remain all his life the humblest tube-crawler, he had dreams of being, some day, Commissar of Subterranean Waterways; more likely, the Socialist Party had looked for, and found, the man who knew more about sewers than anyone else in Warsaw. Kreszewski was evidently that man.

In a brief conference with Berson and Slonim, Kreszewski recommended the manhole K-74, at the corner of Prosta and Wronia, as the most suitable place for an exit. He said he would be ready to go on this mission at any time.

EVENTS MAY 7, 1943. ENTRY MAY 12, 1943. FROM DOLEK BERSON. Berson and Slonim went out into the country to meet Zalman. Zalman was the very opposite of Kreszewski. He was a creature of the forest. Zalman was a representative of the Jewish partisans. He was tall, and though he was very thin, his sunburned face and his touseled uncut hair made him seem a lithe and brutal animal. He met Berson and Slonim, by appointment, beside a bridge about ten miles outside Warsaw, and as they talked, he walked with them across fields of young millet and sorghum. He seemed unable to stand still. He said that although a substantial addition to the forces in the woods would put a heavy strain on their food supply, nevertheless the partisans were eager to receive any who could make their way from the ghetto. Slonim said that he had arranged with his friend Starszczynski for the transport workers to "borrow" two city trucks, which would pick up the refugees at Kreszewski's K-74 at a prearranged time. It would then be for Zalman to guide the trucks to the proper place in the country. When would be convenient? Zalman said, the sooner the better. Slonim proposed the next night, that of May 8–9—at K-74 at five o'clock in the morning. He told Zalman to go to Starszczynski's apartment earlier that night.

Zalman: —— How I hate the city!

Berson asked if arrangements could be made for Halinka to join the escapists. Slonim suggested that she meet Zalman at Starszczynski's.

Having agreed, the three men strolled into the edge of the Lomianki Forest and sat down under a tree and ate a loaf of bread between them and drank a bottle of bimber. Then Berson played some music softly on his concertina.

10

Events night of May 8–9, 1943. Entry ditto. From H. Zilberzweig. Yes, it is ending. One by one the bunkers go. Our bravest friends vanish. We are few. It is almost over. Zilberzweig came to us about two hours ago. Since then I have been talking to him. Now I shall write down part of what he told me.

At about seven this evening, the fighters in the Z.O.B. headquarters bunker at Mila 18 heard sounds of German activity in the street, and the worst of it was: they heard the baying of dogs. They knew that the dogs would find fresh man-spoor leading to the entrances of the bunker, because patrols had been constantly going and coming from and to it. A lookout descended to the bunker and reported that he had seen about forty Germans apparently being quoited around Mila 18, while another party remained in reserve down the street. The Germans seemed to know what they were looking for.

At once fighters went up to their assigned outposts. Yitzhok and others had worked out a kind of defense-in-depth for this bunker, consisting of firing points in the buildings and ruins all around, each of them available to one or more passages to the bunker. Now the points were manned.

Firing broke out at about eight o'clock. Those in the bunker heard one of the dogs run off shrieking and howling, evidently injured. From the sounds of the shooting, it appeared that the Germans were trying to get through to the entrance of the bunker in the ruins of Mila 22, and, in fact, one of the pickets from that vicinity came in agitated, asking for support, and Yitzhok sent four men. But the Germans' firepower was a hundred times that of our fighters, and gradually the Germans forced their way toward the entrance to that particular approach-tunnel. Be it said, however, that it took them nearly an hour.

In the bunker, meanwhile, there was a scene of heightening tension. No one knew at what moment death would come, or in what way. Nahum, the Bund Group leader, suddenly cried out:

—— Take your own lives! Let us die together as brothers and sisters. We cannot let ourselves fall into their hands.

Anselm: —— No! No! Fight to the last man. We must kill *them*, not ourselves.

For a while there was a bizarre debate, and some of the most tested nerves gave way, and tempers were lost. Then Yitzhok shouted everyone down:

—— I am still in command here! Fight until you are dismissed!

Yet there was no one to fight against. There was nothing to do but stand in the damp cave and wait. Shortly, at one corner of the bunker, Zilberzweig saw Ganzener and Ketzl in a bitter, muttered argument, then all at once Ganzener flew at Ketzl's throat, and the two fell on the floor in a terrible, foul fight. Ganzener was choking Ketzl, and Ketzl clawed at Ganzener's cheeks. Others separated the two, and at last it appeared that Ketzl had three vials of cyanide, and Ganzener had wanted one. Ketzl then gave one vial to Yitzhok and another to Nahum and kept one for himself; he would not give one to Ganzener. Ganzener wept and blotted his cheeks on his filthy coat sleeve.

A dog was heard in the entrance to the tunnel to 22. Mendel of Dror ran up the tunnel and our people heard shots. The dog did not enter and no German came; nor did Mendel return. But the Germans had found the entrance, and they came back. Actually the defense was now fairly easy: our people had a passage through two cellars to defend, a narrow way: it would be easy to waylay the attackers, and the Germans, who evidently realized this after their losses, were wary.

Then the most unexpected thing happened. Down one of the bunker's ventilator ducts came rolling a small round object: it fell from the mouth of the ventilator and rolled on the floor. Zilberzweig says he saw Jankiel bend down to pick it up, at which moment it exploded. At once the room was filled with a fog-like vapor.

Zilberzweig says he had heard about the use of gas, and he was of the opinion that it was not poisonous, but was only tear gas. And so very quickly after the gas-bomb went off, he snatched a handkerchief from his pocket, dashed for the water cask at one side of the bunker, wetted his handkerchief, and put it over his mouth and nose. He heard Yitzhok shout:

—— You are free to do what you wish!

Zilberzweig was suddenly face to face with Benz in the misty confusion. He saw Benz put his pistol barrel in his own mouth, shoot, and fall. Zilberzweig heard other pistol explosions, and he also heard coughing and the shrieks of those who were convinced that the gas was poisonous. Many were crowding the exits. His eyes smarted and filmed over, and he began to cough. He could see nothing. He became very confused, and shouted Halinka's name. Beginning to retch, he blundered toward an exit.

Zilberzweig does not know whether it was instinct or accident that led him to the exit to the sewers. At any rate, he heard machine-pistol fire close at hand before he had crept but a few yards in the egress-tunnel: the Germans had evidently penetrated to the cellars adjoining the bunker. Zilberzweig groped his way into the sewer, where, in company with about half a dozen similarly sick people, he coughed and vomited for some time. He knew he must get away before the Germans tracked down the tunnel to the sewer. He moved off. He says he heard some of those in the sewer talking about going to the brushmakers' bunker at Franciszkanska 22, but he strained to remember the directions Rutka had given him for getting to Fein's bunker, and at last, after two hours' work, he did in fact reach us. Our center of command is gone. We must suppose that Yitzhok is lost. We are finished. What was it Yitzhok said?

—— You are free to do what you wish!

What exaggeration!

EVENTS NIGHT OF MAY 8–9, 1943. ENTRY MAY 12, 1943. N.L. At the moment when we had reached, it seemed, the very bottom of the well of despair, we heard the sound of our salvation. Rachel heard it first. In a loud voice she commanded silence, and so urgent was her cry that even the bickerings and contentions of that fractious bunker died down. Then we all heard the sound, in the very far distance—above ground, it seemed—of a concertina.

So that was how Berson had decided to find us! He would advertise himself and let us come to him.

Mordecai volunteered at once to go out and stalk Berson, and he left. We who stayed behind and who knew the real meaning of this concert—Rachel, Rutka, Rapaport, Zilberzweig, and I—wept and laughed and behaved, I am sure, as if we had forgotten where we were. Intermittently we heard the distant music; only once was it close enough so we could make out a tune: *Play Me a Waltz Non-Aryan.* Berson was apparently moving around to protect himself, and remembering Felix's account of Berson's speed and deception in these guerilla concerts [SEE EVENTS NIGHT OF APRIL 29–30, 1943], I could imagine that Mordecai was having a lively chase.

Nearly an hour had passed before Mordecai came in—alone. At first we were alarmed that Berson was not with him, but Mordecai drew us aside and explained secretively that Berson had gone—and we were to go now—to the brushmakers' bunker at Franciszkanska 22, where a party of fighters was making up to leave the ghetto by way of the sewers. Rachel wanted to invite Fein to go with us, and we all felt that that would be only fair. She drew him to our knot and told him our plan.

Fein, patting Rachel on the shoulder: —— No, thank you, my dear. I am busy here.

He indicated with a wave of his hand the noisy, whining crowd in the bunker, and I, for one, could not help wondering for a moment whether Fein's work, of trying to keep his tenants alive, was worth it; then at once I repented my sourness and allowed myself to be moved by his responsibility, which seemed fantastic under these circumstances, and yet was not too surprising in him, when one remembered his bearing during the project of getting Rachel's brother David out of the ghetto. A peculiarly duty-ridden fellow for one so outwardly jovial. I saw Fein bend down and kiss Rachel in an act of gratitude, and at once I recalled Rachel's account of her embarrassment over kissing rude Fein in thanks for his having taken her to stare at David in the window beyond the wall that time. [SEE ENTRY OCTOBER 16, 1942.] Evidently Fein remembered her gesture then. He tried to smile as he kissed her, but failed, in that his face turned rather bleak and his twisted lips seemed purple, bloated, and humorless.

We therefore left and hurried without accident overground to Franciszkanska 22. Though this was to be my last view of the ghetto, I cannot say that I looked around me sentimentally. Here was only wreckage: Jewry fragmented like the bricks of the fallen houses. Only the wall in the distance stood firm and clean. I was bitter and elated: confused, in short. I gave little thought to the landscape. When we arrived at Franciszkanska 22, we found that the brushmakers had left a sentry in the street, thank God, and he led us down quickly into the bunker.

About forty fighters were there assembled. We greeted and embraced Berson, who, being clean, seemed a decade younger then when we had last seen him. Rachel kissed the concertina! Slonim was there. The fighters were a forlorn lot. I thought of the night, just before the battle began, when Yitzhok so proudly catalogued our Jewish potency: twenty-two Fighter Groups! And here: the straggled strength of about one of those Groups. We found a few survivors from the headquarters bunker: the Group Commanders, Jankiel, Benz, and Ketzl (who after all had not used his cyanide: poor Ganzener could have had it!); and three or four other fighters. Yitzhok had evidently perished. Aron, Anselm, Peter, Nahum (so afraid of dying!), Ganzener, Mischa, Mendel, Abraham: lost, all of them.

We met the strange little man, a Polish sewer-worker named Kreszewski, who was to be our guide. He seemed rather surprised at our appearance. Under any but these particular circumstances, we would have been surprised at his. He was a gnome. [NOTE. EDITOR. The entry describing Kreszewski, herein placed under EVENTS MAY 5, 1943, was actually not written until after this one.] Berson was very agitated about getting started. It was now after ten o'clock, and the problem of shepherding forty people past all the twists and turns, around the stoppages, and out to the rendezvous at K-74 by five in the morning, in time for the arrival of the trucks, worried him much more than it did the rest of us. Seven hours seemed to us who know nothing time enough to crawl to Paris in a tunnel. Only the event showed us how right Berson had been, and how wrong we in our casualness.

Kreszewski led the way, Berson brought up the rear. There were forty-three of us, counting our Polish guide. We had five flashlights, which were distributed at intervals along the line. Rutka was directly ahead of me in the line. We from Fein's bunker were fairly near the head of the parade. The man behind me was a former attendant in the Rotblat Funeral Company, who turned out to be an interesting companion: every time we passed a corpse in the tunnel, and we did with moderate frequency, he would assess, sometimes with a mere prod of his foot, sometimes by the smell, sometimes with a touch of his hand, how long the body had been dead: he did not do this in a necrophilic vein, but on the other hand he was not frightened by these bodies, and somehow his rather scientific speculations took a little of the horror out of the encounters for me; it was comfortable to be next to a man who had become so very well acquainted with death. As we went he casually told me some stories about bodies: he called them, in his outlandish professional slang, "sausages."

I had often made short passages through stretches of sewer, but I had never attempted a long trip like this. It was very hard. The slipperiness underfoot, the constant stooping, the necessity of feeling one's way in spite of the intermittent twinkling of our flashlights, above all the nauseating smell, which had a serious effect upon my weakened stomach—I had not foreseen the dreadfulness of the trip in my elation over the opportunity to take it. Sometimes when we took a turn, two or three of our people would become confused, the line would break, and it would be necessary to pass a message all along it to halt and wait, while the strays were returned. The main culverts were over a meter and a third in diameter [NOTE. EDITOR. About four and a half feet.], but occasionally, when we came to one of the rubble-blocks the Germans had placed in a main, we had to cut through on hands and knees to another line by way of one of the lesser cross-drains, which were only three quarters of a meter in diameter. [NOTE. EDITOR. About thirty inches.] In most places, the sewage only came up to our shins, and in the cross-drains it was, thank God, quite shallow.

The trip took us five and three quarters of the seven hours. When we reached our destination, Berson crawled past us to the front of the line. One can imagine the excitement with which we waited for our deliverers. We indulged, even in our sickness and exhaustion, in magnificent plans—for hot baths three times a day, for instance, and for meals that would surfeit gluttons. We spoke of favorite dishes: I heard Berson sighing for *lox*, and I myself thought a sweet *tzimmes* would be nice. I was terrified lest one of my neighbors should declare his appetite for some sausage.

Five o'clock came and went. These were precious minutes, for dawn would soon break. All talking ceased along the line. We waited tensely.

At last, with a sudden clatter, the manhole opened, and we heard a man say in Polish:

—— Are you there?

Berson: —— Forty-three of us.

—— We couldn't get the trucks.

—— What?

—— There was a slip-up about the trucks. We think we can get them tomorrow night.

—— How will we know? Shall we leave a messenger with you?

—— No! It's not safe. . . . I can't stay here.

—— But what will we do?

—— I'll try to be here tomorrow at this time.

The manhole cover clattered back into place. There was silence among us.

11

✿ CONVERSATIONS

EVENTS MAY 9–10, 1943. ENTRY MAY 12–14, 1943. N.L. What could we do? At first the confusion in the culvert was dreadful. Those at the rear of the line who had not heard the exchange at the manhole wanted to know what had happened. Those who had heard the fearful news wanted to discuss it. There was no opportunity for group consultation. Questions and answers had to be relayed along the tube and back. Everyone was nervous, angry, and exhausted.

One thing was clear. Very few of us, if any, would have the strength to crawl all the way back to the Franciszkanska bunker and then come here again the next night: our conductors, Berson, Slonim, and Kreszewski, had already made one round trip this night.

What could we do but wait there?

EVOLUTION OF THE TALKS: One simply had to keep busy. I began by discussing our predicament with Rutka, who was next to me in the line. Almost immediately, I caught from her a curious feeling of heightened sensibility: there was a haunting beauty and vitality in everything she said, similar to the sparkle and life in a woman's eyes when, in broadest daylight, because of excitement, her pupils are dilated as if to see in the dark. Death was our darkness there in the sewer.

I found myself asking Rutka questions which but a few hours earlier would have seemed impertinent; now they were natural, and her answers were natural. I did not take notes on my talks with her and with the others later, but I remember everything she and the others said as clearly as if my mind were a copper plate on which the slightest hairlines and the tiniest shadow-hatchings had been fixed forever by acid. Probably out of nervous habit, I wrote perhaps a dozen short notes on things that happened there in the sewer; I wrote by flashlight. The rest of the time I talked and listened. There was no hurry. Indeed, the problem was to lean our shoulders against the hours and roll them along: now and again I had a panicky feeling that time had stopped, and that we were all doomed to squat for eternity in that echoing, evil-smelling cylinder. Rapaport had a watch. I kept asking him what time it was.

As I talked with one after another of my friends, I began to realize that there was a pattern to our talks. It was not conscious or systematic; nor was it ever explicit. It was indirect, oblique, shadowy.

We were all talking about one question: What has made our lives worth living?

I asked some amazing questions in those hours, but I never asked that one. No one ever said to me: *This* is what has made my life worth living. Nevertheless, I can see that that was what we were talking about.

[NOTE. EDITOR. Nowhere in Levinson's record has the problem of selection been so crucial and difficult as in the presentation of these conversations. (A very few excerpts from the conversations have been moved forward into the body of the text: those passages marked thus: ✿.) Levinson evidently wrote his record of these conversations hastily, and he recorded the talks exactly as they had actually developed, with all their trivia and bewildering detail and confusing shiftiness from person to person and back again. The editor has chosen from Levinson's account of his talks with each individual only a few passages, each dealing with a specific idea or episode. The editor must take full responsibility for this method, and can only hope that, in Levinson's own "indirect, oblique, shadowy" way, it may convey to the reader some kind of answer to the question Levinson felt that the talks posed. The interstitial material, dealing with events and moods in the sewer during the conversations, comes from the notes Levinson made at the time; it has been here interlarded between the talks.

Before proceeding to the conversations themselves, the editor feels justified in presenting a passage from a letter from Rachel Apt, written much later, when Rachel forwarded Levinson's last papers to Palestine. This letter describes Levinson during the conversations.]

[EXCERPT FROM A LETTER TO THE EDITOR FROM RACHEL APT. . . . I was up near the head of the line, with Dolek and the Polish sewer-worker, and we had been there for two or three hours before Noach came along the culvert and first talked to me. I got from him a wonderful feeling of warmth and understanding, and even of gentle humor, and although we discussed the most intimate matters, I felt that it was all perfectly in accord with our mood and with the situation. Noach did not stay with any one person for long—perhaps fifteen or twenty minutes; then he would move to someone else; he would come back again later. He seemed to be *entertaining* us—though of course that was not his purpose at all. Indeed, I don't know how we would have got through that time, had it not been for the thoughts and memories Noach put in our minds. Again and again, as if he were obsessed with the passage of time, he would crawl to Rapaport, and ask the old Socialist to shine the flashlight he had onto his wristwatch, and occasionally, when Noach was quite far from Rapaport, we would hear Noach's deep voice murmuring above the whispers in the culvert: *Rapaport! What time is it? . . .*]

✡ CONVERSATIONS OF MAY 9–10, 1943

6:15 a.m., May 9. Our fear has somewhat abated. Most of us sit crosswise in the sewer-pipe with our knees drawn up. We are accustomed to filth now, and our efforts to stay out of it are not so much fastidiousness as the knowledge that we face a full day's clamminess here: we want to keep as dry as possible. But we will undoubtedly be weary thus. . . .

RUTKA MAZUR

N.L.: —— Rutka, I remember one curious thing. In your labor, when you were delivering your baby, there was a period in which, during each cramp, you reviled Mordecai and seemed to despise him, and then between cramps you praised him and seemed to adore him. Do you remember that?

Rutka: —— I am rather hazy about my thoughts and feelings during my pains. One thing I do remember was a feeling that came back and back: I kept wondering what it would be like to have a baby under normal circumstances—in a peaceful situation, in a decent home, outside the wall. And I kept telling myself that I was really lucky, that having the baby as I was having it was better and more meaningful.

N.L.: —— Can you imagine any reason why you might have talked that way to Mordecai during your labor?

Rutka: —— I suppose that words and thoughts came out of me during the pains that I would not wish to face at ordinary times.

N.L. —— Do you mean that deep down inside yourself you had contempt for Mordecai?

Rutka: —— When you are married to someone, you get to know him very well. Who is perfect? I praised Mordecai between the pains, didn't I? Why are you trying to make me say that I hate him? My feelings about him are mixed, and that is natural, it seems to me, and I think I have been a good wife. We can't be adolescent lovers all our lives.

* * *

Rutka says that even living in bunkers and degradation, and especially during the period when she served as a courier on the Aryan side with Berson, her pregnancy made her loathe herself. Modestly she indicated that she had always felt a certain power in her appearance and in her effect on men. [NOTE. N.L. And justly. I remember in early days the delicate, bluish texture of the skin around her brilliant eyes, her full lips, her lustrous black hair; and especially her liveliness: her rippling laughter.] With a certain shame she indicated that she had used this power to satisfy herself in her relationships with less attractive women —especially with Rachel (as, for instance, when she led the way for Rachel in House Committee and underground work, and in the mutilation of their furs). And when she was pregnant, this female power was gone. She felt weak. Thus on the Aryan side, though she believes she did good work, she was totally dependent upon Berson, and had no power over him. This was humiliating.

* * *

Rutka: —— Listen! I'll tell you a story. On my trip to Wilno as a courier, my contact was a man named Chaim. This Chaim and his wife had had a baby just a few weeks before I arrived, and I wish you could have heard Chaim talk! You remember, the Jews were having a very hard time in Wilno just then, and Chaim had responsibilities: he was the Zilberzweig of Wilno, you could say. He was a tall, gaunt man, a capmaker by profession, and he looked sour—except when he talked about his baby son. I will never forget what he said to me one day: *Rutka*, he said, *you will not fully realize what it is to be a Jew until you are the parent of one.*

* * *

One night in the bunker, when Israel was only a few days old, Rutka says, she woke up from a sound sleep and for a few moments was unable to remember whether she had had the baby or not. She says this frightened her so much that at first she could not put her hand on her belly to find out; she was as if paralyzed. She asked me why I thought her mind had played this trick on her. I said:

—— How should I know?

I wonder if it was because Rutka inwardly doubted whether she should have brought an infant into this world of bunkers, filth, and hunger.

* * *

. . . Best of all, said Rutka, were Israel's feet. In adult life, she says, feet become the least attractive of all the human parts: bony, calloused, somehow vestigial (else why do we encase our once prehensile toes in the leather boxes we call shoes?). But Israel's feet were rounded, pink, mobile, and even on their bottoms as delicate as the skin of his neck or cheek. The softness of his soles epitomized for Rutka his dependence upon her.

Thus did Rutka go over her baby, inch by inch, in memory. She clings to the memory; it is everything to her. I tried to get her to talk about her Hashomer work—or about the day she hectographed Zilberzweig's editorial on the Russo-German war and thought Zilberzweig might make love to her—or about her day-dreams of Mordecai that morning when her cosmetics professor (I remember his name: Kamenhorn! My mind is unusually clear) analyzed common talc—or about the day when she saw her own mother go voluntarily to the *Umschlagplatz*, carrying slippers and candles. But no! Only the baby!

Rutka: —— I will have another. As soon as I am strong enough.

N.L.: —— I am grateful for your optimism.

Rutka: —— This possibility alone makes me optimistic.

N.L.: —— Why are you in such a hurry to give birth to an-other Jew? Haven't you seen what can happen to Jews?

Rutka: —— Noach, I'm surprised at you! Can't you see that that is exactly the reason?

*   *   *

I asked Rutka to tell me what her sensations were when she discovered that Israel was dead in her arms, but she said:

—— Please don't ask me to speak of that.

11:30 a.m., May 9. I can see that thirst will be a serious prob-lem before we get away from here. Our doubled-over position is bad enough, but to be wet and thirsty, increasingly chilled with dampness and dry-tongued with thirst—that is a sad paradox. Yet inwardly we are more comfortable now. For the time being we feel that the danger from Germans is behind us. This confining tube is also a lovely fort. We feel safe. Our friends will come for us in the morning. . . .

Hil Zilberzweig

N.L.: —— Some of my friends have mentioned seeing a change in you during recent months. Have you felt such a change taking place?

Zilberzweig: —— I think I know what you mean.

N.L.: —— Could you describe this change?

Zilberzweig: —— The funny part is: your "friends" think I am less of a man than I was, whereas I know I am stronger and wiser than I was.

N.L.: —— My friends did speak of a noticeable softening.

Zilberzweig: —— No. That is wrong. You see, what has really happened is that I have decided that nationalism is not enough for a man to live by. The "strength" or "hardness" these people thought they saw in me, before, that was artificial: that was my nationalism.

N.L.: —— This surprises me. Aren't you a Zionist by profession? Isn't nationalism your career?

Zilberzweig: —— Zionism has been my only profession. I guess you can say that my "strength" and "hardness" have been professional with me most of my life.

N.L.: —— Why this change?

Zilberzweig: —— I don't know. Maybe just seeing younger men than I, like Yitzhok Katz, who were also "stronger" and "harder" and more nationalistic than I. [NOTE. N.L. This reference to younger men strikes me as interesting, considering the number of times Berson and others spoke to me of Zilberzweig's repeated protests that he was too old to be a fighter: the youth leader growing slightly bald: I recall Berson's analogy of the retiring diva, giving farewell recitals again and again.] It came to me that extreme nationalism can be as frightful in a Jew as in a German. What does Nazi stand for, anyhow?—*National* Socialism. I should not like to survive the ghetto and go to Palestine, only to fall into the hands of Jewish Nazis.

N.L.: —— Do you mean to say you abandon the hope of going to Palestine because of such a ridiculous fear?

Zilberzweig: —— For myself, I abandoned hope years ago— for other reasons. . . . No, I have not abandoned the idea that the Jewish ethical tradition is worth preserving—it is the basis of all Western monotheism, after all; . . . *the Lord our God is One God*—and that the best way of preserving it is to give it a home. No, I have rebelled only against *excessive* nationalism. The religious zealot ends by being (because of his excesses) anti-religious. In the case of the Jews, the national zealot can likewise become anti-religious—and even, in the consequences of his deeds, anti-Jewish.

* * *

[NOTE. EDITOR. The reader is reminded of the excerpts from these conversations printed under EVENTS APRIL 18, 1943, and describing Zilberzweig's thoughts on the eve of the ghetto battle. Those thoughts, the reader will remember, were predominantly *traditional*, and they centered finally upon Zilberzweig's devout father and uncle. The presumption is that they were a culmination of the feelings he outlined to Levinson in the passage above.]

*　　*　　*

Zilberzweig described a conversation he had with Halinka on the day in January when the Co-ordinating Committee decided the Z.O.B. was not yet ready to fight, and would have to postpone action:

Zilberzweig: —— The fighters will be terribly disappointed. . . . (Zilberzweig lay supine on the sofa, with his head and shoulders in Halinka's lap and arms. The pretty girl gazed down on his heavy, tired face with a look of tenderness and pity. Zilberzweig pressed his cheek against her bosom and said:) Oh, Halinka, I thank God for you. You give me strength.

Halinka, pouting and frowning playfully: —— You're not strong. You're like a baby!

—— They'll be so discouraged. Rachel has spoken for days of nothing but the readiness of her Group.

—— Then why did you let the Committee decide to delay?

—— I fought (Zilberzweig lied) against it.

—— Poor Hil!

—— Halinka, I have never known, anything like the happiness you have given me.

Halinka narrowed her eyes, drew back her head a little, and seemed to be surveying her lover, as if he were an utterly new and distant landscape. Then she said pitifully:

—— I have destroyed you, haven't I?

—— Destroyed me? (Zilberzweig closed his eyes and lay limp and flaccid in the young girl's arms.) You have brought me to life.

*　　*　　*

Zilberzweig: —— You see, Halinka became interested in me, and not in one of the available younger men, for two reasons. One was that she needed an education in Jewishness, and our Hashomer work provided that. The other was that, being so feminine, she could see how ripe I was for an education in humanness—perhaps, referring to Halinka, one need only say an education in manness. But you see, even she did not understand the nature of the change in me. She was new to nationalism. It excited her. She could not comprehend that I was turning away from this tight, rigid, dangerous emotion to hunt for the emotions of a universal man. And so it appears that in the crucial days of our history, the lifelong professional Zionist betrayed his cause for the sake of a flirtatious girl. That is one way of looking at things, I suppose. . . .

*　　*　　*

Note. N.L. I cannot say whether Zilberzweig is, as he claims, more a man than he was before he got out of his nationalistic costume, but this much I can say: I used to see in him, and dislike in him, a deliberate, professional pleasantness; his eager smile was one of the tools of his trade. That is gone now. He is pleasant when he feels pleasant; he is rather ugly when he feels morose. I like him much better. This does not necessarily make him a better man, but it makes him more tolerable.

*　　*　　*

N.L. —— You said you decided to search for the emotions of a universal man. Did you find them?

Zilberzweig: —— No, Levinson. Not yet. It is rather hard to find universality within a ghetto wall.

N.L. —— True. You are a failure, then?

Zilberzweig: —— So far. But I can say that I am trying.

3:30 p.m., May 9. The manhole is our parlor. We take turns stretching there: it is possible to stand up full length in the shaft. Luxuriating in the erect position, one can look up and see, like a firmament above, small stars of daylight twinkling in the ventilation-apertures of the manhole cover. Once in a while a truck or a car goes rattling, clank-clank, across the metal disk, and occasionally we even hear a footstep on it. And so we seem to be very close to that society which walks above ground. This is rather exciting. There is less than a wall between us and the world. Only this little iron sky intervenes!

Henryk Rapaport

There were two May Day occasions about which I wished to question Rapaport:

1) Slonim, in speaking of the May Day, 1940, party at Rapaport's apartment, had said that he wondered whether Rapaport had finally, late in his career, begun to doubt Socialism—or at least to doubt whether fallible individual human beings could work together to realize true Socialism. Had Rapaport really come to such a doubt?

Rapaport: —— A man who chooses a career in politics will fail if he believes that his party or his doctrine is perfect, for he is certain to be disillusioned; he will also fail if he sees the flaws and spends all his energy trying to correct them, for he is certain in that case to be cast out. He can only succeed if he learns to doubt his faith and to fight for it none the less.

2) How does Rapaport explain having poured out his despair and sense of failure to N.L. all during the afternoon of May Day, 1943, and then, but a few hours later, having spoken to his party friends in an opposite and fervid tone of triumph and hope?

Rapaport: —— Purgatives are good for the human system.

* * *

Finding Rapaport determined to address me in pompous epigrams, and being on my side equally determined to draw him into an anecdotal way of speaking, I began to spar with him. Since I remembered that during his afternoon of despair with me, he had several times spoken regretfully of the way he had alienated Slonim, I tried to get at him by talking about our friend with the cowlick. To my surprise, Rapaport responded by abusing Slonim. A pretentious fake intellectual, he called Slonim; a conceited and shallow young man. Rapaport really went too far. Personally I have never been particularly charmed by Slonim, but Rapaport went too far. I began to wonder what was wrong with Rapaport. He was not answering me generously and sympathetically, as everyone else in the sewer had been doing: he was sharp, hasty, and unlike himself. It was only after the most dogged work, bending myself in all humility to his harsh mood, that I was able to discover that his stomach, which had troubled him off and on for many years, was now giving him the most excruciating pain. I learned that he had vomited many times on the trip here through the culverts.

Ai! This was a challenge for me. Could I get him to talk himself out of his pain?

I began by questioning him about his belly. I have always

heard of Rapaport's famous weak stomach, but never had I heard him mention it, and I had never heard of his discussing it with anyone else. Now, however, he described with the most affectionate precision the operations of this treacherous organ of his: every tiny sensation, from the dance-like contest between descending and rising waves of his gorge, during meals, to the protesting release into the duodenal torture chamber of more or less digested matter, by his desperate pyloric valve. Rapaport seems to have made frequent inspection tours of his beloved guts, and to have seen for himself the precariousness of his internal machinery. He is positive about his poor stomach, if about nothing else in this world: if only digestion were politics! Rapaport would surely be Chairman of the Central Committee of the Stomach Party.

Lending my wretched, abused ear to his wretched, abused belly, in reciprocal organic pain—thus I gained the old man's confidence, and before he knew it, he was telling me grand stories about himself—and I think he had almost forgotten his hurtful insides.

He told me the story of the Semperit strike, in 1936, when he faced a stoning by strikebreakers and bluffed them down; he told me honestly of his having failed his engineering examinations in the French polytechnical school which he attended; he told me of his accomplishments and errors in days of his "flying squad" work as a labor agitator; he told me . . .

*   *   *

[NOTE. EDITOR. Levinson wrote out several of these stories in detail. Two have appeared in the body of this record: his account of Comrade Boleslav and the missing chocolate (ENTRY AUGUST 1, 1942), and his story about the way Big Ear, the sloppy tinsmith, resented Rapaport's air of superiority (ENTRY MAY 2, 1943). Another follows:]

In a slum apartment in Lodz, one night in 1938, Rapaport sat listening to the personal troubles of a burly weaver named Kamen. Kamen was an Old Socialist, a veteran with Rapaport of work in the early years of the century; but he had somehow fallen behind his contemporaries—he was still, after all these years, no more than the leader of a Group. One of Kamen's troubles was a bad temper. Another was women. Between the two Kamen had now put himself into a sooty cookpot: he had got another man's wife preg-

nant and had broken the husband's nose in an argument over this
adultery. Kamen felt he could have straightened everything out
(except possibly the husband's nose) but for the fact that the
fragile-nosed husband was a member of the Lodz Committee of
the Bund. What he wanted Rapaport to solve was the *political* aspect of his problem. The Lodz Committee cuckold, with his vanity doubly injured, his manhood and his profile both having been
squashed, was determined to expel Kamen from the party. The
case became notorious. One day in the Bund Central Committee
for all Poland—of which Rapaport was a member—an unexpected
fight developed. It revolved around the Kamen case, though that
case was never specifically mentioned. The young man known in
the Bund as Chaver Velvel began to argue, out of the blue, that
the Bund could not tolerate moral delinquency. Rapaport argued
for leniency and understanding. Velvel shouted that personal
friendships should not affect a man's political judgments. Rapaport quietly said at last: "We in the Bund must think of the
whole life of our Jewish worker, not just of his working hours. He
is a man, not a unit of machinery."

*   *   *

With regard to Slonim, Rapaport (his gastric distress evidently having eased) now said he had admiration for certain
things about the young man. Slonim's physical untidiness, his ev-
erlasting cowlick, his intellectual snobbery, his resentment of any
talent in anyone else—these things Rapaport detests, he said. But
the romantic strain in Slonim, the tendency to regard the hard,
cruel events of everyday life as adventures: this gave Slonim a freedom of attitude which Rapaport says he admires.

Rapaport: —— Slonim's great advantage is that social progress is a personal thing to him. It is not an abstraction or a career:
it is a game, an outing, a good time. I wish I had had that view
all my life.

*   *   *

N.L.: —— Which do you think is more important now—
your politics or your friends?

Rapaport (no longer responding in his grand manner): ——
Listen, how can I answer that? When you come right down to it,
I guess my politics *is* friendship. I suppose that is a little too loose

for the Bund: I should be expelled from the Bund myself. And I suppose I am a man without a single intimate friend. And yet: judge me, Levinson. Have I or have I not tried to put human understanding into my politics?

[NOTE. N.L. I find most likable in Rapaport, and most revealing, the fact that he *wishes* to be judged.]

7:00 p.m., May 9. The Rotblat Funeral man detains me as I slither along like a caterpillar past the people in the tube. He wants to tell me more amusing stories about sausages. For once I am a bad listener. I cannot stand it. I want to hear stories about life. One of the people in our party, quite far back along the line, a young girl who survived typhus and escaped once from the Umschlagplatz, died about an hour ago. She lived through all the hardships of the ghetto only to die of that horrible disease called waiting. . . . No! Tell me stories of life—of sensation, appetite, lust, zest, and gladness to be alive!

MORDECAI APT

Mordecai could speak of almost nothing but the wall. Of course he had worked on the wall for three years.

Mordecai: —— We built very well the sections along Zelazna Street. That was in 1941. We were not hopeless then and the physical work kept us too tired to think or worry. I believe you would find the masonry excellent along Zelazna. . . .

Inevitably Mordecai spoke of his feelings of self-blame in connection with having worked so long in the bricklayers' battalion. He holds himself personally responsible for having enclosed his fellows. In this highly charged mood of regret and shame, Mordecai began, in more thoughtful words than I have usually heard him spend, to speak of the wall as an idea.

—— . . . There are two ways of looking at the wall between Jews and gentiles: from the inside and from the outside: there is much to be said on both sides. On the one hand, it can be said that the actual masonry is done by the Jews: the Jews mix the mortar and lay the bricks and complain about the wall, but are sometimes glad to have it. On the other hand, it is the *goyim* who oblige the Jews to build the wall and who supply most of the materials for it; and they are very smug about its existence: without ever going inside it, they assume it is better to be outside and to keep the Jews inside. . . .

Mordecai seemed to ponder a moment. Then he said:

—— Do you remember the time when you and Berson and I exchanged mementos? I remember I was talking that day about tearing down sections of the wall, and I told you I was surprised how easy it was to take it down. That was true. It was amazing. And yet this, too, must be said: it is harder to take the wall down than to put it up. When you are building a wall, the mortar is soft. When you come to demolish it, the mortar has become dry and rigid and adhesive. You have to work with cold steel. Nevertheless, the work can be done. One can even be surprised how easy it is. Of course, as I said at the time, the Germans may have given us rotten lime. . . .

11:45 p.m., May 9. What this did for our morale! There was no more than a teaspoon for each of us, yet we feel we have feasted. Suddenly—terrifyingly—a few minutes ago, the manhole cover was raised. We who were near the shaft thought we had been discovered. Then down to us on a string came a workman's beer-pail, containing soup; and the cover clattered back. No words. Soup for us, who were about to consider sipping sewage to slake our awful thirst! They are thinking of us! What nourishment in that knowledge!

LAZAR SLONIM

I suppose one could scarcely blame Slonim for being obsessed with his successes: especially with his trip to Treblinka. A romantic has to have successes. A romantic is usually both self-centered and boastful. But when I asked Slonim why he has succeeded, whenever in life he did, his answer was not egocentric; indeed, it was rather modest. It contained a whole theory of life (which, however, like all single-layered theories to explain human behavior, cannot quite stand alone).

Slonim: —— I succeeded, whenever I did, because I was thinking about how some other person or persons would react to my accomplishment.

Thus on his mission to Treblinka, as he told me at the time, Slonim gave not a single thought to the meaning of the mission itself: the intrinsic act was nothing to him: what was important was personal: he wanted to justify himself in Rapaport's eyes. Slonim thinks this interplay of human reactions, of approvals and censures and gratitudes and resentments and jealousies and flatteries and generosities and cruelties—this interplay is more important in our behavior than the interplay of ideas. This is especially true in public life, Slonim says. Look at our *Judenrat*! Slonim says that no theory or structure of government has yet been devised that can control this interplay among the governors, to say nothing of the governed, and use it constructively.

N.L.: —— Well, Slonim, you have cut out for yourself a life's work. Invent such a system.

Slonim: —— Listen! I have enough trouble controlling myself.

3:30 a.m. How much longer can we stand this sewer? Can we last another hour and a half, until our rescuers come? To rest from the terrible curved crouch this culvert imposes on us, we kneel for a time, or stand like kine on all fours, on hands and knees, over the putrid river. What time, Rapaport? Can't you make that watch go faster?

DOLEK BERSON

N.L.: —— Do you remember what you thought when you first saw her?

Berson: —— I have told you before: I thought she was an ugly child.

*   *   *

Berson: —— The day—before the ghetto—when Schpunt volunteered as rabbi in Goldflamm's place, and did his dance for the Germans outside Sapir's Hat and Gloves, Rachel was very bitter toward me, because I thought Schpunt had been funny. She called me a fool. I was stung by this. I remember it took me two or three days to get over my hurt feelings.

*   *   *

622

[NOTE. EDITOR. The reader is reminded of the passage from these conversations, placed under ENTRY SEPTEMBER 10, 1942, in which Berson, describing his thoughts while taking a bath after his return from the "Kettle," spoke of having "discovered" Rachel. Rachel had "set the pitch of everyone's feelings" in their group during the frightful "Kettle."]

* * *

Berson said that the one thing about Rachel he never could excuse was her inability to carry a tune.

* * *

N.L.: —— What do you find to like in Rachel?

Berson: —— Well, she seems to me very *natural*. When I ask her a question and she answers me, I don't have to stop and think, Now, why did she say that? She is kindhearted in this natural way, too: there seems to be no self-interest in her generosity. She is very attentive and eager to learn. [NOTE. N.L. *I* observed that quality in her—probably long before you did, Berson!] She is modest and fearless, and she can make people work and fight. Best of all, she is responsive. I think responsiveness is the most pleasing quality one can have.

* * *

[NOTE. EDITOR. Again, the reader is reminded of the passages from this context in which Berson described his and Rachel's first realization of their feeling for each other, the night of Levinson's speech on Peretz (EVENTS APRIL 24, 1943), and his imagined and his real stories of his disappearance with Rachel during the battle (EVENTS APRIL 26–28, 1943).]

* * *

[NOTE. N.L. After thinking about the fantastic story Berson told me to explain his escapade with Rachel, now that I had heard the true one, I became very depressed. The question came to my mind: How much have people been lying to me all these years? How much have I blithely written down as event which was really invented? I could see that some people who habitually lie

623

to themselves could not avoid lying to me. But Berson and Rachel! They are two people who can face the truth! I determined to question Berson further about this.]

* * *

N.L.: —— You told me that you lied about your disappearance with Rachel in order to protect her. Wasn't there a better reason?

Berson: —— Yes, Noach, there was. I wanted to spare you.

N.L.: —— Because you thought I had tender feelings toward Rachel?

Berson: —— Why else?

N.L.: —— That is a glorious reason for lying! I thank you. I love Rachel, but alas! as a brother. You could have saved yourself all that ingenuity.

Berson: —— My lies weren't very good, anyhow.

N.L.: —— No, they weren't.

* * *

N.L.: —— If you had the last four years to live over again, what would you do differently?

Berson: —— That is a silly game. When I was at the Gymnasium, my friends and I used to play another one like it: If-I-Had-a-Million-Zlotys. Playing the game never earned us a single zloty.

N.L.: —— Nevertheless, what would you change?

Berson: —— I have floundered a lot. You used to call me the Drifter. I think I would perhaps try to be more direct and methodical.

N.L.: —— For instance?

Berson: —— Well, for instance, the time for me to have joined the *Judenrat* was right away, in 1939, immediately after I was mistakenly jailed as a deputy councilor. By the time I finally did join, it was too late already. I think I should have thrown myself into House Committee work earlier, and that would have led to joining the Hashomer earlier. I would have thought of some way of protecting Pavel Menkes the night of the manhunt last April when Stefan wanted to turn him in. . . . But, Noach, this is a silly game. I did what I did. Talking can't change anything.

N.L.: —— What about Rachel? Any changes there?

Berson: —— How could there have been any changes? At

first Symka was alive, and I could remember all the good years with her. Does your silly game take those years away? . . . Then afterward it took time for Rachel to grow and change into the woman she became; and I was growing, too. One had to wait for readiness.

N.L.: —— My game may be silly, but it has made me realize the real difference between the Drifter of 1939 and you of today. You're not impatient any more. Then you were in a hurry, because you thought you could encompass everything in your life. You wanted to learn everything and experience everything and be everybody. In a way, that was charming and delightful in you: I used to write in my notebooks that you were zestful. But it also made you seem confused. You did things in fits and starts. You learned as a stammerer talks. . . . Today, you are not in such a hurry. I think you have decided that you can do only a few things at all well, and they are more than enough.

Berson: —— How did you come to this sweeping conclusion out of your game of Give-Me-Back-My-Life?

N.L.: —— Just one small sentence you spoke: *One had to wait for readiness.*

Berson: —— I think I learned patience from Rachel. She has always had so much to put up with. Have you ever heard her complain?

N.L.: —— No. . . . I have one more question: it is one I used to ask you quite often long ago: What is the most important thing for a Jew to do in the face of persecution?

Berson: —— Be himself. Be neither imitative of his persecutor nor try to imagine how a persecuted man should behave. Be himself.

N.L.: —— Is that not difficult?

Berson: —— Yes, because he has to know himself first.

N.L.: —— How can he get to know himself?

Berson: —— Make a few mistakes. There is nothing like an expensive mistake to show a man to himself.

N.L.: —— In other words, it's expensive to be Jewish?

Berson: —— Usually. . . . But now you are making fun of me!

N.L.: —— No, my dear friend. I am dead in earnest. . . . I like your answers better than any you have ever given me.

5:15 a.m., May 10. I tremble. I fear I will die. Our man from above came just now and lifted the manhole cover and said the trucks were still not available. He said he would keep trying. My God! Another day here? Impossible! We will perish.

RACHEL APT

N.L.: —— For a long time, in 1939 and 1940, when I first knew you, I thought you and I would fall in love. Forgive me, dear Rachel, I considered you homely enough to accept my homeliness.

Rachel: —— I know, Noach. I expected it, too. I have always liked you very much.

N.L.: —— Don't talk like that. You sound as if you were trying to console a rejected suitor! Remember: I only *wanted* to fall in love with you. I was not successful.

Rachel: —— Don't be so proud!

* * *

Rachel: —— It is strange. With Dolek, I have never been self-conscious about my face.

N.L.: —— Perhaps your Berson is one of those men who never lets himself have a chance to look at a woman's face. Other interesting features . . .

Rachel (obviously delighted): —— Noach!

* * *

One thing only, in all the years I have known Rachel, have I felt that she hid from me: exactly what her father's "sickness" was, his mysterious "stomach trouble," shortly before he left the ghetto. I remember being very much troubled by the evasive way she dealt with me in connection with that period when her father was bedridden. Therefore, since honesty was now the order, I asked her about it. I got an honest answer, all right:

—— He had his circumcision corrected.

—— Is such a thing possible?

—— Dr. Breithorn had a friend who knew a lot about plastic surgery.

—— So that is what Dr. Breithorn meant in that bitter remark he made to you about your father's having been cured of *the dis-*

626

ease which is transmitted by parents! Had this surgeon of his grown wealthy here in the ghetto doing his little religious conversions? . . . No! I don't wish to hear the answer to that question, even if you know the answer.

Rachel: —— Now do you see why I had contempt for my father—even though I could not help loving him?

* * *

N.L.: —— Berson was the one who first called you Little Mother. Did you feel maternal toward him?

Rachel: —— No, I felt as if he was all men to me: father, husband, brother, and son.

N.L.: —— That must have kept you busy.

Rachel: —— You asked the question; I answered it. Don't mock me!

N.L.: —— Temper! . . . I'm sorry, dear Rachel. I was thinking what might have been if you and I . . . How many men I could have been!

Rachel: —— Brother you could be. The others—I don't know.

N.L.: —— I remember once, when you were talking about how much you wanted to be a mother, you looked right through me as if I were a window. I decided then that I would not make a suitable son. The others—*I* don't know!

* * *

N.L.: —— Why do you think you were chosen a Group Commander of the Z.O.B.?

Rachel: —— My face.

N.L.: —— Nonsense! What recommendation is homeliness?

Rachel: —— It is not nonsense. I believe that it was because of my face that I learned a long time ago to adjust myself to disappointments and to be rather easy about difficulties.

* * *

I reminded Rachel that when she first moved into the Jewish section with her family, she had had very little experience of inner Jewish life. I asked her to tell me what she thought of this inner life, now that she was on the point of graduating from ghetto-school.

Rachel: —— I didn't have much chance to learn about God; I

am rather unclear as to God. But so far as the rest of our religion is concerned, I think there is only one thing: not to hurt anybody. For me the whole of the Torah is in one sentence in Leviticus: Thou shalt love thy neighbor as thyself.

N.L.: —— Even if thy neighbor is a Nazi?

Rachel: —— How else cure him of being a Nazi?

N.L.: —— Maybe there is no cure. Maybe you have to kill him.

Rachel: —— I've tried that, and where did it get me? Where am I now?

N.L.: —— In a sewer.

* * *

N.L.: —— What do you think of your sister Halinka?

Rachel: —— We used to fight a lot.

N.L.: —— Yes, but what do you think of her now?

Rachel: —— I was very proud of her when she became a courier.

N.L.: —— Rachel, I want to tell you something. I've never spoken about this to anyone; I never even wrote this down in my notebooks. I hope you won't be offended. The fact is, Rachel, that for a very long time I thought I was in love with Halinka.

Rachel: —— Why should I be offended at that? Since we are being honest with each other, I must tell you that I am more inclined to laugh.

N.L.: —— Yes, I realize now how funny the idea is. . . . I only thought you might be offended because I tried to love you and succeeded only in becoming secretly infatuated with your silly sister. It was simply her beauty and fragility. I shook in her presence. I used to let my fancy run off with her, and what times they had together—day and night! I was like an adolescent mooncalf. And yes, I realize now that this is so grotesque that it is comical; but, Rachel, it is the only love I have ever allowed myself. Even while it was going on, I was embarrassed about it. I was self-consciously guarded even when I wrote about her in my notebooks. [NOTE. EDITOR. Only once, in ENTRY AUGUST 8, 1942, did Levinson let his guard down. That was the day Halinka was married to Stefan, when he wrote, "I will have no more trouble from that quarter."] Yet even so, I suppose I made a fool of myself. Do you remember the time our staircase became so excited about the affair Halinka was supposed to be having with Gruber? Well, I worked like a slave to clear her name. And then when Halinka went to live with Zilberzweig, I remember I wrote out an elaborate rationalization, in which I criticized Zilberzweig and praised you.

Rachel: —— Praised me? What for?

N.L.: —— For not being jealous.

Rachel: —— You needn't have praised me. That goes back to my face, too.

*　　*　　*

Rachel and I talked for a long time about the ones we have left behind us within the wall, or who have gone away outside: her father, her brother David, Reb Yechiel and Froi Mazur, Rabbi Goldflamm, Felix Mandeltort, Pavel Menkes, Stefan Mazur, Schlome Mazur.

Rachel, who had been speaking of these individuals in a steady voice, quite calmly, but now becoming suddenly very emotional: —— They are dead, Noach. What a debt we owe them! All the rest of my life I will be conscious of them, I will be trying to pay them back.

N.L.: —— Wait and see. You'll forget rather easily.

Rachel: —— No! No!

N.L.: —— Yes, I think so. It is hard to be memorial all the time. And anyhow, it is better to look ahead, I suppose.

10:20 a.m., May 10. They have come. But in broad daylight!

12

Events May 10, 1943. Entry May 14, 1943. N.L. Everything happened so fast that I am still not certain of the exact sequence of events.

It was after ten in the morning. I was talking with Rachel. She was sitting with her knees doubled up under her chin, hugging her legs; I was kneeling beside her. We were three or four meters from the manhole shaft. Suddenly we heard the manhole cover lifted and rolled aside and a voice cried in Polish:

—— Now! Come up now! We have the trucks.

I can say that thirty hours in a dark hole, waiting for a signal, do not prepare one for prompt reactions to the signal when it comes. It took us some moments to realize what was happening. Then, for my own part, instead of reacting in orderly delight, I fought my way to Rapaport, asked him to shine his flashlight on his watch, saw that the time was 10:20, then made a brief note in my notebook! I suppose this was a case of habit taking possession of me.

Meanwhile at the head of the line Kreszewski, our tiny Polish guide, with whom we had been having some trouble (he had brought a bottle; he had been drunk and had been very hard to keep quiet), scrambled up the metal ladder in the manhole shaft, and Slonim went after him. Then in regular order the people in the line began to climb, but they were stiff, cramped, dizzy, and wild, and some had to be pushed, and some pulled, upward. One of the older men fell down all the way from the top of the shaft—he had had his waist out in freedom—and he seemed to have broken his leg and we just dragged him to one side because there was no time to waste. When I reached the shaft, I saw Berson crouching at one side. He thumped me on the back and said something encouraging to me. I gathered that since he had brought up the rear, he was now going to see everybody safely out and round up stragglers, if any, before climbing out himself.

I went up the ladder just after Rutka. There were seventeen rungs. It was a work of great endurance to negotiate them. At the top of the shaft as I climbed I saw a dazzling light: the light of day outside the wall! I counted rungs and concentrated on my footing, bearing in mind the groaning man with the broken leg dragged off into the culvert down below.

How clean the air above!

I got a knee up onto the edge of the manhole and heaved myself out and moved aside to let the next one come. For a moment I was there on my hands and knees, a dripping beast of the sewers. I did not feel that I had the strength to stand up. I blinked and squinted and finally was able to see two trucks by the curb not five meters away. All along the sidewalk I saw tidy people standing, curiously watching. A man was shouting frantically and beckoning. How could one hurry after thirty hours in a sewer? At last I propped myself up on my feet. My head swam. I staggered forward, using all my will to get away from the manhole, so that if I fainted I would not fall back down in that place where I had been so long.

Then I saw Rachel jump down from one of the trucks. She ran to me and put an arm around me and helped me forward. There was a young Pole at the back of the truck to which she led me, and he more or less heaved me up onto the apron of the truck, and then he helped Rachel up.

I kept hearing the word *Hurry,* in both Polish and Yiddish, and I distinctly heard laughter among the neatly dressed people on the sidewalk. I saw Rapaport get into our truck. Slonim went to the other truck. Rutka was with us, and Mordecai climbed in with us, too. We sat on the floor of the truck grinning and weeping. One of the men with us kept kissing the side of the truck.

Down the street we heard a military whistle.

The Pole who had lifted me onto the truck ran around and opened the door of the cab. Rachel cried out to him:

—— Wait! There are more to come!

But the Pole got into the cab and started the engine. We were the first truck and we could see that the driver was also scrambling into the cab of the second truck. Rachel stood up and beat her fists on the top of the cab, and shouted:

—— Wait! Wait! After all this time!

I saw the face of a young man who was just emerging from the manhole, as he realized that the trucks were going off without him. He shouted something toward us in the trucks, bent his head down and shouted something into the manhole, and then jumped out and began running up the street.

We heard more whistling, and then a shot was fired. Our truck was gaining speed. In the very far distance I heard a familiar sound, and it made me look at Rachel, who had slumped down beside me again. I saw that she heard it, too. It was the sound of a concertina. It was playing rather boldly, and the penetrating silvery notes came to us clearly on the sweet-smelling air. We could tell that the tune was *Hatikva.*

LATER. Rachel has been trying to get me to stop writing. But I have some more to put down. Is this the second day? The

631

third day? I have been writing steadily. There is a kind of fog at the edges of my field of vision. . . .

We rode a long time in the trucks. The buildings seemed to stagger and career as we passed them, as if the whole city were giddy and sick. . . . Of course it was only the unsteadiness of our truck.

Far out in the country the trucks stopped and we were told to get out. Some Jewish partisans, who were tan and seemed almost unbearably strong and hearty, helped us down and right there beside the road fed us some bread and tea. I lost mine and I saw Rapaport also spit his up. However, I had another cup of tea and kept it down.

Then we began to walk. I do not even remember the trucks leaving. We walked across some fields into thick woods. They told us it was the Lomianki Forest.

At first we were in a second growth, full of thickets, tangled with vines; then for a time we were among older trees that climbed far above us, while underfoot there were tender ferns and delicate grasses. Again we came into thicker undergrowth among smaller trees, and the canopy over us became torn here and there; we saw the sky; the woods thinned out, and we were among bushes and clumped grass. We moved forward, and the footing became irregular. We entered some swamps. For a while we could step from hummock to hummock, but later we had to wade, until at last we were up to our hips in water and mud—but how clean! Beyond the swamp we climbed once more onto higher, wooded ground. The tanned Jews told us that we were on an island in the swamps. They took us to their camp, on a grassy bank in a clearing among silver birches. . . .

I pluck a leaf from a bush. It has tiny veins. The leaf is almost a perfect oval.

I hear Rachel's voice. She is speaking to Zilberzweig and Rapaport.

—— *Nu*, what is the plan for tomorrow?

A NOTE ON THE TYPE

This book was set on the Linotype in ELECTRA designed by W. A. Dwiggins. The Electra face is a simple and readable type suitable for printing books by present day processes. It is not based on any historical model, and hence does not echo any particular time or fashion. It is without eccentricities to catch the eye and interfere with reading — in general, its aim is to perform the function of a good book printing-type: to be read, and not seen.

Typographic and binding designs are by W. A. Dwiggins.

The book was composed by The Plimpton Press, Norwood, Massachusetts, and printed and bound by H. Wolff, New York.

WAD